NICK SNAPE

A QUEEN IN BLOOD

WARRIORS OF SPIRIT AND BONE BOOK THREE

For Julie

CAST OF CHARACTERS

THE MAJOR PLAYERS

Ecne: an acolyte of Meister Kinst, the alchemical specialist. Ecne has a sharp mind and struggled to come to terms with the Seven's scriptures as their lies emerged. She was attacked by the spirit of Marbhleoir, the Necromancer, on Innealtóir, and still carries the mental scars. She wields Wisdom's crossbow.

General Zendril: mother to the queen, Zendril Weister is a foul-mouthed general who oversaw the Crusade until removed by the Price Consort. Now returned to her role and oversees the Union's northern army.

Gowan: Laoch's First Ranger. Killed by an errant pot bomb and now resides in Leront's heartstone as a spirit.

Laoch: a Queen's Ranger who fought in the Unbeliever Crusade. He rescued Captain Rakslin from a prison encampment, but at the cost of his Spear and brother. In love with Sura, and grieves for her a second time after her sacrifice to save them from the *Kraken* soulship. He carries Justice and a mistrust for Keran and now Nathair, the Spirit Walker.

Mander: once a 'Ser' as part of the royal Honour Guard, he is General Zendril's advisor and lover.

Oisin: a Handren, a human born of the mountains, and an Elite First Ranger. Burned in the fight with Nathair, he barely survived. Bitten by an artifice spider on Innealtóir, he still carries the spirit venom in his soul. Has a strong bond with Ecne. Carries Fate's Bow.

Sergeant Sternath/King Panset: the Union's king who 'abdicated' after refusing to call for the Unbeliever Crusade. Took on the disguise of a veteran, Sergeant Sternath, and fought beside General Zendril when they encountered the Scorpion artifices and the Unspoken. Witnessed the first appearance of the Infected.

Sura: a Schenterenta, a female elven warrior, dishonoured by her suicide attempt and banished from her tribe. A Queen's Ranger and loved by Laoch. She died under Nathair's dragon breath, though maintained her spirit form due to her connection with Honour's spear. She sacrificed herself to the *Kraken* to prevent Nathair and her friends from being captured.

The Captain/Keran: a sea-captain from the realm of Mondrein. His spirit was tasked with riding the Wyrm Ship to search for the dragons of the veil and use them as a weapon against the Constructors. He later bonded with Nathair to purge the Constructor venom in the Spirit Walker's soul.

The Unspoken, or the Eighth: an Inhibitor. She turned traitor, murdering her fellow Constructors and overpowering An Chéad's Spirit Walker. She helped entrap the veil dragon Nathair, and later entered scripture as the Seven's false enemy, thus encouraging the people to prayer. Queen of the Unbelievers, she wears a spiritfire glamour.

COURT

Duke Simeon Weister of Ridth: uncle to the queen, and commander of the southern fleet. Left with Prime Sneed to seek support from the isles of Meres and Khund.

Prime Jacka Vardrin: once advisor to the queen and master of her spy network, he suffered a seizure during the last Soul Tear and is bedridden in Ridth.

Prince Consort Adama: unloved by the queen, she and Lord Penance contrived to have him falsely accused of conspiring with the Unspoken and placed under arrest in the High Lord's House. Since that time, the queen has visited often and suffers due to her betrayal.

Queen Erin Weister: became queen under the direction of the Seven Houses after King Panset's abdication and disappearance. Chosen specifically by Lady Fate and married to Prince Consort Adama. She is aware of most of the Seven Houses' deceptions over the last thousand years, and suspects many more.

OF THE SEVEN HOUSES

Lady Death: her House symbol is the hourglass, and the God's weapon, a scythe. Lady Death fought at Lord Penance's side against Nathair and was severely injured. She helped heal Lady Honour and they are now lovers. Cousin to Queen Weister.

Lady Fate: her House symbol is the spindle, and the God's weapon, a bow. She acts as Lord Penance's most senior partner in the Gods' Council, though she does not always agree with his actions.

Lady Honour: her House symbol is the scroll, and the God's weapon, a spear. Lady Honour was injured by the tainted Wyrding that acted as a beacon to the Constructors. Healed by Lady Death, together they have begun to understand how acting together can prevent the agony of their powers. She mourns Nesca, who showed signs of being an Infected.

Lord Hope: his House symbol is a set of scales, and the God's weapon, a sword. Fought by Lord Penance's side against Nathair and was also injured. He devised message crystals based on Lady Honour and Death's discoveries about paired working.

Lord Justice: quick to anger, slow to forgive, and the youngest on the Council. The God's weapon is a maul, and his House's symbol, a crossed maul and quill.

Lord Penance: High Lord, Overseer being an older title. His House's symbol is a plate bearing the God's weapon – a scourge – laid at the feet of a penitent worshipper. Lord Penance is a manipulator of the Court, the Gods' Council and the flocks. He recognises the strength of the queen, but bears many burdens.

Lord Wisdom: an enigma. Strong-willed in his oversight of the university and the meisters, but weak within the Council. His house symbol is a tome or book, and the God's weapon, a crossbow. He now researches heavily within the Forbidden library.

Seneschal Greeth: Lord Wisdom's seneschal and she now works with Meister Kinst as they devise crystals that can contain various forms of spiritfire.

Sneed: a former High Lord and later servant to High Lord Penance. He acts as a sounding board and is close to the queen, having championed her to Lady Fate. Made Prime after Jacka's seizure, and now with Simeon seeking the isles' support.

UNIVERSITY MEISTERS

Grand Meister Arknold: head of the university, an *engineer*, though she rarely uses that title due to the Houses' dislike for *science*. Working with Gowan to turn the inert veil dragon, Leront, into a trap for the Constructors.

Meister Kinst: alchemical specialist, invented flash (gun) powder and Erin's Wrath, a high explosive. She rails against the constraints of scripture and is now working with Greeth to create spiritfire weapons.

Meister Trizone: a meister of art.

CONSTRUCTORS

Lelion, The Admiral Incarnate: one of the original Constructors who foreswore their bodies in return for eternal spirit life. She is an artificer who built the *Kraken* at the behest of the emperor after the failure of Apso-Tran. She acts as the emperor's second-in-command, though the relationship is fractious.

Lieutenant (unnamed): the Admiral Incarnate's second, whose body was by killed by the admiral after the escape of Nathair from Innealtóir.

Marbhleoir, The Necromancer: left to guard Innealtóir while creating a blend of human and machine, Marbhleoir's spirit inhabited the walls of the great palace. A botched attack on Ecne left part of his soul entrapped and was forced to reveal the location of Apso-Tran, the site of the Constructors only defeat, to Ecne and Nathair. Eaten by Tabharthóir.

Popsilin, Mechanised Inhibitor Captain: has risen in the emperor's favour and now acts as his main, trusted ally for important missions. They worked together to capture a shaman on Mondrein, who later became Tabharthóir's Spirit Walker.

Tarin, Emperor of the Constructors, The Fleshmaster: The saviour of the Constructors. Tarin seeks the Seven Magi who escaped his menagerie. With the veil dragons not returning from their chase, the Constructors had no choice other than to feed on each other. Only after he learned to manipulate the whitefire, could he capture the wyrms and once again ride the veils and feed his people.

Tenith: Popsilin's second as part of a subtler approach to warfare instigated by the emperor.

Viseri, the Great Artificer: another originator and constructor of all the veil dragons. Forever loyal to the emperor, he built Tabharthóir in the hope they would find a Spirit Walker to inhabit the heartstone and return the Constructors to their rightful place.

SCHENTERENTA
Betana Refi Na Partera: leader of the Schenterenta Refi tribe, Sura's father.

Terana Fiotir Na Partera: a tribal leader and Learned. Helped High Lord Penance meet with the Schenterenta tribal leaders where he revealed how the Magi had entrapped their race's spirits in the veils.

Tixar: a warrior and nephew to Terana.

DRAGONS OF THE VEIL
An Chéad: the Unspoken's scarlet-scaled artifice dragon, and the symbol of evil used by the Seven Houses to persuade people to prayer. Newly awakened due to the danger of the Constructors' imminent arrival, he is mute and has regularly consumed human souls.

Leront: the metal dragon who first chased the Seven Magi down and was subsequently dismembered by the Magi. Leront's Spirit Walker remains within the heartstone, where Gowan also resides.

Nathair: the artifice dragon that rose after being fully awakened by the Captain/Keran. Intact and trapped after the Unspoken and An Chéad's intervention a thousand years ago, she fought Laoch and the others until the Captain and Sura's spirit subdued the Spirit Walker. Keran later sacrificed himself to rid the Spirit Walker of its venom, and, in turn, became one with Nathair.

Tabharthóir: the last veil dragon constructed by the Grand Artificer Viseri, awakened by the Fleshmaster after capturing and spiritually torturing a Schenterenta shaman to forge a Spirit Walker for the heartstone.

OTHER CHARACTERS

Captain Mordant: captain of the City Guard, advisor to the queen on military matters.

Láidir: Laoch's brother, whom he was forced to kill after he was caught in an Unbelievers' banefire trap.

Naru: Sura's twin brother, died when rescuing a herd of wild horses from the Handren.

Nesca: a priest-in-waiting who served Honour's House, severely injured during the infected Wyrding that signalled Brandshold's location to the emperor.

GENERAL TERMINOLOGY

Becoming/Quicken: originally *Becoming* was the act of preparing a priest-in-waiting's mind for the use of spiritfire as part of their investiture as a House leader. Later, termed "the quickening", or being "quickened", as the Houses prepared all priests for the use of spiritfire to defend Brand-shold.

Dragons of the veil: artifice dragons built from cogs, metal and wire, powered by a heartstone. This contains a Spirit Walker, the twisted soul of a Schenterenta shaman that hungers for souls and the spiritfire they are made up of. They are hunters for the Constructors, and can fly between realms and slide through veils unnoticed. Also called veil dragons.

Gods' Council: the meeting of the Seven Leaders of the Houses, and now includes the queen.

Inhibitor: thought to be a general term for a Constructor soldier.

Journey: the escape from the Constructors, though scripture describes this as a journey across the sea.

***Kraken*, A Soulship:** a huge artifice designed and built by Lelion. First mooted instead of the dragons, the emperor turned to Lelion after the dragons were lost and he had subjugated the wyrms to find passage through the veils to other realms.

Learned: a person of learning, be it a meister, an acolyte or other such role.

Priests-in-Waiting: senior priests from whom the Lord or Lady of the House will choose a future leader. Sometimes shortened to *the waiting*. Now being *quickened* to use spiritfire.

Realms: multiple planes of existence, where time runs concurrently, but each realm is quite different. During the Sundering, many of the humans who escaped with the Magi ended up in different realms as the veil gate broke apart.

Schenterenta: labelled elves by humans, they are a people with cat-like eyes, pointed ears and dappled ebony skin. They are short in stature and powerfully built, yet retain a grace to their movements. They engage in an ancient form of spirit worship; however, their shamans lost their powers after the arrival of the humans.

Sealgair: hunters sent by the realm of Mondrein, with the Captain, to seek the dragons. Twin-souled warrior magi who wear an armour much like the Inhibitors, to reflect spiritfire.

Seeking (Calling): the emperor and a few other powerful users of spirit-fire, including a Spirit Walker, can use "the calling" to connect with other users over large distances. Constructors use a lower form when near to each other to communicate. A "seeking" is a surge of spiritfire sent out to inform the user of what may be nearby.

Spear: Rangers are arranged into Spears, usually of five or six, who act as scouts or behind enemy lines.

Spiritfire: soul magic. The act of using either one's own spirit or that of another, in the form of energy, to affect the world around you. This energy lies in all living things and can be retained in the bonds of certain crystals. The Magi were specialists, and their spiritfire was coloured by this, and savoured by the emperor.

Spirit Walker: a Spirit Walker is created by spirit torture. The Schenterenta shamans are twin-souled users of spiritfire, formed by one elven twin sacrificing their body to bond with the other. The emperor twists this, injecting a spirit venom that will kill both bonded spirits unless one twin sacrifices themselves to it. Forever in pain, seeking solace and voraciously hungry, the emperor uses these creations to power the veil dragons.

The Constructors: a race of soul-eaters and decadent artificers against whom the Seven Magi led a rebellion, escaping and taking thousands of the Constructors' spirit-dolls and menageries – their humans – with them. It is believed they will hunt down and subjugate the descendants of those who fled.

The Infected: were first created by accident when Constructor spirits tried to inhabit new, but too-long dead, bodies. Insane, slivers of their soul shed like skin, insinuating their way into others and blackening their spirits in turn. If there is blood contact with a human, this insanity is passed on as "soul-pain" and they hunger for souls to ease the agony.

The Patterning: Schenterenta warrior training.

The Seven Gods/Magi: The Seven were powerful Magi bred by the emperor within his personal menagerie. They escaped, taking as many humans as they could with them. On landing upon Brandshold, they wrote the scripture by which they expected the survivors to live. This forbade the study of science and demanded prayer at one of the Seven Houses. After the fight with the dragon Leront, four sacrificed themselves to form the structure of the first veils, only for Nathair to slip through. After her entrapment, with the Unspoken's help, the remaining Magi repeated the sacrifice to form the final three veils.

The Sundering: as named by the Constructors. Seen as an act of betrayal when the Seven Magi escaped the emperor's menagerie and rescued many of the humans used as food. They left by a veil gate, chased by the dragons.

The Unbelievers: those who turned away from the Seven Gods and the constraints of scripture. Often the thinkers and the mavericks, many turned to the Unspoken in the mountains and formed an enclave at Anvil, under her protection. They regard her as a queen rather than a goddess.

Thaumaturge: creators of wonder who can root a Constructor's soul to a new, dead body. Marbhleoir was their leader.

Veils: a layer of spiritfire wrapped about a realm, designed to contain all magic and spirits to ensure what life lies beneath goes undetected by the Constructors. Brandshold's veils are particularly strong, fed and maintained by siphoning soul slivers from those at prayer.

Veil curtain: the protective layer between veils.

Veil glyph: a detection magic that hides within a veil, releasing contained spiritfire should something come through.

Whitefire: spiritfire, but wilder. It can also be tainted by the Constructors.

Wyrding: the Seven bequeathed the Houses a Wyrding Stone, a means by which they can send the drained souls or spirits from their people to the correct veil. The Wyrding Stone is the conduit for this act.

Wyrm/Wyrm Ship: Wyrms are creatures that inhabit the space between realms, feeding off spiritfire that is naturally released. A favourite food of the veil dragons, they were hunted close to extinction. After the Journey, they found many realms were *veiled* and inaccessible. The Wyrm Ship is one such creature that was carved to house the Sealgair and protect the Captain on their hunt

KNOWN REALMS

Apso-Tran: the rumoured site of the Constructors' first major loss in battle as revealed by Marbhleoir.

Brandshold: the realm of the Seven, where many of those who escaped with the Magi settled after the Journey.

Innealtóir: the realm of the Constructors.

Mondrein: The Captain/Keran's home realm where the emperor captured his longed for Spirit Walker.

Repanti: where we first met the emperor and the *Kraken* above the City of Sighs. It is mentioned in book one by The Captain/Keran and the Wyrm ship as a realm they had visited.

BRANDSHOLD
HANDREN MOUNTAINS 
ANVIL
PARTERA PLAINS
JENSE
RUSHOLME
DENT
FARNFORD
ERSTENBURGH
MAKALENA
RIDTH
SOUTHERN REACHES
MERES PORT

Valley of the Unspoken
Pantsil
KHUND
Karak
ISLES OF TEES
ISLE OF MERES
Shelby

I
THE BEGINNING OF THE END

Mist seeped down from the head of the valley, a thick blanket that enveloped the rocky scree and hid the glimmering stone from the moonlight. General Zendril let out a slow breath, mindful to keep the plume from clouding the outer lens of her spyglass as she peered through the trees. The farmstead nestled against the valley floor remained bathed in the moonlight, the few penned sheep on its near side asleep, their heads resting on the ground. The single window on the southern side lay dark, though Zendril hoped the gentle glow emanating from the north was candlelight and a sign of life, rather than the moon's reflection.

A hand squeezed her shoulder, her thick cloak ruffling under scarred fingers. Silently, she glanced back. Mander was pointing towards the western slope, where the hill goats stirred. Bringing the spyglass back up, she followed his direction and caught sight of gentle movement along the edge of the thornbushes. In the moon's shadow, only an experienced eye would pick it out. She had seen enough battles and skirmishes to know its significance.

"How long?" she whispered through tight lips.

"I'm thinking ten minutes at the pace they're moving. First Ranger Yanik knows what she's doing. She'll go in hard and fast if anything changes," replied Mander, covering his mouth to disperse his breath's bloom.

"We need one whole, though for the life of me I'd rather burn all the fuckers to a cinder."

"The Overseer asks much," replied Mander, "as always."

"A necessity," said Zendril, noting a shift in the shadows and a sudden surge of activity among the goats as they skittered off uphill. "Fuck. Are you sure Yanik is up to this?"

Another tap on the shoulder brought her attention back to the farmhouse. The sheep had awoken and were taking a piss while looking around. An edge of fear marred their postures, but no bleating echoed down the valley.

A cry set Zendril's neck hairs standing. An instinctive fear tickled at her soul as three more barely human calls responded. With the encroaching fog and the steep valley sides, she struggled to ascertain the direction, but the panic amid the sheep told all. They hurried to push themselves into the corner nearest the stone building, eyes locked on the scrub to the south, which parted to expose a ragged figure. It approached on all fours, its appearance human – though a second cry from whatever lips remained belied that thought. The sound spoke of hunger and pain, a desperate need bathed in hate. The creature leapt the wooden fence, landing amid the remaining grass on bare feet and bleeding hands, and exploded into forward motion. Its speed set a stone of dread deep within the pit of Zendril's stomach. Wiry arms grasped for the nearest sheep, and the once-human creature buried its head deep into the spring fleece. Blood spurted, black in the night, as it tore away the throat.

Zendril sensed Mander rise, likely to signal Yanik in if she hadn't already noted the animal screams and inhuman feeding.

"Wait," she whispered, one hand raised to her second-in-command and bed partner. "Learn."

Sickened, she watched as a soft glow arose from the stricken animal, pulsing twice before wreathing the *Infected*'s head. The Infected, arching its neck, let go, mouth wide as though releasing what the general's mind interpreted as a sigh of pleasure. The remaining panicked sheep headed for the southern fence, only for three more ghouls to leap upon them. Blood splashed, and the night glowed again.

"Yanik's on the move," whispered Mander, lips barely moving, teeth clamped against the rising tension. "Zendril …"

She raised a hand, all the while watching the Infected feed. "It's fucking war, Mander. And this is just the start. The queen and the High Lord thirst for knowledge about what we face. The meisters too. You saw the Scorpion machines, and now this. Whatever we do, soldiers will die alongside the people they defend. Our role is to make the pain and suffering worthwhile." She turned to glare at her friend and lover. "And I hate it as much as you."

Mander nodded, face set grim and raised his spyglass. "Yanik is in place. She's moved down at speed."

"Good. Now we'll see her mettle. Arrow."

Mander knelt and used the tip of his sword to pry loose a top stone, unveiling the small firepit beneath. With the fire's orange glow lighting his battered features, he bathed a basket arrow amid the small flame until the oiled cloth caught fire. He swiftly grabbed his bow, nocked the arrow, and aimed for the sky above the eastern valley side. With a prayer to Death, he let the arrow fly, blinking away the streak of light that threatened to negate what remained of his night sight.

"They haven't seen it. Or they're not bothered by it, at least," said Zendril, watching as the four creatures clambered over the fence towards the farm building. As one, they headed for the shuttered southern window. Sliding fingers into cracks, they wrenched at the wood. Hoots echoed off the stone valley sides, accompanied by the crack of wood and tearing of metal hasps. The shattered wood cast aside, the first creature tore through the goatskin that covered the aperture.

"Second arrow. Signal Llandon's Spear."

Zendril didn't wait. Rising to her feet, she strode down through the low, wooded copse. Two honour guards – soldiers assigned to her by the queen – took their places at her side, ever present after they had witnessed with her the Constructor's mechanical Scorpions and the Unspoken's dragon. They carried boar spears with crossed bars below the blackened points, and heavy shields across their armoured backs, but they matched the general stride for stride as the second arrow flared above.

Now we see how well these Infected think.

The shimmer of flame lit the sky, forging an orange glow along the top of the fog bank rolling down the valley. Zendril estimated they had fifteen minutes before it enveloped them – time enough.

She and her honour guard looked away as arrows drove into the ground around the three creatures clambering in through the window. Each exploded, the cracks amplified off the stone walls. The Infected cried out as the white flare of the flash powder erupted. A second round of arrows from Yanik's Spear crashed into the earth and the creatures moved, skittering away westwards on all fours as the white light bathed their gaunt cheeks and hollow eyes.

Zendril jogged over to the farmstead. An angry, limping Mander caught up with her, sword drawn, and grabbed her arm. Reluctant, the general allowed her guards to move on ahead, Mander's muttered reminder lost amid her curses. With Yanik's Spear rushing through the farmyard to chase the receding Infected, they reached the southern window to the sound of a battle inside.

"Stay here," she ordered Mander, who complied and signalled his Spear of four to guard the window, arrows drawn. "I need it alive."

Zendril followed her guards to the front of the building. The single window in the front façade was half-broken, and light flickered from within as an animal scream pierced the night. Shadows waivered as the battle raged inside. Zendril drew the key from a pouch at her side. Her hand shook, adrenaline betraying the speed she wanted. Setting the key home, she turned the lock, and gripped the newly made handle before checking on her protectors.

"Ready, *Sers*?"

At the guards' nods, she wrenched the door open and stepped behind the thick wood. A furious mass of flesh and bone roared out, arms flailing, froth flying. Steadfast, the guards drove the boar spears into the creature's shoulders. The white glow reappeared, this time from each of the once-human's joints, as the Infected heaved itself along the weapons' hafts. When its body finally braced against the crossed metal bars, both soldiers shoved in unison and pushed the monstrosity back into the building. Powering onwards, they drove the spear points into the far wall.

Zendril followed as far as the doorway, staring into the wild white eyes of the snarling creature pinned against the wall. Its face was husked, blue lips drawn back over bloody teeth, a dried lump of a tongue flickering behind.

Rabid. As far from being human as is possible. And worse, it spreads the infection at random.

Eyeing the debris within the room and the crumpled figure untangling itself from the corner next to the cold fire, she waited. The soldier's crystal-plated armour shone in the light of the single candle that had somehow survived the battle.

"All right?" she asked, adhering to High Lord Penance's direction and not getting too close as the creature snarled and writhed against the wall.

"Aye, 'twas a mere scuffle," replied Sergeant Sternath, checking over his armour. "But maybe you're right. I might be too old for this crap."

"Don't think you get the choice. None of us do. The coffin is on its way. Lock it down fucking tight."

"What if they need to breathe?"

"Not my fucking problem." The general grimaced and headed off towards the western side of the farm. Mander fell in at her side, his limp pronounced.

"Got it?" he asked. His face screwed up as his left leg hit the ground.

"Yes ... sorry. I—" She glanced over, wincing with him as he limped along.

"You need to stop this, and soon. You can't be reckless. Nor can, you know, our returned monarch. We need you both." Mander stopped and grabbed Zendril's arm. "And I can't be around all the time if you're in the thick of battle. I'm not what I was."

"But you'll keep on trying to be." Looking into the depths of his eyes, a million thoughts merged into just one. "Okay, I agree to be less reckless *if* you agree to something for me."

"What?"

"Get Panset to stop this mummery as a bloody sergeant and do what he's told."

She spun away, following the glow of flame and the cries of frustrated, animalistic anger. Within a few yards, the scrub opened up into a clearing. To one side, a raging single Infected charged at the surrounding Rangers, whose boar spears prodded and probed, trying to force it back into the waiting pit. Yanik stood behind her Spear and let fly with a weighted arrow that slammed into the creature's shoulder, spinning it around. Llandon followed up. His arrow missed as the Infected threw itself to one side, grasped a spear behind its tip and began to pull the Ranger in. But they were well drilled, and a second and third spearhead drove into the rabid beast, shoving hard as the Ranger released his weapon. With a snap of bone, the flailing creature dropped into the pit.

"Me?" said Mander, catching up. "He's a ..."

"A leader we're going to need." Zendril peered into the deep pit. The three Infected surged from side to side, dragging broken limbs and digging at the oil-slick walls. "Because I think we will have two wars to fight."

She signalled to the waiting Yanik and Llandon, and the fire arrows thudded home. The eruption filled the air with burnt flesh and oil.

Mander glanced first at the burning figures, and on towards the fog bank that had finally caught them up.

"Aye, perhaps you're right."

2
AN OATH SHARED

BETWEEN REALMS

Nathair adjusted the beat of her wings. The dragon's metalled skin caught the tendrils of spiritfire bleeding from the veil that wrapped the realm below. They tasted wrong. No, that was not what her blended spirit spoke of. Different. Spiritfire, yes, but of a form alien to her memories.

A challenge?

As much as an ancient female Spirit Walker had faced before? Or her new male human half?

No.

Different.

Nathair adjusted, settling into a rhythm as she – for that was how they both perceived themselves now – tasted the veil curtain, seeking weakness. Though the barrier appeared uniform, Nathair knew it ebbed and flowed like a tidal sea. That was the true skill of the veil dragons – being able to read the imbalance and slip through where it stretched thin.

Not like a wyrm, that tears a rent open, though that was a skill learned late, after the veils were formed and confined their food.

A whiff of memory made Nathair shudder, of the hunt, and the taste of a wyrm upon her tongue. The spiritfire such beasts contained was magnificent. Addictive. Thrilling.

The new Nathair pushed that memory down, imprisoned it behind her own barriers. Together, Keran and she had swept the heartstone clear of past enslavement to a relentless master. For she was now whole again.

'*Laoch,*' she whispered. The thought settled on the man's mind. '*We are near, and we should talk.*'

The sleeping Ranger snorted as her thoughts tickled at his senses, disturbing his dreamless rest. Nathair felt his mind stir, urging the body out of its stupor, and to awaken. Laoch's leg twitched, as did an arm, before he finally threw back the blanket and sat slowly up.

"Keran?" he said, his voice harsh and raw. Laoch reached for the waterskin he'd left by his side at Ecne's insistence, and took a sip. "Keran?" he repeated, smoother.

'*No,*' replied Nathair. '*Keran and Nathair are as one. It is hard to define, Laoch, but as you slept, we have become a true Spirit Walker, kindred, rather than twinned spirits as the Schenterenta would define us. We are now Nathair, though if it eases your mind, I can appear as whoever you wish.*'

"You choose." Laoch stood with a stretch, and eyed Honour's spear with trepidation.

"It is empty," Nathair said, and formed outside the heartstone. Her metal-scaled body glistened orange despite being far from solid. "Honour is no longer within the sigil."

Laoch blinked and raised his chin to stare at the spirit. His mouth moved, but nothing came out.

"I believe Sura and Honour were taken together, absorbed by the *Kraken*. A lost avatar of a god long-departed."

"And now? Why wake me? To make me suffer again?" Laoch walked over, grasped the spear, and spun it until the sigil lay face up.

"Nathair of old would have revelled in such pain, and drunk your spirit with glee afterwards. No, I do not wish to cause you any more grief. But I must know if I can rely on you."

"On me? What is this, you bastard? An accusation? I thought they had all ended with Gowan. Seven Hells, Nathair, I am here and still fighting." His fingers rubbed against the sigil, but no warmth spread across his fingertips. He laid the weapon aside to glare at the dragon spirit. "I have a people to save. Those things in the palace, they were an evil beyond the Unbelievers. Sick and twisted, proof of what you ... what Keran told us."

"Yes. Though the Constructors are far worse. And stronger, faster when fed. That which was Keran yearns for his Mondrein to be safe, as you do for your Brandshold."

"As did Sura. Justice demands I save my people, but I am now honour-bound to save hers. Do you understand, spirit? I'm making a bloody vow." Laoch took a step forwards, eyes still locked on Nathair's scaled face. "You hold all the cards, can ambush us at any time. But if you truly are a Spirit Walker, a shaman, and wise like the bloody meisters, where do you believe the Constructors will strike first?"

"They hurt for what was done to them by the Seven Magi. That I cannot deny. When I left, their anger was all-consuming. The emperor sent all the dragons on the hunt, risked everything, and lost." Nathair's head tilted to one side, while her forked tongue wiped around one eye.

"Pissed off and angry. And stewed for a thousand bloody years while waiting to exact revenge. They'll not be patient. No. They'll go for the Seven and *my* people. Understand?"

"Yes."

"So, can I rely on you?"

Nathair flinched before a smile crept along the lizard-like lips. "A drunkard and a warrior. Have you just turned the tables on the wise?" The smile broadened, scales sliding over themselves as Nathair's cheeks puffed out. "You can rely on me, Ranger."

"Then I make a second vow, for Mondrein. As does Justice."

"Good. A pact made. Shall I awaken the others? We are at Apso-Tran's curtain. We seek a way through, but the veil tastes strange."

—

Laoch awoke Oisin and gently squeezed the Handren's shoulder, the Ranger signal for quiet. The mountain man's eyes flickered open, assessing the room, while his hand reached for the waiting sword.

"We are safe," said Laoch, on his haunches, eyes on Ecne, who slept on. "Still inside the metal beast, though we're waiting to enter a new bloody realm. You ...?"

"Am I okay?" said Oisin. He shoved the blanket away and pushed himself up. "I can still feel the venom, if that's what you mean. But it feels secure, locked away." He rose and rolled his shoulders, then stretched each leg in turn.

"Being aware is good," commented Laoch and, heading over to Ecne, squeezed her shoulder.

"And you?" Oisin stared at the heartstone as he spoke. Laoch assumed he referred to Sura.

"Like shit," he replied, though his face wore a smile as Ecne stirred. He shook her this time, and the acolyte woke with a start, wide-eyed and scrambling for her crossbow. Laoch patted her cheek. "I moved it just in case. Didn't want a Wisdom-sized hole in my chest."

"You could have been gentler," she said, and stretched as she sat up. "That was like the sleep of the de—"

Laoch flinched, but shoved the grief down and forced a rueful smile.

"Laoch, I'm—" Ecne's cheeks reddened.

"Aye. Unthinking. I'll forgive yer once. A second time, and there'll be a dousing of dragon fire from my new friend, Nathair." He stepped away, and the spirit reformed behind him at the mention of her name.

"Nathair?" said Oisin. "You've changed again. Is this final?"

"I believe so," the spirit replied. "Laoch agreed that I should choose my appearance." The dragon's scales once again shimmered, the orange hues filled the room. "We are at the veil curtain, and I have found a thinning, a place of entry. But the veil beyond is strange. It does not match any I remember."

"And?"

"I think it may be raw and unformed. A veil of spirits rather than spiritfire. One placed by my people, the Schenterenta. Entry will be easy; passage will, I expect, be met by fury."

"Fury?" said Ecne.

"Think of a single Schenterenta, an unfettered warrior, and her anger. Then think of just how many more there would be over a thousand years. All that pent-up anger, released on a single veil dragon. It will be a wild ride." The dragon spirit raised a scaled eyebrow. "Batten down the hatches, as Keran would say."

3
ON THE WINGS OF A DRAGON

CITY OF SIGHS, REPANTI

Tabharthóir spread her wings wide, her flight serene, high above the mountains surrounding the City of Sighs. With a thought from the Fleshmaster, the dragon's roar thundered amid the clouds, echoing across the forested valleys below before dying on the wind.

"Too easy, Tabharthóir. You are ready for a challenge." The emperor caressed the heartstone with his ornate gauntlet. A spark of whitefire crackled along the facet and drove deep into the crystal to tug at the venom lacing the agonised Spirit Walker, lashing the spirit with its command. A wing dipped, the other rose, and the metal dragon swept around towards the entrance of a deep valley.

"Yes ... but quicker, faster. No more pretence. I command, and you follow."

The Spirit Walker fought back, railing against the venomous bonds, the shaman's fury and spite thrown against their strength. It brought a joy to the Fleshmaster, the spirit finally giving itself up to the hate he could twist and shape at will. The more it fought, the tighter the venom took hold, and the hungrier the Spirit Walker became.

How desperate your struggles, and how sweet they taste.

The two Inhibitors standing behind him shifted position, their minds locked in with the crystal. They saw through Tabharthóir's eyes, as did the emperor – this the third pair to attempt such a connection. The first two were now with the thaumaturge after becoming overwhelmed by the venom and the Spirit Walker's rage.

Weak, these younglings. Popsilin would have managed, but I need her for another role, and I trust so few … I fear it must be me.

Whitefire surged into the heartstone. The silver-blue dragon dipped down, talons mere feet above the forest canopy, wind rushing over her metalled skin. The beast roared – but not at the emperor's behest – and wheeled up and around. Rather than fight the Spirit Walker's choice, Tarin let the dragon have its head, curious about the change of behaviour. Tabharthóir rose and turned, before diving into the valley beneath the very spot where it had roared, talons extended, razor sharp. The Fleshmaster finally caught the scent.

She hungers and she hunts. Finally.

The mighty dragon drove deep into the trees. Branches snapped and trunks splintered, the crunch echoing through the forest as metal met wood. The emperor felt the talons tear into flesh. Ribs shattered and blood caked the beast's forelegs, bringing a joy that swept through the Fleshmaster and on into the Inhibitors, who screamed their ecstasy. The dragon rammed into the ground, its full weight pummelling into whatever poor animal had been its chosen food. Tabharthóir's neck and head snapped back, and the pocket gave way as the Spirit Walker, in her panic, surged all the available spiritfire into powering her overtaxed joints.

Tarin grabbed at the heartstone. His whitefire latched on and he swathed himself in more. The Inhibitors were not so lucky. They flew forwards and smashed into the heartstone before flailing backwards to ram into the ribbed walls of the chamber. A second crash shuddered through the dragon, a spirit wave, as Tabharthóir roared in frustration. She heaved herself up from the forest floor, anger coursing through her mechanisms. Metal-boned wings spread out wide, slicing through the trees. The mighty wings beat once, twice, and the dragon rose above the canopy, the unrecognisable bloody prize in her talons, the meagre spiritfire aglow as it seeped beneath her scales.

A first kill.

Tarin sensed the spiritfire pocket reform as control returned. With barely a glance towards his broken soldiers, he drove his awareness into the crystal, and a smile crept across his blue lips. The venom had invaded the Spirit Walker, not just wrapped about it. Black, malevolent veins that spoke of control, of anger and, above all else, hunger.

Yes.

A herd of elephant buffalo broke out from the edge of the forest. The huge herbivores had panicked and followed a bull that had lost all reason but fear. Despite a desperate desire to *control*, the emperor gave Tabharthóir permission to feed. She needed little encouragement. Talons drove into the rear of the herd, rending limbs and ripping spines. As blood spurted, the dragon twisted its huge wings, catching the air and, with a little more grace this time, landed amid the carnage. A roar of triumph filled the valley, and the sword-like teeth bit down into flesh and bone, the tongue rasping around her prizes. Spiritfire filled the dragon's maw, and Tabharthóir rejoiced in the feeding.

Tarin forced himself to break the connection. The primal need coursing through the dragon pressed at the boundaries of his own hunger. Leaning over the crystal, he shook his head and glanced at the stricken Inhibitors piled in one corner. The soul-lust crept in at the edge of his thoughts, and he swiftly locked it away.

Now is not the time.

He strode over, grasped the first Inhibitor by the head, and twisted hard. The snap was absolute, and the spirit slipped its root from the body's brain to writhe about the heart, before seeping from the broken chest to enter the waiting gourd. The hunger impinged on his mind again, but the Seven were close. He craved Magi spiritfire far more than that of his own people. A second crack bounced around the room, and another spirit sought sanctuary from true death.

The room sparked as renewed power swathed the walls before soaking inwards to spread among the dragon's many cogs and mechanisms. The skill of Viseri, the Great Artificer, resplendent, as the machinery surged with the melding of her science and the essence of life. Tarin let a smile touch his lips once again and placed a hand against the dragon's ribs. The thrum of *his* artifice thrilling him with its potential.

"*Soon, Tabharthóir, we will feast upon the Seven.*"

———

"What a waste."

"A necessity," replied the newly imbued second-in-command, "according to the emperor."

Lelion faced the Inhibitor, interposing her ex-lieutenant's image over the man who stood there now. A loss. One her own temper had caused. The regret was only assuaged by Lieutenant Spintz's rebirth having been a greater success than normal. Most of her memories had been retained, and she would likely be able to return to duty by the time the attack on the Seven's realm was due to begin.

I hope.

Lelion plugged her bone-white finger into her ear, pulling at it, trying to negate the incessant buzzing. Her new second eyed her warily, perhaps thinking the admiral was responding to his comment, since a fleeting panic twisted his features.

"Yes, as the emperor says. A *necessity*. You will learn, Kankrin, that necessity is sometimes a short-term excuse. Look," she said, sweeping her hand towards the slaughter below. The market square was full of the dead and dying. Inhibitors walked among the bloodied bodies, draining spiritfire, filling their storage crystals with the souls of the living and the dead. "We maximise now, but in a few months, a year perhaps, we could have so much more. Menageries the size of a city could feed our wars. Instead, we create a desert devoid of food."

Kankrin remained silent, arms behind his back, steeling his eyes to the slaughter below. Lelion shook her head, well aware her new second was the emperor's man through and through. A necessity.

For now.

"And when this city is empty, we move on to drain the next."

"As commanded," replied Kankrin. "The *Kraken*—"

"*I know my ship*," cut in the admiral, her hands now gripping the balustrade the Fleshmaster usually occupied. She spun around, letting the anger play across her face. White eyes sparked with ancient power. "And you will do well – *Second* – to remember that." Her hand flicked out. Kankrin flinched, but no blow came. Instead, it alighted on his cheek, and Lelion drew his spirit towards her fingertips. She said nothing, simply held his gaze.

"Yes, Admiral," he said, and a hand thumped over his heart in salute.

Lelion dropped her touch, while the buzz rose in intensity and switched ear. She twitched while Tarin's imposed officer watched intently. Lelion filed that snippet away, but there was little she could change right now. Spirit sleep had been fleeting, and her mind was raw.

"See to it that we are moving when the last feeder is aboard. Now go." She waved towards the bridge. Kankrin saluted again and left, almost at a run.

Lelion scanned the city streets. The first battle had been of conquest, but this had been a massacre. The segmented artifices milled along the roads and cut-throughs, their legs rising and falling in a steady rhythm, draining any errant souls from the remains. They were an old design of hers, scavengers that ensured nothing went to waste. They fed the dregs of a wasteful massacre into the war machine the Fleshmaster demanded as they prepared for the Seven.

"At last. Maybe he is right. They must know we are coming, but not how strong we will be." She watched on as one feeder hauled its segmented body up the tallest remaining building. A multitude of clawed feet hooked the stone until it reached the top. Once there, its upper half lifted into the air, feet waving, and the *Kraken*'s chains dropped to wrap the artifice. A fizz crackled across its segments, and all the spiritfire the contraption had drained from the dead coalesced to speed along the links and fill the crystal at the heart of the *Kraken*.

"And we will bring death and subjugation. And vengeance for the Sundering."

4
THE PAIN OF THE LOST

THE VEIL OF APSO-TRAN

Laoch gripped the seat of the metal-boned chair that protruded from the pocket's floor. The rope wrapped about his chest, and fastening him down, matched the ones securing Ecne and Oisin. The three of them sat staring inwards, towards the heartstone. Each bore the steely eyes and firm chins of those going into a battle over which they had no control.

Laoch wished for Sura's soothing presence at that moment, her certainty. Alive, she had exuded assurance to everyone but him, as she staked her place in the human world and the Queen's Rangers. Upon her death, shod of the burden expected of her tribe, that certainty had shone in her love for him too, only to end with a final sacrifice for all those she cared deeply about. Grief lay at the edge of his thoughts, pressing in, constantly threatening to overwhelm him as he refused Justice's renewed efforts to soothe and calm his emotions. He had made a vow in her name, and Justice understood its faith and power.

"Stoke the fire."

"Eh?" said Ecne.

"Nothing. Mind wandering," replied Laoch. His glance towards Oisin was returned with an understanding nod. "Are we ready? Because I sure as hell aren't." He grimaced, letting a choked laugh slip.

"Oh yes," said Ecne. "Life as a meister's acolyte prepares you for any—"

Nathair dropped, and it seemed as though the pocket floor rushed up to meet them. Crossbows and swords floated, pressing against their restraints, while the heavier water barrels strained and yawed against theirs. Laoch's stomach sat in his throat, threatening revenge for every drop of green-leaf rum he'd poured down it.

"Brace." Nathair's words filled the pocket.

"What in the Seven Hells do you think we're doing?" shouted Ecne, the words hoarse, barely audible, as her lower jaw refused to move.

Screeching broke through the pocket, a rending of metal against metal that set Laoch's teeth on edge and cut through his brain. Unable to think, he gripped tighter, focusing on the pressure as the racket changed pitch, over and over again.

With a thud, one he couldn't distinguish between his heart or the dragon's wingbeat, everything came to a stop. A stillness so opposite to the last few seconds, it forced a shiver up his spine. Sweat beaded, and a whisper swept through the dragon, a soft moan that rippled into the room, rolling, twisting. Wide-eyed, Ecne gaped as she stared at a spot behind Laoch's head. He stretched and wrenched his neck around. His half glance caught ghostly eyes filled with fury. They were locked on Ecne, spite and hate filling the void between.

"They can't get through," said Nathair. "At least ... not yet."

"We need to work on your confidence-building," said Oisin, teeth grinding as he frowned at the apparition. "And that looks pretty much like it's inside."

"A sliver of a vision spirit. Powerless. A seeker, or scout, I think you would name it."

"Knowledge is power," added Ecne, "and this one appears to hate what it knows. Those eyes ..." As she spoke, the spirit spun and whirled about the chamber, bouncing off walls that sparkled with whitefire. Nathair exposed a chink in the room, and the angry scout dived through.

As the last of the spirit disappeared, Nathair yawed left. Vibrations pulsed through the dragon as the pocket attempted to lock them down. A jerk, followed by a drop, and the dragon spiralled downwards. The screech of metal scales filled the pocket, accompanied by explosions that reminded Laoch of the echoes of distant pot bombs. Again and again, the dragon shuddered, and the strain on the spiritfire pocket increased. The Ranger felt his body lift from the chair. Only the ropes held him back.

"Seven Hells, Nathair!" shouted Laoch, frustrated at his inability to intercede, coupled with the acid invading his throat. He glanced over to Ecne, who had fainted, and Oisin, who pushed himself back into his seat, eyes closed, mumbling a prayer. "Oh shit."

—

The air lay thick about Nathair, moist and full of anger. The fog set a fear in the Spirit Walker as the pain spirits emerged, all spite and hate, to ram into her scaled hide. As one weakened, the next hammered in, swathing her scales with boiling frustration, seeking ingress. Not mindless spiritfire, but a form held together by sheer *will*, forged by the demand placed on it. Nathair could taste the taint now, a *shaping*, similar to the many she had performed over a thousand years ago before her soul twin had been ripped from her by the Necromancer's venom. Her spirit-weavings had been formed around the animals of her home, imbued with a sense of family, of protection. These, however, reminded her far more of the Constructors than she liked. Perhaps more than a shaping, a *command*, and despite the signature weaving of a Schenterenta shaman, it was one she feared.

Three pain spirits smashed into her left side simultaneously, and Nathair's panic rose. The roiling anger spilled over her scales, seeped underneath, and as she weakened, found a way in. Nathair redirected her spiritfire, using a vestige to lock down her friends and allies she carried inside the pocket. To ease her fear for their safety before the next barrage. Frantic, she then sent out a *seeking* – a pulse that would crash into whatever lay ahead and reflect back. She shivered, memories of pain assaulting her as a spirit broke through. It scythed into her pocket, desperate to release hate upon those inside. There was little she could do except prevent more from entering.

Fragments of the *seeking* returned. Poorly conceived under the attack, the detail was limited and ill-formed. But no matter. It spoke of one desperate hope, and Nathair entered a death dive towards her chosen spot. As she broke through the low, cloying cloud, a steel-grey sea appeared below. The waves were flat, barely breaking against a black beach.

——

Laoch swore as his eyes followed the boiling mist of hate that battered at the newly formed dome Nathair had erected to protect them. Thanking the Spirit Walker for the shield, he watched as whitefire sparkled at each hit, the acolyte still unconscious and thankfully unaware. Laoch could sense its hate, and with each strike, the whitefire's response weakened.

He slipped out his forearm knife, the small blade's edge honed during sleepless nights. Twisting his wrist, he sliced through the first binding around his chest, and had started on the second when Wisdom flared. Green spiritfire erupted from the God's weapon and shaped itself into a human form to stand between Ecne and the pain spirit. Laoch remembered the battle within the palace library, how Wisdom had defended her charge to the last. A touch from Justice on his mind reminded him he was far from alone, too.

"This may be a short friendship," Nathair roared inside the pocket room. "Batten down. Sorry, but I need to release the do—"

"What ...?"

The whitefire dome gave, and the dragon heaved to one side as everything solid was yanked upwards once more. Bile flowed from Laoch's lips, his throat and stomach reacting to the sudden movement, while the pain spirit seethed towards Ecne. Laoch sensed the clash from amid his own troubles as Wisdom intervened. He cried out, unable to form anything intelligible amid the vomit. Yet, above the roar, he heard Oisin's shout, and blue flared. The pocket turned cyan as Fate and Wisdom enveloped the spirit, consuming and absorbing its anger until none remained.

An ominous sensation invaded Laoch's mind. "No ..." Laoch whispered, and Justice gripped him tight. "Nathair, no!"

—

Nathair arched her neck and back. Scales popped, her spikes clashing against each other as the dark sea closed in. The spirits still rained down upon her, lost in the demands that shaped their will – frenzied, hate-filled. They enveloped her torso and raced along her spine, excited by the newly opened gaps between her metal plates. As the first tendrils touched her metalled skin beneath, Nathair dropped, talons tearing through the waves – the drag pulling her inexorably downwards. Giving in to the inevitable, she folded her wings, and the metal beast crashed into the sea. She rolled as her legs hit the sand beneath, twisting to cover the whole of her mechanical body in the hated water. With a hiss, the pain spirits dissipated. The crystal-laden water drew their spiritfire, seeping away the *will* that held them together. But fear wracked her as the whitefire that gave her life also leeched into the sea. Only momentum drove her on. Her front paws clawed at the water, driving into the seabed below, and she pulled herself towards the beach. Her hind legs sought purchase, meekly scrabbling in the watery sand until they hooked onto the rock beneath. Heaving, her desperation drove strained joints and, with a flap of her dripping wings, she shoved her upper torso onto the dry black sand.

'Welcome to Apso-Tran.'

5
DEATH'S CAGE

THE WHITE PALACE, ERSTENBURGH,
BRANDSHOLD

"I'll be honest, my queen. I am far from comfortable with your decision. We risk much but gain very little." High Lord Penance tapped his stick on the cobbled yard. He pressed both hands on its metal top and rested his chin there. Purple robes rippled in the breeze, the first scent of blossom carried on its wake.

The queen brushed down her riding breeches before stroking her horse's neck, calming the animal as it fretted at seeing a cart entering the courtyard. She let High Lord Penance's words soak in. His constant preparations for what she, and the leaders of the Houses, should do in case of an attack gnawed at her. She had already told him of her decision on that, the stoppered poison a constant companion alongside the thin blade she wore whenever dealing with the war build up.

"We crave understanding, High Lord." Erin nodded to the waiting stable hand, who took her horse's reins and led it away. "And my mother says this creature is restrained. You have advised that it likely infects by bite or wound, not through the air. What is there to fear?"

High Lord Penance chewed gently, letting the junip settle his mind as the juice slid down his throat. Shaking his head, he rapped the cane upon the stone.

"I could be wrong. Perhaps the palace staff, seeing what we face, may cause unnecessary panic? Or it could shed its bonds and attack?"

"On your first point, really? Have you ever been wrong?"

"Frequently. And more so as the realm changes." He grimaced, and a rivulet of purple juice slid down his chin. He lifted a gloved hand to wipe it away. High Lord Penance glanced over to the queen. Her knowing smile diverted his thoughts for a second.

"We need that self-belief, High Lord. Don't let my barbs in. And we agreed that news needed to be increasingly shared, good *or* bad." Erin glanced around, ensuring no one was nearby. "And Lord Hope's *message* stones only show so much, needed as they are."

"A wonder of your making, however much your mother disagrees with such *parlour tricks*." The High Lord sighed. "If you insist, then at least we need your soldiers between you and it."

"I won't disagree. And as I said, it will do us a service for this to be out of the bag. General Zendril and her soldiers face these creatures daily. Word is spreading. Rumours that we are doing something about – what did you call them? The *Infected*? – will only help."

Queen Erin signalled to the waiting sergeant-at-arms. The woman acknowledged the queen's command and marched over to Captain Mordant, who stood, hand on chin, talking to the two outriders who had followed the cart in. The queen masked her surprise as she recognised one of the men – and Mordant's evident joy at their presence.

Panset.

Two Rangers clambered out of the back of the covered cart and waited at the rear as another shoved a box out. It took a second or two for the queen to recognise it as a coffin.

Typical of my mother.

Between the three of them, they used a net to drag their burden across the cobbles to set it down in the centre of the yard, where her palace huntsmen had dragged out a large hounds' cage. They eased it inside and were able to stand the coffin up fully, leaning the head of the box against the large rock placed inside. The whole process fascinated Erin. Their obvious fear and care were palpable, and it soon spread to her soldiers, whose grins at the over-the-top preparations soon disappeared. By the time they'd finished, Panset – or Sergeant Sternath, as he insisted on being known – had donned the crystal armour recovered from the remains of the Smerral attack.

He bowed to the queen and High Lord Penance before approaching the cage.

"My queen, are you sure?" he said as he grasped the metal door.

"With you and my guard, I have nothing to worry about, Sergeant. Proceed." She once again brushed down her breeches and sat upon the wooden throne placed for her convenience.

"As you wish." Gauntleted hands pulled the door open, and he entered. Panset locked the gate and handed the key over to his waiting companion in exchange for a hefty boar spear. Three Rangers, each bearing the same weapon, stood to one side, clearly wary and at the ready. Panset set the spear down and, with a flat-bladed tool, wrenched at the coffin lid while Captain Mordant's soldiers filed in, leaving a gap through which the queen watched.

Splintered wood flew from the cage, and the scent of blossom on the breeze gave way to death and rot, leaving Erin caught between fascination and disgust. With a final crack, the lid gave, exposing the cadaver inside.

Erin stood, unable to help herself. The clearly human body was ravaged and dry, yet the rot smelt wet and musky. Its eyes opened. The orbs were white, flaring despite the morning's light. Its *need* caught her breath and ensnared her thoughts. It glared at her, a bestial growl echoing amid the stunned silence of the courtyard.

"No," said High Lord Penance as he rose to stand by the queen's side.

The creature snarled, eyes flicking over to Panset, who had stood back. His spear hovered between himself and the coffin.

"It lives, yet there was little air within the coffin." Panset prodded at the stomach. The Infected didn't flinch. "It does not fear weapons, and will drive itself onto blades, seeking the kill." He drove the spear tip into the creature's side. A little black blood emerged on the tip. "Yet not mindless. They think."

"Think," said High Lord Penance, taking another step forwards. He ignored Mordant's glance over. "How so?"

"We have witnessed them hunt as a pack. They know what a door and window are, take paths through the forest, seek out loved ones in remembered places. It's as if, somewhere inside, they are still human. But they do not eat. I have no idea how they sustain themselves. They kill, often biting and tearing apart those they catch. But many who escape the attacks still end up like this."

"But not all?" said Meister Kinst, hurrying into the yard, Seneschal Greeth trailing behind with a second priest. "Sorry, my queen. I—"

"No matter," she replied. "Carry on with what you were saying."

Kinst glanced over to the male priest at her side. Erin tried to recall his name.

"Erm, Sergeant?" Panset nodded in reply to Meister Kinst. "As you say, not *all* who encounter them change."

"No."

"Were these wounded? Bitten perhaps?" asked the priest, his hooked nose twitching as he stared at the contents of the coffin.

"As we informed High Lord Penance, not that we could find. Nor claw marks, though each attested they had been attacked." Panset prodded the creature again, exposing a little more blood. "Nor did they have any of this black blood on them. Just torn clothes or bruising."

"Then we surmise this sickness is passed by bite or direct wounds. Like the disease the Khund's claim their giant lizards spread. Mmmm," said the priest.

"That was our thought," cut in High Lord Penance. He took another stride closer, to within six feet of the cage. "And a sickness. An infection. Foul."

"How many are there?" asked the queen, knowing the answer but needing it aired.

"We have hunted and burnt a hundred or more. Rumours are a similar number roam the roads and forests near Pantsil, maybe more. We surmise Rusholme and Dent are clear, but it only takes one to start spreading it again."

A snap of bone greeted Panset's final words, and Queen Erin looked on in horror as the Infected's arm wrenched clear of the clasp nailed over it, leaving the hand and wrist behind. Black blood sprayed, showering Panset and on, towards High Lord Penance.

"No!" she shouted.

Two of the Rangers drove their spears through the cage and deep into the husked body, pinning it to the coffin. The third tracked the errant arm as Panset threw himself backwards. The spear pierced the errant limb at the elbow, and the Ranger rammed the tip into the floor of the wooden coffin. Thick, black blood flowed, and the white in the creature's eyes faded. Panset rolled away, threw his helm aside, and checked his face for any ingress.

Queen Erin ran to High Lord Penance, only for Captain Mordant to step in her way. As she dodged, he wrapped an arm around her waist. Erin tried to wrench herself free, to no avail. One of the Rangers made to move towards the High Lord, eyes filled with horror, until a brief smile flickered. She shook her head, clearly changing her mind, and checked on Panset instead. The High Lord turned. The front of his body was wreathed in a purple glow, his ever-present cane held before him, its metal handle pulsing. Silence lay thick in the courtyard. Soldiers watched on in awe as the spiritfire held the blackened blood at bay. Each drop sizzled, the smell of death and rot masked by ash and fire.

"Damn," he whispered and, with an open palm, sent the remaining spiritfire over Panset's armour. As the last of the Infected's blood burnt away, he let his power drop, shoulders hunching momentarily.

The High Lord turned back to the queen, and the courtyard full of onlookers. "Penance has defended me this day," he said. "Look to your prayers." The yard watched on silence. "Yes?"

The onlooking soldiers' eyes all dropped to the ground. Their hands crossed upon their weapons in front, lips moving. The High Lord glanced over to the Ranger who had come to his aid, and gave her a brief nod. It was returned with a rueful smile, and he approached the queen.

"Clear the yard," said the queen, pulling herself clear of Mordant's arm. His face reddened, and he fell to one knee. "If you think I punish anyone for doing their duty, you are mistaken. The fault lies with me. Now, empty the yard, Captain, except for my Rangers and King Panset."

The rattle from the cage came as no surprise. A glance over to the now definitely *ex*-sergeant was enough to confirm the frustration on the abdicated king's face as his gauntlets wrapped about the bars.

"I know you know, Captain. I saw you conversing. Now that everyone does, *he* can stop pretending and do what this realm needs."

Mordant rose, head lowered, before meeting the queen's eyes. He nearly spoke, lips quivering a little. Then he bowed his head and turned away to fulfil his orders.

"Move out," he bellowed. "Guards, into your secondary positions. Clear this yard." He strode off, shoving and needling his soldiers as he felt necessary.

The Rangers remained, the three spears still pinning the Infected against the coffin's back. She stared at the milky eyes, the jaw that continually widened and snapped shut in a slowing rhythm.

"It's too dangerous to examine," said Kinst, breaking the silence. "Priest Rinkot agrees, despite the Rangers' efforts." As the priest nodded, the queen finally placed the man. He was Lord Wisdom's physician, who had treated Prince Consort Adama after the retreat. Meanwhile, Kinst smiled from ear to ear, likely due to High Lord Penance's exposure.

"As do I," added High Lord Penance. "Duke Panset, if you please?"

Panset shook his head wearily at the expected title of an abdicated king. With a sigh, he approached the cage gate and accepted the key from a clearly amused Ranger. "Keep laughing, First Ranger Yanik, and you'll be overseeing my horse's dung bag."

Once out, with the gate closed behind, he stood facing the cage with High Lord Penance at his side. "We burn them at your insistence. Is Penance able to do that too?"

"Two exposed secrets in one day are enough, your Grace. Both are out in the world right now, whispers flying. Let's not overdo it." High Lord Penance grimaced, his right hand wrapped about the cane top. Though gloved, the exposed wrist revealed completely healed skin.

"Agreed. My queen, may I dispose of this *thing*?" Panset said, turning to find Queen Erin once again on her throne, a stern-faced Captain Mordant at her side.

"This one, and all the others, Duke Panset." She held up a scroll, its seal broken. "I agree with General Zendril's assessment. You have a talent for burning, as she puts it, these *bastards*."

6
BEACHED

Somewhere in the Realm of
Apso-Tran

Laoch dragged himself across the wet sand. Reaching the first of the grassy dunes, he turned over and scanned the ominous sky. A pulse at his side signalled a query. Agreeing, he placed his hand on the sigil of his God. The pommel glowed, and Justice soothed his bruises.

"Seven bloody Hells," he whispered as he noted how the clouds roiled above, the unnatural swirls punctuated by trails of something passing through their lower reaches. "Spirits?"

"I'd say so," answered Oisin, who sat on the first patch of dry sand, Ecne against his knee. Her eyes finally flickered open.

"Shit." Laoch eyed the sky for a few more seconds, then turned his attention to the Elite Ranger. "How is she?"

"She awoke briefly when Nathair hit the sea," replied Oisin.

"*She* is fine. Just a little bruised and wet. What happened?" Ecne shifted, and she strained her neck to look up at Oisin.

"Nathair threw herself into the sea along the edge of the beach," he replied, and rubbed the back of his neck while frowning at the heat. "As to why, I do not know, though the pain spirits have gone."

"In the water?" Ecne sat up and turned back to peer down the beach. The huge dragon lay half in the sea, its orange metal scales dulled at the rear. A faint lustre at the front pulsed in and out. "No!" She tried to push herself to her feet, and staggered a little until Laoch grabbed her arm from behind.

"What's wrong?" he growled, and held her steady.

"Wrong? Look at her. What do you see?" Ecne shoved herself away from Laoch. Though unsteady, she made her way towards the metal dragon. "The part of her in the water."

Laoch looked properly then, focusing on the task and ignoring the trouble above his head. His mind clicked through the illogic of a spirit-driven dragon, to something he knew – a half-doused fire. And that was exactly how Nathair looked.

"She must have gone in the sea to destroy the attacking spirits," he said, glancing at the waterline and the difference in the scales.

"And suffers. We need to get her out," Ecne said. On reaching the dragon's twisted neck, she placed her hands on the pulsing scales. "Nathair?"

"She weighs more than I can even imagine, Ecne. We'd need twenty oxen to even lift the head," added Oisin, catching up. He glanced to the top of the surrounding dunes. "And I don't like that we can't see what's going on inland. The Soul Tear we suffered swept through all our people; everyone knew *something* had happened. I'd guess whoever lives here will be far more aware of such things than we were. Especially after being invaded, however long ago it was. Nathair did not rip her way in, but those spirits saw us as an enemy, and *someone* placed them there on guard."

A sudden sense of danger ran up Laoch's spine. They were one less, and however much losing Sura hurt, the practicalities of keeping them safe had become that much harder. He glanced over at Oisin, then back up the dune, trying to decide who led. Another tangle in their relationship, after the spider bite and the necromancer's influence.

The mountain man dipped his head, fully aware he was being assessed. "It's still there. However much I hate it, the venom is locked down, but far from gone."

Laoch read the frustration in the man's eyes. "Then ...?"

"Aye. You lead until I'm healed. I won't like it, mind. Just so you know that." Oisin slapped him on the arm. "But I wouldn't relinquish it to any other, either."

"Then take the dune top. Scout what's out there and report back. And be bloody careful." Laoch nodded up towards the summit, and the Handren immediately headed up the thirty-foot dune.

Laoch turned back to find Ecne with her head against the dragon's scaled neck, her eyes dancing about. He made to speak, only for a familiar finger to rise and cut him off. Laoch waited, his famed impatience gnawing at his mood.

Eventually, the acolyte pushed herself away from the metal. She blinked before speaking. "She's weak, but there. Her rear legs are paralysed. The sea water leeches any spiritfire she sends that way." Ecne turned her head to one side, fingers drumming on a scale. "I don't know how to help."

Laoch gazed up the beach and towards the dune. Pebbles mingled with sea debris, rope and torn nets amid the odd tangles of driftwood that formed lines along the sand. Something his mother knew well and yearned for often, though she had only ever returned to the docks of Jense with him a few times to see his grandfather.

"There'll be tides," he said. "The sea will rise and fall. I don't know enough to say how far, but that should help. If there's anything of Keran in there, *she* needs to ask *him*."

Ecne leaned against the beast again, her lips moving, taxing Laoch's patience once again. He hated not knowing.

A call caught his attention; not a sea bird. The sound, familiar to him, was likely foreign to this strange realm. Oisin signalled again from the dune's rim, the call insistent. With a sigh as he contemplated the climb, he checked on Ecne. If he went, he left her alone. For all her strength and determination, the acolyte was not a Ranger, and once embroiled in a task, lost awareness of potential dangers around her.

Damn, but I have to trust her. And Wisdom.

"Anything? I have to check on Oisin. He's seen something."

"She's examining their shared memories and experiences. Nathair agrees you have a good point about the tide. They are trying to work out where in the tidal cycle we may be. They will need to watch and learn, possibly a good while. She is hungry too."

"And food means spiritfire. That will help her strength," added Laoch.

"But it needs to be ... to be alive, Laoch. Dead is of no use." Ecne's mouth twisted. "But what choice do we have?"

"None. Keep an eye out while I check on Oisin. Anyone could sneak up on you when your mind's occupied. I won't be long. Keep your crossbow handy."

With that, he turned away, one hand resting on the pommel of his sword, and walked up the dune. The shifting sand made the going difficult and slow. By the time he crawled the last few yards to fall in beside the Handren, he had decided his mother was wrong in her love for the beach.

Oisin pointed. "See the tree line? Those woods are very different from our own. Lush, as if there's a lot of rain and sun here. And there—" He raised his spyglass to check before lowering it again. "There's a wide track running through the middle. Another runs off it, down to a gap in the dunes about a hundred yards that way." He pointed to the right.

"No people?" asked Laoch. He fumbled for his own spyglass.

"None that I've seen. I think we are heading for dusk. The sun is falling," Oisin added.

"That's good. Gives us some time, I hope, and cover for the night. Nathair is weak and hungry, but we think the sea may recede at some point."

Laoch turned the spyglass back on the trees, tracking in the direction he now assumed was northwards. Here, the tree line altered, the plants shorter and thicker at the base. Something moved about their roots. His mind eventually worked out what he was seeing.

"The sea enters the trees there," he said, pointing. "A mangrove, like the one south of Makalena."

"Why is that important? Not a place I would like to visit. It must stink." Oisin wrinkled his nose.

"I've not been, but I've heard stories. Lots of animals – food for our dragon, and unlikely to be many people. Come on. If we start now, we can be back before dusk."

"Wisdom has agreed," said Ecne, placing her hand on the crossbow's sigil. "She will provide what she can if it will help."

Nathair's response was weak, distant, and in her mind. *But remains reluctant while you are alone and undefended, which I can understand. The sea recedes. In a few minutes, my wings will be clear. With Wisdom's help, I may be able to drag myself further up the beach.'*

Ecne smiled, pleased she could finally help. Laoch's comment about her crossbow had fired her mind, but Wisdom's doubts had surprised her. There remained a distrust of the Spirit Walker, borne, she thought, upon ancient memories of its hate and hunger. A thousand years of fear could not be overcome in a few weeks, and harkened Ecne's thoughts back to the Gods' reluctance to help Sura when the whitefire had taken her. Could they have helped? Had they refused because they feared being weakened as Nathair grew strong?

A *thunk* broke her reverie, and Ecne shook herself free of her thoughts. A wooden spear quivered, point down, between her legs. Realisation struck, and she threw herself aside as a second one clanged into Nathair's horned head, the fire-hardened tip shattering against the metal.

Ecne felt for her crossbow, grasped the stock and dragged it behind Nathair's front paw. Then, bringing it to her eye, she sighted along the glowing quarrel towards the southern reach of the beach. A touch from Wisdom on her mind, and the image drew in closer, much as it had at the Constructor's palace. She could make out the humped backs of her assailants, hunkered down behind sea-smoothed rocks. One knelt to peer her way. His shaggy hair was tied back around large ears.

Human.

The cheeks were weather-worn and scarred, the clothes roughly sewn but functional. In his hands was another spear, this one tipped with bone, though there appeared no intent to throw it. Instead, the tribesman was shouting towards her, or possibly the dragon, the spear raised like a challenge.

"Why?" she said to herself, unsure of what was happening.

A shout, a guttural bark, reached her, and another rose from behind the rocks to hurl their spear. It sailed up and over her head to crash below Nathair's crystal eye. Splinters fell. A few landed in her hair.

Ecne was now more confused than ever. "Do I loose?" she asked, hoping Wisdom would answer, only for the question to become moot. A flash of blue signalled Oisin's return.

The spiritfire arrow smashed into the rocks where the leader stood. The light flared, and the man threw himself backwards, accompanied by fear-filled shouts. A second eruption showered the rocks, this one red.

The flare illuminated seven other tribespeople who quickly backed away, dragging their leader with them. They all carried spears, perhaps a knife at their sides on a rough belt. The few words that flew between them were short and barked.

Ecne, deciding against using precious spiritfire to see them on their way, watched until they were lost to her sight around the curve of the beach. A call from behind signalled Laoch and Oisin's approach and, needing to keep watch on the beach, she glanced around Nathair's foot to find the pair of Rangers carrying a large lizard strung up on a pole between them. The range of teeth along its jaw was quite a fearsome sight. However, the stink from their mud-caked breeches was far worse.

"Fresh, pissed-off lizard," Laoch said, and dropped the burden in front of Nathair's head. "And another awaiting our return. Made some new friends?"

"If that was friendly, I'd hate to see them angry. They were aiming for Nathair, I think. And you two are not so fresh. You stink." Ecne pulled out a scarf from her pocket and dabbed at her nose.

"Yeah, tell me about it," said Oisin. The Handren wore a little more mud than Laoch, his cloak and leather armour caked.

"You missed. Can't blame me for that," added Laoch, a grin appearing between his mud-caked cheeks. "Face first. You should have heard the swearing. Put me to bloody shame. We'll fetch the second, Ecne. Watch for their return. This time, you may have to hurt one."

"Wait, I have an idea."

She checked on Wisdom, who once again seemed reluctant, but the sliver of her God still agreed. She set the symbol against Nathair's scales. The green glow increased, and splashed against the orange scales. Her God gave, though slowly, allowing the spiritfire to enter the ancient foe.

'Enough.'

Nathair shuddered. The dragon's jaw pried apart, and the smell of old oil mingled with burnt flesh wafted over them. The neck bent, and with a sideways snap of the jaw, the sword-length teeth bit deep into the lizard, pole and all. As blood squirted, the dragon crunched again, and the rest of the creature disappeared. Whitefire laced her teeth while a glint returned to the crystal eyes.

"Move," said Ecne, just as Nathair's warning flashed into her mind.

She scrambled to one side as the artifice's wings lifted into the sky. A tremor ran along the forelegs, and stricken joints screamed. The feet drove deep into the sand a few yards further up the beach, just as the wings beat down once. A second shudder, and Nathair's wings and legs heaved her another few yards forwards. The rear legs were now out of the sea, the talons digging into the wet beach. A shimmer rode her scales, a wave of energy that rolled along her spine and into the joints of her powerful rear legs.

With her limbs completely out of the steel-grey sea, Nathair continued to drag herself up until her tail was also clear of the water's edge. Spiritfire sparked along her spine, and when it reached the tail's tip, the dragon pushed herself up from the sand.

"Where?" rumbled Nathair's voice.

"That way," answered Laoch, pointing northwards. "There's a mangrove full of them. And the sea is mainly out."

"Good."

And the dragon leapt into the air.

7

A FIRST SIGHTING

OUTER VEIL, BRANDSHOLD

The Fleshmaster placed a gauntleted hand upon the heartstone, and sensed the Spirit Walker's ill ease. Ahead, the first veil curtain pulsed powerfully, its purple taint a threat as well as a promise of the nectar held within. Tabharthóir hovered, sensing the sheer power being held back, and fearful of the skills required to slip between its bonds.

"Emperor?" said Popsilin. The captain prowled at the edge of the pocket, her mind still clouded after Tarin had forced her awake. "Is everything okay?"

"See to your Inhibitors, Captain. Wake them slowly and leave me to focus." Tarin looked over his armoured shoulder, eyes dancing with whitefire. "Yes?" He smiled, and exposed metal teeth laced with the same power. Popsilin's flinch provided more pleasure than he expected.

Hold your emotions, child.

The scuffle of booted feet on the bronze floor signalled her departure to follow his orders, to check in on her squad, whose role could define the future of the coming invasion. Trusting such things to a menial did not come lightly, but Popsilin had shown herself worthy. And so few of the originators survived.

This one I can trust, for now.

The Fleshmaster slipped his thoughts into the crystal and, wrapping the Spirit Walker in a sliver of his soul, demanded calm. The spirit was now one with the mechanics of the artifice Tabharthóir, but with much to learn. As if it wore the metal skin, rather than fully melded with it. But for what they started today, it was the Spirit Walker he needed, not the dragon.

His *seeking* rode a wave of whitefire, as if ripples in a pond, and crashed into the twinned wyrms that preceded the metal dragon. Their collars flared in response, searing the skin, and Tabharthóir quivered. Nothing was more pleasurable for a veil dragon to consume than the sweet, spiritfire-soaked flesh of a wyrm.

"Not for you, Tabharthóir. A reward for the future, perhaps, for when we have the Seven, or their kin, in chains."

A *need* graced his mind in response, a desire. And above all else, a signal that the Spirit Walker was fully his now. A twisted servant of the Fleshmaster.

"Yes."

The wyrms responded to the urging of their collars, sweeping around the veil curtain at the hurried pace only the young use. They tasted and probed while the artifice dragon followed, its Spirit Walker learning from each of the wyrms in turn. They spoke of the ebb and flow of the spiritfire, how it rolled with the surges inside, thickening in places, thinning in others. Each experience added to the spirit's store of knowledge.

Eventually they came to rest, waiting in one place, side by side, their message clear. Tabharthóir swept in, reading their signs, and compared their chosen spot to the curtain that surrounded it.

"Yes?" thought Tarin, and the image spilled into his mind. A Schenterenta shaman flanked by his tribe, each kneeling, a pool of glimmering water at their centre. A song rose, immersed in moonlight that shone back brighter than any spiritfire. The shaman's words wove the light, forming a bowl within which elven spirits whirled, dervishes of joy and energy. With each change in pitch and adjustment of rhythm, the spirits' dance altered, creating a story of beauty and honour that was lost upon the Fleshmaster. It spoke of only one thing to him: a way to the Seven.

The keening rose within the Spirit Walker, blackened by the venom, twisted by the loss of its twin and the desire to feed to sate its grief. The intensity increased, and the dead hairs upon the Fleshmaster's skin danced to its pulse. Tabharthóir spat whitefire towards the curtain. Its impact caused the veil to ripple and the curtain to weaken. And, with a beat of blue-silver wings, she slid between the bonds and entered Penance's veil.

"Yessss ... that scent, the tingle upon the tongue. This I remember as if it was yesterday ..." Tarin writhed, trying to control the urges surging through his body. If he gave in now, he would be lost to the soul-lust, the aroma pervading the veil almost too much to bear.

"So much at once, the temptation... ahhh. But it is woven, used. Old and useless to me. It would melt upon my tongue, a memory with no sustenance." He gripped the heartstone and wrapped himself about the crystal. The strength of its bonds helped to hold his mind steady as he fought the rising lust.

"Fleshmaster?" said Popsilin, eyeing her emperor with trepidation, his desire evident, as she edged into the room.

Tarin wrenched his head round, eyes filled with hunger and, at that moment, unadulterated hate for Popsilin – a meat sack that denied him its spirit.

"Leave," he roared between clenched teeth. "NOW." Power whirled amid the words and whitefire slammed into Popsilin, sending her reeling back into the darkness.

Must quench this before I lose myself and Tabharthóir.

He let his soul seep from the bonded stone, expecting to find the Spirit Walker as lost as he to the soul-lust. Except it wasn't. Instead, the spirit watched him emerge, fascinated. Unnerved, the Fleshmaster sent out a lash of command, whipping his servant, and demanded she seek the next curtain. His dominance reinstated, Tarin steadied his thoughts and built a cage around the lust, locking it down.

Tabharthóir responded to the command, wheeling about to search the curtain and heeding the young wyrms that had swept in behind her to feed. They sent the image of a symbol, one written in spiritfire. A sigil of sheer power that would seek her out, its goal her destruction. The wyrms were too small, and had failed to trigger the glyphs on their first entry to the realm. But they sensed its power, the latent need to destroy all who trespassed.

Heeding the warning, Tabharthóir flew in circles about the next curtain, searching for a weakness. With her newly developed instinct to hunt, to seek entry, she had finally become a true dragon of the veil.

—

"We risk much, Captain. Understand? All seven veils are strong, and signify unprecedented power we must understand if we are to be successful." Tarin stood before the blue-silver scales of his dragon, arms crossed, eyes locked on the captain and her squad. "Mondrein took our ancient Wyrm, and that was but one veil. Learn all you can here about the Magi. And that takes subtlety, yes? The ancient Inhibitor who gave the last of their spirit to inform us of this hidden realm wove a sign of the Seven, an indication they are still known. That they may yet hold power here. I need to know for sure."

Popsilin slammed her hand to her chest, the fist slapping above the heart that barely moved. In there, her spirit retained a shallow root, one that had been ripped and separated many hundreds of years ago by the Fleshmaster himself.

"Yes, Emperor," she said. "I understand."

"Make sure you do. This will be a different war, Popsilin, one where information is near as powerful as the spiritfire we crave. I go to seek your Scorpion scouts and learn what I can. You have but a few nights. I cannot risk being seen, understand? If you are late, then you know what must be done." The Emperor flashed a glare to each of the Inhibitors in turn, his scowl laden with metal teeth. "But the rewards will be sweet, yes? With such power in the veils, I suspect there will be many magi of lower status here. Ones that such as yourselves could feast upon for a millennium, *should* I allow it."

The shift in mood was palpable. The Inhibitors looked to each other before they saluted as one.

"Good." Tarin turned about and headed into the dragon's chest to be swallowed by the shimmer of the artifice's scales.

As he strode over to the heartstone, the Spirit Walker informed him of the Inhibitors melting into the forest, lost to all normal sight in the dark of night, but not to those attuned to their spirits.

"Above the clouds, Tabharthóir," he sent. *"We are fortunate the moon is shrouded here, but it will not be so everywhere. We cannot risk another seeking this close to a city. Likely too many magi to sense our presence; maybe even the Seven. The Mechanised Inhibitor pilots were told to head north, so north*

we go. Let us hope they carried out their duty, eh? And died as a Constructor should, in the service of their emperor."

With each beat of her wings, the dragon rose. The emperor revelled in the power his artifice demonstrated, and the prospect of battling and subjugating the Seven with the mechanised beast. They broke through the clouds, bathed in the half-moon's light, though the presence of Honour's curtain above gnawed at the back of his mind. It had a strange flavour, a merger of something ancient, like his own people, and that of the Magus herself. Each of the other veils had sparked recognition, the initial desire caged by his expectation and resolve, with the heartstone's help. But this was something different, and he hated not knowing. He was close to redeeming all his choices of the last thousand years, to bringing his people back from the cusp of true death and into the glow of the Magi's spiritfire. Once they were under his wing yet again, he could loosen the bonds, free his people from constant war.

If I want to. But not a full return to the decadence of old. We have moved on.

Tabharthóir shuddered and her scales sparkled as a weak pulse of spiritfire coated her plates. The last wave of the *seeking* they'd sent out on breaking through the final veil had returned to its maker. Two pieces of knowledge spilled into the Fleshmaster's mind, but one took precedence.

"What is this?" the Fleshmaster said, hands placed firmly against one facet. "No."

A dragon filled his mind, though it was a mere outline – the spiritfire *seeking* weak and unable to provide detail. Elongated and sinuous, this dragon flew with a grace Tabharthóir could not yet match. The emperor felt a stirring, his thoughts muddled. He had presumed the veil dragons dead, destroyed by whatever magic the Seven had concocted. Perhaps trapped by the Magi's deviousness and drained dry, or blasted from the sky by them striking in unison.

But dead, otherwise they would have returned to their master.

His *seeking* could not lie. A veil dragon flew on, and therefore its Spirit Walker still thrived. An ally, one that would know of the Seven or their descendants, perhaps even fed off them. An opportunity and a gift, wrapped in the scales of an ancient artifice dragon.

"*An Chéad.*"

With a demand, Tabharthóir rode an updraft and headed further north with each stroke of her wings. As the Fleshmaster closed in on his new prize, all thoughts of staying hidden from those below were lost. He shaped a thought, laced with whitefire, and drove it outwards towards the valley. A spear of his will.

And as An Chéad trumpeted his success, tearing a mountain lion apart with bloodied talons, the *calling* slammed into the mechanised beast. The Fleshmaster's will pierced the scarlet scales and penetrated a silenced heart-stone. An Chéad screamed, his spirit bathed in the light of the emperor, his original master. He writhed amid its malevolent power.

The Unspoken, angered, embittered, drove her will into the crystal and quashed the Fleshmaster's demand. Anger gushed from her, driven by a fear of what she might lose.

"Finish your meal," she said. "War has begun."

8

A SILENT CITY

Unknown City, Apso-Tran

"Well? Any thoughts?" asked Laoch, sweeping his spyglass along the smooth city walls that rose above the sand-laden ground.

"I can't climb them," replied Oisin, moving his own spyglass as he searched for a route. "At least, not without a rope tied about a merlon, or from the roof of one of those towers."

Laoch raised his spyglass higher, taking in the battlements and towers that stood, evenly spaced, between them. The level of skill involved reminded him of the macabre buildings of Innealtóir, though these were built with more simplicity and beauty despite their function of keeping everything well and truly out. No one stirred along the walls, something that impinged on his instincts and added a little dread to his thoughts.

"Where bloody are they?" he asked, his voice gruff.

"It is far from abandoned. No place would be so pristine if it were." Oisin dropped his spyglass. "The gates are barred, but no guards. They have a ditch between to prevent direct attack. They prepare for war, yet where is their army? I am at a loss."

"We can't risk Nathair flying over. The fear she would instil if seen will cock up any chance of a friendly conversation," stated Laoch, peering across to where the sun hovered above the horizon. They had stayed at the beach through the day, waiting for their dragon to return from its feast. Sated, Nathair had come back with word of a city whose towers she had seen rising above the horizon a little further to the north. A port, perhaps.

"I'd say we have an hour before dusk. And the clouds gather over the sea; a storm, perhaps. If that sweeps inland, then maybe she could fly over before full night falls." Oisin nodded towards the grey sea and the brewing storm. "A plan, at least."

"Aye. More bloody waiting." Laoch slapped the man on the back. "Stay here. Signal if you catch sight of whoever lives in that ghost city. One thing is for sure, they won't be throwing wooden twigs at dragons."

Laoch slid down the tree to the forest floor. The wet ground sucked at his boot and he swore, the darkness under the thick canopy a contrast his eyes struggled to cope with. The munching of metal and flesh ahead drew him towards Nathair. The dragon sat with forelegs extended, and the Spirit Walker itself stood conversing with Ecne as she roasted something that, until recently, had swung about the trees.

"Laoch," said Ecne, as she lifted her eyes from the searing meat. "Anything?"

He shook his head in response. "Nothing. It's as if they knew we were coming and ran for the bloody hills."

"Maybe closer to the truth than you think," said Nathair, her lizard-slitted eyes falling upon the Ranger. "If they saw me fall, or knew the pain spirits attacked one such as me, then perhaps they hide within the walls. Waiting. I appear as a hunter to them, a predator. We are here because the Constructors lost a battle to these people. They likely see me as a return of their artifices, even if they have not seen a veil dragon before."

"Aye. And we need to know. Oisin suggests you fly above the city when it's dark, or if the storm comes this way."

"Agreed." Behind the Spirit Walker, metal teeth crunched down, the snap of bones not lost on Laoch as the mechanical dragon chuffed. "And if Ecne rides with me, you can stop fretting about her all the time."

Ecne glanced up and smiled at Laoch, who shook his head in response, eyes to the sky.

"Nathair says you've just transferred your worries – your need to protect – to me. I get it. I'm not concerned, but just remember, I have a God on my side." Ecne patted her crossbow. The sigil glowed gently in return.

"I don't know what in the Seven Hells you're talking about. I just know I need that brain of yours, otherwise I have to do all the thinking, and then we're really in the shit. Besides, if I didn't look after you, Sura would never forgive me."

The mention of Sura's name caused Ecne to flinch. Laoch let the flicker of guilt pass. They were, after all, picking at *him*.

"Okay, Ecne rides with you. Oisin and I will get in closer and take a look at that gate."

Ecne placed her hands on the heartstone. Nathair's touch upon her mind established a connection. She found herself drawn into the stone, seeing through the dragon's eyes with terrifying clarity. At the back of her mind, Wisdom pulsed a nagging warning. The sliver of her God had saved her so many times, yet now it felt like an overbearing weight. She was flying, and it was amazing, however much it annoyed Wisdom.

Lightning flashed, crackling from the thunderclouds to lash the grey sea with regularity. Nathair had seeped a little whitefire across her scales as her presence, she said, added an extra ferocity to the storm. Yet she held steady. Compared to the battle with the pain spirits, this was a gentle ride.

The sea met a curved wall of piled rocks ahead, the breaker smoothing the water on the inside as it neared the open mouth of the city docks. Towers loomed either side, highlighted from below by the flashes of electricity ripping into the ocean. The windows were shuttered at the top, though when open, they would have a full view of the approach to the city.

"Warning towers," said Ecne. "Lookouts for errant dragons."

'They are prepared for something, yes,' agreed Nathair. Her gaze alighted on the bobbing ships tied to the docks, their wooden hulls sleek, except for one barrel-chested boat that swayed heavily in the storm.

All the sails were stowed, and some masts had been lowered to the decks. Ecne had little understanding of what such things could mean, but Nathair bore Keran's knowledge.

'They knew a storm was coming, and none of these ships bear the mark of waiting in the harbour long. Their hulls are too clean, no weed marks as if they've been sat. The people are here, somewhere.'

The dragon rose, wings angled to catch the wind, pushing herself deeper into the clouds as she approached the edge of the city and its taller towers. The driving rain splattered on their slate roofs; the metal rods stationed above them taking the brunt of the storm's ire. Nowhere did anything stir.

'Prepare yourself, Learned. This will feel very strange.'

Ecne's eyes flared as her brain flooded with sights it couldn't comprehend. With the barest caress from Wisdom, the scene calmed, and her mind cut through the noise of white glare. Every building shimmered in her vision, each appearing as if built of light.

'They have sealed the buildings with spiritfire. Unless they have a power way beyond us all, even your magi, I believe they have been feeding those walls for centuries,' sent Nathair, the wisp of her words and the bow of her head almost a deference to the power they beheld. *'They hide not just behind stone, but behind spiritfire. They are within, and we must leave.'* The dragon swept on above the city, dipping a wing as lightning struck between the central buildings.

"Leave?" whispered Ecne. Her heart thrummed against her chest. "This is beautiful."

'And dangerous. As it was with Marbhleoir at the emperor's palace. Such power could destroy us. Even me, Ecne. If they release all that at once, I fear the consequences for anything in its path.'

A peal of thunder echoed about the buildings, and Nathair took one last look at the city as she prepared to fly into the roiling heavens.

"Wait!" shouted Ecne, the storm forcing her words louder than she intended. "There, in the centre." She tried to get the dragon's head to turn, though she rode only its eyes. The control remained with the Spirit Walker. "Please, look to the middle, where there is a gap between the buildings."

The artifice dragon continued to spiral upwards, but strained her neck to peer down into the centre of the city. There, a mirror reflected the storm. Lightning flared back off it, black and steel-grey clouds swirling between each flash.

"What is that?" said Ecne, urging Nathair to focus in, though wary of how brightly the storm reflected back.

Nathair responded, her reluctance swayed by the curious feature. As her dragon-sight pulled the object closer, the glare threatened to overwhelm her crystalline eyes.

"It's ... it's ..." Ecne's mind detected Wisdom's tug at her memories, and an image slipped in. A moon pool before a Constructor's house, Sura talking of her people and how such bodies of water were dotted around the Partera Plains. She let the image slide into Nathair, who's growl indicated agreement.

'*We must go. Now.*'

The storm stilled; the rage paused, but its potential hung ominously amid the thick air. An arc of energy sizzled towards the mechanical dragon from a pulsing stone tower, and the accompanying clap of thunder echoed through the streets. Nathair dropped like a stone. The artifice whirled downwards, frozen as if broken. Her cogs and wires stilled. Ecne lost all contact with the Spirit Walker as they dived towards the moon pool, the vision of an orange-hued dragon rushing towards her reflected on its surface.

"No!" she shouted, and braced against the heartstone. Ecne's heart slammed into her chest, expecting her death had come.

Nathair poured calm into her mind. '*I am here,*' came the Spirit Walker's thoughts.

Metal-skinned wings extended, and tipped the huge dragon into a spiral that brought her level with the ground. Talons split the moon pool, scraping the surface and disturbing its calm. She flew along a wide, curved street, folding in her wingtips, her momentum driving the dragon towards the docks. Nathair burst from between two warehouses, her forelegs crashing against the wooden masts of the moored ships. Some cracked, others wavered, rocking in the water at her passing. Splintered wood trailed behind as she emerged above the harbour.

Ecne sensed the Spirit Walker's wariness, the purpose of the twinned towers at the city's docks laid bare by the attack on the dragon. One strike, and they would be in the sea. And this time, the depth would drain her of all spiritfire and hope. True death, and Ecne's likely with it, entombed inside a stricken dragon upon the ocean floor.

Dragon wings beat against the prevailing wind, surging the metal beast out and away from the threat of the city.

"Laoch," murmured Ecne, "and Oisin."

'*On their own, for now,*' replied Nathair.

———

Laoch knelt by the stone pillar at the head of the bridge. To his side was the city's defensive ditch they had spied from the forest. Dry, it was filled with a vicious-looking thorn bush whose tendrils piled in on themselves and then stretched outwards, reaching for light and space to grow.

He signalled behind. Oisin, a cloak drawn over his back and head to dull his shape and appearance in the shadow of the roiling storm, knelt by the pillar on the other side. Laoch signed *wait*, followed by *eyes on*, and squeezed Justice's grip. The God's weapon dulled at his urging, the blade turning grey. He eyed the gateway one last time. The portcullis was down. Its metal, however, was shrouded in a mist he couldn't quite grasp. The air was warm despite the storm, and it made little sense.

Warily, he kept low as he approached, knowing Oisin watched with Fate's bow, ready to cover his back. The lack of guards still gnawed at his patience. The whole situation was alien to what he would expect. A trap. His mind tried to resow the doubt that had become his constant companion since the Unbeliever camp, and the agonising loss of his Spear.

Dark thoughts, and not helping.

Creeping slowly nearer, he watched the right-hand side with care as the guard station emerged from behind the curve of the castle entrance. A heavy, iron-bound door lay shut. Above it, and all along the outer keep, murder holes threatened death. More lay beyond the outer portcullis, and he suspected there'd be a second grill waiting to fall and cage attackers in. Everything screamed of preparation, of a people used to war – or at least, prepared for one.

No challenge came from either above or the sides. With a prayer to Justice, he glanced around the castle wall into the murk of the left side. No door, nor a guard.

Seven Hells, this is horseshit.

With a sigh, he turned back to signal Oisin in, only to flinch. The Ranger sat on the sodden floor; hands clasped around the back of his neck. Two figures in waxed cloaks stood behind him, their arrows at Oisin's back. A third and fourth sighted Laoch. Cat-like eyes locked on his, filled with absolute certainty of his death should he move. Like Sura's, their skin was a dappled ebony, their ears the final betrayal of their origins.

Schenterenta. Elves.

Words poured forth, a flow mixed with harsh syllables that grated at his mind. Whoever they were, they used similar swear words to the elf he mourned. With a glance towards the sky, he raised his hands, surprised to find one of them empty, and a heavy cuff bracelet bound beneath his bracer.

"*Tsen a briken ha,*" said a female warrior, her eyes afire, mouth set firm as she pointed her arrow towards the floor.

Laoch, his thoughts still on Sura, nodded as he recognised the intent of the gesture. He knelt, dropping his knee onto the mix of mud and straw on the stone bridge, cursing. He caught Oisin's glance. The Handren didn't appear surprised at the absence of his sword. The Ranger leant to the side, allowing his cloak to slide away, and there, along Oisin's left forearm, sat a similar bracer. Almost as if their Gods had planned for their ineptitude.

With a grimace, Laoch allowed the warrior elf to bind his arms. She pulled the leather tight, a threat whispered in his ear when he stiffened his muscles in the hope of adding a little give to the restraints. A knife to his back helped him stand up, and the rumble of metal on stone from behind let him know where they were heading next. He was forced roughly around and shoved forwards. Beyond the newly raised portcullis, soldiers waited. Their upper armour shone in the storm, awash with the lightning that cracked overhead. Their certainty only wavered for a second when the peels of thunder were split by the distant roar of an angry dragon.

"Oh shit."

9
A TRAITOROUS MEETING

HANDREN MOUNTAINS,
BRANDSHOLD

The Unspoken remained connected with her scarlet-scaled dragon, the heartstone pulsing beneath her touch as the huge wings beat at the frigid air of the mountain valley.

Do I take a high position, await what comes?

Or circle high? The predator who knows her home, setting the ambush.

"But he will know. A simple seeking will be enough. You were never built to fight your own, An Chéad, but to prey on those weaker. We may face an ending, you and I. The emperor lives, and comes to reclaim his slave."

The artifice dragon touched her mind in return, the memory of his initial response to the Fleshmaster's *seeking* sore upon his thoughts.

"You remain mine, An Chéad. That is good. Here, we are free of the demands of our kind. We do as we will, live as we see fit. I bow to no one, and all bow to me. I am queen in these mountains, with my dragon warrior at my side. I want nothing more ... nor anything less."

She let her other bone-white hand alight upon the heartstone, its pulse in response reassuring. Together, they spied a sharp-edged summit, one she had first perched upon a thousand years before, as she sought her place in this new realm. The betrayal of her people, and the dragon Nathair, had still been foremost in her mind then. The Seven had decreed her a hero and an outcast, and had bequeathed her land they neither owned nor understood. But it had not mattered, for amid the jagged peaks and green valleys, she had healed and grown.

"There, my dragon. We await our former master upon the last place we contemplated our betrayal. Fitting, no?" The Unspoken's mirth broke into glass-like laughter that echoed through the heartstone chamber. *"Yes, there."*

An Chéad hovered momentarily before his sharp talons gripped the rock, scarlet wings beating at the air twice as the sinuous dragon balanced himself, while crystal eyes peered into the fog-bound valley below. The Unspoken knew it intimately. A hunting ground when they first arrived, and now so once again, since reawakening the hungry dragon. She had allowed none of her Unbelievers to settle there, and the few Handren that had bred locally now resided in the belly of her beast. A consequence of High Lord Penance's wish for the Unspoken's dragon to rise and strike fear in people once again. Fear needs to be fuelled, both its conduit and the emotion itself.

"And may their flocks' prayers flow, for war is here. Can you feel it, An Chéad? The emperor approaches, and within an unfamiliar veil dragon. Three have become four. I do not like this. Be wary." The dragon twitched in response, and his tail twirled menacingly before settling back against the ragged rock.

Below, amid the swirl of fog, a pulse glowed, heralding an arrival she had hoped would never happen. The Unspoken had played her role for the Seven, had frightened their people into feeding the seven veils that protected the realm. For a thousand years they had lain undetected, a complex plan she had never expected to work, forged upon scripture and fear of her wrath.

Sheep shepherded by liars and thieves. But what becomes of the veils now?

Silver-blue wing tips broke the surface of the thick fog. The white tendrils furled, wisps wrapping about the metal skin as they carved their way ever upwards. The head was horned and spiked, and the eyes glowed eerily, their gaze focused upon her. The Unspoken sensed the emperor's power and his expectation. To her mind, he waited, ready to lash out should this encounter go wrong. That had been his way over a thousand years ago, when she had first become an Inhibitor, the name given to the few who sought service in return for the emperor's gift of spiritual immortality.

Will he remember me?

As a traitor, I expect so.

But I am a traitor and *a queen.*

The metal artifice emerged from the mist, a roar emanating from jaws that sparkled wetly in the dawn's light. The Unspoken judged the dragon to be longer than An Chéad, the tail whip-like and heavily spiked, its rear legs as powerful as Nathair's. An artifice of beauty and power, that glinted with menace. She shook herself free of doubt, refusing to allow awe of the veil dragon to overwhelm her thoughts. She drew up images of the first time she had laid hands upon the brilliant, scarlet scales of *her* dragon. The power of that connection, the *knowing*.

"We are one, An Chéad. Understand?"

Her own *seeking* pounded from her dragon's heartstone. Not a ripple upon the wind, but a javelin, driven towards the approaching emperor. It slammed into the mechanical beast's head, drilling down into the eyes to invade the silver-blue dragon's own heartstone. A laugh slipped from her, the Unspoken ignoring the nervous edge it displayed.

I face you as a queen. These are my mountains.

—

Tarin flinched, then roared, venting his anger through his hands as he beat at the heartstone.

"Such ignorance!" he bellowed. "How dare they?"

Husked hands slapped at the stone, gripping tight. The emperor attempting to dampen the emotions threatening his mind. Logic and reason were needed, and this Spirit Walker, or whoever rode *An Chéad*, had existed in this land for a thousand years. Perhaps the memories of his rule were distant, or lost amid the Seven's progeny. Reticent and fearful.

"Patience," he murmured through thin blue lips, his thick tongue running across metal teeth. His jaw tightened.

Tarin formed his response, carefully choosing each word before pouring his thoughts into the heartstone to follow the *seeking* back to its originator. He laced it with his power, whitefire crackling amid the placating words – an emperor, demanding his right to dominate.

"Well met. I, Emperor Tarin, thought you lost, An Chéad."

He smiled as the whitefire sparked amid the crystal eyes, sensing the flow of his words and spiritfire drive an attempt to reclaim *his* artifice deep into its stone heart. An Chéad's touch ignited welcome memories. The original, and greatest, of his veil dragons. He had brought the first of the magi to his court, dropped his prize from those blood-red talons at his master's feet. The taste sweet, ripe for the breeding and refinement of their particular flavour. A future they had all revelled in, fuelled by the growing power of his menagerie and his mechanical hunters.

An Chéad remained silent. The ferocity Tarin so remembered, caged, focused. The Spirit Walker mute; its venom subdued.

No longer my slave, but another's.

The Fleshmaster spread his thoughts and expanded the connection. His presence touched upon the inner facet of the stone. And there waited a Constructor. The revelation caused a second twitch of indecision within one usually so certain. An Inhibitor, one of the first given his gift in return for riding the dragons or guarding the magi within his menagerie. The emperor raked through his memories. The time so distant, the name escaped him, though her appearance perhaps not. The vibrant red hair, the glistening skin, pale blue eyes. The glamour the Inhibitor wore portrayed her as she had once been, but the name ...

"You were the pilot," he said, the words spilling unbidden. Annoyed, he continued, "You are *my* Inhibitor, and you ride within *my* dragon, yet I receive no welcome? You should be kneeling, joyful at my arrival. We have a realm to conquer, a people to feast upon and, I hope, Seven Magi to enslave."

Silence greeted his words, though he sensed something deeper on the other side of the stone. It remained distant, until the Inhibitor spoke.

"I would ask you to leave, but that was never your way. This realm is *mine*, as are the people I feed upon. I do with it what I will."

The ferocity and confidence pervading the reply stung the Fleshmaster's raw patience, and nagged at something even deeper. He felt Tabharthóir stir. The rumble of her cogs and wires reverberated within the metal hull, reflecting his own tension.

Admiral Lelion and this woman must never meet.

"I am your emperor, and that is my veil dragon. I say again, you are of my creation. Your spirit life my gift." The words were spat from between gritted teeth, his frustration at being denied barely contained. Husked hands pulsed against the stone. Whitefire arced from his fingertips to wreath the crystal. Tabharthóir beat her wings with increasing rigour up the valley side, the emperor's intent clear as he demanded the sun at their back.

"Yes. In return for service given. Now I serve none but myself, and An Chéad chooses his own path at my side. And I say again, this is my realm, my souls to feed upon, and you are to leave. I share with no one, not even an emperor."

The crimson, metal-skinned wings spread wide as a roar of defiance spilled over into a gush of dragon's fire that lit the frigid air. But, instead of following his silver-blue opponent, An Chéad dropped from the jagged summit and plummeted into the head of the valley.

"Run," spat Tarin, "but you are *mine,* and I will feast upon your traitorous soul and your corrupted Spirit Walker." With the command sent, the Fleshmaster gripped the heartstone as Tabharthóir dropped headfirst, spearing towards the scarlet veil dragon that shimmered in the rising sun. The coward headed for the fog and escape, and they would both be damned if that was to happen.

Tabharthóir roared her defiance, the excitement of the hunt thrilling through her metal-shod soul. The speed of descent belied the emperor's expectations, and the younger veil dragon positioned her forelegs ready to strike. With talons extended, she aimed for the gap between An Chéad's wings. Ripping deep into that spot, the bladed talons could slice through the traitor's metal spine and wire, condemning the dragon to the valley below. Tabharthóir's soul-lust blasted into the emperor, dulling his senses to all but the death strike, the inexperience of the Spirit Walker overwhelming reason.

An Chéad spread his wings, the twitch of wire and the whirr of cogs filling the metal skin with air and fog. He caught the morning thermal, the billowing air rising as it greeted the sun. The mighty dragon jerked upwards, suddenly gaining height, leaving the silver-blue flash of scales to fly on by. Flame shot forth, but not a gout. Rather, one wrapped in on itself, a ball of spiritfire-infused flame that burned into Tabharthóir's right wing. The skin parted, peeling back, as the fireball seared through to splash against her scaled hull.

Tabharthóir screamed, a mix of agony and fear. The Spirit Walker, attuned to its artifice body, suffering the memory of pain much as the Constructors who had built it. The emperor fought the agony, trying to lock down the plethora of sensations assailing his mind and body. He knew they dropped. His thoughts paralysed by a combination of the dragon's pain and his dread. But still he pulled his hands free of the heartstone, and with his mind released from Tabharthóir's, he locked out the fear. Able to sift through his mind for reason and logic, memories flooded in of the Great Artificer Viseri's first attempts at flight. The snapping of machinery, the soul-shifts that left wings rigid and unpowered. Experimentation the artificer had shared with him.

Tarin splayed his fingers upon the stone and a flood of whitefire pierced the crystal's bonds. Domination spewed inwards, a demand for control, and he ripped the Spirit Walker's *will* from its spirit. At that moment, Tabharthóir became his, the Walker's form a mere shell the emperor now controlled. The dragon's mechanism responded directly to his will, and he curled the wings inwards, extending the dive while sending out a seeking to gauge the time and height that remained. A dust-filled breath slipped from his lips as the wings unfurled, mirroring An Chéad's earlier actions. The air caught, and the tear in the right wing widened while the rest of the metal skin held fast.

"Now," said the Fleshmaster, and he tipped the artifice. The topmost wing swept the metal dragon towards the lower part of the valley. A second yaw, and the dragon's damaged wing rose, the adjustment enough to straighten the metal beast to fly parallel to the deepening valley floor. Still they dropped rapidly, and the emperor commanded the forelegs to extend. The dragon bounced from rock to grassy hillock. The stress upon its limbs was immense but, supplemented by whitefire, they eventually caught enough purchase to launch themselves above the taller, tree-clad bulges of land. Ahead, at the end of the valley, the ground flattened out onto a grassy plain. With wings fully extended, the emperor twisted their angle once more to emerge from the remnants of the mist above land exposed to the sun.

Drawing on Tabharthóir's whitefire reserve, Tarin poured most into the damaged wing to compensate for the injury. Storing his hate and need for cold, hard revenge for later, he commanded the dragon to fly up towards the veils and escape.

Piercing the clouds, he flew through Honour's veil, slipping between the bonds designed to keep the Constructors out, not in, abandoning Popsilin and her Inhibitors to their fate.

But I live.

IO

THE COUNCIL OF DREAD

GODS' COUNCIL CHAMBER, HOUSE
OF PENANCE, ERSTENBURGH,
BRANDSHOLD

"No," said Lady Fate, her face red, sweating under her cobalt blue robes. "You can't. It will be the end of ... of everything. It will split this realm to the core, and end all trust in the Houses. In us. There will be no coming back." Her hands pressed down onto the heavy, sigil-inlaid table, whitening as the blood drained away from her knuckles under the pressure. "Please," she said breathlessly.

High Lord Penance bowed his head. His God's sigil stared back from the same table, pulsing fervently, reflecting the swirl of loyalty and pain that addled his mind. The realm had always weighed heavy upon his shoulders, the needs of a people going about their every day lives a mere shadow against the true reality that the veils shut out. He blinked, trying to hold back the dread rising in his gut, and drew on his God for comfort.

"Lord Penance," said Lord Justice, his face as red as Lady Fate's, though his hands were forged into fists under the sacred table. "Is now the time? We are just in the process of building a defence. General Zendril has surprised us all. Duke Panset has accepted his duty in destroying these Infected. If we crack open this new alliance, this new way of working, who will be left to stand against the Constructors? We are here to *serve*, and though I am hot-headed and unthinking at times, I believe strongly in that service. I agonise every day over the lies we weave. Where is the *justice* within it?" He took a breath then, staring down at his fists before looking back to his High Lord. "It lies in justification, does it not? That I ... *we*, deceive our people because *not* doing so would see their enslavement or death."

High Lord Penance shifted his gaze over to the youngest of the seven Leaders of the Houses. How long was it since that Lord had railed against such an alliance?

Has he learned, or is he just spouting back my own words?

"Overseer," cut in the quavering voice of Lord Wisdom, his eyes darting about the table. "When?"

He sighed, knowing that he had given little detail in his rush to explain his thinking. He missed Sneed's calm, the sounding board who kept him on an even keel. All these years, he had prided himself on making considered decisions, however despicable, no matter the self-disgust they caused.

And now?

"Yesterday morning. At dawn. The Unspoken faced their emperor, and a veil dragon she did not recognise. A brief fight ensued after she refused to bow to him." He let the words sit, mulling over how much more he should share.

"So, they conversed? And it is the same emperor as when she served? A thousand years ago?" Lord Wisdom shook his head as he spoke; the enormity of it all weighed heavy on his bearing. "We read and devour the past, searching for answers, and now our history flies in our undefended skies. I ..."

High Lord Penance grasped his cane and slammed the stick onto the stone floor. The echo bounced around the room and cut off the Lord before he could spread any more despair.

"We need to consider the priorities, Lord Wisdom, not bathe in fear. As Lord Justice has already said, we are forming a defence the like of which we never thought possible, and hoped we'd never need. We risk all by holding back from the queen what is truly happening."

"And what we've done," whispered Lady Honour, though the words carried to every ear.

The ensuing silence sat like a malaise about the table, each Lord and Lady contemplating the true, oppressive reality of their duty, revealed to them after years of sacrifice to achieve their status. The High Lord had held the hands of every person on the council, mumbling the words of truth about the Unspoken's real role in their faith. And held them as they wept. The Overseer of faith and Scripture indeed, but not that which was written down – that which kept their people safe.

Until now.

He felt Penance's touch upon his mind, offering no words of relief, just the expectations of a God.

"Can we not deliver a half-truth to the queen, Lord Penance?" asked Lord Hope. "That word has reached us of a new dragon. That the Soul Tear did not announce its arrival because the veils were not torn open but slipped through. Why mention the battle, and that we know of this from the Unspoken? We can see your pain, feel it. But you will shatter this alliance the moment you tell her the Unspoken is a lie. That the very Scripture we build our faith upon was based on a pact between a soul-eater and the Seven. It makes no sense."

High Lord Penance glanced around the table, meeting the eyes of each Lord or Lady. Only Lady Death held his gaze. The rest bowed their heads, though he saw only disagreement in their eyes.

"We understand," Lady Death said, her white hair framing a gentle but worried face. "And I believe your concern stems from Queen Erin's engagement with this council and the effect that has had. May I ask, High Lord, why you want to reveal our greatest deceit to my cousin now?"

He paused, pushing down the inner pain caused by the reminder Lady Death had woven into her words.

Cousin. Yes.

"For all these years, we have spouted the Scripture around an evil and the dragon that embodies it, and then a true dragon appears just when we needed the flocks to believe more than ever. She is not stupid, and Lord Wisdom reports that the queen spends much of her time, when not marshalling the defence, in the Forbidden Library. General Zendril, her mother, has already spoken to her of a meeting with the Unspoken on the field of battle. One that dug up more fears than answers, in truth. Ridth has also been attacked by the Unspoken's dragon, just when concerns arose that the duke may not take our fears seriously. And whatever you may feel about yet another lie, there are too many coincidences for one as sharp as Queen Erin to ignore." As he searched Lady Death's face then, understanding crept into his mind. Her gentle prod had sharpened his thoughts.

He pushed his shoulders back and, sitting up, let Penance fortify his body.

"Word will reach her. The Handren will know. They must have observed what the Unspoken describes. They report of the Unspoken's dragon to you, Lady Fate, do they not? And of the herders taken, not just the goats they tend?" He waited for her acknowledgement. Though it was slow in coming, the flame-haired Lady met his eyes and nodded. This moment, he knew, had always been her greatest fear – the weave cut, the way forwards hidden from her and her distant God.

No – she views it as an unravelling of faith.

"We risk the queen rejecting us out of hand. More, perhaps, turning on us, rallying the people to her. If that happens, the veils will weaken and the Constructors can arrive here with impunity. And remember. The power we – and the waiting, as we quicken them – draw upon will also fade. Faith is our greatest strength—"

"—and our greatest weakness," cut in Lady Fate. "If you tell her, what happens if she chooses to inform her people anyway?"

"She is a Weister," said Lady Death, eyes flickering over to catch Lady Fate's. "If she finds out through others, nothing will stop her from reacting like one and tearing everything to pieces in her path, including us. You tipped our hand when insisting she be the next queen, more so when choosing Adama in an attempt to shackle her.

"When, and I mean when, she learns that the Crusade was one of *our* machinations, that her people died upon their machines and fires for a lie, that the Unspoken has actively killed on the word of the High Lord, what do you think she will do? The only thing that will hold her back is a shared belief we were doing right. Finding out through others will shatter any chance of that."

Lady Fate slouched back against her chair and bowed her head. Tears formed at the edges of her eyes, unseen by all but Lady Death.

Silence returned to the Council table. The High Lord let Lady Death's words settle on each of their minds. She had exemplified all his thoughts, stripping clean the whirl of turmoil and laying the situation out in stark reality.

"And so you believe we should tell her now?" said Lord Hope.

"By the Seven, no." Her words, and the look of apology she sent in his direction, cut High Lord Penance deep, and he winced. "I said our only hope is to make sure she finds out through us. I say we do everything we can to prevent word reaching her, and when something slips through, be ready to jump. But mark this. If Lord Penance is not here, one of us will have that role, and will have to deal with the storm that follows."

"Lord Penance?" said Lady Fate.

The sigh slipped from him unbidden, his heart a lump of iron.

We stand as a Council, and fall as one.

"If that is your word, then, this one time, I will bend. But only on each of your oaths that you will step in to intercept and speak to Queen *Weister* directly should it become necessary. Do I have that?" They all looked to each other, then rose as one and placed their blackened hands upon the table. "Yes?"

And the rainbow of spiritfire poured forth, filling the glyph that lay at the centre. Their colours merged to form a whitefire that sparked before soaking into the metal.

"Sealed."

Remember this feeling. It is what I bore for each of you when you rose to lead your House. Sharing it does NOT relieve the burden; it magnifies it. And my heart hurts for you all.

II
A CAGE OF DISCOVERIES

UNKNOWN CITY, APSO-TRAN

Laoch pushed his feet against the stone block, shoving aside the stale straw and debris that had gathered there after hours of his impatient shuffling. His back rested against the cell wall, its blocks cut as fine as those of the rest of the city walls against which the prison had been built.

The Schenterenta had marched them there without a word spoken, shoving and needling them down a wide avenue that wound its way along the wall. Laoch had already assessed its purpose, glancing over to the edge of the first inner buildings, spying the raised stones on their roofs that served as cover for another line of defence. Everything screamed of a people prepared for war, the trap set for any enemy, and of deep mistrust, likely based on their arrival on the wings of a metal dragon.

Laoch grabbed another handful of straw and squeezed it between his fingers, trying to push down the worry for Ecne that rose in waves every time he stopped moving. She had a veil dragon for company, so why worry? And then there was Oisin, locked away elsewhere; Laoch's calls down the prison corridor met with empty silence. Would the venom rise under the stress? Cause him to act irrationally?

I need a drink.

The scrape of a key broke his thoughts, followed by the door in the corridor creaking open. Booted feet slapped on the stone floor, and he stood, brushing off the straw, setting his stall out to be the *leader* his friends needed.

To his surprise, the female Schenterenta who had bound him appeared. Next to her was a Schenterenta male in black robes trimmed with gold and silver. His ears were adorned with silver tips, the lobes pierced by a silver stud. A chain ran from one to the other. Under his eyes, a metallic shimmer played in the light that seeped from the barred window in the opposite wall.

Royalty?

"*Tena be farda*," the woman said, pointing behind Laoch. He nodded and backed off to sit on the stone bench against the far wall.

"Human," said the other, the words deep and low-pitched. It took Laoch a while before he realised it was a question of sorts.

"Yes," he replied. "I strugg—"

A spew of harsh words fell from the female warrior, silencing him as she stepped towards the bars. The male Schenterenta waited, an eyebrow raised, until she had finished. Laoch interpreted the whole scene as *shut up until spoken to.*

With a stretch of a chin and a hint of an arrogant smile, the man spoke again. "And you understand my words?"

"Yes." Laoch locked down the rest of what he wanted to say, including his choice of swear word.

"Interesting. A dead language reborn."

That caught in Laoch's craw, the implications unpleasant. "Not dead," he said, surprised he wasn't cut off.

"Apparently. Your clothes are also interesting. Ancient." The elf pointed to his cloak. "Your people haven't dressed like that in centuries. Two anomalies. Do you know where you are from?"

Laoch blinked, the question framed in such a way he was unsure how to answer.

"I do," was all he gave, and received a smirk he desperately wanted to wipe from the elf's face.

"And a spark of intelligence. Interesting."

"You use that word a lot. Why so interesting?"

The female cut back in with her tirade, but this time the man raised a hand to silence the elven warrior. He barked a few words, the lilt to his voice one of power and expectation. It reinforced Laoch's view of his status.

"Sarcasm, language, clothing. You are full of surprises. And you arrive on our doorstep at the same time a Constructor's mechanical beast agitates our veil. Are you going to lie to me and say it is a coincidence?"

"Tell me why my language is dead, and I'll answer your question." Laoch crossed his arms, and set his stance with a confidence he didn't feel. In months past, with a glass or two of green-leaf down his gullet, he would have called this bastard out by now. Fallen into his usual trap of foul language and anger when faced by authority.

The elf raised his eyebrow once again, and the smirk reappeared, still certain. "Because we killed it."

Laoch's mind fell away, a vertigo that threatened his body as well as his mind. He steadied himself, arms uncrossed, hands out in front, to the amusement of the Schenterenta noble.

"You seem surprised. Humans are the conduits of the Constructors, the reason they came here in the first place. We made it our purpose to exterminate each one. A few still wander about, and those we find, we *remove*. And here you are, proof that we were right to do so. Interesting, isn't it?"

"Bastard," slipped from Laoch's lips, and the elf laughed.

"I am guessing that's a very unpleasant word. So, you admit you arrived on an artifice of the Constructor's making. Yet you are not one of those *bastards*. So, explain yourself." The elf shifted from his arrogant stance and leaned forwards slightly, eyes focused on Laoch.

"I never said that."

"Coincidences don't happen. And being evasive implies not only are you here with that artifice, but are a danger to our people. How do you think we should react to that?"

The elf spun away in a swirl of black robes. The warrior followed at his side, a final glare catching Laoch's eye as she left.

"Shit."

—

Oisin sagged against the cold stone, arms raised and manacled to the wall. Blood seeped from split lips, and bruises swelled on his cheek and temple. His chest hurt, the thin cotton shirt he wore beneath his armour little protection against the blows that had cascaded into his ribs. He dripped with sweat as pain rushed through his body and set it on fire.

"This is ridiculous, human. I know you speak our language; the oaf you arrived with has already confirmed that. Being stubborn will not help your cause." The black-robed elf nodded, and the female warrior sent another punch into Oisin's side. The blunt knuckleduster smashed into his ribs, though Oisin knew the strike was pulled. Each blow he suffered had just the right amount of power to bruise, cut, but not break bones. This warrior knew her job well.

"All you need to do is tell me where the mechanical beast is. It cannot fly forever. I'll trade information with you. We struck it a blow, watched it fall from the sky. It only just kept itself above the waves. All you will be doing is saving us some time." The Schenterenta smiled, eyebrows raised, arms wide.

Oisin's head lolled, one swollen eyelid shut, the other staring wide and angry back at the noble elf. He judged the distance too far for petty revenge, and more than likely his bloodied spit would hit the metal bars if he tried.

The warrior stepped between them, as if she had read his intent. She cocked her head to the side before an open-handed slap across his un-bruised right cheek wrenched his head around to hit the wall.

"Only more pain is the reward for silence. N'Dika is the least of your worries. I am restraining myself, human. But any more silence, and Sendak here will get to work." The elf sucked in his lips, peering over to what Oisin had assumed to be a shadow in the corner. It emerged from the dark. Taller, broad of shoulder, with arms muscled and heavily scarred as if he'd been practicing his own art on himself. The face was clearly human, though the nose and ears were absent, the scars bubbled and raw. He wore a mishmash of clothing overlaid with a dark brown apron sporting stains Oisin feared to consider.

"Now, before I let Sendak loose, I'll let you have a little think. Contemplate what is to come, and how you can avoid it."

Oisin let a groan slip, blood bubbling on his lips. The glare from the female warrior switched to a grin that sent chills along his spine. She reached out, causing him to flinch, and admonished himself for allowing her that pleasure. She cupped his swollen cheek, and gently slapped it.

"*Shebe te na forkan,*" she said. "Bastard."

And where did she learn that?

At least Oisin now knew Laoch had lived long enough to share his vocabulary.

———

'What are they doing?' Nathair thought, the words forming in Ecne's mind as if she still held the dragon's heartstone. It itched at the back of her head, or maybe that was Wisdom with the usual warning. Either way, it felt weird to be communicating out in the real world and not when seeing through the dragon's eyes. Laoch had spoken of how Sura could talk to him in his mind, and Ecne had put that down to their emotional connection. But she also recalled how the necromancer had encroached on her unconscious mind, trying to persuade Ecne to give up her body, and a shiver ran down her spine.

A gap in the vines that hung from the thick tree canopy framed the Schenterenta who rode slowly in. Three were examining the forest floor intently. The surrounding trees were silent, only the odd call of a strange climbing animal piercing the foliage.

"They are checking the ground, like Oisin and Laoch do when looking for tracks," she whispered.

'Think the words, Ecne, and I will hear them.'

"Yes," she whispered again, and then thought the words, her worries entwining each syllable as her doubts surfaced.

She could feel the weight of Nathair on her mind, and her pause, as if waiting.

Or thinking.

'I cannot read your other thoughts, Ecne. Only those you direct when you think of me. Nor do I wish to hear them. You are so ... young.'

"*I don't know how to take that,*" she thought back, peeved. "*It is good to know. But how can we be doing this?*"

'You have connected with me via the heartstone, much as the Constructors did when I was under their venom. It has a short range; if my memory serves, it is around my length. It was how they called for the dragon's pocket to open up to them. What are the Schenterenta doing now?'

Ecne picked up a little concern in the Spirit Walker's thoughts, which mirrored her own. Laoch and Oisin were late, and it rankled with them both that these soldier-like Schenterenta had turned up. The artifice dragon had landed in the trees as gracefully as she could, but the native birds had called their dissent and taken flight, while the hairy climbing animals had called back and forth about their presence. Someone would have seen that.

Two of the elven riders broke into a conversation, pulling aside some of the leaf litter and pointing avidly at the ground. They turned, one continuing their conversation with a fourth rider on horseback. This one was female, her leather armour carved with unfamiliar symbols. To Ecne, the lilt and form of the words did not reflect the sound and rhythm of the few Schenterenta she had met, but then she knew of human enclaves on Brandshold where their own language had diversified.

The three trackers jumped onto their horses. The talkative one took the lead, leaning over as they followed a path that led away from Ecne and Nathair.

Relieved, she dropped her gaze, only for excited shouts to bounce through the trees. The noise riled the local animals, and the calls turned into over-excited hoots.

'Ecne?'

"They've found something," she said, forgetting to think her words. She raised her crossbow and broke through the vines into the small clearing. Ecne headed towards the right of the path the elves had taken, diving into the thick trees, cursing her lack of finesse as roots and vines grabbed at her limbs. Calming herself, she took a few more steps. The connection with Nathair faded as the spirit gently called for her to be careful.

The animal din continued, the hoots eerie, almost mournful. But in the trees ahead, the cries were pained. Grunts and unintelligible shouts that set her on edge. Creeping closer, she caught sight of the horses milling about a clearing. There were two low huts, their rough structures covered by the wider leaves of the surrounding trees. One lay trampled, the horse nickering as it stood amid the ruins. Its rider had somebody pinned to the ground with a spear. Ecne winced as the elf ground the tip into bone before shoving it deeper. The scream rattled through her, and she instinctively raised her crossbow. Wisdom did not answer with spiritfire. Instead, a touch on her mind called for calm and reason.

The elf withdrew the spear, kicking the person over. Ecne swallowed. It was an old woman, perhaps approaching fifty years, maybe more. The elf didn't hesitate, driving the spear into her throat, the spurt of blood splashing the verdant ground. But it was the look on the elf's face that stole Ecne's breath, the sickening mix of hatred and glee. A cry, swiftly cut off, broke into her thoughts, and she shifted to the other side of a thick vine. Against a trunk stood another human, this one sporting the familiar shaggy beard and hair of the leader who had attacked Nathair on the beach. On the floor next to them lay the pieces of a fire-hardened spear. The elf's curved sword rose. Calmed by Wisdom or not, Ecne brought the crossbow up to her eye.

A hand slipped into the crook of her elbow, dirty and green with scrapes of mossy vegetation. Ecne flinched and swung the weapon around, only for a second hand to catch the stock, preventing it from pointing their way. Four tribesmen emerged from the trees, each holding spears. A fifth, a young girl, knelt next to her, eyes on the scene that played out within the clearing. Ecne didn't feel threatened. The men had had ample opportunity to kill her. They waited, eyes on her. She heard the thud of metal on meat, met with a flinch from the girl at her side, and turned in time to see the old man fall to the ground. His dead eyes remained open, staring their way.

She had no words of her own, only those Laoch had shared.

"Bastards," she said.

The girl glanced at her as tears spilled down her muddied face. "Yes," she whispered, looking back to the bloodied remains. "Bastards."

The girl's hand flitted above her chest, the gestures a pattern of some form. Ecne assuming they were signals, much like the Rangers used, or possibly a ritual.

"Huh," slipped from her lips, and she raised the crossbow, determined to do something. Again, the young girl placed her hand on Ecne's arm and pressed the crossbow down, the look in her eyes pleading.

"No," she said, her gaze flitting back to those who waited behind. "More will come. Death. Watch."

Ecne couldn't grasp how the girl remained so calm, having assumed it was her family who lay murdered upon the forest floor. The urge to do something was strong. Perhaps her time with Laoch, Sura and Oisin had affected her? Their first thoughts were often filled with action and little patience. But the green-smudged hand remained on hers. This was her land, her people.

The elves wiped their weapons on the humans' rough clothing, while the leader dismounted, a wicked-looking blade in her hand. She knelt and forced the old woman's mouth wide before slicing through the tongue. It parted under the blade. She repeated the action with the man, cleaning her knife afterwards on the forest floor before bagging her prizes. Barking orders, she quickly mounted, as did the other elves, and they pulled their horses around to head down a second trail.

The girl looked over her shoulder and raised a hand, a signal that two of the men behind Ecne obeyed, disappearing into the trees. Within a few seconds, a hoot crossed the divide. The girl stood and walked through the vines and leaf litter into the clearing. There, she fell to her knees with her head upon the man's chest, tears now flowing in a river of pain. The sobs tore at Ecne, and she followed to kneel by the girl's side. She reached out a hand, only for a harsh grunt to stay it – one of the remaining tribesmen suddenly in her eyeline, spear raised. Ecne squeezed her fingers shut, heart pounding with adrenaline and sadness.

After a while, the girl glanced her way. As she stood, she took Ecne's elbow, and they walked over to kneel by the side of the old woman. The girl placed both their hands on the bloodied chest. The gaping hole in the old woman's shoulder was raw, and covered in bone splinters. A glow rose from the body – whitefire, though it caused Ecne little fear. There was softness to it – a kindness she couldn't put into words. The spirit absorbed into the girl's hands.

"Mammar," she said. The girl blinked; her face twisted in thought. "Grandma may be the word. She never taught me them all, though we may share more now. Always Mammar to me."

Ecne choked, words sticking in her mouth. Wisdom graced her thoughts and helped to ease the pressure of her grief for this girl.

"Yes, grandma or grandmother. Was that your grandfather?" she said.

"My second father. Ma had me late, a much-wanted girl to follow in her footsteps until the Drach took her too. But now, who will follow me?"

"I ... the elves ..."

"Elves? The Drach? Bastards," she said, then lifted her eyes from her father. "But you came with the giant metal bird, so you would not know. Can you take us away from here? Away from the Drach. There are so few of us now, we could ride as you did. I am too young ... too young to lead."

Ecne stared at the girl. "Lead?"

12

THE SEVEN EXPOSED

SOUTH OF MAKALENA, BRANDSHOLD

Popsilin pushed herself deeper into the undergrowth. The calls of the birds in the forest, the buzzing of insects in her ears, grated at her nerves. She swore, swiping away the multi-legged thing trying to burrow into her armour, its combination of pincers and slime quickly leading to its demise.

"This is the foulest place I have ever been," she whispered through tight blue lips, "bar none."

She flattened herself as the horse ahead nickered, swinging its neck from side to side as it too suffered under the barrage of biting insects. Its eyes watered a little, a signal for the mini-beasts to feast. A human sat astride the saddle, their armour a combination of leather and metal plate, under which they sweated profusely while they rode along the forest trail with five other soldiers strung behind.

"A patrol," she thought, sending it outwards to her squad. *"Calm. Only attack if you are spotted."*

Popsilin assessed their weapons as they rode by – the standard combination of bow, sword and spear. Nothing unusual. And no mark of the Seven that she could see. The horses bore an emblem of three towers on their saddlecloths, but the humans wore the green and browns of typical scouts. She itched to take them down, drain the souls of five and question the last. But it was too soon. The emperor had groomed her subtlety, as well as admiring her ruthlessness, and she needed both to be at their height if they were to find what they needed and survive long enough to inform the Fleshmaster.

The last horse trotted by, baulking at something it sensed. Popsilin immediately went on high alert and raised her handbow, but the rider settled the animal down, patting its neck. He didn't even look to the sides; just rode on as if assuming the forest was clear of threat.

"Wait," she sent. *"Patience."*

It wasn't long before the scout returned, his manner casual, looking down at the ground as if following a trail or looking for something. Popsilin and her kin were far from skilled at reading the subtleties of human body language anymore, but the man was a little too obvious. A shake of the head and he turned back, speeding up to trot back towards his patrol.

If they had been seen, Popsilin expected the rest would already be in the trees watching, or moving in behind them. She sent that thought, and a slew of negative replies calmed her unease.

Relieved, they gathered under a gap in the canopy, with the last of the day's light fading.

"The city lies a few miles to the west of the forest edge. We should come across a few villages on the way if these people act the same as in the other realms. I would much prefer to find word of the Magi there rather than enter somewhere so highly populated." Popsilin looked to each of her Inhibitors. "You will stay in your pairs. Mark well where the emperor will return. If the others fall, make your way back there without being followed. If one has to give their body so the other may get through, so be it. The Fleshmaster promises equal reward for you all, whether renewed or your body survives."

A nod from each, and Tenith led them out onto the trail, with Popsilin in the centre. They kept to the rough trail the patrol had taken, the undergrowth at either side too thick and likely full of delays, whether animal or tangled vegetation. A risk, but it was already dark under the trees. Besides, as the last of the sun dropped below the horizon, their night sight would attune to the slivers of spirit every living creature and plant contained.

The heat, however, didn't reduce, nor did the insect population. The last just changed guard, the nocturnal insects rising from beneath the undergrowth to take their turn at gnawing on Popsilin. She slowly discovered that most insects only took one bite before moving on, her lack of living blood apparently unappetising. Though, something about her gained the little bastards' interest before they discovered that.

Tenith signalled her forwards, and she joined her second-in-command. The trail widened ahead as the trees began to thin out where they had been logged. Her gaze followed the tree line, noting how the rest of the forest's edge was thick with vines, making the trail the only clear way in and out.

So easily guarded, should we be spotted.

The trail led to a relatively flat plain, dotted with tree stumps as far as her spirit eyes could make out. Large animals grazed or slept about them, shifting against one another as the temperature finally began to drop and a breeze picked up.

"*Farmland,*" sent Tenith. "*And logging for wood. There'll be villages around here, all right. Whenever there's work, there's humans willing to do it. Seen it everywhere we've been.*"

"*We need to cover up our weapons and be off this road as soon as we can.*"

She passed that message among her squad, even more wary now they were out of the trees and exposed. They wrapped their light cloaks about themselves, hiding the weapons they bore and the thin armour that would prove little protection if they ran into a magus. She peered into the murk at the side of the mud track, worried at the prospect of walking through the myriad stumps and animals. The track would be quicker; they just had to keep moving and stay clear of that patrol, should it return.

Popsilin ordered a rear guard and ensured they focused on behind and not ahead, then set a steady jogging pace, with Tenith again in the lead. Clouds shrouded the sliver of a moon, improving their chances of spotting danger before it found them. She hoped.

It wasn't long before the first houses came into view, set a good twenty yards back from the road. Animal pens and bird cages surrounded the two wooden buildings. Popsilin noted the rough track that wound its way to the yard.

Weighing up the odds of the patrol returning against more time spent on the road, she signalled the squad to spread out. The Inhibitors paired off and surrounded the two buildings. She waited patiently beside a water barrel stationed near a small patch of ordered plants, watching as the animals stirred at their presence, but not enough to have her worried. That was, until the first bark shattered the silence, followed by a second. Whatever the animal, they had the scent of her Inhibitors and regarded them as a threat. More than that, they had sounded an alarm.

To her surprise, the main door swung open. A man in his middle years, from the age of his spirit, stepped out into the night, framed by the candlelight that glowed from behind. He carried a crossbow in one hand, a small quiver in the other.

"Rampart!" he shouted. "This had better be a real threat, ye bast'rd dog, or it'll be another week in that barn fer ye." The man strode over to the second building and tugged at a handle. As soon as there was a gap, something black and furred sped out. A pink tongue lolled as it careered into the farm's yard.

"Rampart, heel!" The man repeated the command, turning as a second, smaller animal bounded out. This one stayed closer, nose in the air, and locked eyes on a spot Popsilin knew contained two of her squad. The barks increased, and the twang of a handbow, followed by a flare of white light, left Popsilin with no choice. She darted from behind the barrel to aim and trigger the quarrel in one smooth motion. The human glanced her way, realisation dawning slowly. By the time he'd raised his heavier crossbow, Popsilin was on him. She pinned both shoulders to the ground, her knees pressing on his torso. A whimper from the side caused the man to glance that way, and Popsilin took the opportunity to reinforce his fear. A sharp slap cracked the injured dog's neck. She drew its spirit. The white glow wreathing her hand, dancing along her fingers until it soaked into her palm. A morsel, yes, but a point proven. She punched the man, the crack of his head against the ground signalling his descent into unconsciousness.

"Inside. I want whoever is in there, alive."

Subtlety lost, the Inhibitors crashed into the farm building. Popsilin dragged her prisoner inside and slammed the door shut. Within a few minutes, they had checked the upper floor, and a woman she took as the man's mate lay next to him on the floor.

"Guard them, Tenith. The rest of you, out into the night and on watch. Keep away from the animals. They are disturbed enough already."

With that, Popsilin clomped upstairs and examined the farmers' possessions. Eventually she found what she sought within a crafted bedside cabinet, and dropped the thick book, its pages well worn, onto a similarly stout bed. She ran her fingers over the title, where the embossed lettering had faded and cracked.

"The Word of the Seven Gods," she read aloud. "As the emperor said. But Gods?" She flicked the book open. The words merged into a milieu of printed letters that hurt her mind, but the inscription was enough, and handwritten. "The House of Hope, Makalena."

Popsilin went downstairs and selected a kitchen stool. She placed it between her two bound prisoners and sat. With her hand on the man's forehead, she allowed a wisp of whitefire to touch his skull before sliding into his mind. His eyes flickered and, at her behest, Tenith finished the process with a splash of water from the kitchen.

"Wake up," she growled, slapping the man's wet cheek. The eyelids sprang open and Popsilin smiled at the flicker of fear. "With me? Yes? Let me make this short. Your mate is there." She pointed over to his side. "I can feed off her soul just as I did your animal." The recognition in the man's eyes pleased her too.

"What do you want?" he asked, his voice tight and low.

Popsilin pushed back her hood and waited. It didn't take long. Her blue lips and husked skin set near as much dread in the man as her white eyes. "Information. Easy. Nothing too difficult." She dropped the heavy book onto his chest. "Where are the Seven?"

—

The Inhibitor wound back the mechanism until the trigger locked down on the cogs. Fumbling in a hide bag, he pulled out two crystals, dropping one back in and holding the other to the night sky. Whitefire swirled inside. Popsilin watched as her Inhibitor checked that the bonds of the stone remained strong. Satisfied, the soldier dropped it into the thin-barrelled crystal-slinger he'd been carrying.

The moon had long since disappeared behind thick cloud, but none of them needed light to see the spirits of the two guards at the minor side entrance to the walled city. The gate was shut, but they had watched long enough. The crystal slinger and his partner took aim, waiting patiently. After a few minutes, one of the guards rose, nodding to someone behind him. The jangle of keys announced the gate was about to open. A woman walked through, leading a four-legged animal with baskets across its back filled with cloth-wrapped bottles. She handed one to the guard and tapped his cheek with a smile, before guiding the animal silently away towards the collection of hovels that lay a good fifty yards from the city walls. The guard raised the bottle to show off his prize to the other guard, then removed the stopper.

The slingers fired; the crack of the explosive powder like a whip. The crystals slammed into the guard's throat and burned inwards, silencing any cry.

"Now!" sent Popsilin.

The Inhibitors acted with speed. The first pair rose from the shadow of the wall to fall upon the second guard before he could raise a cry, blades slashing deep into mouth and throat. The others swept up the smuggler, slicing her into silence, and dragged her and the placid beast into the wall's shadow.

A precise, subtle strike, but the human guards had been remiss in their vigilance, in their readiness for violence. The five seconds it took for her squad to find a way in meant, however, the city would soon understand war was on the way. She hadn't wanted it to be like this, but the farmer's words had forced her hand.

Gods?

She left two Inhibitors at the gate, cloaked in the deceased guards' livery, to cover their retreat, but it wouldn't fool anyone with any intelligence for long. They hoped the expectation of a locked gate would mean they had some time, enough to follow a soulless farmer's directions.

He had tasted sweet, his fear exquisite, but the woman had nearly swept her away in the soul-lust. The infusion of hate and dread after being forced to watch Popsilin feed upon her mate had been thrilling, a memory filtering in of past excesses in a former body. Her Inhibitors had been required to temper their feeding, taking just a sip of the woman and a few of the animals, with the promise of more on their return to the forest. But first, she needed to see one of these *Gods' Houses* for herself, and perhaps steal a priest.

The streets of Makalena were filled with the scent of the sea, but the docks were not her target. They set off steadily, conscious of time, following the hand-drawn map. With only the odd drunkard or hurrying loner to worry about, they made good speed along the cobbled streets, the skyline dominated by three towers that rose from the centre of the city. Ignoring these, they came to a crossroads, and a wider street that headed east, towards two grand buildings that rose above the stone-built houses. Their ornate facades reflected the description the man had provided. Each was fronted by seven marble steps and as they approached, the entrance doors depicted a dragon in combat with a god.

One of the Seven Magi.

Her Inhibitors prickled at the sight. A mix of awe at finally finding their foe, and fear of what they might be about to face, entering their shared thoughts.

"Wait," she sent, deciding that their nervousness would be too much of a detriment to the mission. *"Watch. Act only on my word."*

Popsilin kept to the edge of the street, eyes on the few lit windows and the odd person, none of whom had any interest in what she was doing. She approached Hope's House, having recognised the scales motif from the farmers' book. The steps were foreboding, a weight falling upon her barely anchored spirit as she took each one. Finally at the top, her hand slid inside her cloak to finger the grip of her handbow as she stared at the huge stone doors. The beauty of their construction harked back to Innealtóir, the carving of such intricacy, it was a stark reminder of what her race had left behind for their hunt. The multiple dragon scales, delicately cut from the hard stone, and the dragon's lines depicted with such care, were all reminders of the years lost due to the selfishness of the Seven. A doubt rose, but Tenith pressed in on her mind. Her second-in-command's query knocking her back into the here and now. She squeezed her fingers into her palms, the gauntlets sparking with a little whitefire to reignite her senses.

Popsilin had expected a darkness beyond the walls. Instead, it was filled with rows of candles, placed as if a wave of light rolled inwards and up, towards the central stone that sat beneath a huge, painted window. Again, the Magus was depicted, one arm bearing the sword her guide had called Hope's Edge, the other, a set of weighing scales, scrolls on each balancing plate – the Word of the Seven.

Sickened, a dread rose in her chest laced with anger and hate. Aware she had made the right decision in leaving her Inhibitors outside, Popsilin steeled herself. There would have been a bloodbath had they seen such reverence for a creature that had left them to starve. A Magus who'd abandoned them to free their people, leaving the Constructors with no choice but to fall upon each other.

"May I help you?" asked a voice that echoed about the chamber. Popsilin turned in surprise to find a woman in yellow robes seated in the rearmost row to her left. "Have you come seeking Hope?"

Popsilin froze, unable to think for a moment.

"Are you with Death's House?" The woman stood. Her spirit was tainted by something strange, as if her soul was composed of many thin layers. Her eyes matched her grey hair, the skin wrinkled, though the purple-lipped smile she bore dropped years from her face. One hand was gloved. She pointed to Popsilin's black cloak. "You are welcome, whether you seek Hope or space to think. Many come here to contemplate their future. That is why our doors are always open."

The priest's eyes rose to the ceiling, and Popsilin's gaze followed. Above her, the dragon once again fought Hope, its tongue long and wrapped about the Magus's sword. But Hope was not looking at the orange-hued dragon. Instead, he stared at the open scroll, lips parted as if speaking.

Nathair.

Popsilin glanced back at the priest, who had stepped closer, and felt the warmth of the candles on her skin. When the priest's eyes widened, she knew her identity had dawned on the woman.

The first punch caught the priest under the chin. The second slapped her ears, and the third sent her to the ground. Popsilin quickly pulled at the priest's robes, exposing the arms and hands. No greaves or knuckle-dusters, no crystal daggers, though one arm was laced with black veins, the wrist black where the glove began. Satisfied the woman was not a warrior magus, Popsilin hefted the woman up onto her shoulders as a cry from the front of the chamber broke the silence.

Popsilin swung about. Two yellow-robed priests ran from the end of the aisle near the strange, inert stone below the picture window. They appeared to be unarmed, but their voices were dangerous enough. They would bring more, and the priest she had captured was the key to the invasion's future. The emperor would pick her clean, and they would know where to strike.

She headed out the doorway and reached the bottom of the seven steps, to be immediately flanked by her Inhibitors. Handbow quarrels flew, the thunk of crystal on flesh soon followed by a flare of light and the smell of burnt flesh amid the screams. Popsilin ran down the street. Infused by the farmer's whitefire, she kept the pace high as Tenith took the lead, taking down any of the nighttime stragglers who turned their way. As she ran down the final street, the tower bells began to peel. Their sound echoed throughout the city, an insistent tone that angered her as it raised the enemy from their sleep. They had done so well, but their luck had run out as soon as she had delayed. She should have acted immediately, not let herself become lost in the past.

"Clear the way!" Popsilin commanded, and was grateful for a swift response. The pseudo guards threw the gates open and dropped their disguises. Kneeling, they aimed their slingers down the street and let loose. The crack of explosive powder echoed around the buildings, swiftly followed by light flares and explosions. Popsilin sped onwards through the gate, the weight of the priest hardly noticeable as the whitefire kept her moving.

"Tenith, take the lead," she sent.

Her second-in-command pounded past, his sword out. They left the road, angling away from the collection of hovels and the people spewing from their doorways as the bells roused them. They entered the dark night, and were soon deep into the farmland that surrounded the city, thanks to the nearest fields being empty of stumps and easier going.

Within a few minutes they reached their first marker stone. Tenith swept up the crystal he'd laid as a guide and headed off towards the second. The third lay waiting at a death-filled farmhouse, the sanctuary they sought before heading into the forest to call upon their emperor.

I bring Hope.

13
WITH TORTUOUS INTENT

Unknown City, Apso-Tran

Sendak scraped the blade across the sharpening stone. The glint of oil along its blade and the crystals embedded within the stone too much of a hint this man knew his craft, however horrendous it was. A heavy breath rattled in the scarred throat to pour forth in a foul hoot from the hole where the nose used to be. The piercing green eyes never left the blade, a tongue tip peeking out to lick his frayed lips as he worked.

Oisin tried to look away, but the leather strap across his head was buckled tight. His muscles and tendons were set hard, suffering after the wait for his torturer's arrival in the dark silence of the cell. He'd refused to answer the second round of questions. The female warrior, N'Dika, enjoying the beating she inflicted, but not the silence he gave back. Eventually the elven noble, who this time introduced himself as Na Pertera Sentil, had sighed and given in to the inevitable. The wait had been part of the torture. Oisin knew this from the tales of the Unbelievers and their fires, and had spent the time calming himself, his hopes focused on giving Ecne time to do whatever she decided. The girl was an inspiration to him. One he would have been proud to have called sister. Should Fate intervene, he aspired to have a daughter just as feisty and wise, if her weave was kinder than it seemed now.

And I still have all my parts.

Silence fell, and Oisin squeezed a little movement out of the head strap to catch Sendak squinting his way. There was a strange look in the human's eye, difficult to place. Perhaps a joy in his role, yet a sadness towards the subject of it. Or a memory of tortures done to him? Oisin couldn't place it, but the torturer picked up the roll of instruments and, easing off his stool, placed them on a stained table next to Oisin's chair. A whistle escaped from the man's nostril as he sat beside the Elite Ranger, and a steady hand landed on Oisin's forearm where the bracer encased his arm. With tongue poking out, Sendak prodded at the metal with a blunt rod, then attempted to slide the rod between skin and metal, to find there was room enough only for the tip. Swapping out to a set of pliers, he dug into Oisin's skin and the muscle beneath the bracer, trying to get a grip, but the metal resisted. Surprisingly, the torturer chose not to dig into his arm for the chance of such a trinket. Instead, he turned Oisin's arm into an unnatural position. Oisin barely felt the new pain amid the throb of his face and chest from the warrior's beating.

Sendak flinched at the sight of the sigil, and eyed the inlaid metal as if he'd found a greater prize. A snort broke from his nose, accompanied by a rivulet of snot his tongue rescued. Reaching behind, he extracted a pointed tool, much like a carpenter's awl, and a wooden hammer from his roll.

"Sendak!" The shout broke the man's concentration, to Oisin's relief.

The elven warrior strode into the cell. "*Shebe te na forkan.*" She slapped the torturer's cheek; the red finger marks were clear against the sallow skin. "*Teska te cantar be.*"

The glare sent her way by the torturer was quickly cowed, and his eyes dropped to the floor.

The elf smiled then, a look that dripped malice, before her eyes fell onto the prone Ranger. She leant forwards and cupped his cheek as she had before, this time raking her nails through the raised welts and bruises to draw blood.

"Bastard," she said. "Bastard *eh Shebe te na forkan.*" She let her cat-like eyes settle on his, then looked to Sendak, who pointedly stared at the cell floor. She tapped Oisin's cheek, then moved to the rear of the cell to watch, arms crossed, a wide smile on her lips.

Sendak shifted back next to him, cracking his knuckles one by one with the thumb on his left hand while collecting the newly sharpened blade with the other. He flashed it in Oisin's eyeline, letting the Elite Ranger see the keen edge and smell the tang of animal oil. Fear bubbled in Oisin, not because he was about to be tortured, but because they were alone. However much he was about to be cut open, his mind lost to pain, even if he were to write the answers in blood upon the floor, there was no one in that cell who understood his words.

This was just a softening. The first step in a long process to leave him as broken as Sendak.

—

"Shame these walls are so thick, don't you think?"

Laoch glared at Na Pertera Sentil. The noble's robes gently shifted as he wafted his arms.

"I was sure his screams would penetrate, but no, apparently not. So, you'll have to use your imagination. Sendak is more subtle than my *nista*, but that does not make the agony any less ... satisfying. So, Laoch of the Queen's Rangers, why do I have a strange human in my midst, riding one of the Constructor's artefacts? The spirit-dolls were all put down out of *our* misery. So, I can only assume the Constructor's plan to return here, and by the abomination that flew over the city, with you at their vanguard."

Laoch crossed his arms and stared back at the elf so unlike Sura and her kin, plains people who followed the horse herds and worshipped at their moon pools under the stars while pining for a lost religion. Despite Sura's aggressive mood swings, which she wielded in self-defence, as a whole, her people were docile, their acceptance of the human invasion part of a malaise. Sura had spoken of their honour and refusal to budge from dying traditions that had driven her away and sowed doubt, since those same beliefs denied their love for each other. But even so, they were a far cry from the egotistical elf standing on the other side of the bars. And, if this silver-eared Schenterenta spoke the truth, the murderers of an entire people – and a representative of those they had strove to find in hope of discovering how to defeat the Constructors.

How? By being bloody worse than them?

And what do I tell them? The truth? Would they help, or just murder us and go back to their hell-spawned life.

"I believe your fellow Ranger may not have long. At least, not with all his parts attached. Sendak is something of a collector. Likes to keep his trophies. I believe he hopes one day to find a perfect nose to replace his own; perhaps a set of ears to his liking." The smile dripped poison, and Laoch knew he not only spoke the truth, but also everything he had claimed was likely just the barrel scrapings of the true reality. They had arrived in a realm where human life meant nothing. Something to be exterminated, crushed. Whether that had started to prevent the Constructor's return was no longer important, for they took pleasure in it now.

"I believe you will kill us whether I bloody tell you or not. I have fought your type before, Na Pertera Sentil," he said, but didn't add *and lost.* "Fanatics who will do anything in the name of whatever shitty cause they have going. You've already signed our death warrants in your own head, and regard us as fucking animals to butcher as you bloody will. Anything I tell you freely, you won't believe until you've tortured them out from me. From us." Laoch uncrossed his arms, trying to hold the anger inside at the piece of shit that besmirched Sura's kin. Her nobility, though wild, lay in far greater honour than the scum who smirked on the far side of the bars.

"Interesting ... As I said, intelligent. Our histories speak of the Constructors' spirit-dolls having such intelligence, yet docile, slaves to the soul-eaters. Those humans they stole from us to feed upon never rose to such heights when they abandoned them. But histories can be wrong – written by the victor, as they say. Tell me, Laoch, how does it feel to have your soul eaten piece by piece?"

Laoch blew out, trying to calm the tremor running along his chest. The elf was letting him have snippets of information, though he was convinced it was deliberate, leading him to reveal something about his purpose. And all the while, Oisin may or may not be being sliced apart. And then there were Ecne and Nathair. What would they do?

"I wouldn't know," he said, his whispered words low and hoarse. Laoch's mind filled with flashes of arrows driven into his Spear, one by one, as they melted before him. "We are not spirit-dolls, whatever they may be, nor slaves of the Constructors."

The noble's eyes glinted as he gazed at Laoch, the slits narrowing in the cat-like eyes. It was the same facial expression Sura used whenever he tried to convince her that the glass of leaf-green was his last.

"And so ... your purpose here? If not as a spearhead or scouts for the Constructors, I can only assume you are here for something far worse. So much so that you keep it to yourself. And, either way, you arrive on the wings of a Constructor's artifice. If you are not with them, I can only surmise it to be stolen, and you will bring them down upon us again."

The words cut into Laoch, the elf making swift, intuitive leaps he knew he'd struggle to keep up with. That was half the problem when dealing with the higher ranks as commander of a Spear. They forever used words when he preferred to act on instinct. Right now, it told him he was being led by the nose to a conclusion the noble had already made.

Just as he had decided they were already dead.

What was worse, he was likely right, and he sensed that vulnerability. If they failed, Brandshold may fall, its people enslaved. And he would have broken his vow to Sura.

—

If it had just been him, maybe he could have held out longer. But venom rode his soul.

Oisin screamed despite himself. The thin cut across his chest sliced through seven others that criss-crossed the skin into the flesh beneath. Sendak, his tongue flicking out as he worked on each painful slice, complemented them by adding a splash of vinegar to the wound. The pain was excruciating, compounded by the acidic liquid that swept along the ragged edges. Each cut was accompanied by a strange gasp from the watching warrior, but Oisin could not see her through the mist in his eyes.

The torturer snorted, and Oisin felt the flat of the blade against his cheek, pressing in. The point nicked the skin, forcing him to look just as Sendak's fingers stroked along the bridge of his nose. A sickening thought crashed in, its vileness insinuating into his thoughts as the man ran the knife along his outer ear.

"I'm sorry, Ecne," he mumbled, the words lost amid the bubble of blood at the corner of his mouth. The warrior elf edged closer as his lips moved. "So sorry."

Sendak shuddered and sat back, blinking. A second rivulet of snot joined the first, this one blood-riven. The torturer lifted his fingers to touch the scarlet liquid and raised it into his own eyeline. A snap dragged his sight downwards to find his hand wrapped about a long, serrated blade that pierced his lung. Despite his efforts, he was unable to prevent it from ripping through rib and meat to expose his inner chest. Wide-eyed, the torturer fell forward, smothering Oisin's left side.

The elven warrior took a step backwards, unable to work out what was going on until she caught the stream of blood flowing beneath Oisin's chair.

"Sendak. *Shebe te na forkan ab dan gorthi!*" she bellowed, and grabbed the torturer's shoulder. The elf pulled him back, more than likely expecting Oisin's ear to be on the table. Instead, the contents of the torturer's chest cavity spilled over the half-prone Ranger. With his arm clear of its straps, a bloodied blade protruded from his bracer.

She jumped back, hand half-drawing the curved sword at her side, and watched as Oisin slashed the leather head restraint. Half freed, he glowered her way, eyes laced with whitefire. The warrior flinched but strode forwards, and her blade struck towards the Ranger's strapped left side. The sword bit into his hip, carrying on through to leave a shallow cut. Wary of the fire in his eyes, she stepped backwards, and Oisin took the chance to free his left arm and whipped the blade towards his feet.

The elf, seeing her chance, chose his death over the opportunity to escape. She darted forwards to slash at his shoulders. Oisin, the venom blinding him, hacked at the strap, but Fate understood the ending the elf's sword heralded and blue light burst from the bracer, searing into the warrior and burning her cat-like eyes. The sword cut only air as pain pierced her brain. Her momentum stayed, she threw herself backwards, out of range of Oisin's blade.

He caught the thump of a body hitting stone while his blade made short work of the remaining strap. Fate's spiritfire coursed through him, easing muscles and joints even as the venom burned at the edges with hate and malice. Two contrasting powers that fought to free him. The blinded elf raised her sword, eyes screwed shut. The sneer was gone, replaced by fear. Oisin stepped in. Fate now within his grip, he cut through the warrior's wrist to separate hand and arm. The spurt of blood rushed across the floor, and he twisted Fate lower, the sword's edge biting into her ankle.

The foot parted, the scream of pain firing the venom's hate to shroud his soul. His third strike rammed into her chest, and the Elite Ranger paused, eye-to-blind-eye with the elven warrior.

"Bastard," he growled, and twisted the blade, shredding whatever lay inside. He drew it out to watch as the elf's life left her. Unbidden, his hand reached out, fingers running through the whitefire his venom-laden eyes saw spilling from her body. A desire, hate-filled, rose in his gut.

14
WE ARE NOT ALONE

JUNGLE, WEST OF THE UNKNOWN CITY, APSO-TRAN

Ecne walked warily towards the clearing, Nathair's grumbled misgivings echoing through her mind. What else was she to do? There was no sign of either Laoch or Oisin, and she had found the one person who could speak their language.

'*We must be careful, Acolyte.*'

She only uses acolyte when trying to put me in my place.

"*I know,*" she thought, breaking out into the nest of branches and trees the metal dragon lay in, "*but she speaks our language, and will have knowledge that could help us find out what's happened. And …*"

'*And? I sense fear in your thoughts. You think your friends lost, that we will have to carry on the fight alone.*' Nathair did not temper the emotions in her voice; a hint of frustration, perhaps anger. Ecne couldn't detect any sympathy, but then, Sura had displayed little.

"It's not as if their spears and arrows can damage you, is it? What have you to fear?" she said aloud, hands on hips. The dragon's mighty head faced Ecne, its crystalline eyes boring into her. The tongue flicked out. It reminded Ecne of a thin metal whip, with barbs along its edges.

'You, above all others, should know that knowledge is power. They may seek to expose us to these Drach. Trade us for something – like freedom.' This time, the thoughts were entwined with emotion – a fear of failing. Images faded in and out: a family, a strong woman surrounded by three boys of varying ages. And in the background, a harbour full of sailing ships.

"Then we must consult, Nathair, and act in unison. I should have asked, but they knew of you. These are the same people from the beach." She placed a hand upon the dragon's snout. The Spirit Walker graced her with a wisp of whitefire that held the warmth of a gentle touch.

'Aye. Let the one who speaks approach. Not the ones with the splinters of wood who are crazy enough to attack a metal dragon. I will speak with her, but not inside by the heartstone. We do not reveal all. I will talk as if a true dragon's spirit. Do not mention our mind-speech.'

"Agreed," she said, nodding.

Ecne waved towards the trail, and the girl rose from amid the undergrowth. Her shoulders, rounded by sadness, shifted back as she walked. Chin raised, she stared at Nathair as she approached. Grunts, dulled by the undergrowth, followed her, and she stopped to lift a hand, three fingers held high, the thumb and her little finger touching. Silence fell, and she placed her left forefinger into her palm, circling it, before heading towards Ecne.

'She is young, her spirit … strong. But something…'

"Show me," replied Ecne, keeping her crossbow pointed at the ground.

Nathair's sight took over hers, and the white spirits spurted into life. Four were now exposed, set in a semi-circle about the clearing. Ecne instinctively knew they were human. But the girl's spirit was different. Nathair grumbled again in her mind.

"What?" she sent. *"Spit it out."*

'Forgive my reticence. I can sense the presence of another – this Mammar, perhaps. But the girl has a tattered spirit – akin to the spirit-dolls, as if she has been fed upon. The soul regrows, sometimes stronger, sometimes weaker. This one pulses with vitality, yet the signs are there.' The artifice dragon stirred, raising its head. Nathair swapped her metal forelegs over before resting her chin again, eyes on the approaching girl.

"You think there are Constructors here? Feeding off her?" Ecne, dread forming like a stone in her stomach, placed her hand back on the dragon's snout.

'That we must find out, and soon. Do not reveal my presence. Speak as if I am a simple, unthinking artifice. A slave to you.'

"Forgive me," the girl started. "I am Q'Noh. And you?" Ecne thought she meant her, and made to speak, only for the gesture to indicate the metal beast her hand rested on.

"This is my dragon," was all she could think to say. "A ... a metal creature that I fly. My name is Ecne. I am a *Learned* among my people. Wise."

Nathair chuffed in her mind, a hint of affection amid the amusement.

"Dragon? I do not know this word, or recognise it from my mother's stories. You fly this? You take us somewhere safe?" Q'Noh now appeared far from self-assured, as if the walls placed around the death of her family had cracked. Ecne wanted to help, but Nathair's warning hung at the back of her mind.

"I don't know whether it is possible, Q'Noh. I would have to think on it. And before I do that, I need my people back. I believe your tribe attacked the dragon and I back at the beach?" Ecne pointed vaguely back towards the sea. The immediate blush to the girl's cheeks an indication she was right.

The girl nodded. "Though not on my or my Mammar's word. They feared it would bring the Drach to the shoreline. Hunting has been scarce, and the Drach have been scouring the Strech in the last few moon turns."

"Strech?"

"The jungle, where we stand. Up to now they have left it alone, but their eyes have now fallen this way. My Mammar feared they had wiped the last tribes out. Many of the lost made their way here." Q'Noh pointed eastwards. "Deeper in the forest."

Ecne mused on that, only for Nathair to send her an image of a snare tightening.

'Leave one place apparently safe for them to go, then you don't have to look far for your remaining prey.'

"Have you seen my people? Two men, dressed like me, with sword and bow." Ecne held up her scabbard and exposed the top of her sword.

"We know who you mean. The two with fire in their arrows. No. But the Drach hunt humans."

"They went to the city. So that is the place we must search." Ecne looked towards the jungle's edge, but the trees and vines hid the stone walls from view. She could sense the city's presence, and Nathair placed another image in her mind – one of buildings that glowed with spiritfire and the strike at the artifice that had come close to sending her back into the sea.

"Then we say goodbye here. You go to your death." Q'Noh made to turn away, and paused as her eyes lifted towards Nathair, a tear forming in one corner. "At least rest first. Eat with us. We can tell you what little we know of the city, for what good it will do."

Ecne made to speak, to refuse the offer, but felt she couldn't despite the Spirit Walker's urging. She patted Nathair's snout and turned to peer into one of the crystalline eyes before she followed the girl.

"Stay here," she thought. *"If you are seen, it will bring the Drach down on these people."*

'I say you are too trusting, Acolyte.'

Ecne gave the dragon a last look, wondering if she was correct, and headed off to follow the young leader, calling her name.

Together, they made their way back to the trail and beyond. A tear-filled Q'Noh said a last goodbye, but didn't enter the clearing where her Mammar and second father lay. She explained that the Drach would return and check if they had been moved.

"Our death rituals have changed since we realised the Drach return to check the dead," she said. "We can no longer give them a proper goodbye." With that, her hands flickered into action. The signals and grunts she used sent the four tribesmen melting into the Strech. "Follow my way. Those behind will hide your clumsy trail."

Ecne bit back the retort when she recalled Laoch's tracking skill. After a good half an hour trek through the undergrowth beneath the humid canopy, they emerged into a small clearing occupied by a roughly built hut much like the ones they had left behind.

"My hut," said Q'Noh. "The others have similar spots in this area. We do not camp together; too easy for the Drach to take everyone. Do not leave this clearing without saying, even for a piss. We have traps about the camp that will snap bones."

The words felt ominous. Thoughts of Nathair's concerns knocked at the confidence she had in her decision to trust Q'Noh. The girl indicated for Ecne to sit, and sat cross-legged beside her, on a log stripped bare of bark. Soon tribespeople arrived, bringing bowls of water, with some spiky fruits and dried fish set on a wide, leathery leaf. Each bowed their head to the girl, accompanied by grunts and flickering hands that the girl responded to with a sad smile before accepting each gift.

"You have questions," Q'Noh said as the last of her tribe left. "I can tell you are eager to ask. If you go to the city, best to ask them now, before the Drach take you. Though, for the safety of my people, I will choose what I answer." She proceeded to drink from a wooden bowl.

"Why do they hunt you?" Ecne picked at one of the fruits, splitting the skin to reveal a dark flesh beneath. Its sweet aroma startled senses stifled by the jungle's plethora of smells.

"Ahhh. According to the tribe, because they are escaped slaves."

"They?" She took a bite. Though not as sweet as its aroma, the fruit sparked her tongue into life.

"*They*. My mother and her mother, and all those before her, can trace their people back to when we were brought here by the Constructors, their Inhibitor soldiers. We came with the soul-eaters. That is why I can talk and they cannot, or at least choose not – I am not sure where that lies now. According to my Mammar's telling, we arrived as slaves, and attacked the Drach and the humans they held in thrall – their army. Many were killed. The Inhibitors took everywhere except three cities. Caintic Sholaimh, where we are now, and Amhrán and Coisir. Though I know not where they lie." Q'Noh took another sip, and a little of the fish, her eyes distant.

Ecne tried to memorise the names, thinking through the girl's words. What she spoke of tallied with Keran's talk of a defeat, and the necromancer Marbhleoir's confirmation that it had happened here, on Apso-Tran.

"So, your people were freed by the Drach?"

Q'Noh snorted. "Freed? No. The Inhibitors died in their thousands, though not their machines. My Mammar did not know why. She knew that the Drach had mourned their impending death, only for it to never happen. We were left in their wake as the surviving Inhibitors ran, to be preyed upon or enslaved by another master. Many of my people saw what was to come and ran – the Drach were too few to find us. But they have hunted us over hundreds of years, murdered my people. Tore out their tongues like they did their slaves' – as a symbol of their power."

"And now you lead?" Ecne skirted what she really wanted to know, allowing the girl to explore some of the grief.

"The Craven, this tribe, respect language. Something inbred from when they were slaves. They looked to us, and my Mammar said there was nowhere else for us to go. I do not know what happened in other tribes. Only that, in the Strech, my mother and all those before her have always led."

"Mothers?" Ecne pondered out loud as she finished her fruit. Now she had a craving for the fish. Not her usual choice, but her stomach growled its response, and she began to pick at the flesh.

"From the men, they took more than a tongue. To keep our people going, we mated with the tribespeople. Usually new arrivals from dead tribes. I do not see how this helps you find your friends. This is the past. If we remain here, the past will die with me." The girl sat back; her green-smudged cheeks streaked with dried tears. "I do not know how to keep them alive. I am too young, and have not yet learned all the lore I need. Much of what remains of Mammar, her spirit now within me, will take too long for me to understand."

Ecne stared at the girl, thinking through her words. She needed to be careful. "You retain her spirit? Is that what the glow was when you touched her chest?"

Q'Noh nodded. "It is more her memories. We were spirit-dolls, slaves to the Constructors. Sharing is what we were bred to do. In this way, we survived when few others have. I ask again, will you take us from here? I am sorry for your friends, but my people still live."

Ecne swallowed the fish. The salty tang made her thirsty, and she tried to use the strong taste to take her mind off the pleas. It wasn't working.

"Help me find them, and I will do what I can. But I won't leave until I know."

"I apologise, but they are already dead."

Q'Noh stood quickly. Her hands flickered, and Ecne suddenly felt vulnerable. She glanced at the fish, a worry forming when as she gazed at the rest of the offered food and drink. Panic set in, and Nathair's warnings surged into her mind. She threw herself off the log, groping for her sword. Q'Noh stared at her. Her hands stilled, looking down at the half-eaten food, then back out to the trees where her people waited.

"We are not Drach," Q'Noh spat on the ground as she spoke. "We do not kill or take what is not ours. Especially from our own."

Ecne flushed and dropped her sword tip. "I..."

"Yes?" The girl approached; her hands suddenly alive with spiritfire. Ecne remained rooted to the spot, fear taking hold of her legs. The smell of death and ancient spirits wreathed her mind as if Marbhleoir stood before her once again.

No. Control.

"You really want to know our history?" Q'Noh reached her side, lifting her fingers towards Ecne's cheek. "Why we need to leave?"

Ecne didn't flinch. Her eyes were solely on the girl's. There was passion there, not evil intent. But, how much damage had been done to her own realm by those who believed they were doing right?

Her throat suddenly dry, Ecne replied, "No. I need to know how the Constructors died. That is why we are here."

The sweet aroma of the fruit broke through the dread, memories of food shared, the girl's disgust at Ecne's unspoken accusations. Gathering her thoughts, she calmed her mind. The girl's eyes now appeared wide and vulnerable – a look she knew her father had hated upon her own face. The fingers crackled with power but didn't touch her, hovering near her cheek.

"Then I gift you what my Mammar retained of that time. What was passed on to her. In return, you will save us, whether your people live or not. This I can do, but only with part of your spirit as a bond." The girl's lips quivered a little, clearly pained by retaining the spiritfire.

"Bond? A binding?" Ecne baulked. The necromancer's offer in the walls of a dead palace pervaded her mind, electrifying her senses.

"A promise, no more. A soul for a soul."

If Oisin and Laoch are dead, Brandshold depends on me.

Ecne nodded, unable to speak, and braced herself as the girl touched her cheek. The spiritfire rolled over her head and Wisdom flared, streaking from the sigil across her neck to form a barrier. Ecne sensed Q'Noh flinch as the two energies met. Wisdom remained as a passive wall, not a threat, but neither did the God move out of the way.

Calm.

She let her thoughts touch Wisdom, the sliver of her God thinning as it understood Ecne's purpose and tasted Q'Noh's intent. The girl's spiritfire gently seeped into her cheek to spread along her jaw and into her mind. It drew on a piece of her there, siphoning a sliver of the soul that lay rooted in her brain. Again, memories of Marbhleoir's attempts to sever those connections threatened to undermine the gift being shared. But Wisdom stood with her – the God that had kept the necromancer at bay long enough for Sura to save her – providing another crutch for Ecne's bravery.

Her soul gift to seal the binding rode the spiritfire back into Q'Noh's hand. The exchange completed, the girl sifted through her Mammar's memories and wrapped these about Ecne's mind. Images poured in of a time hundreds of years earlier.

And Ecne screamed.

15
HOW TO LURE A TRAITOR

Innealtóir, Realm of the
Constructors

Tarin lay on the ornate bed. Metal ribs curved above the Fleshmaster in the shape of intertwining spirits that screamed their hatred up towards their ceiling, and their devotion to whoever spirit-slept on the mattress beneath. Bone-white fingers caressed the first of the devoted, the eyes now barely discernible where centuries of his touch had taken their toll. The bed had been built from an artifice, one that had almost condemned him to true death. Tarin, trapped inside after the debacle at Apso-Tran, had witnessed the pilot Inhibitor's soul being ripped from their body before his white eyes. The grinding noise still echoed in his mind, the pilot's empty cadaver pressing down upon the controls as the machine strode onwards towards the harbour's edge, and the promise of a forever death in the depths below.

Luck and devotion had intervened. The hooked legs had caught on a dry-docked boat, spinning the artifice about, its huge claw snapping down on the hull. Yet the issue of death still remained, his spirit's root within his mind and brain loosening further as a dreadful cacophony tore through his Inhibitor army, heralding the separation of body and soul. How close had his spirit been to caving in? A victim of his own immortality.

The hatch had been torn open and flung aside, and more of the dreadful sound reverberated in the cabin. His mind lost, his spirit so close to losing its grip. A huge claw sheared through the hatchway to clasp Tarin, pulling him free. And he found himself exposed ...

Enough.

The Fleshmaster opened his fingers and slammed his palm onto one of the many metal spikes jutting from the bed's head. The memory of pain shot through his mind, wiping away thoughts he wished could be locked away forever – thoughts that Marbhleoir was supposed to have put to rest with his soulless army of flesh machines.

Except Nathair destroyed them, and now I face another of my veil dragons that has turned on its master.

An Chéad.

Tarin rose from the bed, only to look back at the shroud upon the mattress that retained his shape – just as he had done for the past six centuries. The artifice bed was a constant reminder of how near true death he had come – a blanket of slaughter that hung over them all. And from those ashes, the new Inhibitors had arisen. Young and unfettered by the excess of the past, as many who survived had lost their ancient memories upon the battlefield. The Thaumaturge had grown in status that day. Thousands of new bodies were suddenly needed, and Marbhleoir had arisen to the challenge, he and his people working tirelessly to save as many as they could.

It was my foresight that had the flesh stored, ready. Enslaving rather than hunting. But so many fell that day, lost to us, or stored ready for our triumphant return.

So much harder without my dragons. But now, at last, I have one.

Only to discover the treachery of another.

"Lelion," he said, striding out of the bedroom and into the hallway. "I need to speak to the Admiral Incarnate. Now!"

The scrape of hurried boots below pleased him, but did not assuage his mood. He strode down the white marble stairway, passing the half-empty library and the scorch marks yet to be cleaned. He stopped at the balustrade that marked the chamber below. The room had been cleansed, and the roof was close to full repair after Tabharthóir had torn her way out, the dragon over-infused after consuming the necromancer who had so failed his emperor. The throne sat waiting. Kneeling before it was one of the magi he had taken from the City of Sighs. Not the warrior magus Tarin savoured more than most. Her anger added a certain poignancy to her spirit. No. This magus had the taint he named *union*, which meant nothing to the Fleshmaster. A petty label used to justify the manipulation of power that the magi Solidarity had declared necessary to defend the city. A word, he believed, used to control their people simply so they could draw on their spiritfire.

Drinkers of souls, just like us, but they can't see it. And they name us soul-eaters.

The emperor strode down the white marble stairs and along the curved corridor where his beloved statues stood, each a representation of the flesh he had carved on his way to solving the conundrum of immortality. Despite the many years, each gave him the same pleasure as his eyes flickered across their dreadful beauty – sculpted flesh made stone.

The emperor entered the chamber, striding towards the Inhibitor who held the restraint for the kneeling magus. Tarin gathered the chain on his way past, dismissing the young soldier with disdain. He dragged the human weaver of spiritfire across to kneel before him as he sat on the dragon-winged throne.

Metal-clawed fingers hooked under the chin of the male magus, pulling the man's gaze up to meet his ancient white eyes. He let the fear seep in. The middle-aged human tried desperately to look away, to break the contact. Tarin felt the quiver, knew what was coming, and snapped the man's thoughts into a vice of his own power.

"Piss yourself, and I will eat your soul. Understand?"

The magus nodded, sweat beading on his forehead.

"That's a start."

Tarin unlatched the manacles, removing them from the magus's wrists. He grasped flesh and bone, and dragged the man closer until his dry breath filled the man's nostrils. "This is the time I break you, understand? When I am done, you will be my slave, my spirit-doll. Or you will have fought too long and be useless to me, and I will let my Inhibitors feed upon you piece by piece over a century or more. It is an undefinable agony, I am told." Tarin caressed the man's cheek, letting whitefire grace his skin and roll along his scalp. The essence of the magus's fear was a delight. He was already beaten; he just didn't know it yet.

The Fleshmaster leant forwards and clasped both hands on either side of the man's face. Whitefire wreathed his skull, entering his eyes and ears, seething into the petrified brain. There, it wrapped about the man's soul root and tore it free, shredding the tendril into a thousand pieces and lashing them against the magus's mind.

"Can you feel it? My control? I have your soul in my grasp, have torn it asunder at my merest whim."

Then Tarin rebuilt the pieces, the jigsaw of the man's soul reforming under his guidance. Piece joined with piece at his command, and he reshaped the magus before him. Moulded him. The body shook – muscles tightened, tendons strained with the surge of power. The green eyes clouded, swirling with whitefire, and teardrops dried within the magus's ducts. He sensed the man's resistance fade, and it was now that chance would decry the ending.

However much he had experimented, some human souls could not endure. For decades he had tested on the lost and lonely in his attempts to turn his dreams of forever flesh into one of an immortal, but unrooted, soul. Many had died, more had been broken, their souls rooted too deep, or the whitefire needed too much for the mind and heart to cope with. These were the ones whose souls he found tasteless in the end, and were thrown to the Inhibitors as beneath him.

"It's time," he whispered, and dust from his lips danced upon the whitefire. "Let go."

The magus's head snapped back, the scream silent, yet thrown up towards the repaired dome. Ecstasy rushed through Tarin's dead nerves to fill his whole body with the pleasure of capture. He held the spirit wrapped in his power and drank from its agonised well, the energy infusing every shrivelled cell. It was not the savoured taste of the warrior magus, but it was enough.

Pulse-ridden fingers released the man's cheeks, leaving the skin beneath husked and dry. The green eyes remained clouded for now, swirls of white mingling with pupil and iris as they writhed. His body a rictus, the magus remained completely still. Tarin leaned back to enjoy the pleasure of complete and utter control of a living, breathing man.

"Mine now, magus. I call you spirit-doll, and rename you ... Dis." The tingle of the magus's spirit rushed through Tarin, and he fought to contain the *need* to drink more, to drain the man dry. But a spirit-doll was a precious commodity, and that of a magus, doubly so.

But for you, I have another purpose.

"Clean him up," he whispered, and handed the restraining manacles over to the waiting Inhibitor. "He will no longer be needing these."

Tarin eased back into the throne, sensing the sparkle of the scaled wings around him. He sighed briefly and cracked his fingers wide, a spark of whitefire dancing along their tips.

'Tabharthóir?' he sent.

The artifice dragon murmured in response. Muted, its mind gone, the response was as an obedient beast to its master rather than the Spirit Walker he had so long sought. An Chéad and his *queen* had forced his hand, and now only he could manage the metal beast. The spirit remained fused to the dragon's mechanism, working its parts, feeding as the artifice did, but it was mindless, a dependent child, for it was Tarin's *will* that now gave the spirit shape and control.

And a secret I need to keep.

Tarin's thoughts swept past the Spirit Walker and drove on into the heartstone. The *calling*, focused with his renewed strength, crossed the void between two veilless realms.

"*Lelion,*" he sent, the words wreathed in whitefire, chasing the *calling*. "*Lelion,*" he repeated, "*we need to speak. Now.*"

It seemed like an age before the silence was filled with the admiral's thoughts. Tarin knew the *Kraken*'s commander would be composing her thoughts, shrouding her emotions before speaking. As did he.

'Emperor,' she replied, the thoughts drawn out as if tired. *'You have reenacted the calling. Tabharthóir's training goes well, then.'*

Tarin pushed away the attempt to rile him. She had her spies, and would know he had returned with a dragon in need of repair. If he rose to it, she would score a point in the never-ending search for a weakness. If he remained stalwart, the admiral would regard that as information gained.

"*I have learned much, Lelion. I am sure your eyes have been telling you what I want them to know.*"

Let that sink in.

"An Chéad still flies, Lelion. And in the hands of a traitor. One of the first Inhibitors, Nardelene. Remember her?" The silence ran deep and set Tarin's mind racing. He'd recalled the name, remembered her as someone who'd sought service in return for immortality, but little else. Had she been Lelion's? He sent across a memory, the eyes and hair of the once-human woman, prominent as they had been at their last meeting.

'No,' came the tired reply, and Tarin struggled to grasp whether that was truth or lie. This was likely a conversation he required face-to-traitor-ous-face.

"No matter. She has An Chéad harnessed, and claims dominion over part of the Seven's realm. She does not recognise my rule." Tarin shook his head at the thought of letting Lelion know this, but, as ever, the hunt for the Magi overrode all.

'A complication. And a dangerous one. One dragon is not a match for the Kraken *once we are in the realm, Tarin. But we will be vulnerable on breaking through the veils. And we do not know how powerful the Seven or their descendants are. What about Popsilin?'*

"I left her there," Tarin replied. *"We will look for her when we return. The seeking gave no clue to the Seven, but nor were we targeted by any magus in return. It showed only An Chéad, and one other thing of interest."*

'Ah, so now we get to why we talk. This has to be a success, otherwise all the failures you'd have kept to yourself.' The words dripped with vitriol.

"You run close to the blade's edge, Lelion." Tarin sensed the baulk, the mental flinch. It set more of a worry at the back of his mind than if Lelion had planned the comments. Something wasn't right with his admiral, and it tallied with what Lieutenant Kankrin had relayed. Lelion was struggling, constantly complaining about noises no one else heard.

'Words, Tarin. They spill unbidden.'

"You seem ... distracted."

'No doubt your eyes keep you well informed. I lack spirit sleep, Emperor. Perhaps your urgency causes me such issues. The waste ...'

"Is necessary," cut in the emperor, tired of the same argument. *"We cannot give the Seven time to prepare."*

'You sent the Scorpions, the Mechanised Inhibitors. Chances are they would have been oblivious to us without their presence.' Lelion yawned, and the emperor sensed the dip in the admiral's vitality.

"Chance is not the game we play. The beacon would have been obvious to any magi, the breaking of the veils to release its message more so. But at least we get to my point. The Infected are rife amid the middle reaches. The distraction has worked far better than I thought possible. There lies an opportunity. An Chéad will need to be fed, as Nardelene does."

'Ah. Yes... you mean to starve her.' Lelion sounded genuinely pleased.

"Or at least remove her from the fight. Overwhelm her with the threat of the Infected upon her food source."

'And so, you will need a powerful spirit-lure. A sacrifice.'

"That I already have." Tarin smiled, teeth bared. The pleasure of creating his new spirit-doll ran through his mind, and he let that seep over the calling to the admiral. *"And so much more than that. A trap. How soon will you be ready, Lelion?"*

'A week, if you mean no rest for the Inhibitors. I would suggest two.'

Tarin sighed, leaning back into the dragon-winged throne. *"Let it be two weeks. Then we send in the scouts, Lelion. And the spirit-lure, perhaps. Prepare for war."*

16
DEATH COMES FOR THE CHILDREN

NORTH OF JENSE, BRANDSHOLD

A flame flared against the night sky, catching Duke Panset's eye and causing him to flinch away to save his night sight.

"Cover that lantern," he growled, the words whispered down the line until the light winked out. "Stupid. How many times?"

"Twice, your Grace," answered Yanik. "That I remember."

"It was rhetorical, Yanik."

"If I knew what that meant, I wouldn't be sat here in the fucking dark and damp waiting to burn my own walking-fucking dead." First Ranger Yanik slapped the duke on the shoulder and headed down the line of her Rangers, waving them out towards the western flank of the supposedly deserted village.

Llandon dropped in by the duke's side, his sandy brown hair damp with the spring night air. The Ranger's telltale breath was caught by the scarf he'd wrapped about his mouth.

"Why do I put up with her?" Panset asked, eyeing the First Ranger he'd come to trust over the last few weeks.

"Is that a rhitoracil question, or do you wan' me t' answer?"

Panset knew Llandon likely grinned wildly under the scarf, his gruff accent hiding a sharp but uneducated mind. Unless you counted hunting and killing the Infected. At that, he was a Learned, through and through.

"Maybe you should remind me."

"Easy. She's a fuckin' killer, and 'er Spear would die for you and the effin' queen, your Grace. As would I." Llandon pointedly looked away from the duke as he spoke, focusing on the village. "But ye' can ask agen afta we strike 'ere 'cos this place gives me the eebies."

"Why?" The duke shuffled lower, a raised eyebrow querying the First Ranger, clearly expecting an answer. Llandon rarely gave a view without reason.

"Cos the smell," he replied. "Dry and wet. Usually, when we're too fuckin' late, we only get blood and a whiff of past rot. Not 'ere. Time?"

The duke glanced over to where Llandon pointed. The hood on a distant lantern amid the trees was raised three times in quick succession.

"Time," he said, and slapped Llandon on the shoulder. The man nodded, checking his scarf before heading out to the east and the fire trap they had set. Panset sensed the man's unease, not just in his words, but in the eagerness with which he ran over to his waiting Spear.

Careful.

He, in turn, crept out. The crystal armour he wore was surprisingly light and uncumbersome, though the helm restricted some of his vision. As royalty and prospective king, he had trained from a very young age with the traditional weapons of long sword, arming sword and bow. He had proven his worth on the battlefield despite his abhorrence for the Crusade itself. But for all that, it was his days spent hunting in the wilds that had proven most beneficial. The spear, the true ruler of the battlefield, had become his soldiers' weapon of choice, though it was not boar they sought. No. The Infected, the once-human, were far wilder.

Duke Panset pushed the willow branch fence aside, its cracked posts evidence that something had broken through. The lack of fires and the aroma of cooking was another sign. Eight houses were aligned either side of the rough street, two rutted lines where carts passed through marking the major traffic. Smears splashed across nearby bootprints in the dried mud, black in the poor light, but the telltale spread from spurting wounds confirmed his thoughts of blood.

Keeping low, he was running to the side of the first building when his boot caught on something amid a pile of evergreen fronds. Stumbling, he thrust out his hands to steady himself on the branches. A stifled cry rose from the pile, and his heart both leapt and fell. He dropped to one knee, swiftly eyeing the road and the too-quiet houses. Warily, with his boar spear in one hand, he reached under the fronds. There, his fingers found a wooden lattice. Probing at the gaps, the thin wood shifted. Taking a breath, he raised the grate to be greeted by a second stifled cry. Water sloshed beneath, but his eyes couldn't adjust to see its cause.

"Mista? You dead?" came the whispered words. Hoarse, choking sounds accompanied them.

Panset froze and forced down a sudden dread. Thoughts of his own children, at home safe with their beloved mother, rattled about his mind. It was why he had thought the Crusade a fallacy. But not this war. What if these were his children? The Infected sent to feast upon their souls as if they were mere cattle.

"I live," he whispered. "Hush, I will be back. I promise."

"Please, we're sooo cold."

"I must make it safe. I shall be quick." He gently replaced the lattice and placed the fronds back over the top as their parents must have done.

"As Yanik would say, fuck me."

He glanced up and around, his hand signal more in hope somebody was watching. Turning back to face down the road, a shiver ran across his neck, a bead of sweat suddenly chilled by the shifting breeze. He stood, and was heading for the nearest doorway when a hoot echoed inside, the Infected's call bouncing off the wooden walls before exiting through the shattered window. Panset froze and waited for what always came next.

Answering hoots sounded from along the road. Wood cracked and doors flew open. Infected began to emerge. Husked humans, their skin white. Flakes filled the air at their passing. Dried lips pulled back from dead gums, a multitude of blackened teeth exposed in a chatter that always set Panset's heart pounding. He kept low, eyes upon the street, waiting, hoping they would all spot him.

After all, he was the bait.

"Mista, in here."

The words burned into his mind. Panic forced him to turn around. A girl peered at him from under the raised wooden lattice, one hand beckoning.

No.

They hunted the young first.

Always.

He faced the gathering Infected. All but two were on all fours, noses to the air and sniffing. They were supposed to follow him, run him down, fall upon Llandon's spears and Yanik's fire arrows. And now they had a child's scent.

"I hope, Lady Fate, that you are there for me today."

Panset signalled his intent, hands flickering with urgency. He then planted his feet in a low crouch, wishing he had time to strap on his buckler. Instead, he drove his arming sword into the ground beside him. Fourteen white-laced eyes turned his way, teeth clacking. Hoots spilled from rotted mouths and their smell hit him hard. The dry and the wet, as Llandon had named it.

They charged as one.

Arrows flared in the night. Their flames ruining any hope he had of seeing in the dark. But this was going to be close combat. Too close. And he had not the time to judge the arrows' success. The nearest creature sped towards him, eyes wild, teeth bared as it hungered for his throat. With no other choice, he let the Infected close in, ramming the boar spear through the abhorrent mouth to pierce its brain. It ran onwards, and the head split, whitefire exploding amid the gore. He slammed the metal butt of his spear into the next, catching the creature's throat as the spear tip exited the back of his first victim's skull. More arrows rained in, lighting those that followed, and Panset whipped the spear head down onto a third Infected that sprang over the second. The tip caught its shoulder in mid-air, causing the foul thing to spin, and its filthy feet slammed into the duke, knocking him aside. The boar spear broke from his grasp as he landed amid the branches. The lattice bent, and snapped under his weight.

Panset rolled, not for fear of falling in the well, but in hope of preventing the Infected from doing so. He reached his feet as a third set of arrows struck. Seven of the Infected were now aflame, but not slowing their charge.

Weaponless, he stepped back in front of the horde – having to decide whether to reach for his sword or defend the well. Choice made, with hands low, he hunched down.

A human roar swept through the village, accompanied by pounding feet. Boar spears rammed into the leading Infected, and Llandon's Rangers charged on. Their cross-shafts dug into the pierced bodies, the Rangers' momentum heaving the creatures out of Panset's eyeline. He ducked to grab his sword, and slashed at the legs of the next before grasping the weapon in two hands to spin low and slap into another set of ankles. Bones broke, and both husked bodies hit the ground, hoots of pain greeted by multiple arrows thudding into their heads. Panset rebalanced himself, knowing one of the hated things had passed him, and two remained in front. They did not slow, though their ragged clothing burned as they ran on all fours with him in their sights.

No choice.

He spun about as the Infected landed on the lattice. The wood gave way, and a hungry growl rumbled from the beast's throat as it clawed downwards. Panset threw his sword. The blade spun, and the pommel cracked into the Infected's shoulder. The distraction enough, he drove forwards. Leaping, he wrapped his armoured hands around its head. Teeth scraped against the crystal gauntlet, whitefire arcing across the plates. Panset twisted, but the once-human resisted, its spiritfire-laced tendons refusing to give. So he wrenched backwards, desperately pulling the head and neck away from the well. It snarled and clawed at his arms.

Silence fell, a deathly quiet.

"Fuck me, your Grace."

A splatter of bone and gore arced across his helm as an arrow slammed into the foul creature, before careering on into the night. The resistance at an end, Panset sat back onto the ground, his armour glowing with fading whitefire.

"How am I not dead?" he said to the sky.

"Because," replied Yanik, appearing in his eyeline, hand out, "I'm bloody good at what I do."

The duke took the proffered hand and let the First Ranger pull him to his feet. The last two Infected lay just beyond her, one with Llandon's boar spear pinning it to the ground, the second with the Ranger kneeling on its back, his sword buried deep into its shattered skull.

"And he's quite good too, though he likes to keep it quiet. And if I might say, what in the Seven Hells do you think you're doing, your Grace?"

"Saving the effin' younglings," said Llandon. He got up off his kill and pointed towards the well. Four sets of frightened eyes peered out from under the broken branches.

"What else could I do?" said the duke. He knelt down and pulled the first child from the well. Wet, and worryingly cold, he let her settle on his hip.

"Now that's a rhitoracil question," added Llandon, pointing at Yanik.

"These four need warmth. Fire, blankets, tea! And fucking hurry!" she bellowed.

17
WHEN REALITY STRIKES

FARNFORD, BRANDSHOLD

General Zendril stood atop the scaffold. The wood was roughly cut, but each pole was hammered home with strong pegs and hemp bindings. It stretched for a few yards either side of her. Beyond that, the low earth wall petered out just before it curved around the town. Only where the scaffold stood did it reach a defensible height, around nine feet high.

"It goes so slowly," she said, more to herself than the city mayor who stood, hands behind his back, surveying the same scene, or the meister whose name she had already forgotten, who tapped idly at the planks beneath her feet.

"It does," said the meister, surprising Zendril. She turned to face the general. "But then, we only have *people* to do the job. Perhaps a word with our esteemed mayor, and we could add a few helpful machines."

Zendril analysed the woman's grin. The aged skin and grey eyes hid a sharp mind. Of the outreach branch of Erstenburgh University, it was Meister Pollop who had provided her and the veterans with the detailed town plan of Dent, and her acolyte was working on Farnford's now. The vets had long-since started devising blockade patterns to force any invading army into the narrower streets and well-conceived ambush traps. Only, the giant mechanical Scorpions might not be quite as susceptible to flame and arrow as they hoped. She had at least convinced them that height was to their advantage. Dent was a town of sturdy roofs.

"Mayor Rusin, what's the issue here?"

Stupid question. He's a fucking religious stalwart with Justice's Scripture probably tattooed on his arse cheeks.

"Issue, General? No issue. Scripture is clear that *science* corrupts." The mayor glared from under his stern, square felt hat, the gold brocade of his office swinging to one side. Meister Pollop didn't flinch, just grinned back. Zendril had to assume her reputation had preceded her, and the meister probably fully expected a Weister tirade to hammer the point home.

I hate to disappoint.

"Mayor, if the Unbelievers arrive in numbers, which, with you being so pious, is *very* likely, who the fuck is going to stop them? You can throw a few scrolls at them if you like, maybe hit them with a few words from a fucking book. But they do not care. They will simply use the paper to roast your balls over a fire." Zendril kept her face flat, unemotional, just raising a single eyebrow that had an old burn mark through the middle, thanks to an Unbeliever's bolt.

"Faith," started the mayor, only for the meister to cough. The man's bearded face reddened. "Faith," he repeated louder, "is the only bastion against the Unspoken."

"It won't fend off javelins thrown from their arbalests, or put out the banefires they cast into the centre of Dent. This town will burn, your people will die, unless we get a wall built." This time she stepped in close to the mayor, keeping her eyes on his. "The House of Justice, yes?"

The mayor nodded in response.

Zendril spun about to the retaining balustrade, and peered inwards. "Mander, you fucker!" she shouted. Her second-in-command looked up from where he was chatting with the veterans. "Get me the Lead Justice of the House!"

"Eh?" he said, then read his commander's posture. "Now?"

"Now! In fact, I want all of the *seven*! And bloody hurry!"

"There is no need ..." blustered the mayor.

But Zendril just lifted her hand, choosing to not turn and face idiocy she had no time for. "You use Scripture to decide the fate of your people. I use actions."

———

She stood, one hand on her pommel, the other slipped into her jerkin and against her stomach. Mander sat on the wooden barrel at her side, the two honour guards next to him. The leaders of the seven Gods' Houses stood opposite, facing in towards the town. The almost deferential mayor stood next to the representative of Justice.

"General," Lead Justice began, causing Zendril to glance at the too-young woman from the House of Penance. In all matters, they were supposed to head such conversations unless directed. She took it as a sign of weakness, or pomposity on Justice's side, that matched the mayor's attitude. Perhaps High Lord Penance had been remiss with the outer Houses? "The mayor tells me you wish to use the meister's machines to speed up things. This is unten ..."

Zendril drew out her sword, causing all the leads to take a step backwards. She threw it to the ground.

"The Overseer, High Lord Penance, and the Houses of Erstenburgh have sent you messages to the contrary. I shepherded the priests here myself. You wish to go against the Council's will? Then pick up that sword and defend your people."

"I ... this is ..."

Mander limped forwards to collect the sword from the floor and raised it up for all to see. "This notch here," he said, "was from a metal leg. This one from a metal claw. This," he pointed to a burn mark across the tip, "from dragon's breath. These bastards here—" Mander pointed to the honour guard, who both stood in response. "—the queen's own honour guard, pulled me from the fire, then stood shoulder to shoulder with the general as the Unspoken's dragon landed before us. Do you think a sixty-foot metal dragon gives a flying shit about Scripture?"

"Then why build walls? What good will they do?" asked Lead Penance.

Zendril caught her look. She had been primed, with Zendril out of the loop.

Typical Penance.

"If the dragon comes, we will need ballistae – machines the Gods' Council have already approved. But the Unspoken has more war machines. It is for those that we need the walls and, just as importantly, the ditch before it." Zendril withdrew her hand from inside her jerkin and waved over to three veterans, who pulled a tarpaulin from a waiting cart. On it lay the metal carcass of a Scorpion. Zendril said nothing. She didn't have to. Three of the leads stepped back, stunned by the sight of the bulbous eyes and wicked-looking barbed legs. But four walked towards it: Penance, Fate, Hope – and, to her relief – Death. She had their measure now. She glanced up to Meister Pollop, and the companion she knew had already examined the mechanical Scorpions. They both nodded back.

"Words will not fucking work. Only water, oil and height give you a chance. And my veterans."

"The queen's army ... they must..." said Lead Justice.

"No, we won't. There are too many towns to defend, so we will remain mobile." Despite her distaste for the man, her sympathies lay with his sudden understanding of reality, and that they were to face it alone. "Nor will you be able to retreat to Erstenburgh, or Ridth. Jense, even. Here you stand. Make plans for you families to withdraw to the hills if you must, but they are not to remain in one place."

And may the Seven ensure the Infected stay away. If those fuckers get in, the town will die well before any dragon chows down.

"Now that I have your full attention, Meister Pollop, what do you need?" called General Zendril up to the tower.

"I need quick learners. Ones who can build swiftly with their hands – the basket weavers and rope makers. The smiths would help, though I believe you have those under your charge," said the meister, reading from a scroll as she spoke.

"They do, but maybe I can allow some of their time for specifics." The general turned back to the leads of the Seven Houses. "Your acolytes, and many of the priest-in-waiting, will fit the meister's requirements. You know your flocks, so get looking."

"We have not ..." started Lead Justice.

"Yes, we have," interjected Lead Penance, stepping forwards, Lead Hope at her side, who held out a fist-sized crystal. Within its facets, High Lord Penance's purple image swirled. Next to him, a red-faced Lord Justice.

"You wish to speak to them directly, or shall I interpret your bullshit for them?"

Zendril laughed, and a smile crept onto her face.

"I'd choose the latter, if I were you."

———

"Why the show?" asked Mander, scooping up the stew with a wooden spoon. He slopped the mixture of vegetables and rabbit into his bowl, and dropped into a padded chair in front of the fire. He sighed despite the commandeered four walls around them, and stretched his leg.

"Quicker than, as Lead Penance put it, all the *bullshit*." Zendril slurped at the stew, the taste setting her senses alight. As in most things, the people of Dent had taken her by surprise. Stubborn until turned, then they were your friend until proven wrong – and their food was a delight despite its dour appearance.

"Was it wise, revealing those bloody Scorpion things?" Mander chewed, refusing to let any of the stew escape his lips.

"It was you who told me rumours from the surviving vets had hit the taverns, Mander. Ale and rum are a fast way to spread word around, and this was a swift way to get my fucking point across. The army will not be big enough, so we must be on the move. The towns will need to delay whatever is coming. The veterans are answering the call, but they are old or carry wounds, be it in the head or the body. Giving them a place to defend is best. We will need time to assess what these town-loving bastards can do, and how they fight." Zendril let the spoon pause a second as she savoured the taste, her mind wandering over the consequences of her words.

"I know the plan, but we are sacrificing people, whole towns. Giving them up. It doesn't sit comfortably, Zendril. Not at all."

"War is fucking shite, whichever way we turn. I need to save as many as I can. At the moment, we plan as if the attack is coming from the north. If they arrive in the south, then Mandrich has the pleasure of taking the fight to them. But he won't." She dropped her spoon, licking her lips. Changing her mind, she approached the steaming pot with her spoon again. "He'll sit behind Ridth's walls, as will the Duchess of Makalena, and if there are no dragons, rely on the fleet to save them if needs be. I urged him to send Rangers into the hills and forests, even the Southern Reaches, at a push.

Whether he will, well ... It depends on how much my daughter and the High Lord decide he needs to know. The truth is fucking scary, Mander."

"But you think the north?"

"Me? If the Infected and the Scorpions are any hint, then yes. But I've been wrong before."

"Woah, is that a Weister I can bloody hear? No ... it can't be." Mander smirked, and set his bowl aside.

Zendril shook her head. She dropped the hot spoon and took the man's hand. She stood and, drawing him up from the chair, headed towards the back room.

"Fuck knows why I love you."

18
A POISONOUS REMEDY

Unknown City, Apso-Tran

Oisin threw up, his stomach churning with a hunger that sat there amid the maelstrom of acid. His back arched as the venom raced along his nerves, demanding he feed upon the soul that wavered about the elven warrior.

Fate engulfed his mind, swallowing his rabid, venom-infused thoughts. Disorientated and torn between two paths, the Handren fell to his knees and screamed. Black-veined, acrid vomit speckled the floor. And, as the last of his agony spilled from his mouth, he saw it move, squirming as if a worm in a puddle. Sickened, he retched again. Once finished, he reached for the elf's blade and scraped the foul mess from the floor, flinging it against the far wall. It writhed before it stilled.

"I ..." The word croaked from a burned throat. Oisin swallowed hard, trying to wash away the acid, when the iron-bound door screeched open. A leather-clad foot came into view. Oisin recognised the cut of the jail guard's boot. He grasped for his knife, only to remember he had a God's weapon. With a mere wisp of thought, Fate coalesced into her favoured form. The arrow flared as the elf entered the cell corridor, eyes intent on the wall opposite, where the keys lay. The guard's left hand was wrapped about them as he peered over his shoulder – a cat-like eye taking in Oisin and the flaming green arrow.

The mountain man caught the nervous eye-flick towards the door, and loosed. The arrow tip drove into the Schenterenta. The guard grasped at his throat, but spiritfire had already burned through, and he collapsed as his neck gave way.

"Now what?" said Oisin, staring at the keys that swung slowly on the hook.

An image popped into his mind of a strange house, and stone doors held fast by an internal lock. A now-lost spirit elf helped them enter. He nudged at Fate's sigil, rubbing the spindle with a plea in his mind. Within a minute or so, they had worked together to form a hook long enough to retrieve all the keys. With a sigh, urged on by the stench of his vomit and a creeping sense it still quivered, he opened the cell, returning only to collect the warrior's sword and knife.

Sore, his body wracked by the ministrations of the now-dead Sendak, he gently eased his way towards the sole door. He slipped it open a crack, wincing before looking through to find a set of stairs rising to his left, and ahead, a door much like his own. With the head of the stair passage dark and silent, he twisted the handle opposite and felt it give. Opening the door, he listened through a gap, expecting to hear Na Pertera Sentil. He was greeted, instead, by silence. He had lost all sense of time, but assumed the latest beating had been the herald of morning, and Laoch would be suffering the noble elf's presence.

The smell was certainly better than in his own cell. Less vomit, blood and crap. No moaning either. He slipped through the door and closed it with care. As silent as his pained legs could manage, he approached the second cell, the first empty of all but old straw. Peering around the dividing wall, he found Laoch lying on a wooden slab, eyes to the wall.

"You sleep on your other side," whispered Oisin, trying to keep the pain out of his words. "And snore like a pregnant cow."

Laoch rolled onto his back, one eye on the Elite Ranger. "The first thing you do is insult me ... By the bloody Seven, Oisin ..." He got to his feet, hands quickly on the bars. Oisin felt every cut and bruise as his friend surveyed his face and body.

"Heh, is it as bad as it feels?" Oisin asked.

"That depends if you feel like you've been hit by a bloody battlecart and blown up by Erin's Wrath." Laoch reached out a hand. The Handren dropping the elf's sword to grasp it in return. "If I'd known ..."

"You'd have what? Charged in to rescue me, risking your death as well as mine. We have a job to do, Ranger. And besides, I lost a little weight in there. The venom ... I think Fate took her chance and expunged that crap. Not all, but most, I think. Though we both tire."

"Looking at the battering you've taken, I'm not surprised. You wouldn't happen to have the keys?"

Oisin held up the collection he'd brought. Each had its own strange, lined symbol upon the grip. He ran through three before he alighted on the correct one. The welcome scrape of a mechanism turning brought a little relief.

Laoch exited and gently gripped Oisin's arm. "You gonna hold out long enough for us to get out?" he said, his mouth twisting as he caught the tang of blood on Oisin's cinched jerkin.

"I hope to. This isn't my blood. I may have hacked my torturer back in return. Can you remember the way?"

"Well enough."

Laoch's tight smile gave Oisin a little confidence, and he handed over the warrior's knife. "Then lead on before we are discovered."

Laoch slid the knife into an empty sheath. His eyes stared into the distance, a little red seeping in at the edges, and his arm bracer reformed into his favoured short sword. He headed for the door, gently pulled it open, and surveyed the dark stairway beyond.

Oisin dropped in behind, his stiff body lulled by Fate's touch, which eased the aches enough for him to keep pace. He held his God's bow low, the string undrawn, but knew Fate was ready. He fretted about his exhaustion. While some muscles ached from being in one position so long, the rest were bruised and battered from the warrior's ministrations. Still, Sendak's cuts were sore, but not deep.

Stop complaining. Focus.

Laoch ascended, each foot gently placed on the next stone step as he led the way to the upper floor. Here, another bound door waited, its fit precise except for a small gap beneath. Light played there, warm, yellow and flickering.

"Still night," whispered Oisin, receiving a nod from Laoch, who placed his ear close to the door and signalled his intent. The door was hinged inwards. Laoch gently lifted the latch before steering it open a crack. He signalled two guards, both seated, and Oisin readied his bow. Laoch crashed through the door and took three strides before driving his blade through the back of the first guard's neck. Cards fell to the table, bloodied, and the guard slumped forwards. Oisin loosed. The blue arrow seared over the first guard's shoulder to burn into the face of the second. Cat-like eyes shrivelled as the heat took hold, and Fate's arrow burned its way into his skull. Both died in near silence, though death's aroma would alert others. Laoch strode across the room to a second door and set his shoulder up against it, listening.

Oisin followed, and scavenged his sword and equipment from where they'd been stacked along one wall. He gathered Laoch's gear too, all present except for the spear he held so dear. The mountain man quailed at that. Would Laoch leave without it?

I doubt it.

"Anything?" he asked.

Laoch raised a hand for patience. After a pause, he shook his head and turned back. He eyed his bow and quiver, eyes sad, before collecting his armoured jerkin and putting it on.

"Laoch," said Oisin, only to receive a glare in return. He recognised that look, and swore under his breath. "I know what you're thinking, but ..."

"I get you out. You fuck off and find Ecne and the bastard dragon. If I follow, then all's good. I'm not leaving without Sura's spear." The Ranger finished hooking his jerkin into place, placed the quiver at his hip, and slid the spare sword into a waiting scabbard. "You understand what faith is, how an oath works, more than most. I go without it, my spirit is hollow. Worthless."

"We have a people to save."

"Aye, we do. No one asked me though, Oisin. Nor you. We just took it on because we swore an oath to a queen and the Houses. The right thing to do, despite all the shit thrown my way. And I will honour it, but without ... without Sura who gave herself for us. That spear is the last link I have. Something to hold me together so I can fulfil what's expected of me." Laoch's eyes flicked to the floor, and over to Fate's bow. "You have faith in Fate, and I in Justice. The difference is you have a good soul, whereas mine shrivelled in an Unbeliever's banefire."

Oisin paused, eying Laoch. He'd heard the stories, though like all fireside tales, there was bound to be embellishment and exaggeration. Was this the time, halfway through an escape?

"Your brother?"

"Aye, Láidir. And the others. Murdered, yet still living as the flesh fell from their bones. You don't heal from that. Never." Laoch looked directly into Oisin's eyes, much as he did when Sura took his sole attention. "Ever. But you look for something to ease your soul. I thought it was at the bottom of a bloody bottle, but no. It was in the eyes of an elf. I never held her, Oisin, not once. Never will. But that spear is the last thing I have of her, and without it, I fear what I will do – whether I'll collapse into the *nothing* I was, or the rage will take me. Neither will help save our people."

Oisin glanced towards the door. His mouth twisted into an uncertain smile, and Fate tugged at his mind. The weft and weave pulled his sight towards the table and the pile of cards. Under the slumped form of the dead guard, a ring glinted. His ring, the single, worthless stone set within it the mark of his status amid the Handren. He pulled the guard back and collected the ring, wiping it down before slipping it on. A simple comfort from home.

The smile hurt, but he let it widen.

"Laoch," he said, and pointed towards the guard he'd killed with Fate's arrow. His friend rolled the guard clear of Honour's spear, the relief on his face palpable. "Torturers *and* thieves. Not quite the allies we sought."

Laoch wiped the weapon clean and slid it into the sheath on his back. A weight seemed to lift from his shoulders.

"Lead on," said Oisin. "Let's find a way to the gates and get out of this hell hole."

Laoch turned away. Justice shimmered red along the sword's edge, reflecting the fire in the man's words. He edged the door open, pulling it inwards to peer out into the dark. They could see little, their eyes unadjusted thanks to the candlelight inside the guardroom. Laoch became aware of Justice's glow, and dulled the weapon before stepping out into the passageway that led to the road they'd been marched along. At the street's edge, he peered around both corners.

Oisin closed the door behind on Laoch's signal, and took station. In the mist, small pinpricks of light could be seen along the shrouded, empty street. It remained uncomfortably warm, and the silence of the city was only disturbed by the hum of insects as they hunted any exposed skin.

Laoch signalled for Oisin to cover and, keeping to the buildings along the far side, he moved fifteen yards further down. Oisin began to follow just as he disappeared into the mist, and soon caught sight of the Ranger waiting for him at the entrance to an empty alleyway.

"Nobody," Laoch whispered. "What's...?"

A bell rang, its pitch low and thunderous, echoing through the night and barely dulled by the mist. As the last reverberations faded, another sound filled the air. Low and sonorous, it came from deep within the city. It tugged at Oisin, penetrating his chest to reverberate within the hollows of his lungs and stomach. His whole body matched the pulse of the sound. Laoch's hand alighted on his shoulder, only for Oisin to detect the same hollow echoes running through his friend.

Another change of pitch, and his fingers tingled as if numbed on a cold night. The note tugged at his heart, and its beat began to match the weird, musical rhythm that echoed through city and man.

"Is this prayer?" Laoch asked as he stared down the vacant alleyway. He stepped out, following the sound.

Oisin gripped his arm, a flick of his head towards the alley indicating Laoch needed to be cautious. "It reminds me of something," he said, "though it escapes me. Where are you going? We need to leave."

Laoch shrugged Oisin's hand off. "We have to see what's happening. Remember, we are here to learn how they survived. This may be important, Oisin. Then we get the hell out." Laoch stepped away. Keeping to the edge, he headed down the alleyway. The mist lingered even here. Not wanting to lose him, Oisin followed. Fate tugged at his mind while the deep, musical note pulled at his heart.

They reached a second, wider street, which appeared to form a circle around the city, and then a third. Each step drew them closer to the deep music, while the eerie presence of the fog and the lack of people continued to gnaw. As they emerged from the alleyway, Oisin began to understand that what they heard wasn't one instrument, but many, layered atop one another and woven with a multitude of voices.

A thought dropped, a memory.

Nura.

When the Handren had brought the corpse of Sura's brother, Nura, back to her tribe, they had been greeted by song. A procession through the hide tents, accompanied by the raised voices of his tribe. A deep, vibrating song that rose and flowed through the procession. It had not stopped the entire time they remained there. Day and night, somewhere in that camp, it rose and fell until they left.

It must have been Nura's lifesong.

"Laoch," he whispered.

The damp mist and song masked his words, and he hurried, racing from building to building with the eerie emptiness gnawing at his senses. Laoch finally stopped, though in plain sight, his head haloed by the glow that emanated from beyond him. Light wavered to the rhythm of the song, the voices sonorous and multi-layered, each note designed to underscore the next. Its deathly beauty was evident, but Oisin was in no mood to appreciate it. Laoch seemed unaware that he was exposed, and as he caught him up, Oisin shoved the Ranger into a doorway and grabbed for the man's hood.

"At least try to stay alive," he said.

Laoch stared back at him, eyes a little glazed before the light returned to them, edged with Justice's red. He shook himself and placed a hand over Oisin's heart.

"Can you feel it?" he said, eyes wide. "The pull?"

Oisin blinked, keenly aware of the sincerity in Laoch's eyes. Anyone who didn't know the man may have taken it as fervour. "No," he replied, but Fate graced his mind, and he followed the thread she showed him to an image of a heart bound by thin, venomous black chains. Not all the poison had gone. "But I understand."

Oisin gazed over his shoulder. The song remained strong, and his eyes were stung by the white light emanating from whatever lay at the entrance. He could make out the backs of many heads, hair short, ears protruding to points, big and small.

He released Laoch and pulled his own hood up. To one side, a set of stairs led to an upper doorway, into what he assumed to be a house. He took the first step, and then Fate drove him on, and Oisin found himself at the top, staring towards the centre of the city. His heart railed against

Fate's chains, but they held him fast, urging him to *see*, while dread crept in as Laoch ascended.

Is he strong enough to see this? Am I?

Oisin was drawn back to the sight below. Hands gripping the balustrade, the vision producing a sense of strange vertigo. The mist glowed around the city as whitefire rose in a hemisphere above the moon pool, wavering to the rhythmic fall and rise of the Schenterenta's song. The light illuminated the huge crowd, all of whom stared inwards, mouths wide, lips moving as the layered lifesong entered a strange, structured pattern. Discordant at first, it struck Oisin like a hammer until his body became attuned to it. Fate wove a thread around his heart, a cord that linked to his mind, and his spirit pulsed to the powerful rhythm. A man immersed in song, mind, body, heart and soul.

"A lifesong," he whispered. "But for who?"

And staring out into the spiritfire-lit night, he knew. And it sickened him to the core.

The light sucked back from the centre of the moon pool to reveal an elf in black robes, silvered edges glowing with spiritfire. Na Pertera Sentil stood before an altar. A naked human man lay upon it, his hair hacked back, beard roughly shaven. To one side of his head rested his bloodied tongue, cut out by its root, while blood flowed from between the man's lips. The Schenterenta noble spun slowly about, hands raised, moving in time to the song – or perhaps directing it. A fist-sized crystal was held aloft in one hand, its internal glow wavering to the rhythmic beat. The elf took it in both hands and the rock shook, vibrating faster. Whitefire lashed at the elf's hands. But he remained strong, bracing himself, and slammed the crystal down onto the man's chest.

Oisin expected a crack of ribs, a shattering of bone. But that would have been a mercy. Instead, the voices dropped to a low background murmur, broken by a silenced cry from an agonised soul. Dread wrapped Oisin, and he sensed Laoch tense as the prone human's back arched, the spine seemingly pushed beyond possibility. The man's spirit tore from the body, tendrils rooted in heart and brain stretching before snapping loose. The seething form was greeted by a roar from the crowd.

Na Pertera Sentil bellowed, the crystal raised in triumph, and the song ended in absolute silence as the soul was drawn into the stone.

"Seven Hells," said Laoch, one hand over his heart, the other, sword in hand, braced against his head. "What in the Seven's bloody name was that?"

"Probably the most hateful and evil thing I've ever seen," replied Oisin, his thoughts numb. "And we were looking to these for help?"

19
TO TREAD LIGHTLY

APPROACHING KARAK, KHUND, BRANDSHOLD

Prime Sneed leaned against the mast, the ship rocking beneath his feet as it had for the last few weeks since leaving Meres. The sea there had been blue and sanguine, the short trip over to Meres Port from Ridth a well-trodden trade route that had been a pleasure until they had faced the merchant prince of Meres Port. Santanini's steadfast refusal to accept the rise of the Unspoken and the Unbelievers had not taken the prime by surprise, the Isle of Meres being far removed from the Crusade in the north. They had sent a token force made up of mercenaries and untrained youths, who had been used mainly as guards and reserves should they be needed. The fact many had left their post when the tide turned in the war was a moot point with the prince. As he had explained at least twice to Queen Weister, it was not really their fight, as the isle was secular in nature.

Sneed had nodded at the prince's flowery words and token promises should the word of dragons be true, and sat back as Simeon drowned the poor prince in his own rhetoric. By the time the Duke of Weister had finished, the prince was still not an ally to be relied upon, but was at least aware how much aide would be coming their way should the Unspoken's dragon fly south: approximately none. And nor would Simeon be allowing the southern fleet to risk being under the dragon's breath should the isle become desperate.

Of course, Sneed knew well enough that the Isle of Meres' status as an associate member of the Union meant they would never come under threat of expulsion, their wool and weaving the finest in the human-occupied lands, their wine famed. At least the worship of the Seven flourished amid the unmoneyed, offering hope while being milked for taxes. Though, right now, Sneed could understand the desire to remain in such a warm and welcoming land.

Here, the sea was a dull grey, the waves high and swells deep, with the promise of a cold death should you fall overboard. They had passed Khund's forbidding mountains a few days ago, and were now riding the waves towards Karak, the isle's capital city and home to the Khund Oligarchy. The complete opposite of Meres, it was filled with zealots and oddballs who took the Seven's Scripture to the extreme, with every form of science or invention analysed for blasphemy. They had the wheel, the sail, and had since stood still for nearly six hundred years. Even their grain was ground by hand, always with one hand on Scripture, the other on their souls.

But they remain hardy and driven, their seven armies unmatched in their zealotry. If King Panset or, later, the prince consort had called them to arms for the Crusade, then perhaps the outcome would have been different. Instead, they had feared what would happen should they find our people lacking in faith.

The duke's flagship, the *Wither Born*, finally made it around the headland. The harbour breaker came into view, and beyond that, the secondary walls of the harbour itself, with the promise of calm waters and, perhaps, a night's sleep.

Horses I can do. Ships? No thanks.

"Pining for the land, Prime? The thrust and parry of the Court over the swell of the sea?" Simeon's smile had been painted on his face since they had first come aboard ship. For all the man's reputation, well-earned as it was, Sneed had seen a new side to his once-friend and student. The man was as comfortable aboard ship as any he knew. Perhaps the root of his surliness lay in being tied to the land rather than the duties of a duke.

"You know well enough that I am. How you can enjoy such pitching and yawing, I know not."

"Hah, you were loving it around Meres. What's the difference?" Simeon goaded, his smile widening.

Sneed could not help himself but rise to it. Perhaps their friendship was on the mend? Though there had been difficult nights between Meres and Khund when they had hardly spoken a word. "Warmth, glassy seas and a short trip."

"And a false welcome and little warmth at the other end. Santanini is about as honest as a lead coin covered in gold leaf. At least here you will have honest, if blunt, answers."

They both eyed the harbour as it came fully into view. The multitudinous ships resting there ranged from basic skiffs to the small Khundish fleet the oligarchy kept as a protection against pirates and any other threat posed to its piety. Behind lay the ships of Penance, four warships that boasted oars as well as sails. The competition to man such a punishment ship was rumoured to be vicious.

"This is only my second time here," said Sneed, "though I have met with their delegations annually in Erstenburgh. I understand you enjoyed their welcome a little more often?"

"If you mean I indulged in the gambling houses of Hope and the warmth of Fate's embrace, then yes. But to my understanding, the House of Honour now heads the oligarchy, and such delights are reserved for the patrons of the Houses only."

"Honour does. And that may well play to our advantage, Simeon. And you will need to be the dutiful duke."

"Beholding to his queen's prime, yes? No doubt regale them of tales about the Unspoken's dragon. I do not know which way they will fall, Sneed, after being snubbed for the Crusade. Word was they talked of the heresy of the Houses back then. What will they make of things now?" Simeon's smile had slipped. Sneed noted the Weister sneer.

"Just words. Penance ruled then, and they eventually agreed it must be the Seven's punishment for their sins. Though the Khundish House of Honour ..."

"Did not," finished Simeon. "And we are going to need them, are we not? Hence, I bring a third of my fleet as a sign of its importance. I will order them moored in the lee of the wall, but away from the harbour in case they take our intent wrongly. You can only get so much across by bird, and the fleet can be taken in two ways. Either the import, or the intent to enforce."

Sneed's toes were cold, white and argumentative. The stone floor beneath them offered more punishment, and he eyed the thin line of carpet between his feet and the prayer stone with trepidation. Sucking in a breath, he took the first step, using a little of his spiritfire to deliver warmth to his toes and praying such interference went unheeded. This House's lead, as befitted the head of a secondary House, had taken upon themselves the title of Superior. It had been the first sign the Khundish were moving away from the interpretations of Scripture laid down by the Erstenburgh Houses. The second had been the attempt to break away completely, only to pull back when news of the Unbeliever enclave at Anvil had risen.

Superior Penance watched carefully as Sneed enacted the ritual, keeping his gait straddling the thin carpet, refusing its comfort as he walked through the magnificent prayer chamber to kneel upon the stone. No one in a Khundish House refused to give upon the prayer stone, for all were equally sinful and deserved whatever their God decreed. In addition, the priests' sufferance was seen as a gift. Luckily for Sneed, some deference was allowed for a member of Court, otherwise the scourge would also have been in use.

He knelt upon the stone and felt his soul part, a sliver sliding between the crystal bonds to reside with whomever else had given that day. He had to admit, it lifted him somewhat, a moment of shared faith he had lost when the true cause behind the Seven Houses and their Scripture had been revealed at his investiture. The day his faith had been broken, then rebuilt upon the need of a people.

Superior Penance laid a gentle hand on Sneed's shoulder and squeezed, the fingers like iron, cutting through the cold and slight numbness caused by the gift-giving. Sneed leant back on his haunches and stood, steadying himself on the offered arm.

"Thank you, Superior," he said, a little more hoarsely than was his intent. "It felt good to give penance again."

"Hah," replied the older man, his beard and the tufts of hair upon his scalp, snow white. "Whispers tell me you're not one for ships, Prime Sneed. So, reconnecting with the land can do nothing but good. Come."

The man, Sneed placed him as mid-seventies and as fit as any he'd met of that age, led him towards the stairway so like that in his own God's House. It proved a little less worn as they descended and, unlike the one in Erstenburgh, the Superior's rooms here were much deeper. However, the effort to get there kept Sneed warm enough. Along the way, the Superior recounted the recent history of the oligarchy. All known to Sneed, but perhaps a sign of connection he was going to need.

Eventually, they entered the Superior's austere quarters, including the circular table and the smaller Wyrding Stone that lay in the middle. As with all the subsidiary Houses, the lead, or superior in this case, supported the gathering of souls, though they gifted theirs to their Lord or Lady in Erstenburgh via the Wyrding Stone. That was as much as they knew, their faith in their Gods not stained by the truth. The fewer who knew, the fewer would break under the strain.

"Sit, sit, Prime. Ale?" asked the older man. The Khundish ale had already been opened and allowed to breathe, as was their way.

"Your ale is far too strong for my disposition, Superior." Sneed raised a hand, placating.

"Nonsense. Besides, this is brewed especially for my House. A weaker strength, more for fortifying the soul. This is what we share with young and old instead of those barn cakes you dole out. You should try it. Might bring a few more of the flock to your prayer stones." The glass waving his way magically filled, Sneed took it with a smile and a shake of the head. The first sip was slightly sweet, yet filled with a sour berry aftertaste he rather enjoyed. True to the superior's words, his senses reinvigorated as the warmth spread from throat and stomach.

"See? I can tell by your eyes. I have a crate or two in the back. I'll have them aboard your ship for your return. Possibly a brew or two for the High Lord, eh? Maybe it'll encourage the *lad* to visit some of the more distant Houses."

Sneed grimaced at the word *lad*, though the superior seemed not to notice, or possibly care. Clearing his throat before taking another sip, he set the glass down. "This has been a pleasure, Superior. But we have business of great import."

The change was palpable. The jovial superior, who had taken him quite by surprise, switched to a stern-faced elder, eyebrows knitted, cheeks sucked in. It was a moment Sneed instantly regretted. The Khundish were, by reputation, so hard to read. In that moment, he understood why.

What opportunity did I just miss?

"Business. Yes," said the Superior. "A few words have already reached our ears about what your business may be. Word of the Unspoken and her dragon. That Ridth has been attacked. And, if conjecture is correct, Erstenburgh too, though you have closed many mouths about that. Yet there is undoubted truth in the Soul Tear. Our people suffered as much as yours."

"Most of it tavern talk, I'm sure," replied Sneed, "but close to the truth. The Unspoken has risen again, and there has been confirmation of her dragon. Killings near Ridth, and a sighting in Ersten Forest, where the beast attacked the High Lord. And a third in the north, where word came before we departed of new, evil machines. I have evidence with me that the Unbelievers have a reflective armour, which they wore, as you say, in Ersten Forest."

The old man leant back in his chair, throwing down the last of his ale and setting the glass aside. "And the Soul Tear? What of that?"

Sneed tried not to lick his lips, nor stare up to the left as he spoke. "An act of the Unspoken. We think she transported her Unbelievers in this way to the forest. The world felt the ripples of the magic."

"Magic? Not machine?"

"Let us say, the Eighth acted in a way we do not understand. Is that easier to swallow?"

"For the oligarch, yes. You were High Lord, Sneed, when our people were *dishonoured*." Again, Sneed winced. "Our righteous armies were denied the opportunity to fight the heathen bastards and their machine-loving witch. You and the Gods' Council were as much to blame as King Panset for that denial. Do not think for a moment that we have forgotten. Or that I have forgiven."

Sneed shivered as the atmosphere in the room turned as cold as the floor. "No. On that we agree. Yet you did not secede from the Union. If I am to convince the Oligarchy of what they face, it would be useful to understand why. Not that which is written, but what remains unsaid."

"That is easy, Prime. Faith. Unshakeable belief that our Gods and their chosen ones are acting for the greater good of our people. That you had reason for denying us." The old man squeezed his hands together upon the circular table, eyes narrowing as he watched Sneed.

"Those are words for your people, your soldiers. What are the words for the House superiors? Your unspoken thoughts."

"That King Panset was weak of faith and would rail under the gaze of our House generals and be proven unworthy. That basking in the power of our belief would have been too much for his armies, and they would fall when they understood that they also were as unworthy as their king. And we were proven right."

"Yet you remain within the Union," said Sneed, now leaning forwards, eyes intent on the superior.

"Many believed that we should secede, go our own way. And yes, it is still for debate. But in the face of the Unspoken, one walked the path of faith and devotion before her people. You ... *we* may finally have a monarch worthy of our devotion again. To your credit, Prime Sneed, we understand Queen Weister was your choice. And for that alone, you have the ear of the Oligarchy. But use it wisely. This time, the test may well be whether the Union is worthy of *our* soldiers' faith, rather than the other way around."

20
A WALL OF SPIKES AND STONE

House of Penance, Erstenburgh, Brandshold

The prince consort dabbed the quill into the pot of ink, carefully checking the nib until satisfied it would not spoil the paper. Queen Erin closed her book and watched as his tongue slipped between his lips, touching each corner before a sparkle lit his eye and the scratching began again.

She had sat for half an hour, the monotonous sound of Adama's writing a light relief from the clamour for her attention outside Penance's walls. Captain Mordant and Grand Meister Arknold had declared the wall defences as strong as they could be, the scaffolding holding the new ballistae having been reinforced since a trial led to its collapse. Arknold had failed in her attempts to design a useful system for moving the huge crossbow-like machines, and Mordant had provided the fastest means via bricks and muscles. At least the smaller arbalests, mounted on stationed posts, had proven viable.

Yet, despite each minor success, another pile of papers, contracts and demands would fall upon her new table, awaiting her attention. Assistant Prime Bertin had proven her worth in many ways since Jacka had left and subsequently been taken ill. But paperwork was not one. Where Jacka had the confidence – let's say over-confidence – to act in the queen's name, Bertin did not.

The queen sighed, stood, and placed her hands softly on Adama's shoulders. She squeezed, and the consort stopped writing, letting ink-stained fingers fall upon hers. A moment of tenderness that had run through these brief times together. Occasions that had not punctuated their previous life.

"Did you send it?" he asked, patting her hand before bowing his head to write again.

"I did. I am sure Simeon's seneschal will appreciate the treatise. The general may be more of a critic." Erin gave his shoulders a final squeeze before backing towards the door.

"Hah. Mandrich will listen, nod sagely, and likely go his own way. At least he is consistent, and would treat your mother's words in exactly the same way. You leave so soon?"

"I must. There is much to do. I have to inspect the City Guard, at the captain's request. At least it means a little less reading." She waved the book, though she knew he would not recognise it. It was as forbidden to him as to anyone else outside of the Gods' Council. If they knew she had purloined it, likely even the Union's queen would find herself shut out from their secret library. Though she might not be so quiet about it.

"Thank you for … for these moments. They help me heal, though I know you cannot see it."

An unexpected tear appeared in the corner of her left eye. Erin wiped it away before moving to his side. She laid her hand next to his and pointed towards the notebook. "I sense it in your words, Adama. The flow, the rhythm. I see the clarity in your eyes. You are coming back, and I will be here as you heal."

—

She waited for the carriage to pull fully up before giving her leave to Penance's seneschal. The paired horses pulled them towards the city's main entrance, the walls on either side festooned with a variety of metal and wooden scaffolding. Some rose above the walls, and these she constantly regarded as particularly vulnerable, though she knew the grand meister intended to talk her through their purpose today.

The streets and market squares remained busy. Her subjects going about their daily lives, fully aware that a threat to their faith and their lives loomed. The evidence lay in the ballistae and arbalests on the walls, the trebuchets around which they milled. Only the storage barrels were off-limits, their contents broadcast throughout the city as volatile. In fact, they were full of sharp rock and metal cut-offs, with no one willing to risk Erin's Wrath amid the city just yet. But familiarity with such dangers kept the people sharp, and the fascinated children under the watchful eyes of their parents. They just played amid the rocks and stones piled on the other side.

As her honour guard cleared the way ahead, her unannounced sweep through the city was met with waves and smiles. She kept her countenance relaxed, joy-filled as she strove to appear calm for her people. Meanwhile, on the inside, she railed at the sheer number who sought safety within the walls, and the fear of how many they could help when an attack came. Supplies were growing, all dried and carefully stored, and the wells were constantly monitored.

But for all that, it was soul-eaters that were coming. Creatures she now understood had once been human, who had severed their inner spirits from their bodies in their search for immortality. Her home, Ridth, had been a city full of tales of horrors. The serpents of the deep sea, the dire wolves of the mountains. Yet they loved, more than any, the tales of the vampire. The more she read from the Houses' Forbidden Library, the more she understood the root of such stories. The Constructors were soul-vampires who sought to feed upon her people, threatening an eternity spent as the puppet of something so inhuman. Or worse, the prospect of mere emptiness, your soul taken, used up. The *you*, the spirit that defines you, simply *ending*. For a people who expected their souls to join their brethren in the veils, such a finality held far more fear than death itself. It was this that drove the Overseer and the Council to the lies and deceits they showered on their people.

An absence, an emptiness. A nothing. What greater fear is there than an ending?

"My queen," said Captain Mordant as the carriage door opened. The palace servant moved away to allow a modicum of privacy.

"Captain," she replied, and stepped out onto the hastily built gangway she assumed was for her. Below it was a swamp of spring mud and wood chippings. "I am ready," she said, slipping off her cashmere shawl to don a uniform jacket. The cut was exquisite, but the style deliberately functional. She was here as head of the Union, and the rank placed upon her since the consort's incarceration.

"This way, Your Majesty. I think you will be pleased with the progress. Meister Kinst awaits us. The grand meister has been called back into the forest. She assures me she is fully briefed."

"She would," replied the queen with a smirk. "And if she didn't, she would likely talk with so much conviction, you would have thought she designed the whole thing herself."

Mordant entered the lift box behind the queen, and on his signal, the contraption rose in the lee of the castle wall buttress. At the top, they alighted onto the walkway; the stone was widened by layers of planks sat upon the protruding scaffold. She could make out three of the ballistae and two of the smaller, more mobile arbalests as she looked to the west, with a similar arrangement to the east.

"Impressive," she said. "And I assume they can be adjusted for distance and angle?"

"Physically, by manhandling them, yes. Those on the corner towers have been mounted on turntables, but there is not the space for such ingenuity on the walls." Mordant pointed towards the waiting meister. Kinst was busying herself with one of the ballistae, an irate-looking soldier arguing with the meister as seneschal Greeth looked on in amusement.

The queen approached, and the soldier stiffly saluted as she'd been instructed a thousand times by her captain. Meister Kinst turned and bowed her head briefly in deference, alongside Greeth.

"Meister Kinst. I've been told you have something worth seeing? A return on all my expensive investment, I hope."

"I do hope so, Your Majesty. Greeth?" she said. The woman stepped forwards to remove a metal cap from the front of the three-foot-long quarrel Kinst had been fussing over. It exposed a crystal. Its purple and aquamarine glow took the soldier by surprise.

"Heh," Kinst said. "Greeth has been working on a variant of Erin's Wrath in solid form." The meister winked at the queen, who paused for a second until she put Greeth's role and the stone together. A lie for the soldier, though rumours of the High Lord's *magic* had swept the city. That's where the High Lord was now, manipulating in the background, trying to get the priests of all the Houses to turn the incident into a powerful rumour mill about a gift from the Gods – and a timely one. To achieve that, more had to be revealed.

"Now, Operator Worster here will assist in its third test." The meister stepped back, ensuring she and the wall guards were to one side and out of harm's way. "Release."

Worster freed the hooks upon the ballista. The thick bowstring and curved arms thrust the quarrel out, over the walls. Queen Erin watched its flight intently. The metal javelin dropped as it arced over the gap to the forest, and smashed into an already dishevelled-looking target. The wooden façade and straw bales erupted with greenfire; splinters flew a good twenty yards, clattering into several other targets set at various distances from the tree line.

The eruption was met with a roar from the onlooking guards, and slaps on the back all round for Greeth, Kinst and Worster.

"Impressive," said the queen. "And these, err, new versions of Erin's Wrath? You have a large supply?"

"Not yet. It drains resources quickly," said Captain Mordant, gently shepherding the party towards the walls after dismissing Worster.

Kinst nodded. "The priests-in-waitings' ability with spiritfire is improving. Each day we can imbue more of the crystals. Seneschal Greeth here has been a... ha ... a godsend, so to speak. But if any attack comes soon, we will quickly run out. I suggest the focus should be on the Unspoken's dragon."

"And on Erin's Wrath itself. Arknold talked of its use with the ballistae." The queen looked out over the settling cloud of ash and straw.

"That has been less successful. We lose much of what we send. A better use would be in the trebuchet, with a more solid pot. Though the captain has a secondary idea. One far simpler, if I can sort out the contamination issues."

—

The first clasp of her tunic pinged open as her ringed fingers pushed it apart. The second demanded her attention as her thoughts wandered to the waiting hot bath. She hated being served. As queen, Erin had always seen herself as the servant of her people, not the other way around. Her insistence on changing alone was only thwarted when protocol demanded a high degree of formality and complexity in her choice of clothing. Her dressers had learned soon enough that their time was after her bathing, and only on her call.

The soft knock at her chamber door came as a surprise. A rarity in a world of formality.

"Yes?" she said, knowing no one dared enter unless commanded.

"Sorry, my queen. You have an urgent visitor. Visitors," came the boy's timid reply. "Assistant Prime Bertin has sent me to request your presence."

Sighing, Queen Erin did up the one clasp she had managed to undo, and glanced over to the steaming bath with frustration. Shoving it down, she approached the door and opened it with controlled care so as not to startle the servant.

"Visitors? At this hour? Tell me – and no, there's no punishment for inaccuracy. Just for silence, Vianti. Yes?"

The boy bowed his head, eyes to the floor. "It is a First Ranger, one who rode with Duke Panset, and some urchins. In the off-chamber."

"Urchins?"

"Handren," added Vianti. "Four of them. Wide-eyed and tired, but excited to be here. The First has spoken to Assistant Prime, and she sent for me. I know no more."

"This had better be worthwhile. Keep the water hot, Vianti." Queen Erin had taken no more than two steps before one of her guards moved in beside her, and another behind. Within a few minutes, she had reached the smaller throne room they used as a meeting chamber – or the off-chamber, as Vianti had named it.

Her lead guard checked the room before allowing her in, and she felt his tension beneath his armour. On entry, she recognised First Ranger Yanik, the woman's self-confident aura doing the introductions way before her words. She bowed low, and dragged the four urchins down to mimic her actions.

Erin found herself grateful that her two guards had taken station outside. A weight filled the room as Yanik returned from her bow, her expression disturbing.

"Queen Weister..." began the First before Bertin glanced over to silence the Ranger.

"The Ranger has some disturbing news, brought on the tongues of these Handren children. I thought it a morning matter, but she has a note from the duke insisting on its importance." The assistant prime handed over the short letter with its broken seal.

Erin read it before looking to the Ranger and her charges, who huddled together. She placed the letter on her chair as she stood. "Call for food, Bertin, and warm drink. Now, if you please. Then leave, and take my guards with you."

She turned back to Yanik. The woman's eyes were full of discomfort. When the food arrived and Bertin made to leave, Erin whispered to Bertin that they would talk after. Visibly upset, the assistant prime bowed and left.

That, I must rectify. But this ... this ...

"Sit, eat, and talk with me awhile."

The children looked to Yanik, who nodded, taking her own seat at the queen's table. Now a place for the commoner.

"Tell me what you saw ..."

21

IT IS WITHIN THE WORDS

UNKNOWN CITY, APSO-TRAN

Laoch shoved Oisin behind the pile of offal, only to yank him aside again as more booted feet walked past. The Elite Ranger scowled, but crawled into the gap between the stone bins, shoving his back against the wall before glaring back.

"We should have gone while we had the chance," he spat low and hard.

"We needed to see. It …" A sadness took over Laoch's eyes, the turn of his mouth sour.

"Sura. It reminded you of Sura. I know. But she would not want you on the end of one of these bastard's blades. And now we're …"

"Fucked, yeah. But we learnt something. What we saw … There has to be something there we need." Laoch drew his knees out from under him and rose onto his haunches to sight along the outer edge of the bin. More legs and feet hurried past, but there seemed to be no hue and cry.

Their escape was still likely undiscovered. Or if it had been, the general people of the city were not the ones looking for them. At the end of the ceremony, after watching the soul death of a mere human, the elven citizens had turned, almost as one, and headed back to their lives. That was when they had run.

The clamour in the main street seemed to be receding, the main body of the crowd heading for bed, Laoch hoped.

"We need to leave now," Oisin said, and grabbed Laoch's arm, "before dawn. Once it's light, there will be nowhere to hide."

"Aye. But think on it, Oisin. They fear the dragon and more coming like us, or the Constructors themselves. The gates will be under greater watch than ever, and the walls too." Laoch spat, and rubbed it into the cobblestones. "I say we head for the harbour."

"That'll be guarded too."

"Yes, but it's far harder to keep an eye on everything going on in a harbour. Comings and goings all the time. Fishing and ship husbandry wait not for the moon but the tide. The busier, the better." Laoch eyed Oisin, who peered out into the quietening street, then nodded.

"You can find the way?"

"Follow the smell of the sea. And I think these streets are designed to encompass the harbour. Follow one of the inner circles and I think we'll find it if my nose lets us down." Laoch took one last look at the Handren. "With me?"

"Yeah. But I'm no sailor."

"Hah, nor me. But I sink well enough."

———

Laoch sat upon the edge of the harbour wall. Below him, the dark swell of the sea rose and fell. There hadn't been much of a breeze to lead the way, but he had been correct in his interpretation of the streets. The cloak wrapped around him had been stolen from a fisherman's drying line. Its stink of smoke and curing vinegar assailed his nose more than the fish, covered by gauze, that lay on the racks behind him. It kept the flies off his flesh, but hadn't deterred the little bastards from trying, and he was forced, far more than he liked, to swipe away the swarm that collected around any exposed skin. At least he had a damn fine excuse to raise his hood and keep a scarf wrapped about his lower face.

Hate this bloody place.

He tapped his boots on the seaweed-infested wall, and reached inside the cloak to draw out a wooden pipe he'd found discarded on a vinegar barrel. He made as if to fill the end, all the while watching the dual guards who paced along the sea wall, their dark uniforms highlighted against the gentle glow that emanated from one of the harbour towers. It reminded him far too much of the whitefire that had taken Sura and swept her away, to be consumed by the *Kraken*.

Laoch flickered his hand and cracked a knuckle, receiving a sharp flap of a window shutter in acknowledgement.

Noted.

Below him, and about thirty yards to the right, a small fishing boat rolled with the incoming tide. A lone fisherman worked the nets, readying them, Laoch assumed, for going out. Probably at first light, though Laoch knew that some preferred to leave beforehand, depending on their intended catch. The elf had paid him no heed, Laoch having positioned himself just behind a stone mooring to avoid any eye contact. If the elf hailed him, the plan was done, and all would end in blood.

Well, more blood.

The tap of boots on stone rose in volume amid the harsh words being passed between the two guards as they strolled towards him. A knock of a shutter, and he began to count the steps. Unlike in the forest, where Oisin and he were masters of the ambush, an exposed harbour only had the masts and stowed sails to mask their intent.

So, hide in plain sight.

His internal count hit seventeen when the guards' harsh conversation rose in intensity, though the tone appeared not to be laced with threat. Laoch was sure the words were directed his way, so he raised his pipe, waving the thin end behind and back towards the guards without turning his head. More words followed. When Laoch's count hit twenty-one, he heard the expected thud of an arrow.

On the turn, he sprang to his feet, his right leg driving him forwards despite the slime underfoot. He grabbed the surprised guard by the chin and, slamming the Schenterenta's jaw shut, sliced through his throat and into the artery. Not waiting, he pulled the Schenterenta down next to his compatriot. He drove the knife into the guard's heart and stretched to ram the blade into the back of the second guard's neck. Justice glowed, and Laoch felt the God's satisfaction.

Oisin was soon at his side, and swiftly they lowered the guards over the wall, dropping them onto the ledge below to be swallowed by the tide as it rose. Far better than risking the splash. Laoch ducked behind the mooring stone, eyes on the fishing boat. There was no sign of the fisherman, but neither could he see any reason to be alarmed.

Oisin touched his shoulder. "Nothing the other way. The second set of guards will be suspicious in around five minutes," he whispered.

"But we don't know about the towers," Laoch replied, finishing off the Elite Ranger's thinking. "We go now."

He set out low from behind the mooring stone, Justice unsheathed and bloodied, but with no giveaway glow. Laoch stopped by the boat's mooring. Oisin glided past to take up station just past the stern.

Laoch waited, listening for movement, and was rewarded by the scrape of shoes on varnished wood. The elf emerged from a low cabin door, a slice of bread between his fingers smothered in something orange. The fisherman bit down, wiped one hand on his trousers, and returned to the net.

With a thought, Laoch's short sword wavered and reformed as a bow. He dropped softly to the deck. The elf stiffened, and his neck twitched before he began to turn. A hooked netting knife nestled in his hand, designed to strip and slice, and no match for the soft glow coming from Laoch's arrow. The elf glanced over to the cabin door, drawing Laoch's eyes despite the need for silence, just as a slim hand appeared above its edge.

"*Yeg*," the fisherman said as he strode forwards, hand out towards Laoch. A warning, but for who?

Laoch twisted as an elf emerged, her ebony, dappled skin reflecting the tower's glow. The cat-like eyes narrowed in concern as they flicked from the fisherman to Laoch, a cry ready on her lips.

Laoch froze. His mind's eye filled with the possibility of an arrow driven into the side of her head. Scarlet would flare from within her nose and mouth, a brief flame of Justice Laoch did not feel. The woman would fall, slamming her head upon the wooden step before lolling back into the cabin.

Laoch shook his head, clearing Justice's demand from his mind. At the lowering of his bow, the fisherman pulled the woman clear of its line of fire. Only a yelp filled the cabin's void as he pushed her behind him.

"*Yeg ne bart freen,*" the elf said, the whisper low and guttural. He had a hand up, palm out, placating, as the net blade dropped to the floor. The scuffle of boots from behind let Laoch know Oisin had dropped onto the boat.

"Laoch?" he said.

"Keep watch," growled Laoch, his mind reeling as Justice haunted his thoughts. "Inside," he said, and waved the tip of a glowing arrow towards the cabin. He repeated it as he edged around, making it clear what he wanted. The Schenterenta responded by shuffling to one side. A low whisper from the male quietened the woman, and they walked backwards and down through the hatch, the fisherman's gaze never wavering from Laoch's as he followed.

The cabin below was rudimentary, a table set against one side with two small benches attached. On the other sat a pile of woven crab pots and a sap-lined tank.

Laoch indicated for them to sit, and realised that the woman was much younger than he had taken her for. The baggy clothing and ruffled hair hid someone of significantly fewer years than Sura. He gathered a buoy line and threw it over to the male – the father, he now assumed – and indicated the girl. His reticence was clear. The tears on the girl's cheeks and choked sobs didn't help. The elf stepped back after tying the last knot, hands wide, a pleading expression on his face.

Laoch took a breath. Staring at the girl, the image Justice had sent played through his thoughts, juxtaposed by the act of ripping out a man's soul upon an altar. How do you tally such things together, make decisions where the innocents could die alongside those who condoned murder? He held no doubt they had likely watched the ceremony, urging the sacrifice, giving their permission – possibly, their adulation. Yet in this moment, they were simply people again. But so were the Unbelievers who had forced him to kill his own Spear. His own brother.

"Seven fucking Hells," he whispered.

"*Ne?*" asked the elf, his hands out wide again.

Sura would have done it clean. But he was not Sura, and he had an oath to keep.

His way.

Fuck me.

"You," he said, and pointed to the fisherman, his arrow flaring red. "Up." He gestured towards the hatch.

The elf's eyes flicked towards his daughter.

How in the Seven do I do this?

He chose the father. Pulling back on the bow string, he allowed Justice to add a lick of scarlet to light up his face.

"Now." He indicated the hatch again and made to follow. "Oisin?" he called.

The Handren appeared at the hatchway, gesturing the fisherman up.

Again, the elf looked back at his daughter, and then to Laoch.

Who am I?

Laoch aimed the arrow at the girl. Her eyes widened, barely contained yelps slipping between her lips. The arrow tip sparked with redfire, but Laoch's eyes were on the fisherman.

"Now," he growled.

It was enough. The father turned away and headed up the stairs.

Laoch eased back the string and briefly lowered his eyes to the floor, sucking in a breath. Desperate for a drink. Yearning for the gentle touch of Sura's fingers on the back of his neck, the gentlest of spirit kisses to let him know everything was okay.

But nothing was okay anymore. Death was everywhere he went, and he was a provider of its touch as much as anyone else.

A sniff from the girl brought him back. Her eyes were on him, red-rimmed amid the green, with widening pupils in the centres. Laoch looked either side of the cabin and settled on a piece of rough-spun clothing. Hating himself, he approached the girl. Her sobs were now silent. He placed a finger to his lips, hoping she understood, and then to hers.

"Sorry, but I must."

He mimed placing the cloth in his mouth, and relief swept over him when the girl opened hers in response. Again, he apologised, and balled the cloth before tying it in, making sure her nose was clear. He checked her bonds, tightening here and there, loosening others, before he placed the back of his hand against her cheek. The last time he'd been this close to one so young, he'd chopped into their neck outside a poacher's cabin with a long-lost short sword. Taken their life and blamed a poor Ranger for it. It had been the rum, he knew that. Running from himself. But what would *that* version of him have done here?

Probably fucked it up, and they'd both be dead. And I'd be knee-bloody-deep into a new bottle.

The creak of ropes being pulled, and the stomp of feet on the deck above, brought some relief. He moved towards the hatch, but stopped and gestured for the girl to be calm. She blinked her tears away and nodded.

Laoch headed up the stairs. He considered closing the hatch and decided against it. If he and Oisin needed to be out of sight, it was the best retreat. By the time he had picked up the hooked netting knife, the boat had begun to draw away from the harbour wall. The elf jumped back aboard, the mooring rope looped and stowed seconds after his bare feet hit the deck. He glared at Laoch, a stubborn hate in his eyes. Laoch repeated the placating gesture, pointing back down to the cabin. His heart thudded at what this elven father must think of him.

The fisherman leapt over pots and ropes to head his way. Laoch gripped the bow and raised it just a touch, but stepped away from the hatchway. The fisherman dropped to his haunches and peered into the cabin, locking eyes with his daughter.

It was a brief glance, but apparently enough. The elf stood to face Laoch. Laoch didn't raise the bow nor allow himself to flinch, but held the father's gaze a few seconds before responding with a dip of his head. The Schenterenta's lips twisted, and he broke eye contact. Laoch headed towards Oisin, who was kneeling next to the single mast. The fisherman ignored him and hauled on a set of ropes.

"I need a drink."

22
REVELATIONS AND CONTEMPLATIONS

THE STRECH, APSO-TRAN

E cne snorted. The half-snore half-choke woke her to a strange tingling against her cheek.

Memories flooded back. Too many, and far too quickly. Vertigo swamped Ecne despite her being prone on the ground. Her stomach heaved, and she retched in response, but everything was dry and empty. She tried to rise, but the vertigo kicked in again. Her gut finally surged, and she was sick upon the leaf litter.

'Acolyte?'

The thought cut through the maelstrom in her head and provided something to grasp on to as her mind drowned. Taking hold, she pulled herself clear of the chaos as her stomach heaved again.

'Ecne, it is normal. Calm.'

"Normal?" she thought.

She risked opening her eyes, and, despite the foul sight, her brain and eyes began to work in unison, confirming she was neither falling nor on a precipice. At least, not a physical one. Ecne leaned backwards and recognised a tingling sensation, this time upon her hair and forehead. As her eyes adjusted, she touched her neck, only to find a fabric there, a gauze. Finally, she understood the gloom.

'Q'Noh placed the blanket over you, said it was the best protection from the insects. I have to agree. I think some of them could bite through my scales if they were in the mood.'

Ecne lifted the gauze clear to find a collection of determined, yet stuck, insects of all varieties hanging from the fine netting. Many still fluttered or waved angry limbs – she knew how they felt, as her brain instigated a headache to join the nausea. Ecne took a long drink from her waterskin, and watched Nathair as the dragon chuffed next to her, eyes glittering in the dawn's light that broke through the canopy.

"I don't remember getting here," she said. Screams echoed in her skull. The smell of blood and old death assailed her nostrils. "Only that it was all too much."

'Q'Noh spoke to me. Tried to make contact. Pleaded for her people. I believe she is genuine. Her spirit, though sore and deeply scarred, is true.'

"She reminds me of the priests. Not a zealot, but driven. She ... She ..." The nausea swept over her again. The clash of steel upon a crystal eye. A shattered head flying through the air. Brain and bone splattering her face, the drops wet, the shards pricking her skin. And that scream ...

Ecne found herself on the ground again. A gentle, metal talon tapped at the forest floor at her side. She blinked, and scaled, ethereal feet appeared in her eyeline, soon followed by the concerned face of the Spirit Walker.

"She has given you memories. I can see them in your soul. They are part of you, yet not. A gift, and likely a curse. When Keran and I bonded, we shared the same as this. But the more difficult times ... Ahh, they hurt all over again. Except we could face them together. Watching my twin sacrifice himself while Keran held me, and I with him as his nieces and nephews drowned. Once shared, the pain didn't diminish but was more tolerable. It did not lessen their importance, for memories shape us, but it helped us to make sense of who we are now. Maybe ...?" Nathair held out a hand, twisting it so the palm was up, expectant. A scaled eyebrow rose above a human eye that glittered with whitefire.

If Laoch and Oisin are dead ...

Ecne took the hand, and felt a strength there reminding her of how Laoch had spoken of Sura's touch. She stood, and Nathair placed both hands either side of her head, eyes seeking permission. Ecne nodded, and bonded with another soul for the second time. Q'Noh's gifted memories poured from her.

The sky tore asunder, spirits falling, fading as the Soul Tear rippled across the realm. Strange birds – no, artifices akin to the dragonfly she had examined in Innealtóir – broke through the clouds. Except these were insane, twisted things that bobbed and bounced upon impossible wings. Where the mind tried to place normality, be it a pair of bird wings or the four of a bee or fly, there would be six, or three. Some spun; others rowed like oars, cutting through the air. Crystal facets peppered their outer hulls, and where Nathair had scales, these had glinting metal skin.

The sky darkened before lighting with the crackle of spiritfire, white and ominous. More of the weird and wonderful appeared as flying machines, bearing legged and wheeled cargo, swooped, dropped or spiralled to the ground to disgorge their macabre machines. The Soul Tear faded, though its ripples echoed among the surrounding spirits. And then, chaos.

Ecne shook, her soul railing as Constructors poured forth. The vanguard wore the crystal armour she knew and, despite the mirrored appearance that crackled with whitefire, they seemed almost normal amid the chaos. For the horde that followed was a nightmare incarnate. All her fears of monsters in the night made flesh, bone or metal. A wave of horns, antlers, claws and twisted bodies, accompanied by the hoots and ravings of madness. The turmoil had no true form, no rank or order, except for the crystal-armoured vanguard and the separation of artifice from the chaos of the Constructors.

An army usually attacked as one, yet this maelstrom of insanity was fractured, parting into groups that chose their own victims.

Ecne flinched away, but Nathair's gentle insistence brought her back, attempting to focus her mind to seek what gift Q'Noh had meant to impart. Limbs were torn from bodies. Bone splinters flew. Gore-splattered families were spared, only for their souls to be ripped from their bodies and eaten as their bodies died. Hatred, desire, need and lust rolled over each village and town, consuming all in its path, or tearing apart at whim.

And, at the periphery, the vanguard waited. Disciplined, their war machines stood watch.

'These are the true enemy now, Ecne. I sense the emperor amid them. Changed. Aware of what his people are. He stands guard amid the soul-lust. This is new to me, for he once would have been at the centre of the excess. This, we should fear.'

"Please," sent Ecne, *"can you take the memories away? I can't ... no one can."*

'I am sorry, Ecne.' The thought cradled her mind, gentle, yet cold. *'This is a shared burden, not one to shed. It is necessary. Your sacrifice to save our people. You must remain strong amid their lust for life and joy in death. I will try to help. Perhaps darken the irrelevant as we look for answers.'*

The touch of the Spirit Walker upon her soul sent a shiver along Ecne's spine, the claw tips like hot nails into her mind. She fought, pushing away the spirit's touch, denying access.

"No!" she screamed. *"No."*

Nathair withdrew, an apology whispered in Ecne's mind. *'I can do no more.'*

"Then get this done, Nathair. Quickly, please."

'Perhaps a calling,' the Spirit Walker said. With that, a pulse of whitefire crawled across Ecne's skull, flickering in the increasing light before driving down into her mind. The shock was absolute. The smell of flesh burning, the taste of blood and ash upon her tongue, merged with a stretching of her spirit. Her soul, rooted in heart and mind, still raw from the necromancer's attempts to cut it free, opened up to Nathair, desperate for the moment to end.

'Here,' whispered Nathair. *'Yessss, here.'*

The battlefield before the city fluttered in the heat of fire. The broken and the damned lay shattered before the walls, flesh and bone torn asunder. Dead, soulless eyes watched the circling machines that dived and spiralled in their lust amid the thermals. Aboard the collection of fearful artifices that waved claw and bladed limb towards the city walls, the weird pennants barely moved in the breeze. Stillness reigned, the groans of the near-dead silenced as the feeders crawled among them, sucking the last vestiges of their spirits. And along the shattered walls, the Schenterenta waited, eyes dulled, weapons blunted.

Pain hovered above the elves, a miasma of loss and agony Ecne could almost touch. A hum rose, a mournful dirge that wavered until the soldiers upon the broken stone added their voices. It cut through the dread. The song galvanised the few who stood ready to lay their bodies and souls down in defence of those that remained. Each voice pierced Ecne, adding layer upon layer of grief tempered by the joy of having lived. In her mind's eye, Sura's spirit stood proud amid the throng, Honour's spear at her feet, lips parted as she joined the lifesong, the pattern and weave of sound she had honoured the dead with back on Innealtóir.

The scene held Ecne's heart in cold thrall. A people about to be decimated, their souls drunk or twisted to the Constructor's whims.

'Not so, Ecne,' whispered Nathair. 'My people's spirit is rooted deep, yet slides from us when we so choose. It sustains a Constructor, but it is the human spirit they crave more than any. This isn't a battle for food, but for domination and control. To take a realm, to milk the remaining humans like animals with no interference. To sate their lust for death and mould this world in their image. And I was once their vessel for doing such things. The shame ...'

A horn sounded. Spiked wheels and metal limbs dug into the bloodied earth, driving the ghastly collection of artifices forwards. From behind, the crystal-clad Constructors pounded across the battlefield, their lower halves drenched in the blood of their foes, their upper halves glinting with whitefire. The wave of metal and ancient, animated bodies crashed into the waiting elves, shattering the thin line. Death entered the city.

Ecne expected the dirge to cut off, the song to end as those who mourned died upon spike and blade. Instead, it heightened, and more voices joined. The song's volume filled Ecne's mind – joy in life, and the sorrow of passing written in pain upon the wind.

A flash erupted from the centre of the city, a flare so bright it stung Ecne's eyes. Q'Noh's memory rippled, pulled and stretched. Whoever's eyes she watched through were now filled with blood and fire. Pain struck. Not physical, but a spiritual agony Ecne remembered well, as it emanated from the walls of the Constructors' palace. The souls, stretched thin like the sap of a tree on the brink of snapping, ready to set them free. A last, lingering glance about her brought a singular joy as Constructors writhed upon the floor, and as she tumbled to the ground, hope shrouded her mind.

Nathair removed her spirit hands, mindful of Ecne as the acolyte's eyes fluttered. *'Ecne, are you with me?'*

Ecne staggered, only just catching herself before she fell into the remnants of last night's dinner. With her hands upon the dragon's metal-scaled foot, she leant against the artifice, welcoming its cool touch against skin and cloth. Ecne emerged from the memory of a nightmare into a bitter reality.

"Did you see it?" she asked, the humid air tight in her lungs. "Nathair, did you see?"

"Yes, yes, I saw," replied the Spirit Walker.

"That flare, the spiritfire. Whatever that was attacked all the Constructors at once. It must have been that ..." Ecne shifted herself against the dragon's paw to examine the Spirit Walker's conflicted expression.

"No. Well, partly. The spiritfire woven in the song *was* born from the moon pool, but it needed to be filled first. It was a magic of immense power that rippled through the Constructors. Akin to the Soul Tear." Nathair crossed her arms in front of herself. "One I cannot see helping us."

"Why? You saw. They fell almost as one."

"They did not all die, Ecne. But ..."

"Say it, Nathair. What filled the moon pool? What is the weapon we need?"

"The lifesong," replied the Spirit Walker, looking directly at Ecne. "It was filled with the love and joy of life. It was not deliberate, Acolyte. They weren't trying to kill the Constructors. They were singing their own lifesongs, adding their final verse, a farewell as they faced their deaths. So many at once ... it tore the Constructors souls from their ancient, dead bodies. Forced their spirits to depart. They did not all experience true death. Many would have found sanctuary. But it was their undoing."

"This is hope, Nathair. Surely this is what we came for?" Ecne pushed herself off the dragon. "Maybe you are too close to it now, but there must be a way to use this. Sura spoke of moon pools on Brandshold. What about Mondrein?"

"Different. Something I need to explore with Keran. But remember, Ecne, Sura said the moon pools meant little to her people now. They are just gathering places. The shamans have lost their spirits."

23
MACHINATIONS

"What in your Seven Hells am I doing here, Lord Penance? This is anathema to me. It stinks of human piss and that cheap crap your people drink ... *bear*, is it?"

"Beer, or ale, Terana. In my youth, I spent many a day and night in places like this."

High Lord Penance peered around the dingy, smoke-filled tavern, counting to himself the number of punishments each of the denizens deserved for the state of the tap room. He couldn't deny Terana was correct in her assessment. He had seen much worse, however, though not in the last twenty years or so.

I may have to break an oath or two if I stay much longer. Becoming a habit.

He scratched at the beginnings of the beard he'd let grow over the last few days and ran greasy fingers through his recently shorn hair. His hand – and body, for that matter – perhaps as healthy as when he'd last been in such a place. All due to beseeching his God about the necessity of anonymity when dealing with the likes of Geral.

Hiding in plain sight. Who would believe the High Lord was sitting having a pint in this … how would the locals describe it? … Ah, shit 'ole.

"How much longer? I need an open space soon, or I'll start to crack," Terana whispered into the sweet-smelling mead she'd ordered and not drunk. "And the looks. Why am I here?"

"Because they'll remember the Schenterenta, not the man. You said you would help, and help you are. Anyone who recounts this will talk of a sour elf who hated her drink and complained constantly." The High Lord's eyes lifted to the serving woman at the bar, her dress the cleanest thing in the entire tap room. She had run a cloth over a jug, one she had tipped upside down, and now she reached for a second that she placed upright next to it. Dropping the cloth on top, she turned away to serve a complaining customer.

"You're in luck," he said. "That's our cue. Time to go." He rose from the cracked stool, one hand on the table to ease his suddenly complaining hip.

"About time." Terana stood and placed the mead on the table, choosing to glare at anyone who dared meet her gaze.

They exited the tap room into a side alley, and both took a relieved breath despite its relative stink. Rubbish-strewn though it was, it bore no comparison with the tavern.

High Lord Penance pulled up his cloak's hood and eyed the wet cobblestones as the drizzle fell. He wished for his cane, but the whole city knew of his fabled stick. There would be no greater sign of who walked the rubbish-strewn streets than his slow, painful gait.

"This way," he said, and headed for a second alleyway that branched off towards the west side of the outer city.

Terana fell in beside him, her hood up. At least the grumbling had stopped. He didn't acknowledge the beggar who knelt with their back to the alleyway wall. Instead, he simply dropped a bronzed coin into the cupped hands before moving on. After ten yards, a soft glow emanated from beneath a thin wooden door. A pair of diagonal scratches lay at its base, as if scraped by a boot.

High Lord Penance, Overseer of the Seven Houses, knocked once before lifting the latch to be greeted by an inner door one yard further in. This one was iron-bound, with no apparent lock. Terana moaned behind him, her sighs echoing off the dank walls. Shaking his head, he pulled out a dagger from its sheath at his side and tapped at the door. A shuttered window slid open, and he passed it through.

"Aye, it's him," could be heard from behind the door, and multiple bolts later, it opened outwards, forcing them to step back and setting them off balance. A giant of a woman waited on the other side, her leather armour-covered frame filling much of the corridor. She glared at them both, then flicked her head for them to follow and strode down the stone corridor. Another guard walked in front and knocked at the next door.

After a few more bolt scrapings, light filtered out. High Lord Penance blinked when the female guard exited the corridor and the brightness from beyond flooded in. They emerged into a scented room. Smoke curled from incense sticks that burned upon a mantlepiece above a fireplace.

"You can go, Sherma," said the man who sat at a wide oak dining table. The plate set before him was filled with fresh fruit. "And you, Esquin. But listen out. Our guests won't be staying long."

High Lord Penance eyed the smiling speaker. His leather jerkin was beautifully cut, yet clearly old, and his cloak brocaded with a faded silver thread. He still looked to be in his late forties, with his beard trimmed and bright eyes. But the burn along his scalp, barely hidden under the skull cap he wore, marred his attempt at neatness.

When the others had gone, the man rose, and knelt upon the floor, head bowed.

The High Lord placed his hand upon the man's shoulder. "You do not kneel to me, Geral. Not before, not now, not ever. Unless, of course, we are in the House." He smiled, the warmth caught by Geral, who let his hand fall upon the Overseer's. He stood, and they drew each other into an embrace. "You look surprisingly well for a dead man."

"How many times can one person die, eh?" He looked over to Terana, lowering his head before raising it to greet the Schenterenta with his gaze. "And well met, Terana Fiotir Na Partera. I hope your tribe thrives with the herd. I go by the name Geral."

Terana smiled with real joy as she breathed in the incense, and allowed her own eyes to greet Geral's. "Hah. A man with manners and honour. You would do well to learn from this one, Lord Penance. *Sha ne be ceran.*"

"I won't admit to knowing what you said, but thank you. Sit. I hope the incense is to your liking. That, at least, came on advisal from the High Lord." Geral waited until they both took up the waiting chairs, and offered the fruits to Terana. "As a guest, you should partake first. However, if reluctant, I can taste whatever you choose."

"My paranoia stopped with the incense," replied Terana. "And your manners." She took some grapes. High Lord Penance likewise. Then, licking her lips, she spoke with a sideways glance at her companion. "But, beyond all the manners, who are you? I know who the High Lord said you are, what you do. But this ..." She spread her arms wide. "... does not match the vision I have of a thief and a smuggler."

"Is that what he called me? Probably about the nicest thing he's ever said." Geral looked over to High Lord Penance, who returned it with a shake of the head and a smile. "I am his brother-in-law, if truth be told. Though that was one of the many sacrifices I've seen him make over the years. I am his eyes and ears out in the wilder regions of the Union, and yes, you could say I dabble in theft and smuggling. But as a mummery. I serve the House of Penance, and in turn, all the Seven."

"Brother-in-law?"

"My sister is ... was ... the High Lord's wife before he entered the House." Geral raised a hand, cutting the conversation short, clearly deciding after a glare from the High Lord, that he had divulged too much. "Enough, I think. To business."

"Yes," said the High Lord. "First things first. Terana Fiotir Na Partera, Geral and you will need to structure an escape plan. A way to smuggle the queen, and anyone else deemed important, out should the Constructors overrun the city. This is my greatest priority. Should Erstenburgh and the other towns and cities fall, many will need passage away from human settlements."

"As agreed, Lord Penance. And I am here because you want to demonstrate the trust you are placing in me," said Terana, a little fury in her eyes.

Geral smirked. "She really does know you, eh, High Lord? It has been a long time since I saw anyone but my sister read you like that. Yes, Terana. Now we have met, I am also placing my trust in you. Though I doubt there will be much call for my trade when we are all on our knees in thrall to those that come."

"Good. Then we all know where we stand. I can work with this man, High Lord." Terana placed both her hands in her lap.

"You said for all the towns. That is a lot of work, and coin," Geral eased back in his chair, miming a hefty bag. "A lot."

The High Lord sighed and placed both hands upon the oak table as he leant forwards. "Agreed, focus this task on Erstenburgh. Prepare the ways. The queen is the priority. But if the city is to fall, we need other ways out of the city."

"Such as your crypts?" Geral raised one eyebrow, the smirk disarming the High Lord.

"Yes, such as those."

"Have you thought of something a little wider than that? As a sewer rat, when I get corralled, I run before I need to fight. Think on it. Why wait to be herded?" Geral's smile dropped. "Rats survive when others don't, High Lord."

"Wise words," said Terana. "The herds show the way. They have space to run free, and if corralled, panic." Her expression mirrored Geral's as she gazed at the incense burning above the fireplace.

"I will think on that, though it goes against my own instincts, and those of the Gods' Council," replied High Lord Penance, and reached for another grape.

"Battles are not won by Councils," said Geral. "Only by leaders."

The High Lord bristled and thrust back his shoulders. His eyes flared. "Are you questioning the Gods' Council, Geral? I thought you loyal to the Seven."

"Always. And I ... have carried out some despicable but necessary acts in the name of the Seven. As have others." Geral's eyes flicked up to meet the High Lord's. "But I know what I know. If I had lived a thief's life listening to counsel, I would have died a long time ago."

The High Lord held Geral's gaze and sighed. "I will consider your words. As to the second set of business..." The High Lord pulled out a pouch and placed it on the table with a jangle. "It is time I listened to our queen. I need word spread, Geral. Throughout the city, and on into the Union. In every tavern and taphouse. To the north and the south."

"It's a long time since I last did that. Sneed was the High Lord on that occasion, with word of the Unbelievers' sacrilege." Geral sighed, brushed his head and pressed at the burn scar upon his scalp. "And that did not go so well."

"With foresight, he would still have made the request, Geral. Understand? Your sacrifice, and those of our army, were a necessity. It pains Sneed and I, all the Houses, for what we did. But the flock was wavering. If we had not ..." The High Lord leant forwards and, taking Geral's shaking hand, squeezed it. "I know the cost; I wear that shackle upon my soul."

Geral grasped both of the High Lord's hands. "We serve because we understand the burden. What do you want me to do?"

"Spread word of the Infected high and wide, the truth within the rumours. It must be the north first, to make them wary, to let them know how to defend themselves. A decree from us will be met with disbelief in the outer regions, and those in the cities will presume they are safe behind their walls. No one is safe, Geral. No one."

"That I can do. Is that all?"

"No." The High Lord drew his hand back from Geral's, and let it light with purple spiritfire. Geral's eyes widened, his jaw worked, but no sound came. "That the Seven walk again through us. That they have granted us the power to defend ourselves against the Unspoken and the Infected. That the magic we call spiritfire is real, and we need their faith in us."

"I heard... from the guards. But I did not believe ..." Geral's fingers reached out, tips close to the High Lord's own. The spiritfire arced, crackling across the distance to wrap itself about Geral's hand. His eyes widened further as he twirled his sparkling fingers.

"It is real, and the people need to understand why it has come. The bleatings of the priests are listened to, but again, in the outer reaches of the realm, many will deny it as more words to drive them to the prayer stones. That is all good, until one of our priests-in-waiting begins to show such abilities and they panic. And they will. War is coming, and we will quicken all we can. If we set the seed now, make the people understand that we act in good faith, order will be maintained."

"If I hadn't seen it ... Madness. Will it all look like this? Each priest?"

"No, Geral. They mark the colours of the Houses." The High Lord paused briefly, looking to Terana. Though not for answers. Inspiration. "White is the mark of the Unspoken and those we fear who follow. A whitefire. Understand? It also marks the Infected, and any of their other servants. I had not thought before, but spreading both rumours together may work to our advantage."

Geral nodded, and High Lord Penance, grasping the man's hand again, drew the spiritfire back into himself. "It is limited, Geral. Finite. But the more the people pray ..."

His brother-in-law nodded. "Yes, yes. I see. Is this why you walk so well now? This spiritfire? Has it healed you?"

A sour expression fell upon the High Lord, the sliver of his God more distant than he wished. A yearning sat in his heart. Had he grown dependent?

I dare not answer that question.

"All but my soul, Geral. That will only heal should we save our people from what's coming."

24
A FATE SEALED IN BLOOD

Queen Erin paced the contemplation chamber, assimilating facts and supposition into myriad possibilities, all of which tore at her mind. *A puppy dog, fed scraps and lies.*

She strode over to the white stone wall that lay at the northern end of the room, staring at the doorway that led to her personal prayer chamber. Fate's dragon, inlaid into the oak door and entwined with the God as they fought for supremacy, glared back. She shook her head and let her hand rest on the handle a while before biting at her inner lip and yanking it open.

Inside, the chamber was unlit except for the deep blues that cascaded through the stained-glass windows. Their colours, shaped by the fading sunlight, shadowed the stone floor. Erin let her fingers run along the tops of the two sets of pews, remembering the first time she had entered to pray as the queen-in-waiting. Word of King Panset's abdication had rattled the Court and Houses, his refusal to engage with the Crusade tipping, it was believed, the Gods' Council to force his hand. She knew better now.

The then-High Lord Sneed had fought for him to accept the necessity of a religious war, and the king had turned away. It served the Houses to think he had been forced out, his family and himself almost struck from history as they disappeared from the realm. It was then they had turned to her, at Lady Fate's insistence, though her ex-master Sneed had endorsed the decision wholeheartedly.

A choice of political expedience. A new queen to be carried along on the religious fervour whipped up by the Houses, and the rise of the Unbelievers. Rumours rife of their growing numbers, their treatment of the faithful and their plans for expansion. Examples of their science heresy suddenly coming to light, and the Unspoken's evil, that whipped them on.

Erin stopped before the prayer stone, hands clasped in front of her. Hues of cyan and aquamarine played upon the surface from the glass depiction of the stout dragon on the eastern window. She eased in a slow breath, the sense of peace she had so enjoyed within the chamber in those early days lost amid the stress and pressure of keeping her realm safe.

But from whom?

"My queen?" The voice from behind wavered at a slightly higher pitch than the last time they had met. As a new queen, she wouldn't have spotted the signs of stress. But loss and lies soon make a person learn or wither.

Weisters don't wither.

"Lady Fate," she replied, looking up towards the depiction of their God upon the west-facing stained glass window. "I expected High Lord Penance."

"He is busy, Your Majesty," said Lady Death, causing Queen Erin to turn around, her concerns immediately heightened.

Two to replace one?

They faced each other in brief silence. The two House leaders stood in the doorway, Vianti hovering behind. She nodded to him, and the lad left. Erin cast her eyes to the waiting ladies. In her mind, this was her House, the Court her priests. And, at this moment, these two felt like intruders.

Who bows to who? Has anyone ever described the etiquette within a royal prayer chamber?

Lady Death broke the moment, displaying a slight deference to the queen and, in turn, Fate's chamber by declining her head a little. "May I?" she said, and Queen Erin indicated she could enter.

Lady Fate's choice was hidden by her cousin's entry, but it mattered not. Despite this Lady's higher role on the Gods' Council, Erin now suspected why Lady Death was there. Whatever was to come, it must be connected to the conversation they had had those few months ago in Fate's House. Where a burden shared was a burden multiplied. Glancing back at the usually radiant red hair and blue robes, the cast to the Lady's demeanour appeared faded, tired. Far from the powerhouse she so often portrayed.

A new façade, perhaps? To hide behind.

Erin moved to one side, returned the pained smile Lady Fate sent her way, and allowed her past to engage in the brief ritual of arrival with her God. By her side, Lady Death – her cousin – watched Erin intently. She could sense her gaze, the search for answers.

When Lady Fate finished her intonation, the weight of the room suddenly felt oppressive, wrong. It pressed in on Queen Erin's thoughts, dulling her mind to the possibilities that had whirled through it beforehand. It soon passed, and her certainty of purpose returned despite Lady Fate's tear-filled eyes.

"You are thinking this is not the best place for this conversation," said her cousin, her words drawing Erin's gaze. "But I think Fate's chamber is the most apt. The weft and weave of our Gods, the Magi, is coming to a decisive branch. A junction of thinking."

"You know why I called the High Lord, then? Do you have spies everywhere, cousin? Is there no act or decision I make that the Houses are not watching?" Erin caught the twitch of Lady Death's eyes towards Lady Fate, the subsequent look away accompanied by a redness to her cheeks.

"We have been preparing for this day, though we hoped it would never arise. And no, this is not word from your palace servants nor those who worship at our Houses. Taverns are the hotbed of gossip, and First Ranger Yanik likes a drink or seven. Her talk of the Infected was welcome, and that is where the Overseer is now, sowing such seeds on your advice – and of the spiritfire we wield. May we sit?" Lady Death looked to the pews. "It has been a difficult few hours, and my bones ache."

Queen Erin had to smile at that – an old saying from their shared youth. Designed, perhaps, to put her off guard, but also a reminder of their shared humanity. She allowed it through her emotional armour.

"Yes." She looked to Lady Fate. Her eyes were red-rimmed, lips stretched thin, as if whatever was contained inside had to be held back. "Sit, Lady

Fate." She pushed down a compulsion to touch the leader of her House, to break all etiquette between them and provide some comfort.

But what is she holding back? Or am I being played once again?

They each took a pew and faced one another. A meeting, without the barrier of a formal table between them.

"Yanik spoke of four children who she and Duke Panset saved from an Infected and ravaged village. That they were Handren younglings, already refugees from their own hamlet in the mountains." Erin nodded at Lady Death's words, keeping her eyes to the floor so as to not betray her thoughts. "Their village bore witness to two dragons of the veil. I assume ...?"

"Yes, they spoke of it." Queen Erin kept her counsel, letting her cousin add the detail. A battle of words.

"Then you know the Unspoken saw the other dragon off. That she fought, and won."

"So. The Constructors have found us, yes? And the Unspoken, who slaves a dragon such as theirs, fought it." Erin paused, waiting. But Lady Death added nothing more. "Yet you are not surprised. More to the point, you are here, without calling a Gods' Council, to discuss what happens next. You knew."

Lady Fate spluttered, her body shivering. The Lady of the House of Fate wrapped her arms around herself like a child. Erin caught Lady Death's concern, but she made no move towards the visibly distraught woman.

"Yes. The Handren are Fate's flock. News of the Unspoken and her valley comes to us through them."

"Those who remain," uttered Lady Fate, her wet eyes dripping tears upon the floor as she rocked forward. "The Unspoken's dragon is hungry ... Penance ..."

"No," said Lady Death, and she took to her feet, hands pulsing.

The red-haired woman's glare caught Queen Erin by surprise. They sparked with blue spiritfire. The magic arced around her eye sockets and boiled away the remaining tears. "I can't stand this anymore. I can't. The Un—"

"Lady Fate, no." Erin's cousin took a stride towards Lady Fate, hand out. "This is not the way."

"But it is. Fate demands the weave is cut and started anew." Lady Fate directed her gaze towards Erin. "Queen Erin. The Unspoken is a lie. A pretext. The children speak true. The Eighth was a Constructor who helped in the defeat of Nathair. Her dragon is of the veil, too. In return, she was gifted the mountains and ..."

"Please, no," repeated Lady Death, her hands now pressing against the sides of her head.

"... took on the role of the Eighth. Of the Unspoken."

The maelstrom in Erin's mind slowed as the pieces slotted together. The anomalies in the Scripture, the histories the Seven Houses had buried so deep within the Forbidden Library. The Eighth was not a Magi she could find no mention of, but a soul-eater. And her people ...

Food.

"My mother spoke of how the Unspoken helped when the Constructors attacked. Destroyed these *artifice* Scorpions. I assumed she intervened as she sought to dominate all of Brandshold's people, as the Scripture and the tenets warn us. And that the soul-eaters are therefore our common enemy. You are saying this is true, but ... but this is because *she* is one of them, a Constructor traitor. And you allow her to feed on people? On us?"

Lady Death closed her eyes and nodded; her lips thin. On opening them, her gaze settled on the blue-robed woman who still sparked with spiritfire. She was mouthing something Erin was unable to make out. Lady Fate rose quickly, gripping her hands in front of her before sliding them over her upper arms once again, tightly holding herself in. She shivered.

"I must ... go," said Lady Fate, stiffly declining her head. "Your Majesty."

"No, you may not leave. You cannot drop such a thing on me and then walk away, Lady Fate." She broke etiquette and grabbed the woman's arm, pulling her around. Spiritfire flared, a crackle of power that pulsed through her fingers. Stunned, she yanked her hand away.

Shock rode the flame-haired woman's face before the sadness flowed once again, mouth wide, hands reaching out towards Erin. "No, no, no. I am sorry, my queen. Please ..."

Erin stared back, unable to process what had just happened. Lady Fate cried out and ran for the doorway, ignoring even Lady Death's calls.

Her cousin turned to her, an apology on her lips cut short by Erin's wide-eyed look of shock. "I must go to her. But we need to talk again. Soon. Before your thoughts cloud all your judgements."

"No. You will stay, Sucreta. You will remain and tell me all. Or by the Seven, I will pull your Houses down brick by deceitful brick. I am the

Union's queen, and without me, for all your power, you will fail. Sneed is *my* prime now. General Zendril has *my* army. The city is defended by the meisters. And Captain Mordant is under *my* orders. Your errant ex-king stands as *my* duke between the Infected and our people. If I so much as whisper at disquiet with your Houses, the people will listen because I am *loved*."

"I warned them," Lady Death said.

"Warned who? The Gods' Council? I am a member of that Council, cousin. Did you warn me? Or was this yet another secret?"

Lady Death shook her head. "I advised them that, should you discover the truth, this was how it would go. Threats that no doubt you will carry out unless sense can be sown first. That the Weister anger needed to be subdued before the stubborn streak kicked in."

"I am your queen, Sucreta."

"That is *not* my name. I am Lady Death. I carry the burden of the Seven on my shoulders, and the pain of the people in my heart. Every day I am amid the flock, sharing my love for them, hiding the agonies, placating those close to death yet still draining their souls so others may live. I am a figure of hate in my own mind and if I don't seal that away, find some love somewhere, then our realm will fall to the soul-eaters. So yes, the Eighth is a lie, and it eats at us all, especially Lady F—" Lady Death paused, eyes widening. A tremor twitched at each corner.

"Erin, please. I need to get to Fate's House. Now."

—

The carriage pulled up at Fate's House, the horses sweating and anxious. Queen Erin's honour guard tethered them, and two took station beside Fate's huge, intricately carved doors. The others fell in behind the queen and her cousin as they stepped out of the carriage. Lady Death rushed up the seven steps. The moon's rise cast a ragged shadow as the queen followed more cautiously. The great doors were ajar, and a wail echoed amid the blue-dark interior. By the time Queen Erin had entered the Prayer Chamber, Lady Death was kneeling at the front, next to the plinth and its prayer stone. The mournful cry was from her cousin. Lady Fate's glorious red hair was spread across her bloodied knees, and from Lady Fate's neck, dark, scarlet blood seeped. The woman's lips moved, the sound unheard amid Lady Death's sobbing. In her hand, a spindle glowed azure as the blue spiritfire seeped slowly into the prayer stone.

Queen Erin's honour guard sought to press ahead of her, but Erin's whiplash glare caused them to part. She knelt next to her cousin and took Lady Fate's empty hand. The green, watery eyes glanced her way, the lips still shaping words. Erin knelt in, trying to listen, her other hand squeezing Lady Death's knee to reassure and silence her cousin.

The words were soft, but certain. "Forgive us. Forgive me."

No.

She lifted her head. The back of her hand graced the Lady's sallow face, ignoring the blood. A final sacrifice. Even in death, she had chosen to give herself to her people upon the prayer stone.

But forgiveness? No.

However, I am now a player of games, with my people's survival the prize.

"Yes," she whispered, despite the cold stone in her chest.

The last of Lady Fate's soul poured into the stone, and the spiritfire died.

Erin took a moment before releasing the dead woman's hand. She stood, eyeing the blood that now stained her dress, and her cousin, whose tears spilled onto the scarlet blemishes along her robe.

Without a word, she turned away and walked down the aisle, her honour guard striding behind. With chin up, she exited Fate's House, carrying a new burden upon her Weister shoulders.

25
A Fate Sealed in Lies

The White Palace, Erstenburgh,
Brandshold

The silence hung heavy. High Lord Penance kept his hands upon his cane as it rested on the Council's table. Across from him, the queen had her hands upon a box unlike any he'd seen before. It was made of iron, of that he was sure, austere and worn as if it had witnessed many a role before the one it found itself in now. He had tried, on entry to the queen's throne room, to gain sight of whatever faded sigil lay on its lid, but with no success. Since taking his seat, no words had passed. The queen merely stared at him, her demand for quiet absolute in her bearing.

How far we have come.

He lasted another minute before he sighed and collected his cane, intending to make his leave.

"Sit," Queen Erin stated, her tone allowing no recourse.

How long had it been since he'd sat in this very room, making threats about the meisters Kinst and Arknold? Overseer, indeed. That mantle was fading. And probably about time. Lady Death had described the queen's tirade before they had sought out Lady Fate, each word recounted with the same venom he saw in the woman's eyes now.

If she had knowledge of spiritfire, I believe the Seven would have their match.

He sat down and waited for the tongue-lashing that would surely come.

Queen Erin opened the lid, drawing out an inner box of wood. Upon it was the sigil of the Queen's Rangers.

High Lord Penance winced. He *had* seen this box before, or ones similar. One was carried by each regiment's commanding officer.

"Congreave," the queen said, reading off a small wooden plaque shaped much like a domino. She slid out more. "Persun, Wolfe, Bartlett ..."

She reached for another. The High Lord raised his hand for her to stop. "Please, Your Majesty. There is no need. Every name in that box deserves honour. I understand that."

"You know nothing of honour, Lord Penance. You have a House dedicated to its name. It has the stink of betrayal and deceit scrawled on its front door, as does every House of the Seven. I thought, when I learned of the Constructors, that there was more. But these ..." She lifted the box, tipping the remaining hundred or so plaques onto the table. "... bear my taint. They fought in my name, died with my Crown upon their lips. This man ..." She drew up one plaque. "... Láidir, died, screaming, at the hand of his own brother to relieve the agony of the Unbeliever's banefire. For what? Your lies? You sent my people to their deaths as a ... a ..."

"Necessity."

"A charade. A mummery of murder to trick the people into prayer."

"Lady Death said you would work it out eventually. Do you think this sits well with us, Queen Erin?"

"*Weister*, Lord Penance. From now on, you address me as Queen Weister, for that is who you have awoken." She slammed the lid shut, her steely gaze burning into him.

He licked at his purple-tainted teeth, feeling the spaces between where Penance had healed the rot, but could do nothing for the already broken or disintegrated. "Queen Weister, I ... There is nothing I can say, is there? You know of our burden, our choices, how it degrades us. You know. And all that you feel is right. It marks you as human, as does the trauma it causes the seven Lords and Ladies. There is no way to put such things into words."

"Six," Queen Weister replied bluntly. "The six. And I have Lady Fate's blood on my hands. I understand the weight." She sat back into her chair, eyes searching the plaques but finding no answers. Her gaze flicked up to fix upon his. "It has been mine to bear since you first revealed the partial truths. Do I make all these deaths worthless? Their forsaken souls, lied to and sent to their deaths, a waste?" She stood, shoving her chair back. "But know this. When this war is finally fought, and we fall in defeat or stand victorious, it will be the last of the Seven. Your Houses will fall. Your time has come to an end."

"On that, we agree," he whispered, eyes on his cane. Penance flared at his words. "But if our people survive what is to come, then it is built on the sacrifices made by all those who preceded us. We, the Gods' Council, want nothing more than an end to our role. But be careful what you wish for, Queen Weister. If we do survive, the people will still need belief in something. And to know of *all* the sacrifices made so that they alone survive, is simply the shifting of a burden, not a negating."

He waited, expecting the Weister anger and stubbornness to deny his words. But Sneed and Lady Fate had been right. They had chosen this slight, young woman to replace a king who had refused to accept the Houses' word, expecting her to bend, yet grow stronger. Had Lady Fate seen what was to come, how the weft and weave would form?

What did Lady Death recount her saying? 'Fate demands the weave is cut and started anew.'

He stared at the queen, and the calm mind of the Overseer, the great manipulator, made connections. Lady Fate had been able to scry glimpses of future pathways, and had understood what choices faced the queen once she learned of the Unspoken.

She knew she would teeter on the precipice.

Not a suicide steeped in despair, but a sacrifice.

High Lord Penance stared on, aghast at the choice Lady Fate had made.

"High Lord?" said the queen, concern on her face despite the anger. "I—"

He stopped. What could he say? The truth? This bundle of spit and fire had demanded to be told everything, yet could she handle the sacrifice Lady Fate had chosen, had foreseen? That her own suicide was the demonstration of her burden that would tip the queen their way, despite what the Seven had done for a thousand years to the people she had sworn to serve.

"Sorry, my queen. But ..." He looked at her then, really looked. "I would ask that you are not too hasty in what you do next."

"If you mean I should consult with the Gods' Council, then that *demand* lies with us all. Is there any more I should know? Any truths unturned?"

"Yes. Though they lie with me, and me alone. I have caused the deaths and ordered the murders of a multitude of people since the Crusade, in the name of our people. I have requested the Unspoken kill and pillage to make the realm aware her dragon is awake and a threat. That rests with me, my queen. I am the instigator – to the horror of the Council. More of a monster than the Unspoken and her dragon. That is but the tip of what I am prepared to do to ensure this realm does not suffer the fate of the soul-eaters, these vampires, and their desires. I am not asking for forgiveness, nor understanding, nor for you to share such pain. Only that you see the truth in it, and that when this is over, give me peace."

Queen Weister pressed her hands into the Council table, searching his face, perhaps for remorse or more lies hidden within his words. Saying nothing, she turned away and walked up the white marble steps towards her throne. She stood before it, her back to him, shoulders shaking. "Leave me, High Lord Penance. There are to be no more Council meetings without my presence. I expect to be consulted on all matters pertaining to the coming war."

"And the investiture of the new Lord Fate?"

"Lord?" she said turning. "There has not been a Lord Fate in a few hundred years."

"I understand the *becoming* is likely within a few days. At least this time, when I reveal the truth of the role, he will already be aware of all we have had to do in the name of survival – except for what you just learned."

"Am I required?" He noted the twist of her mouth. "Of course I am. I must be seen to support the Houses, to feed the veils. Tell me, Lord Penance, what happens when they smash through the veils? Where will all those prayers and souls go? Will they not feed the soul-eaters?"

High Lord Penance blinked, the tangent catching him off guard. "Those in the ether will be lost. Our understanding is the cost to the Constructors of breaking through will be heavy. And though the veils *may* fall, we work towards them self-healing, to make every entry as painful as the first. But after that ..." And he explained what a magus could wield, why the

Constructors prized them so. When he had finished, he bade his leave, at least having healed some of the distance he had been forced to put between them.

His thoughts wandered to Terana and Geral, and more words that he hoped would make their task a little easier. But amid the chaos of what was to come, he couldn't shake the feeling that the one who truly mattered had been left, agonised and alone, in her own throne room.

"Such is the enemy we face, that it rips those who we respect apart."

"High Lord Penance," called the palace servant from behind as he entered the courtyard. Surprised, he turned as his carriage pulled up. The young lad was not alone. By his side was an acolyte of Hope, and a soldier wearing the colours of Makalena. "My apologies for calling, High Lord, but Acolyte Hinsten has been waiting for you."

"Me?" he replied, eyes on the nervous-looking soldier.

"Sorry, High Lord. Lord Hope believes you need to hear my message immediately." The acolyte nodded towards the servant, who left. "And perhaps the queen." He licked his lips and looked around before stepping in close. "Lead Quantain has been taken. Kidnapped, or killed, we are uncertain which. She has always insisted on our House being open to all overnight, for those who may lose Hope during the darkest hours. A few days past, someone came. A warrior wearing black, and masked. The priests believe she was female. They struck the Lead and took her."

"The Wyrding Stone?" asked High Lord Penance, hand clutching the acolyte's arm.

"Safe. But Renga, the priest-in-waiting, was called away for Lord Hope's crystal experiments. We have no other who can use the stone. The Lord has rectified that, sent one of his newly trained waiting back with Renga and Sergeant Amina's troop." The acolyte nodded towards the waiting sergeant. The man's grizzled face and stark expression were a warning there was more to come. "Amina, if you will?"

The sergeant straightened his shoulders and puffed out an armoured chest. "They had the meister's flash powder, for sure," he said, eyes darting from the High Lord to the floor and back. "And more. Whatever they used caused a flash of light, a loud bang, and burned through whatever and whoever they hit. When they ran, they didn't care whether they killed townsfolk or soldier. And ..." The sergeant looked to the acolyte, who grabbed a leather shoulder bag that lay across his back, checking they were alone again before lifting the flap. "We found a farmhouse. The people inside ... I am ashamed, High Lord, to say we desecrated the body, but it was important."

Inside lay a hand, the skin white, husked. Exactly how the wielders of spiritfire appeared when they drained too much of themselves. Not an Infected. No rot yet.

"Was everyone in the farmhouse like this?" he asked.

The sergeant nodded in response. "I have a few shattered quarrels we recovered, and an odd crystal we found embedded in the leather of one of my soldiers." The man licked his lips. "Though I do not want to touch it. It glows ..."

"White," cut in the High Lord. "And you are right not to touch it. Who else knows? Have you sent riders to General Mandrich?"

"Yes. Captain Steppi sent riders to Ridth and all the outlying villages. Is this the Unspoken's doing?"

"It is. And I fear she must have reason for taking your House Lead, Acolyte Hinsten. Perhaps a soft target. I am afraid I am about to make you feel even less comfortable, sergeant. Wait here." The High Lord strode back into the palace entrance, a growing unease wrapping itself around his heart. Just inside the doorway, the servant waited.

"Vianti?" he said. The boy jumped at his name. "Yes? You must inform Assistant Prime Bertin that I require an urgent audience with the queen and herself. Urgent, you understand."

War has come.

26
TO BUY A LOYALTY

Western Coast, Brandshold

The memory played constantly through her mind. Her tongue licked over her metal teeth, darting across moist lips. The thrill of that first taste had enraptured her spirit, her ancient soul surging through her body as if it were truly young again. No human nor the banal spirit of a Schenterenta had ever tasted so *alive*.

At first, it had been just a taste, to sate her curiosity. To discover for herself why the emperor and the originators so coveted the magi. But then the lust had taken her, the priest's spirit so enthralling, Popsilin had dived into her depths. She had drawn and drawn, each time meaning to stop, to let the magus recover. But it had been too much, the woman's cries in the throes of death goading her to drink the last of her spirit. She had finally experienced a magus, one whose soul the emperor craved.

The memory of such lust had not left her despite the days that had passed. Popsilin had bathed in that soul. And now she needed more.

The steady splash of armoured feet through water cut across her thoughts. Tenith returned with another of their scouts to the stream-cut valley by the sea's edge. They had travelled north at night, on foot, bypassing Makalena after the emperor had failed to show for their retrieval in the southern forest. It had been the spur for her to question the priest, and Popsilin's discovery of the wonderful depths of her soul.

She rose from behind the boulders at the stream's edge, assured by Tenith's blatant approach that no human was there to pry. "Well?"

"There's a road a little way in from the coast. Perhaps half a mile or so. It heads north, as far as I can tell. There's not much traffic along it now." He peered up at the darkening sky, furrowing his brow. "I'm thinking, if we travel alongside it, we'll hit a few homesteads along the way."

"You grow hungry, Tenith?" she said, tapping the side of his head.

"Aye. We all are." He didn't add *unlike some*, but she suspected that was exactly his thinking.

Was this how it was during the Sundering, when the Magi escaped? Each of us looking on the other with first jealousy, then hunger. This ... need ... Ahhh. Without the emperor, we would have perished, eating our own until no one remained. Yet he abandons us, sacrifices my vanguard and plays games with the admiral incarnate. But he was right. There are magi here, and perhaps the Seven. But just for him?

"The emperor tasked us with a secondary target if he did not return. That is what we do."

"More magi?" Tenith asked. An unusual bitterness laced his words.

A thought intruded into Popsilin's mind, of the Inhibitor way: the strongest survive. Was he about to challenge her here, now, when they were on the cusp of an invasion? Take her mantle and do the emperor's bidding, while accepting the plaudits?

"Perhaps. But we know of them now, and have left those words for the emperor to find on his return. We know of their Houses, where the strongest magi sit at the centre of their web. We know they decry machines except for one they call the Unspoken, and that the veils are so strong due to their *faith*. With this knowledge, *I* will rise alongside the emperor and take the loyal with me."

Tenith glared at the scout at his side, masking his thoughts. The Inhibitor saluted Popsilin before scurrying off into the dark.

Popsilin squeezed her fingers, imagining the soulreaver in their grasp, striking Tenith down if she had to.

"The loyal? We are abandoned here with no knowledge of when the Fleshmaster will return. If we die here, who will rebirth us? We look to you, Captain, to keep us alive. But your eyes are wild, and you seem elsewhere. Since you fed upon that priest, I worry where your mind is." Tenith couldn't remain still as he spoke, feet digging into the earth, fingers pulsing.

"Are you questioning my judgement?" Her hand alighted on the grip of her soulreaver. An unfair match against his Inhibitor weapon, but that was the point. You earned the right to wear one, and fought to keep it.

Tenith stepped back, hands up. "No, Captain. But ..."

She whipped out the sword, tip wavering inches from Tenith's chest. The whitefire glow sparked at its edge, strangely tinted with a yellow glare.

Tenith dropped to his knees, head bowed, hands well away from his weapons. "You cannot afford to lose me, Captain. You have so few of us."

She guided the tip under his chin with enough pressure to force him to his feet, the outer layer of his flaked skin parting.

"I do not mean to kill you, Tenith." She forced her *will* into the sword, the weapon designed to drink a soul becoming a conduit for a sliver of her own. It slid between Tenith's parted skin, the yellow taint entering his body and invading his mind. She waited. The fear in his white eyes soon receded, taken over by a yellow fire swirling in their depths. She leant forwards to whisper in his ear. "That is a drop of what I offer in return for your *loyalty*, Tenith. This is what the magi provide, and it is glorious. Stand with me, and we will have our fill. We do the emperor's bidding – until we don't."

"Yes," he said, the words dripping from his suddenly moist mouth. "Loyalty, Captain."

Popsilin stood and gripped his forearm with her free hand. His eyes whirled a moment before settling, his tongue running along wet lips.

"Is this ... what it's always like?"

"I do not know. But I intend to find out. And along the way, we complete our task." She untied the bag at her hip and opened the top wide. The crystals inside flared with whitefire. "We head north. Feed on the way."

"The others?"

"Yes. Let's spread a little loyalty, shall we? But not too much. Just a drop."

27
HOPE UPON A MEMORY

BEACH, THE STRECH, APSO-TRAN

Laoch spluttered, and shoved the large, mottled green seaweed aside as he dragged his feet clear of the water. He hauled on the rope, a sense of duty forcing him to carry it through the sand-filled water towards the lone rock that protruded above the beach. He wrapped it around the rock, finishing off with his favourite knot before turning back to survey his handiwork.

The fishing boat lay on its side, the sail stowed before they hit the sand bar at low tide. Oisin had the girl, Yeg, and the fisherman walking in front, heading towards him.

Being human. Making honourable choices when we can.

The elven fisherman's tired, angry face brought a grin to Laoch's. He had no doubt he remained perplexed at still being alive, but couldn't help being annoyed about his boat. The girl, however, remained quiet, her countenance softer towards them both. Yet Laoch trusted her the least. Sura was always at her worst when silent.

Oisin pressed them both down into the dry sand next to the rock, then stepped back and away from the elf's glare. "This is enough," he said, looking to Laoch.

"Yeah. We leave them here. They'll find a way out of the bonds. There's enough sharp rocks further along the beach for them to free themselves. We go …"

The cry from the trees where the beach ended brought him up short, Justice suddenly in his hand and formed as a bow. Oisin had already knelt, the blue glow of Fate lighting his face as he drew the string back.

A figure appeared from behind a wide tree. Animal skins covered their shoulders and legs, and a familiar-looking spear gripped in their hand. He shouted again, the words, if they were words, guttural and hoarse. The gesture, however, was a common language. The human was waving them towards the trees.

"Thoughts?" said Laoch, one eye on the suffering First Ranger. The sea had taken its toll on the cuts that swathed his body.

"Last time they threw spears. This time they are acting like we've drunk rum around a fire together."

"That is not how I act after green-leaf," replied Laoch. "And I could use some right now." He caught the pained expression on his friend's face, made worse by Fate's blue glow.

He needs rest, and time for Fate to help him heal.

"One of you is Laoch," came a cry from the wooded edge. "The other Oisin." Both names were spoken in a strange manner, the inflection wrong. But at least it wasn't elven. Two tribesmen stepped out to join the one who had gestured. Between them was a teenaged girl. "Ecne spoke of you both. I told her you would be dead in the city. No human is allowed to live." The girl waved them over. "We can take you to her, and the metal bird."

Laoch stood, lowering the arrow though keeping it ready should he need Justice's wrath. "You have Nathair?"

"Have? I don't think anyone *has* that beast. But I know them. I ate with Ecne a day ago." The girl walked towards the forest and threw a glare back over her shoulder. Laoch knew that look. Hatred, but not for him. The bile was directed towards the two elves at his feet. She uttered something, and the tribesmen strode down the beach, their intent clear.

Laoch took a step to stand in front of the fisherman and his daughter, the bow raised a little. "No!"

The girl stopped at the trees' edge, shoulders slouched, and turned around. "They are death-dealers. Drach who tear our spirits from our bodies. They find us, they rip out our tongues to show we are not worthy of speech. Kill our people without mercy. They seek an end to our race, Laoch." The weary look on the girl's face seemed odd. That, and the fact she clearly led whatever tribe this was.

"I know. But we are not like them. I kill without remorse when I have to, girl. But I do not take lives when it is unnecessary."

The girl scowled. "Ecne said she may have a way to take us from here. That the dragon could help save my people. But she needed to find you first, and whatever the Drach used to stop the Constructors. I gave her that. Now I give her you. And you want more?"

Laoch sucked at his lip, trying to work out the truth amid the girl's words. "I can't murder people who have done me no wrong, or who are not in my way. So yes, I ask for more."

"They would spit and roast you in return, Laoch and Oisin." She shook her head, but the guttural grunts that followed stopped the advance of her people. "This is the last that I give, but they will be taken elsewhere. Released at the far edge of the forest. And will have to take their chances that others don't kill them."

—

Ecne squeezed Oisin tight, the hug producing a huge gasp from the mountain man.

"Let him go, Ecne," Laoch said, clapping her on the back. "The poor bastard was sliced and carved for dinner back in that bloody city."

"Sliced?" She touched Oisin's face, the bruises there purple and black.

"Tortured. They took it all out on him."

Oisin pulled away from Ecne, though he patted the acolyte's cheek as they separated. "I'm fine. Fate is helping, though that sea water stung." He lifted his blood-stained shirt to reveal the criss-cross of lacerations that glowed blue. "Feels weird, but I'm on the mend."

"Fate says he was close to being carved up," said Nathair. The spirit shimmered beside the metal scales of the dragon's front paw. "That this Sendak had plans for your nose and ears."

"That was the impression I got. But that is in the past. Q'Noh said she gave you memories, as a gift, Ecne? That she showed you the Constructors' defeat?"

"She did, though Nathair has shared much of that burden. It was painful, as if I was there. It was the ..."

"The lifesong," cut in Nathair.

"And the moon pool," finished Ecne. "Together, they tore the Constructors' spirits from their bodies."

Laoch and Oisin looked to each other, surprise mixed with their shared memory.

"We witnessed something like it," added Oisin. "These Drach tear spirits from bodies, just like Q'Noh told us at the beach. We saw them do it to a human, and it was in a huge moon pool, bright with power."

"And the song." Laoch shook his head. "The whole city sang throughout the ritual. So yes, these things tie together. Nathair?"

Nathair crossed her arms, the scales over her eyes rising and falling as she blinked. "What are you asking, Ranger?"

"Can we use this? And if so, how?"

"You are the Spirit Walker, the shaman. The Drach must have been engaged in a ritual you understand?" Oisin caught Ecne's glance towards Nathair as he spoke. A clue that they had already discussed it.

"It is not as simple as that. These Drach are of Schenterenta heritage, it is true. But our people have been spread across the realms for longer than any spirit can remember. Our rituals have diversified." Nathair's hands uncrossed and she ran them down both sides of her neck, stroking the scales there. "I would need help to build the ritual. To work with other shamans. It could be done, I believe. But there is more than that to consider."

Ecne clasped her hands, rubbing them together as she spoke. "We think the Drach moon pool was already energised by spirits, much as you saw. However, when the Constructors attacked, those spirits within the pool must have been the souls of their own people. It is where the Schenterenta souls congregate after their bodies die. Brandshold's moon pools are empty. You heard Sura. They know not where their spirits go, and they mourn this, entombing their dead in caves in the hope they will return. However, Nathair knows where they are."

Oisin stared at the Spirit Walker. A shimmering pattern of red ran along the scales on her cheeks and upper chest.

"I did not put them there, Oisin of the Handren, so expunge such thoughts. The flight through Brandshold's veils was pained, the venom strong, but I sensed something that could be the souls of Sura's tribe. Her presence made it more prevalent. I believe they are trapped within your inner veil."

"You mean Honour's veil?" said Laoch.

Nathair nodded, her tongue flicking out to sweep over one of her eyes.

"You believe this, Ecne? This cannot be true," said Oisin, his look almost pleading.

"I don't have to. Once Nathair voiced it, Wisdom almost choked in my mind. It is true, Oisin. Though Wisdom does not hold all knowledge, the Magi remembers the sacrifices. Their spirits formed the structure to hold the veils. Wisdom, Fate, Justice and Honour were the first to make the sacrifice. Honour's inner veil curtain draws in the spiritfire freed on death. All death."

"Spiritfire? As in, the souls that survive when the body dies," added Oisin. "But the elves? It is ... Ahh ... And they never knew? The trauma of those people." He shook his head, eyes downcast.

"It explains much," said Ecne. She glanced towards Laoch, who was staring at the ground too, head bowed. "But it may not help us. If Nathair can devise the ritual for Brandshold's Schenterenta, we still have to solve the riddle of how we return them to the moon pools."

"But there is no other way?" asked Oisin. He moved to stand by Laoch, and gripped the man's shoulders. Laoch glanced up, forcing himself to acknowledge the Elite Ranger's presence. He squeezed Oisin's left hand. It didn't make the pain any less, his thoughts on lost Schenterenta spirits – and on one in particular.

"You will not like my solution," said Nathair. "Least of all Laoch." She waited until he broke away from Oisin's gaze and looked to her. "Mondrein."

"Hah, as ever. Everything points back to Keran's wish. I swore I would defend your realm after saving ours. Is that not enough?" Laoch didn't have the energy for anger. The talk of Sura and lost souls had dampened his mood rather than enraging it.

"To which I agreed. But now, we have a reason. The shamans there can help me form the lifesong ritual, and discuss more of the moon pools. Mondrein does not use such places. There was never enough land upon the islands. They could help us, whereas we know the Drach won't, and the Schenterenta on Brandshold can't."

"Mondrein," said Ecne, nodding and trying to catch Laoch's eye. "And what about Q'Noh?"

"Why not? Every-bloody-one else wants to go there." Laoch spat upon the ground. "But Q'Noh and her bastard tribe stay asleep until we dump them somewhere with no bloody elves."

"Keran remembers enough islands devoid of Schenterenta from before he left. Some of those may still be empty, though I hope they can fish, and enjoy eating weeds."

28

TO TEAR A SOUL

SOUTH OF JENSE, BRANDSHOLD

The duke passed the spyglass over to Llandon. The Ranger's sour expression matched his own as the mist wove its way between the trees ahead. The pine needles there dripped moisture, the darkness beneath them a death trap for anyone foolhardy enough to enter.

"Without Yanik, I'm ain't so sure I wanna try this, Panset," Llandon said, the spyglass giving no clue as to where the Infected were hunkered down. "I like Michala 'n all, but she's no' ready to lead a Spear."

"None of us are ready when we face these things, Llandon. And there's more every day. For every Infected we burn, another two rise in its place. More." Duke Panset eyed the copse, stress building up yet another unwelcome headache. "We can wait them out, try to pick them off when they emerge. But the longer we wait, the less time we have to mop up any others in the area. Time we don't have."

"Aye, s'right. Reck'ning it's five miles to Jense, yeah? You thinkin' that's where they're 'eadin'?"

"It's not a straight line, but they're hunters, and there's a lovely meal corralled inside some stone walls, just waiting to be unwrapped. If they get in there, we're ... we're ..."

"Fucked." Llandon handed the spyglass over. "We can go in, Duke. But we don't know 'ow many are in there. Prints show maybe five or six, but the rain ... It's a risk." Llandon ran his dirtied fingers through his hair and down his face as he sighed.

Panset could see the man's tiredness. Felt it himself. Their hunt had been drawn out. The call for more Rangers had been heeded, but was now delayed due to a second Infected outbreak near Dent. He had thought them so close to removing the scourge. He'd had to send Yanik to advise rather than return from the palace and help them mop up the dregs.

He swore quietly. A grin from Llandon caused him to chuckle in return. "Send Michala in. Your Spear covers the hills to the south and east. I'll keep mine here, to the west."

"Are you sure?" They both knew his Spear were strung out, having been at the vanguard of most of the skirmishes with the foul creatures.

"Yes. It's on my head."

Llandon nodded and slid back from the thick, rotten pine trunk they had been leaning on. He ran off into a small stream valley, signalling as he went.

"And you stay close, Arjon. Yes?" The duke glanced behind. Hope's priest was silent as he knelt on the wet grass. "You are not to engage the Infected, understand? What you carry is far more important than any of us."

Arjon raised an eyebrow, his bald scalp wrinkling as he did so while he attempted a serious expression. The young priest was the most jovial person Panset had ever met, though he had a sad suspicion that was all about to change.

Panset signalled his six Rangers to take station ahead. The soldiers kept low as they crept out from under the sparse trees in the pairs they had become accustomed to. If one got scratched or bitten, the other had the fateful pleasure of ending their partner before they turned.

Shaking his head, the duke raised the spyglass to catch Michala's signal. The newly promoted First Ranger spread her Spear out in pairs as they edged slowly down the slope towards the pine copse. In their hands, wooden torches smoked and spluttered, resisting the mist's attempts to douse them. Panset scratched at his scar, unease hunkering down beside his headache.

"Something's wrong," Arjon said.

The duke looked back over his shoulder. The man's grin was gone, face slack as he shook.

Panset gasped, the air catching in his throat as he stared. A second Arjon seemed to hover just outside his body, like a perfectly formed shadow that glowed against the wet grass. Stretched outwards, away from the priest's body, the elongated form shimmered towards him. Panset spun around to catch sight of his Spear, frozen in place, their spirits similarly straining from their bodies, fear etched on the ghostly faces.

He stared down at his own hands, turning them over and over. His own soul began to separate from his body, lifted as if blown on a strong wind. It screamed, open-mouthed, mirroring his own fear. Yet through it, another, greater dread, rose. Hoots and cries from the copse echoed loudly, and the Infected burst forth, their bodies rippling, raging with whitefire. They tore through his Rangers, teeth ripping through flesh as claws stripped meat from bone. They did not stop to feed, but bounded on, powering towards him.

Like a statue, he awaited his death. The hoots closed in, pounding his ears as an Infected leapt the rotten trunk. Someone slammed into his back, hard, and he pitched forwards into the muddy ground, his soul howling for what he had lost.

———

High Lord Penance pushed himself back into the carriage seat, attempting to ignore each bump in the street that vibrated through the wheels and up through his pained back. The sigil on his cane glowed a little and, accepting Penance's offer, the seep of purple spiritfire flowed along his nerves to ease his spine.

The drums continued to beat, their heavy bass adding to the thick atmosphere hanging over Erstenburgh. Outside the carriage, blue-robed acolytes were roped together by single cords, their intertwining dance tying a multitude of weaves that miraculously came undone as they ducked and wove their way along the road. The royal carriage followed his, draped in the blue ribbons of the queen's faith and as homage to Lady Fate. Inside seethed a bitter woman, maddened by the Seven's machinations, but as wrapped in the cords of fate as the dancers themselves.

"How far do I push, Sneed?" he said, wishing his friend and servant were by his side. "She is stronger than all of us, yet we lay our deceit at her feet almost as an offering, expecting her to bear the weight of our pain." He stared out at the deathly silent crowd, their heads bowed in deference, many with blue ribbons wrapped about wrists or hair. "And what will the flock do when the Constructors come? Can I keep you alive? Your children, your future?"

He pulled out the aged letter from within his robe, the seal long broken, lips moving as he read once again. He knew each swirl of the quill, each letter and word, and felt the pain of its meaning upon his mind. A purple tongue slipped into the nooks and crannies of his cracked teeth, trying to push back the memories of when they were whole, of the time before he wore the robes of Penance.

"I would be lying," he said with a snort, "if I said I did all of this for you, daughter. I only knew the truth of my role when Sneed quickened my mind. But, perhaps, you and your mother are the blessings that sealed the duty of what I bear. If I had one wish, it would be that my actions give you a future free of servitude to those that come."

High Lord Penance's finger shook. The letter fell from his hand as he grasped at his cane. He felt his God's touch, anchoring him to the sigil as his soul raged in heart and mind, battling the tug of the Soul Tear. "No," he whispered, lips barely moving. "They come."

⸺

Queen Erin Weister clutched the chain around her neck. Her fingers turned white as the blood drained, heart aching while her sharp mind set afire. With her spirit stretched thin, ethereal strands of her *self*, her spirit and *will*, battled to remain rooted in her mind and pained heart. She gasped and leaned forwards, focusing on her soul before throwing herself back to scream defiance, sucking her spirit back in with sheer force of will.

"I refuse!" she shouted and forced herself to her feet. She grabbed at the door handle and looked out the curtained window. Vianti writhed on the street, the boy holding his ribs, eyes wide with fear.

"No!"

She shoved the door open and, missing the step in her hurry, fell, only for a strong arm to wrap about her waist. Captain Mordant, his soul shimmering but contained within his body, his face stoic, held her still.

Erin placed her hands on his shoulder and levered her feet to the ground with a pained "Thank you" on her lips. She knelt beside Vianti, clutched his face as his body shook, and whispered whatever words came to mind. As he calmed, she glanced upwards, her already-whirling mind assailed by her people's panic. The gathered crowd either lay in distraught heaps along the street edge or stood weeping. Tears spilt, not for the loss of their Lady, but for the agony of the Soul Tear. To have seen yourself – what composes your being – ripped from you to waver upon two strained roots and threatened with oblivion – an ending – was too much for many to bear.

Erin stood, blinking. Then, without doubt or fear, she strode into the crowd, her delicate hands reaching for those upon the floor, lifting, talking. A smile of reassurance here, a touch there. And, by her side, a captain with both desolation and pride in his eyes.

High Lord Penance dropped from his carriage step, the tap of his cane upon the street barely audible above the clamour of the crowd. A shake of his head at the sight of his queen amid her people, and he turned to the tangled acolytes, his eyes dancing over each one. "Your queen is doing your job," he said, "and mine."

He took one last look at the aged letter and slid it inside his robe. "Look to your Houses. Solace is to be found there!" he bellowed, and with a spark of spiritfire, he raised his glowing cane and entered the crowd. "Your Gods have granted us the power to help. We are here for you."

—

General Zendril held Mander, gripping the man tight. His sweat-stained body shook against hers as their souls rippled above the bed. She bit down on his shoulder, fear taking hold of her senses as the blankets glowed with their combined spirits. Mander's fingers pressed against the flesh of her back, and she took reassurance from the strength they displayed. With a shudder, her soul slid back inside her body. Cold seeped along her spine and into her mind. A dread.

"Mander?" she said, pushing against his chest. His heart beat fast, and she grabbed his face, pulling it down, searching his eyes. "Mander?"

"I'm okay," he croaked. His eyes betrayed him, however, and Zendril's own heart quavered as she watched his struggles. He patted her hand and pushed himself away to sit on the edge of the bed and lean over, gasping for breath as he held his chest.

"You're a fucking awful liar." Zendril pushed herself up next to him and laid her head against his scarred back. "How bad?"

"Can't get rid of me that quick," he replied, the words strained as he squeezed her thigh. "We have a war to win. You think …?"

"What else could it be? I had better check on the camp. You are under orders to stay here." She grabbed her clothes from the tent floor, and eased up from the camp bed, eyes on his until he nodded in agreement.

She dressed quickly, exiting the tent to the mournful sounds of her army. Horses neighed with the stress while soldiers rolled out of their tents or staggered down the rows, fear etched upon their faces.

"Don't start fucking moaning!" she shouted, striding down the first line of tents. "Look to your mates, your platoon leaders. Check on everyone. I want a fucking roll call in ten, understand? Get moving!" She grinned manically as the orders passed from line to line, shoved at those slow to respond, glared at others who appeared lost in their thoughts of the Soul Tear. "Move!"

"General," said a voice to her side. The sound was meek and mild, far from the rough soldiers and veterans who busied themselves about the camp. She paused, a hand signalling for patience as she surveyed the camp. Satisfied, the general faced the waiting priest.

The woman's blonde hair was tied back, strewn with grass and twigs from wherever she had been when the Tear had hit. Her blue eyes were troubled, and she chewed slowly, purple juice gathering at the corners of her mouth. The priest lifted her hand, displaying the oddly shaped crystal that sat there. "General, you need to see this," she said, her voice wavering, barely audible.

"I have not the time for parlour tricks, woman. Can you not see the disarray? As soon as I give them time to think, they'll be harking back to your lot, wanting a fucking prayer meeting and holding sodding hands. You know what that Soul Tear heralds? What's fucking coming?"

"I do," she said, and splayed her fingers. Hope's yellow spiritfire played across the crystal. "As does the Overseer, and Lord Hope. That is why I am here, General. And I say again, you need to see this." The anger flared in her eyes, tinged with yellow, and the crystal glowed strongly in response.

"Put it down, priest." Zendril glared around the camp, eyes falling on a hapless major who was ordering the nearest section of soldiers into line. "Demartis, I want them lined up and singing my fucking praises in ten minutes. I'll be back." She grabbed the priest's arm, shoved the glowing hand down and indicated towards her tent. By the time they had both ducked under the flap, Mander was dressed in his uniform, adding to her already roiling anger.

Saving her fury at her bed partner for later, she swore under her breath.

"Now?" the meek voice asked.

Zendril thought it hid more steel than she had expected.

The hand flared. Yellow light filled the tent as the priest opened her hand. Hovering above the crystal, Panset's bloodied and mud-splattered face appeared. His lips moved, though no sound came, but General Zendril could read the fear and agitation in the duke's face.

"You need to use our skills wisely, General. We can communicate almost instantly if we have the opportunity, though it drains us. I showed you the duke's face so you can trust what I'm about to tell you. The Infected were driven rabid by the Soul Tear. They cut through most of the duke's Rangers, but did not feed. They infected them, then ran. He says they headed off in the direction of Jense."

"Jense? How far from the duke is that?"

"He said five miles."

"Two hours by foot. But if they are on the run ... By the bloody Seven, if they get in..." said Mander as he slipped on his last boot.

"Okay, Priest ... err."

"Kendul."

"Kendul. Is there anyone at Jense with one of the crystals? A way we can warn them? We are two days ride away, six by foot, maybe more. They're on their own. If Panset makes it there before the Infected, they may not recognise him with his face scarred." Zendril looked to the roof of the tent, boot tapping as she worked through the possibilities.

"The Lead Hope of Jense has means. I can try, but we are not paired. I cannot guarantee I will get through." Kendul sat on the bed and pulled up her legs to sit cross-legged. "I need quiet," she said, raising her eyebrows.

Mander grabbed the general's elbow. "Come on. It proved useful once. Give her a chance. And we need a backup. Two days ride? I reckon I know someone who can knock half a day off that."

—

"Calm, An Chéad. We knew this day was coming." The Unspoken sensed the Spirit Walker's agitation. Memories of the emperor's previous arrival and attempts to subjugate them both stirred in its thoughts. *"We prepare. Watch. Understand his strategy. The humans will expect a war much like how they fight. All manoeuvres and counter-manoeuvres. But they do not know Emperor Tarin and how far from their own thinking he is. And nor do we, anymore. We must understand his tactics before we act, or we risk losing everything."*

The metal dragon opened its maw, the cry from its metal throat deep and thunderous. The small city of Anvil had paused below them. Its people – her herd – lost amid the Soul Tear. They were no more immune to that than they were to the Inhibitors that would surely follow in its wake. Their hopes lay in the machines they built, and the faint possibility the emperor may be satisfied with feeding upon the people of the Union. But this, she doubted.

He was never one to be sated. Always wanting what was just out of reach.

"Come, An Chéad. Let us assess what our pets have built."

The dragon roared again and spread his metal-skinned wings, catching the wind from the palace balcony. The mighty beast leapt and tipped his wings to descend in a spiral towards the valley floor, and the smoking towers of the two foundries. Where once they had tinkered, the Unspoken had urged them to build. But they were no Constructors. Their skills and knowledge had been held back by Scripture for so long, and the Unspoken's talents lay elsewhere.

Even so, we ready as we must.

Talons alighted upon the tiled floor as fetid steam rose from An Chéad's nostrils. The Unspoken checked her glamour, and exited, entering Anvil's city square to talk to her pets. To reassure them their souls were still their own.

Well, *mostly.*

———

Gowan stirred from her spirit sleep, suddenly finding the heartstone's bonds claustrophobic. They lay tight, constricted, as if trying to squeeze her out of the great crystal. She sent her spirit mind out amid the stone, seeking Leront, thoughts querying what was happening. As she neared the centre, ripples bounced amid the bonds, a disruption she recognised from the dream she had been awoken from. And again, a sense of displacement threatened to overwhelm her.

Eventually, Gowan emerged amid the withered forest where she had fought Leront. The hill rose ahead, and Gowan swiftly made her way there as the tree branches waved to the pulse of the strange ripples within the crystal. Jumping the stream that wrapped the hill, she ran past Leront's tail, expecting to find the dragon sleeping as it normally did. Instead, its tail twitched in a familiar rhythm. When she reached Leront's chest, the same pattern inflicted a deep fear into Gowan. Across the green scales, a black, viscous poison seeped. Foul, malignant, the power spewing from it drew Gowan in.

'*No,*' was her last thought.

———

What am I?

Where am I?

"*Who am I?*"

The hum restarted, a rhythm that rose and fell, weaving a pattern. Each piece slotted into her mind. The sounds became words, the words phrases and eventually, lines of memory.

A song.

A lifesong.

My lifesong.

The lines built into verses. From birth to childhood, from the joy of being a twin to the grief that wreathed such loss. The touch of a man's fingers upon her cheek, to the first flash of spiritfire to break upon her comrades-in-arms.

"I am Sura, and I am home."

She whirled in on herself, seeking each element of her *will*, sensing their closeness as the crystal's bonds locked her in place. But the lifesong made those connections, wove them tight. More spirits were held fast around her, but their will was absent, stripped bare, their *self*, their *being*, lost amid the stone.

Is this Nathair's heartstone? No, no, I defended it. Remember, remember ...

I was drawn back and stretched thin, sucked into a whirlwind of whitefire into ... into ... the Kraken. *So why am I whole?*

'*Because we are one. Bonded. We are Honour, and this is my veil. We must leave before we are consumed.*'

"Consumed?"

'*My veil attacks the soulship; it needs spirits to keep it flying, but also as a defence. It draws upon this store to feed that. Prepare.*'

"How?"

'*We must do as the ship does. Draw upon the spirits, grow stronger. And then, when we are called upon, we can maintain our being, our will.*'

"That is abhorrent. I am not like them."

'*We are needed so all our people will not end like this. These spirits are mindless, already lost. This is our only chance. Or it is an ending.*'

"I cannot ..."

Sura felt around her. Every part of her spirit touched on others that shared or neared her bonds within the stone. Each was absent, bereft of thought, of mind. They did not retain the madness of some she had met on Innealtóir, more akin to the lack of will displayed by the artifice they had discovered in the mansion house. She let a tendril of herself touch upon theirs and drew a little back, subsuming it into herself. Nothing railed against her, nor fought. Just an entity whose *will* had been stripped. An absence. Formless spiritfire. She took a little more, a piece from each, growing in strength as she stamped her *self* upon them.

'*We must be quick. The glyph ...*'

Sura was torn free, ripped from the bonds that held her tight and thrown into a current of whitefire that boiled out of the massive crystal. She was forced into the brass hull, squeezed and stretched until she was expunged onto the soulship's surface. Everywhere was fire, orange hued and angry. A creature whirled amid the flames, tail flapping in pain, the bone around its head scarred and livid with burns. It writhed, and a soul scream slammed into her new form, tearing at her spirit. Those others at her side, the absent, were shredded, their tendrils sliding away from the ship and dissipating into the veil. Sura roared, her *will* strong, defiant. The lifesong responded and thrummed through her body, holding her fast. A huge explosion swept into the soulship, and the noise briefly drowned Sura's lifesong. As she recovered, the metal and stone collar that restrained the burning creature shattered, and the body exploded into meat and hollow bone.

Sura sensed Honour's urgency, the need to draw away from the brass hull. A sliver of power thrown outwards grasped something that writhed about the meat of the dead creature. A tug of familiarity flowed along the tendril, dragging her clear of the soulship and out into the angry veil that had spurned the ship's presence.

"Who? What?"

'*Calm,*' said Honour. '*Quiet until we are away.*'

And Sura-nista of Betana Refi Na Partera, a Spirit Walker once split asunder, swam within Honour's veil while the spirits of her kin wrapped her in need and yearning.

Home.

29
AND SO IT BEGINS

WEST OF MAKALENA, BRANDSHOLD

Lelion stared at the brass deck, throat tight and thick with whitefire while her head throbbed.

"Leave me alone!" she bellowed, and shoved the bridge crews away, arms spread wide to ensure they stayed back. "Let me be. I am fine."

My head pounds, the bridge spins, my dead innards rail against me. But that abhorrent noise has finally passed. A relief for which there are no words.

A wave of tiredness swept through her spirit, the roots sagging against her mind. A sense of age settled onto her thoughts. She glanced up at her Inhibitors, who remained staring at their admiral as she shook upon her knees.

"Get to your stations, now! We are over water, you stupid bastards. We falter here, you condemn all those we carry to an eternal grave. Move," she growled, dragging one foot underneath her to plant it on the deck.

The crew moved, taking their places. The noise of dials and solid buttons being twirled and clicked was welcomed by Lelion, now the infernal buzzing had stopped rattling about her skull. She pulled her second leg under her, and grasped the rail to pull herself fully up. The viewing window whirled across her eyesight before settling into a slightly less disconcerting

double vision that finally merged into one picture. Ahead lay a city –
Makalena, the emperor called it, its port busy and walls low. Tarin had
warned of their priests, the possibility they could be magi. But easy meat for
the *Kraken* soulship, and an opportunity to feed her engines before they
moved on.

The unease at their entry, however, had shaken her belief these people
were as defenceless as the emperor claimed. The veils had been strong, the
final, orange-hued curtain tumultuous. And the glyphs had decimated one
section of the *Kraken*'s armour. Along that side, they had lost many of their
chains and all her vision crystals. Two decks had been penetrated, and the
Inhibitors there burned to a crisp by the furious spiritfire that had seeped
in.

"A decision to be made," she said out loud, gripping the rail hard as she
eyed the city.

They had been seen. The people below were emptying the port, running
to wherever they felt safe.

And that would be nowhere.

"Burn their ships, then sweep past the walls. Keep our starboard side
facing away from the city. Show no weakness. We pass by and establish a
foothold first."

"Admiral ..." Kankrin started. "The emperor—"

"Is not here, Kankrin." Lelion reached out and cupped the man's jaw
despite his flinch. "I am tasked with this invasion while he attends to other
matters. Now, sweep the walls after burning their pathetic wooden ships.
Put the fear of their fucking fate into them, and find me a place to land.
Understood?"

"Yes, Admiral," Kankrin replied. His white eyes flared as he raised an
eyebrow. A mistake.

"The fuck you do." She grasped his chin, snapped her second's neck,
and yanked the head fully round. The grind of strained vertebrae echoed
through the suddenly silent bridge. As she imbued whitefire through her
arms, all the pent-up hate and frustration over her lack of sleep and the
infernal buzzing poured into this one act. A final snap greeted its release,
and with a sigh, she let the body fall. The twisted head stared back at her,
white eyes dulled.

Inhibitor Ranket reached behind his back, pulling out his gourd.

"No. This pet of the emperor's can enjoy eternal death, Ranket. Get me Lieutenant Spintz, and tell the fucking thaumaturge that *I* think she's ready for service."

"Yes, Admiral," replied Ranket. He spun on his heels and headed out of the bridge.

"Are we in position yet? Yes? Now let's give these future spirit-dolls a show that'll have them cowering in their beds and make their spirits taste all the sweeter for it. Move."

The soulship spun gently about, chains twirling underneath on the port side, the metal hooks glinting in the last of the morning sunshine. Its brass hull shone, the whitefire glow beneath giving the ship a countenance of beauty – in the admiral's mind.

But not theirs. Look at the fear in them. Such a joy.

The first of the city's arbalests released, the spinning quarrel lancing towards the brass hull.

"Hah. Give them a show, Henar."

The admiral licked her lips, and her teeth clacked together as whitefire lashed out from the hull, streaking into the quarrel. The metal spike was glowing white hot by the time it struck the hull, where it shattered into a thousand pieces. A second arc of whitefire smashed into the offending arbalest. The weapon's wooden frame set alight, the two operators screaming as sparks showered their armour.

"Welcome to your new masters. Hah, burn those bloody ships and get us on past. Make sure they don't see our damage. I don't want any magi getting big ideas."

"Such a pity," said the Fleshmaster, running a metal-edged nail across the pale cheek. "You taste so sweet, magus. Your kind are such a delicacy, addictive in a way. I had forgotten just how strong your souls are, how such a spirit becomes a *need* rather than a *desire*." He opened his hand and tapped the cheek of the wide-eyed magus.

"If I had known that such a bond felt like this ..." the magus replied. He pressed his cheek against the emperor's withdrawing hand.

"Hah. Your kind changes. Never satisfied with how things are. Always wanting to break away to seek something more. But that is not such a bad thing. The Sundering taught me an important lesson: that I should not get too attached, too immersed in the spirit-dolls and their gifts. It was because of your kind our people fell, long before the Sundering itself. We had become decadent, reliant on the dragons and our spirit-dolls, unmindful of the world around us. Such is the life of an addict. We played our games, magus, made our machines shaped from the souls we fed on. Yet we were nothing."

"I am here to serve, Fleshmaster."

"That you are."

The emperor removed his hand and placed both against Tabharthóir's heartstone, seeing through the dragon's spirit-sight. The mighty dragon flew just above the water. A city lay to the east, across a thin strip of sea. It glowed with human life, rife with spiritfire and hope. Seven buildings pulsed with power that leaked from their wide doorways. Popsilin's message had been found. His Mechanised Inhibitor captain now heading north to fulfil her next mission. Fortuitous, in a way, as she remained an unknown amid the chaos he and his Inhibitor army were about to rain down on this realm. But she had left him the memories of the priest, of the Seven and their web of Houses. And their purpose.

The Seven have laid down a scripture, built their veils, suppressed a people. I taught them well. However, those walls to keep me out have made them weak, dependent. First, I must temper the traitor to the north while we take back what is rightfully ours.

He lashed out, grasped the back of the magus's head and dragged him closer while maintaining one hand on the throbbing crystal. "See. Look beyond the walls."

Tarin sent the images deep into the spirit-doll's mind. Tabharthóir's sight penetrated through the city harbour and on, towards its walls. Beyond that, the glow of living souls thinned out. Some walked the walls, others waited at the gates or wandered along the road beyond that. So few, yet.

"You see?"

"No ... no ..."

But then he did. A deep glow, full of hate and bile. Whitefire blackened by burning ash, roiling within a body of living skin and bone. A chaotic mass that boiled along the city's approach road. Tarin could feel the magus's inner sickness at what he saw, a thought much like his own when he had first seen the effects of taking a body too soon.

"They come for you. Understand? They are like beasts in a desert, desperate for a drink to quench their thirst, to ease their pain. They sense a beacon of hope, and it is you they hunt. Yet, between you and them lies a city. I offer them an oasis full of delights, more to infect, and when they are done, magus, they will remember what guided them here. You. A spirit-lure." Tarin let those thoughts settle on his spirit-doll's mind. "You are my bait. Serve me well, and you may sit at my feet when I rule this domain."

"But ..."

Tarin poured his will, etched with whitefire, into the magus's mind and broke the last vestige of resistance. He would not taste so sweet, but needs must.

"Yes, Emperor."

"Good. Now you understand my power, and your task. I only hope Lelion understands her role as well."

A purple tongue slid over his metallic teeth, licking his now-moist lips, and he watched through Tabharthóir's eyes as his plan played out.

The Infected had grown in number. Perhaps they had emerged from hiding since his battle with An Chéad. The lure drew them in, their hunger and need building as the potential for salvation within the broken magus's soul shone bright. Following a blackened instinct, they tore into any human and animal travelling along the road. Teeth gnawed upon exposed flesh, nails ripped at bare legs and arms. But they fed little, desperate to move on, to get to the lure that promised release. For every encounter, another was soon added to the horde, the infection infusing their spirit with soul-pain and hate. One by one, the road filled, the hoots and screams rose.

Tarin smiled, his skin able to flex in response as the magus's glorious spiritfire flowed through his body. He watched on with glee as the city guards realised what was boiling their way.

Will they close the gate in time? Oh, so close ... I can taste their fear, their confusion. Do we run? Bring the portcullis down, leave those outside to be eaten. Such ... pleasure.

The mass of flesh slammed into the dropping portcullis, the metal tips shattering bodies, piercing skulls and releasing the dread-filled souls inside.

More came, scrabbling at the metal, heaving and lifting with inhuman strength as others crawled beneath. Arrows flew, burning oil spewed from above. But there were too many. Tainted spirits driving sacks of flesh and bone. The Infected dragged and pulled themselves inside the city of Jense, their hoots resonating amid the screams.

"I have arrived, and this city is *my* sacrifice. Do not blame me for this ending, but the traitor, Nardelene. The one you name the Unspoken. You were right to revile her, for it is her theft of An Chéad that has sealed your fate."

He glanced at the slack-jawed magus, his white-rimmed eyes dancing amid the dragon's spirit-sight. "Come, magus. It will not be long before you are needed once again."

30
A CHANGING OF THE GUARD

THE WHITE PALACE, ERSTENBURGH,
BRANDSHOLD

"It has begun," stated High Lord Penance. He stood beside his chair at the Council, eyelids puffed from lack of sleep. "Hope's House in Makalena and Jense have called for help. But this ... this is beyond imagining. We thought it would come on dragon's wings, perhaps the limbs of Scorpions after General Zendril's encounter. But this?"

Lord Hope rose and took his place beside his High Lord. His eyes searched the Gods' Council – each face stern, eyes downcast, hands clasped together and resting on the table. "Makalena reports a huge ship of a gold-coloured metal that floats in the air, chains hanging beneath. It burned their ships but passed them by, and settled in the farmland beyond. They report it is the size of the White Palace, maybe larger, and their soldiers and artifices spew forth." His hands shook, and the Lord clasped them together, cracking knuckles as he did so. "And Jense ... I have no words. The Lead there died screaming, Hope's House invaded by the Infected.

She spoke of a horde, a riot of malevolence. I have never seen such ... such dread. I fear the city is lost."

"All of it?" asked the new Lord Fate, his red hair combed back from his lined face, the features of his sister so familiar to the Council. "That is impossible. Ten thousand people live there."

"Closer to twelve thousand," cut in Lord Wisdom. "Many moved south after the Crusade, fearing the Unbelievers' retribution."

"Duke Panset and the few Rangers left to him are scouting the city walls now. With him is a priest, Arjon, who carries a message crystal and survived the initial onslaught. He talked of a malignance, a power he could not describe, leading the creatures like a distant light in the night." Lord Hope gestured to the queen.

"General Zendril is aware and marches that way. Her horsed Rangers will be there within the day, we hope," she added. "And General Mandrich is considering splitting the southern army."

"No doubt looking to shore up Ridth," said Lord Justice. "Not that I am saying he is wrong to do so. But half the army, say, five thousand men? Will that be enough? To my mind, such a small number would be marching to their deaths if this ship is as big and as powerful as it seems."

The queen's hot stare fell on the Lord. "Or do we leave a city alone to defend itself while we cower behind our walls? Those are my people. Your flocks. They face an enemy we do not understand." She grabbed the table as she stood. "I thought you stood for Justice."

"Yes, my queen. But for all," the Lord replied. "I have spoken before about my haste in matters, and now I would counsel a pause to think before acting. The general certainly will, my queen. I am sorry, but there are lives at stake – more than just the soldiers'. All those they would save should they stay alive."

"You suggest hiding behind walls?" the queen spat, her face reddening.

"No. I suggest we observe, report, and formulate a plan. I am willing to take my waiting with me, to intercede where we can. Even buy time for the general, if need be."

"No," said High Lord Penance, his words echoed by Lord Wisdom – to the man's own surprise. "Everything we know and have read points to magi being a primary target, Lord Justice. We cannot sacrifice a key ... resource in this war."

"I understand, High Lord. But with my queen's permission, I would still ask that we are deployed. Though it galls me not to be at the forefront of any defence, my understanding of the Constructors could be vital in any observations. Queen Weister is correct in her view – we need to communicate, to coordinate our actions, otherwise we would still be unaware of these events. If I can take more of Hope's waiting with me, disperse them amongst his army, and also analyse their tactics, it can only be of benefit."

The High Lord could not drag his eyes aways from the young Lord. The flash of scarlet in his eyes, the stiffness in his face an indication of the self-control he was trying to manage.

Geral was right. I am not a war leader.

This is not my time.

He broke his stare and looked to the queen. He slid his cane from the table, hands flexing against the sigil on top of its handle.

But if it is hers, then I must take the role of counsel to temper the Weister in her. If she will have me.

"My queen," High Lord Penance said, but his eyes roamed the room, taking in each of the Lords and Ladies in turn. "This is the war that all here have prepared for over the last few months. We are now, I believe, a War Council. And for that, someone must lead. Someone who will listen, take advice, and make decisions that send soldiers, townsfolk and priests to their deaths." He stepped away from the table and leant his cane against his leg. Fumbling beneath the robes swaddling his neck, he eventually lifted a silver chain over his head. Below it hung a seven-pointed star contained within a circle.

"That leader should be you." He approached the queen, offering the pendant that glinted in the sunlight streaming through the slitted window. "I bequeath you the title of Overseer. We – and I – are yours to command."

"Lord Penance, I don't—"

"It is written," cut in Lord Wisdom, "that in times of crisis, when the Council decrees, the office of Overseer can be passed to one deemed worthy. It is not written that they *have* to be a leader of one of the Houses." Lord Wisdom rose from his chair and knocked his hand upon the table, his face set hard in a manner only the meisters had ever witnessed. "I, for one, agree with the High Lord. We will be blinded by our faith, by the years of hiding our intent. I say yes."

Lady Honour stood, as did Lady Death by her side. Both knocked on the table, their eyes on the queen. "As do I," they said in unison.

"I agree," added Lord Hope, "as long as the High Lord's words are heeded." He also stood, and glanced over to Lord Fate, who raised an eyebrow and rose to stand by his side.

"That leaves the hothead," smiled Lord Justice as he pushed himself up from his chair. "I apologise, High Lord, if I caused this decision." He knocked on the table.

"Apologise? No need. A spur, perhaps." High Lord Penance turned again to face the queen. "With this, we are yours to command. Only should *all* the Council agree, will it be rescinded. We place in you our trust, faith and hope. Will you accept?"

He watched as her gaze flickered around the table, her search for a chink of dissent at his choice. It brought a smile to his face, briefly exposing purple teeth and allowing the smell of junip to pervade the space between himself and the queen.

His queen.

"I do," she said. "Until such time my people are safe."

"Spoken as one who understands," said Lady Honour, "what we truly stand for."

High Lord Penance lifted the chain over Queen Weister's head and set it around her neck. The pendant settled upon her chest. The seven Houses were now hers to command.

The queen took the Overseer's symbol in her hand, feeling its warmth as she examined each element. "This does not mean I forgive any of the Houses' dealings," she said, eyes lifting from the pendant to lock with the High Lord's, before sweeping the room. "However, such a reckoning can wait until our people are saved. Now we must blend science, faith and spiritfire to their best end." The queen's posture altered, her shoulders set higher, further back, her impact on the room shifting once again. "High Lord Penance will serve as the conduit for your thoughts outside of this War Council, as is his right. Right now, we have to act decisively." She glanced over to Lord Justice, who acknowledged her. "But with caution. Lord Justice, I agree with your intent, and I urge you to split your *waiting*. A number to act as a guard for yourself, the rest to accompany the battlecarts I will send behind you. My understanding, from meisters Arknold and Kinst, is that we have a good number, with more to follow. General

Mandrich will have need of them if the talk of these machines is correct. Lord Hope?"

"Yes?"

"How many of your waiting are in the south, and can use the message crystals?"

"As chance would have it, my queen, there are two within the city of Makalena. I have four more who I could send to General Mandrich, now he is more willing to utilise them." Lord Hope let a reluctant smile slip as he eyes flicked to the ceiling. "I believe you could have a strong influence there. General Zendril has, at least, finally understood their potential."

"Ready them." Queen Weister paused, her hand still upon the pendant. "High Lord, I would seek your advice on the next step."

"If I may suggest, my queen, a recess then, if decisions will be made that the Council needs to hear afterwards?"

—

She sat upon the edge of the pew, hands clasped upon her lap, heart beating a thousand times faster than she thought possible. The pendant at her chest instilled a strange combination of weight and expectation. Yet, there was also comfort.

A right.

"Are you okay, Queen Weister?" High Lord Penance asked as he closed the prayer chamber doors. His cane tapped each tile as he walked the short distance to sit opposite.

"That does not matter, does it? I am still undecided whether you acted in your own self-interest or that of the people." She continued to stare into her hands, refusing to look up. "Mistrust is not a great place to begin your new role as counsellor."

"Hah. Once you open a box of vipers, you always expect each box after to be full of them too. And then, when you forget to check, another surprise arises. Such is life, and I accept whatever judgement you decide." His chin sat upon his hands, which rested on the cane top. His usual pose, though his eyes were softer than when she'd first seen him sit that way.

"Tying up my thoughts in words seems to be your speciality. I will need plain speaking, Lord Penance. You forced me to change, to take on the true mantle of my family lineage. Weisters have not the patience for any other way. And now this." She clasped the Overseer's symbol, rubbing a thumb along each arrow. She could feel, along the circle, a tiny representation of each House's sigil.

"I don't often act on impulse, but I believe it was, and is, correct. I am not a warrior, except within my faith. You are, though I urge you to listen to our counsel and consider the value and power of each of the House Leaders." He let a rueful smile slip, his chin lifting from his hands as he tilted his head. "Is this what you wished to discuss?"

"No ... Maybe." Her lips twisted, and she looked at him, slowly shaking her head. "Two things. I believe that the Infected are a threat to the north, the Constructors to the south. It feels like a plan to squeeze Erstenburgh between the two. Except ... the Unspoken. The talk of the fight between dragons, it does not sit well with such a plan."

High Lord Penance nodded, his smile fading. "You mean, there is more to come?"

"An unknown. If my mother taught me anything, it was to always watch your back. Like your box of vipers, once you open the box, your mind is always on it until you forget. And that's the day you are bitten. There is more to this. I would wish to have someone of power present there, able to advise and act, who understands the Constructors and their motivations."

"Advise your mother? Then they must have an indomitable spirit." The smile reached his eyes this time.

"You mean, like a member of the Weister clan?"

High Lord Penance nodded. "Hah, yes. May I suggest Lady Honour accompanies your cousin? If, as you say, there is more to this, our new learning shows we act best as a pair. Especially against the force of will that is your mother."

"What about Lord Justice? I sent him alone."

"He has a connection with Mandrich. The general worships Justice, and they converse often. I believe that will be enough. They have trust."

The queen rose and held her hand out to the High Lord. He paused to catch her expression before accepting the offer and rising to stand in front of her.

"Our first joint decision. Good. Now, Lord Penance, tell me of this Geral I have heard whispers about."

31
TO SEE THE FUTURE

PEATFIELDS OF JENSE, BRANDSHOLD

The bloodied edge caught at the breeches before slicing through to the husked flesh. The knee bone split, shards scraping against the blade as the sword chopped through and into the ground. The Infected flinched, its hoot cut off despite the fingers wrapped about Llandon's arm. Filthy fingernails searched for any exposed flesh where the Ranger's armour had split. Duke Panset drove his dagger into the Infected's right eye and on, into its brain. Whitefire fizzed as he withdrew the weapon, and the once-human creature toppled to the floor as its lower leg gave way.

Panset stepped away, leaving Llandon to extricate himself from the lifeless arms. He swung his sword over the top of the kneeling Arjon's head as a second Infected entered the hut. The blade bit deep into the Infected's skull, shattering bone, spraying brain matter and whitefire in equal measure. The Infected's momentum took it onwards to land where Arjon had been kneeling. The duke gave the creature a kick. The lack of response eased his mind as he slammed the door shut and dropped the wooden bar.

"Llandon, the window," he said.

He didn't wait to see if the First Ranger complied. He dragged Michala up from where she lay in the corner, dropped his sword and wiped the gore from his dagger before slicing open the material along her upper thigh. The bruise beneath was livid and blood-stained, the teeth marks prominent.

"Fuck," he said.

He was making to rise when the woman's hands gripped his. "Kill me," she whispered, the horror of her own words showing in her pained eyes. "I can feel it seething inside. The hate. Kill me, please."

He pushed her arm away, his breath heavy, refusing to exit his lungs.

Llandon, bow in hand, grunted as he peered out a slit in the cloth covered window. Panset desperately wanted to turn around, to seek Llandon's approval. Or perhaps in hope the man would take his turn in the death-dealing.

Instead, he knelt, only for Arjon to take the woman's hand instead.

"First Ranger," the priest whispered, throat tight, words barely audible. "Look to the duke."

Accepting her fate, Michala blinked and faced Panset. Arjon placed one hand at the side of her head. Yellow spiritfire flared between his fingers, strong, its arcs of power barely controlled as they rode her neck and down her body. The smell of burnt flesh assailed the duke's nose, and the twist of fear and hate rose in his stomach. It was the second time the priest had produced such magic – the spiritfire. The first had saved his life.

Arjon fell back against the rear wall of the wooden hut, his breathing ragged.

"Thank you," said Panset. He wanted to reach out and squeeze the acolyte's shoulder, but the man's drawn cheeks, the jovial countenance long gone, kept him away.

Now is not the time.

The yellow spiritfire faded. Michala's empty skull stared back at him, mouth wide in a final, soundless scream. He couldn't help himself. He leaned forward and eased the lower jaw closed, refusing to let the pain overwhelm him.

"The bastards 'ave gone, Duke. Moved on. I can't get me 'ead round it. They just 'it and run." Llandon wiped his leaking nose across the back of his torn armour. "What's 'appening?"

"How far to the city?"

"Reck'n half a mile. This is the last storage shed fer the peat." Llandon kicked the pile of rolled up mud next to him. "Ten minutes."

"Are we clear?"

"As far as I can see 'n' hear." Llandon glanced over, mouth twisting when he spotted Michala's burnt shell. "We runnin'?"

"No. We are Queen's Rangers and have a duty. Are you with me, priest? We have to see what's happening. We need to report it, understand? Do you have enough of this spiritfire left to get a message through?" The duke pulled at Arjon's shoulder, wincing as the man turned to face him. His mud-stained cheeks were riven with tears. But he nodded. Panset grabbed him by the arm and pulled Hope's priest to his feet.

"Cover our exit, Llandon." He grasped Michala's sword, sheathing it while holding his own.

Letting out a breath to calm his heart, he lifted the wooden bar and pulled the door open a crack. The hoots echoed in, but distant and fading. The duke exited, Arjon close behind. After a signal, Llandon followed. They headed up the short trail littered with piles of peat and darkening blood to arrive at the approach road to Jense. Ahead, the city glowed orange and red against the darkening sky. Flames licked the walls, towers barely seen above the ash and smoke. Panset imagined the people inside, holding out for a bastion of hope as the city fell under the ravages of tooth and claw.

What if it were my family in there? What would I do?

Survive.

Hold out, but for whom?

Llandon appeared at his side, down on one knee, arrow nocked as he stared ahead, eyes averted from the fire.

"Watch ye' night sight, Duke. Gonna need it if we fekin' goin' out on the town." The gap-toothed smile took Panset briefly by surprise. "Got some killin' to do. Reck'ning there's some folk that need a 'ero in there. Know any?"

"Not handsome ones." He shook his head. "Cover us."

The duke headed off, sword low, searching side to side as he crept along the road. The twang of a bowstring alerted him, and he threw himself down at Llandon's cry. He found himself next to a legless Infected. It dug its broken fingers into the cracks of the road, dragging itself towards him. He had just lifted his sword when a dagger slammed into the creature's ear. Whitefire glowed briefly about Llandon's grip.

"Missed the bastard," he said. "Up."

He pointed ahead and Panset stood, sword in hand, as figures dived under the slightly raised portcullis. They pummelled at the dead Infected pinioned beneath the portcullis spikes, dragging themselves clear. The twang of Llandon's bow was met by a short hoot as his arrow slammed into the mouth of a chasing Infected. The husked creature collapsed into the gate before rising again, shattered jaw flapping as it gnawed at the metal bars. A second arrow drove deep into its nose, and the Infected spiralled to the ground.

Escaping townsfolk ran their way, panicked and wild. Panset pulled Llandon aside. The three men and a woman ran on by, heading for the woods.

"Nothing we can do," he said. "And there'll be more. We need to get them out. The rest is up to them. And we have to see."

"You can't," said Arjon, both hands covering his face. "You can't let any out. If just one gets free, this will only start again." The priest squeezed the bridge of his nose and wiped his fingers onto his already bedraggled sleeve. Sadness weighed heavy on his shoulders. "Even those who just ran by could soon fall to the infection. Like Michala. Do we know when she was bitten? How long it took?"

"I—"

The situation tore at his heart. At the portcullis, a child raved, her eyes wild and white, scrape marks across her neck and scalp. In one hand, a straw-stuffed doll, while the other clawed at the metal bars. She was surrounded by at least ten more, all of them lost. They ignored each other, their focus solely on Panset and his group. A scream from behind, long and drawn out, drew their attention away. The ravening group around the girl turned back to the burning city, hooting. Some dropped to all fours, while others pushed their way past, grappling with their own as they sped deeper into the city. Only the girl remained, and was wriggling through the dead pinned by the portcullis. Blood-matted fingers dragged her clear of the bodies, and she released a strangled hoot of success.

Panset's heart pounded.

Is this the future the Seven held back from us? Is this a taste of what will become of our children. Our families?

She charged, the doll forgotten, eyes filled with white madness. Llandon's bow rose, but Panset pushed the weapon down and stepped forwards. The slash of his blade ended the threat, and, perhaps, the last of his humanity.

He stared at the ragged mess upon the ground. The girl's hand twitched as the seeping whitefire dispersed. He took a breath, sword hanging by his side, memories of battles with the Unbelievers rattling through his mind. The sword stroke that had sliced his face, smashed teeth from his mouth. The blade he had taken to save another, only to see them fall under the next.

"Duke?" asked Llandon, hand resting on Panset's shoulder. "Are we goin' in? 'Cos this is our chance."

Panset felt the weight, the burden, shift. He shook his head and began walking over to the gate.

"Clear the bodies. We bring the gate down." He glanced over his shoulder at the priest. "How long did Zendril say?"

"The riders should be here in a day. The army, maybe four, or three if she can drive the, ahem, *fuckers* any faster," Arjon said, with no trace of a grin. "She did mention others may arrive sooner. Queen's Rangers."

They reached the portcullis and Panset kicked the doll aside, unable to cope with its presence. Together, he and Arjon cut and dragged the bodies clear while Llandon stood guard. The final slam of the metal points into the waiting holes was a welcome relief. Beyond the inner-city walls, heat pillowed, the smell of burning flesh and wood hanging in the air. But still the hoots echoed, the screams of the soon-to-be-Infected ringing through all their minds. Shadows flitted, silhouetted against the flames as people ran or Infected chased their prey.

The duke gripped the bars, staring inside, struggling to tear himself away. "There is a southern gate, I believe. That must be our next target."

"And northern and western," added Arjon. "Smaller, but no less well-used. This is my city, Duke Panset. Those are my people, though this does not ease the pain. We must try to contain this."

Llandon's eyes lowered to the ground, unwilling to look upon the city. "Aye," the Ranger said. "They are already wi' the dead."

"We stay together and watch each other's backs. Hope we get some help soon. I say we sort the southern gate first, then the western." Duke Panset took one last look into the burning city before heading south into the flat, open grass field surrounding the city. A killing zone.

Of little use when your enemy is already inside.

32
AND ON TO WAR

ERSTENBURGH, BRANDSHOLD

"How many is that?" asked Meister Kinst, examining the iron binding around the tip of the large wooden stake that protruded from the back of the battlecart.

"A dozen are ready, and the Erin's Wrath is loaded in the carts behind," Greeth replied as she lifted the large bag of crystals into a waiting soldier's cupped arms. "Take care with these. You watched the binding, yes?" The soldier, eyes wide, nodded as he carried the bag up the open steps and into the battlecart.

"Good," continued Kinst. "And they have spread these out, yes? Not all bunched together?"

"I explained what would happen should one go up, so yes. Stop fretting and finish up the last binding. Lord Justice will wear a path in the courtyard by the time you're done."

"For my acolyte, you are very bossy," said Kinst. She patted the binding, then the cart behind it containing Erin's Wrath. Memories of the last time they had prepared in this way filtered into her mind, memories of Ecne's fussing bringing a sad smile to her face.

"Acolyte? You wade in dangerous waters, Meister Kinst."

Greeth grabbed the last bag of large crystals and walked to the rearmost battlecart, its armour plate wet in the evening drizzle. The tethered horses waited calmly, nickering as the woman passed. She handed the bag to the waiting female soldier, and sighed. "That's it. Done."

"Are we ready, Meister Kinst?" bellowed Lord Justice. The clop of his horse's hooves rang loudly in the yard as he rode up.

Meister Kinst took a step back and waggled her fingers in the air as if counting things off. "Ballista quarrels loaded – there are a dozen each. That's two dozen per battlecart. Six loads of potted Erin's Wrath. And the ram crystals are prepped for each cart and aboard. Greeth has sent cut quarrel tips for crossbows too. Those will have to be worked by the general's fletcher. We had too much to prepare. There are about a hundred pot bombs per battlecart as well. If you want a gentle word of advice, go easy, Lord Justice."

"We do not have the time, Meister. I wish we did. We will spread the carts wide apart." He grimaced as he looked down the line of horses and their drivers.

"About a dozen yards, at least," added Kinst. "And keep the *waiting* clear." She winced at the Lord's glare, but held her ground. "We all have a value, Lord Justice. Scientifically as well as spiritually. Greeth is sending one of her people with you. Someone who has worked the powders' production and knows how to handle them. They also need to be kept clear, understand? Lose them, then the effectiveness of these new weapons will be wasted."

"Science," said Lord Justice, wheeling his horse away and riding down the line of carts, "will be the death of us."

"Suppressing it may well have killed us first," whispered Kinst, eyeing Greeth, who just shook her head. "Come on, woman. We need to replace all we stole from Erstenburgh's stock. No dallying. I feel the need for a drink, and an old friend."

—

"Gowan, what is wrong?" Grand Meister Arknold yawned and continued to tap at the iron bolt on the table with a small hammer. The heartstone glowed Fate's blue, the pulse quickening until Gowan emerged. The spirit looked weak, faded. Arknold could see the walls through Gowan's body for the first time since meeting the dead First Ranger.

"Leront has become difficult," Gowan said, her glow muted, pulsing softly in tune to the heartstone. "As before, when the Constructor's beacon tore through the veil after Nathair emerged. I wish High Lord Penance would keep us informed. It is hard for me to understand the Spirit Walker's moods without knowing what is happening outside of this cage of ribs."

"War," said Arknold. "I told you."

"But Leront is keening and angry. The frustration comes in waves." Gowan flickered in and out. "I am worried my control may slip."

The grand meister put her hammer down and scraped the repaired chair back as she stood up from the makeshift workbench. "Slip? You said ..."

"Everything was fine before the last Soul Tear. I had him locked away, and though I am stronger now, he draws from something. Or maybe whatever calls to him is forcing him to greater strength."

"You think he is called?" Arknold leaned back to sit on the edge of the bench. "Like the beacon you intend to become to draw them to our trap?"

"Yes ... Now I think on it, that's it. Not deliberately. But each time Leront catches the presence, he reacts. Like he can't control himself and must respond. He has a wound."

"A wound? How can a spirit have a wound? You weaken. We have spoken on that before. But that affects all of you." Arknold watched Gowan flicker at that, the spirit nodding. There was something odd the grand meister couldn't put her finger on. A change.

"This is different. It is like his outer skin has been sliced open. If it was exposed, that which is Leront would pour out. Like blood. It is sealed by something ... malevolent. I think it is the seal that forces him to react." Gowan blinked and ran a hand through her hair to nudge aside the Ranger's cap she always wore. She chewed her lip as Arknold walked closer.

"And this is important? I can see it bothers you. Why?"

"Because it is like a darkness, a stain on Leront. Don't get me wrong. I have no intention of letting him free of it, even if I knew how. I remember the battle we had when I was first released from my body. Now he has awoken further, I fear I would stand little chance."

Arknold stretched her arms out, daring for the first time to place them close to Gowan. "You are formed of spiritfire, yes? A soul that has been released from the body, yet somehow retains its form, remembering who you were."

"*Are.*"

"Sorry, *are*. And it is this that Leront used to power his metal dragon body? Yet he is, himself, formed of the same substance. And once was a Schenterenta shaman?"

Gowan nodded.

"And you say this wound is sealed by a ..."

"A poison. I know that sounds ridiculous, but the more I think about it, the more it appears to be that. Imagine an ink-black fungus that suppurates in the wound itself. Leaking evil." Gowan shook her head, her hand again on the back of her neck as she stared at the floor. A pulse from the heartstone was matched by her own before she faded away.

Arknold's concern at her absence grew until Gowan flickered back. "Leaks where?" Arknold pursued the thought. "Into you?"

"No, back into Leront."

"Feeding his shaman spirit poison constantly? Like a drug? Keeping Leront compliant, you think?" Arknold drew her hands back, but this time Gowan reached out and placed both her hands upon them.

"I can show you, if you agree."

Arknold blinked and withdrew her hands, but quickly changed her mind. Her curiosity called, an unquenchable need to know despite her misgivings. She let Gowan touch both hands.

Warmth spread into her fingers, and she sensed Gowan's spirit as it bled along her nerves and onwards, into her mind. Her sight faded into a riot of colour, the world glinting in a rainbow of metallic hues. They swirled, tying each other in knots, only to slide away and crash again into another. Amid this maelstrom, a Schenterenta appeared, its legs twisted so one knee faced inwards, the other out. Their shoulders were bent, eyes white and streaked with black. Against its chest, where a human heart would beat, sat the malevolence Gowan had spoken of. It pulsed hungrily, a foul thing. At its edges, a black ichor seeped into the Spirit Walker's skin.

"Leront?" Arknold said.

The face turned to her, white eyes rolling in their sockets. And the Spirit Walker slid into her mind.

"Do you see what I sssee, Grand Meister?" whispered Gowan's voice, though with a sibilant hiss Arknold struggled to remember. *"That we are but food, and the mastersss have returned?"*

Arknold quivered. The black tendrils invaded her mind, squashing any other thought beyond their demand. She slid from Gowan's touch and placed her hands upon the heartstone. She gave of her soul to the Spirit Walker within, gasping as it drew from her.

"Enough," said Gowan, and pulled Arknold from the heartstone.

The grand meister blinked, her mind fogged. She expected to see Gowan holding her. Instead, the spirit flickered between the twisted shaman and a white-eyed Ranger. A sickness invaded her stomach, soon quashed as Arknold's mind broke amid the waves of subjugation pouring into her head. She was Leront's in mind and body, to use as he wanted.

"Yesss. Enough. Now fetch me a priessst. I remain ... hungry."

33
A CITY OF THE HORDE

"You must leave now!" shouted Llandon, and pulled at the city guard's arm.

The huge woman shoved him off and wiped the gristle that covered her hand onto the wall. "Fuck off, coward," she growled, and checked her palm. Satisfied, she collected her hooked axe from where it leaned against a trough, and tapped the haft on the floor in some weird ritual. Before her lay the chopped remains of six Infected, their skins husked, their eyes fully white. "These feckers are not passing me. And you're not shutting the fucking gate. Now, either stand with me or fuck off." She didn't look at the Ranger, just prowled ahead, moving her weight from foot to foot. Panset had to admire her bravery.

Llandon backed away, shaking his head as the woman's axe fell again, splitting an Infected's head as it charged her. She ripped the axe clear, and as the inhuman beast fell, tapped the floor again.

"I canna ..." said Llandon, his eyes pleading with the duke as he walked the final few yards to the narrow gate. "Please."

"We must," said Panset, and he grabbed the double set of chains piled at the side of the gate. "Check the guardhouse, Arjon. Find anything I can lock these with if she won't give up the key."

Arjon ran for the doorway, kicking away the limbs and torso of an Infected that had met the guard's axe. The duke passed Llandon and ordered him to watch Arjon. They needed to send word soon. The southern gate had already been locked, the guards there having thrown the keys through the portcullis as their final act, their eviscerated bodies splayed against the bars.

He approached the large guard, who still bounced from foot to foot, eyes locked on the curve of the dark street ahead. A shout, fear-filled, echoed along it. Feet thudded on the cobbled road. By the time Panset was six feet behind her, three figures had rounded the corner, clothes bloodied but their eyes clear of the white. Two were women, their feet bare, the third, an old, frail man. The women pounded towards them, half-dragging the man, whose face remained slack, as if he'd seen all the evil the world could throw at him in just a few, short hours.

"Run," shouted the female guard, and stepped to one side to let them hurtle past. They ran straight towards Panset. His breath caught in his throat, eyes roaming all three for slashes or bite marks, his head screaming at him that he couldn't let them go free. It was when the man looked his way that he knew he could never win. He'd seen too much, been changed forever by the malevolence they faced. His heart hurt. Llandon's pleading rang in his ears as he raised his sword to strike.

A roar shook windows and gates alike, cutting through the night's screams to drain his will. The women stopped, unmindful of Panset's intent, and stared into the sky over his shoulder. A metallic dragon beat at the sky above with huge, silver-blue wings. Maw open, its sword-like teeth reflected the red and orange of Jense's fiery demise. Trailing behind, the metal-scaled tail lashed at the city walls, knocking the stone merlons deep into the cobbled streets.

The Seven be damned.

"Fuck me," Llandon swore, the bow in his hand briefly forgotten.

The dragon roared again. A whiplash of whitefire arced across the sky, greeted by the howls and hoots of the creatures below. The cries merged into a wave of sound that rose and fell to the rhythm of the dragon's wings.

"Nooo!" bellowed the guard.

Panset spun to find her covered with the Infected. The creatures tore at her arms and bit at her cheeks. She kicked out, ramming two of the foul things together, their skulls splintering as a third tore a chunk from her arm. Blood spurted, but the axe remained in her hand. She kneed the thing in the chest and, as it reeled away, brought the axe down to slice through a shoulder and down, into the ribs. She yelled in frustration and stepped back from the mess surrounding her, only to find the duke's sword protruding from her chest. He ripped it clear and, as she staggered forwards, he chopped down upon her neck. She landed amid the gore of her kills, silent.

"I'm so sorry," Panset said, but had no time for grief. He scrabbled for the gate keys, pulling them clear of her pooling blood. More hoots echoed along the street, the sound of a growing mob heading their way.

"Llandon!" he shouted, running for the gate. "Get Arjon out of there!" He glanced over his shoulder as the long shadows of the mob streaked around the corner, the slap of feet upon the cobbles and the howls indicating they had little time. "Now, Llandon!"

He ran. Llandon appeared ahead of him and shoved Arjon through the small gates. No more than a cart's width wide, they serviced the coast road and the incoming trade. Double gated, rather than a dropped portcullis, the Ranger was already pulling an outer gate closed when Panset reached him. He dragged the other shut, and Arjon wrapped a single chain about the inner bars while Panset's unsteady hand slid the key home on the third try. The horde scrambled over the murdered guard, the first reaching the inner gate as Panset heard the lock scrape, He thanked the Seven as it engaged. Bloodied hands slammed through the bars, groping for him, desperate to spread their vile gift. Llandon pulled the duke clear of the raw fingers and their promise of infection.

White eyes burned through the Rangers' souls, the Infected's hunger striking them like a physical blow. A third roar rumbled across the glowing sky, followed by a sweep of dragon's fire. The ravening mob plunged into immediate silence. Stillness chilled Panset to the bone, compounded when the horde turned as one to stare into the sky. They rocked backwards, mouths open, and released howls that assaulted his ears and churned his stomach. The tide broke, and the Infected turned away from the gate, pushing and shoving over each other. Chaos descended, the once-human creatures crushing others beneath, ripping at any limbs and heads in their way as they desperately followed the dragon's path.

"No—" came a choked off cry.

Panset spun about, sword raised, ready to defend his people. Llandon stared back at him. The slack-faced old man chewed upon his thigh, blood spilling down his lips as his eyes rolled back. Hands shaking, Llandon slid an arrow from the quiver at his hip and drove the tip deep into the man's eye. Whitefire swirled along his fingers as he withdrew the haft, and held the bloody tip up to his own eye. Panset strode forwards, crushing any thoughts with his own scream, and thrust his sword up through his friend's jaw.

Arjon cried out, but his pleadings cut off, silenced. As Panset turned, yellowfire died upon the priest's fingers. The two barefoot women had slashed his throat. As the priest slumped to the floor, Panset took two steps backwards, giving himself space to face this new horror.

A hand wrapped around his ankle, forcing him to look away. The female guard's fingers had dug into his boots, stretching through the bars as she lay, bloodied and dishonoured, upon the floor.

"Fucking coward," she said, blood bubbling from her neck. "Die like one."

Panset slammed the hilt of his sword into her wrist. The crack of bone signalled the release of her fingers. Angry and bitter, the duke slashed back towards the Infected women, expecting their attack. But they weren't there. A glance to the north revealed them running alongside the western wall, heading north. The sky was aglow with the flames from the burning city, punctuated by the occasional streak of dragon's fire. Amid the loss and pain strangling his reason, he knew they followed the dragon's call.

But northwards. Why?

The duke, self-loathing gnawing at his soul, drove his sword into the remainder of the guard's neck, giving her a final release and finishing his murderous act.

Llandon still knelt on the floor, blood pouring from his neck and jaw. Another death on his hands. Panset searched for the tears, but they refused to come. He swore, blaming the Seven as he hacked at his First Ranger, making sure he would not return to haunt the duke he had served so well.

Finished and sickened, he forced himself to search Arjon for the crystal the priest had used to contact the general. He had no hope of replicating the act, but knew they were rare and vital in this bloody war that had exploded into existence. A small success amid all the blood and loss.

"North," he whispered. Zendril needed to know of the dragon, and the Infected it clearly commanded, as well as their heading. And the queen, that twelve thousand souls had been lost today.

Twelve thousand and one.

He swiftly rifled through his dead companions' pockets and bags, collecting food, water, and a couple of pot bombs Llandon had scavenged after the Infected attack back at the copse. With his friend's bow in hand and quiver at his hip, Panset set off at pace, tracking the women's path through the ash-covered grass along the city walls.

After a half hour, the sounds of the Infected within the city rose in fervour. The duke guessed the numbers were gathering, trying to follow the silver-blue dragon that, to his relief, remained out of sight. Fires still raged, but much of the screaming had stopped. Just howls and hoots blended with the roaring of the flames. And an odd, repetitive thud he could put no purpose to.

With little cover, the killing field swept clear of all possible hiding places on General Zendril's orders, he dropped low as he rounded the north-west portion of the city wall. Here, the noise of the crowded Infected faded to the occasional squeal, and Panset dropped into the grass. Forced to crawl, his bow and readied arrow in one hand, he inched forwards until something glinted above the ground ahead. As his eyes adjusted, he realised it was the dragon's tail, the spikes catching the orange flames menacingly as it hung in the air. Infected clawed at the dragon's taloned hind legs, biting at the metal scales, shredding their hands as they appeared to attack the huge beast. The tail swung along the ground, a whiplash that tore through the Infected, smashing bodies, limbs and innards flying.

Are they fighting?

The tail continued its path, the dragon's body turning while the hind legs dug into the earth. A huge thud vibrated through the city walls as it struck. The hoots inside became a long howl. The tail rose again, thrashing through the air, sending Infected flying as it whipped once more into the city wall. The thud was less dull this time, accompanied by the crashing of stone and the squeal of metal.

Panset inched forwards, eyes only for the dragon and the battering it was giving the city. A third, then a fourth strike sent stone dust flying to spark in the heat of the fire. As he closed in, more of the Infected reached the silver-blue dragon, clambering over its forelegs or clinging to the metal-skinned wings. The dragon shivered and threw the once-human creatures off, their howls filled with hunger and frustration. It then leaned forwards, sending another powerful swipe of its tail into the remains of the city entrance. The towers collapsed, spilling their stone, and the remaining wall followed suit. The dragon raised its head to the fire-lit sky and emitted a roar of triumph before leaping into the air. Three wingbeats fanned the heat, the waves rolling over Panset as he watched the beast rise into the night. The metal beast wheeled about and, with a second rumble of triumph rolling over the city, turned northwards.

The tears finally came, forging rivulets in the ash and blood that covered his face as a mass of Infected humanity poured over the smashed walls. The old and the young, the hale and the misshapen, desperate to follow the dragon that had released them. Like beer from a keg, they erupted from the city in their hundreds, their thousands. They only looked forwards, to the north. Uncaring of the devastation they left behind, trampling the weakest underfoot, many still burning from the fire within, yet unmindful of the pain.

Or not feeling it.

A hoot from behind him set ice in his heart.

34

OF HONOUR AND REDEMPTION

"Is this wise?" asked Lady Honour, nudging the collection of bags Lady Death had piled against her bedroom chamber wall. "You should be travelling light."

"Those are not clothes," replied Lady Death, tutting all the while as she gently shoved the last of her clothes into a backpack. "Medical equipment, soothing potions, and one of Lord Hope and Meister Kinst's messaging crystals."

"That is not what I meant. Is it wise leaving Erstenburgh and the Wyrding Stones behind? I have no second who is ready to act in my stead, like you. My veil ..."

Lady Death pulled at the pack's cord and shoved it off the bed. She then faced Lady Honour, and reached out to touch the corner of the woman's lips. "Is that not why I'm here? Tonight, we heal our veils as best we can so, should there be more Constructors arriving, they will suffer under our spiritfire and glyphs. After that, what more can we do here? The prayer stones will gather the offerings, store them ready for our return should they be needed. There is no more reason to keep feeding the veil."

Lady Honour looked to her blackened hand. The fingers, almost healed, the constant pain in her wrist receding. Since they had joined in the union of spiritfire, their bodies had begun to heal despite the burden of their task. Yet, it seemed wrong that the thieves of souls should no longer be marked as such. Lips twisting, she took Lady Death's fingers in her own and ran them along her cheek.

"First you worry when you can't heal your veil, then when you heal yourself. Certainty needs to be your guide. Are you certain of me?" Lady Death lifted Lady Honour's chin, her startling, blue-flecked eyes locking with her soul partner's.

Lady Honour smiled in return, her own hand tracing the fingers that lay on her cheek before reaching out and drawing Lady Death in. They kissed while the thrum of their hearts harmonised, the roots of their souls slipping free and entwining, whirling about the room as their bodies eased onto the bed. The drum of their heartbeats echoed from the walls until the black and orange of Death and Honour plunged into the waiting Wyrding Stone.

Together, they rose through the floors of Honour's House, tore free of its huge tower to swirl ever upwards into the dark of the clouds above. Once through, wrapped and intertwined in the pure joy of the merger of their spirits, the veil's wound called them. Ripples of soul-pain rolled along the inner curtain. The paired souls following the agony back towards the gaping hole that bled orange spiritfire into the sky above the ocean. With a thought, they drew upon their House Wyrding Stones, calling on the slivers of souls stored within. A bounty stolen, but so needed. Encased in the threads of power, they drove inward, seeking and finding the pathway that had been cut through the veil. There, Honour's glyph lay dormant among an unrecognisable, cancerous cloud of ash, flesh and bone. They passed by to reach Death's curtain, which had also been torn asunder. Together, they channelled their flocks' gifts of spiritfire and eased the ripped curtain together. Weaving around the wound, stitching with a thread forged by the combined souls of the people they were sworn to protect.

Once complete, they returned to Honour's glyph, inert amid the cloud of whatever it had destroyed. It was clear the God's structure had failed, the forging of the magical symbol overwhelmed. And they had not the skill to rebuild it. They whirled about it once, a combined sadness sitting upon them, when something changed. The veil roiled, Honour's orange churning in hues of tangerine interspersed with the dreaded white. It pressed inwards, causing their entwined souls to squeeze tighter, until a strange touch of mind and spirit alighted upon them both.

"I—" began Lady Death, only for her lover's touch to silence her, the joy within it striking at her spirit heart.

'It is my God,' she whispered. *'Yet not. Something more.'*

The current hastened, seething, the white in ascendance until Honour's orange burst from its centre. Fine, vibrant threads of the God's power spreading wide to lace the white.

'She seeks refuge, away from the veil.'

"How?" whispered Lady Death, only for Honour's urgency to overtake her, and the combined souls dropped towards the curtain's wound.

'Follow,' said Lady Honour.

The white and orange whirl flowed their way, leaving turmoil in its wake as it bludgeoned through the veil. Lady Death and Honour exited the wound, turning to watch as the boiling mass emerged into the skies above Brandshold. A hum began, the vibration rippling through their souls, their spirits rising and falling in line with the rhythm. As it grew, the hum broke out into definable voices – into a song. A song of the Schenterenta.

It ended, as suddenly as it started. The combined white and orange fire swirled in on itself, the head eating the tail until it formed a tight ball that exploded outwards, throwing streams of spiritfire across the sky.

Lady Death and Lady Honour hovered above the sea, watching the souls fly into the night. All except for the one that waited before them. The swirling mass took form, becoming a female Schenterenta. Her skin a dappled ebony, hair a shock of grey, and eyes as wild and cat-like as any they had seen. An orange halo glowed around her, a mark of Honour's touch.

'Laoch?' the elven spirit asked.

And the entwined spirits replied with a "No".

The resultant howl was adjoined by an eruption of light. When the angry, jagged arcs dissipated, Sura had vanished. Only the howl of pain remain, echoing in the distance.

"What happened?" asked Lady Death, a touch upon Lady Honour's mind.

'*She freed the stolen,*' replied Lady Honour. '*Took back the Schenterenta souls my veil curtain took from the world.*'

"*We showed her the way.*"

'*A thousand years of denial and religious pain that brought a race to its knees, my love, is not redeemed in one simple act.*' Staring at the wound in the veil, Lady Honour clasped her hands, her thoughts, perhaps, on a rebellion her God would likely approve of.

"*We cannot dwell on this now. We must heal your curtain before our Wyrding runs dry,*"

Lady Death tugged at Honour's mind, sharing her thoughts about the urgency needed.

'*No. Honour's time has passed. What remains has merged with Sura. There will be no more veil in Honour's name. The rent allows any Schenterenta spirit a way to escape. I can no longer allow their entrapment when Honour herself helped pull them free.*'

"*Each of the other six will be repaired tonight. All those gifts, the souls of your flock, will be lost.*"

'*We must find a different way. You are the healer among us. I believe in you.*'

And Lady Death felt the weight of Lady Honour's burden, the pain of denying a race their beliefs, and knew she must. The pain over Nesca and the beacon were minor compared to what gnawed at her lover's heart.

"*I will try.*"

—

"Be careful. I said careful."

Meister Suerese, his wispy grey hair flying high above his ears, wagged a finger at the servants who gently eased the strange contraption through the throne chamber's doors. The squeal of the wooden wheels on marble tiles grated at Queen Weister's ears, which she graciously ignored as the mix of teenaged girls and boys huffed and puffed under the meister's direction.

"Yes, yes. Better," the meister continued, guiding them to a stop next to the Council table. "Now lift the material together, or the section will crack. And that will not do." He fussed around the four nearest the table and, as the heavy wooden base edged onto the lip, clapped his hands excitedly together. With a final shove, the Handren Mountains locked into place above the Partera Plains, and the huge map of Brandshold was complete.

Well, nearly.

"That's it, run along. Acolyte Pietra awaits your return for the models. Chop, chop." He clapped behind them, this time in urgency rather than joy, then made a hurried bow to the queen before exiting via the ornate filigree doors.

Captain Mordant approached the map, hand scratching at his thick moustache as he began wandering around its edge.

"Amazing, isn't it?" said High Lord Penance, rising from his chair to join the captain. "And you say he has built a complete model of the city?"

"Aye. A huge boon for my plans," said Mordant. "And we've been working on some adaptions to the city street runs, creating dead ends and fire traps. I believe he has rather enjoyed it, though I do not think he understands its import."

The knock at the door caused them all to turn. The meister was waiting nervously.

The queen realised the man had engaged all her servants already. "Enter," she said, and the meister did so, followed by the gaggle of servants, each carrying various bags. Once the models of the cities and towns were in place, and an estimate of where Anvil lay, the meister bade his leave. A final bag was left waiting on the table.

"And these?" said High Lord Penance.

"Toy soldiers," the queen said. "My father's collection. And Meister Suerese has arranged for a few more to be added. His acolyte is firing them up now. Captain Mordant?"

"With pleasure," he said, a brief smile of pride brushed away as he coughed. The High Lord and the queen watched in fascination as the captain of the city guard organised the map.

"Going by the meister's rough scale, High Lord, we hope to judge movement times. Meister Yanpet was more than willing to adjust the calculations for me once I mentioned your name."

High Lord Penance coughed with a rueful shake of his head. "Who plays with words, my queen?"

"I do not play." The queen turned to Mordant. "Thank you, Captain. Now we have a near complete picture of the task ahead. All we need are Pietra's additional figures, the new players on the board. With General

Zendril and Mandrich out in the field, I will need a military advisor by my side. That will be you, Captain Mordant, until such time the city is attacked. My mother has great respect for your insight, though she didn't quite use those words."

"I accept," he said, shoulders thrust back.

"Of course you do. Ensure you have a competent second, Mordant, who can run the defence of the city should I require your time when most inappropriate." She handed over a sealed letter. "This will be their commission, and are to carry it at all times. This second letter is for you. It contains specific orders should the city be overrun."

"Yes, my queen." He bowed his head, and gently eased the letter inside his uniform. The High Lord watched from the side, an eyebrow raised. The queen ignored him, and was turning back to the door as her servant, Vianti, appeared. After a quiet word, Acolyte Pietra, her brown eyes wide, sweat beading on her smooth skin, shuffled in with a bag she carried with great care.

"Thank you, Pietra."

The middle-aged woman bowed low, her lips moving, though no sound emanated. Erin interceded and placed a gentle hand on her shoulder, a smile and a thank you passed as she took the bag from the mute acolyte, allowing her to leave.

"These are for you, High Lord Penance." She placed the bag at the table's side, and eased the top open to expose the clay models inside. She lifted out an exceptional likeness of the High Lord, cane and all. "You say you are a resource not to be squandered. So, place your Lords and Ladies on the map, the waiting and, above all else, where the messaging crystals are in use. You bequeathed me the title of Overseer, High Lord, and Meister Suerese's work will allow me to do such a thing." The queen drew out a model that glinted in the morning's light from the palace window. "But perhaps you should start with the Unspoken, yes? Where do you think she might be right now?"

35
FATEFUL MEMORIES

THE WHISPERING ISLE, REALM OF MONDREIN

"I'm not sure this is a good idea, Ecne." Laoch spat into the sea, the water splashing back as the wind whipped at the waves. "It looks like it's been bloody deserted a fair while."

"Nathair insists," replied Ecne. "And to be honest, I'm not sure we have a choice." She pulled her green robe tight as it flapped in the sea breeze against the leather armour underneath.

Oisin kicked at the tangle of driftwood that lay in his way as they walked side-by-side along the sodden beach. Dead weed ranged out before them along the tide line, up to the wrecked ship they were headed for. Masts lay shattered on the sand dunes, the sails fluttering manically in the wind. One side had taken the brunt of whatever the wooden ship had hit; the hull caved in across the waterline.

"You know this, Laoch." Oisin eased his shoulders, gently rolling his neck as if expecting his skin to be sore. Yet only the tightness of the thin scars remained. "As soon as she caught sight of that wreck, there was nowhere else we were going. The fact she let us approach first is more of a surprise."

The heavy beat of wings caught Laoch's attention, and he peered back over his shoulder to catch the orange-hued head of Nathair lifting above the dune. The crystalline eyes were focused solely on the ship. On the third and fourth beats, the dragon's front legs reached out to soften the landing. With a crunch of the broken ship's timber and aged driftwood, the hind legs sagged into the sand as the artifice dragon folded its wings.

"Yeah. Real patient," Laoch said, punching Ecne gently on the arm. "S'pose Nathair has joined up with the right bunch of people, eh?"

The dragon's neck extended towards the ship. She peered into the shattered hull before lifting it to examine the forecastle. The nostrils sniffed at something, and the tongue slipped out to wrap around the ship's fore balustrade. The metal, whip-like fronds slid along the soaked wood, and drew back into the dragon's maw. The head turned to peer along the beach towards them, a chuff emanating from its throat that Laoch took as *hurry bloody up.*

He broke into a jog despite his misgivings. When a sixty-foot dragon requested a little speed, perhaps it was best to comply. Especially when that didn't even include the tail.

Nathair's spirit emerged from the dragon's chest, her glow intermittent, pulsing with an urgency.

Or was it pain?

"It is her ship," said the Spirit Walker, taloned hands reaching for the splintered hull. Sadness sat heavy on her shoulders, the inability to touch the broken ship clearly upsetting the spirit.

"*Her* ship?" asked Ecne, to Laoch's relief. The acolyte and Nathair's connection, he sensed, was about to become important. "Whose?"

"Surena. Keran's wife." The spirit dragged her eyes from the dark hole in the hull and over to Ecne. Sadness welled in the corner of her lizard-like eyes. An impossibility. And, Laoch suspected, a mummery.

"That is hard to believe," he said, and Oisin grabbed his arm, pulling him back with a hard glance. He shrugged the Elite Ranger off. "The first thing we come across on his beloved Mondrein is his wife's ship?"

Nathair seemed to increase in size, her scales stretching. They scraped across each other as the spirit glared at Laoch. A lick of whitefire arced across her talons as she took a step towards the angry Ranger. "Do not judge what you do not know, Ranger. Keran believes it, and he is part of me. Is *me*. I can feel his yearning, his pain. This was his ship, and we can taste her presence. And the whitefire of the Constructors. Think on that, human, before constantly judging others."

Laoch bristled, hand twitching above Justice's pommel. He sensed his God's wrath, the sliver of power denying he was right. Which only annoyed him more. Oisin's hand fell on his shoulder and Ecne's in the crook of his arm.

"Calm," she whispered.

Oisin squeezed.

"It would make sense. Surena brought Keran here for his sacrifice. Watched as they tore his soul from his dying body and forged him into the Captain to wander the realms in search of aid. They knew the Constructors would come. That my master's captured wyrm had tasted their realm's veil." Nathair crossed her arms tight, talons clacking against her scales. "She was aware the shamans were here, understand? That there were Spirit Walkers on this isle."

"So, the Constructors followed her here, or made her show them," Ecne said, and eased her hand out from Laoch's, who spat on the floor, before looking away to the ship. She walked over to Nathair, anguish in her eyes as the spirit's grief rode the connection between them. "You think she is dead?"

"Of course, and her soul drunk while she watched. And those of their … our … children."

Laoch flinched, failing to blink away grains of sand that irritated his eye. He used his hand to rub them away. "I am sorry, Nathair … Keran. I'm too bloody hasty … A fuck-up at times."

"Agreed." Nathair turned back to the ship. "I would judge three weeks, if time passes here the same as your realm and Innealtóir. I would ask that you search the ship."

Oisin slapped him on the back. Laoch nodded and turned away, heading for the breach in the hull in the hope of finding a way into the main part of the ship. "Ecne, stay here. Keep an eye along the beach."

With Oisin at his side, they sloshed through the dregs of sea water that festered in the interior, eventually climbing past sodden bails and bobbing barrels to reach a set of steps that rose at an awkward angle. They climbed through the ship. Initially, they found little of interest.

At length, they returned to the beach with a shattered, black crystal helm, its sheen lost. Laoch threw it to Ecne, who weighed the helmet in her hand as she surveyed the cracks.

"Light," she said. "It looks similar to the Constructor armour we've seen."

"Their taint is upon it. So we have, at least, confirmation of my first thoughts. I have a fear settling in me, Laoch, that the damage has already been done. The Constructors have been here, and my guess would be in search of shaman."

"Innealtóir," said Ecne, mirroring Nathair as she wrapped her arms around herself. "The dragon. The dragon in the palace. Sura said the heartstone was missing. Do you think ...?"

—

Laoch's spyglass brought the village's devastation into focus. The houses had been partially burned or torn apart, the fires long gone cold. The drying racks lay shattered upon the sand, and fishbones were strewn everywhere. A few gulls still milled about amid the ruins, searching for an easy meal.

"Thoughts?" he said.

Oisin, by his side, grunted in response as he peered through his own spyglass.

"Long gone," he eventually replied, and sighed as he brushed sand from between his fingers. He looked over his shoulder towards Ecne, who stood watch by the orange dragon. "Q'Noh said the sea was filled with spiritfire around their new island. That it would mask their presence. At least we have achieved something good by coming here."

"Except we now have a pissed off dragon grieving for their family. Keran and Nathair were adamant we come here from the start. Look where it's got us. The Seven be damned, we are no nearer saving our people. For all we know ..."

Justice erupted into a scarlet glow, and Laoch flinched away, thinking he had enraged his God with his curse. Sand churned beneath his feet, whirling into a dervish of grain that whipped at his legs. A hand emerged from the whirlwind and grasped his ankle. A second appeared, a wicked-looking blade in its grip. The slash aimed for his calf.

Laoch overbalanced as he tried to kick out at the knife, and fell backwards. Oisin, however, was faster, and his boot smashed into the wrist, snapping the bone with a crack. A pained scream came from the hole, but Oisin ignored it. Grabbing hold of the injured hand, he twisted the wrist back. It gave completely, the grinding of bone causing more screams to echo from the hole. Laoch shook his leg free in time to catch another movement in the sand. Discarding the spyglass, he drew his short sword. Justice pulsed, and a fiery glow shadowed the Ranger. He drove the blade down into the sand, but the tip never reached its target. A hard wind pummelled into his chest, heaving him backwards. Pain erupted in his ribs, rapidly spreading through his limbs. Laoch's agony found no release through his mouth as it slammed shut, his whole body twitching as his nerves pulsed with agony.

Nooooo.

—

When Laoch awoke, the sky was black and filled with the pinpricks of distant stars. His head pounded, refusing to let him enjoy the sight. As he tried to sit, every muscle and tendon screamed their dissent until he finally managed to push himself up from the blanket. Blinking, his agony restarted as he wiped the sleep from his eyes, and the gritty sand that had wheedled its way in.

Oisin sat across from him, munching on a skewered fish. The aroma dragged back memories of Laoch's mother.

Mouth salivating, he pushed himself up from the ground and hobbled over, each movement soothing his body after an initial protest. Oisin moved aside to make space on the driftwood log, and handed him a second skewer. Laoch pressed the flesh of the fish against his lips and, satisfied it would not burn his tongue, took a bite.

"Not going to ask?" said Oisin, chewing happily on his fish.

"We have a sixty-foot metal dragon. Either it came to the rescue or it joined forces with whatever bastard attacked us. Either way, this tastes too good to waste." Laoch spat out a bone, picking another from between his teeth before returning to the fish.

"True. They are Schenterenta. A few survivors of the Fleshmaster's attack, and a shaman." Oisin grinned. "That was her pain spirit you danced with. Looked painful."

"I remind you that you carry the spider's venom, and you were begging to die outside under the sky. Did I joke about it?" Laoch chewed some more, a half smile on his lips.

"Maybe you should. Sorry."

"You broke some bastard's wrist. Did they forgive that?" Laoch glanced over the few remaining flakes of his fish. Still hungry, he wolfed them down, licking his fingers.

The Handren shook his head a little.

"He hasn't, no," replied Oisin. "But the shaman read your spirit and your connection with Sura. She ordered him to stand down, and the four others who were tracking us. Come on, there's more fish. And you should meet her."

Oisin stretched and helped Laoch up from the log. They crossed over a patch of dune grass, a fire's glow pulling them towards the sea's edge, where Nathair rested with her metal head upon her forelegs. The Spirit Walker stood by one of the crystalline eyes, talking animatedly to a short, cloaked elf. As they got nearer, Laoch could make out the unnatural twist to her shoulders, the curved left leg supported by an ornately carved staff. The spirit glanced his way, and the shaman turned, one milky eye weeping, the other glinting in the firelight.

"You are Laoch," she uttered, the words slurred but ringing with the harsh tone of her kind. "Recovered?"

"No," he said. Oisin handed over a searingly hot fish from the fire. "That was bloody painful."

"Ah, not so much as it could have been." The shaman turned about fully; each step supported by the staff. "If I had not touched your spirit, it would have killed you, no doubt. Nathair tells me of her, this Sura. But I want to know more, Laoch. I ask your permission to touch your soul again."

"Why not just use bloody words? Sura is my memory. Mine to hold on to." Laoch spat on the floor, half-turning away before catching Oisin's eye. A small shake of the Handren's head caused Laoch to look again towards the shaman, only to find Ecne staring at him too.

We all grieve, you selfish bastard.

But it's my pain.

"Because I, Rensta ad li Tark, ask. Nathair has explained as best she can why you are here. She is preparing to share the memories of this Q'Noh, who you dropped on one of our islands. It appears you need aid. To convince me to help the riders of a Constructor artifice that resides in our ancient stories as a thing of evil, I will need persuasion." The firelight glinted in the woman's sole working eye, but it was the other that held Laoch. It swirled, whitefire lacing across its inert centre.

Laoch kicked at the sand, swore, and approached. "How?"

"Like this." The shaman's right hand reached out; fingers spread to sit gently over his heart. He felt first the pull, then the rush of the shaman's touch as it whirled inwards. Justice flashed in his mind, and suddenly a barrier lay between the elf's spirit and Laoch's.

"Hah. I have a protector," he said, smiling at the shaman. "My God stands by my side."

The shaman's face twisted into a smile. "Not a God. A shadow of a human magus, perhaps. But a protector it is. May I?" she asked.

Laoch felt the two touch, a meeting that flared in his body, briefly, before Justice withdrew. Gently, Rensta entered his heart and flowed deeper, up into his mind. She shared his moments of joy, pain, refusal and stubbornness. The loss and grief, mired between Sura's emergence as a spirit. Each moment she touched upon, he felt the elf's warmth spread through his mind.

"Love," the shaman murmured, and her hand moved from his heart to his face. "And I thought you a stubborn bastard before I touched your mind." She tapped his cheek. "For one so wild, she chose well. Despite you being a human."

Laoch blinked, and the shaman withdrew from his head.

"This Sura was a twin, yes? Born to be a shaman, but her twin died before their time. Nathair tells me she bonded with one of your ... magi ... Honour, was it?"

Laoch swallowed, shaking his head at the memory. "Yes. I carried Honour's spear, much like I carry Justice. We had little time after the *Kraken* arrived, but Nathair believes they had joined somehow. The spear lies within Nathair, but the God's sigil is empty."

"A Spirit Walker, then. Twinned with another soul."

"I had not thought of it that way," said Nathair, scales over her lizard-like eyes rising. "But possible. I am joined with Keran, as you know."

"Why is that relevant? She is dead." Laoch spat again, hands on hips, the skewered fish forgotten as he stared at the shaman.

"Because Spirit Walkers are resilient, human. When our bodies pass, our twinned spirits survive for however long our lifesong is remembered. That is our fate. To advise and help our people for as long as we are needed. Often, until the birthing and training of new twins. But at times, even beyond that, if the tribe requires it. Should her song be sung …"

"Do not fill me with hope," Laoch growled, and turned away, almost throwing the fish into the fire before changing his mind. He stomped off, following his own tracks, shoulders tight.

"He has a point," said the shaman, glancing at Oisin. "But so do I."

"The shamans on Brandshold are powerless," said Ecne. "Sura told us they have been unable to command the spirits since humans arrived. Many of her kind have turned away from the old ways, but they still store their dead in caves, waiting for when the spirits return."

"That is sad, but also ill-educated. For that, I do blame the humans. Sorry, but your magi had great power, this we know from the ones who arrived here. They could do wondrous things, travel the realms as the wyrms do to rescue your people. But they wielded that power without thought for consequences. We taught restraint to the lesser magi who arrived here, and we were in harmony until the Constructors found us and desperation took hold. I would guess that something these Seven Magi did caused the loss of their spirits, and the spiritfire."

Ecne approached the shaman, conflict flickering across her face. "And that is why we are here. Are you ready, Nathair?"

"I am. But first, that which is Keran within me wishes to know of his wife and children. On your beach, their ship …" Nathair trailed off, staring into the night sea beyond the ship.

"I wish I could help, but we found the ship adrift on a weedfield. The hull finally gave as we brought it through a gap in the reef. There was no one aboard, only evidence the Constructors had likely attacked it first. Surena had brought the Repanti shaman here in their time of need, and your Keran, in the distant past. I surmise they attacked for that reason."

Nathair shuddered, her scales rolling. Beneath the shimmer, Keran's face briefly appeared before fading away. "I am ready, Rensta ad li Tark. And thirst for revenge."

"As do we all," said Oisin and Ecne together. There came a growled agreement from further away, where Laoch sat atop the dune.

The twisted shaman looked towards Laoch, and turned her ear towards the flapping of a broken shutter against a ruined shack. "Yes. As do we all."

36
PRAY FOR ME

NORTHERN GATE, JENSE,
BRANDSHOLD

Panset's eyes refused to open. He tried to brush away the gum sealing them shut, only to discover the numbness in his arms and their outright refusal to move. With throat dry, and a weight upon his chest, his breath was short and shallow. And the more he thought of it, the more panic began to seep in. He attempted to draw in air through his nose, but whatever sealed his eyelids had clearly covered his nostrils too.

"Seven Hells, I've had enough," he whispered, the rasp unrecognisable to his ears. His lips scraped against a cloth that pressed into his mouth, irritating him further. Something pulled at his ankles, firm hands that grabbed at his boots. His first thought was of a thief, here to ransack his dying body. His second was to kick the bastard.

His toe connected with something; a moment of joy cracked his dry lips wide.

"You fucker," said a muffled voice. "Hey, Silus. Got one for the pit. Bring the rope."

—

The arrow drove into the tumbled thorn and scavenged branches, its basket of flash powder igniting on impact. The oily bush lit immediately. Hoots and screams bounced off the outer city walls and shattered stone. A lick of fire crawled up the ragged clothing, blackening skin before reaching the Infecteds' heads, where what remained of their hair caught first. Yanik watched long enough to know this batch of Infected had been confined to the veils, and turned her eyes to the Rangers in her Spear. She signalled, and the long-shafted spears prodded the townsfolk of Jense into the hastily dug, shallow pit.

"Don't let the fuckers out," she said, and threw more orders to keep the Spear tight and on task. One slip and they could be scratched or bitten, and another one would be lost to the pit.

Smoke billowed from beyond the city walls, Yanik thankful the ash and thick clouds hid the horrors she knew lay inside.

"Yanik!" her second, Silus, shouted as he pulled at the reins of his distressed horse as they cantered up. They had tethered the rest upwind, nearer the beach. The animals were jittery with the smells emanating from within the dead city.

"I told you to keep the horses away from here," Yanik replied as she removed the string from her bow and slid it into the strap across her back. "We can't risk losing any. Zendril will have your knackers if we can't keep her informed."

"The duke," panted Silus, his face twisted somewhere between relief and outright exhaustion after the charge to the city, only to find Jense lost to madness and death. "The fucking duke. He's alive."

"Bitten? Scratched?" asked Yanik, the first hint of something positive energising her thoughts as Silus shook his head.

"No. Been in a fight, all right, but he checks out clean. Though he wasn't bloody happy at stripping off." Silus examined his saddle, expecting a tirade for shaming a duke.

"He'll fucking get over it. Better than a burn pit to see if he howls before he hoots. Off."

Yanik waited until Silus had slid from the saddle, then mounted the nervous horse, pulling at the reins to wheel away from the city. In the distance, Mertens waved her way, and she kicked the horse into action.

"Keep 'em focused, Silus. No bloody accidents."

———

Panset lathered the bar of foul-smelling soap against the hard bristles, and scrubbed at every inch of bare skin. His face was already raw after removing the grime and blood of the two women who had died at his hands. Flashes of how close he'd come to joining them in the race to the north kept sliding into his mind. Llandon stabbing the old man, Arjon's throat, ripped apart. Worse, the guard's face as he dealt her the final blow.

"Done?" asked Yanik. She threw the spare underclothes her Spear had mustered over the sheet strung between them.

"I'll need several more scrubs before I feel remotely clean," he replied.

"Cleanliness is over-fucking-rated. Once you give in to it, you never feel right. Embrace the shit, and you can carry on with your day." Yanik smirked. Panset was unable to tell if she truly meant it. "Though I don't blame his Grace for wanting all that crap off."

"Very kind," he said, shoving his raw legs and arms into the clothing and tying them off. He yanked on the hose for each leg before donning the leather armour some poor soul had cleaned for him. "How far away is the general?"

"Two days, at least. Depends on how hard she marches. The cavalry will be here by noon, at a guess." Yanik admired the bite marks in the arm greaves, shaking her head as she threw them over to Panset. "Orders?"

"I want you to send a messenger to the general." He bent down to collect the waiting crystal, and held it up. "I want someone who can use one of these to follow the Infected. We need to know where they are going, and why."

"We tagging along?" said Yanik, looking towards the burn pit that smoked merrily away. Half her Spear were sat back from its edge, watching, the other half with eyes on the hole in the city wall, arrows stabbed into the earth ready for quick retrieval.

"There's no one better. But first, the city. We wait on the cavalry, then we go in."

"The general won't like that, risking the Queen's Rangers and all." Yanik smiled at the duke, the effect more than a little scary. "I like it."

—

Panset wiped the ash from his eye, scraping the sleeve of his thick coat across his eyebrows where more had gathered. He shuddered to think of the ash's origins. Behind him, Yanik was bent low, her arrow nocked and ready. The House of Hope stood at the top of its seven steps, broken bodies upon the white marble steps. The huge, ornate doors were wide open and blood-spattered. The city had proven eerily silent on their journey in, the Rangers only required to put trapped Infected out of their misery or send the few survivors scurrying along the main street to be greeted with caution by the waiting cavalry. The horror of their surroundings had long since been dulled by the repetitive death.

Panset waited, letting Yanik martial her Spear into position before approaching the doorway. Each step felt like a trial. The last two Houses, those of Honour and Fate, had been empty of anything alive. He peered inside; the darkness punctuated by shafts of light streaming through the elaborate windows. No candles flickered, nor braziers lit. He swore, slid between the doors and moved to the left-hand side, sword in hand, as Yanik went right.

The wooden pews were splintered, their backs covered in circular scorch marks. Others clearly had been alight, but doused. Amid the rows, bodies lay bloodied and torn, but none twitched or moved as they passed. The ash-filled air cloyed to his lungs, the atmosphere heavy. His skin began to crawl.

The duke glanced over to Yanik. Her sideways movement along the wall indicated she was also on edge. She glanced from row to row, her eyes on each of the dead as if they would rise again. He shook his head, trying to clear the thoughts of Llandon, the pits, all of it. He bit down on his lip, drawing blood, but the pain sent those thoughts into the void.

Once parallel with the prayer stone, the air thickened, warm and heavy. The dust pulsed in a rhythm of strange waves that raised the hairs on his skin. On the other side, out of sight of the door, a yellow-robed priest lay on the floor, one aged hand upon the stone. Yanik signalled from opposite him, bow poised, watching the open doorway to his left that led down into the priests' cells. It gave some comfort as he bent low, sword in hand and a battered buckler on his left forearm. An ache entered his body as he approached the priest. Tired muscles protesting, he kept going until a yard away from the body. Once there, the air held him back, pushing him away like an invisible wall that stretched from the stone to the stairwell entrance. Panset tried to push the sword through, the light from the window glinting off the blade. The air around the priest sparkled a golden yellow in response. Memories of Arjon's spiritfire purge made him blink and, distracted, his foot caught against a candleholder that rolled noisily away.

The body twitched, head lifting to turn his way. At first Panset saw the husked cheeks, the shrivelled fingers that flexed against the stone, and drew the sword back ready to strike. But the brown eyes caught his, a fleck of yellow amid the rawness. Not white, not seething with hunger and hate. The mouth opened, and purple drool spilled onto the floor. Panset sensed the air wall collapsing inwards.

"Behind," shouted Yanik, and he spun. An arrow sailed past him to thud into the forehead of an Infected at the top of the stairwell. It hooted and staggered back. Blood and brains flecked its yellow robe, and the white eyes rolled. Frustrated hoots bellowed, hands clawing from behind at the dying Infected. Panset ran, planting his boot in the creature's midriff, shoving back. Contorted hands clawed at the leather but failed to grip, and the body gave out. The Infected toppled backwards. Panset, kneeling, dropped his sword and reached for a pot bomb from Llandon's stained pouch. He threw, hard. The clay shattered against the wall two-thirds of the way down. No eruption followed, and the duke swore as he hurled the last of his alchemical treasures. Fire and smoke whirled back up, the noise harsh but welcome. The hoots cut off and Panset stood, buckler out front and sword in hand, waiting for anything that would come barrelling up the stairs.

Two of Yanik's Spear soon arrived at his side, one with a bow trained on the doorway, the other armed and ready as he was. "Watch for any more," he said, and turned away to drop beside the priest. He brushed the grey hair away from the sweat-stained brow, revealing a woman of middling years. Her tired eyes spoke a thanks her lips could not form, and she fainted, consciousness deserting the priest as the smell of burning flesh rolled up the stairway.

"You know her?" asked Yanik, eyes on the stairwell as she approached.

"No, but the ring on her finger marks her as a seneschal."

"Means nothing to me," said Yanik with a shrug, though her voice was strained.

Panset hefted the woman from the stone and placed her thin body upon the sole remaining pew by the side of the prayer stone.

"A priest-in-waiting who has reached an age beyond choosing often takes a new post. A teacher, or in this case, an administrator for the House." Panset used the woman's robe to wipe her face clear. Checking her pulse, he frowned, and shook his head.

"So why she look so fucked? And alive, for that matter?" Yanik flinched as an arrow sped down the stairs, a thump and a thumbs-up from the archer producing a fearsome smile.

"I'm guessing she used spiritfire to keep her Infected priests back. I know as much as you, Yanik. But she's alive, which is more than they are." He placed his hand on the prayer stone, feeling its warmth. It set an unease inside him he couldn't identify. A nagging he didn't have time for.

"The Wyrding," croaked the priest. The woman's raw, brown eyes were on the smoke-laden stairwell. "The stone," she said, one hand dropping on Panset's forearm. "It must be protected. They all must be protected." She looked to him then, urgency in her husked face. "Each of the Seven Houses, understand? They contain a stone in the head of the House's chamber. They must be guarded, and each of the prayer stones."

"We are here for the survivors, not fucking stones," spat Yanik, turning away and heading off to the stairs. "People, not sheep."

Panset stared after her, a feeling in his gut that the priest had touched a nerve. The woman's hand squeezed Panset's fingers, a tickle of yellow light easing across his knuckles. "The stones *are* for the people. Understand? They must be retained. They cannot be lost."

Panset shook his head and removed the priest's hand. "If I am ordered to by my general. Right now, the priority is to save who I can, though we will sweep the Houses first."

"That is good, at least. I ask you to sit me on the prayer stone, Ranger. Until such time someone searches for the Wyrding below. I cannot rest until I know it is safe."

Panset's eyes glanced up to the chamber ceiling. Hope and a dragon staring back. His life had always been in Fate's hands, but right now he took no comfort in any of the Gods. Still, he owed Arjon something. The man's death should count.

"Okay," he said, and lifted her down to the stone. The crystal pulsed, and a warm glow encapsulated the seneschal. He detected the merest shift in her skin. He turned away, thoughts creeping in as he grabbed his sword.

From where is this power? Gods do not kneel and pray. People do.

"Yanik," he said, "we're going down there."

"We?" she said. "Fucking marvellous." She hit the archer on the shoulder. "Check before releasing while I'm down there, you fucker. Yes?"

Knocking an arrow, she took a look down the steps. Bodies lay shattered, limbs protruded everywhere. She eyed Panset's heavy coat and gestured towards the stairs.

"Dukes first."

37
PLANS WITHIN PLANS

MAKALENA, BRANDSHOLD

Lelion pressed her bone-white hands onto the brass balustrade, gripping the metal tightly, while her white eyes roamed the potential battlefield. The *Kraken* hovered above the edge of the forest to the south of Makalena, the trees behind the soulship either felled or burning as the Inhibitors ensured their line of sight in all directions. Stretched out below the ship were the Scorpion war machines, the usual vanguard of their attacks. Their tails were raised and claws held high as their pilots went through final inspections. She could smell victory on the air, taste the fear emanating from the city spread out like a spirit-doll before her, ready to be taken by the throat and have its spirit torn out.

"When?" said Lieutenant Spintz, her arms rigid behind her and back straight as she eyed the city and the burgeoning ranks of armoured humans strung across the upper walls.

"When I say, and not before."

Because my beautiful soulship is injured.

"How long before the ornithopters are airborne?" Lelion asked, moving over a few feet to look east. In that direction, a strip of land had been levelled completely, and eight of the dragonfly-like aircraft waited while another's wings beat rapidly upon the grass. Inhibitors moved swiftly about them all, tools in hand. Their shouts echoed over the breeze.

"Two are already flying reconnaissance. They have gone east, as you requested," replied Spintz, a small smile quickly squashed as Lelion looked her way.

"Good, good. We need another two waiting when they return. I want at least one of them in the air at all times, patrolling the eastern flank. Reinforcements will come, I am sure. No one will have missed the violence of our entry, Spintz. Nor can they miss the smell of shit from this city. They await their deaths. Little do they know what we will truly do to them." Lelion wrung her hands in an attempt to squash the tremor of excitement.

"Are you okay, Admiral?" asked Spintz.

Lelion glanced back, one eyebrow raised, a growl suppressed on her lips. She couldn't afford to lose Spintz, either in body or mind. "This is exciting, Lieutenant. So yes, I am wonderful. But I will be more wonderful when we crack those walls open and rip their souls from their bodies." She leaned forwards to peer over the front of the soulship to the Inhibitors who had set up station below. They had arrayed a line of long-barrelled machines, each dug a few feet into the ground, the metal gleaming in the spring sunshine. "I think it's time we tested those walls, yes? Keep them undercover and away from any tempting thoughts of survival. Grind them down."

"The soul-gunners are ready, Admiral. They report we are beyond the range of their primitive machines." Spintz smiled, her hand pressed against the chest of her uniform. "You wish to give the order?"

"Yes," said Lelion, "I do." And she sent a thought spiralling through the *Kraken*, the command jumping from crystal to crystal to resolve into the gunner captain's mind. The acknowledgement brought a metal-toothed smirk to the admiral's lips, and she tensed against the brass rail, anticipation thrilling her heart and mind.

The whine sent a shiver up her spine, the shouts from the Inhibitors overshadowed by its pitch as the first soul-cannon prepared. The admiral awaited the moment of release, her body poised until it erupted with pleasure as the crystal shard spun from the barrel and streaked across the divide. The white flare that trailed behind was a poignant reminder of the

City of Sighs when they had first got word of the Seven's realm. The crystal projectile smashed into the wall about halfway up. Whitefire splashed wide, crackling amid the joints, Lelion imagined the tiny fractures that would spread from the point of impact like cracked ice. The cheer from the prey aligning the walls ignited a knowing smile.

Hope? Such a good place to come crashing down from. Their spirits will taste so much sweeter.

Lelion snaked a hand out to clasp the kneeling woman at her side. Her hand slid down the back of her neck, and Lelion revelled in the quiver of anticipation. She drew the Mondrein captain's spirit up through her body, taking just a sip that tingled in her fingers. Enough to sate her need, and not set the emperor into a tirade.

Keep them safe, for now, he said. I think he really meant her as a gift, otherwise why trust me? Words for this woman to make her fear taste so much sweeter.

A young lad whimpered next to his mother, and a smile crossed Lelion's lips. Fear bled from his soul, and she couldn't resist letting a single finger run along the bridge of his nose before drawing it down to settle above his heart. His mother threw her head from side to side, anger coursing, spirit afire as she fought her chains.

"This is just the beginning," Lelion whispered. "You will watch a world suffer that you helped bring to ruin, while we feed on your family. By the end, you will beg for release, and I will not allow it." She drew upon the boy, his whimper music to her ears. Lelion sensed Spintz's disapproval. Her second was well aware of what angering the emperor would lead to.

But I do so enjoy it.

A second soul-cannon fired, dragging Lelion away from the feeding in time to see the projectile crash into the wall. Again, as she had expected, the wall held. But she knew what the weapon could do. Had been part of its design as they scaled up the crystal slingers. She licked her dry lips.

"Patience," she said out loud. The waiting ornithopter finally rose into the air, wings beating steadily. "I want them to circle the city. I need to know the range of their arbalests and ballistae. Should there be any magi around spouting spiritfire, they are to withdraw. Understood?"

"Yes, Admiral."

"Good. And split the vanguard. I want half the Mechanised Inhibitors on the eastern flank with a division of the foot soldiers. The scouts are to report directly to them, then me, understood? They are protecting our flank from potential attack. And Spintz, *feeders*. We won't require them here just yet. Yes, send four of my little darlings with them. We won't be needing them until the walls fall and we reap the city."

The lieutenant left, and Lelion regarded the city as another spout of whitefire laced the walls. She gripped the rail, fighting the urge, the scent of dread from the woman calling to her.

"Perhaps just a sip."

I detest this.

The dragon's crystalline eyes caught the sun's rays as they bounced off the perfectly circular pool that sat, ominously, five miles ahead. His stomach roiled, the memories battering at his mind sending a long-dead nervous system into turmoil. He drew a little spiritfire from the magus who waited patiently at his side, causing a murmur of ecstasy from the spirit-doll.

Pity your bones will soon be spread across the mountains.

"We give this a wide berth, Tabharthóir. Those waters are not for us."

The dragon spread its wings, flapping once to drive its body to the west as all four legs ripped into the grass plain. Behind, the horde of Infected spirits rolled along like a river of hate and sickness. Hungry, desperate to sate their twisted bodies and ease the pain running through their souls, they trailed the metal dragon and its master. But their calling was for the spirit-doll inside, who shone to their spirit-sight like a lighthouse upon a grass sea.

The Spirit Walker mithered, worries rising in ferocity despite its mind having been torn away during the altercation with the Unspoken's dragon. The Fleshmaster pulled the Spirit Walker's thoughts into his own and felt the pulse of the Schenterenta. Those of bland spirit who occupied every realm, whose shaman he had so long craved. They rode upon beasts in the distance, shadowing the dragon and its poisonous treasure.

"There are no shamans among them. We ignore them for now, Tabharthóir. But we must avoid the moon pools. I think it is time." He released a weak seeking, a mere wisp of power that brought no immediate threat back.

"Come," he said, and the magus followed, eyes wide and a huge smile at the prospect of what might happen next. In the next part of the pocket, just before the chest, sat a bejewelled, metal insect some twelve feet long. As they drew closer, it became apparent that much of its length lay in the dual set of folded, gossamer-thin wings that sat against a narrow fuselage. Tabharthóir's chest shimmered, exposing the plain and a flat circle of trampled grass. The emperor pressed both hands against the artifice while the slaved magus gawped. Whitefire sprang the machine into life and it trundled forwards on its six legs to exit the dragon. Once outside, the sunlight sparkled off encrusted wings while strands of gossamer-thin wire, interlaced with tiny crystals, swirled with pinpricks of whitefire.

Tarin ran his hands along the nose of the fuselage and the wings sprang wide, flapping in dual pairs independently of one another.

"In," he said, and lifted a transparent canopy.

The magus blinked briefly, but the emperor's demand overcame his mind and he clambered inside the cockpit. The Fleshmaster clicked home a strap and placed the back of his hand against the man's cheek. "You are strong, understand? The spiritfire runs through you like lava, and it calls to anyone who wishes to feast upon the sweetest of souls. What you are about to experience is both beautiful and horrific in equal measure. Remember me as your last thought, and I will be forever ... your master." He drew a little from the magus, savouring a final taste, thoughts slipping to the last of the Repanti magi awaiting him on the *Kraken* as he dismissed his latest pet from his mind.

The canopy snapped shut. From the front, Tarin could sense little other than the artifice itself, the new crystalline plates – similar to those of the Inhibitors' new armour – working wonders. From behind, however, the spirit-lure's soul raged. He forced himself to step away before soul-lust swept reason away.

Vibrations thundered through ground and air, signalling the imminent arrival of the horde. With a word, the bejewelled insect flapped vigorously, rising into the sky as mechanical wings beat at the air. The gentle seeking he'd sent out rolled back over the emperor, a touch so soft he doubted anyone but himself, or one of the Seven, would notice its caress.

"Be my beacon," he whispered, and turned on his heel. The horde was closing in, their hoots and squeals rolling across the grass as they sensed their quarry. Frustration boiled over in the mass of flesh, hands tore at the nearest spirit-infused meat, be it theirs or their neighbours', as the damselfly ornithopter took to the sky to hover temptingly above the ground.

Tarin strode into Tabharthóir and commanded the pocket to close. Mindful that everyone they crushed or lost to the soul-lust was one less to occupy the north, he sent the artifice on its way to the human city, and its traitorous queen, with a thought.

"And now, to battle."

38
BRUISED SOULS

General Zendril strode through the mud churned by her soldiers. Mander hobbled at her side, the slippery surface sucking at his strength. The hastily erected tents flapped in their rows, surrounded by the ditch and raised earth wall capped by wooden, outward pointing stakes cut from the nearby woods. The other two-thirds of her army were stationed a good few miles away, towards the eastern Partera Plains. Far enough to have time to react should those with her be overrun by the Infected.

"I don't have a clue about the bloody logistics," pleaded Mander. "I'm a fucking soldier, an honour guard. Not a bloody general." He pulled at Zendril's arm, lost in his frustration and losing decorum.

"I don't want you to be. Major Demartis has that in hand, and more. But the vets will hold the green bastards together, and the vets need you." She eased his arm off, tempted to take it in her own but knowing full well they were being watched and judged. "I need someone to lead, make the fucking hard decisions to come if I am ordered north." She winked. The sly grin winding Mander like a coiled spring, as intended. The bluster overtook his words as she strode off into the tent.

Inside, he grabbed her arm again, ignoring Lady Death and Lady Honour, who sat with the duke and a yellow-robed priest around a trestle table. "North? You can't be serious?"

"Deadly," she replied. "Now, act like a fucking honour guard and stand quietly while the important people speak." Zendril turned on her heel, taking in those who waited with a shake of her head. She bowed to Lady Death and Lady Honour, a grimace reserved for the haggard-looking Panset and his companion. The seneschal, now cleaned up, appeared healthier than the duke.

"The city wall is as secure as it's ever going to be. We've staked the outer perimeter, set fires at intervals, and barricaded the remaining gates." Zendril sat, easing back into the collapsable chair. She raised a hand to the seneschal, who had moved to interject. "The Houses have been sealed, four guards set within each for now until decisions are made."

"Then you need this." Hope's priest collected a wooden plinth from the floor and lifted a large yellow crystal from her lap to place it in the centre.

"Thank you," said Lady Death. "A full Wyrding will enable all to engage. If you would, Seneschal Reekan."

The woman nodded and placed her hands upon the large crystal. The pulse of yellow turned golden in the tent, and the priest's eyes mirrored the hue as she stared into the distance. As the light from the crystal coalesced, Lord Hope's face appeared first before the picture pulled outwards to reveal High Lord Penance and the queen by his side. Unlike the smaller messaging crystals, they all could hear Lord Hope's greeting as he acknowledged his seneschal.

"Duke Panset," said the queen, her lips twisted by sadness. "For all else that has happened, I am glad to see you survived. I hear of the loss of many of my Rangers, and I share your grief."

Panset swallowed, pausing before nodding in reply. "Yes, my queen." He looked to the wooden table, Lady Death's hand resting his arm.

"Do not blame yourself. This is a horror beyond anything we imagined. We understand the city is lost?" continued Queen Weister.

Zendril took that as her cue. "The people, yes. All that can burn has turned to ash, but the majority of the stone buildings remain, as do all the Seven Houses. The northern wall has been breached, however."

"All the people?" asked High Lord Penance, leaning forwards.

"There are some who holed up or were lucky enough to avoid the madness," said the general. "But few. The fires have consumed many of those that were ... were killed. But not all. I fear disease if we do not burn the rest soon. The duke reports a silver-blue dragon breached the walls, and the Infected followed it north. Thousands upon thousands of them."

"North?" said the High Lord, glancing over to the queen. "Not east towards Rusholme? Nor south towards us?"

"No," said Lady Honour. "And Duke Panset's description matches that of ..." She glanced around the room, and her eyes settled on the shimmering image of the queen before taking a breath. "Of the beast that the Unspoken fought."

The queen flinched, and Lady Honour sensed the tension in the tent increase.

"Is this something I should know?" Zendril glared at Lady Honour, barely holding in her anger as her mind struck off the list of swear words she couldn't use before two of the seven. She gave up. "Because you are asking the fucking impossible if you think we can fight an enemy when you withhold information from your fucking general."

The silence that ensued was punctuated by the duke, who stared at Zendril, before returning to the image of his queen and the High Lord. Pain twitched across his face. He rose, kicked the chair away, and stomped out the door. Zendril contemplated following him, ripping off her uniform along the way.

"General," said High Lord Penance, licking his lips before continuing. "Your queen has only just learnt of my deceit."

"*Our* deceit," said Lady Honour, Death nodding alongside her. "We all carry burdens we despise, General. My House included, as do all the Seven."

"There is far more, Mother," said the queen, her eyes hard, face set firm. "And knowing all would just cloud your judgement. You can't walk away from Brandshold's need, and nor can the duke. You will do your duty, as will I. The Seven have layers upon layers of lies they have revealed to me. Some, but not all, to you. You must trust that the decisions I make are now as the queen *and* as the Overseer. I command the army and the Houses. There will be retribution for the past, but right now, we must deal with the present."

"Overseer?" she said, the word shocking upon her lips. The monarchy and the Houses as one? The thought wouldn't sit right in her mind. Her daughter held a power not seen in the realm since the Seven laid down the Scripture. "Daughter?"

"No. Not until this is done. I am your queen, and your Overseer. And you will trust my word, follow my command, and do your duty. As will the duke."

"Fuck me," she whispered, the words falling unbidden before she could catch herself. She made to kneel, head bowed.

"That is not the general we need, Zendril. Stand up, take your burden, and save our people. You can swear, beat, shout and rail as much as it takes. While you do, General Mandrich faces a huge force to the south. One brought on a flying ship. And this ... horde heads north. Decisions need to be made, and soon."

—

"No, leave me be."

"The general requires your presence, Your Grace." Mander stood at the tent entrance, the wind catching the flap above his head, the smell of ash and burnt flesh riding the air. "Now, sir."

The duke rolled off the camp bed, sitting up to stare at the ex-honour guard. "You heard?"

"Not my place, Your Grace," replied Mander.

The duke grabbed a boot, sliding it on. "You heard, but have you put the pieces together? All of them? I know Zendril confides in you, Mander. And I know you would never betray such an oath when you stood with honour at my side. But think on what was said back there."

"Again, not my place, Your Grace." Mander's eyebrows twitched, and he looked away, trying not to catch the duke's eye.

Panset frowned, standing with both boots now on. "Lead on."

They crossed the central area. The crisscross of prints from humans and carts made it heavy going as the sun touched the Partera Plain at the horizon. Mander held the general's tent flap open. The duke ducked under to be greeted by the general, now alone. On the table sat a jug of green-leaf and three glasses, one already half-empty.

"I don't drink," said the duke.

Zendril sniffed, reached down by her side and lifted a bottle of Meres red; the intricate silver label reflected the brazier's firelight. "Not what I heard," she replied.

"Where in the Seven Hells did you acquire that?" said Panset, taking the bottle from the general's hand.

"Mander's been saving it. Stole it from your reserve when you fucked off and abdicated. Said it was the least you could do for him after his years of service." Zendril sent a smile Mander's way, receiving a rude salute in return. "Sit the hell down and have a drink. I think, as you are now an honorary Ranger, I outrank you."

Panset shook his head, brushing the chair clean before sitting back to admire the bottle. It had already been opened; the cork, he now saw, sat beside a clean glass.

"It's been uncorked for an hour," said Mander from behind, taking up the third chair as Zendril kicked it out from the table. "If I remembered it right."

"Near enough." Panset picked up the cork and drew in the aroma. "I missed this, above all things. This, and the steam baths." He poured himself a small glass, lifting it gently to his eyeline and swirling the purple liquid. His nose dipped inside the glass before taking a sip.

"Good?" asked Zendril.

"Delightful."

The general lifted her own glass and knocked back the leaf-green. She poured another shot for Mander and herself.

"A toast?" she said.

"To whom?"

"To my daughter, the queen and fucking Overseer of the realm."

Panset spluttered, catching himself before losing any of the revered wine. "Overseer?"

"She asked me to sit you down and ensure you understood the implications. I am sure you already do. Religion and the monarchy as one for the first time in a thousand years or more." Zendril leant forwards, raising up her glass. "Join me, Ranger."

Panset raised his glass, a reluctance in his eyes. "To the Overseer," they said together, Mander joining in.

"So, why leave? What revelation did I fucking miss?" Zendril set the half-empty glass down. "Mander read your reaction, remembers much of your time as king, but won't fuckin' tell me a thing. My daughter won't let me know anymore either; says it will colour my judgement. Yet I hate not knowing, you understand? So, this is either a request ..."

"Or an order?" finished the duke, pouring himself another small glass and setting the bottle aside. "In Jense, the seneschal kept the Infected back using spiritfire."

"This I know."

"But she drew it from the prayer stone."

"Erin told me all about the veils. That the purpose of the Houses was to hide from the Constructors and their dragons. This is not news." Zendril drank the rest of her glass. Mander mirrored her and poured another before sighing, a look of resignation in his eyes that Panset caught.

"He knows," said Panset. "Mander has put the pieces together. Feeding the veils, yes? I always thought the Crusade was an excuse for the Houses to drive the people back to the prayer stone, to kneel and subjugate while our people died. I considered it another expression of their thirst for power. It is why I refused to lead my people to die, and was forced to abdicate. It never felt justified, despite High Lord Sneed's mummery. A lie. Tell me, Zendril. Are we to guard our borders or chase the horde down?"

"Hunt them, burn them before they turn back ..." she replied, the glass paused close to her lips.

Panset shook his head and took a sip of the wine. "I believe the deceit goes deeper, General. I think the Unspoken, the Eighth, is exactly that. Another like the Seven, and no true threat."

"We met her," said Mander, "and her big bastard dragon. She took down the machines, the Scorpions that brought the ... the first Infected."

"She told us we had new enemies, and they couldn't have us as we were hers ... Are you saying she is ... that the Crusade was the *deceit* the High Lord spoke of? They sent our people to die against their machines and the banefire as a ... a symbol?" Zendril picked up the bottle and slammed it down again.

Panset leaned in, squeezing the general's forearm gently, then collected the bottle and poured her another shot.

"And now we go to save the Unbelievers," Panset said.

———

"We need to do this in the morning." Lady Death's posture remained stiff, the nightdress she wore beneath her hastily added robes hanging just above the tent groundsheet. Her face flushed, and for the first time she let the general see uncertainty in a House Leader. Behind her, Lady Honour parted the tent curtain. Zendril read anger in her posture as she slipped on her orange robes.

"Is that rum on your breath?" said Lady Honour, wrinkling her nose. "Are we able to conduct a proper conversation about our failings with you half-cut on the green-leaf?"

"Just tell me," Zendril said, and she pushed Mander away, who had nervously approached the swaying general from behind, "the fucking truth."

Lady Death glanced over to the ex-honour guard. The concern on his face brought her up short. The pad of more boots in the mud signalled Duke Panset's arrival.

"There are many truths," she replied, holding her hand up as Zendril attempted to bite back. "No riddles, General. The Unspoken's dragon is a weapon we need against the Constructors. You have seen its power first hand. That is why the War Council believe the Infected are going north, to keep the Unspoken busy while they tear us apart from the south. Their emperor rides that silver-blue dragon, and lost his first battle with the Unspoken. Lost, understand? It all fits. And before you ask, no, I cannot live with myself, and nor could Lady Fate. Her death was suicide, General. You understand? She told your daughter, my cousin, of what we had done, and could no longer live with the pain."

"I—" Zendril said, and swayed again, the anger fading into a numb silence. Mander took her in his arms, nodding apologetically towards both Ladies.

Lady Death watched them walk away as Honour held her, fear in her heart that the revelation would destroy one of their greatest assets. The pair passed Duke Panset, who stood aside to let them by. When they had left, he glared over to where she stood, Honour holding her close as she shook under his haunted gaze.

She had no words for him. How could she?

As he left, they remained in each other's arms, holding on tight for a moment longer.

"The High Lord has received no word from the Unspoken? Nothing at all?" said Lady Honour. The shake of the head in response set ice in her veins.

"Silence."

39

FROM THE ASHES

JENSE, BRANDSHOLD

"Clear the way." Mander pulled back on the horse's reins as the animal shied away from the creaking rope and tackle towering above them. "Now."

The townsfolk, stunned, eyes still narrowed against the sunlight, trailed in his wake. Zendril counted twenty-two. That would be around three hundred in all rescued over the past few days. In her mind, each one was a win. Each soul pulled from the rubble and ash of Jense spoke of the durability of human life. Hope amid the madness that had befallen the city. A hoot echoed back off the tattered city wall from where she observed the repairs, soon cut off by the thwack of a sword and the smell of burning oil and flesh.

"That the last?" she whispered to herself. How many times had she asked that recently? The general shook herself and waved Mander over. Her consort, relieved at not being sent to advise the standing army, had gladly swapped leadership for the death throes of the city. Not that it left the duke remotely happy, but the queen had spoken, her new title of Overseer causing as much shock as the ensuing logic in her decrees.

"Another twenty-odd," said Mander, dropping carefully from his horse and onto the ground. He wrapped the reins around a handy stone and hobbled over. Behind him, the assigned squad of soldiers led the survivors with gentleness and care towards the makeshift tented camp and the prospect of food, warmth and safety. "But they have seen much. I swear, for everyone we saved, we found another who took their own life rather than relive what they saw."

"Maybe the queen is right sending Panset in pursuit," Zendril gritted her teeth rather than belittle the comment with her confusion. "Everything is fucked up, Mander."

"Then we do as we are told. We rebuild the wall, set a defence for the Seven Houses, and move on to reinforce Erstenburgh. If the queen and the High Lord are right, the threat comes from the south and not the north. Mandrich will have to show some mettle, not sit inside walls that can be breached." Mander waved towards the hole where the northern gate used to be. Zendril eyed the shattered stone that had freed the Infected to race northwards.

"There's no wall that can suffer such an attack as Panset described and still stand. None. Our only hope is to wear them down, deny them for as long as we can. Hope they tire or grow desperate." The general spat on the ground, and rubbed the spittle into the dust-covered soil with her boot. "Harry them. If the cities fall, we must be ready to accept that a standing army is simply a target for their dragon or those Scorpion machines."

"Maybe the Unspoken will help."

Mander flinched as Zendril's glare fell on him. "You were there, Mander. You listened to Captain Rakslin, saw what they did to our Rangers. The burnings. Are they a people you think would come to our aid? We are dealing with liars everywhere we turn. Deceit that runs deep on both sides, that basks in the blood of our fallen."

"I believe in your daughter, Zendril. And for that, I stand ready with my sword, with whoever fights at my side. And for all the bleating of an old woman, so do you. Fuck it, Zendril. You want to see reason, come and search this ruin for survivors. I know how bad the Crusade was, lived it through the eyes of the queen-in-waiting. And I tell you now, this is far fucking worse."

Mander shook his head and limped away to join the line of refugees walking, open-mouthed and fearful, towards the waiting camp. He took a swaddled baby from a bent mother, let her wrap a bloodied arm about his shoulders.

Zendril felt a tear form and angrily wiped it away. "Fucking men," she said. "Don't bloody need them. Talking sense and shit."

She glanced back to the wall, where a huge block of stone was being pulled up from its base. A carefully built contraption made the job easier than anyone could have expected, one of Wisdom's priests working with a surviving meister to keep everything moving.

—

Lady Honour strode through the rubble-strewn street to the seven steps that led up to Honour's House. Each step was marred with blood. The bodies of the fleeing and the already-infected had been dragged to the side, the fires set to cleanse them finally dying down. But the stench pervaded the air, seeping into her clothes and mind. Lifting her chin, she pulled back her shoulders and, despite the heaviness that lingered there, took each of the seven steps with the confidence dictated by her role amid this madness. On reaching the top, the doors appeared to be as blood-stained as the steps. Skin and nails left behind where desperate people had scraped at the stone, seeking sanctuary from the death that harried them.

Or to get inside and feed, spreading their filth like my poor Nesca.

She knocked her spear butt, the weapon of her House, against the stone. Though inert, it was the one she had trained with since first taking the robes. The rhythm she beat received a rapped response, and after a few seconds, the carved doors opened and the smell of roasting meat overcame the stink outside. The soldier stepped aside, his helmet reflecting the orange of the fire. There was some fear in the way he glanced back at the fire pit his men had built to the rear of the chamber.

"Sergeant Steen, calm. I understand." The soldier nodded in response, his cheeks reddening as he glanced to the floor. "You are Justice's man?" she asked as she stepped through into the heady atmosphere near the fire.

"We all are," the sergeant replied.

"Good. Then I will let Lord Justice know how you guard my House with honour." She peered over to the stairwell. The darkness there foreboding.

The sergeant caught her look. "It has been cleared, my Lady. Most of the priests had gone to the aid of those outside. Lead Untha waits in her chambers."

"Thank you."

She moved towards the stairwell, but not before making sure each of the soldiers received an acknowledgement. At the top, she peered down the stairwell. Duke Panset had described the horrors beneath Hope's House, of those trapped, their souls desecrated, or those who had taken their own lives rather than become what slavered at their doors.

She had touched Nesca's mind, seen the evil that lay there. All she had heard about the Infected spoke of a low cunning, and the memories of hunting their own people before moving on. Nesca had kept that hunger locked inside, contained by her will until Death took her. Had she succumbed, she would have had the opportunity to infect all of her House, maybe even Erstenburgh itself.

How close we came to defeat before we even started.

The stench of fire and ash washed up the stairwell. Lady Honour began the steady walk down. A ball of orange spiritfire lit the way and shielded her from the stink. A glow slid under the first doorway she came to, and she opened the scorched door to be greeted by a line of three braziers, lighting the corridor beyond. The heat threatened to overwhelm her. By each brazier, leaning against the walls, were lines of wooden torches.

Lady Honour passed down the corridor and knocked upon Untha's door, the sound deadened by the crackle and spit of burning coal. A tremulous voice bid her enter. She opened the door to find Lead Untha sitting at her desk, the House's small Wyrding Stone by her side.

Untha rose. The wisp of grey about her brow was new to Lady Honour, her eyes far harder than she recalled. But then, she had survived where her priests had not.

"Lady Honour." She made to bow her head, and the cowl slid aside to reveal a livid red scalp, the hair gone. Lady Honour stepped forwards, open-armed, and pulled the woman close. She felt first the tremor, a shudder that preceded the tears, sobs that tore at her resolve. Lady Honour squeezed her friend since their time together as priests-in-waiting. Eventually, the crying receded, a tide of pain released. Untha drew back, turning away to wipe her face upon a streaked cloth that sat ready on her table.

"I am sorry, my Lady." Lead Untha wiped her face one last time before dropping the cloth upon the table. "It was … I don't know where to begin."

"Sit. You tell me what you need to, but I have seen what remains of the city with my own eyes, so nothing will surprise. And after, we will talk of the Seven Houses in Jense, and the plans the Overseer and War Council have in mind." Lady Honour sat, indicating Untha should do the same.

"Plans? The city is in ruins. I thought you were here to take us back." Her friend's eyes widened as realisation slid in. "You mean to stay?"

"The queen is now the Overseer, on the High Lord's, and the Council's, word. Between them, they see the protection of the Houses as essential. The High Lord is insistent that the prayer and the Wyrding stones have a part to play. We are to maintain their security as our priority, until such time they declare otherwise. I am not privy to why, though we face an enemy that drinks souls and feasts on spiritfire. The Houses shield such power and the stones they contain. Moving the stones would reveal their existence to their veil dragon."

"I don't know if I'm strong enough, Lady Honour. I … I have only just come into this power after being *quickened*." Untha squeezed her hands together in her lap. "It is why I survived. I was forced to kill my own priests, burn them as instructed after being bitten, or when they turned. In the end, I locked myself away. It was a foul thing."

"It is the same for everyone else, Untha. Raw power kept the seneschal of the House of Hope safe, and the Infected clear of their prayer stone. Another defended Duke Panset to the end. I am here to help, to teach all the Seven Houses in this forsaken city. My given role, and one I welcome. I just wish we had more time."

And I fear for another.

40
WHAT WAS ONCE LOST

REFI MOON POOL, PARTERA PLAINS, BRANDSHOLD

High Lord Penance shimmered in the camp light, his sheer purple hand clasped to the cane that helped maintain his spirit form. Tixar waited beside the flat, grey stone upon which the Wyrding crystal stood, the one gifted to the Schenterenta tribal leaders in the hope of opening a dialogue. That felt like years ago now. Since then, the veils had been pierced, and the healing of Penance's curtain had proven costly.

I hope the strain does not show.

The night was lit by spring stars. A gentle mist upon the plain barely masked the string of the brightest still visible. Brighter than usual, because the veils stretched and heaved in their healing. A little thinner, a little less powerful, but perhaps a deterrent should the Constructors have more evil following in their wake.

He leant on the cane a little, hoping the hint at his discomfort would somehow get through to the Schenterenta warriors who stood patiently about the firepit. The moon pool behind glinted, catching the odd moment of starlight, its beauty lost on him right now as his patience rankled.

He opened his mouth to speak, only for the circle of warriors to part and Betana Refi Na Partera to enter. Aged, his face weathered by decades upon the plains of Partera, there was still a smooth grace to his movements. High Lord Penance knew of the Patterning, a word often mentioned by those who spoke of Ranger Sura after he had recently delved into her past. It was the ease of her movements, the swiftness of strike and counter strike that each Ranger spoke of. That, and the quick anger they mentioned every time Sura's name arose. He had seen some evidence of that in Terana, the female elf now following Betana into the circle alongside the other tribal leaders.

They each sat upon a stone, the scratch marks and scars of old moss adding to the sense of age and ritual that pervaded the circle. High Lord Penance, focusing on his impatience, calmed his thoughts and allowed some of the purple spiritfire to ease his nerves.

Am I too reliant?

"High Lord," Betana started, his voice husky, a rasp that mirrored the wind the plains were famous for. "Your enemies have come. We felt the Soul Tear, yet we sense the spirits of humanity have lessened, not grown. Our clan warriors have told of something—" The aged tribal leader seemed to search for a word, his eyes sad but distant. "—abhorrent that travels at speed across the plains."

High Lord Penance flinched. He eased his position against his cane, wished he could sit and think on those words rather than have to respond immediately.

Am I getting old? Slow?

"And you know these are connected, I assume. The Constructors arrived as I said they would. They brought with them an infection."

"Of the spirit," interrupted Terana. "A foulness to which we can put no other name than *Bás Anam,* soul-death. They cannot be cured, only their bodies killed, for their spirits are already lost."

High Lord Penance stopped, a thousand thoughts pouring in at Terana's words. He could make no sense of the sudden dread that took hold, and he wavered, his spirit body flickering in and out before Penance, drawing on the Wyrding Stone itself, solidified his form.

Terana made to move forwards. A hiss from Betana stayed her, though the concern in her posture remained as she locked eyes with the High Lord. He felt control return, and acknowledged Terana's concern with a pained nod. They had been through the Wyrding together, and despite her competence, they both knew the effects left one stretched, one's soul strained.

He held up a hand. "I apologise. Those words have struck a chord I cannot quite hear, and I need to think on them."

"Why?" said Betana, the huskiness gone as he raised his voice. "Kill the body, and the poisoned soul will be absorbed by your veil as it has absorbed the souls of *our* people for a thousand years."

High Lord Penance frowned. "Likely," he said. "But first I must tell you of Jense, of what is happening in the south. We call the horde travelling your plain the *Infected*, for simplicity. I think you know they come from Jense. The city is devastated. Few survived the infection. It is passed on by scratch and bite, we believe, and not through the air."

"Spirit contact," said Terana. The warriors nearest to her murmured briefly before Betana raised a hand for silence. "Living blood."

"That sounds right," Lord Penance continued. "We have killed many before by burning, or a shattering of the brain."

"We have watched," someone from the line of warriors cried. Tixar stepped out from the group. "Seen and used your technique with the ones who wandered onto the plain. Your Rangers, despite being human, are skilled. *We* can keep the plains clear of their filth."

"But not the horde," added Betana. "Their numbers are too great, the risk too much. And our horses fear their stink. They are deeply connected to the spirits and sense the infection, so even skirting the edge and whittling their numbers holds dangers. And the dragon of your legends? It has gone. It sent its child into the sky, and *it* leads them now."

"Child?"

"A metal beast like it, but smaller. There is a power to it, strong. A twisted spirit, but not sick. It is this that your Infected follow with fervour," added Tixar. "I saw it fly. This dragon went south."

"Then I must go back immediately and let the queen know."

"Not yet. There is more to share, Overseer," said Betana.

High Lord Penance shifted his feet. He mulled over correcting their use of his former title, but changed his mind.

"First, your intent. The horde go northeast, towards the city of the Unbelievers. To Anvil. There is nowhere else so many could feed. You have sent part of your army in pursuit, why?" Betana stood then. The warriors beside him whispered as their leader leant upon his staff.

High Lord Penance kept his face neutral and forced his mummery to the surface, hating himself though the lie to come had some truth. "If they overrun Anvil, we would face a horde twice the size, maybe more. Then where next? Pantsil? Dent? Even your beloved Partera? They appear mindless, yet the Constructors manipulate them to their ends. We plan to smash them against the walls and valley sides of Anvil." Terana made to speak, but he carried on, cutting her off. "What the Unspoken and the Unbelievers will do, I do not know. But we cannot risk the infection reaching that city."

Betana twisted his head to one side, his cat-like eyes focused on the High Lord. He remained silent before gently sweeping his gaze around the circle, locking eyes with each of the waiting warriors in turn. Once the circuit was complete, he faced the High Lord again, eyes reflecting the firelight. "We will not join this fight, Overseer. We will stand as protectors, as Terana has requested. Should survivors of your folly enter the plains, we will do the same if their spirits are clean. We offer no more than that at this point. But the clan warriors gather, the horses remain at our call should we decide to do more once our spirits are at peace."

"Peace?"

"Peace." Betana smiled and, if possible, stood straighter. Torchlight flared behind him, taking the High Lord by surprise until his spirit sense rose. There was a power to that light, one he recognised.

Betana stepped aside and an elven woman walked forwards, her garb setting his mind afire. She wore the cloak and armour of a Ranger, and as he peered closer, he realised that, despite his initial assumption, they were not whole.

A spirit.

She dropped the cloak's hood. A shock of grey hair spiked upwards, the skin on her face and hands aglow with a familiar orange. He felt Penance's pull, a link that spun across the divide between them.

"Sura?" he uttered.

"Sura-nista," corrected Betana. His hand landed upon the spirit's shoulder.

Landed. It did not pass through.

"I don't understand ..."

"Sura has returned to us, and has brought many of those we lost to your veil. They are ill-formed, and we must sing the lifesongs to make them whole." A murmur rose around the circle. A hum rang out from those standing behind the warriors. "Each tribe has had their spirits returned by the one we mark as the greatest of Spirit Walkers, Sura-nista, my beloved daughter. And for that, her lifesong will be sung by all the Partera tribes. We will be as one again."

"I still don't understand. Nathair? The dragon's fire? Honour and Death spoke of you, but ..."

Sura ghosted closer, a knowing smile upon her lips unmatched by the ferocity in her eyes. "With permission," she said, "let me show you."

A crackle of yellow spiritfire danced across her fingers, infusing the air between them. He felt Penance's touch, one of agreement upon his mind. At his nod, the elf's fingers laced the back of his head. Images poured in, Sura's words and thoughts explaining all she had seen and died for. Her love for Laoch shone through it all, and the sacrifice she had made at the last to enable a shred of hope.

Staggering backwards, his spirit form fell to the ground, knees upon the grass of the plain. The final memory, of her people – the Schenterenta – lost and denied their faith, struck an agonising blow.

Gentle hands took hold of his own, drawing his fingers away from his face as she knelt down and locked her gaze with his. "Laoch will come. He bears Justice. Ecne holds Wisdom, and Oisin cradles Fate. They have a dragon of the veil who, at the last of our time together, I believe wishes this realm well. Whether it is enough with the *Kraken* at your gates, I do not know. But I believe they will come, and will wield the weapon they seek."

High Lord Penance stared into the Spirit Walker's eyes, his thoughts upon her words. But his mind's eye could only see the might of the *Kraken*, the machines of death and destruction it contained. About them, crystal-armoured Constructors walked, their weapons rife with spiritfire, their hands preparing artifices of claw and wing, blade and wheel. Infused with hunger and a certainty of victory. The finality of setting foot in the realm of the Seven they had come to subjugate, to feast upon.

Despair rode that ship.

"It will not be enough."

And Penance agreed.

41

KNOCK KNOCK

MAKALENA, BRANDSHOLD

Dust rode upon the breeze across the steel-grey sea to the west of Makalena. Stone chips swirled with ash, a scent of fear and desperation amid the mix that thrilled the emperor as he stood upon the *Kraken*'s foredeck. Its brass hull vibrated softly, the metal outer blurring as the speed of its movements increased.

It is time. The first of their cities to give their gifts to my Inhibitors.

Tarin raised his hand, flexing husked fingers as he gazed upon the city walls. From here they looked strong, the humans inside and along its battlements confident their mighty walls would hold. He let a smile slip, his thick tongue playing across the top of his metal teeth at the thought of what was to come.

"Now," he said to the admiral incarnate, who waited impatiently behind him.

A pulse of weak spiritfire swathed the *Kraken*. The white magic spread out like ripples in a pond. Each Inhibitor dropped their helms in place, or closed the doors of the artifices waiting below. With the signal sent, the *Kraken*'s hull shook, and stilled. Silence reigned as if the realm held its breath. Until a pulse of nerve-shredding sound thundered across the killing field. Shaped by whitefire, it focused upon the walls, smashing into the stone fractured by the soul-cannons.

"Science conquers all!" bellowed the emperor, slamming his fist into the brass rail.

The southern wall of the city erupted into dust, spewing inwards to shower buildings in a grey shroud accompanied by the screams of those caught in the explosion.

"Vanguard," he said, turning to face the captains waiting for his orders, "Advance. Take this city. Be mindful of the magi, for they have more power than those you have faced before. Any engagement, and you send for aid."

He turned away, dismissing them. His sole focus was now upon the Scorpions, whose legs clacked, rising and falling as the Mechanised Inhibitor vanguard started its advance.

Popsilin would have been so eager to be in command of her Inhibitors. But should she succeed, I will give her the honour of a new position.

Tarin glanced over his shoulder, to where Lelion's glare waited for him. *An admiral, perhaps?*

The Scorpions entered the range of the humans' simple war machines. Rocks flew as the trebuchets released their first volley. The Fleshmaster could not help but smile. "Throwing rocks, Lelion. Stones!" He proceeded to laugh, the anticipation of victory drawing long-forgotten joy.

The first rock crashed between the two lead Scorpions, skidding across the grass before rolling towards another. The artifice sprang to one side and let the stone roll harmlessly by, to more laughter from the emperor. A second and third volley entered the air, whistling through the sky to crash down behind the first Scorpions, thudding into another. A howl swept across the field as orange flame erupted from the artifice's hull. Smoke billowed, and the emperor waited, fingers gripped to the brass rail. For all their successes in battle, few other realms had used explosives such as these against them. The other Scorpions ground on, limbs dragging them ever forwards as more trebuchets released their loads. The smoke cleared with the breeze, and a smile cracked the Fleshmaster's lips. For the Scorpion powered on. Char crossed its bubbled window, perhaps a dent on one side, but the tail whipped angrily, thirsty for what lay inside the city.

The vanguard spread wider, leaving greater gaps as more payloads filled the air. Most missed, with just a few striking home. None of the Scorpions faltered, and as they advanced, the first of the soul-cannons opened up, firing between the artifices, their spiritfire smashing into the gap in the city wall.

A roar went up from the rows of waiting Inhibitors, foot soldiers desperate to join the fray as death released the spirits they craved into the air above the human city. Another wave of explosives rained down. On impact, the Fleshmaster sent the order across the battlefield. The Inhibitors charged, their run timed to coincide with the reloading of the simple machines, while the Scorpions were within yards of clambering up the breach.

Will they wait?

The first flash of spiritfire answered his question. Scarlet hues ripped through the gap and smashed into the lead Scorpion just as it crested the topmost stone, tearing open the exposed underbelly. The ferocity of the explosion took the Fleshmaster by surprise. The impact of the bolt's ripples spread deeper than just the physical destruction across the vanguard, causing a hitch in their leg movements as the pilots hesitated.

Tarin spun around to rest his lower back against the rail. "We have a fight on our hands, Lelion. This is what you craved. And it will be glorious. Can you taste it? Such power we thought lost to us forever. But there are no coincidences. I was right."

Lelion glared back. The emperor smirked, making sure she watched.

Annoyed that I returned in time to lead the charge? Know your place. Soon this world, and those magi that remain, will be at my feet. And then, Admiral, we shall end this feud.

The Scorpion had collapsed onto its back, flames pouring from its ruptured hull. In the last throes of what passed for mechanical life, legs flailed at the air, while bubbled eye windows shattered. Equally broken Inhibitors had been flung to the ground, their whitefire souls desperately seeking their gourds.

A second Scorpion, far more cautious, reached the summit, and a third joined to flank the edges of the breach. They entered in unison, claws slicing apart any soldiers they faced. As human blood sprayed across their hulls, smaller flashes of spiritfire crashed into their hulls. At first, the emperor was confused. He associated this purple spiritfire with memories of great power. Yet the closer he looked, the more he realised these were planned attacks, the magic acting as a lash to wrap the Scorpions' forelimbs.

"Look to beneath!" Tarin slammed the thought into Popsilin's replacement.

The new Mechanised Inhibitor captain jolted as the words speared into his head. Another powerful bolt raged upwards, a magus releasing their power from underneath a tangled artifice, at the risk of a shower of molten metal and hot crystal shards.

Furious, the emperor spun on his heel and sent a single, frustrated thought into the admiral's mind. He heard the responding cry to lower the *Kraken*'s chains. As the ratchets spun out below, he dropped through the deck hatch to grasp the first of the chains and descend towards the ground. Taking a second in hand, he glared at the city as a rainbow of spiritfire and quarrels flew in equal measure, raining down on the Scorpions and the advancing foot soldiers.

She should never have split the vanguard.

Tabharthóir waited. The great silver-blue dragon poised, ready to leap into the sky and pour death upon the city. Her sword-long teeth, shining with whitefire, gnashed as departed spirits floated across the battlefield. Tarin swung towards the scaled chest and let go of the chains to sail into the dragon's pocket. On landing, he sent a command spiralling into the heartstone, placing his hands upon the crystal as the dragon's scream ripped through the air. Pistons heaved, wires and cogs strummed with power, and the metal beast leapt into the smoke-filled air.

Rising above the killing field, Tabharthóir's glowing eyes took in another round of trebuchet missiles as they sailed over the solid walls. Marking those for later, the Fleshmaster ordered her to fly below the south-western wall. Metal quarrels and javelins clattered against the creature's back and neck until she hovered level with the battlements. Whitefire ignited, and the flame flowed across those who had dared fire upon her. Humans turned to ash, skin sloughing from their exposed limbs, their armoured bodies cooking as the emperor took his revenge. Tabharthóir flapped once, her body and tail drawing in the spirits of the dead, filling her limbs with energy that whirled through her machinery.

His petty revenge complete, the Fleshmaster peered through his dragon's spirit-sight to take in the glow of the magi defending the gap. He baulked in surprise when he found their innate power low, each linked by a web of spiritfire to those around them. Another release of the purplefire whip fascinated him, the lash of power greater than that held by the magus who wielded it.

Almost as if …

Crystals … yes. Like our quarrel tips and slingers. But as stores. Clever.

Tabharthóir extended her wings and stalled in the air to drop onto the stony ground. Razor-edged talons wrapped about the magus, his purple robes spraying with blood as the talons pierced his torso. The dragon roared and sliced the magus apart. Their tainted soul erupted from roots in the heart and shattered brain, and slid under his scales, filling the metal beast with an energy beyond measure. But it was a mere fleeting pleasure. The Fleshmaster scooped the delight away from his slave and absorbed the magus's soul.

"Yes," he said, low and quiet, his mind suddenly filled with an ecstasy he struggled to contain.

No. Control.

And the huge mechanised tail lashed out, sweeping across the breach. Razor-sharp spines sliced through armour, meat and bone. A splash of scarlet spiritfire thundered into the dragon's rear leg just as multiple black limbs extended over the top of the gap, claws grasping at any who dared to defy them as the Scorpion vanguard dragged themselves over.

Tabharthóir stretched her neck, searching for the source of the attack. Her head lifted level with the woman whose spirit glowed red. Her face defiant, she lifted a crystal in both hands, screaming as more redfire surged outwards. Tabharthóir ducked. The desperate magic seethed across her neck and scorched the scales around her spines. The dragon opened its maw, forked tongue lashing out to wrap the priest before she bit down, swallowing her scream as she feasted upon flesh and spirit.

"This is my city!" bellowed the emperor, his mind wallowing amid this new drug. Tabharthóir, caught up in the lust, trumpeted her pleasure to the burning sky while the *Kraken* loomed at the fringes of the doomed city.

Lelion admonished herself, trying desperately to squeeze down the emotion railing against her ancient Constructor spirit. For a thousand years since the Sundering, they had awaited the chance to take their revenge upon those that left them bereft of hope and food – a vengeance for forcing them to fall upon their own people in desperation. Here they were, the emperor now at the fore of the battle, tearing through the Seven's progeny and those of the slaves they had rescued, and it felt ...

Hollow. But why?

She contemplated the realms they had taken as they clawed themselves back from self-inflicted extinction under the guidance of the Fleshmaster. His emphasis had always been on the work of either the Great Artificer Viseri or Marbhleoir, the necromancer of flesh and machine.

But where does my name sit among these? Is my name on the lips of the Inhibitors? Will it be me they call to when this wretched city falls? Or the Emperor Tarin, the Fleshmaster and his artifice dragon?

"How will I be seen? Worshipped?" she mumbled, before quickly side-eyeing the bridge crew who appeared not to have heard. Lelion shook herself, attempting to clear her maudlin, and forced herself to watch as Tabharthóir reared back and poured death and destruction into the city. The Scorpions strode past, claws bloodied, tails thrashing as they tore the defenders apart and feasted upon the souls. They were at the balance point of soul-lust. She could feel it, see it in the way they charged into the city, their discipline abandoned as the Fleshmaster himself fell prey to its addiction. For hundreds of years, Tarin had stayed his sword, guided from the bridge of the *Kraken* as they took realm after realm. Lelion had thought it a reaction to Apso-Tran, that moment when the emperor had come so close to falling to the Drach's evil magic. It had cost them Viseri, the artificer sacrificing themself to rescue his beloved emperor – and with that one act, they had all thought the time of the dragons had ended.

Or so we thought. And now they return. Where will I and the Kraken *stand in the new age to come?*

"If I let this pass, they will tear the soul of this city apart. There will be nothing left. And who will defend you? Who will stand in the way of any army that comes while you roil in ecstasy? And what of the Inhibitors who stand in reserve, or the vanguard I denied such glory to watch our flanks? How will they react, oh emperor of mine?"

"Admiral?" asked Lieutenant Spintz, her body ramrod straight. Her white eyes, however, roamed Lelion's face as she sidled in. "Are you asking me for counsel?"

"Counsel? Hah. No, Spintz. But how does this scene play out for you?" she replied, spreading her hands towards the clamour of battle that was disappearing into the city.

"I ... I do not have an opinion," she said, her dry cheeks stretching as she attempted to keep her thoughts from her face.

"You do. We all do," Lelion continued. Her eyelids fluttered as she sent her spirit deep into the *Kraken* and her waiting crystals. She drew on the thoughts of her crew. The artificers and thaumaturges. Those who sweated upon the engines, and those who guarded the burgeoning menagerie. Their surface thoughts were all on the victory to come, on taking this realm. On the triumph the emperor led them towards.

Lelion sagged and shook her head. "The captains are to maintain a reserve, Spintz, ready to reinforce the flank should an attack come. They are also to set a rearguard at the walls. How many feeders remain?"

"Five, Admiral."

"Set them at the ready with the rearguard. I fear they will be needed more than originally planned, but we must harvest the souls as best we can. We have the soul-cannons to replenish, and the ornithopters to maintain."

Such divisions could be dangerous. Maybe now is not the time.

42

ACCEPTANCE

REFI MOON POOL, PARTERA PLAINS, BRANDSHOLD

Sura sat on the cold ground in her solid spirit form, Honour drawing strength from being back on Brandshold. The plains grass whispered in the breeze, its caress a gentle reminder of her past. The times spent amid her people at this very spot by the moon pool, waiting in expectation for those who would join them in the lifesongs. The drink, the sacred food, the sharing of joy, be it a birth or a death, that they sang for that night.

Of course, the spirits never came. Hadn't for a thousand years, and the celebrations became focused on the bonding of the tribe with the present more than the past. Not that the shamans were happy, but what choice did they have? At least the traditions maintained their status, though the young, like herself, always sought to *see* the truth rather than be *told* it. And now she was the very thing – a spirit – that she had denied existed.

She eased backwards, resting her head against the grass slivers. Her shock of grey hair mirrored the silver moon that hung above. It drew memories of Laoch and the White Palace. How they had broken into the garden and fought the unalive, and later, the necromancer. It had been their last time together before her sacrifice. And now, once again, she cast a faint moon shadow as she stared up into the sky.al

"Where are you, Laoch? Is Ecne safe, and Oisin healed? I hope Nathair still carries you."

The cold, spring night failed to nip at her lips and nose, a sensation she had always loved, lost when her body died. It was only here, with a lull and time to think, that death truly struck home. Amid the family that celebrated her return, pain and grief, only soothed by Honour's touch, rode their love and welcome.

'It begins.'

Sura grimaced, her peace at an end as Honour's thoughts touched her mind. The drums began a low, steady beat that would rise and fall with the intensity of the songs to be sung. She sat up and stretched threads of her spirit to hover above the tribe as they walked hand in hand to the pool. The light of the moon washed the plains, its reflection mirrored by the still water to fill the night sky, blinding all to anything but its glory. A beauty she had never appreciated before, a binding of the tribe both in spirit and in bone.

"Bonds I never knew I needed, nor wanted."

'The young often take time.'

"No, Honour. Our spirits were just tales around the fire. The shamans powerless, the lifesongs jubilant but empty of substance." Sura drew all that was her, back in. A sensation of joy mixed with distant sorrow pervaded her thoughts. "And though they rejoice at their release, there is an underlying fear that each soul has been too long departed. That they are just one among many. So, they start with the tribes. My father has decreed with the other elders that we will sing for the people first, hope to draw them to their tribal moon pools. Tonight, across the plains, the Schenterenta sing our memories." Sura bowed her head, and spirit tears fell to the earth, wisps of spiritfire that dissipated upon the soil.

The drumbeat stopped. Only the whistle of the Partera wind penetrated the silence as her tribe encircled the moonlit pool and waited. Expectant faces basked in the silvery cast of the night, eyes shining. Smiles upon faces that Sura had assumed, in her youth, had long forgotten where joy lay.

Hope.

The old shaman stepped forwards, her back twisted at its base, her neck cricked to one side where a horsehair mane trailed down her back. Ferena, the one who had woken her by the cliff edge, anger and fear upon her face when she realised Sura's intent.

Did she stop me that day, or did I faint from fear and loathing? And still, I died.

The crone's mouth widened, and a guttural yelp emerged as she bellowed the tribe's name. "Refi," she said, repeating the word over and over, the drumbeat starting beneath to carry the sound across the pool. The tribal elders took up the call, pinioning the sound with their low timbre, and soon the whole tribe joined the song. It swept along on the wind. The tone changed as Ferena led the tribe's song on its dance through time.

In the past, these were just words sealed to their fate by Honour's veil, the moon pool emptied by its draw upon the dead. But today, they had Honour's gift, shared by Sura.

Sura felt the tug, a pull at her heart and will, and let herself fall into the flow of words. The sweet whispers of her mother flooded into her mind, a memory of unfettered joy only a child could feel. Being part of a family and ensconced in love. And by her side, her brother, his gentleness of touch belying his swiftness to raw anger. Sura sang, words that, for the first time since Nura's death, spoke of the joy of belonging amid her people.

And Honour's gift stirred amid the moon pool. Mist formed on the surface, coalescing into delicate spirits that pulled on the armour of flesh and bone as they looked upon Partera. The forging of their collective tribe, the original spirits born and clothed in flesh, all acted out for the first time in a thousand years. As Sura and the tribe sang, the mist showed their meeting with the great horses, their gift to the shaman who maintained the moon pools at such spiritual, emotional and physical cost. Each verse, sung from memory, drew on the recollections of the old and the young; even those who had strayed from the spiritual path. Many had fallen asleep at their mother's breast to these words. The Song of the Refi, binding them in love and tradition despite the struggles of the young to believe. And now they watched in awe as their faith was restored.

'*Sura,*' whispered Honour, only to be ignored as Sura immersed herself in the lifesong of the tribe. In her mind's eyes, Nura stood before her, still proud, his shoulders back, the smirk on his lips as he hovered before her. He wore the same dark clothing as when he had disappeared into that fateful night, though now clean of the mud and hoofprints. Bones mended, purple bruises healed. Sura let her love flow, reaching out.

'Open your eyes.'

Sura blinked, fearing the image of her twin would be lost, only to find he floated above the moon pool. His spirit pearlescent in the light, eyes cast her way. Pinpricks of whitefire swirled, weaving around him, brightening with each pulse of the drum, every word that was sung and gifted to the night.

Sura felt herself drawn, a calling that thrilled through her body. The possibility of becoming one with her brother amid the moon pool, of joining the others who now glowed in the moon's light.

'No, Sura. Now is not your time. Rest will come.'

Honour's words rattled about her mind, an ugliness that railed against the promise of entwining with her twin's soul. In frustration, she pushed at Honour, trying to undo the bonds they shared, until a gentle touch fell upon her arm. Nura stood before her, the smirk gone, his eyes locked onto hers.

"Nura," she whispered, the song forgotten.

"You found me ... us. All of us," he whispered back. "Sing my lifesong, Sura. Remember the good ... and the petulant." The smirk returned, and with a final touch, he glided back to the pool. Spirits whirled above the water, wrapping themselves about Nura before the Song of the Refi bonded them all with the water of their tribe.

Sura's heart welled.

Am I filled with joy or sadness?

For a moment, the moonlight faded, and sheer dark circled the pool. The Song of the Refi came to an end, the beat stopping to the reverberation of a final, soulful note.

Ferena raised her arms to the air, fingers spread wide. "Refi!" she cried, and the tribe echoed her as one. Silver light erupted from the water, its beams glimmering amid the tribe.

Sura felt a presence, a strength that pressed in around the tribe. The dull thud of a new rhythmic beat resounded, and the ground thundered to the sound of hooves.

A murmur rippled through the gathering, and they turned as the Partera herd entered the light. The wickers and neighs of the horses drowned out the words falling from shocked lips. The herd came to a stop, pawing at the ground with eyes that shone in the reflected moonlight.

'Your tribe has healed,' said Honour. *'And now there is more to do.'*

"More?"

But as Sura spoke, a wicker from behind drew her attention. Hot breath fell upon her cheek, thick lips nuzzled at her neck, and as she looked over her shoulder, black eyes locked with hers. The Partera stallion pawed at the ground, bowing its head before rearing back, its mane shimmering in the silver light.

Sura pushed herself to her feet, one hand gently nuzzling the stallion's chin, the other stroking its ear and cheek.

"I don't understand, Honour. Nura ..." Sura paused, drew all of herself inside, and realised the truth. "We are twinned. We have been chosen. But why now?"

But she knew. The eyes of the Partera were sorrowful but accepting. Honour's own grief needed a release, now that Sura's had been resolved within the moon pool. The Partera stallion had accepted Honour, and in so doing, had acknowledged the pain the sliver of a God held.

'Many of my people suffer, their infected souls in poisoned torment. Today, I have gone some way to repaying a debt to your tribes, for it was my veil that swallowed your people's spirits. But now I ask for your help. Your tribe has refused, and that I can understand. But you and I may have some role.'

"North," said Sura. "I will get there quicker as a spirit," she said, and nuzzled the horse. "But one day we will ride the Partera Plain together, free of burden."

—

Popsilin blinked away the light spot from her white eyes, annoyed that she'd let the eruption of whitefire take her by surprise. She peered away from the moon pool and the tribe gathered there. The drumbeat wrapped her withered heart in cold fear. A memory, one that all her kind who had been ripped from their husked bodies on Apso-Tran saw only in their nightmares. It pulled at her rooted soul, tearing at its pretence of permanence. Reminded her of the fear of true death. It had been before the walls of a long-forgotten city, a hateful song that swathed her body and yanked her soul from its shallow roots to send it spinning into the ether, helpless. She remembered the paralysing dread as she swirled above her inert body amid thousands of her kin.

Many empty bodies had fallen upon their gourds, shattering the fragile pots. Others had stolen those of their comrades, fear shutting out any other thought but the desire to live on. In her nightmares, she always took refuge swiftly, relief infusing her body. But the drumbeat said otherwise. The song that echoed from the hollow where the moon pool lay, pulled the truth from her denials. Her own gourd had lain broken, shattered by her mirrored, crystal armour as it struck a stone block from the city walls. At her side, a chance for life presented itself, the gourd of her Inhibitor comrade exposed and ready. She had raced his soul for that refuge, ripping his spirit from its entrance in a desperate bid to survive.

The first of her kind she had condemned to true death.

But not the last.

Popsilin, drawing upon the last vestiges of the priest's spiritfire, cleared her eyes as the dreaded song abruptly ended. Darkness fell, bleak along the edge of the grass plain nearest the human town of Rusholme. Not fooled, she hissed a thought out to her squad to keep their eyes down. The sudden explosion of light that ensued did not leave them blind and exposed, thankfully. When she dared look again, the foul elves were laughing. About them, horses milled, their usually dark eyes reflecting the spirit light that poured from the moon pool.

"Captain?" whispered Tenith at her side.

"We wait," she said, and pulled the bag off her back. She rummaged inside and drew out the emperor's gift. A mottled crystal, black and white spiralling inside in an unending dance she often watched before going to sleep. Another six of the precious stones remained in the bag. She had no idea how many they would need, nor whether those she had would be enough. But Popsilin had her orders, and she would follow them. For now.

"Hold," she sent. *"We wait until they leave."*

Their responses came, agreement bonded in the sharing of the magus-cum-priest's spiritfire. These were her Inhibitors now. Loyal, hungry for what they had shared together. But their travels, filled with fear, had revealed a more wary people up north. Food had become harder to come by. Clearly the war had begun. They had crossed paths with the taint of the Infected the day previous. Now, having experienced the song of this realm's elves, she understood why the emperor had set her this task. Though what the crystals did, he had not shared.

A poison, perhaps? But if that is true, they will surely come hunting for those that seeded it.

In the hollow, the tribe split apart, the elves milling amid the horses, or walking back together towards their tented homes that flapped in the distance. She could taste their joy – anathema to her – but remained patient until the remaining Schenterenta had left the pool behind. Only two remained, one a gnarled, old man, his body shape familiar to her. It smacked of those they had hunted in the caves of Repanti, and later on Mondrein. Yet there seemed little to fear here. The shaman's spiritfire appeared no stronger than any others in the tribe. By his side, a younger elf waited. At length, the shaman turned away from the pool, hobbling towards the camp.

The temptation to capture another user of spiritfire sat strong with her. Their knowledge of where the other moon pools lay was likely invaluable. But such an act would draw attention, and reduce the number of pools they could reach.

Balance.

Popsilin signalled her squad out, sending them wide to circle the pool and on guard. She and Tenith kept low, their cloaks helping them merge with the grass in the dark. Eventually, they neared the pool and crawled the last few yards to its edge. Once there, she could sense newly imbued souls within the water. But nothing made sense. These were not the newly dead she had expected. Yet, there were so many within the pool, swirling as if exploring a new home. Her presence seemed to alter their pattern yet, much like the water barrier prevented full knowledge of what lay inside, they appeared to only be disturbed by her, not fearful as she would expect. Almost as if they were ill-formed, much like those they had left behind on Innealtóir, whose *will* had faded over time.

With Tenith on watch, she drew the crystal from her bag and threw it into the centre of the pool. As it flew, the stone's facets caught the moonlight, glinting with menace before landing in the middle. It hit the water with a soft plop. The surface appeared to part, almost as if refusing to touch the crystal as it dropped below the surface.

Popsilin pulled at Tenith's arm and they withdrew, his eyes on the camp, hers on the inert moon pool. Of all the things she expected to happen, absolutely nothing hadn't been on her list.

They reached the hollow's edge, and she recalled her Inhibitors. Once together, they headed for the tangle of bushes and their stowed gear, her thoughts flying on where they should go next.

Having collected their equipment, they unburied the Schenterenta Tenith had captured earlier – the one who had given away the location of the moon pool under painful duress. Popsilin smiled as she withdrew the hollow shoot from his mouth, pleased that Tenith had reminded her that they needed to breathe. Amid the blood of his broken teeth and nose, he had managed to stay alive, and his soul remained fresh. She placed her hand upon the young man's neck and drew his terrified spirit to the surface. She drank. Despite its blandness, she revelled in his soul-death as she took her due. When replete, she sat back and let Tenith draw from her in turn before the others, too, fed.

They are mine, but I will need another magus if they are to remain that way.

43
A Dragon's Horde

The Unspoken failed to relax into her chair, but not due to the cold hardness of the marble that went unregistered by her dead nerves. No. The unease lay with the man who faced her now, hands shaking and gripped tightly together lest the tremor spread to his body. At first, she thought it was An Chéad, the scarlet dragon shimmering in the first light of day as the sun cascaded through her palace veranda. But no. The man's gaze had barely glanced towards the metal dragon. It was fixed on her. The sallow skin beneath his thick fur robes alive with fear as his spirit quaked.

What has the emperor wrought? Was I mistaken to shame him as I did?

"For my own sake, that of the Eighth, the Unspoken, speak, Dathair, before I decide to end your suffering a different way." She kept her smile light, the glamour responding to her gentle thoughts, and not the newly awakened concerns that sat heavy around her dead heart.

"My queen," he started, wringing his hands, almost melding his feet to the cold, stone floor in an attempt to hold himself together. "Anvil is under attack."

"Attack? My senses would scream if you were in peril. If you speak of the Handren, they watch from above as you build, Dathair, and then they run off to little Lady Fate and squeal like stuck pigs. They are not worth the bother." She gestured with her long-fingered hands. The nails glistened, reflecting her dragon's metallic scales. It did little to calm Anvil's mayor.

"Not the Handren. Though they see, and I am sure run to their ridiculous mistress. There is a ... a stampede of ... people. I do not know any other word ... once-human but now not. Thousands. They had reached the valley entrance when I left. By now, I fear, they will be approaching the walls. We have not heard from the outer patrols, but there are reports that their steam-carts were overrun. The horror ..." Dathair clenched his teeth together, and nervously brushed back the circle of grey hair around his bald pate. "The people of Anvil did not want another war, my queen. The last was dreadful, the evil perpetuated on both sides despicable. But it comes to us."

The Unspoken pushed herself up from the suddenly annoying throne and her graceful feet flowed down the step. Long fingers lifted the mayor's chin from his chest. "Have I not looked after my subjects, Dathair? Given you the chance to flourish? To grow? Beyond a few skirmishes and a war we never asked for, I and my lineage have kept the peace for close to six hundred years. I provide sanctuary, while the sheep who follow the Seven have cowered upon their prayer stones, whipped their own bodies and suppressed creative thought. I warned you war would come a few months back. Your preparations have been appropriate. What else do you ask of me?"

The mayor glanced over to the inert dragon before licking his lips. "Come see for yourself. You spoke of another dragon. One that would lead an army of ... of soul-eaters. You have always been true, as were all those that sat upon the throne before you. This is not what you warned us of. This is something more."

More than Tarin? What madness has he unleashed? And why no word from Penance?

"Leave. I will follow, Mayor Dathair. This had better not be an exaggeration. My time is precious." The Unspoken waved him away, and waited until the mayor had exited the throne chamber. She watched through the arched, open windows as his ornithopter dropped into the valley. A fleeting memory from a distant past, on another realm, tugged at her mind as the feather-light wings caught the rising air that swept up the valley side.

"Siggler," she whispered. The sound slipped across her husked tongue and between metal teeth. "Here, now." The intricately carved door swung slightly, the stiff-backed guard rattling as he approached to stand before the queen. She shook her head as thoughts of the Seven's Crusade seeped into her thoughts. What had it really achieved? Stronger veils and stored spiritfire, yes. But her kin had still come seeking the souls she alone had fed upon up to now, and found them, despite the Seven's efforts.

Maybe I should have taken control when they died. Ruled this realm, fed as I wished. But then ...

She turned away from the guard to stroll out onto the veranda and drink in the glory of her valley. Her gossamer dress whipped about her in the bitter wind. Ice crystals formed wondrous clouds above the mountain peak, reflecting the sun's light. Myriad colours that filled her dead heart, urging it to beat.

Too late.

"Siggler."

The guard approached, and her hands sparked with whitefire. The guard's glamour fell, and a white-eyed, husk-skinned apparition replaced the guard. Its teeth were metal, but the soul inside was withered and near death, as she liked to keep it. The clank of armour had been replaced by a Ranger's garb, that of the Burners. Hated for the atrocities they had committed in the Unspoken's name by the Unbelievers, nearly as much as by the followers of the Seven, she had declared them outlaws and cast them from Anvil when the war had ended in stalemate.

Or hidden them until needed again. They are costly to make.

She let a tendril of whitefire wrap the creature's head, awakening the spirit trapped within. One she had tortured to the point of insanity, breaking it until it only knew the Unspoken and her bidding. A spirit-slave in all but name, wrapped in a sliver of her soul.

"Here." She dug a crystal from the palace wall. Its glow was low in the dawn's light, but powerful enough for the task ahead. "Awaken the others. I may have need of you."

An Chéad swooped through the valley, the metal bones in his wings straining, skin billowing as he yawed to one side. The city sat proudly below, its towers bursting upwards from tree-laden streets that ran straight and true. Though smoke belched from chimneys and sat heavy in the cold air, the smog soon rose to form a muddied cloud that hung above the city. A new blemish to the Unspoken's second-favourite valley.

But needs must, An Chéad.

The dragon's sight informed her of the hundreds that lined the walls, and the many who waited upon building roofs, their steam-javelins and artifice ballistae ready for a different dragon. One that had not yet come. The Unspoken urged her metal dragon over the walls as the cheers of her people echoed up the wide-mouthed valley.

Dust rose ahead, thrown from the ground that drummed with the thunder of thousands of feet. A wrongness swept into An Chéad's heartstone as he neared. Disgust swathed the Unspoken's mind, crashing along the deep connection she held with the Spirit Walker. A poison that threatened to overwhelm her seeped from the foul horde that charged towards Anvil's walls. Buried deep within it was the taint of the Constructors. Not the venom used to quell and subjugate the Spirit Walkers. No. This had the oily texture of soul-madness, when another invaded an occupied body. The Sundering had seen Constructor fall upon Constructor, first the frenzy, then the feeding. Some, close to death, had tried to enter animals, others their deeply hidden menageries that had avoided the Seven's machinations. Such attempts, without a thaumaturge or the emperor's aide, were doomed.

This is how it feels. But more so.

The Unspoken drove a whitefire barrier into the pervasive madness, blocking the connection between An Chéad and the thousands of souls that festered and hungered for respite as they ran fervently towards the city. Relief swept through her, and she relaxed, despite the wedge that now reduced their shared senses to a level akin to her human subjects. Spirit-blindness.

An artifice came into view, flying barely above the ground, wings flapping desperately to keep it ahead of the horde. Obviously a machine built by her kind, it appeared similar to the ornithopters her people flew, though with far greater complexity to the mechanism. Over-elaborate and struggling, she could not read its power or discern what lay inside. Acidic whitefire raged across her body as her frustration grew.

"Do they chase, or does it lead? What secrets are in there, An Chéad?"

The dragon, as mute as ever, allowed a sense of concern to swathe the Unspoken.

"Knowledge is power," she sent in reply.

The scarlet dragon wheeled about on her thought, a roar emanating from the wide jaws. A lick of whitefire ignited, and a gout of white flame spewed forth. The dragon flew above the front of the horde, pouring fire, igniting limbs and clothes. The creatures hooted in response, leaping those that turned to ash, pushing past those whose legs continued to run as the flame consumed their bodies. For the thirty they burned, a hundred took their place, feet pounding into the ground as they drove on towards the ailing ornithopter.

"Now," thought the Unspoken, and An Chéad turned again, wings carrying him past the machine, only for them to spread and catch the wind. The dragon was yanked around, and spun to land before the struggling artifice. Chest scales shimmered and the machine flew straight into the dragon's pocket. Another roar, and the metal beast's tail whipped around. Spines shattered, hips snapped, while cogs and wires drove An Chéad back into the air. The front of the horde leapt, groping for the dragon's legs and feet. Their bodies tore open as they slid along metal scales, or sliced apart as hands and limbs sought purchase upon the talons. Two strokes, and he was clear of the defiled spirits, surging up and along towards the city walls. Behind, the Infected did not miss a beat. Angered, frustrated that their prize had been stolen from them, they charged onwards towards the waiting city.

The Unspoken withdrew her hands from the heartstone, the tremors hidden by her glamour, but not from herself. She could still taste the vile spirits upon her tongue, the bitterness of so many pained souls. Their reaction to An Chéad had caused consternation in her thoughts. But no fear lay there. They had attacked en masse, falling to the dragon's natural defences. But there was ten thousand, maybe more, all charging towards her city to prey upon her human herd.

"This is the emperor's gift, An Chéad. He has sent an army to stay my intervention, to hold me here to save my people. And I do not know if even I am enough."

The Unspoken squeezed her fingers, quickly checking that her glamour held despite the underlying stress, and entered the next room. There, the artifice had crashed against the wall, wings forever broken. The paper-thin skin shredded, as were the limbs and struts. She let her hand glide across the crystal-clad front, sensing the strength of the bonds and the material's lightness. It felt strangely inert, dead, and bereft of any spiritfire residue. Moving on past, the whispers of High Lord Penance's Wyrding suddenly swept over her. Distant, just an echo, but there. Blocked by this infernal machine.

Desire hit the Unspoken like a hammer blow, a surge of *need* that swept through her body to overwhelm her mind, demanding the soul-lust that had last taken her at the human manor house. Desperate for satiation, she tore into the wings, ripping them away, only to be greeted by a shattered canopy, its crystal shards sprayed upon the object of her sudden desire: a human whose powerful aura demanded her need.

A magus.

She had avoided the magi for centuries, surrounding herself with the Unbelievers.

Keeping such lust at bay.

Helpless in his thrall, she fell upon the flesh, every part of her body sodden with the allure of his power. Mindless, the Unspoken bathed in a shower of blood and spiritfire.

An Chéad screamed. Whitefire dripped from his mouth, tongue lashing. He soared over the city walls while the people below cheered, hope in their voices at the dragon's flames that had erupted in the distance. But the dragon flew on, sweeping past tower and chimney, breaking through the smog. Seeking sanctuary as his master lost her mind.

44

On Awkward Wings

APPROACHING ANVIL, HANDREN
MOUNTAINS, BRANDSHOLD

Panset brought the horse to a slow halt, mindful of how hard he'd pushed the animal and those following behind over the last few days. The grass on either side swayed, yet ahead it lay trampled, tens of thousands of footprints flattening the plains as far as he could see. Hoots carried on the breeze, mingled with the thud of boots and bare feet, raising soil and dust as they beat at the earth.

"We are close," he said, turning back to face Yanik's Spear and the cavalry behind. They were no match for what lay ahead, but cleared a pathway for the army that marched under Major Demartis' demands. Lady Death rode at the centre of Yanik's Spear, protected as best they could. She kept the major's priest informed of their progress. That, and helping in the despatch of the trampled Infected that remained a threat as they crawled ever onwards towards Anvil.

"Spread out. There are more broken Infected ahead. Miss none, as any we leave could fall upon us in the night, or on the army that follows. One bite or scratch, and this horror starts again." He wheeled his horse about to face the cavalry officer, Marshall, who had railed against his orders briefly before encountering the first of the injured Infected. The woman was now zealous in her duty, with a much-needed methodical approach, and a keen eye to go with it. She nodded, and spread her mounted soldiers out, boar spears in hand. They followed behind as the duke urged his tired horse forwards once again.

It wasn't long before the head of Anvil's valley rose from the plain. The high-sided hills formed a passage that had dramatically reduced the Crusade's effectiveness, funnelling the Union's army towards the higher valley beyond and, eventually, the walls of the city. A folly to attack when the people behind those walls had trebuchets and ballistae ranged and ready, with banefire set to burn those who dared try. But that was against an army that cared for its soldiers, zealots or not. The Infected were as different an enemy from the Union army as possible, and the Unbelievers were about to get a shock. Should just one gain entry, the infection would take hold and the whole of the Union would face a fearful army from the north, even as the Constructors invaded Makalena and beyond.

"Fucking mad this, Duke, eh? Racing to help the scum." Yanik laughed as she spoke, her grin set firm. "Fuckers burn the skin from our comrades' backs, and now we're off to save *their* faithless skins. What's the word? Erony?"

"Irony, Yanik. Not so sure it's the right one. Scandalous may fit better, aye, Lady Death?"

"Your jibes are lost on me, Duke Panset. But if they help you heal, carry on." Lady Death eased her horse next to his, keeping her voice low though she gazed ahead. "But the more you speak ill, the more you fracture confidence in the Houses. And without that, all will be lost. Whatever you may think, it will require the spirit of our people, as well as their flesh and bone, for any to survive what comes." She glanced over to Yanik, who pretended not to have heard, but she had. The grimace told all.

The duke shook his head and refused to speak, the anger only hardening the shell around his heart. Shouts from behind and to the left drew him away from his thoughts, with cavalry outriders gesturing Panset over. On approach, the smell worsened to a foul mix of burnt oil and flesh. The earth was scorched, with bodies amid the ash, recognisable where limbs remained untouched, or a few bones had survived the heat. It was the second time he'd seen and smelt such devastation.

"Dragon's fire," he said, trotting up to view the patch of burnt grassland that stretched for twenty yards or more. Yanik's Spear spread around, searching the edges for any hidden Infected.

"Agreed," said Lady Death. "I remember it well."

Panset glanced at her, one curious eyebrow raised.

"I fought Nathair, Duke. While you hid in the north, I fought a dragon by the High Lord's side."

A cry from a mounted soldier stopped her from saying more.

Yanik rode across to the Ranger, a good fifty yards in the distance, and dismounted. The First Ranger clambered onto a raised area Panset had taken for a rock outcrop. The woman kicked at something before turning and waving them over. With the remaining Spear riding as guard, an upturned metal contraption came into view, appearing much like a battlecart but devoid of horses. A pair of heavy wheels were attached to metal rods, which in turn had sets of machinery the duke could make neither head nor tail of, including a chimney that spouted at the top. Yanik loosed an arrow through a shattered window. The thud as it struck something inside was unaccompanied by any response. No yelp or a feared hoot.

"They're fucked inside," she said, turning away to stare at the mangled machinery at the rear. "I guess this is from bloody Anvil? Didn't help them much."

"Looks like they were heading back," said Panset. He raised his spyglass, focusing ahead. "I've lost the rear of the horde, but I think they'll be in sight of the walls within a day, as they do not rest."

A scrape of metal upon wood sent a trickle of fear along his spine, a dread that the cart was not as empty as Yanik thought. He spun, sword sliding from its sheath, and headed for the far side of the artifice. Lady Death was already there, her robes shining with a black flame. In her hands, a scythe that glowed with the same fire. It pulled him up short, only for the twin hoots of the Infected to bring him to his senses. The thwack of an arrow hitting home was joined by the shattering of bone and reaving of flesh as Lady Death's weapon cut through a charging Infected from shoulder to waist. As it fell, blackfire welled from its eyes, nose and mouth, boiling away wisps of white spiritfire. The other still ran, Yanik's arrow embedded in its skull. A second arrow hit an eye, accompanied by the crackle of Death's black flame as the Lady backhanded the scythe's outer edge into its side. The two Infected halves spun away as the weapon burnt through flesh and bone. Panset recovered enough to drive his broadsword into the base of the creature's skull as it hit the dirt. A third and fourth arrow whistled over his shoulder, ramming home into the undercarriage of the cart. Panset turned about, readying his sword to defend against teeth and claw, when searing heat followed the arrows' path. Blackfire erupted along the shoulders and neck of a third Infected, white eyes boiling as the husked tongue fell from an open mouth that hooted in agony. The thing collapsed in the open hatchway, the blackfire fading as it turned to ash and bone.

"Fuck me," said Yanik, waving her thanks towards the Ranger who had dispatched an arrow at the hidden Infected. "Maybe we should stop baiting her, eh, Duke?"

Panset watched as the last of the Infected's skin released the blackfire, only to turn about to find Lady Death watching with just as much intensity. Admittedly, the black shimmer about her robes and hair helped.

"Flesh, bone and spiritfire, Your Grace. The price we pay. Look to the sky. Something comes." Lady Death pointed towards the gathering clouds, where a contraption beat at the air like a bird. Clearly built, not born, his mind could only place it amid the machines and science of the Unbelievers.

"Yanik!" he shouted, and she needed no more bidding. Yanik and the rest of her Spear were off their horses and readying their bows. "The new arrowheads, Yanik. Let's introduce our science to the Unbelievers."

"Wait," said Lady Death, stepping in front of the duke.

"They don't know why we're here. We should take no risks. But hold your arrows unless I command otherwise, Yanik."

He looked about. The cavalry that had spread wide on the hunt for the Infected drew together to the south-west, around Marshall. Pleased, he watched as the strange machine approached, its path directly in line with them. Lights began to flash at the front.

"Signals," said Yanik, her bow partially drawn back, the crystal tip hardly wavering. "Seen them use mirrors and shuttered lights before, up in the foothills."

"You know what they say?"

"Naah. Too busy killing the fuckers." Yanik smiled, winking at the duke. "But I'd say they'd usually be dropping some of their shit on us before signalling."

"Agreed. Stay wary." The duke shook his head at what he was about to do, then raised his arms and waved towards the approaching machine. The lights flashed again, and the weird contraption dipped a wing. It began to spiral downwards for a minute or so before straightening up close to the ground. To his amazement, the wings locked steady and what he now saw as wheels broke through the grass to trundle along the earth to a stop.

"Stay here and keep me covered. And make sure the horses stay calm," he said, and checked his sword was loose before striding towards the contraption. He'd taken two steps when he realised Lady Death was by his side. He was about to argue when the top of the machine, a canopy of glass or thin crystal, lifted upwards. A woman wearing the mixed green and brown hues of an Unbeliever uniform rose from her seat at the front. Anxiety immediately beset the duke, and he heard mutterings from those behind. He lifted his hand, signalling calm, and carried on. After all, he had Death at his side.

"I am Duke Panset," he said, loud enough to be heard, he hoped, over the machine's weird, rhythmic noise. He kept his hands away from his weapons.

"Your Grace," replied the woman, her oily hands raised to show they were empty. "I am Irina Dathair. Rin, if you will. I have been sent to ascertain your numbers and your purpose. But these creatures, there are so many." She peered back in the direction of Anvil. "Our scouts say you were following their path."

"Scouts? We saw no one."

"Then they are good scouts. You follow and kill any creatures you come across. I have been sent to find if you are chasing them our way, or hunting them. The difference is key, you understand." She appeared to notice her dirty hands for the first time, and proceeded to wipe them on the legs of her uniform.

"And?"

"I could not tell, so I landed. I am, of course, not at any risk, as *we* have a dragon."

"And near twelve thousand Infected rampaging your way. I'd say your dragon might be busy." Lady Death took a step towards the contraption. "Duke Panset is here ahead of our army. They intend on attacking these creatures against your walls while you destroy them from above. You cannot let even one into Anvil, you understand? Each bite and scratch spreads their infection, poisons the soul. Everyone wounded will have to be burned alive or have their skull shattered. They attacked Jense, and now they come for you."

"And Jense survived?" the woman said. "But you worry for us? Odd."

"Survived?" Panset pointed towards the horde. "Those *are* the people of Jense, understand? Only a few got inside Jense's walls and spread their filth. I saw them with my own eyes. After only a day, they left, having infected the entire city. And were led here to attack your city by ..."

"By?"

The woman waited, but Panset decided against saying any more. How much did they know about the Constructors? Would that sound even more insane? And he doubted Lady Death knew all of High Lord Penance's machinations. "Look, think on it. They get into your city, the horde doubles in size, and then it goes onwards to the next, and the next."

The Unbeliever nodded, clearly considering their words and glancing back towards her city. "You have an army following? That is something our scouts will ascertain. If you are here to help, perhaps you should parley with the mayor. Explain to him your intent."

"How?"

The woman gestured behind her. "I will take you."

Panset felt Lady Death's touch upon his arm as the offer struck home. They both turned back towards Yanik, who vigorously shook her head.

"Coordinating an attack would increase the chance of success?" said Lady Death. It was both a question and a statement.

"Yes."

"And we need the Unspoken and An Chéad." Lady Death caught his querying look. "Her veil dragon. That is my task, as well as the destruction of the horde. I will go. Mind the priest with the army. I can speak to you that way." She turned on her heel and headed to the flying machine with the determination of a Lady of the Seven Houses.

Panset sighed.

"Life's a fucking bed of roses," said Yanik, spitting on the valley floor as she fully relaxed the bowstring. "I'll go if there's room."

Panset considered joining Lady Death, but knew his going would render the army, inexperienced in fighting the Infected, leaderless. The major, even the general, had but a fraction of his knowledge. But this was Lady Death.

Someone had to go.

"Okay, Yanik."

"O-fucking-kay? You're supposed to argue that she can look after herself. Fuck me, Duke. I thought you liked me." Yanik grinned, sliding the arrow back in the quiver at her hip and noticeably checking the bag on her other side. Unstringing her bow, she strode towards the artifice. "Don't die while I'm gone."

"Same back at you. Keep her safe."

Lady Death dropped into the seat behind the Unbeliever, the woman demonstrating a set of straps to keep her in place. Yanik clambered up, swore, argued, and squeezed in behind Lady Death to lie down somewhere inside. The air around Lady Death shimmered and she appeared to shiver, pulling her robe in close.

"Maybe she fears the machine as much as Yanik after all," he said, taking care the soldiers did not hear.

The canopy dropped, and the machine's rhythm picked up. The wheels bumped along the ground. Unable to watch the artifice take one of the Union's most beloved people into the city of the most feared, Panset turned away, repeating his orders to keep the horses calm.

"At least I know why they sent me and not Zendril," he said to the waiting Rangers. "She'd have killed the Unbeliever on the spot and danced on her grave after setting that artifice ablaze. Okay, back to scouting ahead. And you heard; we're being watched. I want to know by who."

45
NO TIME FOR PATIENCE

"I cannot. My tribe need me. We have much to recover after the Constructor's attack." Rensta ad li Tark ground her freshly cut staff into the ashes of the fire, examining the end. She blew at the embers that glowed at its tip, and patently avoided Laoch's gaze, infuriating him.

"My people need your knowledge. Sura's tribe, all the Schenterenta of Brandshold, need what you know. They will not listen to a drunken, dishonoured Ranger any more than trust a dragon of the bloody veil. Your words will hold weight, whereas they will laugh us off." Laoch got up off the gnarled driftwood he sat on, gripping Justice's pommel at his side. He appreciated the warm glow, but Justice offered him little comfort. The sliver of his God railed against the shaman's words, fanning his own frustration.

"That, I cannot help. I have seen Nathair and Ecne's shared vision. Lived the life of Q'Noh's ancestor as a spirit-doll, and seen the near-fall of these Drach. I do not deny these things, Laoch of Brandshold. But, beyond placing the knowledge within Nathair's spirit as to how to reenact the lifesong ritual, I see no place for me at your side. Whereas here, I do." She shoved the stave back into the fire, a slight smile of satisfaction crossing her face as she ground it deeper into the embers.

Laoch stared at the top of her head, trying to calm the storm brewing at his hip long enough to think clearly. Oisin waved, the Elite Ranger carrying three hooked fish in one hand. Laoch's eyes beseeched the Handren to join in with his efforts, and tilted his head towards the shaman. The mountain man sighed and handed over the fish to Laoch. With a grimace, he settled himself next to the preoccupied shaman.

"I take it your answer remains no," he started, placing both hands on his lap, his face aglow with the deep red embers of the firepit.

"Correct," she replied. Laoch growled at that, as he proceeded to gut the first fish on a nearby stone. "And it's a decision made in logic. Your world is very different from mine. I have seen how the moon pool worked upon Apso-Tran. I have adapted the ritual appropriately, and locked it into Nathair's spirit mind. She can reproduce this for your shamans. I am unneeded and have work to do."

"What happens if the ritual fails?" Oisin pressed.

"They take your world, drink your souls, feed their machines and come here. I know the argument, the tangents that such a decision will lead to. I am not blind, Ranger Oisin. Just ..."

"Fearful," said Ecne from behind, her quiet arrival making both Oisin and Rensta flinch. "Is that not right?"

Laoch looked up from his preparations, the pieces of Rensta's reluctance slotting home. "Of what?" he said, the fish now on a skewer as he approached the fire. "Of the Constructors? You should be bloody afraid, as the Seven Hells will be a joy compared to what they promise."

"No," said Ecne. She walked around the fire, peering at the shaman over the heat haze as Laoch placed the fish over the embers. "Not the Constructors, or at least, no more than we all do. Nathair says it is her she fears."

Rensta ad li Tark lifted the stave out of the fire, shaking her head as she slowly blew the embers that helped harden the tip. Laoch assumed she was going to remain silent, but Rensta looked directly at him. He saw the fear there, and was taken aback by the emotion writ large upon her face. It was clear she had suffered much. The creation of a true shaman, a Walker among Spirits, was a dreadful process.

"She is wrong. Though again, I can see the logic. I fear what has happened to Nathair, and in turn to Oisin and even Sura. There are two souls within this body, Laoch. Two. One sacrificed its body to entwine within mine. My sister, who I love, loved, gave her soul unto mine, and together we live in harmony inside this twisted body."

"You fear the venom? The poison that rides my spirit?" said Oisin.

Rensta reached out and squeezed his forearm, her smile tight. "Not in the same way, but yes."

"More, the second sacrifice," said Ecne, her eyes hazed in the fire's light, but Laoch was sure he could detect a hint of Nathair's lizard amid her pupils. It gripped at his heart to see what was happening due to their connection, though he stayed his words. "To enslave the Spirit Walkers, they introduce the venom, threatening to kill both spirits unless one sacrifices themselves. You fear spirit-death." Ecne squeezed her fingers against the bridge of her nose, blinking. "Of course you should. You are a shaman who has touched Nathair. It is Nathair's enslavement and the death of her twinned soul that you truly fear."

Laoch eyed Ecne. The tears streaming down her face formed rivulets and washed wayward sand from her cheeks. He turned the fish, one eye on Oisin, knowing the Handren couldn't help himself. As expected, he rose and pulled the acolyte in close, letting her sob against his chest.

"I do not understand," said Rensta ad li Tark. "Why does my pain and fear cause you such emotion?"

"Ecne has a close link with Nathair and whatever is left of Keran. She has seen what you saw of Q'Noh, and the loss of ... of Sura. We witnessed the horrors of Innealtóir, and of Apso-Tran, where the elves have twisted themselves into something as bad as the Constructors themselves. Yet through it all, we have remained as honourable as we could."

"Are you saying my choice lacks such devotion? Such honour?" Rensta sprang with surprising speed to her feet, the staff in one hand, eyes locked onto his. "I do not rise to false words, human. I have offered what help I can. And you can prod my faith and beliefs as much as you will, but I will not risk such a heinous thing upon my sister and I. We have sacrificed enough."

"But they will come," said Ecne, her face red, cheeks still wet. "They will not stop until every realm is under their thumb, every spirit enslaved to their will."

"Then I will prepare my people. You may succeed or delay the inevitable. Time that is precious." Rensta turned on her heel and froze to the spot. Nathair's snout wavered behind her, the dragon's crystalline eyes locked onto hers. The shaman's shoulders trembled as the artifice dragon shifted to its haunches to expose a shimmering chest.

"She remembers," said Nathair as she disembarked from the dragon's chest. "Rensta remembers the wyrm's pain when she, and the other shaman, lured it to Mondrein by causing a rent in the veil. She remembers feeding the souls of her own people to the creature, lulling it to sleep with the calming spirits they crafted. She remembers carving the skin and bone of the creature, and embedding the Sealgair for their journey."

"The wyrm agreed. A pact was forged."

"After you had mutilated it. Only *then* did you explain your purpose. Ashamed when you realised the creature had intelligence, a language of its own. And it was also when you realised Keran was needed in case the wyrm chose a different path. Another sacrifice." Nathair's scales flickered, reshaping. Keran's face now peered back at the shaman as she bowed her head.

"We have all suffered under the yoke of what may come, Nathair. You are a Spirit Walker, once a shaman. Yet it was your twin that made the sacrifice so you may live. Not you." The shaman's anger and shame competed for dominance in her slitted eyes. "I do not judge. Maybe they thought you would be the stronger, would eventually resist the venom as you appear to have done. They would likely judge their sacrifice worth it. And now that you stand before me with a dragon of the veil at your back, so do I."

"Yet you refuse to see it through," said Nathair, but the words were Keran's, and his eyes flared white with power.

The shaman sat back down; shoulders bowed. "I was supposed to go, but I feared death, and ... and the consequences of being caught. One of us enduring soul-death so the other may live only to serve in agony – it was too much. In the end, the tribal shamans chose a human. You, Keran." Rensta twisted her crooked neck to peer up at Nathair. "And you have proven worthy. But I cannot ride the dragon ... I can't."

Laoch drew Justice, hating himself, and took two steps to the right at speed. Twin, elven arrows pummelled into the firepit, sparking the fire into life as he rolled away. A third arrow whistled in the other direction – this one flaming blue – and the cry of pain as a result, sadly welcome. He powered up the dune, his leather armour glowing red with Justice's light. Another arrow slammed into his chest, hurling him backwards down the dune. A scream greeted a second of Fate's arrows, and Laoch, the bait for Rensta's guards, rose from the sand with an ache in his shoulder. Ignoring Justice's ire at exposing himself, he checked that the elven guards still lived as Ecne dragged an unconscious Rensta into the dragon's chest. Nathair's lizard-like eyes glinted red as she followed them in.

He understood her fear.

But they had no time to ease it.

—

"How long?" Laoch asked, checking the shaman's bonds were loose enough to not cut off her circulation. Satisfied, he rolled her up against the metal rib of Nathair's chest to be greeted by angry, desperate eyes locked onto his.

"A week in your time, I believe. Or thereabouts." Nathair, her body rippling with the whitefire drained from the weedfields, crossed her arms as she gazed at Laoch. "You wish to spirit sleep?"

"We need to be fresh," said Oisin. "We should rest for some of the time, at least."

"Aye, and some time to plan and prepare best we can." Laoch pulled down Rensta's gag. The shaman spat in his face. The purple spittle slid down his nose.

"Next time that will be green, Laoch the Dishonoured. And I will burn a hole in your face to prove there is no honour inside."

Laoch knelt back, wiping away the spit with the sleeve of his cloak. He replaced the gag with a little more force than necessary. "Okay. You can answer with bloody nods. Nathair plans to put us all asleep in a while. She calls it spirit sleep. You know what that is?"

Rensta glared back, the faintest of nods in response. Laoch noted the narrowing of her eyes.

"No one will hurt you or your sister. I will guard you with my spirit and bone, shaman. You hold the key to my people's lives, as you likely do your own. I'd lie and say I feel like shit for taking you, but I don't have the time to feel anything right now." Laoch made to rise, but changing his mind, reached for the shaman's gag. "No spitting," he said, pulling it down.

None flew his way, though vitriol poured from every one of her pores.

Laoch met her eyes. "I lay in a cell not knowing my friend was alone and having his skin peeled next door. That has sat with me every bloody day since. Yet I know, if I had the choice, I'd not turn away the discoveries we made in return for his pain."

"And if Sura stood before Nathair again, Laoch the Dishonoured, would you have made the same choice? Would you have allowed her to burn in the dragon's fire to save your people?"

He stared back, mind spinning as, once again, Sura fell under those dreadful flames. "I ... she would have killed me if I hadn't."

But that's not the answer, is it?

She sacrificed herself for all of us when the Kraken *struck. But would I give her up again, given the chance?*

Rensta broke contact, looking down at her bonds. "At least we have something in common. I wish to sleep, but should anyone encroach on my body or our spirits, your realm can suffer in your Seven Hells."

"Agreed." Laoch nodded over to Nathair. The thin-lipped grin he got in return exposed fangs at the corners of her mouth. Luckily, the shaman's eyes hadn't left her bonds. Nathair briefly faded, and in turn, Rensta's chin slumped against her chest. Laoch eased her into a more comfortable position on the bed roll he'd provided.

"What did she mean by 'green' spit?" asked Ecne, rolling out her own mat. "Sounds nasty. Maybe we should search her, just in case?"

"She's tied," replied Oisin. "And I feel bad enough already."

He shook his head as Laoch shrugged and proceeded to check through her pockets, asking Nathair what each strange pouch, box or item was. Most were the paraphernalia of rituals Nathair understood. Only the single roll of a leaf tied with gut was unfamiliar. He sliced it open while Ecne watched, exposing a green, foul-smelling powder. Ecne wrinkled her nose, eyed Laoch, then drew out her boot knife. Taking a sample, she dripped a little water onto it and watched the violent reaction as it sizzled and spat.

"Acere," she said, and wiped the residue on a cloth, only to find the tip of her knife had rounded, slivers of the metal edge now residing in the material. "Stronger than I've ever seen. I used acere, a vinegar, from wine and spirits, to clean our equipment. Stronger ones to activate some of Meister Kinst's more stable concoctions. She really would have had a look inside your head, though it would have likely killed her too if she held on to it too long."

Laoch raised an eyebrow towards Oisin, who held up his hands in response. "I wouldn't be giving her that back anytime soon," he said. "But she'll know it's gone."

"A choice between my face or a little more hate. I'll tell her you took it. She likes you." Laoch grinned and eased himself down onto his own roll. "Wake us in four days, Nathair. Then we go to war."

46
OF STEAM AND SPIRIT

APPROACHING ANVIL, HANDREN
MOUNTAINS, BRANDSHOLD

Lady Death held her breath, calming the beat of her heart which threatened to break out of her rib cage and run for the hills. The difference between Wyrding, her spirit flying apart from her body, and real flying caused her a fear she thought only reserved for the histories around the Constructors. And to cap that, she felt odd, as if being watched. She glanced back, but couldn't catch sight of Yanik, who lay against the floor of the infernal machine.

The fragile artifice beat at the air. Soon they came upon a sight that took her mind off the rhythm of the wings. Below, the Infected ran. Whether child or man, mother or grandparent, they raced with unrelenting purpose towards the walls rising in the distance. They were, to her senses, near death, their souls ravaged far beyond the condition Nesca had suffered before her death. Flayed, driven, and desperate for a nourishment that lay on the far side of the walls, the riot of bodies ran on.

"They are closing in," said Rin, eyes on the walls. "And soon in range. Do you see the marker posts?"

Lady Death looked down, searching amid the flailing bodies. It didn't take long to pick out a line of red-tipped posts that spread across the valley, about a hundred feet in front of the horde. "Yes."

"That's steam-javelin range."

The pilot eased the ornithopter to the left, bringing the machine far too close to the valley wall for Lady Death's liking. She returned to holding her breath.

"Here they come," Rin said, and removed one hand from a control stick at her side to point ahead. Lady Death peered into the sky. Within a second or two, she caught the flight of spears that sank to crash into the front wave of the Infected, piercing limbs and torsos, cracking skulls and splitting brains. She guessed thirty may have fallen. At such a distance, an army may have stood back, waited, tested the range and perhaps assessed the numbers sent their way. The Infected hooted on, scrambling over any injured. A tide of hunger, uncaring of those that fell before them. A second volley of javelins cut through the sky, their arc bringing them thudding down into a mass of flesh that ignored their impact.

"Powerful," said Lady Death, gripping her seat as the ornithopter finally came into full view of Anvil's walls. "But they seem not to care."

The Unbeliever stayed silent, her hands back on the controls, her knuckles white.

"Only one needs to get inside, you understand, Rin? My flock and those of the other Houses are down there. My people. And they were taken from us forever. There is no cure. Your soul just withers and dies. They seek relief in feeding off others, but it never quite sates the need, the desire, or salves the pain. Where is the Unspoken? An Chéad needs to burn their bodies, strip their spirits clean."

Lady Death scanned the top of the city walls. Amid the familiar ballistae, four long-barrelled machines pointed towards the valley floor. A lick of fire burned at each open end. A gout of flame erupted from one. Banefire that poured onto the ground a few yards out from the metal city doors etched with a huge hammer and anvil. The grass burned – a sign of hope, perhaps. But walls can be scaled, and the city lay exposed to the valley walls on all sides. An army would flail against those and likely be driven back, but an unthinking mass of once-humanity simply would not care.

The ornithopter dipped over the walls, lights flashing. The artifices huddled below belched steam in response. With the aircraft clear, they released another barrage of iron over the walls. Lady Death shook her head as more machines came into view. Some she recognised – trebuchets and ballistae – and others appeared as bastardised versions. Each pointed upwards from the lower city buildings, watching the skies, steam rising from their rear.

"You expected dragons, and got death on foot instead." Lady Death gripped the top of Rin's seat as the ornithopter shook. The new rhythm brought them down towards a cleared space where another three of the winged contraptions sat, waiting. But it was what lay beside them that struck Lady Death dumb. A patch of the soil lay scorched, and in its centre, a scarlet dragon, curled in on itself, metal scales wrapped tight and rigid. The head was locked under the front paws, talons exposed, their edges blood-red. Twelve soldiers stood around the frozen An Chéad, stock still, swords drawn, watching their approach with malevolent interest.

The ornithopter rumbled as the wheels of the machine hit the earth, to Lady Death's intense relief, and it rolled to a stop. Rin leant forwards, head upon the canopy. It took a moment for Lady Death to realise the woman was crying. Her sobs echoed through the cockpit. This soldier, all spit and confidence, had been reduced to an emotional mess, as if she could no longer mask what her bravado hid. Lady Death laid her hand upon the young woman's shoulder, assuming she was overwhelmed by what she saw.

"Rin? An Chéad? What's happened?"

"We do not know. The Unspoken came to our rescue, as she always has. We knew she fought and swallowed something out there, though we know not what. An Chéad has not moved since he returned, and the Burners emerged. That was why I was sent to see who was coming. I apologise for the lie, but ..."

"Is anyone going to let me the fuck out, my Lady. I can't feel my fuckin' arse."

—

The crowd pressed upon Lady Death's senses. Their physical presence was not unlike that she faced as the head of her House, but their stress and fear squeezed in on her, a need filled with dread that simultaneously called to her disposition while drowning her in hate. Many among the onlookers had clearly seen what approached outside their walls, and they regarded her with hope as she stepped down from the ornithopter. But more wore the expressions she expected – of those who had run from the oppression of the Houses and their Scripture, had chosen the Unspoken's lands as a sanctuary, and now faced the judgement of the Lady of Death.

She waited as Yanik unfurled herself, flinching at the cussing – which cut out immediately the Ranger clapped eyes on the silent crowd. Lady Death knew Yanik would rather a sword and a last stand against the antipathy of the horde, than suffer the stares being thrown her way.

Somebody pushed themselves clear of the crowd. They wore a long tunic over tough breeches, their hair grey with a large bald patch. He walked over, feigning more confidence than he clearly felt, stopping just before Lady Death as she brushed her robes down. Rin's feet met the ground behind her, but she avoided the temptation to check on her state of mind.

"Lady Death," said the man. The deft bow of his head surprised her, considering where they were. "I am the mayor of Anvil in the Unspoken's name. My name is Dathair."

"This is all very strange for everyone," replied Lady Death, her first glance for the mayor, the next swept the crowd while she projected her voice. "I am not here for any other purpose than to crush the malignant horde that rushes towards your walls." A murmur ripped through the miasma, and the Unbelievers glanced towards each other as if looking to see who trusted her words.

"It is true, Father," said Rin, taking a position beside Lady Death. "As far as I saw, they were killing those wounded at the rear. They have a Duke Panset with them, and he says an army follows with the same intent."

Lady Death waited on the mayor's response amid the sudden clamour from the crowd – the word *army* being passed from lips to lips. A shiver ran down her spine.

"*Duke* Panset?" said the mayor, his eyes widening. "And an army marches to our wall?"

Lady Death nodded. "The duke has returned due to the Infected's attack on our people. Should we not take this somewhere quieter, Mayor Dathair?" She side-eyed the crowd. Their presence pressed in even more, as precious time slipped by.

"The people need to know your intent, Lady Death. You represent all they have run from, and fear."

"More than death?" She looked over to Yanik, who had positioned her-self behind, only to ease beside her now, hand wavering near her pommel as she eyed the crowd. "If they get through, they will turn all your people into ones such as them. The Overseer fears they will sweep through all of Brandshold."

The mayor looked over to where An Chéad lay curled up on the ground, the unmoving Burners standing guard, watchful of the crowd. He licked his lips and scratched at his bald pate. "I ... You are here on Penance's word? Of all the Houses, Lady Death, those here would trust yours the most, and his the least."

"The army comes to help. *I* come to help. And Penance is no longer the Overseer. That title has been passed to the Union's queen to fight those that follow – the Constructors. The Infected that approach your walls are their creation."

"Fuck me, people," said Yanik, her face flushing. "Send Rin back. Get her to scout the Union's army. Let her tell you what's missing."

"Missing?" replied the mayor.

Lady Death caught on, surprised at the woman's insight. "Siege artifice," she cut in. "They follow at speed, Mayor Dathair. No trebuchets, nothing more than mounted ballistae. No weapons that would trouble your walls. They are here because the Infected swamped Jense, not to lay siege to your city."

"Jense? You say they took Jense?" Fear and angst rose from the crowd, mirroring the mayor's worry. He spun about, arms wide to the people behind. "Who here has family in Jense?" Hands shot up, shouts joining them from further behind. He turned back. "Most here will have family or past friends there, from before the Crusade. What happened to them? How many survived?"

Lady Death's heart crushed tight, and she blinked at the mayor, before her gaze settled on the crowd that waited on her words. These were the people they had sent the Union's army against, forged them into the role of the enemy. Built a dread of the purported evil they spread amid the flock so they could drain them dry. Ordinary people. It had been so simple. Words around a table, sending out their own to die against the distant fires and artifices of the Unbelievers. Just folk who believed in something different, and had chosen a life under the wing of the Eighth, and forced to kill by the machinations of the Seven Houses.

A reality that caused bile to sit at the base of her throat, threatening to burn her soul, but still leave the sin of what she had done behind.

What is evil?

Lady Death raised her voice, sweeping the crowd, forcing herself to look into the eyes of all that would look back. "Just a few Infected took all of Jense in one night. Those are the people of Jense out there. Twelve thousand poisoned souls that turned north at the behest of the Constructor's silver-blue dragon. They come for you, and should just one get through, Anvil, and likely all the Union, will fall." She strode forwards, passing the wide-eyed mayor, feeling the pain in his soul as he worked through the consequences of her words. The crowd parted as she approached An Chéad. A few bowed their heads while others looked away.

Emerging from the back with Yanik by her side and the mayor trailing, Lady Death came to a halt in view of the scarlet dragon's single, exposed eye. It appeared inert, but she was a wielder of spiritfire and could sense the power inside.

The shell may be inert, but the dragon is much as Nathair was when we met. More so, the spiritfire stored inside is vital, and high.

"Unspoken," she said, and laced the words with power, spearing them towards the dragon's metal-scaled head. "You are needed."

A Burner moved, hand upon the sword at its side, adjusting position to stand in her immediacy. It locked eyes, and inside, Lady Death flinched. There was a coldness there. Not hate. An indifference to who and what she was. The impact struck her, and she let a tendril of her power slide amid the air, unseen, to wrap itself around the man who wordlessly faced her. She tasted an old soul, one tethered to the body before her, but which had resided in many others.

A Constructor. No, lesser, yet it appears human.

A spirit-doll, perhaps?

Curiosity demanded she dig further, but this was not the time and place. Besides, revealing what lay at the heart of the Unspoken's power was not going to go down well with the citizens of Anvil, especially with the Infected at their gates.

Thoughts of Lady Honour seeped into her mind – the warmth of her touch. Something to ward off the chill of the Seven's chosen, and devious, ally. She shivered again and spun about. The mayor and his people stared back at her.

Yanik came to her rescue. "Looks like your dragon is a bust. Anyone here fought an Infected before? Anyone?" She smiled, a ferocity in her stance as no one answered. "Well, I fucking have. Who do I need to speak to so that all you fuckers will listen?"

47

TO SUP UPON A CITY

MAKALENA, BRANDSHOLD

Tabharthóir ground the bodies between her sword-like teeth, and threw them into the air, swallowing what remained of the flesh and bone. Spirits tore from their dying hearts, nourishing the dragon as they poured into the heartstone. Tabharthóir bellowed in triumph as her talons gripped the stone of Makalena's inner castle walls.

"*Settle,*" thought the emperor. "*You have fed enough.*"

The dragon shook her head, the ripple flowing down the central spike before her tail lashed the limestone walls. Her back legs bent and eased to the floor, and Tarin exited from her silver-blue chest, soulreaver laid casually across both shoulder and neck as his armour gleamed.

Prostrate on the ground, with black-armoured Inhibitors on guard behind, lay the Duchess of Makalena, and an old magus who wore the orange robes of one of the Seven. Tarin remembered the purple lash of power others in such clothes wielded, and stretched out a tendril of his whitefire to roll along the chained magus's back. The man's spine arched as pain rode his nerves, his agonised spirit tasting all the sweeter for it.

The Fleshmaster approached the pair, a spark of life amid the devastation wrought upon a castle that guards and servants had defended to the end. Strewn amid the blood lay the soulless bodies that had fed the victors.

Tarin let the point of his sword sway before the duchess, enjoying her squeal as it touched upon her ear and neck. "Look at me," he whispered, his words hard and expectant. The duchess responded by straining her neck backwards. Red-rimmed eyes stared at the Fleshmaster, who laughed at the streaks of soil and ash across one pampered cheek. "Kneel."

The duchess followed the command, her hands free of the spirit-manacles her companion bore. With head bowed, she awaited her fate.

"Many of your people cower in their houses or cellars, waiting for a rescue that will never come. Ever." He had expected more from their royalty; defiance, maybe. But she had crumbled, the foundation of her right to rule shattering amid his words. The tip of his soulreaver alighted beneath her chin, and he raised her head so that her eyes met his white-eyed gaze. "My Inhibitors feed upon your wounded. Few will survive. But there are those that could serve us, become spirit-dolls at our beck and call. For this, we gift them life, but this is your burden, Duchess. Do you wish your subjects to die in their homes, or live?" He let the soulreaver draw upon her spirit, a mere sip of her sorrowful soul. "See, in a way it is a relief. A draining of the pain. Go with my Inhibitors, call for your soldiers to stand down. Free your people from the threat of death and accept the yoke in return for life. Yes?"

The faint nod was enough, and brought a metal-toothed smile to the Fleshmaster's husked face. "Take her to their enclave against the northern wall. Accept their surrender and kill their officers. Then parade her through this pathetic city and gather those who live and answer her call in the market squares. And then ...?" Tarin raised an eyebrow to the Inhibitor captain, whose smile was grim but accepting in return.

"House to house, Emperor. And any magi?" The captain waited, knowing his priorities.

"Any you find in the slums of this shithole need to be brought to me first. I have shared the broken and the wounded." Tarin eyed the captain. "That is enough for now, is it not, Captain?" He accepted the salute, knowing full well the balance he had to tread in feeding his army just enough to keep them sated. But the magi were his, and his alone.

We are close. Letting soul-lust run rife could end that.

He watched the duchess being dragged away, and waited until the captain had passed through the smashed gate before squatting down in front of the magus. He grabbed the manacles about the man's wrists, sensing as the sliver of the ancient Spirit Walker bonded to the metal squirmed at his presence. Confident that it restrained the magus from exerting his spiritfire, he raised the man up by the chain and forced him to his knees. His straggled, long grey hair was streaked with stone dust and ash, his face dry, skin cracked. Evidence of just how far the magus had pushed himself in the defence of his city.

Or in fear for his soul.

"You, I have a purpose for."

—

Tarin stood amid the bloody puddles of the pockmarked street. A Scorpion of the vanguard squatted at his left, its tail swaying ominously above the armoured hull. On his right, a feeder crawled through a narrow side-street, draining the remnants of any spirits that flittered amid the ether while its many feet crunched through the litter of war.

"I feel so at home here, magus."

The ornate doors at the summit of seven steps rose fifteen feet. Upon them, a dragon, talons poised, a spear buried deep into the dragon's chest, battled Honour. Yet the eyes belied defeat, even as its maw stretched wide, teeth bearing down upon the lone figure.

"Hmmm," said the Fleshmaster, and dragged the magus up the seven steps. The man pulled against him at each rise, bringing a little joy to Tarin as he thought of how many more may be inside. A tingle started around his heart and brain – an expectation of the feed to come, perhaps.

Or of the secrets that lay inside. Popsilin has whetted my appetite.

He slammed the magus into the left-hand door, gauntleted hand still wrapped about the chain, and pulled him up eye-to-eye. "Get me in," he spat. "What did Popsilin's book name you? Yes, priest. Get me in, *priest.*"

The man trembled, searching the white-eyed monstrosity before him for hope. Each shake and quiver was returned with a smile. Then he shook his head, grey hair falling across his brow. "No."

"No?" roared the Fleshmaster, and clamped both hands down upon the priest's head. Whitefire surged through his leathered muscles, urging his fingers to crush the man's skull. "You will do as I command, or ..." He squeezed.

The magus's eyes bulged, the pressure building as the bone flexed. "No."

The emperor slammed the man's head against the ornate wall, breaking his hold before the magus's impudence overcame his reason. Blood bubbled from his scalp to seep down his neck. Tarin glared at the manacles and debated whether to remove them so he could subjugate the bastard's mind.

He needed into the House – all the Houses – desperate to see what Popsilin had hinted at. But more than that, what the Inhibitor had missed. The Houses stood strong, their stone and foundations fortified by spiritfire over a thousand years. How much more lay inside, he could not calculate, but spoke of a power he needed to have, if only to deny the magi the opportunity to wield it against him. The Seven had contained their power, hidden it from everyone, including him. The crystals the lesser magi had used to lash the Scorpions hinted the Seven had knowledge of the heartstones, and had steered it to their own ends.

"I don't make such mistakes twice," he whispered, eyeing the manacles. A decision made; he snapped them open. Heaving the magus against the door, he poured whitefire into the man's mind. It struck a barrier like none he'd met before, orange-hued and immersed in faith. Images of a scroll upon which the Seven Magi's words were written forged the wall's foundations. Tarin shaped the whitefire into a thin point, and the tip rammed into the defiant wall, piercing its centre. His hate and desire flowed through the rent and swathed the priest's mind.

"I see ... you talk to the others. You have your own calling crystals, magus. That I cannot allow. Fear of the unknown is my greatest weapon."

Spiritfire gathered there, a mere flicker of orange light amid the vacuum of the magus's drained soul.

Tarin laughed, the sound tumbling from his dry lips at the pathetic display, and waited for the magus to attack.

But nothing happened. Instead, the magus burned out his own mind, searing all he was. Memories, self, his *will*. All that was left was an empty skull. The splutter of spirit that remained, tasteless, mere sustenance at best.

"Nooooo!" The Fleshmaster wrapped his hands about the magus's head and crushed the skull. Bone shattered as his fingers dug deep. He cast the corpse aside, infuriated. Stepping back from the ornate doors, he glared at their defiance as Honour stood strong against the veil dragon.

Can my dragon break through? If I assault these doors with Tabharthóir and fail, how will I look?

The feeder skittered out of the alleyway and dragged the dead magus's body away – scrabbling the body below its segments to drain the wisps of bland soul from within. Tarin scowled, knowing full well Lelion used the artifice to watch and inform. The admiral incarnate rarely missed an opportunity.

Lelion.

The emperor faced the waiting Scorpion and sent a thought spiralling into the pilot inside. The response was swift. The artifice strode down the street, tail lashing the air as it headed towards the breach in the city wall.

"Let's see if Lelion's soul-cannons can break in, yes?"

He strode away from the door and, containing his frustrations, headed for Tabharthóir. The Inhibitors were systematically searching the area around the inner castle, and he passed a market square containing row upon row of townsfolk sat upon the ground, huddled amid the detritus of battle as guards watched on. The numbers had tripled from earlier, and he could hear the cries of the search squads as they battered into the homes. It returned a little joy to his dead heart.

On reaching the veil dragon, he took flight with his mood lifted a little. He circled the city once, pleased to see the Scorpion had reached the line of soul-cannons and that word would be passed soon enough.

Whether Lelion would be angered by their requisition or not, he didn't ponder on. Right now, she was rather busy, and smug with her own foresight.

48

TO TEMPT AN ADMIRAL

MAKALENA, BRANDSHOLD

L elion placed the vision crystal back into the slot she had fashioned next to her simple, fluted brass chair. The images still streamed in her mind, the shadow of the ornithopter's wings tracking the ground as the craft flew above the human army.

"Pah," she spat, ignoring those of her crew who turned to check they were not the target of her ire. Swearing, she pressed the crystal home and whitefire crackled. The images now appeared in the air, glimmering in the centre of the bridge. Lelion flicked her eyes over to the waiting, lightly armoured Inhibitor pilot. "How many?"

"I'd estimate around five thousand, maybe a few more. They have horsed archers and heavy ballistae stationed on higher ground." The pilot pointed to a section of the picture and waited for it to shift position. "Here," he said. At that point, the images fizzed with scarlet spiritfire and shorted out.

"A magi attack?" asked Lelion, rubbing her chin, one elbow on the brass armrest.

"I think not. The ornithopter did not miss a beat. But they were there, all clad in red. When I turned around to fly over again, they were gone." The pilot shook his head. "Whether they disrobed and dispersed, I do not know. There were carts nearby. Maybe they hid in those?"

"Twenty, you say?"

The pilot nodded.

Lelion chewed at her lower lip, the hard teeth scraping the husked lips. Dried skin floated about her face.

Do I wait? No.

"Order the other two ornithopters to scout the flank and rear. I want to know what comes. You are to fly back to the emperor, tell him of what you have seen." The admiral popped the crystal from its holder and flipped it over to the pilot. "Inform the Fleshmaster we guard no longer – the *Kraken* goes to war."

The pilot saluted and strode off through the outer bridge door. Lelion followed, embracing the spring air as she proceeded to the bow of her soulship, where the two adjutants waited. Light rain fell, filling the sky with glistening motes. Undulating farmland stretched outwards before the *Kraken*, crops sprouting from tilled fields downtrodden by the boots of the Inhibitors she had assigned, or the feeders that trailed through mud and bush with no care. A small village burned merrily to their left, the people there either fled or fed upon, their corralled animals crying in fear as the *Kraken* loomed. Along the rise of some low hills ahead, an army waited. She could smell their fear, taste the miasma of dread upon the rain that alighted on her armour.

"This is to be a glorious day, adjutants. There is nothing I like better than reaping the souls of the foolish."

Lord Justice strode along the cracked stone ridge, tracking the artifice beasts whose long limbs scuttled easily across the ditch at the base of the low hill. They were spread out, perhaps ten yards between each, but driving towards the centre of General Mandrich's waiting army. A flicker to his left drew his attention. Flags were raised, red and blue, and the first twang of a ballista was soon followed by several more. The heavy javelins cut through the rain, the first crashing into one of the scorpion-like creatures. Cheers rang from the watching soldiers as the tip exploded, smoke rising from the top of the metal artifice. More thundered into the metal hull, and as many again hit bush and field in equal measure. As the spiritfire cleared and the smoke drifted, Lord Justice could see the dents, or cracks, in what he took for armour. Each of the struck scorpion-like machines stuttered briefly before driving on.

"Ready the carts!" he shouted, and squelched through the increasing mud to stand behind the first two battlecarts. Their rams stood proud from the front, the crystal at each tip shrouded by a metal cap. Soldiers waited behind, hands on the cart's wheels, ready to heave. More javelins flew. The echoes of their explosions were dulled by the rain, but definitely closer. A choked roar cut through the noise, and he heard the clatter of long spears and pikes along the hill.

"Come on, General." Lord Justice wiped the rain from his brow and watched the skies. "Got to be soon."

Flags rose, double red.

"Remove the blocks!" he commanded. "Heave!"

Lord Justice slammed his shoulder into the rear of the nearest cart, mirrored by one of his priests-in-waiting on the other side. With a surge, the wheels broke free of the cloying mud and rolled forwards. He chased the battlecart far enough to see the hope it contained career towards the artifices that had reached halfway. Four more rolled further along the hill, half of the allotted carts. The rest, Mandrich insisted, were held in reserve at a fallback position.

Lord Justice prayed; his hands clasped together. The three Scorpions below his position paused, their bulbous eye-windows peering up the hill as the carts hurtled downwards. At first, he thought they would hit, but each machine scuttled to the side, their limbs shoving them clear of the carts' paths. His heart sank, and lifted again when the twang of the smaller ballistae sent tipped quarrels flying. They struck the carts from behind, driving through the open rear to pierce the Erin's Wrath stored within. A powerful eruption swept over the hill. Lord Justice squatted, head turned away, and covered his body in redfire to redirect the heat and smoke. When he rose, one of the artifices had been torn open, the legs on one side obliterated, hull exposed. Sparks shimmered, wires and cogs growled as the remaining legs flailed in the mud. Something human-shaped dropped from the ragged hole, their crystalline armour wreathed in burning, sticky fire.

"I hope you burn in the Seven Hells!" he roared, and as the smoke cleared, a second Scorpion lay on its side, legs flailing. Smaller quarrels rained down, the flashes barely lighting its armour as the third machine's tail pulled the flailing Scorpion back onto its feet. Further along the hill, he counted three more downed artifices that he prayed were out of action. The remaining half powered up the hill, claws snapping in front, tails poised to strike.

The major's horn sounded; the note mournful to Lord Justice's ears. "More sacrifice."

Horses reared, straining against the weight of the heavy ballistae as they moved away from the battle – their retreat a declaration of Mandrich's intent to save previous resources. A wave of soldiers poured down the hill towards the machines. Behind them were three of Justice's priests-in-waiting – the bait – their spiritfire bolts flashing outwards to slam into the hulls of the remaining artifices. Word from Makalena had described how the Constructors and their machines focused on the destruction of priests first. The Lord was straining to see when hands clamped on his shoulder.

"We must go now, my Lord," said Antar. Her eyes were tight, angry, the female priest clearly as frustrated as he was. "We must leave."

Lord Justice peered back down the hill. The noise and clatter of the attack hid the few who had volunteered for the assault. Most had family in the city that burned in the distance behind the huge, floating ship that heralded the pain to come.

"A test, no more." Spiritfire surged as he raised his hands, only for Antar to press them down.

"You will draw their attention. You need to save your spiritfire for later in this battle," she said, turning away.

Screams rolled up the hill, cloying at his ears. Lord Justice knew he couldn't leave. Ignoring the departing priest, he ran for the rocky ledge where the waiting released deliberately feeble bolts of redfire towards the bloodied Scorpions. He dropped in, panting, readying just as he knew the waiting did. He spared a glance over to the line of pikemen. Their ranks split as half ran for the next defensive position to cover the retreat. A cry from his left, and the first metallic foot slammed into the ledge. The whirr of cog and wire drew the metal beast's second leg over the top of the rock. The priest positioned there grasped the crystal within her fist, and the raging spiritfire wrapped itself about her hands. He could see the strain, and desperately wanted to help as gore dripped from the Scorpion's underside.

She released.

Raw energy crashed into the underbelly, melting metal, cracking the thin crystal. Her face lit with manic glee until the last of the crystal's power faded. Justice sensed her drawing upon her own soul.

A clang broke his focus as a metal foot slammed down at his side. A pierced head, the dead eyes staring at him in horror, quivered upon the limb. He threw himself onto his back, hands splayed before him and the raw power of his God poured into the Scorpion's hull. One of the priests-in-waiting joined him, and they worked together until hot metal sloughed from the armour and the hull gave out. Screams from the waiting by his side ended as the molten armour seared through his throat. Lord Justice stared, horrified, while about him, redfire kept the weight of the artifice back. Hands scrambled over his shoulders, attempting to yank him away, to only succeed when more spiritfire wrapped his own to lift him clear of the machine.

"We need you, Lord Justice. The flock, the general and your priests." He heard Antar's words, but they barely registered as she pulled him away from the smouldering corpse.

Back on his feet, the bulbous, shattered windows of the artifice faced him. An armoured Constructor, still alive, flailed at the straps that kept him in his seat, helm battering the window while flames licked the cabin. Lord Justice sensed his relief as the straps finally tore. He drove his redfire-wrapped sword through the window, and onwards to pierce above the Constructor's throat guard. Hate roared along the weapon, boiling whatever lay inside, and a foul stench wafted from the shattered window. He felt the body die, but not the spirit. Already detached from the liquefied brain, it withdrew from the heart, seeking refuge. That scared him more than the death-dealing machine it rode in.

Leaving his molten sword inside the morass of the dead Inhibitor, he turned to leave, only to spot the dark, roiling wave of Constructors that ran towards the hill's edge. Their weapons glowed with whitefire, giving their countenances an ethereal and malevolent beauty amid the carnage littering the hill. As if the fields of his homeland were awash with spirits.

Skittering among them, he got a first sight of the segmented beasts his priest had reported before sealing themselves away in their House. Many-legged, they drank the shreds of life that remained among the dead and dying, and chewed their way through flesh and bone.

"And there is more to come."

He backed away, battling self-loathing as he ignored the cries of the wounded upon the battlefield, condemning them to a fate he dared not imagine. He ran, Antar and his guard at his side, retreating towards the secondary line of pikemen. On reaching the far side, he grabbed his horse's reins and mounted as the Constructors struck the first line of defence, the clamour of battle immersed in whitefire. Pained howls mixed with silent death as the Constructors attacked the soldiers behind the long weapons.

The original plan had been for archers to line up behind the pikemen, driving their crystal and flash powder arrow tips into the enemy's armour while the pikes kept them at bay. But as word of Makalena had spread, the general had become more cautious. An innate fear of the artifices had focused his tactics towards reducing their numbers, though the cost would likely be high.

Lord Justice wheeled his horse around and galloped away, the remaining priest-in-waiting at his side. The reserve pikemen strode backwards on their captain's order.

Maybe they would survive.

—

The *Kraken* hovered high in the darkening sky behind the admiral, the strangled cries of dying humanity cut off as the feeders drew upon their souls. Lelion, savouring the agony, tried to block out the sight of the shattered Scorpions strewn across the hill.

"A trap," said the adjutant as he trailed behind. Lieutenant Spintz winced at the man's words.

Lelion stretched her shoulders back, rolling her neck. The cracks pierced the silence upon the hill. She turned to face the adjutant. She had to admit, the Mechanised Inhibitor knew what was coming, but faced it like a Constructor. She decided there and then that, with resources so scarce, he only needed a reminder. She imagined the soulreaver tearing through his chest and downwards, eviscerating his body. She packaged it up and slammed the imagery into his mind. The adjunct collapsed to the ground. A whimper slipped from husked lips.

"Yes, a trap." The admiral looked to Spintz and shook her head. "Gather whatever you can and set the artificers to work. We may be able to cannibalise enough parts to rebuild a few."

"And deal with the weakness they exploited," replied Spintz, matter-of-factly.

"No. Not enough time, I fear. But perhaps we can adjust those the emperor retains, yes? It will slow the Scorpions down, mind. So, it will be *his* choice to make." The admiral flinched as a creeping sense of power raised the hairs upon her neck. She looked towards the brow of the hill and began striding up the slope. Two guards hurried to keep up. The lieutenant scurried to follow as Lelion quickened her pace.

"Yes, Admiral?"

"Something ..." she replied as she reached a battered, torn Scorpion upon the rocky outcrop. Lelion called to mind the burst of spiritfire that had taken it apart. From a distance, she had assumed a major crystal, like those Tarin had described in use within Makalena. But now?

Lelion entered the rent in the back half of the artifice. Spintz followed to find her digging among the ruins of the motor. She emerged, drawing a dull, smooth stone from its heart.

Lelion frowned, and whitefire poured into the stone, lighting the broken hull. Amid the boiling energy, a red streak writhed. Lelion's lips pulled back in a metal-toothed smile. She wrapped her hands around the stone and immersed it with more whitefire before handing it over to the lieutenant.

"I want the ornithopters up and searching for the source of this spiritfire. Each is allowed a taste, understand? So they know who they seek."

"One of the Seven?" asked Spintz, her white eyes wide.

Lelion shook her head. "No. I believe them to be long dead. But a powerful magus nevertheless, and a beacon. Yes."

"And the emperor?"

The admiral paused; her dried lips drew back before she looked at Spintz. "When we have word," she said. "Perhaps."

49
A MEMORY FOREVER SCORNED

THE UNIVERSITY, ERSTENBURGH,
BRANDSHOLD

The High Lord squeezed his eyes shut, squinting as he opened them again to look upon the charcoal pictures – superb recreations of the mosaics that adorned the veil dragon Leront's inner walls. Perfect in every detail, yet still he could name the artist simply by her style. But, that was just as a husband should.

"Are you going to hang around all day, cluttering my mind as much as my work room?" Meister Trizone bustled by, face flushed, hands waving in front of her as she gestured at the High Lord. "Clutter."

He sighed and drew in a long breath as he nestled his chin upon his cane. He scanned the words below the meister's recreation, lips moving as if to display their importance – but they both knew he wasn't here for anything to do with the finds within the House of the Seven.

The meister brushed away dust from a stool she produced from under her worktable, and eased herself onto the seat a few feet from him. Her hands rested on her lap, though her knees bounced as she eyed him.

"Speak. I cannot abide your silence," she said.

"They're coming," High Lord Penance said, dragging his eyes from the depicted dragon to rest upon his wife. Her blonde hair was now streaked with grey amid the darker charcoal dust. Her eyes sparkled blue, and the hard set to her face failed to belie the beauty he always saw within.

"And you have prepared. It's what you do. A nudge here, a bribe there. A threat when needed and, at rare times, a love shared." The knees eased their constant motion, her hands whitening as she pushed them down to keep herself still. "If you are here to check on me, my thoughts are far and away from here. But I suspect you know that."

"I know where she is, yes. But you do not."

Trizone winced, her eyes wet, expectant.

"Things have changed ... War has come, but to Anvil, death. The Infected are at their gates, and Yanik has entered the city alongside Lady Death."

Meister Trizone rose from her stool. The slap across his face was harsh, stinging. "Bastard," she said. "Why did you not let her join your House? It would have been the end of my fears, if nothing else."

Refusing to touch his cheek, he let the pain seep in. He pushed his God's touch away when it tried to interfere.

This is my pain, mine alone.

"I watched her give upon the prayer stone that first time, Maria. And saw what it cost. I would have been unable to see her under the scourge, nor learn the truth behind the Seven. Had she looked upon me with realisation of what I, and those before me, have done, I would have snapped." He bowed his head before pulling back his sacred purple robe and rising from the chair.

"Does the duke know who she is?"

"No. I don't think she does anymore, either. She told me what she thought of me before Geral smoothed her way into the Rangers." He reached for the door and looked back. "If they come, Geral has passage for the queen away from here. I want you to go with them."

"Another bribe? Or am I an annoyance that is simply in the way?" she bit back, her face set hard. The High Lord recognised her usual attempt to restrain the torrent of emotions. She stood and kicked the stool away before resting her hands on the worktable. "This is my city. I live and breathe this University, and those Learned who share a love of life. I would wither anywhere else. At least here ... the memories remain *bitter*. I fear leaving would simply wipe away the pain, just leave those fond moments. I refuse to depart this world remembering you in a good light."

High Lord Penance stared at his wife's back, the strain in her shoulders, the flush to her neck. He grasped the handle of the door, and the hinges creaked amid the silence.

"Save her, Petr. If you can do one thing where you place your family before others, save our daughter." The words were hoarse and filled with need.

High Lord Penance paused, blinking away the moisture that formed at the corner of his eyes, and wrenched the door open.

—

Queen Weister sat at the War Council table, her back pressed into the high-backed wooden chair, trying to allay the tension building in her stomach. The table felt empty without three of their number, four if you counted the High Lord, though the tapping echoing through her throne room doors signalled his approach. Vianti entered and nervously looked around, clearly expecting her to be on the throne and not seated at the table. She nodded to the boy, and he waited until High Lord Penance entered before departing.

The queen eyed the man who approached the table. What felt like a thousand years ago, he had held sway with an aura and demeanour that demanded compliance. Now healthier in body, his spirit seemed to weaken day by day. If she knew no better, she'd have sworn he'd been crying. A glance around the table was enough to understand that all but Lord Fate held the same concern. Only when she caught the High Lord's eye did his countenance change. His back stiffened, eyes and face suddenly set in the same, age-old manner she remembered before the world had fallen apart.

"My apologies," he said, his voice strident as he placed his cane beside his chair and sat. "Had some business to attend to."

The queen decided against biting back, for what could be more important than the protection of the realm?

"Then we begin," she said. "Lord Hope?"

The man nodded; his yellow robes resplendent as he stood. He had, oddly, taken to adding crystals to his collar and cuffs, and they glistened as they reflected the light streaming through the windows. "General Mandrich reports a successful battle with the Constructors outside of Makalena." He picked up the relevant models, placing them on the map. "They succeeded in destroying some of these Scorpion artifices with Erin's Wrath and Meister Kinst's spiritfire crystals. He has withdrawn with minimal losses to a secondary position, but he fears the tactics employed may not work a second time. These *machines* appear to have a weak underbelly. Lord Justice confirms this. He engaged directly in the battle." Lord Hope coughed and eyed the queen from under his eyebrows.

"Directly?" asked the High Lord, leaning forwards.

"He reports using his own spiritfire to take down a Scorpion, Lord Penance." Lord Hope flushed a little. "Against both your orders."

The queen shook her head, more at High Lord Penance's concern than the hot-headed Lord Justice's actions. She understood exactly why he had done it; her own fingers itched at her own inaction.

But that is not my calling.

"And Makalena? You have any reports at all?" asked the queen. She stood and sidled around the table to place herself beside the city in question.

"We know now that both this silver-blue dragon and the denizens of the flying ship attacked. The city fell in hours once they broke the walls." Lord Hope held out his hand. A crystal lay in his palm and, as he spoke, a strange weapon appeared above it. "They used these weapons to assail the walls. The soldiers thought no damage was done, but they kept hitting the stone in one spot. We understand they shattered after a foul noise rose from the sky ship, and the battle was over once the Scorpions entered the city. My Lead reports the loss of many of the waiting and those lesser priests who had been quickened, but they bought the Houses time to secure their doors. None of the Seven have yet been breached, but now no word reaches us of the city itself."

"Saving themselves is all well and good, but what about my *people*, Lord Hope? If the city fell so quickly, surely many survived?" The queen stared at him.

Lord Hope, licking his lips, glanced over to the High Lord, who nodded once.

"The queen is now the Overseer, Lord Hope. No secrets. She must know and *see* all." The High Lord placed his hand upon his cane. The touch of the sigil eased the tiredness in his face.

The crystal burst into life again, replacing the strange weapon with a view from on high. "This is what the Lead sent before they sealed the House of Hope." The view of the devastation was thankfully brief. Alleys littered with the dead. A strange, segmented metal beast crawling along the street below while black-clad Constructors followed, pushing bedraggled, weeping citizens towards an open square. They watched, horrified, as one of the Constructors clamped a hand to the back of a screaming man's neck. There was the unmistakable shimmer of whitefire rife along the crystal greaves before finding an ingress into the Constructor's armour. The man shrivelled, his skin sucking inwards, facial skin drying out. The Constructor discarded the remains – whether alive or dead, they could not tell – and spun about, gauntlet raised to shield his eyes as he looked up towards them. The image immediately died.

The queen blinked at her welling tears, her tight, thin lips clamped shut until she slammed her hands onto the table. "We need to know where they are headed next," she said. "And the townsfolk must leave."

"Abandon a city?" said Lord Wisdom. "What if it's here? The library? The University?"

"My people and your flocks. Unless we can destroy those weapons, the walls are useless. Their dragon can fly over, burn whatever it wants with only the ballistae to prevent it. I suspect this flying ship can do the same. But they don't. They choose to break the walls, crack the city open. Why?" The queen glanced from Wisdom to Hope, Fate and Penance.

"My guess is, they seek food to feed their army. To keep as many alive as they can," said Lord Fate. "But there is nowhere safer."

"The horde," cut in the High Lord, a slight twitch to his face as he spoke. Geral's words spilled into his mind. The people were not like the fleeing sewer rats he'd mentioned, but more a herd to be milked. "With them out there, our flocks will be exposed without walls. I see what you are saying, Queen Weister. If we remove the townsfolk, spread them wide and away from the city, more may survive. I agree. But we must also ensure the Infected cannot get to them. Duke Panset and Lady Death hold the key to such a plan."

"Agreed. And, despite my misgivings, we need them to free the Unspoken and her dragon. Without them, if the Constructors choose to fly into the cities, I see little hope." The queen lowered her gaze to stare at the map. "So many soldiers, but against these artifices and weapons, I fear we must plan to leave."

"There is another hope, beyond that of emptying the cities," said the High Lord, a little more sparkle to his eyes. "The first is the return of Sura-nista – at least, her spirit form – to her tribe. She rode the dragon Nathair alongside two Rangers and Meister Kinst's acolyte. She brings talk of the Gods' weapons that we are missing, and the turning of Nathair to our side. I hold her memories and believe she speaks truly, that this dragon seeks a weapon with your Rangers, and may come to our aid. Whether they will succeed or even return in time, I cannot say. But it is hope."

"Is this the Laoch the ladies Honour and Death spoke of?" asked Lord Wisdom.

"The same. And Oisin of the Elite. Sura believes in them, but it is the dragon that may be the key. If the Unspoken does not hold her end of the bargain ..."

The members of the War Council nodded, aware that no sign of the Unspoken's dragon had been reported by Panset as they neared Anvil's walls, and Lady Death had not yet returned from the Unbelievers' city. It didn't bode well.

"Even if this Laoch and Nathair succeed, we should prepare for them to fail. Or at least, find ways to provide more time. Do we agree that we should consider emptying the towns and cities?" asked Queen Weister, looking around the table.

"Well I, for one, am in complete agreement," the High Lord said, averting his eyes from the other members of the Council. An act the queen caught, piquing her interest. "Though we need the horde extinguished if we can. And the Houses must be protected for as long as possible."

Lord Wisdom made to speak, but changed his mind under the queen's glare.

"Then, as Overseer, I charge you with helping where you can. I understand the preparations you make to defend the Union and this city, so all I ask is that you keep your dissent to yourselves and prepare where you are able. Lord Wisdom, you may call upon my staff with regard to the

Forbidden Library, should you need help. Is there anything else? No? Then we meet again tomorrow if there is word of General Mandrich or Anvil."

As the Council departed, the High Lord rose slowly from his chair and approached the queen.

"I would beg a favour of the Overseer," he said. "A selfish one, if I may."

50
THE BURNING

Anvil, Handren Mountains,
Brandshold

Flame flowed from the strange, barrel-shaped weapons, liquid bane-fire that set alight clothes and flesh in equal measure as the Infected charged the walls. Yanik shivered, dread running up her spine as the odour of the foul mixture wafted into her nostrils. Many a Union soldier had spoken of its vile ability to stick to skin and burn its way in, with water unable to douse the heat and flame. She had witnessed it once, from afar. The swirling ball of death, hurled from a distant trebuchet, rolling amid the cavalry that covered the Consort's retreat from the valley. The scream of the horses, the agonised cries of the mounted soldiers begging them to help as they ran.

"Fucking hate that shit."

Leaning against the central stone that marked the gate position below, Yanik spat. The Unbelievers cheered as the first streams of banefire cut through the pressing horde. Choking, oily smoke rose from the pyre that stank of cooked flesh. Through the rising cloud, the banefire appeared to have little immediate effect on the Infected, but Yanik knew from bitter experience it would continue to burn on through cloth and flesh. More javelins flew over the wall. The metal rods slammed into the baying horde, piercing whatever they struck. But they were weapons designed to kill soldiers and horses, not the once-human. Trebuchets – at least, whatever these weird versions the Unbelievers used were, with their coiled metal cogs and springs – released balls of explosives to smash into those Infected who pressed in from behind.

"What will run out first, their banefire, or the twelve thousand people of Jense?" She spun about. Twelve Unbelievers were waiting and eyed her suspiciously. The last group for her speciality pep talk. "Okay. You bastards need to adapt your spears, right? No boar in the mountains, but these fuckers act just like boar. They don't know when to die, and keep running up the bloody shaft until they bite your effing nose right off. So, you need a spar about here." She pointed to a place about a forearm's length from the spear tip. "Strong enough to hold them back while your mate smashes the head. That's what ends them. The head, got it? Burning them works eventually, but again, boil their fuckin' brains first. Any questions?"

"What happens if you get bit?" asked one, their arms clearly wrapped in extra cloth and knotted with twine.

"Pray … ah shit, you don't do that … hope someone loves you enough to end you there and then. If not—" She looked over the wall. "—jump. You get bit, scratched, anything that draws blood, you're done. You hear me? You won't care who you love, hate, fucked last. None of that. All you'll want to do is get to them and hurt them too. Now spread the word."

Yanik left the last of her training groups with a manic grin and headed for the lift system. She trusted it far more than Meister Arknold's, having watched the weight of weapons and soldiers that it took. She climbed in without hesitation, only for a cry to go up further along the wall. Reversing course, Yanik ran, feet pummelling the walkway just a few yards behind the group she had just spoken to. They reached one of the banefire weapons. The cogs beneath it were clogged with a cloth that had worked its way into the machinery. Two of the Unbelievers were tearing at it with a set of pincers while another pointed down below. Yanik was forced to the side, but could see enough to confirm her worst nightmares. The last banefire stream had fizzled out, and the horde was up against the wall. Those behind were climbing up onto them, and the next after that even higher. Within seconds, they were halfway up the wall, hoots ringing in her ears as more streamed forwards to join the rising throng.

Yanik stepped away to let the arriving crossbow-wielding soldiers aim and release. Behind each one, their second wound another crossbow and handed it over, ready to take the empty one to reload. The quarrels struck. Most tore Infected from the walls, their hoots fading as they crashed to the ground, only to rise again. But more clambered to take their place, and Yanik could see where this was going.

"Hoy!" she shouted. "Line up, you bastards!" Yanik grabbed the Unbeliever with the extra padding, pulling him back into a line that she bullied into position. "You've no crossbar, so if you can't smash the head, shove them over. Failing that, you drive it fucking home and send the spear over with them, understand?" She spun about and grabbed one soldier from the line. "More spears, now. Failing that, long poles or pikes even. Get me? Anything to shove them over."

Yanik turned back. The crossbows were silent as they backed away from the wall. "Ready?" she shouted.

And the first head appeared over the parapet. The white eyes burned with hate as they narrowed, the hair ash upon the raw scalp. Dried, spindly hands gripped the stone as three quarrels slammed into its upper skull. Whitefire crackled and the eyes flared before rolling back. The creature toppled away. Cries of *pick your targets, one for each*, rang from behind Yanik as she drove her spear into the next Infected. The tip smashed the nose, driving upward into the eyes and brain. She shoved, hoping the dead thing would slide from her spear, but it barely moved. To her surprise, another spear lashed out and sent her victim sailing out into the choking air. Yanik noted the padded forearms of her new partner, and with a fierce grin, set to work on the next vile head that appeared.

After five chaotic minutes, and with arms tiring, relief finally came with a shout from behind. The two teams split apart, a mix of spears and crossbows on both sides, stabbing and releasing, as the banefire weapon finally wheeled about. The flame ignited, only for an Infected to clamber onto the overhanging barrel in its desperation to reach those on the wall. The banefire flowed, igniting the pinnacle of the clambering once-humans. Fire spread swiftly down the pyramid of husked flesh. Multiple quarrels slammed into the lone Infected as it clawed its way towards the end of the barrel, hands red and raw with the heat, hoots spilling from its gnarled lips. Two spears drove in from the side, cutting deep into the creature's hip. And Yanik struck. Her bloodied spear tip smashed into the neck, driving on through to splinter bone and brain, bringing an end to the Infected. She turned about, the relieved grin on her face crashing as she stared at her padded partner. Ragged arms were wrapped about his waist while teeth set in a shrunken face bit into the unprotected skin at his neck. Blood spurted, covering the Infected, and hoots of joy greeted its success.

With a "Sorry" upon her lips, she gazed into the blue eyes of the Unbeliever and drove the spear into his head. A shove sent the soldier flying backwards, wrapped in the arms of the gleeful Infected. Oily flames spurted and banefire wreathed the bottom of the wall, thankfully shrouding the scene below.

"Fuck," she said, and shook her head clear of any maudlin.

Turning away, she found herself surrounded by the remaining Unbelievers. She paused, not knowing what to expect, until one held out another spear. The Queen's Ranger took it with a nod of thanks, noting the fierce set to the woman's eyes. Today, their world had changed and there was no going back, however much the old scars hurt. The two cohorts returned to the centre of the wall, their thanks thrown over shoulders as their captain called them back.

Yanik walked away and took the lift, spinning the handle until she reached the foot of the wall. She strode out through the milling soldiers operating the weapons they had termed *artillery*, and on towards Lady Death, who waited impatiently before the Burners and their drawn swords. All the while, those blue eyes sat in her mind's eye, the fear and thanks in them as she condemned the Unbeliever to his death.

A penance, perhaps. Her father would be proud.

"No change?" asked Yanik, stating the obvious with a smirk she didn't feel.

"None. How's it looking out there?" Lady Death replied, the growl of more flames from the city walls greeting her words.

"Hard to tell. The banefire works, but these fuckers don't die straight away. And they climb so bloody quick. I have a creeping unease about it all. If the walls can hold out until the Union arrive, then there's hope we can cut the bastards down from the rear."

"Or the Unspoken and her dragon from the front, if we can rouse her. I need to get inside." Lady Death squeezed her hands together, raising them up as if to rail against the Burner standing in front of her. To her surprise, the guard sheathed his sword and moved towards Yanik.

"You stink," he said. "Of venom and hate. The same stench that rises from the far side of the walls."

Yanik wanted to step away. Avoid the foul creature that addressed her. Lady Death had described the Burners as being as far from human as the Infected battering at the walls. But she held her ground, thoughts immersed in the prayer stone of her father's House, and the flash of spiritfire he had wielded in the White Palace courtyard. The glowing, purple shield he'd shaped with a single thought as she watched poisoned blood fly towards him from a caged Infected. Maybe it wasn't so great in the Rangers, but she had the power of Death on her side.

"The same stench the Unspoken should be putting to a fucking end," replied Yanik.

"You, I trust. You are weak of spirit but strong of mind, unlike this bitch," said the Burner, a grin on his face as Lady Death flinched. "The Unspoken has no trust of a magus dressed as a priest. You may see, warrior. She stays here."

Yanik twisted her lips. "Been a funny fucking month, you know. My Lady?" she said.

"It's a start." Lady Death grasped Yanik's shoulder and gently pulled her around. "We need her out of there, Yanik. And soon. If what you describe happens again, then it only takes ..."

"One. Yeah, I know." She made to walk forwards when the Burner's hand landed briefly on her chest. Yanik knocked it away, a sneer on her face. The Burner returned a fearsome grin, and pointed to her sword and the quiver at her hip.

"Fuck me." Yanik undid the buckle of her sword belt, dropping the scabbard, followed by her bow and quiver.

"And the armour," said the Burner.

Yanik's eyes flicked to the sky as she tutted. She undid the clasps of her leather jerkin, dropping it to the ground. The inlaid plates clanged against the stone. Cold nipped at the exposed scars along her upper arm, and beneath her flapping tunic.

Lady Death flinched, her fingers reaching out, but not touching the old wounds. "Penance's House?"

Yanik grimaced. "For a while. I find prayer hard to come by now, mind you." She glanced over to the huge metallic dragon. "Got room for another in your flock?"

"Always."

"Yeah. It'd make my father happy, but it'd feel like a betrayal. And that runs too much in my family. Let's get on with this before my nipples fall off in the fuckin' cold, yes?" She glared at the Burner, who stood aside.

The dragon's scarlet chest shimmered, and Yanik tried not to think of its significance. Together with the Burner, she approached the red-scaled chest, expecting a door to open. But the Burner pressed onwards, and was half inside the chest when he beckoned her in.

"Fuck me backwards."

Yanik expected to clatter into the scales at any moment. Instead, she found herself in a room that smelled of dust and age. A pile of bedrolls and the detritus of army life were gathered around a strange artifice. It held similarities to the ornithopter the Unbeliever Rin had flown, but much smaller, more delicate. The Burner urged her on, and she entered a second room. At its centre was a plinth with a huge crystal inlaid. Curled up on the floor, in the same repose as the dragon, was a white-eyed monstrosity wrapped about a ragged ball of cloth. No, not cloth. There was a body inside, though it appeared dry and long-dead.

What did I do to deserve this?

Apart from being born to two of the most screwed-up people in the Union.

"So, what the fuck do you want me to do? Tickle her awake?" whispered Yanik, eyeing the husked hands and face of what she assumed was the Unspoken. She circled, keeping a body-length away out of habit. Eventually, Yanik could see straight into the white eyes. The orbs swirled like thunderstorms.

"What happened?" she said, looking to the Burner.

He appeared ill at ease, an unmistakable shift to his body language despite his stiff nature. His head tilted to the side slightly. "She was taken by the soul-lust. The magus triggered something within her."

"Soul-lust?" Yanik peered back at the body, trying to work out what in Seven Hells that could be.

The Burner adjusted his position, deliberately setting his back to the bundle upon the floor. There was a twitch to his eye that set a shard of fear in Yanik. "It is ... addictive," he said, and his eyes lit. Whitefire crackled over his face, flickering in and out of focus like two drawings super-imposed upon each other. Beneath, he appeared much as the Infected, though his skin was whiter. Dead. But the eyes held reason, thought. She took a step back, her hand reaching for an absent sword.

The Burner spread his hands wide. "I know what you see. Soon – if the memories the Unspoken shared with us about our creation are true – all the Burners will lose their glamours. I fear Anvil will collapse at that moment. Word will spread of who the Unspoken truly is, and hope will be lost. We must awaken the Unspoken from her stupor, and soon."

"So why me? Lady Death—"

"Is a magus. I know enough to understand it will not end well. You will need to be a conduit between the two."

"Oh, fuck off ..."

51

TO AWAKEN THE DEAD

The sword tip drove into a neck, severing the spine, releasing a poisoned soul into the ether. A final hoot died upon the lips of the Infected as the duke removed his boot from between its twitching shoulder blades.

The cavalry had split. Half were now dismounted, hacking at the injured stragglers who crawled and limped their way to the walls of Anvil. Occasional flares erupted from the city. The smell of banefire, oil, and the heady stench of burning flesh wafted across the crumpled grassy plain. The duke swore, raising his spyglass as one corner of the city wall blackened with climbing bodies, only for the fire to erupt again to prevent the breach. Unbelievers ran across the walls, taking up new positions whenever another of the pyramids began to build.

"Marshall!" The duke raised his hand and spun about. He was pleased to see the other half of the mounted cavalry heading his way. The officer at their lead pulled her horse close by, and was debating whether to dismount when she caught the duke's eye and merely lowered her head.

"Any word?"

"Major Demartis has a detachment of a hundred of the fittest, two hours away. The rest are still a day's march." The woman's face was stiff, the auburn hair beneath her helm twirling in the thermal breeze and the stink of death.

Panset nodded. "Thoughts?"

The officer looked across to the walls, blinking out the soot and ignoring the hoots as more wounded Infected died. "I fear the night," she said. "I don't think we can risk any approach after dark. Even setting up camp will cause issues." She wheeled her nervous horse around.

"Then we take a step back, recheck the area before nightfall, and camp in fours. Come first light, we resume."

The officer nodded and eyed the valley ahead. "It is too wide here if the horde breaks before the army arrives. If they turn back and head for an easier target, or whatever lured them here fails, we will be swamped even with a hundred new soldiers."

"If that happens, the Union is done. Pick a line, Marshall, and we fortify it best we can until the major arrives. Send word that he is to advance until he can seal the valley, and ready whatever Erin's Wrath he has. Dig spiked ditches and raised mounds, but be ready to attack on my word. Understand?"

Marshall nodded. "And if the dragon comes?"

"Then pray to the Seven that the Eighth keeps her word."

———

Lady Death held Yanik's face in her hands and stared into the woman's eyes, seeking an answer to her question.

"What are you not telling me? You are no priest, yet there is a flame in your soul. You cannot let go of Penance, yet you must embrace Death if we are to work together and awaken the Unspoken. The truth, Yanik. You have a wall harder and thicker than Anvil's." Lady Death's spiritfire danced along her fingers, her gentle touch one she frequently shared with her flock as they faced their fears of dying, of entering Death's veil. She could feel the reticence, as strong-willed as any.

"Don't you have secrets you want to keep, my Lady?" Yanik's hands embraced Lady Death's, waiting for those caring eyes to release hers. But to no avail. She let out a sigh when the silence broke her down. "I am the daughter of Meister Trizone."

Lady Death withdrew her hands, the sparkle of black spiritfire quenching as her lips parted. "You are High Lord Penance's child?"

"Do I look like a bloody child? I have been knee-deep in fucking death since I joined the Rangers, my Lady. Child no more. But I still can't let go of my birth House, or my calling, which he denied." Yanik gripped Lady Death's hands, placing them back on her cheeks. "Now I know why he had them turn me away. I see it in the bloody burdens you all carry. But I *need* my faith if I am to ... to cope with all this ... this shit."

"Knowing helps," said Lady Death, and she cupped Yanik's chin to lift her head back up. "Knowing the reason, I can try to work around it." She glanced towards the Unspoken. "Ready?"

Yanik nodded.

Lady Death eyed the Burner, whose faint nod she took as agreement. "Hold my hand, and place the other on the Unspoken's head. Whatever you do, don't let go, either physically, or when I take your soul."

"Take—"

Lady Death stretched her spirit, cursing the lack of a Wyrding Stone and the denial of her God's weapon as the roots in her mind and heart gripped tight. She poured into Yanik, sensing the trepidation mixed with dread of the creature she touched. Lady Death used a little of herself and the black spiritfire wrapped about the Ranger's spirit, shaping her soul into the conduit the Burner demanded. Together, in a much weaker form than when she and Lady Honour rode the veils, they eased towards the Unspoken, only for the barrier to the Eighth to remain strong, defiant, rejecting them both.

Lady Death let Yanik go, allowing her soul to spring back into heart and mind, when a touch caressed her spirit. Gentle, cold, but not uncaring.

'I can help,' whispered in her mind, *'though the Burners will not thank you.'*

"Who?" thought Lady Death, only for an image of a cold shell to enter her mind. A barrier, bonded much as the crystal armour the Constructors wore. One that deflected spiritfire. It thinned as it touched her spirit mind,

and Honour presented herself, entwined with a Schenterenta filled with a desperate yearning for a man called Laoch. *Sura.*

'Let me in. I know you are familiar with Honour, and she will help willingly. The Burners fear the Unspoken will wake to a magus and feed. That is where I come in.'

"Sura? But..."

The sensation along her skin was overwhelming, the hairs rising as the sliver of a God graced her body. It lacked the power of Death's weapon, yet the inner strength of Sura's *will* gave it a sense of certainty and confidence she could not deny. Lady Death opened herself up and Sura entered, gently tugging at her soul's roots, easing them out with a song that both thrilled and calmed her thoughts. She sensed Honour amid the elven spirit, but the two were as one – bonded. Together they surged into Yanik, letting her spirit rest, calming her mind and ensuring she maintained physical contact come what may.

Together, they entered the Unspoken. The wall of the Eighth's will still held firm as they swirled against it. Lady Death prodded and probed, seeking a weakness.

'Force will not gain you entry. Knowledge will,' said Sura, her spirit fading, thinning. She merged with the wall, leaving an outstretched, beckoning hand. Lady Death took it, and felt herself stretch as the bonds of her *self*, her *being,* loosened. A fear crept in, soon lost as her mind failed to hold the thought, only to reform on the other side as her *will* bonded her back together. A mountain valley spread before them. Lush and green, the sides aglow with an ever-rising dawn. A dragon roared – the trumpeting defiant, angry – to echo along the valley walls. Sura stepped forwards, a spear in hand, feet set firm in the lush grass as the scarlet beast rushed over the fruit-laden branches of a tree. Again the roar, this time accompanied by a gout of dragon's fire.

Sura waited, the spear held firm and high. Flame burst against her, and the elf, swathed in orange spiritfire, let the fire envelope her. Lady Death baulked, shocked at the loss of Sura. But Honour's light cut through the flames, a sheet of spiritfire that forced the dragon's flame into a seething ball that was drawn into Sura's spear. The elf twirled the weapon into a new position, a defiant smile upon her face as she spoke.

'The Unspoken is unfocused, in a haze. Senses a danger, but not what it may be.'

Sura crouched, waiting, until the scarlet dragon returned as it swept across the sky to her left. Whitefire raced along the dragon's tongue, but Sura leapt, not prepared to wait for the flame that was sure to follow. In awe, Lady Death watched the spirit slam into the beast's chest and disappear. Instinctively, her hands prepared a blackfire shield of her own. The dragon roared, neck twisting back, its flame forgotten as it searched for the elf. The wings became unsteady, their beat uncertain, and the head twisted to snap at its own forelegs in desperation.

The dragon's wings locked solid and no longer caught the air as it spun about. Lady Death rushed forwards in panic, running through the trees towards the distant palace as the air filled with heat and oil. A crash reverberated from behind, the screech of metal upon stone chasing her through the trees as shattered rocks bounced all around her.

On reaching the far edge of the copse, Lady Death looked back. Through a newly made gap, she spied Sura emerging from a twisted pile of scrap that swirled into a mass of chaotic whitefire before fading away on the mountain wind.

'*It is done,*' said Sura. And as she approached, the spirit held out her arms to envelope Lady Death. Wrapped about each other, they rode the wind to the glistening palace upon the valley side. In the glow of a permanent dawn, they entered the intricately carved doors to emerge into a throne room with wide, open windows that framed the sun. The Unspoken, her white eyes blazing, sat upon a spiked throne, its spears rising like compass points. A chaotic power roiled beneath her husked, bone-white skin, pulsing in a strange rhythm, twitching each muscle. A heartbeat that encapsulated her entire body.

'*Your turn,*' said Sura, and Lady Death strode forwards, a memory forming in her mind. That of the flame-haired Unspoken. Long, graceful fingers, smooth porcelain skin, the glint of malice to her ice-blue eyes. Her hand cupped the back of the Unspoken's neck and, with that imagery, she entered the chaos of the Eighth's mind. Lady Death shaped and formed the sludge, and amid the soul-lust, found its true cause: the hint of venom amid the spiritfire the Constructor had gorged upon.

"*Like Nesca, but more subtle. Hidden.*"

She reformed the ancient spirit, drawing out the poison, wreathing the evil in black spiritfire as she had seen Honour and Sura do. She had not the skill to save either Nesca or the Unspoken, but she could at least contain this poison long enough to enable the Eighth to emerge from her addiction. What happened next, she could not control.

Lady Death released her hand, and Sura was suddenly at her side, the spear once again held ready before her. The rhythmic pulsing stopped. The skin settled, changing, as if someone repainted the Unspoken as they watched. White eyes turned blue; the skin of her arms emerged pristine in a wave of porcelain white. As her body filled out, the horror of a desiccated Constructor was replaced by a stark, icy beauty. Eyelids fluttered, and long fingers gripped the metal armrests of the Unspoken's throne.

'*Time to leave,*' said Sura.

They wrapped about one another again, spirit on spirit, and left.

Lady Death released her grip upon Yanik, and the Ranger slowly awakened from her stupor. Lady Death moved, grateful to step away from the Eighth and her dreadful body, yet the coldness remained, a shiver running down her spine a reminder of Sura's presence.

"Come away," Lady Death said, guiding Yanik. "She will be disorientated when she awakens, and will not want to be seen."

The Burner stepped beside them. "I feel her stir," he said. "You have succeeded. But as the magus says, you should leave until the Unspoken is fully awake."

"Not a morning person, huh," stated Yanik, rubbing her aching hands.

Lady Death led the Ranger out of the room and onwards, through the shimmering rib cage of the metal dragon. Once past the outer ring of Burners, she looked back upon the scarlet-scaled dragon. Her arm hairs were still standing on end.

"Did you feel her?" asked Lady Death, facing Yanik. "The Ranger Sura? Did you sense her presence?"

"You mean there were more of you walking over my fucking grave? Hope she wiped her feet." Yanik smiled, but the grin dropped when Lady Death didn't return it. "You serious? Sura? Fuck me. Now you're going to say she's not dead."

"No, she has definitely left her mortal body. Did you know her?"

"Only by reputation – as fierce and angry as they come. Think she had a thing for Laoch, who must also be dead. You're not going to tell me he was dancing in my head as well? Now there was a man with a past. Shit, if he was here, he'd be chopping these bastards into mincemeat." She glanced over to the Burners, who were all stirring, half-looking back over their shoulders as An Chéad's chest scales rippled.

"The Unbelievers?"

"Them, but mainly the Burners. Going by what those on the city walls say, it was those bastards that did all the torture during the Crusade. They forced Laoch to kill his own brother, and his Spear. Burned them alive. If he was here, there'd be no fucking diplomacy to be had. Not even sure that effin' dragon would stop him." Yanik spat on the floor, suddenly wide-eyed as the beast's giant, scaled foreleg stretched out. "Hope you know what you're doing, my Lady. That is going to be one ancient evil with a giant fucking hangover – and a pissed-off dragon – that you just woke up. I seriously pray she really is on our side."

The dragon's head rose twenty feet into the air, the crystalline eyes aglow. The maw opened, exposing the rows of razor-edged teeth. A roar emanated from the depths of the beast's throat, and was greeted by a resonating cheer from across the city.

"Me too," said Lady Death. "I hope your father has it right, otherwise we may be swapping one ancient evil for another. Or getting both."

52
AT ODDS

Makalena, Brandshold

The Fleshmaster grimaced as the gunners whirled the brass wheels set on either side of the soul-cannon's rear, his expectation rising as the barrel dropped into position after making its way through the detritus of the broken city. The delay required to make the modifications to enable the mighty weapon to roll through the narrow city streets had tested his patience as the taste of victory rolled about his mouth. Yet, the artificers had brooked no argument. The soul-cannon was a necessity as they moved on to the next city, and therefore a precious resource, only replaceable with a return to the forges of Innealtóir. And so, to ensure they didn't damage it, the careful alterations required meant taking their time. They had worked tirelessly through the night, enhanced by the souls the Fleshmaster had supplied to keep them going.

But now...

The soul-cannon flared, and whitefire crackled across the encasement around its rear before surging along the shortened barrel. The first bolt exited the muzzle to whirl through the air, sending out arcs of lightning. The smell of ozone drowned the stench of death oh-so-briefly as the seething bolt lashed the doors of Makalena's House of Honour, the whitefire racing along the stone. Tarin's dead heart responded to the surge of his ancient spirit as his expectations reached their peak. The soul-energy petered out at the edges of the doors. The gunners wound down the soul-cannon and raised their goggles as they approached the huge doors. The Fleshmaster strode over, booted feet stomping up the marble steps as the artificers placed a strange box against the stone where the bolt had struck. In a fit of irony, they had aimed for Honour's head.

"Well?" he growled, hands gripped behind his armoured back.

The Inhibitor tapped the crystal window on the box, showing her compatriot, who shook his head. She eyed the emperor warily before speaking. "The stone resists," she said. "Like no other. Except, perhaps, that of your palace."

The Fleshmaster placed his hand upon the doors and contemplated using Tabharthóir once again, only for the admiral's face to seep into his mind, wearing that disrespectful glare she had so perfected, waiting for an opportunity to challenge.

"Could you make it work?" he asked, his dried tongue flicking out as he spoke.

The female gunner looked back at the adapted weapon, and biting at her lip, peered at the gap in the city walls above the rooftops. "We have a city full of whitefire, Emperor. Given time, I cannot see the stone resisting forever if we feed the soul-cannons enough. But it won't be quick."

"Take what you need," he said, and sent instructions to the Inhibitor pilots in charge of the feeders. *'The whitefire for the soul-cannon first, the* Kraken *second.'*

———

'Why? You need the Kraken *if you wish to move artifice and Inhibitors at any speed. This is fool—'* Lelion stopped, the flare from Tarin's eyes bringing her up short as they blazed in her brain.

The emperor sneered, letting his anger spill into the admiral's mind before squashing it. With a sigh, he sent his tempered thoughts through Tabharthóir's heartstone. *"It is a fool that leaves such power behind them. These Houses have a purpose. I believe them a store to power their veils. Imagine it, Lelion. Each House, flavoured with one of the seven Magi's specialties. Such spiritfire would gorge your* Kraken *and lead our army to victory."* The emperor deliberately set his features aglow with whitefire as he hovered in Lelion's mind. *"And with the losses of the Mechanised Inhibitor vanguard, we may have more need than you think."*

'My artificers have rebuilt four of the Scorpions,' Lelion replied petulantly. *'Delay could be dangerous and give the humans time to dig in, perhaps make more of their explosive weapons.'*

"I made no mention of delay. We will need to run the Kraken *on what you have gathered, unless you fear the damage suffered by your ship is too great?"* The emperor paused, his smile menacing. He carried on when Lelion didn't bite. *"We leave a force here to ensure the cannon can do its work and take the next city to feed your soulship. What word from your ornithopters?"*

'There are two southern cities. One on the eastern coast – smaller, lower walls, and a small standing army. A second, the pilots believe is the capital. Their walls are taller and stronger than this Makalena, and they envision a greater number of weapons along them. They have split their meagre army into three. One third is in reserve, the others guard the ways to each city.' Lelion sent the images the ornithopter pilots had shared, though the emperor sensed an unease – a gap in the information that he'd need to consider later.

"Then the path to victory is obvious, Admiral, is it not? You head north to this capital. Tabharthóir and I will scatter the army to the east, force them back to their meagre city to await their fate. Pitiful." The emperor's face twisted a little, eyes narrowing as he awaited the admiral incarnate's response.

'Agreed.'

The emperor stirred and shifted position, uneasy at how quickly Lelion had accepted moving on. Something was not right, but Lelion liked her games.

'What of the Schenterenta?' the admiral continued.

"As with all the other worlds except Apso, they appear meagre and ineffective. Popsilin has her orders, just in case. My worry is that we have not come across any of their more capable magi. Perhaps they await us in this capital city, in which case, the sooner we attack, the better."

'Then we agree, for once. I will make preparations to leave.'

The emperor ended the link and stepped back from the stone, anger and frustration milling about his thoughts despite the plan.

Always watching my own back can be so tiresome. When the Magi fall, and this realm is ours, a reckoning will be needed.

"*Tabharthóir*, rest. In the morning, we go to war."

—

"May I ask why?" asked Lieutenant Spintz, eyes locked on the outer deck.

Lelion knew the twitch at the corner of her mouth was a sign she awaited the admiral's ire. Her silence was deliberately painful as she stared out on the burning city against the night's deep black sky.

Fear holds you in thrall, as it does the rest who serve me. But for the power I offer ... I need unyielding loyalty.

Eventually, Lelion stirred, pushing herself away from the balustrade. "Because we will take this magus for ourselves, for my glory and the *Kraken*. With such a prize, we could make the repairs we need and still empower the engines. Strengthen our position should the emperor's eyes turn our way."

"You fear he will?"

The admiral incarnate nodded. "I would. It is our way, Spintz. I am a threat, as he is to me. There will be a reckoning, put on hold for hundreds of years since Apso-Tran. Only the hunt for the Magi has kept his mind from wandering my way – and his need for my soulship. What happens when it is no longer required, when we take this world and what remains of the Seven? You think he will share the Magi with me? No."

The admiral eyed the woman chained to the rail, the one she had been tasked with keeping alive by the emperor since he returned from Mondrein, and for no good reason that she could see. But she did taste so good. Lelion licked her lips. "I am sick of doing his bidding." She approached the sea captain. "And when he decides to crush me, Spintz, he will dispense with all of you. He will not risk your loyalty to me."

The admiral placed her hands upon the woman's neck, sliding them behind, drinking the fear in her eyes.

All the sweeter as she fears what I will do with her younglings.

The admiral smiled. "I will not be gentle with your children. Perhaps I will cast them to the crew. Would you like that?"

The woman's soul filled with agony.

The neck snapped. The thought of the emperor's anger thrilled Lelion near as much as the pained soul she drained from the dying body.

"Yessss. A reckoning. No longer will I be told what to do."

53

A King's Irony

Approaching Anvil, Handren Mountains, Brandshold

I t was that moment when life comes crashing in. When you knew the world would end, and that you would not live to see it.

Almost a relief. A release after the horrors of Jense.

The hoots silenced; the pyramids tumbled to the ground. No Infected cloyed at the stone or clambered over each other in a desperate need to get inside the walls of a tiring city. For two days the horde had fallen to the flame and spears of the defenders upon the wall. The barrages of javelins had pierced the Infected as regular as a meister's clock ticked, the banefire filling the air with choking ash and the constant stench of burning flesh and bone. But as the javelins lessened, and the banefire weakened, he feared for the city.

It only takes one.

The duke, the cavalry, and the one hundred or so tired soldiers who had rushed to the city's aid watched on as the horde paused. The whoosh of javelins fell silent, the twang of the trebuchets paused, and banefire did not pour. The scorched, scarred walls lay quiet, wreathed by smoke.

"Have they taken the city?" he whispered, not daring to believe it. He raised his spyglass, only to find tired Unbelievers upon the city walls. Their faces wore smiles, while they fell to their knees, wrapping their arms around one another. Tears flowed, but none screamed nor tore at flesh. The city endured.

Then, to the duke's horror, the horde turned their way.

White eyes flared. And the hoots rose once again.

Shouts echoed, cries of soul-pain and frustration borne upon the feet of the once-human horde. At first, Panset thought he imagined the rumble and the fear it induced, but soon understood that it was the pounding of feet, running their way.

Dread squeezed his fingers white against the brass of the spyglass. "Sound the retreat, Marshall!"

"Duke," said one of Yanik's Rangers, pointing back to the wall, his own spyglass still watching. "There!"

Panset raised his spyglass again, framing a waving figure upon the wall. A Ranger in Union garb, her hair tied back, hands signalling for him to look behind. The duke shook his head. Yanik. The irony. The woman whose survival he'd recently been ordered to ensure via the priest's message crystal was probably the safest of them all.

"Got one thing right," he said as he turned about.

A roar rolled over the cavalry as they prepared to mount. The horses reared, frothing at their mouths in fear as the soldiers fought to keep hold. The scarlet dragon swept over, its maw open, forked tongue hanging loose. The artifice dragon wheeled left, whitefire pouring from deep within its throat as it turned the first of the Infected to cinders.

The cavalry horn sounded retreat, and the riders forced themselves onto their terrified horses, calming the animals as more fire burst through the rising smoke. Those whose horses had fled were pulled aboard to ride pillion, and the cavalry began their withdrawal. Panset grabbed his own reins, his mind on the foot soldiers, who had not yet moved, their captain standing amid the ranks as the archers prepared their bows. By the time he was at their side, the dragon had turned back, more whitefire pouring from its maw to tear through the running horde.

The archers loosed, and Panset turned his horse about as Yanik's Spear followed the retreating cavalry.

"We retreat, Captain," he shouted above the roar of flame.

"We do not have the energy to run," replied the officer. "We stand and fight. What that creature misses, we will take down." More arrows flew as burning Infected emerged from the scorched grass. Some crawled, others limped, all were aflame.

But none can pass.

His scar itched in the heat while duty gnawed at his resolve. His need to lead, to see his soldiers to safety. But then he spied the priest, and Panset knew Fate called. Another sacrifice in the face of the Unbelievers. The duke dismounted and hauled the priest up from the ground as he tried to focus on his crystal.

"Go," the duke said, shoving the reins in the man's hands. "We need you safe." He drew his bow from the saddle and, not looking back, entered the defensive circle formed by the soldiers. Their weapons were light – broadswords and bows – their armour leather with a mere buckler shield as protection. But their hearts were stronger than any he had fought alongside. Whitefire flared amid the smoke and grime, though he didn't have time to contemplate the Unspoken as the hoots and screams rose in intensity.

Aim, loose, nock, and aim again.

Half the soldiers waited at the archers' sides, stepping out to chop and decapitate. Gore-covered blades despatched the once-human as they strove to feed. Those soldiers who fell to bites or scratches, the captain killed. Running from edge to edge, ending his own and letting no other do so while he had the strength to lift a sword.

And still they came.

As Panset loosed the last of his arrows, a cry went up. Archers, short swords in one hand, were pulling at the captain, dragging him back inside the circle as an Infected crawled up his legs. The bite was swift, teeth penetrating the woollen weave of his leggings. The duke dropped his useless bow and drew his sword as an archer ended the half-burnt Infected. Without thought, he split the captain's head in two. A sickness grabbed his stomach, a grief that threatened to overwhelm him. Yet more of the horde appeared from the fume-filled battlefield, uncaring for his inner pain.

"No," he whispered, watching as a soldier from the ring of sword and shields fell, soon followed by another.

A horn sounded, the thunder of hooves overriding the hoots, and from behind, the cavalry charged. Curved blades chopped from side to side, driving into the advancing horror. The duke knew the outcome. This was not an army to be battered under the hooves, nor parted for an army to pour through the breach. The Infected grabbed, scratched, bit and tore. The weight of their numbers bore the horses down and pulled the mounted soldiers from their saddles. For every five or six of the Infected despatched, a cavalry soldier rose, slavering in their place. Hungry, and needing to sate the pain in their souls.

"To me! To me!" Panset shouted, and the remaining soldiers pulled in tighter. Shoulder to shoulder, stabbing and slashing at limbs, neck and head. Those of the cavalry that had survived the first charge formed their own small circle, but were soon swallowed beneath the mass of flesh that pressed in.

The duke assumed the role of the captain, killing those that fell, ending the possibility of a soldier turning on their own. As he chopped down into the fifth, Marshall stood before him. A livid cut spliced her face, her nose hung ragged, bite marks upon her cheek and shoulder. Her clawed hands slashed at him, aiming for his grip on his sword. The nails raked his glove, and the duke stepped away, eyes beseeching the soft leather to be in one piece. Blood lay there, whether Marshall's or his, he could not tell, with his hands numbed by what felt like hours of combat. Marshall took another stride in. The soldier at her side drove a short sword into her hip. An arrow flew over Panset's shoulder, the Ranger's fletching spiralling the tip into the officer's forehead. Panset reeled backwards as the white eye burst, tearing the glove from his hand.

Beneath, blood welled from a cut as the soldiers about him fell under tooth and nail.

Panset grabbed the pouch he'd been saving, clutching the bag above his head. As the horde crashed in, he smashed the pot bombs upon the blood-covered ground, praying to Justice that one would ignite.

Metal wheels rolled over the field of burning corpses, crushing limbs, shattering dead spines as steam rose from its chimney. The artifice rolled onwards with three more behind, each powering their way through the piles of the dead. Ballistae swung on top, their heavy quarrels occasionally released to strike those bodies that twitched or crawled to the sides, while the wheels ended those in front.

Onwards the machines chugged, wreathed in the ash and smoke. Above, An Chéad flew in ever decreasing circles over one spot upon the battlefield. The lead artifice turned that way, leaving the others to scour for any of the Infected that remained. Eventually, the metal dragon landed, and the steam cart waited until the dragon's fire made the area safe before pulling up alongside. The hatchway opened, and the Unbeliever soldiers exited, soon followed by Yanik and Lady Death, her black robe crumpled.

"Fuck me," said Yanik, eyeing the metal dragon, its scales dull amid the smoke and ash.

The chest swirled and shimmered, and the flame-haired Unspoken strode out. She scanned the circle of dead Union soldiers, her face set hard before she wrinkled her nose. "Your ex-king lies beneath. Though I think you will find little left but his ring."

Lady Death glared at the Eighth and made towards the pile. Yanik pulled her back and pointed towards the horizon and the Union banners that pierced the sky. "That's your job," she said. "Making sure none leave this fucking furnace. Leave the duke to me."

"I—" started Lady Death, but caught Yanik's eyes, red-rimmed and angry. "Okay."

"Your army is being careful, destroying any of these Infected they come across," said the Unspoken, indicating towards the Union banners. "My people will do the same. When they meet, they do so as allies, Lady Death. At least, until the emperor has fallen."

The Unspoken smiled, the leer fearful, and re-entered the scarlet dragon. With a trumpet to the fluttering, ash-filled sky, the mighty artifice leapt into the air. Heavy wingbeats drove the charnel stench across the death-filled valley floor.

"You catch that? Until the fucking emperor has fallen. I don't trust that bitch, pardon me saying," Yanik whispered, glancing over her shoulder at the two Unbeliever soldiers who waited beside the steam cart. She threw them a smile. "And if she releases the Burners anywhere near our army, it'll be an end to any bastard alliance. Just sayin'." Yanik turned away, and used her spear to dig at the remains.

Lady Death pulled at her robe, her heart heavy, and turned back to the chugging steam cart. It would cause a stir amid the approaching army, and especially with Major Demartis. One glance up to the sky, however, put paid to any deeper concerns. If they were still approaching with a thousand years of representative evil in the sky, then a steam cart was probably at the bottom of their list.

"I'll need to be up top," she said as she approached the guards.

Yanik appeared beside her, hand held out. She pressed the duke's ring into Lady Death's palm and looked away, wiping a hidden tear as she entered the cart.

54
SOLACE

ERSTENBURGH, BRANDSHOLD

The queen's breath billowed in the sharpness of the spring morning, dragon's breath that rose and expanded above Erstenburgh's walls to merge with that of her city guard. The faint memory of a nightmare slipped from her mind – a lake filled with the blood she had shed, the souls of those she had forsaken. She ran her hand over her chin and up to the bridge of her nose, attempting to squeeze the image away. It refused to leave.

Captain Mordant stood at her side, one hand resting on his pommel, the other slipped into the scabbard's strap.

"My queen," he said, eyes fixed on the north road and the dancing pennants of General Zendril's army that marched towards the city. "You could not have known from which direction the attack would come. You cannot blame yourself."

Queen Weister shrugged and rested both hands on the city parapet. "I hold no blame. There is not the time, Captain. The Infected were a far greater initial threat to the Union than the Constructors to the south." She turned to face Mordant, brushing an errant lock of hair out of the way. "Mandrich was the right choice. Tactically astute in terms of open war, defensively minded, and not afraid to sacrifice his soldiers if he could gain advantage. But against such beasts as my mother and the duke have faced, he would have been unable to grasp the impact of failure. No chance to withdraw and lick your wounds when the injured rise to lick them for you. Lose the battle, you lose the war."

"Then?"

Queen Weister blew out a slow breath, watching as the last dregs of the northern army rolled up with their supply carts and piles of cut wood. "All we can do is buy time in the hope our ancient enemy keeps a bargain, Captain. Or run, abandon the cities and spread my subjects across the north and prolong the hunt. I see little hope in either option. But that is between you and me. Where General Zendril's thoughts lie with this is what truly concerns me."

"I will follow your command to the end, my queen. As will all that guard Erstenburgh."

And I fear, Captain, that the end is closer than you think.

"By your leave," he said, cheeks reddening.

The queen waved Mordant on, knowing the urgency of sorting and organising the needs of the five thousand soldiers, the majority of whom would be camping amid the killing field around the castle, with a few to be billeted in hastily built wooden quarters in the palace grounds.

Queen Weister and her honour guard walked along the castle wall, watching as the many layers of the army's hierarchy organised the soldiers and their equipment into campsites. She had studied, under Sneed, the processes of how to keep an army moving, motivated and, above all else, ready to fight. So many factors to consider, none less than the predictable nature of boredom and fear. The constant waiting, stretching out endlessly before you, suddenly punctuated by a rapid call to arms and the potential of facing death.

And her mother, the great General Zendril, who had added humanity to her organisation. Demanding discipline, but in turn understanding what being a soldier really meant. A strange blend of pride and duty. Many of those below had faced the aftermath of Jense with neither rest nor time to heal from the horrors she had merely glimpsed in a crystal.

The queen reached the lift on the western wall, and took the opportunity to descend with her honour guard by her side. There, her carriage waited alongside the mounted guards.

"Calmly," she reminded the driver.

She stepped inside and sat where she could be seen through the window. As the pair of grey horses trotted towards the makeshift camp, each soldier or labourer who got out of their way, or gawped from the side of the road, received a glance. A moment of being seen by their queen. Being aloof, a symbol of power for her subjects, was for another time, another place. These were scarred soldiers, and the honour was hers.

Just off from the centre of the rapidly widening camp, a large tent flew the pennants of the Union, Erstenburgh and Ridth. The carriage pulled up. The foot servant dropped the steps while her honour guard stood waiting. In her newly made uniform, the Overseer stepped out of her carriage. Seven coloured bands formed the thick belt from which her plain scabbard hung, each marked with the sigils of the Seven in silver. About her throat, the seven-pointed star of her office lay against the lapel of deep blue cloth. On her head, a simple circlet was laced into her hair.

She strode through the chipped bark in her black, leather boots to rest upon the rough mat at the entrance to the general's tent. The flap flew back, Mander taken aback as he unexpectedly faced his queen, while all about, the soldiers had paused in their duties to gawp.

"My queen," he said, caught between a kneel and a bow.

"You dare kneel, Mander, and I will make use of this sword, ceremonial or not." She waited. Mander's lips curled into a smile before he bowed his head and looked back over his shoulder. "She suffers doubt. Jense ... the Unspoken. Zendril needs a purpose, my queen, with certainty. An enemy she can grasp."

"As do we all, Mander. Lead on." The general's consort nodded, turned about and pulled aside the inner curtain. "General," he said, standing to attention. "The queen."

General Zendril leaned against a sturdy, wooden table. A map was laid out in front of her, stones keeping the corners pressed down. One glance was enough for the queen to turn back to Mander and her waiting guards.

"Leave," she said. Her gaze expected no argument. She waited until they left before approaching her mother, whose stiff posture and tired eyes spoke for her. "Go ahead. They are not here. You can rant and rave all you want. Get it off your chest."

Her mother shook her head and glanced down at the waiting chair. "As this appears to be a family chat, are we dropping any formalities, my queen?"

"Sit," she replied, and her mother dropped onto the chair. Erin took up her own while brushing down her uniform breeches. "Get on with it, and then we can deal with what needs to be done."

Zendril tentatively reached out, her rough fingers stroking the Overseer's pendant, and shook her head. "Seven lies, not Seven Houses," she said quietly. "And now you lie with the Eighth. The greatest deceit of them all." Her mother ran her fingers along each of the points before she eased back into her chair.

Queen Weister adjusted the pendant, making sure it sat where it felt most comfortable.

"Panset is dead." Zendril's eyes filled with tears. "That bastard went and got himself killed to make me feel even fucking worse."

"Dead?"

"My pet priest just got word from Major Demartis. He held the line when the horde turned away from Anvil's walls. Died beside his soldiers." The general sighed and clasped her hands together to contemplate her palms. "Should have been me."

"No, it should not. And though I grieve him, Mother, what news of the Infected?"

"The Unspoken's dragon burned them to ash. Eventually. Lady Death was there. Speak to her. My words will be coloured by ... by ... I don't know what to feel, daughter." Zendril's' eyes left her hands, and she glanced up. "How are you able to function amid all these lies?"

"Just as you did when you first decided to remain an officer. You stood against my father until he bent to your will and agreed to continue your commission. Strong, stubborn, and loved." Erin leant forwards, placing her hands into her mother's. "You raised me to be what I am. To be queen, to stand strong against the tide and bend with the wind."

"The latter was Sneed and your father," replied her mother, a slight smile lighting her face. "I'll take credit for your backbone, though." She squeezed her daughter's hands, and their eyes met. "Tell me you are doing the right thing. That the Unspoken and her bloody dragon will stand with us. I need to believe."

"If you want certainty, High Lord Penance believes it. And the fact Lady Death and Demartis still live are proof enough the Unspoken has restraint. Beyond that, I can give no assurances. Just belief that, despite all their machinations, the Seven Houses are truly acting to save us from the Constructors.

"Makalena fell in just over a day. A day, Mother. Mandrich and Lord Justice have given them a smack, but no more. They are coming for us, and whatever sliver of hope we have, I will take. Even ... even if it costs my soul to do it."

Her mother's eyes widened, and she released a hand to touch her daughter's cheek, catching the single tear. "Mine first," she replied, taking the queen of Brandshold's Union in her arms. "They will have to strip the spirit from my body before I let you fall."

The queen stood at the edge of the great table, the beauty of its map and the detailed models laid before her, reflecting on all that vied for attention in her mind.

"I can set defensive lines here, along Maclin Ridge to the southwest," General Zendril said, pointing a long stick towards the outer edge of the forest. "It's the only rise on the approach to the city. Low, but enough to give us some advantage. Mandrich has split his army three ways for mobility, with the mounted troops stationed between. I can see the logic. He intends to harry rather than face them head on."

"They can just fly over," said Lord Hope. "We planned for a dragon, not a sky ship. If they wanted, they could just bypass any army and attack the cities."

"But that would leave thousands of soldiers at their back. Whatever happens, they want to feed off *people*. To do that, they will need their army on the ground. From what's been reported, the sky ship is ailing at the rear. If that is the case, they will not ignore any force capable of attacking it from behind." Zendril put her hand to her chin, eyes poring over the map. "That includes Mandrich's soldiers on the route to Ridth. If the sky ship is heading here, where is the dragon heading?"

"You think towards Ridth?" asked Lord Fate, pulling back the sleeves of his blue robes as he leaned towards the coastal city. "Does it make sense to split their forces?"

"It's a dragon," cut in Lord Wisdom. He tapped a book he had carried from the Forbidden Library. "It can go where it wants, when it wants. All our histories point to the Constructors as hunter-gatherers who turned to farming. They want to herd us in and beat us down until we surrender. I have been buried in the library since our queen talked of abandoning the city. I am no tactician, and the thought of leaving everything behind galls me to my very soul. But ..."

"Abandon?" said the general, immediately looking to the Lord before turning to the queen. "Why?"

"They want us trapped. To think we are safest behind our walls when, in fact, we have built our own prison. A present wrapped up in a little bow," replied the queen, casting her eyes to the table. "If we abandon the cities, run to the plains, the forests, even the Handren mountains, then we force them to expend time and energy on the hunt."

General Zendril leant on the table edge, fingers spread, lips moving as she spoke each city's name in turn. "And Ridth?"

"If we are right," cut in the High Lord, "what do you think the dragon would do?"

Zendril blinked and walked around the table until she came to rest nearest her home city. Her treatise on its defence had been her pride and joy, but dragons and sky ships were never part of the plan. "Fuck me, I'd drive the army inside the walls. Seal them in. You wouldn't even need to wait around, just the threat would do it. Once inside, you narrow any escape routes."

"And attack from the sea," whispered the queen, her thoughts on the prince consort. "If they had such ships."

"Not ships," said Zendril. "If I was a dragon, I would burn the bastard fleet to ash. A fucking prison, indeed."

"Do we have contact with Ridth? The Houses?" said an agitated Lord Fate, who rose from his chair, unable to keep still. "We must warn them."

"No," said Queen Weister, her eyes aflame. "We need them to stay, to hold the city and their dragon's attention. We need time to empty the north. They must stay behind their walls while we waste the Constructors' time and resources hunting us."

"And what if they turn back? Decide Ridth is easy prey?" added Lord Fate.

"We need to offer them something more desirable. Something the emperor can't resist." The queen glanced to High Lord Penance, whose grimace and brief nod confirmed their agreement. A daughter for a diversion.

Lord Wisdom glowered then, his balled fists pressed against the table. "You mean us? The Seven? You want to use us as bait?"

"A lure, only if their eyes turn back to Ridth," said the High Lord. "Am I right, Overseer?"

"Only if needed. We must plan for every eventuality, and such a distraction may give Ridth a chance."

55
TO CAGE A PEOPLE

Metallic skin bulged as the huge wings beat downwards, catching the air, pushing the veil dragon on towards the rising, green hills. Below, a ribbon of road crossed a muddy-looking river that wound its way between fields and open grassland. The silver-blue dragon snorted, mirroring its master, who watched the spring day pass by without thought or care.

The seeking swept back into Tabharthóir's heartstone, the pulse of whitefire attracting the emperor's attention from his musings on Lelion, and the ease with which the admiral had agreed to attack the north. The seeking crept into his thoughts, and he placed his hands upon the heartstone, filling his mind with Tabharthóir's spirit-sight.

The main road split and reformed ahead as it passed a village. The glow of life filled the emperor's mind and Tabharthóir stirred, thoughts of feeding impinging on the Fleshmaster's musings.

"Patience," he said aloud as he focused ahead. "All will come to us in good time."

The hills closed in, and with them, the weaving valleys that protected the city beyond. It was from high on either side of these vales that the spirit-sight declared the presence of humanity. Of food. Waiting to be dominated, to have their future shaped to the emperor's will. He guided the dragon to head south and, dipping a wing, they wheeled about.

"Now," he said.

The Spirit Walker's response was filled with desire as it trumpeted into the sky. With the glow of appetising souls afire in their spirit-sight, the dragon's tongue sparked, and the whitefire lit. They dived, and the spirits below bubbled with fear and dread. These emotions wove their way into the waiting souls, and eager dragon fire flowed over the throng. Screams echoed in Tabharthóir's ears, the pain of the burning thrilling the Spirit Walker, urging it to feed. Tarin wrestled back control while taking joy in the maelstrom of fire and death below. He commanded Tabharthóir onwards, to rise high above the valley, to be *seen* and *feared*. Once achieved, the dragon dropped again, wings tight against the metal-scaled sides, more flame hurtling downwards to wreathe the other side of the valley. As smoke rose and meat cooked, the mighty wings spread wide, caught the heat and brought the dragon to a stop as he crashed amid the burning. The dragon's teeth crunched bone and sinew while metal scales resisted sword strokes and spear tips to gorge on the dead and dying. Spirits spiralled along its body, filling the heartstone before spreading wide to fuel wire and cog. With another roar, the metal beast thundered into the air and rose above the destruction.

"Yes," said Tarin, who swiftly built walls around his rising lust as the Spirit Walker gorged. "We have a purpose, Tabharthóir, beyond that of feeding. Calm yourself."

The dragon beat at the thermal rising from the fires, cutting across the heat to emerge amid the next valley. Heavy quarrels flew, their tips exploding against her metal scales. Blue spiritfire spat and arced across the dragon's chest, seeking a way inside. Others flew wide, while one pierced the dragon's outer wing. Under Tarin's orders, Tabharthóir dropped low with a roar. More javelin-like quarrels sailed their way. One glanced off a foreleg, the sting of the strike causing the dragon to flinch, but no more. He drew his taloned feet forwards and, on cresting a rock formation, the razor-edges tore into the ballistae beyond. Wood and blood splattered the rocks, and the dragon's tail lashed as the soldiers behind spun their primed weapons to attack. Spikes ripped the thick ropes, parted flesh, sent the metal javelins flying harmlessly into the distance. The dragon bit down and severed the running soldiers' heads from their bodies, drinking their spirits before once again leaping away. Blood trailed in Tabharthóir's wake to splatter the ground in a drum beat that signalled defeat.

Horns blew to signal a retreat, but the emperor had already called Tabharthóir away. "We cannot kill them all. They are food, no more than that. But it is always wise to ensure you have plenty of your herd left to breed."

The huge metal beast surged through the smoke and ash, silver-blue death leaving terrified victims to run for their lives.

Go and seek the sanctuary of stone walls to quiver behind until your new master finally comes knocking.

"Ah," he said as Tabharthóir's spirit-sight pierced the billowing smoke to spot a thin line of yellow spiritfire spurt north from the valley below. "A calling, as I saw in the magus's mind. They use a crystal to focus. Ah, they know now what we do, but not what we do next. End it, Spirit Walker."

And Tabharthóir roared, and a blanket of spiritfire spewed forth to shroud the sky and dissipate the magus's calling before he wheeled away.

⸻

"You are to withdraw." Antar peered into the crystal she had paired with a priest in the House of Hope. "Return to Erstenburgh. The War Council want you at their table."

Lord Justice looked to the blackening clouds. The sky ship of brass and whitefire blotted out much of the sky as it made its way above the village. The sight galled, though the buildings had been emptied of life by Mandrich's soldiers just hours beforehand. It appeared like the model on the War Council table, impossibly small beneath the Constructors' ship that trailed menacing, hooked chains, snagging any life that had not run from its path. Be it cow, bird or human, it did not care. They hung, impaled upon the hooks, twitching as the very life was drained from them.

"You're not going, are you?" Antar said as her hand ran along her horse's neck to calm the snorting animal.

"I need you to go, to explain what you've seen. Take my place." Lord Justice brushed away the rain that ran down the lip of his helm. "Be my second, with the seneschal as your hand and eyes. Protect my House."

Antar patted her horse again, pulling at the mare's ears as the palomino whinnied in fear. "You are sending me away while you stay to die."

"There is no Justice if I am not here. I cannot let the remaining priests-in-waiting fight alone. What Lord of Justice would I be? The burden is yours. If I do not return, the seneschal has a letter for you, and the High Lord is always ready to help each who take on the mantle of a House." His eyes had not left the sky ship, certain he could feel the malevolent presence aboard watching him back. He dropped his eyes to his own horse before turning to meet Antar's gaze. "You still here?"

"Stubborn man," she replied, and pulled the jittery horse's reins about.

"Lord. I'm a stubborn Lord. And I believe I just made you my replacement," he smiled. "A bit soon, but war does that."

Antar urged her horse away, refusing to look back. She spoke to each of Justice's waiting on the way past. Reaching the last one, she leant over and wrapped them in her arms before taking her leave.

Lord Justice looked along the line of the depleted army, smelled the fear and dread the sky ship instilled as whitefire crackled beneath its hull, spewing lightning into the cold evening. Burnt air caught his nostrils upon a suddenly warm wind that carried with it the sound of metal limbs. He peered across the churned fields, punctuated by the regimented stone of the southern Queen's Road. The slope was minimal, not enough to give them an advantage, and certainly not enough for the remaining battlecarts to be deployed in the same way. The Scorpions rounded the edge of the village. Nearly as tall as the houses' eaves, they scuttled by, tails waving ominously as they bypassed the village.

"Shit," said Lord Justice, and he looked along the clanking line of soldiers, seeking the signal flags that still indicated to hold.

The first eruption tore the wooden beams and thatched roof from a rear house, initiating a cascade throughout the village. The mechanised Scorpions leaped a good five yards to the side to land with claws ready, bulbous windows towards the burning village.

"It failed," he said, taking little joy from the few Constructors whose bodies had been tossed into the air. "They sent in their foot soldiers first."

His horse stamped its forehooves, chomping at its bit as the scent of oil and smoke rolled over. Two priests-in-waiting arrived by his side, the remainder of his guard, as ordered by the queen. He looked over his shoulder, and was pleased to see the rest of the waiting had left to join their designated cohorts.

Two of the flags dropped, repeated down the line of soldiers, and a third rose. Whips cracked, and the cohorts parted, the squeals of fearful horses filling the air. Battlecarts hurtled between them, four horses hauling each of the weighty transports as their drivers lashed and shouted at the frightened animals. Six carts, and at least ten targets. Not good odds.

Lord Justice heard the roar go up, the beat of sword and spear upon shield as the flags changed. The first wave of arrows sailed overhead towards the Constructors' foot soldiers, who emerged from the smoke. This close, he could see them pounding through the fields and along the road, buckler shields on one arm, an array of glowing weapons in the other hand. The arrows fell like bloody murder. Those with crystal tips flashed as they struck, while those with baskets filled with Meister Kinst's alchemical concoctions exploded. Some of the rampaging army staggered, but few of the Constructors fell, their black armour having reflected the spiritfire or absorbed the hit.

A wave of Constructors took to their knees as one, their long weapons pointed towards the carts. Flashes sparked and horses screamed, dying as whitefire exploded in chests or heads. They stumbled, dragging those that lived down with them, and the carts smashed into the chaos. Erin's Wrath tore through the empty battlefield, the shattered metal armour of the carts shredding little but horsemeat and the flesh of the drivers. The eruptions' echoes rolled like a miasma over the waiting soldiers near to Lord Justice, and hope drained into the churned earth.

The kneeling Constructors raised their bucklers, and a second rain of arrows clashed against crystal plate or steel shield. A few fell, impaled through gaps or lucky strikes. But then they turned the long weapons upon them, the flash of explosive powder haloed against black-clad bodies. Union soldiers died along the line, bones shattered, limbs smashed, while whitefire pierced their armour and ended their cries as it burnt inward.

The heavy stone that was Lord Justice's heart broke and anger boiled out, a lava he could no longer contain. He didn't see the Union flags change above the dead and the dying, but amid the haze, it was the urgent shouts of the charge that spurred him on. His horse spurted forwards. Along his left arm, a round shield bearing Justice's sigil. In the right hand, the maul he so wished contained his God.

Amid the smoke of the battlecarts and the blazing village, a Constructor stood in his path. Shouts and cries echoed across the battlefield, punctuated by clashes of metal upon hardened stone, yet still Lord Justice kept his focus. His horse's hooves beat the ground as he charged, and when the Constructor looked his way, it was far too late to raise their long weapon. Lord Justice's maul shattered both helm and the skull inside. A flash of whitefire enveloped his weapon before dissipating into the ether.

A crack resounded nearby. The Lord turned to see the flash of a quarrel swirling his way. He yanked on the reins, only for the shaft to drive into the horse's withers. A bright flash ensued, and the stink of burning horse flesh assaulted his nose. His horse reared in pain and fear, and as its hooves regained the ground, the animal collapsed, throwing Lord Justice forwards. He tucked his head and arms inwards, denying the urge to stretch out and protect himself. The leather and plate armour along his neck and shoulders absorbed the blow, and he rolled amid blood and soil to land, filth-covered, upon his back.

He moved instantly. A sword cleaved the ground where he had lain. Scrambling amid the shattered crystal armour, his hand clasped the dead Constructor's weapon. Lord Justice rolled onto his back and raised it as a barrier. The Constructor's sword slammed into the metal barrel, and the vibrations loosened the Lord's grip. He kicked out. Both feet smashed into the ankles of his assailant. The Constructor toppled forwards, sword slashing at Lord Justice as he flung himself to one side. The sword's edge bit at his helm and sheared off the metal guard. His soul shivered, a tug at its root that instilled a sudden fear. To the soldiers who fought at his side, these were simply the enemy. To a Lord of the Seven Gods, these were the soul-eaters. And one had so nearly taken a bite.

He rolled back and rammed his fingers into the Constructors neck, between the throat guard and helm. Husked skin, dry, cold and unyielding, lay beneath, and he poured his hate-filled spiritfire into the creature. The inside of the helm lit scarlet, and fire and flame poured from the eye slots as the white eyes boiled.

Lord Justice pulled himself away, anger urging him to stand and drag his bloodied maul from the ground. The battle raged about him, humans fighting soul-eaters face-to-face. So few of his fellow soldiers still stood. A sudden fear prickled at his neck, and he spun about. A metal limb slammed into the earth, followed quickly by another and another. Bulbous glass eyes stared his way, the snap of twinned claws indicating its intent. He took a step backwards and raised a hand. Redfire wreathed his fingers. The bolt, swirling, sparkled a scarlet that lit the ground as it sizzled through the air. It rammed into the left-hand claw, shearing the lower blade. With glee, he raised his other hand, and his writhing hate appeared in a ball of angry redfire. He threw it towards the Scorpion. One bulbous eye shattered under the assault, the crystal shards tearing into the white-eyed face inside, shredding skin, piercing one eye. But the lips beneath that eye grinned, and the creature yanked the lever in its hand. The metal tail whipped downwards, and crashed into Lord Justice's shoulder as he attempted to dodge. Lord Justice felt the bones shatter, the surge of pain overwhelming his senses as he hit the ground. A squeal of metal signalled his expected end. The agony was too much as a weight landed on his back, shoving him into the blood-soaked ground. The metal limb pressed harder, forcing the air from his chest. Unable to suck in a breath, panic assailed his mind. Redfire banked within, raging, ready to spew forth, to deny the Scorpion victory, when a boot crashed into his head and the world spiralled into oblivion.

—

"We have one," whispered Lelion, hands wringing as she watched the pathetic human resistance from the *Kraken*'s deck. "Victory tastes so sweet."

56
WHEN DUTY CALLS

ERSTENBURGH, BRANDSHOLD

"Captain? It is time," Queen Weister said, looking across the killing field and the trees beyond at the shadow that loomed in the southern sky. "We have done what we can."

"My queen, please, I beg you to leave."

She squeezed her fingers hard against the cold stone of Erstenburgh's walls, her neck flushing red. She glared at the man, but he had already turned away, knowing her answer.

"Close the gate!" ordered Captain Mordant, and watched as the last straggler was shoved out from under the portcullis. "Now!" He got down onto his haunches and ran a hand over first his sweaty neck, then through his greying hair. He flinched when a soft hand fell upon his shoulder.

"I either leave here as a victorious queen or in a box of *my* choosing. Either way, my soul is mine, Captain. I serve my people best by being here."

The captain stood, blinking away his emotions. "The Seven Houses ..."

"They believe the Constructors come solely for them. But the Constructors have an army to feed, and for that, they come for our people. We both know the power of a figurehead, Mordant. It works both ways. A rallying point, one we can use to steel our soldiers against the darkness.

Our task is to delay, to let as many of our subjects fade into the forest and the Union as possible. To hide, buy time. Maybe this Laoch will come, or some other miracle. But you and I are practical people, Captain. What will happen if I live? What will the people do?"

"Rally to you."

"Come together and become an easy target. Sheep ready for the slaughter." The queen turned back to stare at the closing shadow, and licked her lips as another appeared beside it, wings beating. "We are to defend to the last, even if I have to stand with shaking sword in hand before their emperor to buy a single second. But promise me this, Captain. Do not let them eat my soul, meagre as it is. That, I could not abide."

Shouts echoed from below – the gruff voice of a meister's complaints about lowering the portcullis, accompanied by Mander's calmer requests that it be kept closed. Erin smiled to herself and shook her head while taking the lift down. Her honour guard accompanied her, leaving Mordant to walk the walls. He would be checking for the hundredth time that the artifices were oiled, and as ready as the soldiers under his command.

"Why are you still here?" Erin asked Meister Kinst as she exited the lift. "Your queen and Overseer has given you your orders to leave."

The meister bowed her head, chuffed, and flicked her eyes to the sky. The small horse beneath her was jittery as it halted on the stone floor.

Mander, clearly annoyed at the meister's reticence, spoke up. "Perhaps you could ensure this one does as she is commanded?"

Erin raised an eyebrow and returned her gaze to Meister Kinst, who squirmed. She kept her regard upon the meister, and the woman eventually sat up straight in her saddle.

"My queen, there is call for my services. Rangers have come across something in the forest. Greeth is not here, so I must—"

"And where is Seneschal Greeth? She was to stay and support the defences. Ensure the crystals and Erin's Wrath were ready," Erin replied, uneasy at the meister's words.

"Meister Kinst sent her away," said Mander. "That's another reason we are arguing. She sent Greeth in her place. My soldiers guided the seneschal out an hour or so ago, with a cart full of books and equipment."

"My research," said the meister. "It needs to be saved should the city fall."

"Which *you* were supposed to rescue by heading to Pantsil, not Greeth, who should remain with her House." Erin glared at the meister.

Kinst flinched. "The forest. I am needed."

"A lie," cut in Mander. "And a poor one. No one has called for you, Meister. One of the Ranger Spears is guiding families to the east, my queen. Meister Kinst seeks to join them, leaving us to our fate."

Red-faced, Meister Kinst looked away and harrumphed. "I am not a coward, my queen. It's the grand meister." She looked back at Erin. "Under High Lord Penance's orders, we set a trap, as you know. But in all this furore, no one has checked on her in a few days, maybe a week. There are others there – priests, some of the soldiers..."

"Yet I have just seen the Constructor's dragon from the walls, Meister Kinst," replied the queen. "We have need of your knowledge."

"Exactly. Arknold needs to know."

The queen grimaced and adjusted the Overseer's pendant before she looked the meister in the eye. "No. As you have seen fit to make yourself indispensable, you stay and help defend my city."

"My qu—"

"No, Meister!" Erin bellowed. The yard before the southern wall fell into instant silence. "Everyone who remains is here to defend the Union and this city until the very last – including *me*. You are one among many, as is the grand meister. We thank you for all you have done, but your duty is not at an end. Now, return to your role. War is coming, and you will wield your science as the Seven wield their faith."

Kinst flinched and shook her downcast head before turning her horse back the way she had come. The queen huffed, exhaling a long plume of dragon's breath that rose on the cold spring air.

"And why are you here?" Her harsh words were accompanied by a glare directed at Mander.

"Honestly, Your Majesty? General Zendril sent me to find out why this Greeth had left. In truth ..."

"She hoped you'd be trapped here, and that I'd send you away with some of my people. Ensure that you lived."

Mander nodded.

"Open the portcullis!" the queen shouted before turning back to Mander. "I thank you, and the general, for your service to the Union and the Crown. Choose your own path."

"My queen," replied Mander. He bowed his head, then urged his horse towards the gate, and exited beneath the still-rising portcullis. His horse trapped neatly over the stone bridge beyond before heading south towards the general.

Erin's lips twisted briefly, holding back a sudden and overwhelming awareness of Mander's love and loyalty. Annoyed at herself, and how such weakness could be viewed, she reset her expression and looked along the central street towards the Houses of the Seven.

"My carriage," she said. "We go to Penance's House."

The tap of the cane echoed through the chamber while the allocated priests-in-waiting who remained inside cleared up the blood and flayed skin of the last mass before they sealed the House. High Lord Penance eased himself next to Amarnta as the female priest attacked the stains as readily as she had her depleted flock. She wrung the cloth out into the bowl, the water running red as the blood dripped.

"They fear what is to come," she said. Her tongue slid over purple-stained teeth, but she did not look up, focusing instead on the task in hand. "That their souls will not be taken by Penance, not squirm under the scourge, but instead kneel before a new master."

"And you?" the High Lord asked gently.

Amarnta stopped scrubbing to look at him. "I have faith that you will lead us along the righteous path, High Lord. That your decisions have always been for the good of the ragged flock. I believe in Penance, in you, and in the gifts we have been bestowed." A wisp of spiritfire flickered along her fingers, burning away the bloody water that lay on her nails. "Such gifts have a purpose."

"We cannot let the House fall, Amarnta. You know this?" he said, letting an urgency enter his voice.

"I understand." She glanced behind him. "The queen, High Lord, waits upon the last penitent's step."

The High Lord's cane pressed into the stone floor. "At last," he whispered, and glanced back to Amarnta. "You believe that I have always acted for the good of our flock?"

"Yes," replied the priest. "With love, and with pain."

"Then understand that what passes now is for all of our sakes. I will ask of you something you may reject or deny, but believe me when I say, it must be done."

"As you ask, I obey," she said, her eyes flashing purple. A small sliver of junip slipped from the corner of her lips.

The High Lord nodded, his face set grim as he balled his fist on top of Penance's cane. He began to talk as the queen waited impatiently. When he had finished, Amarnta was silent. After a quick glance towards the queen, she dipped the scrubbing brush back into the bucket and carried on her duties.

The High Lord bowed towards the queen, enabling entry, and she walked along the aisle, avoiding any glances towards the looming dragon depicted upon the ceiling. Her honour guard waited just inside the doorway, eyes outwards, armour gleaming in the candlelight of the interior.

"My queen and Overseer," the High Lord said as she approached. "The War Council is due in an hour, so I apologise for the request."

"I thought Prince Consort Adama gone, High Lord," she replied. "I sent a guard and servant, and they have not returned."

"He refuses until he has spoken to you."

"Then lead on. We have little time. The sky ship waits where the hills and forest meet. I assume they are preparing an attack, and soon. Did word reach you of the dragon? Of Ridth and Mandrich?"

The queen walked on by, forcing the High Lord to hurry. A sliver of spiritfire warmed his hand and rolled on to ease his joints.

"Yes, though I hoped they would commit more of their forces that way. But we know the power of a single dragon, don't we? Why else did we gamble on the Unspoken?"

He lowered his eyes to the floor as his cane struck stone a little harder than normal.

"Her treachery was always part of your Scripture, High Lord. Perhaps that fiction speaks truer than you thought. How many died with Panset to set her people free of the Infected, only for her to be absent during our time of need?" The queen paused at the first step and drew in a breath. High Lord Penance didn't miss her attempt to calm her shaking hands.

"A failure that can be put down to me. I put my trust in her," he replied.

"No. You advised *me* to put *my* faith in her. And I listened. It cost lives and time." She began to walk down the spiral steps. "But there are always gains to be seen in such a loss. I have ordered Demartis to evacuate the villages and towns on the way to Pantsil. To seek the southern fleet if any remain, and in turn, Prime Sneed and Duke Simeon – assuming they weren't foolish enough to return to Ridth. Beyond that, to seek refuge upon Khund." The queen's leather boot landed on the final step. She paused and eyed the passage ahead. "A standing army that may help protect an outpost of whatever remains of us."

"Should not the War Council ..." he started as she spun about.

"No, because there are too many plots you still keep from me. I still feel *used*, High Lord." The queen remained in the doorway, eyes narrowed, demanding his attention. "Adama left. I know this. Drugged by my servant as he waved his pen about, swearing he would defend me to the last. You bring me here on another pretence, and my sense of deep mistrust tells me that beyond those doors lies Terana Fiotir Na Partera, or whoever you feel you need to use to *persuade* me to leave."

"I—" The High Lord paused as he recognised how meagre his plans had become. "Geral, though he knows not that you refuse to go."

"You were right to make me the Overseer. Your time has passed, your motives without the shield of Scripture laid bare." A noise echoed down the steps, a sharp intake of breath and the smell of aged wood burning.

"Done, my queen." The words echoed down from the staircase entrance above. A scrape of metal armour on stone accompanied the voice. "Though she fought like a wildcat."

"I should have you flayed before the people, but you'd likely enjoy that, and so few remain to watch. What is this mummery, High Lord? These games? What purpose does it serve to have me out of the city other than to weaken my soldiers' morale?" The queen clenched her shaking hands. What the High Lord had taken for stress was barely contained anger. The door ahead creaked open. Geral peeked out, and a pair of elven eyes regarded them both from over his shoulder. Tixar.

"A rallying point," he replied, "for those that survive."

"And we gather again? Ready to be corralled. It was you who supported me when I suggested we should empty the towns and cities. You, High Lord. Why would we gather again and draw the Constructors down upon us? Why sacrifice my soldiers, Ridth even, to repeat the same mistakes?"

He sagged, legs stiffening upon the step under the queen's furious gaze.

"Perhaps I should show you. If you would?" He indicated towards the corridor. Erin rolled her eyes and backed away as armoured feet stomped down the staircase. The honour guard emerged just behind the High Lord, another waiting close by.

"Do not harm them," she said as she pointed to Geral, who had opened the consort's cell door in trepidation. "See them out of the city. If I see their faces again, it will be swinging from a gibbet with their innards upon the ground."

The High Lord tapped his way towards the Gods' Council chamber. He wished Sneed was waiting for him on the other side.

I should never have sent him to Ridth. How much easier it would have been to have another who knew by my side.

He let his palm sweep across the chamber door, purplefire merging with a steel binding along its edge. The clank of physical locks resounded, and he pushed the door open with his cane. With a glow from its tip, more spiritfire arced out, setting the crystals in the ceiling alight with a stunning luminescence. He stepped aside.

"I am not going into yet another trap," the queen replied, her eyes full of wonder as she stared up at the ceiling's beauty. "Are those ...?"

"They are the stars as they were when the Journey ended, and we Landed upon Brandshold. Soon after, the veils were formed, and many can no longer be seen. A reminder of what we sacrificed, among so many other things." Twisting his head with a purple-lipped smile, he gestured into the chamber, but at the queen's refusal, entered himself, increasing the light until the chamber was fully lit. He placed his cane upon the table and commanded it to transform into his God's weapon, the scourge.

"There are strands to the glyph inlaid in this table, and a stone set in its centre. Jacka provided you with a drawing – which you altered, I believe – for the copy in your throne room. I do think the map was a far better use for it." He turned to face the queen. "Each House has its place upon the God's Council table. This is not about hierarchy, Overseer, but about *power*." He let a little of his own rise in his voice, imbuing his skin and hair with a crackle of his soul.

"More politics," the queen replied, though her voice was less certain than it had been in the stairway just a short time before.

The High Lord shook his head. "We have Seven Houses in each of the cities, my queen, most brimming with our flocks' spiritfire." He sat down, and steepled his fingers as he stared at the stone set in the centre of the table. "The Seven set one to be High Lord or Lady of the Council. One whose life was always in penance for a choice they may have to make. All my machinations and manipulations – and of those before me – were with the aim of saving our people, and so that such a ... a horrendous act would never have to be taken. A final solution." His hands opened, and he found himself burying his face within them. Tears formed that the High Lord could not hold back. Sobs racked his body.

To his surprise, he sensed Queen Weister, Erin, sit by his side. The warmth of her arm that wrapped his shoulder sparked through him like a shock. It burned away the pain, encouraged him to slow his breathing. To calm. A buttress against the storm.

By the Seven, this woman.

"Should we fall..." he started, fingers wiping the remaining tears from his cheeks. "Ah. Let me start again ... The Seven knew that the others who fled the Constructors with them so long ago had reached safer realms. So, a final sacrifice was prepared. The penance – a sacrifice of spiritfire – was gifted to the High Lord by the other Houses whenever the Gods' Council met. Nigh on a thousand years of gatherings to feed a glyph, one that is linked to every House in every town or city. Should I trigger the glyph, there will be an eruption like no other. Imagine a whole city on fire with Erin's Wrath. It will cascade through Brandshold and set the sky alight. It will wipe out the cities and towns within which they reside, and much beyond."

"Including Khund and Meres?"

"I do not know." He shook his head. "Khund's link is tenuous. Their Houses have not given for hundreds of years. Meres, no. They give lip service, but no more." He glanced over to Erin, who eased her arm from his shoulders. "I thought I was strong enough to do this. But, each time, you chip away a piece of my inner armour. Strip the High Lord of the Seven Houses of his resolve. This is why the Scripture was written. The Seven meant us to be devoted, unthinking in our faith, for one such as me to simply sacrifice everything without doubts." He let his hand fall upon the scourge and drew it closer. "I thought that, when you suggested emptying the cities, my resolve would remain strong. That if I could persuade those I cared for most to leave, it would come easier. I understand Yanik survived and has been assigned to Demartis. My wife has been bundled into a cart and sent on her way. Only you and the other Lords remain, and we are the bait to lure them in."

The queen remained silent, leaning back, her hands now gripped in her lap.

"I know you retain little trust in me. That for every layer you peel back, another lie is in your way. You have reached the core – one that even the Seven Houses do not know. How could I have shared such possibilities with Lady Fate? The slightest hint at the destruction I could wield in the Seven's name would have had her scrying the weft and weave of our future, and no doubt had her blood spilled upon the prayer stone long before she eventually took her own life. You were her choice because of your strength. She saw in you, as did Sneed, what I wish I still had." He looked to the queen then, spiritfire burning away the threat of more tears. "We are to be unmarried, divorced from our children. To have no attachments except to our God. And why?"

"So you could make such a sacrifice." The queen shifted in her seat. "The Unspoken has abandoned us – a failed plan – and our people flee. The more time we buy, the further they are from what you suggest – this final solution. And I still believe it best. And what of this Laoch? Is that a truth?"

The High Lord nodded. "Sura was convinced. Her belief in the man is unbreakable. But time is against us. And you have seen the death the sky ship brings, as have I. What weapon can destroy such a ship other than what I wield?"

"You would have once said faith," replied the queen. As she stood, her eyes fell upon the metal glyph that now took on an ominous quality. "We buy time, High Lord. We stand fast, ensure as many of our people survive what it is to come as we can. A duty we both swore to uphold, though we have walked that path in very different ways." The queen headed towards the door, one hand pressed against her heart, the other resting on the pommel of her useless sword.

"And the glyph?"

"You are to stay away from the walls and the fight to come. You remain here. Seal the doors when they break through into the city. With my blessing." She looked back from the door as she pulled at its inner handle. "And your Overseer *commands* you to use the power at your fingertips when all else is lost."

57
WHAT DEPTH YOUR SOUL?

JENSE, BRANDSHOLD

'*Death lies here,*' Nathair whispered in Ecne's mind. The acolyte repeated the words to Laoch and Oisin.

"Where are we?" said Laoch. "Can you show us?"

Nathair glistened briefly in the heartstone. Whitefire formed and dissipated as a scene akin to winter emerged.

"Snow?" said Oisin, stepping closer to the stone.

"White ash," replied Ecne. "Like that thrown from the fire mountains in the Southern Reach."

"Or an entranceway to a palace," growled Laoch as he recalled the memory of Nathair burning the unalive. "Where are we?"

Nathair altered her neck, pushing her head up so her crystal eyes could settle on the scorched, shattered walls, and the sea harbour covered with an oily residue. The skeletons of burnt ships lay amid the ruin.

"It's Jense," said Laoch. "We are too late." He took a breath. Dread constricted his chest, squeezing the hope he had clung to. "Are they here? The Constructors?"

Ecne's eyes emptied, as if she were a million miles away. Her hands pressed gently against the heartstone, and her lips moved. "Nathair senses none of the Constructors nearby. But a magus watches us from the northern wall. There is some life, but so little. Wait." Ecne swallowed, and her pupils widened further. "The magus sends a calling, as Nathair names it. A message."

"Of what?" cut in Oisin.

"One word ... Sura."

—

Sura's world shifted. Her tribe continued to strip the tanned hides from the conical roofs of their tents, yet they flashed in and out of focus. Her inner balance wavered, then failed, and she fell to the ground, only for her hands to disappear into the stony top layer. She caught herself and strengthened her link with Honour, pulling herself free to roll onto her back. Terana stood above her, concern on her face as she knelt by her side.

"Are you okay, Sura-nista?" she said, gently reaching out a hand to lay it upon Sura's chest. "Your ... your heart, it races."

"Heart?" replied Sura, and dragged herself onto her knees, her hand upon her breast. "My soul ..." Her eyes widened, the slits drinking in the sky as her head pulled back. "The sigil has returned. Laoch ... Laoch has come."

"Where?" asked Terana.

"To the southeast," she replied, and let her spirit senses follow the tendril of Honour's link.

"Jense," said Terana. "That city is dead."

But before she could say more, Sura was gone.

—

Nathair stretched her orange wings wide, filling the metallic skin with air and a pulse of whitefire to land upon the churned road two hundred yards from the shattered northern gate. She wrapped her tail around her rear legs, lifting her front to expose the glimmer of her chest scales. Shouts arose on the stone barrier erected along Jense's breach. The crystal tips of ballistae prodded forwards, aligning their flight with that metal chest.

"Better hurry," the Spirit Walker said as she emerged from the heartstone, "before they lose whatever raw patience they have left."

Laoch was already in the next room, clearly on edge as he impatiently waited, tapping at a metal rib bone. When the chest wall faded, he passed through to the outside. Oisin and Ecne struggled to keep up. More shouts, carried on the sea breeze, followed their arrival. A glow, orange and pure, rose from among the broken stone, and a woman wreathed in its spiritfire made her way down the pile of rocks that had once been Jense's walls. Trailing behind her, Laoch noted a mix of House robes and soldiers, each more wary than the Lady. He understood their ill ease; the stench of charred flesh and houses pervaded the area. A malaise that must sit heavily on those who survived.

They met on middle ground, and were ten yards from each other when a fearful soldier requested Lady Honour stop. She bid them wait, only for Laoch to fall upon his knees when she turned back, a spear offered in both hands. Lady Honour signalled to those behind, and bypassed her inert God's spear to place a hand upon the Ranger's fingers where they gripped the butt.

Laoch twitched, uncertain, and raised his eyes to meet Lady Honour's. "It is no longer mine," she said, and moved aside. Behind her, a spirit solidified. Elven eyes locked with his, and Sura enveloped his soul with her own. Warmth spread, calming his insecurities, drawing him out of the depths of the despair he'd thought locked away.

"It is me." A whisper in his ear. The softest of caresses against his cheek. He rose, pulled to his feet by the need that burned away his disbelief. Gentle fingers touched his lips, and where a warm breath of the living should be, spiritfire flowed.

"I—" But no words would come as her kiss removed all thought.

"We're here too," said Ecne, staring intently at the ground.

Sura parted from Laoch, though tendrils of her soul refused to leave his presence, stretching, holding on to what they had both feared lost. While she swept Oisin and Ecne into her arms, her soul held him still.

With a welcome shared, Sura returned to Laoch. He lifted the spear again in open hands, waiting. Sura took it in both hands, her face shining. An orange glow emerged from her chest to wreathe the weapon in spiritfire that danced along the shaft. Honour's sigil erupted into life, and to Laoch's surprise, the weapon faded, disappearing completely to reappear strapped against her back.

"She *is* Honour now. They are one, and more capable than I ever would be," said Lady Honour. "And, as you can see, there is need."

Before she could say more, Sura wrapped herself into Laoch's arms, head against his shoulder, before releasing him again.

"Jense," Oisin said, and tilted his head towards the scorched stone of its walls. "What happened?"

"The Infected," replied Lady Honour. "A disease of the spirit that took them all."

"All?" said Ecne, her mouth dropping. "All? There must have been ten thousand souls living here." She gawped at the wall, blinking. "I knew people here at the university outlier."

"They're dead," interjected Sura. "Their souls were already lost to *Bás Anam*, the soul-death. All of them have been burned at the walls of Anvil by the Unspoken's dragon. A threat ended, while the Seven talk of worse to the south. Did you find it? A weapon, a way to end this?" She looked to Oisin, and back to Laoch.

"We hope so," said Laoch, though he flinched at the mention of the Unspoken. "But how we use it is another bloody matter. We have brought someone you both need to meet."

—

The moon pool reflected the grey clouds while raindrops set ripples crashing into each other along its surface. The wind stirred the shaman's robes as she leant on the wooden staff. Aged eyes stared at the water with Sura waiting impatiently, Laoch standing nearby. But Sura's focus was on the new shaman at her side.

"Rensta ad li Tark," whispered Ferena, her horsehair mane damp in the rain. She looked to the sky and shook her head. An hour ago, it had been filled by a dragon. Her people, already disturbed by one discovery, had wanted to flee, only for the herd to refuse to leave. The camp had emptied, the tribe now hidden somewhere out on the plain, and the scaled beast loomed somewhere behind.

"Yes," said the Mondrein shaman. "*Ad li Tark*, of the Ghost Isles."

Ferena's tilted head nodded. One hand pressed into her back to relieve the pressure there. It popped loud enough to make Sura wince. "And you agree with Nathair, the Spirit Walker, that these Constructors are fallible? That a lifesong saved this other realm?"

"The Drach? Yes. I witnessed a scrying. I watched as the song bore their spirits from their bodies. Thousands fell; few had the strength of will to survive, and those that did, fled."

Ferena faced her counterpart, chin set firm while her eyes danced over the other shaman. "And yet you arrive to find it was a wasted journey." Ferena knelt and swished her hand through the grey water. She licked her fingers, and flinched. Holding them up, she spotted tiny crystals, like sand, sitting on the tips.

"No? How? You are so far from the sea?"

"I do not know. The herd went to drink but turned away. I thought them sated, but no." Ferena glanced over to Sura and shook her head. "A problem."

Sura stirred, only for Laoch's hand to snake under her arm and gently pull her back. He marvelled at how she paused at his touch, and admired the brief flare of her anger as she glared at him.

"Leave them," he said.

"Something is wrong," she growled, and pulled away to stride over. "Ferena? What is happening?"

"The moon pool has been poisoned. Salted."

She bypassed the two shamans and dropped to her haunches next to the pool. Since seeing Nura, time had passed in a whirl. She expected to be able to feel him amid the water, his soul more formed than most because her *will*, her *need*, had helped to shape his spirit.

"He's not here," she said, a single finger disturbing the surface of the pool. It felt odd, thicker. She faded, spreading herself thinner before letting her whole hand enter the water. "No," she said, shaking her head. "He is here, but weak. So weak. Empty."

Laoch knelt next to her and reached for her arm. For the first time since her return, he found her form to have no substance. Whatever words he had, he choked back.

Sura broke her focus and strengthened her spirit bonds, reforming. But not for his sake. "This is wrong," she said, eyes briefly locking with his.

"How ...?" Laoch replied.

"I am not sure." Sura broke eye contact and strode off. "I do not understand."

Laoch trailed in her wake, only for Ferena to stand in his way. "Do not follow, Laoch. She knows, but cannot accept. The spirits are fading. The water cannot hold them."

"They are leeching," cut in Rensta. "We have the weedfields in the sea on Mondrein that bond much of the spiritfire. You do not. And so, we are lost." She turned to Laoch. Sadness and anger played across her features in equal measure. "And my forced journey here, wasted if all the other moon pools are the same."

Sura passed through Nathair's chest, entering the pocket with a determination the waiting Spirit Walker must have recognised, as it immediately emerged from the heartstone.

"What do you see?" Sura demanded. "In the moon pool."

"I have not looked. You asked me to keep an eye on your people, due to their fear," replied Nathair.

"Look," she said, eyes flashing with orange fire. "Now."

Nathair's scales slid around her face, pulsing once before opaque lids flickered over her eyes.

"I see nothing," the Spirit Walker replied. "You said you had returned your people's spirits, yet there is so little here. No, that is wrong. There is something but it is so ... weak."

'*Unbonded. Slippery, draining. Like ...*' said Honour. Sura repeated the words.

"Seawater," finished Nathair. The Spirit Walker's face went still.

Sura spun, rushed out, and pulled an exasperated Laoch away from Oisin and towards the pool. Ecne already stood there, watching. The two shamans separated. Sura plunged her hand into the pool, and spiritfire arced through the cupped water. She sensed so little in there.

She held her cupped hand out to Laoch. "Taste it," she demanded.

Laoch ran his fingers through the water and licked them. "It's salty," he said. "Like Ferena said."

"Is it like the sea? Does it taste how you remember?" Her eyes narrowed, hands on his head. She drew upon the memory he began to conjure, trying to feel and taste what he did. Frustration boiled as she failed to understand the sensation.

"Sura, what are you looking for?" said Laoch. "Help me to understand."

"I can't put it into words," she replied. "I am sorry." Her hand touched his cheek, then she slid her own memories into his mind. Of the void, the blackness. The loss of self among the myriad souls locked in the *Kraken's* crystal. How a distant memory of life and song was the only thing that remained, sung over and over. The faintest part of her, winding like a thread about the hope she didn't understand. Thoughts, fleeting, gone as quickly as they fluttered in. Partial memories – a laugh, a fist, blood and burning. Wind rushing through her hair. The touch of his lips. Nothing but a whirlpool of disconnection. But, amid it all, the lifesong bubbled. Trapped within the bonds of stone, one she could neither touch nor hear, smell or see. But taste. Yes.

Laoch sat back, mind reeling from the swirl of thoughts and emotions. Yet, through the loss and emptiness of a void, the metallic taste of her crystal prison remained.

"Yes," he said, stumbling as vertigo hit. His hands dropped to the grass to steady himself. "Like that."

"Then they knew," growled Sura, and grasped Laoch's face, locking eyes. "They knew what you sought and prepared for it. The Constructors destroyed the moon pool. We are lost."

58
IN LOVE AND WAR

SOUTH OF ERSTENBURGH,
BRANDSHOLD

"Loose when ready!" shouted Zendril, and the flag rose. Within a few seconds, the ballistae crews to her east and west released their metal javelins. As they flew at an angle above the edge of the forest, the general counted each one. "Fucking hit," she said through gritted teeth, eyes switching to their target. The three artifices parted, metal wings dipping and flapping at the air. Scouts. Eyes that would inform the sky ship and the bloody dragon of the locations of her soldiers. They were ponderous machines, and she had waited agonisingly for them to enter range.

Two split wide. The third was slower to react, and javelins pierced its wings. As it dipped, another with a crystal tip struck the hull, and the flying machine erupted in a brilliant green flame. Another round of metal bolts flew, the secondary ballistae having awaited the artifices' attempts to adjust. This time, multiple bolts struck home, and a cheer rang amid the remains of the general's army. Smoke billowed from the failing machines and they spiralled downwards. The sounds of their crashes deadened by the trees as they struck a few hundred yards ahead of the ridge.

"Move the ballistae out," she spat, and her command team raised the flags. She eyed the sky ship hovering above the muddy fields that abutted the forest. In its shadow, the Constructor army gathered, the milieu of black armoured foot soldiers massing as the Scorpion machines, she remembered, and hated, prepared.

"What are they waiting for?" asked Mander. Lifting his spyglass, he surveyed the scene.

A roar echoed across the southern edge of the trees, a blast that rolled over the canopy, bringing fear and flame to the minds of the waiting Union soldiers. Another rumble, and fire billowed from the south-eastern trees. Screams replaced the roar, and trees burst into flame, as the mighty dragon flew across the sky. Black smoke trailed in its wake, boiling into the air. The beast swept directly overhead, and the stench of burnt oil and ash beat upon the ensuing wind. Guilt hit Zendril like a wave. She had known the dragon would target any threat; a risk she had accepted with the ballistae crews' lives.

"That," said Zendril.

A second gout spewed upon the woods, accompanied by the cries of her ballistae crews.

"Just hope some live. Give the signal."

"Are you sure?"

"Give the fucking signal. We scatter, form units, attack the bastards from the sides. No holds barred. Focus on them bastard Scorpions and the crystal slingers that devastated Mandrich's units. And pray to the Seven we delay them enough. Now!"

The command flags waved, and from all around, the shouts of cohort officers boomed. Drilled soldiers melted into the woods, their packs and pouches filled with their remaining hope.

"Make my daughter proud," she whispered, only for a heavy hand to fall upon her shoulder. "Don't get fucking maudlin. You should not be here. Can't you take a bloody hint?"

Mander squeezed. "There's me and a couple of old friends who need you alive."

Zendril shook her head and glared at the two honour guards who had faced a dragon at her side, and lived. "Fuck me," she said, and picked up her own pack. The clink of pot bombs inside made her wince. With a last glance down towards the advancing Scorpions, she started to jog towards the nearest path into the trees. "Let's get this done."

—

"There." Mander pointed into the clearing.

Metal limbs clattered into the shattered branches, lifting the Scorpion's hull over the still-smoking tree. Arrows struck the artifice's bulbous windows. Ineffective, they pinged away. The machine grabbed a thick branch in its pincers, throwing it out of its way before taking another step. More arrows scraped along the hull, and the machine turned to whip its tail into the leafy top of a tree twenty feet away. The tip hit something solid and blood spurted across the greenery, followed by the body of an archer falling to crunch against the ground. A dozen foot soldiers swarmed in from behind the Scorpion. Most were armed with glowing swords or heavy maces, handheld crossbows at their sides, but four carried one of the dreaded long weapons. They instantly took a knee, and the weapons swept the trees ahead. Two fired, and whitefire exploded amid the undergrowth.

This was the moment Zendril had waited for. The camouflaged ballistae released. The heavy metal bolt sped across the clearing and rammed into the Scorpion's lower right side. Greenfire erupted – the colour of Wisdom, and Greeth's power – and rocked one side of the huge machine into the air.

"Now!" Zendril ordered.

Two sacks of pot bombs flew and struck the suddenly exposed underside of the machine. The first hit with a clunk and fell to the floor, lifeless, accompanied by a bout of vicious swearing from Zendril. It cut off as the second sack exploded. She threw herself to the ground as flame, blood and shattered crystal armour peppered the undergrowth.

Adrenaline pumped through her veins as she pushed up from the forest floor. Amid the carnage, metal limbs flailed, striking whatever was in their way. Half the Constructors lay in pieces, as dead as they got. The others were already on their feet, crystals flying from their strange weapons. Whitefire erupted, and the cries of the ballistae crew cut through the smoke, ending any hope of a second bolt.

The remaining Constructors ran their way, weapons drawn, shields strapped to their arms. Zendril's two honour guards spun out from behind a tree, bows drawn. Their arrows glanced off armour and shield; the crystal heads exploded, but the greenfire washed over to little effect. They dropped both bows to draw their swords. A mace smashed downwards, its glow eerie under the canopy, to strike the arm of the left-hand honour guard. He screamed, bone crunching beneath his shattered greaves. His half-drawn sword clattered to the ground. A strike smashed his chin, sending his helm flying, and he crumpled to the forest floor.

Zendril's broadsword pierced the Constructor's hip, scraping beneath the joint and ramming into the soldier's spine. No scream came. Instead, the crystal-clad soldier brought their buckler down on her extended arm. Zendril released her sword and bent her arm to prevent a shattered elbow, taking a bruising blow in its stead. Doubling over, she drew her boot knife, and sprang up to ram it under the Constructor's helm. The blade ground against jaw and gristle, grating against the skull to enter the brain. Whitefire surged along the blade, wreathing her hand before skittering down the dying Constructor's armour. She withdrew the knife, only for amazement to threaten her resolve as the glow entered a gourd strapped to the soldier's black armour. She lifted a boot and crashed it down to shatter the container, anger fuelling her efforts.

The general gathered her broadsword, swore, and struck at the Constructor engaged with the second honour guard. The blade twisted off a shoulder plate but, distracted, the soul-eater turned slightly and took a sharp kick to the knee from her guard. Zendril lashed out. One blow smashed the arm, another the wrist, and the Constructor toppled. The general's honour guard drove his sword into the back of its neck, and whitefire rolled along the blade.

Zendril smashed the butt of her sword into the waiting gourd. To her renewed astonishment, she watched as the glow balled in on itself before shooting off towards the wreck of the Scorpion.

"Fuck me. Don't tell me they come back, Mander," she said, looking around the smoke-filled clearing.

She blinked, heart pounding. "Mander?"

She swallowed. Closing her eyes to hold herself in. Her hand quivered, pressed against her chest, when a metal gauntlet touched upon her arm.

"Dead?" she whispered, afraid to speak the words out loud. The explosion, the blood. A squeeze came. "If I look, it will be the end of me. I have my army."

"If you don't, will you forgive yourself?" replied the honour guard.

"Forgiveness? I'll forgive when I'm fucking dead." She grabbed at the pouch at her side and checked the last of her pot bombs before raising her sword. "Time is the only currency we trade in."

She strode into the clearing. The three crystal slingers had been reduced to just one, who was on his feet, watching the trees ahead. Zendril's pouch smashed against the soldier's back with a swear-laden prayer. It exploded, hurtling the broken mess into the undergrowth. Zendril ran on, eyeing the whitefire that flowed from the sack of steaming meat to swirl across the forest floor towards a dead slinger. It surged over the cracked armour and, as she watched, made a failed attempt to enter the intact gourd. With a wicked grin, her pommel cracked the container open. A splurge of dying light her reward. The whitefire whirled about in apparent uncertainty before driving towards the Scorpion.

"To me," she shouted. "To me."

A few blood-stained, mud-covered soldiers emerged from the trees, many wounded, all sore from battle.

"The containers!" she shouted. "The gourds on their backs. Crack every one you see. Spread the word. We kill as many of these fuckers as we can, then smash those bastard things, so they really die. Understand?" She lifted the pieces of a broken gourd from the Constructor at her feet. "Get the word out, then get back to your killing. Go."

She watched briefly as they left, and turned to her waiting honour guard. "You are sworn to the queen, yes?"

"Yes."

"And by her order, I am to buy as much time as we can. That is correct?"

"Yes, General."

"Then, by my order, and therefore the queen's order, you are to leave me the fuck alone and take these pieces to Erstenburgh. Understand?" She waited for the bite back, her eyes hard. "Under-bloody-stand? Head north, find a horse, kick some fucking upstart cavalry officer off if you have to, and get your arse to the city."

"Yes, General." He went to leave, but turned back. "It's been an honour to serve you, General. And ... and Mander."

"It has. Now piss off."

The guard disappeared into the trees.

She walked over to the bloody mess within the undergrowth. Falling to her knees, she drew the man she had loved more than life up to her chest, and wept.

59
A FIRST TASTE OF ECSTASY

"Foolish," the emperor spat, anger in his eyes. His white fingers pressed harder against the heartstone, the husked skin stretching at the tips as he searched Tabharthóir's vision to see the single ornithopter, swamped by the metal bolts slung from the city walls, spiral towards the ground. "Why are the young so reckless? Slow and sure. Judge their range carefully."

The artifice crashed into the western field about the city, the remnants of a hastily cleared camp catching with the whitefire that boiled from the machine. A crackle of white lightning raced upwards, the traces reaching Tabharthóir and channelling into the emperor's thoughts.

"What is this?"

He let the pilot's last sight fill his mind's eye. He had expected an image of the city, humans quivering on their walls, magi ready to hurl their precious spirits at the oncoming onslaught of his Inhibitors. But no. The pilot had clearly wasted its current body by spying on the empty forest. On trees.

"Useless," he whispered, and dismissed the churned mud along the spiderweb of paths that spread outwards from the human city.

Tarin guided Tabharthóir to fly parallel with the southern wall, and at its end, banked right along the eastern side. The Fleshmaster and his slaved Spirit Walker then continued to fly a gentle inward spiral, eyeing the simple machines built to throw metal bolts or hurl rocks.

As the first javelins flew towards them, dipping a few yards from the dragon's wing tip, the emperor laughed.

Yes, they have shown more acumen than those we have fought before, yet still they crumble and mither behind their walls.

"Let us hide them from their pathetic spiritfire callings, Tabharthóir. No word is to pass in or out. Let them quail in ignorance for when we move on to the next city."

The dragon roared, and her huge wings pounded at the air as she rose high above the walls. A second bellow was filled with a stream of whitefire, which fell like a curtain of rain across the city. The Fleshmaster enjoyed the last taste of fear amid the human souls before Tabharthóir's breath poured down upon them, hiding them from their spirit-sight.

A necessity.

Tabharthóir dived, wings tight against her body, her jointed tail snaking behind. Her crystal eyes flashed white, and she dropped from up high where the ballistae could not aim. Whitefire caught on her breath to ignite flames that poured down upon the southern wall. Her metal-boned wings extended, tail swinging like a rudder, and she swept fire and hunger down upon the humans and their pathetic machines. Some bolts, small and accurate, flew. Tabharthóir sensed their path, but she travelled far too fast, and they struck her along the rear. Red and yellowfire erupted from small crystal arrowheads to scorch her silver-blue, rupturing a scale or two.

The Fleshmaster snorted, tasting the power of the two magi who had bequeathed their spiritfire to the crystals, and marked them as future delicacies to hunt down.

"Come. Let us finish the battle to the south before the admiral makes a mockery of our superiority. That is enough dread for them to chew upon."

———

The Scorpions gathered in the burnt centre of the ridge. Eight remained of those sent into the attack, most with hulls that bore the scorch marks and scars of battle. Their claws waved, and each took one of the human soldiers between their pincers. The cuts were swift, bodies and limbs flying as whitefire briefly laced the bloodied limbs, only to be absorbed into the machines. The Inhibitors beat the rest, smashing knees and hips until they crashed to the floor. And the claws gripped again, sliced, and fed.

Lelion, forcing herself to look away from the refuelling, turned to set hungry eyes upon the manacled man who knelt at her feet.

"You taste delicious," she said. A single, brass-covered finger alighted under Lord Justice's chin. "You are mine, and mine alone," she whispered.

Lelion drew a little from the back of his head, the flavour of the spirit a delight upon her body. "Redfire," she mused. "My first taste. And it will not be my last." She patted the human magus's face, and a wicked smile exposed her metal teeth.

His lips moved as if he made to speak. And with that simple thought, the manacles acted. The insane Spirit Walker that inhabited them quelled any rebellion it assumed could possibly be an attempt to draw upon spiritfire.

"No. I don't care for anything you wish to tell me. This is not torture, magus. This is subjugation. My Inhibitors will take your pathetic city, and we shall feast upon your people for eternity." She grabbed the manacles and spun him around. Before him, a dreadfully thin woman, her skin like dried, cracked leather, lay pinioned to the hull, her scalp exposed as the wind tore tufts of hair from her husked skull.

Lord Justice pulled his eyes away, unable to look upon those that were pinned next to her.

"This is your future. The younglings struggle to sustain me. I contain such age, such power. I want something more, magus ... I could take you as my own spirit-doll, your redfire at my beck and call. What say you? Ah, of course. You cannot speak." She pulled upon the chain. "I will take that as agreement."

Brass gauntlets wrapped about Lord Justice's head, and whitefire poured inwards, tearing at his mind and the root of his soul. The admiral forced Lord Justice to taste the many spirits he had consumed in the past.

Young and old, they had all died in fear and pain. Lelion revelled as dread set about the young Lord, along with thoughts of his God, the great Magus who, in turn, was but a lie. A facsimile of reality that provided little strength despite the Lord's desperate need to escape the sweet, sweet offer the admiral incarnate drilled into his head.

"Be mine, feed me, and you will know joy. To pleasure one such as I will become your life. No burden to carry, no lies and deceit to sustain. Be mine, be mine ... and mine alone."

Lelion revelled as Lord Justice built a wall of faith in his God, and it crumbled beneath the untruths. And again, when he constructed a wall of justice for his flock, a belief in what was true to him, only for it to crumble beneath his selfishness. In its place, he devised a bridge, and the admiral incarnate filled with elation as the Lord swept doubts aside amid the flood of need and desire.

"My hunger is at an end."

Lelion released the magus's head and stepped away, her teeth bared with a howl of victory she hurled into the air. Redfire danced upon her gauntlets, and she drew the spiritfire inwards. The sigh was long, drawn out, the pleasure palpable as leathered joints eased, tendons soothed and her mind was set afire.

"Mine," she whispered, and ran the back of her hand along Lord Justice's jaw. "Forever."

"Admiral," said Lieutenant Spintz, her white eyes to the deck. "The emperor is returning."

"Good," replied the admiral, and reluctantly left Lord Justice to approach her favoured viewing position. "Let him play amid the battle. It will appease him and ensure his opinion of me is lowered even further." She looked below briefly. The refuelled Scorpions now rampaged in pairs amid the forest a few hundred yards from the ridge. A feeder scavenged the pile of body parts, its segments quivering as the cloud of whitefire rose from the dead.

"Are you with me, Spintz?" The admiral spoke without looking. "Are you?"

The lieutenant looked over to the manacled man. "I ..."

The admiral turned about and reached out a brass gauntlet that sparked with redfire. "Taste," she said.

Spintz grabbed the hand. The dead tongue slipped between her dried lips to lick at the fingers. Her eyes rolled and her head fell back, redfire weaving lines among the white.

"I am generous, Spintz." She let another arc spurt along her fingers to dart into the lieutenant's open mouth. "To those who are loyal."

Spintz could not speak as her back arched. Her body shook until the ecstasy passed. The lieutenant squeezed her fingers into her palm, and marvelled at the flexibility of her skin. "I am loyal, Admiral."

"Yes. Of course you are."

—

Dragon's fire enveloped the forest canopy. Leaves fluttered on the hot wind, lifting until charred into white ash that swirled about the sky. Tabharthóir strode on. Talons ripped burning trees aside, flinging trunks as she cut a pathway towards the spirits that glowed in her sight. She bellowed, and they withered under her demand for their subservience. Dread and fear added a savoured tang.

The dragon peered into the smoke and, swiping with her left forefoot, scythed through the undergrowth. Flame and blood exploded in its wake. Whitefire rose from the maelstrom to seethe about her scales and seep inside.

"They attack from behind," thought Tarin, and urged Tabharthóir to respond. The thick tail hovered briefly above the ground before lashing out. The barbed tip crashed into the ballista that had been hurriedly wheeled in and aimed at her side. The metal spikes shattered wood and bent metal, and swept on to crush bone. With a thought, the tail whipped back, striking the other side. Trees splintered and their burning branches fell upon the advancing soldiers. Shouts and screams were music to her ears, and the dragon shivered as her body drew in the souls of the dead.

"Focus," ordered the Fleshmaster. *"Do not get caught up in the feeding."*

Spiritfire struck the dragon's jaw, splashing yellow against the silver-blue metal. Tabharthóir's head jerked back in surprise. Tarin crushed the anger and soul-lust the spiritfire caused, and sought the magus via the dragon's sight. Peering through the smoke, he found the glow, which pulsed ochre as it ran. Weaker than those they had met at Makalena, but a new delicacy – and a minor threat – nonetheless.

"There, Tabharthóir. You may feast upon it when we are done."

The dragon trumpeted. Her cogs and wires surged with whitefire, driving the metal beast through the trees on the hunt. As brittle branches shattered and stouter trunks were squeezed aside, Tabharthóir lurched ahead, forcing her way through. Loathe to burn when it could mean the loss of such a morsel, she ripped into the ground, increasing her speed as her belly dragged along the burning grass.

The smoke cleared as the scaled dragon broke out from the trees onto a slope that rose towards a set of low hills. The ochre glow had stopped, but halfway up, a human in yellow, torn and bloodied robes, waited. The hood flicked back to reveal an older woman, a sneer upon her face. Tabharthóir's spirit-sight flickered. The soul uncovered by the robe was white and seething. And it was not dread, but fury that boiled inside. The woman's gauntleted hand flicked open, exposing two clay pots.

"Not the source," said Tarin, suddenly wary.

Yellowfire crashed into the dragon again, this time from the side. Tabharthóir whipped her head around to catch sight of the magus. This one bore the scars of battle, a tiredness in their soul echoed in their drawn skin and glazed eyes. A second bolt flew, weary, and the female magus collapsed to her knees under the strain. The dragon trumpeted, tail lashing as she charged forwards.

And Zendril Weister, general of the northern army and mother to a queen, crashed the pots into the hole at her feet. The thin clay lining that separated two alchemical concoctions cracked, igniting the small pot bombs as they hit the boxes buried below the soil.

"Fuck it," said Zendril, and the world bathed in Erin's Wrath, searing her body and tearing into the belly of the metal beast.

60
CHEATING DEATH

THE WHITE PALACE, ERSTENBURGH, BRANDSHOLD

Queen Weister handled the broken metal pieces of the strange container, twirling them about her fingers. The exhausted honour guard sat at the War Council table at her insistence. Beside her, Lord Wisdom mithered, desperate to get his hands upon the Constructor's container. He was almost dancing from foot to foot before she finally handed them over.

"Thank you, my queen," he said, and his green robes swished as he descended the steps to sit next to the honour guard. His fingers flickered swiftly over a book already laid open on the table, while a further pile awaited his attention nearby.

"And you say Mander is dead?" she said, eyes downcast, her thoughts upon her mother's grief. The honour guard nodded. Ash and blood streaked his cheeks as he hid his eyes.

With Mander gone, what will she do?

"You are to rest." The queen rose from her throne, taking each step down to the table with deliberation, to stand before the guard. She held both his hands in hers. "I know you have seen much, but this evil comes for my people. Your people. I can offer you no more than respite, Ser." Queen Weister looked across to her waiting servant, barely masking the shock when she saw the boy Vianti awaiting her words.

"Vianti! I sent you away," she said, fighting the swell of pride in her chest.

The boy bowed his head, lips twisting but unable to speak.

She blinked away a forming tear. "Find a room for this man, Vianti, if you please. With warm water. And ensure he is fed."

Vianti lowered his head again, clearly relieved, and led the honour guard away.

"Any thoughts, Lord Wisdom?" she said, and took the seat on the other side of the Lord.

"Some. It pains me to admit it, but I would want the grand meister and Meister Kinst for such a discussion." He held up one piece of the gourd. The inner side glinted in the throne's light. "I will seek out Kinst later, perhaps. The books hint at the immortality of the Constructors, that their bodies were, in fact, already dead, but animated by their souls. That they need spiritfire to replace that which they burn up. Their food."

Queen Erin shuddered, already aware of such things, but recalling the sight of her beloved forest burning while the sky ship hovered at its edge.

They come to feast upon our souls.

"From what the Ser speaks of, perhaps, when the body is destroyed, their spirit can live on awhile. These are crystals embedded within the metal, much as those Kinst devised for our weapons." He flicked a page, blowing out his cheeks as he did so. "Nothing is written here about such containers that I remember reading, or that my priests-in-waiting have brought to me as a discussion point."

"But if we kill them, and they can come back, then we are lost." Queen Weister said, her shoulders slumped.

"They will need another body," replied the Lord. He flinched, shocked at his own words, as the queen glared back at him.

"There are thousands of dead laid out in the forest at our Union's service, who have bled a lake of blood for our people, Lord Wisdom. They have bodies *enough*." She stood. Clasping her hands to help hold in her resolve. Her uniform sleeves, smart and unbloodied, wrapped about her wrists.

A lake of blood, and I am drenched in it. Yet my body is clean.

"My queen," said Vianti, having silently reappeared at the throne room's ornate doorway. "Captain Mordant bids you to the walls."

—

"There." Mordant handed her the spyglass. Queen Weister peered into the falling darkness, lit only by the fires of the battle to the south. "See it?"

"The forest burns," she replied.

"At the south-eastern edge, where the hills meet the trees."

Erin brought the spyglass round, adjusting the elongated tube until she found the sundered earth and scorch marks across a strip of grassland. Amid the embers, silver-blue scales glinted, reflecting the eerie orange of the nearby flames.

"They hurt it? Why have the priests not been in contact?"

"By the accounts of my soldiers, a huge explosion lit the sky. When they saw where, the dragon had begun to rise from the ground, but unsteady, and flew to the south." Mordant pointed towards the sky ship. "Towards the ship, they believe. It has galvanised the city guard upon the walls. A little hope that will spread through the city, no doubt." Mordant ran his hand across the top stone of the wall.

"Some good news, at least." She handed the spyglass back to the captain, gut churning at the last sight she had taken in. Long, segmented artifices scavenging between the trees. "But that battle is over, Mordant. If Zendril's priests send no word via the crystals, then they must be dead. We will be next."

Shouts resounded from the western wall, and flags rose from the nearest tower.

"Excuse me, my queen, I am needed," Mordant said, and tilted his head towards the commotion.

"I will come walk with you, Captain, and talk to those along the wall, if I may."

They proceeded along the southern walkway, her dual honour guard at her back as she spoke to each watcher upon the walls. Mordant, impatient, eventually strode ahead. By the time she reached the tower, he was deep into an animated discussion with an officer of the watch. The woman saluted, turned away, and bowed to the queen before taking her station again on the wall.

"A problem?" she said.

"A patrol is returning; their scout claims they have Lady Death among their number." Mordant rubbed at his grizzled chin, shaking his head a little. "I thought her to the north, with the Unspoken. She has a Ranger with her – Yanik."

"So did I. And Yanik? I ordered for her to be sent east with Demartis. You know who she is?"

"I remember the name ... was she one of the duke's?" he said and gestured towards the lift.

"Yes, and the daughter of the High Lord." Mordant didn't miss a beat, but she caught the sudden tension in the captain's shoulders. "Cut from a different cloth, by all accounts, but just as stubborn."

"I apologise, my queen. Major Demartis did make it clear that First Ranger Yanik was to accompany him." Lady Death shuffled into her chair, and picked at the plate of cheese and bread. "But she's as devious as her father." The white-haired Lady glared in Yanik's direction, who merely shrugged and shovelled more cheese into her mouth. "She hid in the rear of Rin's ornithopter. Rin left us along the Queen's Road to the north, unsure of what welcome she would receive."

"Likely a javelin in her infernal machine," replied Queen Weister. "We have been scouted with such artifices by the Constructors, swiftly followed by their dragon. Perhaps you can shed some light on where the Unspoken is if, as you say, she flew this way."

"I cannot," said Lady Death. "But I don't fear her joining forces with this emperor. There is a hatred there, fuelled further by the threat of the horde and what this Fleshmaster tried to do to her people. I would not suspect an attack. Indifference, however, I would not put past that creature."

Yanik coughed and withdrew a piece of crust from her mouth, a semi-apologetic look on her face. She received a glare from Lady Death, but the First Ranger ignored her, only to come under the queen's withering gaze.

"Fleshmaster? Is that what she names him?" Lord Wisdom asked as he passed the pieces of the gourd over to Lady Death. "I suspect that, when the Constructors' bodies die, their spirits are contained within these in the hopes of gaining another body. Fleshmaster? Mmm."

Lady Death picked up the gourd pieces and focused on the crystals along the inner wall. "After entering her mind, I would certainly agree that the Unspoken could pass into another body and control it. Her Burners, I thought to be spirit-dolls, but they held her taint within them. Yes, that would make sense. And I can see the importance." She handed the pieces back to the anxious Lord, who gathered them in front of his open book.

"We need their deaths to be final," said the queen, her eyes glistening, "otherwise all this blood will have been for nothing."

"We have Laoch and the veil dragon Nathair, my queen. Has Lady Honour not been in contact? They have returned, though I have heard no news since. I would have thought Lord Hope, at least, would have informed you."

The queen sat up in her chair and leaned forwards, her eyes a little more eager. "Lord Hope has been in constant contact, pulling many strings, but is likely at rest as we speak, readying for the battle ahead. He suffers, thinking his waiting have fallen to the Constructors. And more now, in General Zendril's last stand." She pushed herself up from the table. "But still, we have had no word. Do they bear a weapon?"

"I understand they carry those of the God's weapons that were thought lost. And a hope that a Schenterenta they travel with may have the key to destroying the Constructors. But how, I do not know. My Lady Honour, however, felt their strength. She believes. We have to believe."

"Time paid for in blood and souls." The queen pulled her hands in towards her chest, lacing her fingers over her heart.

61

AT HONOUR'S HOUSE

ABOVE THE PARTERA PLAINS,
BRANDSHOLD

Sura sensed the calling long before Honour touched her mind. Her spirit rippled as the weak, but focused, spiritfire pierced the dragon. She gasped and fell to her knees. The strangeness welling from the contact akin to when Honour's spear had returned through the veils.

Laoch hunched down, well aware that the glow emanating from her meant physical contact was futile. He sensed as her spirit reached out to anchor upon his. No words passed, but he felt the shift like a Soul Tear.

"We are called," said Sura, and her spirit body rippled. "Lady Honour has news."

"The last moon p—" began Laoch.

Sura's glare cut him short.

"They are dead to us, Laoch," cut in Rensta. "Useless. What is one small pool compared to that of the Drach?" The shaman squeezed her hand against her staff. "Take me home."

"No," said Sura. Her spirit floated up from the floor of Nathair's pocket. "Not until the Constructors are dead, or our world is. Lady Honour would not call if it was not urgent." She approached the heartstone and placed her hands beside Ecne's as the acolyte rode Nathair's sight.

"Can you hear her?" asked Sura.

'Now you touch the stone, I can,' Nathair replied in her mind. *'Think only of her.'*

Sura brought the Lady's image into her spirit-mind's eye, and Nathair latched on. The heartstone swirled, and soon Lady Honour formed within the crystal. Her eyes were drawn and red-rimmed, her cheeks sallow.

"Lady Honour," said Sura, and the woman's eyes glazed, "can you hear me?"

The image seemed to shift, and the Lady appeared larger.

"A Wyrding Stone," said Sura quietly. "You called, Lady Honour, and I have answered."

"Sura. I fear Erstenburgh is under attack. I sent a calling to inform of your arrival, but it has returned unanswered. I have tried again and again, but the Wyrding cannot get through. Lady Death knows of you, however, and goes to the city; I only hope she can get in." Lady Honour's image trembled a little.

"Then we must go. We have the God's weapons and a veil dragon. We can make a bloody difference if nothing else." Laoch caught Oisin's eye, who nodded in return. Ecne, though, was lost within Nathair's sight.

"There is something of more importance," said Lady Honour, and her image grew again. "My House in Makalena, it comes under attack. The Lead reports the doors are failing. I fear they have but a few hours before the Constructors gain entry."

"Your House?" spat Laoch. "I'm talking about a bloody city full of people. We go to Erstenburgh, fight for our queen and the Union. Tear the bastards a new hole and spit on whatever life they have left."

'You have not changed. Listen!' sent Sura.

Laoch's skull thrummed with the command.

Lady Honour closed her eyes, apparently speaking through some form of pain. "All of the High Lords feared this would happen. It has always been written that the Houses be sealed, the prayer and the Wyrding Stones preserved, kept from the Constructors lest they drain the spiritfire of the stone and veils. They would gain such power."

"Say that again," said Rensta, the shaman eagerly approaching the stone and pushing past Laoch, "for one who does not understand your ways."

—

Nathair dipped low beneath the sightline of the city walls, with the sliver of a moon at her back. She glided, daring a beat of her wings every few seconds, as Makalena came into sight. The port lay in cinders, the other half of the northern fleet blackened skeletons against the grey walls of the harbour.

"I can see them," said Ecne, her hands bone-white as she pressed against the heartstone. "They burn in the night, their spirits afire." There was disgust in her tone and a sneer on her lips as she turned to Laoch. "They gorge."

Laoch closed his eyes, trying to push the words away lest his anger rise and colour his judgement. This was a time for a clear head, with Sura already angry at his outbursts.

"Facts," said Oisin, and he walked over to place a hand on the acolyte's shoulder. "Just tell us what we need, Ecne. Lock the emotions away."

'I count a hundred or so,' thought Nathair.

With more calm to her voice, Ecne repeated Nathair's words to her friends.

'Many watch along the walls, or in the gap. But there is a cluster near a market square. The whitefire is strange there.'

"Then that's where we go," said Laoch. "You are to clear the walls, Nathair. We will take those who attack Honour's House."

"Agreed," said Ecne.

She released the stone and knelt to collect Wisdom's crossbow. Laoch couldn't help but smile at the acolyte's determined expression as she checked the weapon.

"Shouldn't you say something poignant, Laoch?" asked Oisin. "A rallying call."

He smiled, hand on his pommel. "Sura?"

Sura solidified beside Laoch, spear in hand. "It's time we took the war to these bastards."

"Like she said."

—

Laoch watched Ecne's fingers, each disappearing into a fist as her lips counted down. The connection between her and Nathair would soon be out of range, but if the veil dragon spoke true, zero would signal the start of her *distraction*.

Ecne's final finger dropped, and her hand closed about the grip of Wisdom's bow. The roar of an orange dragon erupted across the city walls. Laoch sensed a shift in the atmosphere, but not a rising dread.

After all, they have their own dragon. One that feeds on humans, not Constructors. Unlike ours.

Flame pierced the night. The first flash of whitefire from Nathair's nostrils lit her dragon's breath, the bilious flame reflecting from her outstretched wings as she hovered above the southern wall.

On cue, Oisin loosed. Fate's arrow, in its helical spiral, seared across the marketplace to slam into a Constructor's neck. The sizzle of old meat filled the square, and Wisdom's green flared bright as it struck a second of the Constructors, alongside a rotting pile of the dead. The other four turned about, and Oisin and Ecne released another round of their Gods' redemption. Oisin's arrow struck home, whilst the rest dived for the stony ground covered in detritus that had once been alive.

A raging spirit emerged from the mound of discarded humanity. Her spear drove into the skull of a prone Constructor. Sura twisted, and an arc of whitefire and ancient brain burst from the shattered helm. She kicked out at another, striking at their neck. The resultant crack was welcome, though not a killing blow. By the time she'd withdrawn her spear, the final Constructor had risen, a glowing mace in hand that he twirled her way. He didn't get a second chance. Justice drove through the soul-eater's back, severing the spine. Sura's smile towards Laoch spoke more of revenge than pleasure, and she thrust Honour's spear into the flailing Constructor, whose broken neck became the last of its troubles.

Laoch and Sura dropped side by side, their Ranger training cutting through the emotions of their first act of revenge. Across the market square, six Constructors were stationed about a strange, humming artifice. A circular section nearest the Constructors glowed, whitefire swirling within the brass through sectioned windows. Attached was a thick tube, directed towards Honour's House, from which a fiery bolt sizzled across the ten-yard gap to smash into the carved doors. The Constructors, however, paid no mind to the effects. Their white eyes instead peered upwards, hands pointing at the flames that burned along the southern wall.

"South," thought Laoch.

Sura acknowledged and faded, then ran through the stinking mound with, he hoped, little awareness of what she did. He signalled Oisin in the same direction, and for Ecne to remain with himself. As they both moved, the Constructors split. Two remained where they were, and removed a tarpaulin off a set of heavy, pulsing bars. One lifted a single lump of the glowing metal, while the other rodded out a similar, inert grey bar from the brass sphere.

Laoch had no intention of permitting another shot upon Honour's scorched walls. With Ecne taking aim by his side, Justice responded to his command, and an arrow flared in his newly formed bow. The Constructors had locked in the metal rod, and were now pulling levers at the rear. The swirl of whitefire increased in intensity within the small windows.

"Loose," growled Laoch.

Wisdom's green and Justice's red lit the market square. The two Constructors sensed the attack, and turned about, hands reaching for their weapons. Their cries cut short as spiritfire raged inside their shattered helms.

Laoch was on the run before they hit the floor, Justice lighting his way as it reformed into his preferred short sword. He slashed downwards and removed the first head, crushing the second with his boot. Again, the white flared, forming balls of spiritfire that boiled and seethed out of the bodies. Unlike in Innealtóir, where the whitefire of the unalive had merged into the palace floor, these stopped along the Constructor's back and entered a strange metal container.

"Fuck that," said Laoch, and he brought Justice down upon both gourds.

"Laoch!" Ecne whispered loudly, and he spun about.

The southern side of the market was aglow with Honour's light. Two Constructors lay dead upon the floor while the others faced off against Sura and Oisin. The crack of a whip cut through the silence. The weapon lashed towards Sura and her spear, and wrapped about the shaft. The Constructor pulled, only to stumble slightly as the metal lash gained no purchase. Laoch couldn't help but laugh at Sura's smile as she solidified and ran for the clearly shaken Constructor.

"They'll take them down," he said, and turned back to the infernal machine. He picked up the prod from beneath a dead Constructor and shoved one end against the glowing metal bar. It gave with a heave. A second, and then a third ram shoved the glowing metal completely clear of its slot. The weapon's hum changed into a whine, with the rod inert on the ground.

"Ecne!" he shouted.

The acolyte released a quarrel that slammed into Oisin's opponent. She looked back, noted Laoch's frustration, and ran over.

"The metal rods feed it. The levers fire it," he said. "Kill it."

Ecne nodded, her eyes already working over the controls and mechanisms to seek an answer. As she placed her hands upon the levers, the eastern sky lit with Nathair's flame. The huge dragon swept across the tops, to the welcome cries of pain and anguish from the soul-eating defenders. The additional light, however, caught something malevolent marching on a hundred legs along the street. Something eerily familiar.

"A bloody feeder," Laoch said. "Hurry, Ecne. We haven't long."

A shout of pain and another of victory resonated from behind, and Sura and Oisin were soon by his side.

"It's heading here at a fair pace," Oisin said, and he looked to what Ecne was doing.

"We'll have to deal with it," said Sura. "If the doors are as weak as Lady Honour says, it may well be able to take them down."

"Aye, and there's bound to be more of the bastards out there." Laoch wiped sweat from his eyes, mulling over their next move. "Ecne, how long?"

"I have no idea what I'm doing, Laoch. The only thing I can think of is your usual method," replied Ecne, hand on chin as she examined the levers. Lips moving, she sidestepped the biggest lever to peer closer at where it entered the machine.

"My method?"

"She means hit the bloody thing. And hard," said Sura, smirking.

"Very bloody funny."

"I meant it," said Ecne, and reached out to tap the top of a lever. "I can fire it, if that'll do."

Laoch glanced down the street to where the feeder was closing fast. Its segments ebbed and flowed while the ripple of feet carried it inexorably on towards them.

Choices.

"Then we move it. Sura, we need time." Her cat-like eyes flared orange in response, and before he could add more, she had gone.

Laoch, together with Oisin and Ecne, moved to the rear of the cannon.

———

Sura reformed in the centre of the street, planting Honour's spear on the blood and debris-strewn cobbles. Townsfolk had bustled to work along its paths. Carts and horses had taken their foodstuffs to market – or their owners to whatever tavern they sought. A strange life to many of her kind, but one she had come to love as much as the Partera Plains. All about her, faint spirits swirled, their memories gone, their *will* faded. They were being slowly drawn upwards in a race against the feeder that hunted them. She could sense their despair, for that was all that was left of them. Yet far above, Honour's veil waited, its curtain ready to accept one and all – and to see them on their way.

'I can feel their pain, as I did your people's,' said Honour.

The feeder's back arched in a wave of movement, the segments rippled as each set of feet pummelled into a street layered with the agonies wreaked upon this city. Each time, a flash of whitefire entered her spirit-sight, a hint of what the artifice contained – and its purpose.

"A harvester of the dead," she growled.

'A feeder of the weapon used to try and destroy my House.'

Sura smiled, eyes fierce. Her body glowed a fearsome orange that lit the sides of the street. A hitch entered the feeder's momentum, a sign it had seen her. She waited. She was a tempting morsel, after all.

The artifice surged, stretching, upping its pace. With a patience borne of being part-God, she refused to move, enticing the machine onwards. As the feeder neared to within ten yards, she noted another change in its movement pattern. The rear moved much further forwards than the front, a high arch forming in its centre.

Readying herself, Sura crouched, waiting.

The mechanical creature thrust forwards, foremost limbs reaching for her, mandibles scything the air.

Sura leapt vertically, spun once, and landed upon the creature's head. It reared back, frustrated, seeking the elusive food.

As tempting as striking at the armoured head was, she ran, her feet flying over the crystal segments to dodge between the spikes that littered its back. She felt the segments heave and twist. Honour informed her that the feeder was turning about, on the hunt for a prey that refused to stand still. Sura attempted to send her spirit senses deep into the centre of the beast, only for them to bounce back from the armoured segments.

"Honour?"

'The crystal is too strong, and very unlike that of the veil dragons. More akin to this black armour we have seen. It rejects spiritfire.'

"Or contains it." Sura reached the artifice's end, the snap of mandibles to her rear speeding her along. The last segment and the tail whipped up, trying to fling her into the air. When it failed, the fore section pulled itself up a building. Now in too awkward a position to catch the flailing elf, the feeder dragged itself higher and twisted around, forcing the rest of its body to turn awkwardly back on itself as it sought the delicious spirit on offer.

Sura decided to take control and faded away, only to reappear on the street, facing the huge artifice.

'Firing. Move!' came the thought from Laoch.

The bolt lit her spirit-sight and Honour railed, a sudden dread washing over the sliver of the God. Sura threw herself to one side, her physical form blinking out before she hit a wooden door, and hurtled through into the building beyond. Noise pierced her thoughts, though she was unsure if real or spiritual, and her spirit vibrated. The violence kept her on the floor, her mind splitting apart, hanging at the edge of a loss of reason as spiritfire roared outside.

In silence, Sura stood once again at the precipice, a wind whipping at her cloak, contemplating the leap. To join her brother in death.

She was no longer that person.

The noise and pain stopped. Sura's spirit, stretched like tree sap, responded to her will – and Honour's presence – and reformed. She stood tentatively, suddenly aware of the room she found herself in. At its centre, husked, drained bodies clung to one another. A family. Their eyes were dark holes. Fingers, now mere bone, still wrapped about those they loved for a final time.

They were empty. Silent.

"This ends," she whispered, and burst out through the door.

The segmented artifice reared into the air as it writhed in pain. Though Sura could see little damage, her spirit-sight caught whitefire gleaming from the crystal armour. Tiny veins that laced each segment. Fractures. The butt of her spear struck the nearest, and the crystal shattered to expose the mechanism within. The creature's limbs flailed, trying to pull the wound away from her vengeance.

Sura threw herself inside the mechanism.

62

A SUNDERING

SOUTH OF ERSTENBURGH,
BRANDSHOLD

Tabharthóir tore into the Scorpion. Whitefire laced each bite as scrap metal rolled down the dragon's throat. In the heat of its magic, scales forged within the beast, cogs soldered and healed, wires rebound as the Spirit Walker worked. Beneath the looming power of the *Kraken*, the last of the emperor's veil dragons renewed its strength while its master fed upon the soulship.

The emperor drained the Repanti magus dry, leaving nothing but a drop of their existence at the heart of their soul. They would recover, but it would take months. By that time, he would have all the Seven's offspring to feast upon. With a sneer, he took the last drop because he could. The flavour held less savour compared to the magi on this realm, but the nourishment was required.

Tarin let the husked body slump to the wood of the outer deck, and his eyes roamed up to the drained bodies nailed to the *Kraken*'s gleaming hull. He shook his head, a scowl upon his replenished lips.

A push here, a nudge there. Each a challenge, but never outright. You vex me, Lelion, yes? Your time is coming.

The admiral incarnate approached, a smirk upon her lips. At her side, the Mechanised Inhibitor captain who had replaced Popsilin. "A problem, Tarin?"

The emperor glared in response, but forced any thought of reprisal down. After all, he had left the sea captain and her younglings with Lelion as an annoyance, nothing more. The admiral looked well fed, and the death of her charges perhaps explained her good mood. It usually showed in her acquiescence to his orders rather than the bitter acceptance of his demands.

Though, there is something ...

"Our way to this city is clear, their pathetic resistance quashed. There is no problem except the losses you incurred," he said, letting a smile curl at the edges of his lips.

"Acceptable," said the admiral. "You wish to report, Captain?"

The Mechanised Inhibitor captain shuffled his feet and raised his white eyes from the deck to take in the two powerful Constructors. The emperor could smell the fear, and revelled in it. "Yes, Admiral. My Inhibitors report only a few Scorpions are inoperable. Most of those damaged could continue in a limited role if required, though the preference is for some additional time to action repairs. Just one feeder was destroyed. We lost five hundred Inhibitors, however. The foot soldiers took the brunt of the human resistance."

"Admiral?" said Tarin, the Fleshmaster not suppressing his glee at the failure. "Acceptable?"

"They use alchemical explosives, Tarin. You know this, though their stock must surely dwindle soon. We came across few magi. Unlike you." Lelion's lips twitched, clearly fighting another smirk. The emperor's spirit boiled.

A crack of bone and tendon resounded across the deck as Tarin balled his hands tight before spreading them wide. "I will take that, Admiral." The Fleshmaster closed in, his teeth exposed in a snarl. He noted as the captain's hand shifted to rest upon the pommel of his soulreaver, but ignored it for now as his dust-filled breath fell upon Lelion. "But you push and push."

The deck shook with vibrations that rose through the soles of his feet. A scaled head lifted high above the emperor, crystalline eyes staring down with malevolence at the admiral. Tabharthóir filled the remaining space upon the *Kraken*'s deck, and Tarin revelled in the slight tilt of the mighty soulship beneath his dragon's considerable weight.

"And eventually one of us *will* break." The Fleshmaster snapped his fingers, and Tabharthóir roared into the night's sky. One forefoot pawed at the deck, scoring the wood and brass. The screech cut through the air. "And it won't be me."

Tarin backed away from Lelion, but his white eyes never left the admiral incarnate. A second click, and teeth scythed down to slice the captain apart in a puff of dust and bone. His lower body collapsed to the deck, and the dragon tossed the upper half to land at the admiral's feet.

"I want the soul-cannons to start their work before sun's rise. Their walls are high, the stone thick but ill-bonded. No more delays, Admiral. The feeders are full, the *Kraken*'s stores high. Break those walls. We have the Seven's progeny to extract from their houses to feed *my* needs."

The emperor strode over to his dragon and entered the repaired chest. With a bellow that shook the bridge windows, the veil dragon leapt into the air.

—

"Six," said Lelion as the dragon disappeared into the night. "You only seek six of the Magi now." She glanced at the remains of the captain's body, her white eyes veined with redfire.

The bridge's brass door slammed shut and Lieutenant Spintz emerged. "Does he know?" she asked, and grimaced as the captain's whitefire poured into the waiting gourd. A white shadowed by a wisp of red.

"I do not know, but any other converts need to be kept out of his sight. Your test was at least worthwhile." The admiral glanced back up into the sky. A sliver of a moon appeared fleetingly from behind the cloud, but the dragon was absent. "How many?"

"All but one were willing, once they had a taste of the Magus," she replied, absently running a finger along her lips. "And they will soon turn their eyes your way, I am sure. When?"

"It must be before he gains any of the stronger magi, the progeny of the Seven. You have tasted the power of just one of their number; we cannot let him have any of the rest. We do as he says. Take control of the city. If the magi hide in their Houses like in Makalena, we strike then, when he is at his weakest." The admiral strode over to the deck rail and peered down into the milieu of Inhibitors and artifices below. In their centre, a dragon lay curled in on itself, its scaled head resting on taloned forefeet.

"And Tabharthóir?" Spintz asked as she joined Lelion at the brass rail.

"He hides it, but I believe the Spirit Walker suffers. Why else would he insist on being the veil dragon's pilot? Every war, every battle, he has stood here and spouted orders for his own gain. He claims it is for us, for the Constructors, but he is seeking revenge on the Seven for turning from his light. He burns with hate, and only lifted us from the darkness of the Sundering to fulfil his vengeance." The admiral looked to her lieutenant. "Kill the Fleshmaster, and Tabharthóir will either be as a kitten, or turn wild and flee. Both serve our purpose."

63
ON A WING AND A PRAYER

MAKALENA, BRANDSHOLD

"Sura!" Laoch called as he yanked apart the pile of cogs and wires to peer inside the shattered feeder. "I think it is dead." He dropped the pieces on the street, only to reach for another set of tangled wires. Ferocious noises clanged from within – a crash of spear upon metal and stone as the elven warrior continued to berate the machinery. "Honour's House!" he bellowed, and the battering came to an end.

He stepped away from the gap, and was pleased to see Sura emerge. The fury on her face dissipated as she locked eyes with him.

"It is done," he said. "And a fine bloody mess you made of it."

"It will not be done until the last Constructor dies," she replied, and kicked aside the pieces he'd dropped. She strode off towards Ecne and Oisin, Laoch in her wake as she approached the cannon.

"It did for the feeder's armour," Ecne told her as she strode past. "Weakened it, as it has the door."

Sura walked on to the seven steps of Honour's House. She

placed her hand upon Honour's head amid the scorch marks, and her body stilled. When Laoch finally caught up, all four were at Honour's door. The elf's lips moved, though the words were not of the Schenterenta, but human. Then she knocked a pattern upon it and waited.

"Oisin," said Laoch, "there'll be more Constructors coming. We need time until Nathair is done cooking all the bastards on the walls."

"And Ecne?" Oisin tilted his head towards the acolyte.

"Go with Oisin, Ecne. Keep us clear. And let Nathair know we need Rensta when you can."

Ecne lifted her crossbow into the crook of her arm and set off with Oisin. The Elite Ranger directed her to cover the entrance to the square.

The doors parted, and orange light spilled out.

"Lady Honour?" said a male voice, though its owner remained hidden.

"No," replied Sura, and a sliver of orangefire swept from her hand and into the gap. "I *am* Honour."

A surprised gasp led to a swiftly opened door. The robed priest, wreathed in Honour's spiritfire, fell to his knees, eyes wide. His lips moved, but no words came as he stared at Sura.

Placing both hands upon his shoulders, Sura released the smile that had stolen Laoch's heart so long ago. "Stand. We have little time. Lady Honour sent us to stop the attack upon my House, but our need is greater than that. I need to see the Wyrding Stone."

"I—"

Sura followed up her smile with the withering look Laoch also knew well, and the priest stood quickly, bowing. "This way," he said.

They headed down the central aisle and towards four other priests of varying ages, who stood by the prayer stone.

"Are all your Houses like this, Laoch?" Sura said, her gaze focused on the large crystal the priests clearly guarded. "With such a stone?"

"The ones I've been in, yes. Though the Houses of Erstenburgh are larger, the prayer stones thicker." He looked at the dragon depicted upon the ceiling – Honour, with spear in hand, fending the beast off. "And all with the Unspoken, in some form, on the bloody ceiling pressing down, spreading fear. That doesn't even look like you, you know."

Sura glared his way, half smiling beneath her ferocity. "You made your choice. Change your mind, and I can rip your heart out and take it with me." She nudged him and pointed towards the prayer stone. "I need Rensta right now. If her thoughts are right, moon pools and prayer stones serve a similar purpose."

"Aye." Laoch glanced at the priests. The one who'd met them beckoned Sura onwards. With a nod, Laoch left. He strode out the door as the glow of Fate's arrow lit the adjoining street, soon followed by another. Ecne waited beside the strange cannon, her eyes directed towards the other entrance to the square, but in reality, focused on nothing. On calling her name, Ecne blinked once and signalled up. The flap of metalled wings filled the square with gusts of cold spring-time air. Laoch backed away, and Nathair squeezed into the available space, her wings spread wide. The shimmer of her chest heralded Rensta's arrival, the shaman's walk marred by her twisted back as she exited.

"Rensta," he called, beckoning her over, "Sura is inside. Ecne, what's Nathair doing now?"

Ecne slipped into her thoughts again, then pointed north. "The Constructors are running for the northern gate. She intends to … eat."

"A fine choice," Laoch replied, and turned to follow Rensta inside. A glance over to Oisin confirmed the Handren maintained watch.

Sura stood before the prayer stone, her faded form pulsing with orange-fire. The priests were all on their knees, eyes fixed on her, a mixture of rapture and fear upon their faces. Rensta nearly choked on her way in and soon stood by Sura, eyeing the crystal the priests had guarded.

"Yes," she said, and her hand landed on Sura's arm as if it were fully formed. Whitefire flashed between them, and Laoch gawped as two spirits rose from the shaman. They were beautiful, ethereal in form, yet shining with vitality. They intertwined as they rose, their faces always focused upon the prayer stone, and a gentle hum reverberated from the crystal. As the intensity increased, the priests shuffled away, though their attention remained on Sura.

Laoch's heart began to vibrate as the thrum echoed through his chest and skull. It pulsed rhythmically, in tune with the stone, and his soul stretched, the roots in his heart and mind drawn towards the crystal.

Like a Soul Tear.

It ended suddenly. Rensta's twinned souls poured back into her body while Sura solidified. Laoch took a moment to steady himself, hands on his knees, but kept his eyes on the pair of Schenterenta. Their broad grins stoked the hope that thudded in his chest.

Sura's eyes shone bright. "Yes," she said, and pulled Laoch in close. "Hope."

"The Wyrding Stone," said the male priest, and thrust a cloth containing a fist-sized orange crystal towards Sura.

Sura's fingers lingered on Laoch's arm before she broke contact and took the stone. The orange in her eyes flashed, mirroring the spiritfire that rushed up her wrist. Sura frowned and her face contorted before it slackened. Suddenly, there were two faces interposed over each other. One human, the other, Sura's. Not fighting for supremacy but merging.

"Take it," whispered Sura, and the priest wrapped the crystal back in the cloth. Sura doubled over, holding her arm, which pulsed briefly black before orangefire swept the discolouration away.

"You okay?" asked Laoch, and moved towards her.

Rensta swiftly blocked his path. "Careful," the shaman said before lowering her arm, cat eyes locking on his. "There's too much power there. It is unfocused, ill-formed. Have patience."

After a few seconds, Sura stood straight, a hand, palm out, raised to show him she was fine, though her lips quivered in a way he recognised. "It will work, Rensta. But not from here. The Wyrding burns because it fights itself." She looked to Laoch. "The filling of your veils runs against the bond of the stone. Your Houses suffer for what they do, do they not?"

"I—" began Laoch, but the male priest stepped in and pulled back his robe. His right arm was black, stirring Laoch's memories of the few Lords and Ladies of the Houses he'd met.

Sura grimaced at the withered limb. "And I know why. Your prayers and the Wyrding Stones, they are connected?"

The priest nodded. "These, yes. But not those of the Erstenburgh Houses. They are fed from the prayer to the Wyrding. The waiting believe there is it too much power in those huge stones for any of the Lords to truly control."

"But they are connected to here? Each of the Seven Houses are linked to their own outliers? That is how Lady Honour knew you were in trouble, but the connection with Erstenburgh has been blocked?"

Sura's words were greeted by the priest's agreement.

"If the lifesong is to work, it must be focused on where the Constructors are. The more central the song, the more we will ensnare." Rensta hobbled closer to the prayer stone. Bending over, she placed a single finger upon the highly polished surface. "But there is such power here, Sura. This can be done."

"But by whom?" said Laoch, only for a scuffled noise in the House doorway to catch his attention.

"Laoch, we need you!" shouted Ecne. The urgency in her voice was punctuated by a flash of blue from behind. "We have a group of Constructors under shields, approaching. And Nathair is out of range."

"Work to do," he said, and pulled Justice free. The redfire along the sword's edge crackled into life. "Decide what we need to get done, and bloody soon. If Erstenburgh is cut off, the queen is in danger as well as the people. For all we know, we are too late." He ran for the door, Oisin's shouts beyond it encouraging him on.

By the time he'd descended the steps, Fate glowed blue along Oisin's short sword as he faced off against two Constructors. Another had Ecne trapped in the market corner, and the sword in their hand had an evil about it Laoch struggled to define as the weapon pulsed with whitefire. Decision made, he charged that way, flinging a thought towards Sura and hoping it would slide through the doorway somehow.

Ecne blocked an attack from the Constructor. Sparks of whitefire flared against Wisdom's green. She took a step backwards, desperately avoiding a kick the Constructor aimed at her knee, only to stumble against a limp body on the floor. Falling back, she raised Wisdom as the evil weapon crashed downwards.

Too late.

Laoch screamed in anger. Ecne's death was in that weapon.

Wisdom burst into flame, the light so intense it seared Laoch's sight. He careered onwards. His shoulder slammed into the Constructor's hip and took them to the ground.

Eyes burning, his arm and Justice were trapped beneath the crystal armour. Though his own weight added to the problem, fear of the Constructor's sword kept him in place. Justice's angered redfire slid off the plates that held it fast. The God's frustration built, urging Laoch to move. To release them.

Sudden heat from the foul sword washed over Laoch's neck as the Constructor slammed the pommel into his back. Pain hit his *being*, and the root of his soul was drawn sickeningly towards the weapon. The pommel lifted and struck again, and Laoch's heart hurt as his spirit stretched at the root. The demand of the Constructor's sword was too much to resist.

More heat swept over him, but a third strike didn't land. Crystal shards clattered against his back and a gasp of remembered pain bellowed in his ear. Laoch rolled away, his sight still full of hues of green, blending with Ecne's shadow as the acolyte struck again and again at the Constructor.

"Die, you bastard!" she shouted. A crunch of bone was rewarded with the glare of whitefire, warping Laoch's vision once again.

Laoch rolled onto his hands and knees, blinking furiously at the dark ground in the hopes it would help clear the spots. "Help Oisin," he growled while pressing fingers deep into his eye sockets.

"Sura has that covered," Ecne replied, and knelt down near his face. "Wisdom blinded the white eye, and by the looks of it, took you out too. It should pass soon."

"That sword," said Laoch, finally rising to his haunches. A final blink cleared all but one of the eye spots. "Don't touch it, but have a look. Did you feel it pull at your spirit?"

A noise cut through his words – Sura and Oisin shattering gourds around which balls of whitefire roiled. Laoch looked away and squeezed the bridge of his nose as a few blind spots reappeared.

"Wisdom spoke to me, told me to be wary of it. I didn't feel a pull, but if Wisdom was helping, then perhaps whatever it does was blocked." She stood and, using Wisdom, poked in the ruins of the Constructor to expose their weapon. "Is it of use?" she muttered. Laoch got the sense she wasn't talking to him.

Ecne nodded as if to herself and drew out a cloth from her bag. By the time Laoch had gained his feet and his vision had cleared, she had used the cloth to collect the weapon and sheathe it, taking the belt and scabbard. She shrugged at Laoch's querying look.

"You can add it to your artifice spider collection," he said, sheathing Justice, "and all those cogs and wires you hoard."

"Nathair requested those, just in case." Ecne looked to the sky. Dragon's wings sent smoke streaming across the sliver of the moon. "And she comes."

"You have a lot of voices in your head, girl," said Oisin as Sura re-entered the House. "Any of them make more sense than you?"

Ecne threw Oisin a glare clearly drawn from Sura's repertoire. The Elite Ranger held his hands up, his smile forcing Ecne's seriousness to crumble into a laugh. "Yes. They make far more sense when you block out some old man's wittering."

"She's fine," added Oisin, and grinned at Laoch. "I wouldn't fret too much about her. Though that glare might be a worry. Too much dragon spirit and Wisdom in her moods I can handle, but when she adds a pinch of Sura in the mix? Dangerous."

Ecne shook her head, and as Nathair's wingbeats echoed across the rooftops, they headed into Honour's House, towards the sound of elven singing.

64
WE STAND AS ONE

ERSTENBURGH, BRANDSHOLD

The soul-cannon spun up. Whitefire crackled within the sphere until it emitted the crystal shard. It streaked across the killing field, a whirling dervish that smashed into Erstenburgh's southern wall. A wave of whitefire rolled out from the impact site, the stonework appearing to ripple. There was no cheer from the Constructor soul-gunners. Instead, they hammered out the metal bar from the centre of the sphere to land amid twelve other spent lumps. A second cannon fired, soon followed by a third, as the sun passed its zenith.

"Do we know how long we have?" asked Mordant, turning to Lord Hope, who peered through a strange-looking spyglass towards the weapons.

"Makalena reported a day of bombardment before they went silent." The Lord lowered his spyglass and looked over the western section of the forest in what he judged to be the direction of that broken city. "I think they block our vision crystals, my queen. Even those we sent north to Pantsil no longer answer. Their evil lies like a malaise over the city."

"Then we are alone in our fight, Lord Hope. Until the Constructors enter the city, I bid your priests to watch the skies for dragons. Theirs and the Unspoken's – or perhaps even this Nathair the High Lord has put store in. It would be a short-lived irony if we were to strike against our own salvation." The queen allowed a faint smile towards the Lord, who bowed his head and left to reaffirm what his priests were already doing.

"We are encircled, but they do not attack," said Mordant, his hand held tight against his chest as he turned to the queen. "As at Makalena, except there the threat of Mandrich's army split their forces. Once the walls are down, it will be street by street until they reach the walls of the palace."

"You are to defend the Houses before the palace, Captain, as I have already stated. We are to buy time for the Seven to act, or the Union will fall as we do." She laid a hand on the man's shoulder, catching his gaze. "I put my trust in you and your city guard. You have prepared for this; they know what to do. I am not their goal, Captain. Even if I was, you must put your trust in me and in what I command."

Mordant squeezed his eyelids together, looking to his queen before sweeping his gaze across the city and the brightening southern walls. Arrayed on every tower and wall, scaffolding held Arknold's ballistae at the ready, crewed by soldiers who had trained for weeks in their roles. Along three of the four walls, a few guards remained on watch, with many more beneath the highest walkway and shielded from dragon's breath.

He checked the buildings, most with ladders waiting upon their roofs. About them, thieves and street fighters languished, ready for when their particular skills would be needed. Scum who had volunteered to defend their home city on the word of a gang leader they named Geral. And finally, the trebuchets and their piles of rock, off-cast metal and – most precious of all – the Erin's Wrath hidden beneath tarpaulins.

"Yes, my queen," he said, and settled his gaze upon the central street arrayed with barricades and the stout but ornately carved Houses of the Seven. "We know where the last stand will be made. It will, at least, be easier without our people in harm's way."

Another crash of crystallised stone upon the southern wall caused a wave of whitefire to flow over the top. Its glow lit the whole wall. Two more crashed in, lower down, and echoes stretched across the city as the bombardment continued.

"Now I ask a favour of my queen." He turned to her, his eyes red and aged, taking her in, arms out wide. "To leave the walls, to seek sanctuary with the Seven." He raised a hand, daring to cut the queen of the Union dead as she made to speak. "I, and my soldiers, will fight for you and this city to the last. But the moment you fall is the moment that resolve will crumble. Go to Fate, or Penance if you see fit. Let us focus on what we do."

"I—"

"—wish to die with a sword in your hand and one of your mother's swear words on your lips, I know. But that is not your role here. As long as you are out of sight, our queen and Overseer is presumed safe, and we can get on with the job of killing our enemy."

Queen Weister harrumphed; her return glare filled with irritation, yet honoured by the man in equal measure. "May the Seven stand with you, Captain."

"My queen and Overseer has my sword and heart, and Justice my soul," he said, hand back upon his chest. "And I will be forever grateful for both."

—⸻

The tremor and sudden release fascinated Yanik. She watched as the weight dropped swiftly, propelling the trebuchet's great arm at impressive speed. As it sprang upwards, its load creaked within the sling and flew high over the southern wall. She imagined the stone crashing into the killing field, bouncing forwards to knock aside the Constructors like jugs in a tavern.

"Five yards short!" came the reply from the spotter, with responding grumbles from the team resetting the machine.

"Still too far," echoed back, and the spotter put his thumbs up as he returned his spyglass to the south.

Yanik shook her head and rechecked her equipment for the hundredth time. The Ranger Spear she had been assigned to had memorised the streets about the southern wall like the backs of their hands over the preceding weeks. Her knowledge was scant, but her skills desperately needed. No longer the First of her dead Spear, she only cared for the chance to fight the creators of the Infected horde who threatened an even worse fate for those left behind.

She stopped, fingers poised, as she checked the fletch of an arrow. Silence had fallen – the boom of the Constructors' weapons had stopped. The city held its collective breath, Yanik included.

"Abandon the southern wall!" The command came from above, Captain Mordant's voice strident in the deathly quiet. The warning bell rang, its import picked up across the city. A cacophony of panicked voices all with the same thought. The remaining townsfolk – those who had stayed to feed and house the additional soldiers assigned to the city guards – ran for cover, while officers demanded readiness and courage.

Yanik missed the comfort of Duke Panset's determination – his drive to do what was right – and General Zendril's stubborn resolve. But, above all else, she missed Mander's quiet confidence. And for all their collective efforts to stem the tide of the poisoned horde, the Unspoken had not come. What lay beyond their walls now hungered for their souls with weapons she could not understand.

Signal flags waved along the walls.

A low hum, ominous, tainted with evil intent, filled the air. Malevolence glowed like a mist above the southern wall, a pulsating light that sickened Yanik.

The throb of sound and light brought a dread-filled pause to the city.

A hand gripped her arm, and she turned, expecting someone to have orders or a word. Instead, the First of her Spear had simply reached for the nearest human comfort he could find. Yanik examined the man's face, looking for the fear that could lead to panic and poor decisions. Undecided, she turned away as the pitch changed and the hum's intensity increased. Her chest, feeling suddenly hollow, began to vibrate. The discordant pattern set the beat of her heart racing.

"Calm," she whispered, and placed her hand suddenly on the First's and squeezed back.

The malevolent light flashed, and a crescendo of sound and vision roared across the city, a wave of malice that pulled at her soul. In Yanik's mind, the streets filled with the spirits of fallen comrades beseeching those still alive to release their pain. The whitefire left a bitter tang in the air.

"So much death," she said.

And the world turned grey.

The southern wall shattered. Stone and dust billowed across the city as the ring of protection was breached. The choking, swirling clouds swept through parallel streets and across into adjoining lanes. Yanik turned away, burying her head into the crook of her arm as she had when the horde burned before the walls of Anvil. Coughs and splutters marked the dust's passing, and as Yanik cleared her eyes and nose of it, light broke through. She blinked, swiping away the dust that had settled on her lashes, staring into the void where a wall had once been. Beyond the breach hovered the sky ship, the crystal-crusted lower half dulling after its work was done. Before it were the machines Mander had spoken of: giant Scorpions from her nightmares, with metal limbs that drove into the grass and pincers out front, steel claws ready to slice your head from your body.

She drew a breath, eyes roaming over the black-clad soldiers lined up beyond the Scorpions, their armour gleaming in the sun's light. Not a mote of dust upon them. Clean, shining and – according to Captain Mordant – ready to repel both blade and the priests' spiritfire in equal measure. And lastly, and never still, segmented monsters, their mandibles scything the air as if they could taste the human souls from where they waited.

"By the Seven," said the First.

Yanik whipped her head about to glare at the man. "No. This is what the Seven fought against. These are the evil that would take your body, mind and soul, and feed upon them on a whim." She stepped away from the man, eyes sweeping across the four others in the Spear. "They murdered Jense, turned them into the hungry dead. Twelve thousand souls, families whose spirits were so poisoned, they fell upon their own children." She took a breath and calmed her heart, knowing her fear was spilling into the words. "Fear and despair are your enemy, understand? You flinch once, you run instead of stand, dither instead of act, they will hunt you down. Play with you like a cat with a fucking mouse. Find where your family hides and eat their fucking souls. You understand? You give no quarter. None! Kill these bastards any way you bloody can. You can either piss yourself and wait for slavery, or you can fucking fight." Yanik paused, suddenly aware she was being watched by more than her Spear. She spun about. Six more Spears, sprinkled with veterans and cutthroats, had stopped to listen or peer down from rooftops.

She blinked, unsure of what to do next.

"You were at Jense?" said a scarred female Ranger, the mark of banefire across one side of her head.

Yanik nodded.

"As bad as they say?"

Yanik wiped her nose clear of the cloying dust before locking eyes with the veteran. "Worse." She spat on the floor.

The veteran turned to her Spear. "You heard 'er, ye feckers. One of ye bast'ds pisses themselves, I'll rub ye bloody nose in it. We're not here for the bloody Seven but ye bloody kids. Hear me?"

Yanik watched as the woman turned away, eyes sweeping the others as nods and grimaces were sent her way. The Rangers disappeared into the streets and alleyways, while the cutthroats scampered away across the rooftops.

"Man the breach!"

Mordant's words were taken up at street level as the bells sounded again. Yanik stared through the hole, stone piled upon stone spilling into the ditch that surrounded much of the city. The smallest of barriers as the squeal of metal pierced the cries. The first of the metal limbs lifted, reaching forwards, and a hundred more joined as the Scorpions started their journey. Above her, the sound of booted feet upon the topmost walkway signalled the arrival of the city guard. They took station along what remained of the southern wall, and turned the surviving ballistae the way of the artifices. With that, the first wave of rocks flew overhead.

"Fuck."

———

"Captain!" The barely audible shout reached Mordant's ears. He swivelled his head to catch sight of the priest running towards his western tower. With his yellow robes wreathed in dust, the man stopped within shouting distance to point and yell, "Dragon!"

Mordant, shielding his eyes from the high sun, gazed at the huge artifice that beat at the frigid air. "Signal the target," he growled, and the flag bearers selected and waved their pendants, mingled with the shouts of more watchers.

There was little sign of an injury, its wingbeat steady until they locked into a dive.

"But, thank the Seven, not from above this time, where we cannot aim."

The twang and release of a heavy ballista quarrel gave the captain some satisfaction. More followed, spiralling northwards towards the silver-blue monstrosity hurtling towards them. The first three dropped below or to the side, their crystal heads useless as they dipped towards the empty forest.

The fourth clipped the machine's chest. A flash of blackfire marked it as one of Death's.

The dragon roared, and spiritfire wrapped about its metal scales before sliding away into the ether. The artifice didn't miss a beat.

"Keep them firing," he ordered, and the artillery signalman waved his flags while Mordant spoke to his companion, whose signals were solely for the walls. "I want them under cover," he said.

The bells pounded a different rhythm, and the raised flag alongside sent three walls of guards racing towards the ladders.

"Sir?" said the waiting guard.

Mordant knew what he was asking. "No. We hold. It heads for the western wall."

More heavy quarrels flew. Mordant winced as they missed their agile quarry. But then the final one struck a trailing leg. Again, Death's black wreathed the scales, rewarded by flashes of silver-blue metal that burst into the air behind the diving dragon. Still the metal beast dropped, and a flash of whitefire from its snout ignited a river of flame that poured down upon the wall.

Mordant waited, stock still, eyes scanning the walls. The screams started. Those guards still on the ladders burst into flame and flailed at the fire as they toppled backwards into the streets below. More cries came from beneath the walkway. Fewer than he feared, but more than he wanted. The shadow of the dragon passed over the end of the city to the smell of scorched wood upon the hot wind, and continued south to disappear behind the sky ship that hovered, inert, above the forest.

"It'll come back," he growled out loud, and leaned forwards to place both hands on the stone of his tower. He watched the Scorpions marching towards the breach. "From the east, or perhaps the more likely is the south. Ready yourselves."

The air whistled with rocks and pots as the trebuchets' second round of missiles arced above the southern wall. The Scorpions, clearly aware, paused their movements. He sensed them watching, judging, with the spacing between each carefully calculated for sudden manoeuvres. As the barrage hurtled towards them, they moved, their coordination breathtaking as the rocks drove deep into earth and grass. Erin's Wrath, however, was not so easily cowed, and explosions rocked two of the multi-limbed machines. Smoke rose from one, and another's crystal windows shattered.

They barely missed a stride, however. Their pace increasing as they once again headed towards the breach.

The two surviving ballistae upon the southern wall fired. Their heavy quarrels were harder to pick out, but they struck home. Redfire arced from one, blue from another, and the Scorpions stuttered.

Mordant prayed.

And beseeched.

One succumbed to Justice's rage, the redfire ripping through its hull where a limb joined. Whatever lay inside suddenly vibrated, and the artifice collapsed to the floor, legs twitching. The second's fate was more unclear. It stuttered onwards, clearly injured, yet apparently determined to keep moving.

Shouts caught his attention, and his signalman pointed. Smoke billowed from the south-eastern corner of the wall. The dragon's head appeared above the stone, wings spread wide, beating hard to keep the beast in the sky. Fiery breath poured across the southern wall, cooking the nearest ballista crew. The gout of flame rolled onwards to engulf the second crew beyond the breach. In a proclamation of victory, the dragon roared, wings thrashing at the air to lift its bulk above and away from the wall.

Heavy quarrels flew from the inner towers. Two struck their mark, the explosions wreathing the dragon's chest in Greeth's greenfire. A few scales shattered to expose skin and ribs, the silver-blue plates melting under the impact. The dragon's head swivelled about and the crystalline eyes flashed. Mordant knew it had marked those towers for its next pass as the attack dissipated.

Whitefire emerged from beneath the scales to wreath the metal creature and, to Mordant's amazement, the veil dragon rose higher and higher with each beat before twisting lithely away from the walls. Two smaller quarrels hit its tail, their flashes of power merely lighting the creature's spiked end as the limb whipped back to strike one of the wooden artillery pieces. The machinery splintered into matchsticks as its broken crew flew like rag dolls off the wall.

"Evil bastard," he spat. "Signal the tower ballistae to reload, fire, then run. It's coming for them. The northern and eastern walls are to take cover in case the dragon changes its mind. Now!"

Mordant paused, his mind on the southern wall. It would fall, but how much to sacrifice to fill the breach?

We need time.

He yanked at the yellow robes of the watcher who still peered out across the eastern forest, his strange spyglass obviously declaring no danger lay out there.

"I need the priests," he said. "At the breach."

"This is expected," said the woman. Her eyes filled with yellowfire as she exposed the crystal in her fist. "I will inform them they are to engage."

"I am sorry," he said, eyes cast to the stone floor of the tower.

"We serve the Seven, and we knew it would be required. You wish them all? They stand ready." The priest, still and focused for so long, eyed the captain as she jittered from one foot to the other.

"Two waves, as we trained."

"It will be done." The crystal lit with a muted glow. The shroud the Constructors had laid upon the city subdued the connections, but those who waited were close. "Deploy n—"

The priest fell silent, her wide-eyed gaze fixed on the sky behind Mordant.

"Down!" Mordant shouted.

Hot, oily breath flowed across his back and neck, punctuated by the beat of wings raising the dragon above the eastern wall. Signalmen threw themselves to the stone floor, cries of fear amid the clatter of flags, as the priest's hands came together. The air lit with yellowfire as she struck out at the dragon's open maw. But Mordant's fate was sealed. A tickle of whitefire kindled the dragon's breath and searing heat ignited his uniform, incinerating the cloth and heating the armoured plates to cook his flesh beneath. With hair set alight, his eyes boiled in their sockets while his melted flesh sloughed to the floor. Mordant fell to his knees, collapsing in flame upon the eastern tower.

Hope's priest stood unscathed upon the tower, her spiritfire stalled as true, terrifying dread took hold. Crystalline eyes flashed and a long, metal tongue wrapped about the woman and drew her in. Sword-like teeth bit down and massive, metal-skinned wings flung the silver-blue dragon away from the walls in a trail of blood and whitefire.

65
FORGOTTEN HOPE

ABOVE ERSTENBURGH, BRANDSHOLD

"*A mere snack compared to the delights to come,*" the emperor thought, revelling in Tabharthóir's surge of pleasure as the magus's spiritfire infused her heartstone. With a second thought, the Spirit Walker savoured a last taste before waves of spiritfire crackled about her limbs and hull. Cogs and wires eased with the renewed energy, wings beat stronger, while scale and metal healed.

They swept across the eastern forest, the dragon dipping a wing to head north and upwards. Tabharthóir cut through the air to finally turn about with the city spread wide before her. Rising, with the magus's tang upon her spirit, the dragon roared and dived, adding momentum with her wing beats as she arrowed towards the veiled city.

"*Yes, Tabharthóir. Beneath our shroud lies the spirits of thousands, and among them, the magi quail, ready for our wrath. Vengeance is so close.*"

They flew above the northern wall, the ramparts now bare of soldiers, though four hefty quarrels darted Tabharthóir's way from the central towers. The emperor had expected the response and, with wings spread, the dragon jagged first left, then right. One of the metal javelins struck her neck. The scales there absorbed the impact. Greenfire spread across the rest, searing, seeking passage beneath and into the heart of the artifice. A spurt of whitefire crushed the attempt, and Tabharthóir, responding to the emperor's urging, wreathed the towers in her flame. The simple wooden machines caught light and burned to ash under the onslaught as their crews fled or cooked.

"*Yessss. Show me,*" the Fleshmaster commanded.

The dragon's eyes took in the breach. The first of the Scorpions were clambering towards the summit of broken stone. This time they were more wary, aware of the dangers that may lie inside. But with the dragon's own shroud disrupting its spirit-sight, Tarin could not tell where the magi where waiting.

"*A curse and a blessing,*" he thought.

The dragon's muted response favoured the former. Angry, Tarin suppressed the thought. Arrows rained upon the metal artifices as the dragon soared above, only for something much heavier to strike her wing. The dragon dipped slightly before recovering. The ensuing crash of rock and explosions that rocked the rear of the Scorpion vanguard hinted at what had struck them.

The Fleshmaster sneered, realising the Inhibitors on foot were being held back. That Lelion waited for the Scorpions, or himself, to put an end to the barrage from the city.

"*So be it,*" he thought, and brought Tabharthóir down low, forelegs extended. The surge of whitefire thrilled him as Tabharthóir's talons latched onto her target. The heave of her wings drove the dragon and her prize into the sky, the effort far greater than the emperor had expected. However, the veil dragon responded to her master's demands. Higher it flew, wheeling about, wings pounding at the air over a portion of the still intact southern wall.

With glee, the talons opened, and the writhing, angry feeder they had stolen plummeted amidst the wooden machines that had kept the admiral's Inhibitors at bay.

"Coward," he said out loud as the feeder crunched into the nearest trebuchet. Head lashing as it wriggled to regain its feet, the rear segments rolled across soldier and machine, feet flailing at anything in its path. With a final surge, the artifice righted itself, and mandibles sliced open the nearest of the trebuchet crew as they scrambled away. Blood spurted, and the feeder's body thrashed against the toppling trebuchet.

The last thing the emperor saw before crossing the western wall was the artifice's rear segment scrabbling for purchase on a slippery tarpaulin. Barrels and clay pots rolled out from beneath, spinning about the wreckage as the feeder fed.

—

"What has he done?" The admiral glared at the distant dragon as it left the city behind. Spintz made to answer, but changed her mind when whitefire sparked across the admiral incarnate's brass armour.

"Answer," the admiral snarled, whipping about to pour her frustration towards the lieutenant.

"Accelerated the attack," Spintz replied. She waited, hands gripped tight behind her back, as her body tensed.

"I can see that. Why?" The admiral shifted position, frustrated she couldn't see into the city, couldn't see what the feeder was doing. More anger bubbled as she remembered all but one of the ornithopters were downed or under repair. The humans had proved resourceful, and it gnawed at her that they were relatively blind except for the Fleshmaster's dragon.

"Either to stop the explosive attacks and free the Inhibitor foot to go in, or to draw away the magi to take the feeder down, or ..."

"To piss me off. Say it."

"To piss you off while achieving any of the above." Spintz took a step backwards, while Lelion's angry whitefire crawled over her brass armour and arced outwards, seeking an outlet.

The admiral witnessed several flashes within the wall gap. Purples clashing with blues and greens. Smoke rose, and the screech of metal expanding against metal throttled her next tirade.

With a thought sent to the Inhibitor captains, she ordered the first and second divisions towards the southern wall, holding back the third as something tickled at her mind. As she watched the Inhibitors pound across the divide towards the city wall, she thought it was the return of the dreaded humming that had sent her half-mad. It grew in weight and import, a distant voice demanding her attention. She leant her elbows on the rail, trying to focus, when the captain of the pilots ran over from the starboard side of the soulship.

"Admiral," the captain said. "Can you sense it? It is pilot Inhibitor Crena. The emperor's shroud has blocked her thoughts, but the urgency is clear."

The admiral shook her head, pushing herself away from the rail as she tried to concentrate. The emperor's actions had limited the range of their thought commands, much as it had muted the humans' message crystals. A loss and a gain, considering the Inhibitors, when close, could still act in unison. Now she knew who was trying to make contact, she focused her mind, quelling the redfire that still swam in her ancient veins.

Images seeped through, mired in the green of the forest canopy. As she focused, Lelion could make out shapes running between the trees. Their shields were adorned with stylised images of the Seven. They carried long hooked spears and wore light armour. And they kept coming, line after line. As the pilot Inhibitor glanced upwards, Lelion made out the *Kraken* in the distance, hovering next to the smoking city.

"An attack," she whispered, her throat dry. Dust filled the air about her lips. "From the east." She grabbed Spintz by the collar. "There's an army coming on foot, running through the forest. Get the third to reinforce the eastern flank. Now."

Lelion turned back to the city and searched the skies for Tabharthóir, only for a silver metal tail to whip over the eastern wall. It lashed downwards, ash and smoke swirling as it raked the battlements. A rainbow of power lit the smoke from below, flashes that scorched the silver-blue scales, rocking the artifice in the air. But the tail still slashed and lashed, scattering soldiers, tearing apart the remaining ballistae. More spiritfire was hurled towards the dragon's flank. Most missed as it dropped over the northern side of the city.

Lelion swore and kicked at anything she could find along the deck. Within three strides, she was upon the redfire magus. Hands hovered over his head, a decision to be made.

"Ahhhhh!" she screamed, hands clenching as the need burgeoned. She shoved the man to the deck and stepped over him.

He will taste the magus upon my spirit. Too soon.

Glaring at the family pinioned to the hull, she took their last in turn, unable to delight in their deaths as urgency pounded in her ears. Prepared, she ran onto the bridge and placed her hands on the crystal that waited before her chair.

'*Tarin!*' her thoughts, strengthened by a child's soul, shouted. '*Listen. An army comes from the east. From the east.*'

She felt the muddiness of the Fleshmaster's shroud but cut through the murk, seeking the dragon's heartstone. An absence was returned, a *nothing*.

"Ranket!" shouted the admiral.

As the Inhibitor approached, expecting orders, she drove gauntleted fingers into his throat. The whitefire screamed along her arm and down into the crystal.

'*Emperor! An army to the east.*'

"*Must I do everything?*" came the sneering reply.

66

ON ZEALOTS' SHOULDERS

ERSTEN FOREST, ERSTENBURGH,
BRANDSHOLD

Sneed's purple lips bubbled with the junip, the juice spilling from the corner of his mouth as his horse trotted through the trees. With roots and undergrowth a real concern, he'd found himself overtaken by the leading cohort of the oligarchy's army. The House of Honour had their shields strapped to their backs, swords and daggers sheathed. But their major weapons shone from within, filling the forest with the zealotry that seeped from their pores, spiced with the dishonour of being denied their right to join the Unbeliever Crusade.

The journey had been fraught with arguments between the fanatical soldiers of each House. Once they had landed at Pantsil, the seven generals had been forced to keep the camps separate and ringed by the priests. These were the seconds to the Superiors, who had remained behind on Khund. Quickened, Sneed had found himself once again the tutor he had been in a former life as they explored their new skills with the spiritfire. They were raw, and it worried him, especially after the forced march the generals had insisted on.

Dual horns, like heavy thunder, resounded through the trees, and Prime Sneed reined in his horse as the charge towards war became real. The soldiers of faith spread out, taking cover, eyes searching ahead, while the undergrowth swayed or snapped underfoot. Commands brought on the breeze indicated the soldiers of the other Houses along each flank were doing the same.

He dropped from his horse and led it beneath the tree canopy. Duke Simeon joined him, placing a calming hand upon his own mare's neck.

Whispers were passed backwards, followed by a stillness mirrored by the forest's silence. Sneed's horse jerked its head and blew through its nose. He ran his fingers beneath the mare's eye and along her jaw. The horse nuzzled him in return before rearing up ever-so-slightly. The leaves stirred, a breeze sweeping through that exposed the sky above. The wind rose in intensity, and there was a rhythm in its gusts that tightened Sneed's already dry throat. Murmurs spread from the soldiers to the north, and as Sneed watched above, he caught the first glint of metal. A wing tip. And as he gawped, more of the dragon emerged with each beat of giant wings against the sky. The huge head moved from side to side, staring downwards as the crystalline eyes searched the trees.

And it can be for only one thing. Us.

He glanced about him, sensing the zealotry rise – the desperation to fight. The air beneath the canopy crackled with their desire to expound their faith, yet dread gripped his heart. He knew belief was no shield against such devastation. They would burn amid the dragon's fire as they declared for the Seven, all hope of relieving the city and its citizens lost under burning ash. It was clear to him that their hope lay inside those walls, amid the Seven Houses and the queen he loved.

"Simeon," he whispered, and grasped the duke's hand. "Save Erin. And thank you for the forgiveness."

The Duke of Ridth blinked, taken aback. "I haven't—"

But Sneed had already mounted. He squeezed his legs tight about the mare's flanks and directed the horse towards the south. With a snap of the reins, the horse, desperate to get away from the smell of danger above, was spurred into action. He kept the reins tight, aware that one misstep could lead to a fall or a lame horse.

Sneed drew upon his spiritfire, the junip in his body a catalyst for the ease of its gathering. From heart and mind he centred his spirit, balling a sliver of his soul into a roiling mass, a beacon of purplefire that burned bright beneath the trees. As fearful hooves drove them onwards, he burst into glorious light, a purple glow that filled the canopy to spill out into the sky.

The responding roar shook the leaves.

I give you what time I can.

Shouts rose from behind. Swords beat against shields, and the oligarchy charged. Sneed dodged between the trees, steering his horse, trying to prevent the expenditure of all the animal's energy in a panicked flight from the hunter above. A calming tendril of his spiritfire rolled along its mane, swaddling the gap between the mare's ears to soak into its mind. The animal settled, calmed, and they connected as if one body. The rapid, jarring movements smoothed, and together they flowed over the uneven ground. Sneed resisted the temptation to up the pace and, instead, focused on keeping whatever cover he could between them and the dragon's oily breath.

Sneed ranged his senses out, but felt them curtailed, mired in a shroud of white that suppressed and denied. Drawing a little from his reserve, he attempted to pierce the spirit mist, only to stop as the horse yanked its head in a sudden jolt to the right. Something sizzled past his ear, followed by a second and a third that struck trunks and exploded in dazzling white splinters. Constructors appeared from behind trees and bushes, their armour black and shined to perfection. Instinct took over, and he went with the horse, accentuating the shift to the right and lengthening the stride, a prayer to Penance on his lips.

Constructors meant the dragon wouldn't strike. He just needed to avoid those too.

But he was wrong.

Dragon's fire bathed the forest ahead of him, charring the trees. Leaves curled and turned to ash. Twigs burst afire, and branches caught. A Constructor collapsed amid the pitiless flame. Black smoke billowed from beneath their helm, accompanied by an agonised scream that carried on the searing wind. The Constructor's death a symbol of the dragon's intent. Sneed forced a calming thought into his horse, stymying its instinct to swerve violently away to the south, where more fire lit the trees. He yanked the reins northwards, towards the city. Hooves clipped the charred Constructor's legs, causing the horse to shy again and scrape against a tree trunk. Pain slammed into Sneed's knee and hip, the impact twisting his joints askew. He walled off the agony, masking the pain with spiritfire, and urged the animal onwards.

Shouts rose from behind, soon drowned by the clash of metal upon metal that rolled through the trees from ahead. Voices beseeched the Seven to render their sword, axe and mace with the power of their chosen God. Prayers blessed their spears and pikes, strengthened their shield arms.

Sneed burst from the trees to emerge onto the grass plain beneath a huge shadow. Providing a brief joy amid the numbness, the Oligarchy's soldiers had cut through the Constructors' defensive line – the ones he himself had careered through – only to come face-to-face with charging Constructors on foot. Between them and Sneed, three huge centipede-like artifices writhed.

Crossing the plain at a steady speed, he headed for the fray, where human and Constructor fought hand-to-hand. But it was the great shadow that stole his breath as the horse's hooves pounded at the churned earth. A massive ship floated above him.

Floated.

Chains swung below it, their links wrapped about people he had sworn to protect, hooks that crackled with whitefire piercing limb and torso. An embodiment of evil that, even as a servant of Penance, he could not have envisioned. His horse stumbled, and his hip and knee cut through his block to scream their pain. Only his experience gleaned from years hunting in Ridth kept him aboard, and, hating himself, he threw more spiritfire into the panicked beast's mind.

He had a decision to make, and little time. Head for the city and possible sanctuary, turn towards the Oligarchy's army and fight for whatever brief time they could gain, or head for the Constructors' western flank that charged towards the Oligarchy's incursion.

A fearsome roar from above made his mind up. With his horse now under his control, he rode in a long, lazy curve towards the onrushing Constructors.

"Farewell, High Lord, and my queen," he said, and patted the horse's lathered neck. Hot wind struck his back, and he wrapped himself and the horse in his purplefire. A target. He waited for the rush of dragon's fire, but it never came. Instead, talons like curved swords wrapped themselves about his arms and chest, crushing, cutting. The horse screamed as metal ripped into its rib cage. The mare stumbled to the ground, blood spurting from its side. Yet Sneed hung in the air. His lungs constricted, and the talons squeezed tighter as he dangled just a few feet above the ground. For a second, he thought he had failed, but the Constructors ahead had started to panic, the front of their charge towards the Oligarchy splitting apart as the huge dragon flew their way. Amid the stench of oil and blood, he felt the dragon shift, starting to rise as its wings beat at the air.

With a sigh, he let the last of himself go. He was no match for the High Lord – far too aged, and bereft of a God's weapon – but enough of a beacon to draw the dragon away from the hope he'd brought. The purplefire, his remaining soul, drew in on itself. His skin dried in an instant, cheeks sucking tight, eyes fading. And with a final cry, he let his power go. The talons burned under the onslaught. Purplefire crackled, seizing mechanical joints as the last of Sneed's soul rolled up the beast's limbs and dived under the scales. For a moment, the silver-blue dragon stuttered in the air, missing a wingbeat. Talons scraped the ground, scything the mud to catch upon the rock beneath. The artifice drew in its wings, giving up the fight to stay in the air, and wrapped in on itself and around its prize. The dragon of the veil hit the ground in a roiling mass of metal.

Tabharthóir smashed into the advancing Inhibitors, her weight crushing hundreds beneath her body. Their screams mingled with the thunderous wave of metal that skidded across the ground to crash into the trees beyond. The dragon lay still, unmoving for the briefest moment, before its tail unfurled. The long limb flapped against the ground until the back stretched and the mighty creature righted itself amid a quiver of its spine. With no look towards the carnage wrought upon her own people, the dragon's neck bent back, and bit down upon Prime Sneed, the prize, with undisguised relish.

—

Amid the battle, the duke fought with the same methodical anger that he had lived his life. The Constructors had weapons that flared with whitefire to break shields and shatter armour. From the malignant swords, a mere cut caused death as the injured writhed in agony. Witnessing whitefire drawn out from a poor soldier, sending the Constructor into a rapture, set dread in the duke's heart.

A flare caught the corner of his eye. Amid the circle of soldiers and priests within which he fought, Honour's orangefire ignited for the first time. Sneed had often spoken about such things on the sail over from Khund. About how the magic had always been there, hidden within the soul. But he had also spoken of its dangers, beseeching the Oligarchy's priests to be prudent, to not wield such power unless all else was lost. Thousands still fought at their side, and though they lost two or three for every one of the Constructors they killed, there was still hope.

Soul-magic lit the sky, and a Constructor fell as its armour failed to deflect the strike. More bolts flew, the accumulation filling his small area of the battlefield with a rainbow of light. They were the priests of a zealous religion, and not to be outdone.

And as the act hit home, the duke turned to see the crystalline eye of a dragon fall upon his circle. Sneed's sacrifice seemed pitiful beneath its glare.

It brought one thought to his mind.

Prey.

"I forgive you ..." he uttered, and roared into battle.

67
A STING IN THE TAIL

ERSTENBURGH, BRANDSHOLD

Yanik released her arrow and dropped below the edge of the roof's lip. Nocking another, she knelt to send a second shaft into the savage battle. The small crystal tip exploded with Fate's blue. When she rose for a third time, she expected her target to be dead next to the multi-limbed artifice. Instead, the Constructor clambered up from the rubble, black armour scorched where her arrows had struck, but nothing more. Time and again, the Constructors had demonstrated their mechanical prowess, with Kinst's arrowheads only proving effective should they strike a joint or an unknown weakness.

"Fuck me," she said, and released.

This time, her shaft drove into the back of the Constructor's neck as they bent to clamber down a large piece of the wall, searing into the widened joint. With a yip of glee, Yanik ducked when the bluefire drove into the shattered joint. The resultant scream cheered her no end, but a metal claw landed within inches of her head. The pincer's pivot point creaked with effort, then tore the stone lip of the roof away. Yanik tumbled, the roof collapsing as the roof joints crumbled under the onslaught. She hit the ground hard, and rolled to one side as more of the roof followed.

Hands grabbed Yanik under her arms. The angry Ranger swung a fist towards whoever had dared, only to stop when she recognised her First. Beside him, the rest of the Spear were on their knees, loosing arrows into the breach. The artifice had moved on, snapping a city guard in two with little effort on its way to the far end of the street.

"Get fuckin' off," she said, and stretched for her bow amid the rubble. The upper limb had snapped, and she kicked it angrily away. Her eyes fell upon the still-smoking Constructor. At his hip was a handbow and quiver. She grabbed both and assessed the weapon's easy mechanism. She loaded a quarrel, and drew her short sword in her off-hand before changing her mind and swapping them over.

"The breach is lost," said the First. He signalled his Spear. "Time to be bait."

They fell in and, with Yanik covering the rear, spun off into the shattered house, exiting through a half-filled doorway into a back alley. They pounded down the street, taking two right turns before coming out onto a main road that ran through the centre of the outer city. Flashes of spiritfire lashed across the street from the windows of a shop. Two of the Scorpions were advancing on the shop front, each with four Constructors behind, bucklers up. They left them to it, the third Scorpion that exited the rubble their chosen target.

Yanik eyed the roofs along their side of the street, seeking and finding the chalked "X" with a circle around it. The entrance underneath led into a butcher's shop, and was wider than most. She took station at its edge, her handbow cocked and ready.

The rest of the Spear advanced on the Scorpion, loosing standard arrows. Once the artifice noticed them, claws snapped their way, and the artifice scuttled about to face them head on. At the First's command, the remaining Spear ran back towards Yanik and waited for the charge. Yanik sensed the shift in the artifice, the twitch of its legs. Unlike an animal, where you could gain a hint of its intent from the eyes, an artifice gave nothing.

It surged forwards. The First turned, and slipped on the gravel-like rubble before regaining his feet. A hair's breadth from the lashing claws, he dropped a sack, and spurted for the protection of his Spear. His eyes suddenly widened and his chest burst open. The Scorpion's stinger emerged from amid the broken ribs, dark blood and torn lungs wrapped about the tip.

"Shit," said Yanik, and took aim.

Amid the shock, two arrows slammed into the sack. A little too early by her judgement, as the Scorpion's bulbous windows were barely above it. Nothing happened, and when two more shafts slammed into the inert material to no effect, Yanik took aim once again. She had little experience with crossbows, never mind one so small. They were a pick up-and-fire weapon, however. Those in the army who couldn't gain the muscle needed to handle a bow of any power or range had shifted over to crossbows after the failures of the Crusade. Another win for the meisters.

She pulled the trigger, the twang of the cord more powerful than she expected. Luckily, she had assumed the shaft would fly straight and true, with only a small dip over the short distance. The crystal head of the quarrel tore into the sack. Whitefire exploded, but was soon engulfed by the pot bombs it contained. The eruption lifted the front of the artifice from the ground, limbs flailing as they disconnected from the stone. Yanik waited, the smoke and dust preventing any clue as to the condition of the machine's underside as it crashed back down.

"Fuck," she whispered.

The wait clawed at her thrumming heart. Across the street, the first of the Scorpions had rammed its tail deep inside the higher shop windows, withdrawing with a priest of Death skewered through the shoulder. To her surprise, the tail dropped behind, rather than drag the priest to die upon its claws. She didn't get to see what happened next, as her personal nemesis pulled itself clear of the searing pot bomb fire. The tail lashed menacingly, and four of its functioning limbs forced the damaged artifice onwards at a far quicker pace than she liked. Yanik reloaded and waited for the order to withdraw.

"What now, Yanik?" The words were shaky and hoarse in the dust. She looked back. Four expectant faces, all desperate for a leader.

She shook her head as realisation hit, and indicated towards the butcher's rear entrance. "We stick to the plan. Pulsen, Martin, take the door. Fenir, Roden, the alleyway. I'm last out. When I pass you, fucking run."

She didn't wait for confirmation, eyes on the artifice as it made surprising progress towards them. She slowly backed into the shop, checked her quarrel, and wished for her own bow. By the time she was inside, metal claws had torn away the window frame, shattering the remaining glass. The Scorpion did not stop. She could see the twin sets of black armour inside the bulbous eyes, their intent solely on her. Each time she checked her footing, or looked from side to side to ensure the way was clear, the long metal legs had forced the artifice closer. The smell of hot oil and burning explosive filled the shop, coupled with the screech of metal upon stone and wood.

One of the Constructors gesticulated her way, slashing a hand across their throat as the other slammed two metal rods forward. The claws lashed out, wide open, and whipped towards her body with murderous intent. Yanik threw herself backwards. The pincers sliced the tip of her ponytail as it flew up. With a scream of defiance, she aimed and released the quarrel. It drove into the "X" scrawled on the ceiling, but Yanik didn't wait. She spun onto all fours, feet scrabbling for purchase as she threw herself out of the beckoning doorway.

Erin's Wrath erupted. Pulsen and Martin slammed the reinforced door shut behind her, but were unable to wedge the stout wooden block in time. The door smashed open and the explosive roar washed over Yanik's back. Heat seared her armour, and the remains of her ponytail set alight as she rolled herself into a ball. The alleyway walls rang with impacts, and something briefly wet showered Yanik before the heat boiled it away.

Once the initial wave of the eruption had rolled over, she unfurled and beat at her remaining hair. Martin stared at her, eyes wide. His lower half lay across the doorway, and was shredded with pieces of crystal armour. He coughed once. Blood streaked from the corner of his mouth, and the light in his eyes slid into the void.

Pulsen lay at his side. Her armour was scorched, with a few shards embedded into the leather, but thankfully there was no blood that she could see. Her face, however, spoke of the horror the young Ranger had witnessed.

"Move, Pulsen!" Yanik shouted, and grabbed the woman's arm to yank her up. At first the Ranger resisted, her eyes dull, until she responded to the force of Yanik's command.

Keeping low, Pulsen bypassed Yanik and headed out of the shattered alleyway. Yanik scrambled back, apologising in her mind as she scavenged Martin's still-functional bow and his remaining arrows. Without a word, she closed his eyes and followed Pulsen out of the alley. A right turn brought them back onto the street.

Here, the ground was littered with the dead and dying, and behind the dual Scorpions, she could see further artifices bypassing the street, spreading out in search of more roadways to penetrate the city. Black-armoured Constructors followed on foot, their weapons sizzling white. The only contrast was the line of manacled priests of many hues, bloodied and injured, robes scorched or torn. They were being led back towards the breach, whitefire whips cracking above to lash them onwards.

"We gonna help them?" said Fenir. "They saved us from the Eighth. Now it is our turn."

Yanik spat on the ground, clearing the heat and dust. The last of the line of priests wore purple, and their scalp was red with blood. They glanced back their way. Yanik could see none of her father's fire in their movements.

"No," she said, and turned away to eye Fenir and the others. "We have our orders. We defend the outer city until we are called back. Then the Houses. Whoever is out here fights until their last, be it priest or fucking Ranger. Understood?"

A clank made her swing around. The two Scorpions that had captured the priests were beginning to shift along the street, one on either side, their bulbous windows ominous as they swept over the destroyed shop and the broken, pinned metal limbs beneath it. A scuttle round and one peered down the street, a foreleg waving their way.

"Fuck, they've sussed us. Move!"

Yanik ducked back into the alleyway, switching to the right, only to be called back by Fenir, who took the lead. He took the third alleyway in that direction and shifted right again, and pointed to the roof. With a nod from Yanik, he shouldered his bow and clambered up foot and handholds she could not see. A clatter soon followed, and a ladder dropped. They climbed up; the Spear gathering the stored arrows and pot bombs hidden on the rooftop. Finally, a pause and they took a welcome swig of water.

As the fresh liquid cleared her parched throat, another explosion rocked the city – Erin's Wrath tore through two roofs to the west of them. Black smoke and flame poured upwards, and across the rooftops, city guards and ex-cutthroats swarmed away from the blast. Another win, but the sights along the city street had taken Yanik aback. Each win was at such cost.

From her position, she could see the ebb and flow of the enemy as they moved about the city. How the ripple of defenders would congregate, launch an attack, then withdraw. She placed markers in her mind. The Constructors were sticking to the main streets, advancing where they had the most advantage. A war of attrition, but despite their control of the rooftops, their weapons were fearfully ineffective against artifice and Constructor armour.

"Yanik," said Pulsen, pointing back towards the breach, and the ominous sky ship that hovered the other side, waiting to release the next wave of attacks. Dragon's breath rose above the eastern portion of the wall, gouts followed by a trumpet of victory that sent a shiver down Yanik's spine. Amid the flurry of ash and smoke, a torn and scorched orange flag wavered upon the wind. It was not one she recognised.

"Anyone know it?" she asked, pointing.

Pulsen had already drawn out her spyglass, lips moving as if talking to herself. "One from the isles," she said, and lowered the spyglass. "Khundish, I think. And Honour's House."

Yanik washed out her mouth again, watching the flag when another roar rolled over the city from that direction. The silver-blue machine of dread rose higher with each flap of metal-skinned wings. Caged within its talons, priests in robes of many colours writhed. Alive, screaming.

"Fuck," Yanik said. "Can this get any bloody harder? Ready yourselves."

She looked over two alleyways towards the main street, where twin Scorpion tails swung above the roofline, occasionally dipping down to strike out at someone below. They were the only defenders on the rooftops on this side of the street.

"Get us across, Roden. Fenir." She nodded towards the remaining sack of pot bombs stored ready for another Spear, should they fail. "Bring them all."

68
A VENGEANCE SOUGHT

An Chéad's scales shimmered as she broke through the clouds. The sun's rays lit the water droplets as if sparkling, scarlet jewels encrusted her body.

"We rise again, An Chéad. Unbroken. Cleanse yourself of the smoke and charred flesh."

The Unspoken sensed the Spirit Walker's agreement, and the dragon dived into the clouds, seeking those heavy with moisture. The freshness wiped away the horrors of Anvil. The spirits of the Infected were foul, inedible, and the memories of their demise from flame and talon still hung in her heartstone.

Renewed by their visit to the Unspoken's palace, and having fed there upon the spiritfire she leeched from her subjects, the dragon beat at the darkening cloud to emerge above a human town. The Unspoken gazed through An Chéad's sight at the deep ditch and high earthen wall that now surrounded the human dwellings. Yet, no lamps were lit, the houses stark and streets empty.

"What do you see?"

And the Unspoken immersed her mind fully into the dragon's spirit-sight, expecting a healthy glow huddled deep within each house, the humans hiding within their walls of stone and soil as the emperor marched on. But the town glowed with little whitefire, unlike the woods and surrounding fields. There, the souls sparkled like ripples in a pond, spreading outwards, leaving their stone walls behind.

"They leave, but to go where?"

She blinked, the film of dried skin wiping her white eyes but not helping with her disbelief.

"Humans always group together, An Chéad. Like the herds on the plains, seeking solace and protection in each other. This is … worrying."

The Unspoken urged the artifice dragon onwards. The steady beat of his wings dragged them over emptying villages, and a second town where only the wisp of the occasional soul remained. Fear struck her dead heart, though the why of it only slowly crept in. As the herd dispersed, food would be much harder to come by. The hunters who had become farmers of souls would be forced to expend far more effort.

"Anvil, An Chéad. We cannot let such thoughts reach our people. My herd. When our bargain is as complete as I see fit, we must act upon this … this betrayal."

They swept over the last town and flew above the great forest of Ersten that spread out towards the distant city. Amid the trees, streams of whitefire shimmered, human souls weaving their way in all directions except south. It took a bite from her ancient spirit. Such madness had to be stopped.

A darkness shrouded part of the forest at the very spot where it opened out onto the human's main city, a black spot in their shared sight, and one of a Constructor's making.

"The emperor," whispered the Unspoken, her poise shaken by the power of the shroud that encapsulated the city. "He blocks all spirit-sight. He must think we are coming, An Chéad. We must remain wary. He knows us now."

She urged the dragon to the west of the spirit shroud, ordering the artifice to circle and survey the events around the city from afar. Cautious.

Careful. As they swept out to the west, they could see fires along the city walls and, in the distance, towards the south, a mighty ship hovered.

Dust choked in her ancient lungs.

"You see it? It is huge. Such an artifice, I never thought possible. The whitefire it would need ..."

Her words trailed off as they caught sight of the Inhibitor army pouring into the city. Far more organised than any of her time. The artifices, consistent and efficient, the soldiers regimented, and their black armour gleamed menacingly.

"I..."

Below the huge sky ship, humans lay burnt upon a killing field, their souls eaten or being scavenged by the victors. A roar cut through the noise of battle. Triumphant, hidden by the shroud and the city walls, the emperor's silver-blue dragon leapt into the air.

The Unspoken's confidence ebbed. First the huge sky ship, which at that moment had not responded to their presence, and now a well-fed and victorious veil dragon. Still convinced they had not been detected, she peered to the south, and the smoke and ashes of the human army amid the trees.

"They are failing, An Chéad. What use is an alliance if one side is so under-powered and the enemy is not? I say we sit back and watch from afar. See if there is an opportunity ... and save our own herd if not." A tremor from An Chéad sent her senses reeling, and the dragon swept its neck backwards in search of the emperor's artifice. The dragon had expected it to be below them, perhaps heading for the sanctuary of the Constructor ship. Instead, the sky was empty of all but the ashes of the city and the looming presence of the giant floating artifice. A dread rode through the heartstone, and at the Unspoken's insistence, An Chéad beat her wings with increased urgency. Three mighty lashes of the metal-skinned limbs saw them break free of the spirit-shroud and out above the forest.

The Unspoken sent a seeking, but too late. Talons ripped into An Chéad's back. Sword-like and razor-edged, they tore at his scales and the metal beneath. Only the artifice's sudden drop saved him, the talons tearing free before they could slice the vital machinery that heaved his mighty wings. The emperor's dragon followed them down, its back talons slashing at An Chéad's wings. The limbs reverberated from the attack, and he pulled them in. The snap and crack of joints, and the thinner, finger-like limbs that kept the wings taut, revealed the damage wrought. Most, but not all, now lay flat against his body. The Unspoken's dragon rolled onto his back, his own talons flashing upwards. They raked along the silver-blue dragon's exposed underbelly, digging in where damage had previously been healed. The resultant roar signalled An Chéad had scored deep, and a final slash cut into the tail's first joint.

They were falling fast and, with the advantage gained, An Chéad curved his back, head bent in an arc towards the burning forest below.

"How bad?" the Unspoken asked out loud, and her senses dived into the machinery. They whirled just as her dragon did as it spiralled towards the earth. She swiftly spent spiritfire to drag the most tortured metals together, healing joints with a desperation borne from the fear of what chased them towards the ground. "That is the best I can do."

Still An Chéad plummeted, the Spirit Walker relying on the damage he had imparted and a hope the emperor was not willing to risk a kill so close to the ground. At the very last second, he tipped his long neck and raised his head. With tail lowered, he spread his partially mended wings. Scales flew off, ripped away by the force of the air as it battered the damaged wings. A scream of metal reverberated through the dragon, and a moment of fear pervaded the Unspoken's connection. The dragon's chest crashed against the upper branches, and his feet trailed along the earth before An Chéad gave a mighty heave to shove himself back into the air.

The dragon beat swiftly, adding to their momentum despite his injuries. Desperately needing to know where their enemy was, the Unspoken sent another seeking, one that clashed against the emperor's own as his dragon wheeled away and headed back towards the city.

The emperor's words echoed through the heartstone. "Keep running, traitor. But I *will* find you and eat your soul."

The Unspoken shivered and let her head drop to rest against the heartstone.

Eventually, she cast their spirit-sight to the south, then to the west and the distant isles that could keep her fed until the sky ship and its emperor found them both. It would mean abandoning her herd, but she had given much of herself in their defence already. It was futile to fight on against such odds.

"Take it slow, An Chéad. Keep clear of the shroud. We turn north to feed on our herd, then westward. Our time here is done."

69
A SONG OF HOPE

THE SEVEN STEPS OF HOPE'S HOUSE,
ERSTENBURGH, BRANDSHOLD

"Captain Mordant fell to the blue dragon," said Lord Hope. "After that, I lost contact."

The queen peered into her hands, finding nothing there that would help. For all her efforts, and that of Mordant and his plan, the soldiers defending her city were now leaderless. Each unit knew their role, and had the right to act as they saw fit. Once the Constructors were in the city, Mordant had known there would be no way to communicate, to lead them as one army. Despite all the fanciful bedtime stories of a single hero leading an army to victory, in truth, a war was won by tactics and reason. He'd understood this, and prepared for it. Readied the defence for his own death.

Yet still such a loss struck home.

Amid her rise to be the true queen of the Union and Overseer of the Houses, he had flowered from the petty city captain she had first met to a man devout in his determination to save their people. He had seen in her a *calling*, and risen to it. Now he was another casualty, another whose blood had been spilled in her name. At least he was relieved of the burden of watching his people chained and fed upon by the soul-eaters.

"My queen?" Lord Hope gestured towards his House doors. "He requested you remain out of harm's way."

"*I* make those decisions, Lord Hope. I decide when I am in harm's way or when my people need me. I am here because he felt me a distraction – and rightly so. But whatever happens out there in my beloved city, they will come for me. And *you*."

A flare of distant spiritfire caught her eye. A dragon's wings raised the Constructor's artifice above the southern walls. It trumpeted a victory, and though she could not see what it held, in her heart, she knew. It held the city's soul, torn from her people, within its grasp. An ending.

So be it.

"Ser," she said, rising from the seventh step of Hope's House. "I wish to be with the High Lord."

The honour guard stepped aside and followed his queen as she walked down the steps and headed off towards the House of Penance. She stopped, looking back to the Lord, who watched after her. "Inform each of the Seven that they are to be ready, Lord Hope. That what comes will make all their lies and deceits mere lines in the sand that I not only cross now, but erase from history. I thank you for your service."

"I don't understand," he said, his voice a barely audible whisper. But she could see that he knew.

"For all the High Lord's machinations," he whispered, "we have always known." Lord Hope sucked in a breath, attempting to hold in the thought of what was to come. Eyes filled with tears. "Penance is due."

—

Meister Kinst scurried along the street, dragging the cart behind her. An acolyte of Wisdom shoved at the cart from the back. The boy was barely into his teens, but had proven a worthy labourer for the ageing meister. Together, they had ferried the last stores of ballistae heads from her workshop in the university, only to discover the weapons had been destroyed by the dragon that flew above. Its cry echoed across the screams of agony and death that filled her beloved city.

Having changed direction for what seemed the hundredth time, they emerged at the market square to the sight of broken trebuchets. They were strewn across the area, and amid the wood and wires lay the broken crews, bodies limp, eyes distant. The devastation tore at Kinst. The mighty machines of Grand Meister Arknold, reduced to matchsticks.

"How?" she said, and peered from machine to machine, seeking an answer. There was none immediately apparent.

The sounds of battle were several streets away, and she had come hoping to at least provide a final set of useful ammunition for the trebuchets. They walked slowly onwards, the piles of broken machinery divided by a line of the dead. Their bodies were limp, their skin dried to the bone. Eyes stared soulless, lost, to the sky.

The whimper from behind brought Kinst up short. She had seen the dead. Experimented on them, no less, with her potions and alchemical concoctions. But not her young charge. It was only then she noticed that the cart felt heavier. She soon found the lad had stopped at the edge of the square, and was doubled over and vomiting against a wall. She understood his fear, but blocked it out. Somewhere out in the forest, Arknold, she expected, had likely given her life for this cause. She couldn't let that go to waste.

Kinst dropped the cart next to a barrel. A smile crossed her face as she recognised the stencil on its side. The more she looked among the detritus, the more barrels she could see.

"I will show you *service* and *duty*. If the world is to come to an end, let it be lit by my greatest invention. The pinnacle of *my* science. After this, the Houses will have to accept it is the future. If we survive, that is.

"Boy, when you've stopped introducing your breakfast to the street, we have work to do."

<hr>

The tap of cane upon stone echoed through the prayer chamber. The High Lord cast his eyes from side to side as he looked upon the rows of pews. He recalled the lashes, the bloodied scars. The cries of joy and ecstasy that mingled with those of pain and punishment. He paused, ignoring Amarnta and her sullen glare, the bandage across her head now cast aside.

The cause of her injury rapped at the door again, the pattern and rhythm familiar. The spirit-lock let him know who awaited the other side.

"A moment," he murmured, and glanced up at the gallery above the pews. He thought of the sadness at his daughter's first giving, the gift to her God feeling so false upon his mind that it was a burden too far. How could such a simple thing bring the joy of sharing, and the pain of betrayal? If she had remained in the service of the House of Penance, he doubted he would be stood at these doors, waiting for the word of his queen and Overseer.

Yanik.

Hopefully long gone.

He nodded to Amarnta, who swore before turning away. A sliver of purplefire graced her fingers. A skill that, less than six months ago, only he, as High Lord of Penance, could wield.

How times have changed.

The doors cracked open, and the queen's honour guard surveyed the chamber before stepping aside despite Amarnta's seething glare.

"My queen," High Lord Penance said as Erin appeared in the doorway.

Her look spoke of war and pain, and impending death. She had come to stand by his side as they murdered their people in the hope that no other realm had to suffer at the hands of the Constructors.

Or, perhaps, to ensure I have the will to do so.

Such strength.

Penance flared in his hand, the sliver of his God suddenly expectant of what was to come.

No. It does not flare for her.

He slowly turned about and stared down the aisle. There stood Geral, whom the queen had sent away after she had discovered his intent. His brother-in-law stepped aside, allowing Terana Fiotir Na Partera to enter the chamber from the stairway. The Schenterenta fixed him with a glare before she took in the Union's queen. She bowed her head just a little.

"High Lord?" asked the queen from behind him. "We have been through this. I die with my people."

"This might be hard for you to believe, but this is nothing to do with me. Terana?" he said as the elf stalked along the aisle; her eyes locked onto his before switching to the queen's.

"I come in the name of Sura-nista and your Ranger, Laoch," she said. "I bring you hope in the words of the lifesong."

———

"What is so important, Sergeant, that you drag me from my house?" Lady Honour dropped her yellow robes to the dusty floor, brushing off the stone chips and debris that had accumulated during the climb up the shattered wall.

The sergeant waited patiently for her to finish, before asking Lady Honour to look for herself.

"Oh," she said. "I suppose telling me about it would have pushed believability a little too far."

She placed a comforting hand upon the veteran's shoulder while her eyes swept Jense's northern approach, which remained covered with the ash of the dead. Amid the death, powerful horses pawed at the ground. Upon their backs were more Schenterenta than she had ever imagined. And at their head sat a metal dragon. The glow of the God's weapons greeted her as Rangers appeared from its chest.

"What do we do?" asked the sergeant, eyes wide as the Partera horses shook their manes and whinnied.

"Do? Whatever they ask, Sergeant. Whatever they ask."

———

It tore at her heart. People milled about the city, going about their business as if the world outside could be blanked out by their high walls. Their spirits untainted except those who grieved for their lost soldiers.

Do they not know what comes? Or do they hide it from their minds, an impending fear, best suppressed?

'No, Sura. They exist the best way they can.'

'I want to fight, Honour. To stand beside Laoch and defend our people.'

'Really? I said you would change. That you would face challenges, and in the end, you may not choose Laoch over what you have become. This is duty as much as standing in the face of the enemy with your spear in your hands. You know this. Laoch knows this.'

'You do not know me as well as you think. I will do my duty, but when it is done...'

'It is never done.'

Sura waited until the crowded Ridth street emptied a little, the people bustling towards the market or home. The only sign that war had come was the whiff of burnt wood from the port, where the fleet had been caught in the harbour.

Trapped.

She coalesced before the first step of the House of Honour, eyes gleaming orange as she strode up each one. The doors were open, striking her with the pain and death she had witnessed in Makalena and Jense. There, the Houses had locked themselves away. Not to hide from what was happening, but defending a last bastion under the orders of the High Lord. Yet here, they remained open for worship.

Sura reached the top step, and the surge of power that spilled from the open door welcomed her and the sliver of Honour that bonded her spirit. She let Honour flow outward, immersing her aura with the God's light, and walked in. Along each row, worshippers knelt with heads back, eyes cast upwards to the dragon carved into the ceiling. The Eighth, the Unspoken. An effigy of evil, created by the Seven to keep a people's minds on prayer. To give willingly.

And now, it is time to use that.

Sura widened the light, her God's shadow stretching along the aisle and spreading across the chamber. She levitated to float above the tiles as she swept towards the prayer stone. Each row of worshippers she passed sprang to their feet, words of faith and Honour spilling from their lips. The murmur rolled through the entire chamber, and the priests engaged with the prayer stone stopped and stared.

"Honour," became the single word from the worshippers, repeated over and over until Sura paused before the prayer stone, her light now so bright, the priests shielded their eyes. Sura, or Honour as she presented to her worshippers, whispered soothing words as the worshipper upon the stone was drawn away by a gawping priest. She hovered higher above the stone to stare down upon the awed flock. Her eyes pulsed with Honour's light, and spiritfire laced her words with power.

"My people, I bind you with Honour's words. Your faith has been astounding, but now I, Honour of the Seven, who bound you in tenets and Scripture to worship, call upon you to spread my words across the city of Ridth. We are to use that faith to rid our world of the evil at our gates. My gift is a song of worship."

The chamber shone with Honour's light, spiritfire that Sura drew from the prayer stone and drilled into each of the flocks' minds. A song of a life well led, of passion, love, death and failure. The highs and lows. The cry of a newborn entwined with the passing of the aged, the first kiss upon chaste lips to the passion and grief of love lost.

The hum echoed about the chamber, a rhythm that ebbed and flowed as lips and tongue wrapped about their individual words. Their lives merged as one, into the lifesong of Ridth.

"Take your song," Sura said, "and a piece of me with you. Share it among the faithful of all the Houses. Let the Seven celebrate life as one." She stretched out a hand, and the priest at her side grasped it in her own. Her eyes lit, spiritfire igniting within them. "Take this gift to each of the Seven Houses," Sura placed a hand upon the head of the second priest. Orangefire arced along her arm to wreath their skull. "They must open the doors to the faithful, let them sing their new song of worship. When the hour is dark, the Seven will provide a light amid the void."

—

Lady Honour placed her hand upon the ornate doors. She had witnessed much in Jense that had sickened her, yet the destruction wrought upon this city, upon Makalena, hit harder. Piles of the dead lay all around the square of the Seven Houses, rotting. Discarded rag dolls of meat that had once contained the souls of her flock, each spirit torn from heart and mind to be used as a tool, or to feed the evil that now assailed Erstenburgh's walls.

She sensed the ill-ease behind her, and looked over her shoulder at the lines of Schenterenta that had travelled with her aboard the veil dragon – how strange her new world was. Their eyes were calm despite their words, and she recognised their horror at what they saw. They had viewed the destruction of Jense from the outside, but not the careless death the Constructors wielded as if all life was theirs to take as they saw fit.

Her spiritfire weaved its way into the scarred stone and the lock beneath. A rap upon the door, and a male priest opened it wide. She smiled, and spreading her arms, pulled the priest into a warm embrace.

"It is time," she whispered in his ear before pulling back. "We have the Seven's work to do. Are the other Houses ready?"

"They are, though what you propose is … unusual."

"There are no people left here to worship, to trigger the Wyrding and the prayer stones power. To channel it as the shaman said, we will need help. They have come in our – and their – time of need."

Lady Honour stepped aside to allow the twisted Schenterenta to approach the priest. "This is Ferena, and she has a song to share."

70

A LINE CROSSED IN BLOOD

ERSTENBURGH, BRANDSHOLD

"There is to be no let-up, Lelion." The emperor strode through the *Kraken*'s bridge and on towards the admiral, who sat, deep in thought, upon her command chair. "None."

"The Inhibitors along the eastern flank need time to feed if you wish to minimise casualties, Tarin. They fought off the attack, but their numbers are depleted. Without spirit sleep or feeding, they are weakened. You know this."

The emperor bypassed Lelion to take a place where he could peer out of the bridge windows. Lelion could sense his tension, and revelled in it.

For all his bluster, he seeks to drive our people onwards because the dragon needs to recover. How far do I let this charade go?

"Their magi were ... pathetic," the Fleshmaster replied. "Nothing compared to what we will face once we reach the inner city. We must weaken their remaining army, then prepare for that battle."

"We? So you will join the fight?"

"*I* must prepare. Tabharthóir needs to rest if we are to be victorious, yes? We have run off the traitor, but An Chéad is powerful. We must be ready if he returns." The emperor's white eyes blazed.

The admiral incarnate flinched, squashing the sudden fear that rose amid her spirit. His anger was internal. Or, perhaps, another more unusual emotion.

Does he fear An Chéad? Or their magi?

"Send in the sixth, and the feeders." The emperor flexed his fingers. The creak inside his gauntlet was evident in the sudden silence of the bridge.

"They defend the northern approach, and are reinforcing the east after the attack," replied the admiral, taking to her feet. "You would expose us to more surprises. First you blanket the area so we are spirit-blind, and now you take away any defence should an attack come."

The emperor took a step towards Lelion, his hands balled into fists, pulsing.

No. He fights his anger at not ending the traitor. Tabharthóir is young, and has perhaps exposed him to too many of the magi they took – a little soul-lust in the mix.

The slap came fast, and the admiral incarnate hit the floor. The Fleshmaster's ornate gauntlet shredded the skin of her cheek, and memories of expected pain stung her mind.

"You will *not* question your emperor." He turned to the waiting captains. Each stood straighter, eyes staring ahead. "Recall the sixth and send them into the city. I want the feeders inside those walls now. Order the remaining fifth to the north. If they are too weak and pitiful to respond, send their officers to Tabharthóir."

Lelion stared up at the Fleshmaster, shock at his audacity and ignorance keeping her on the floor as the captains of the foot and Mechanised Inhibitors departed. Hands eased under her armpits, and she glared upwards to find Spintz there. She shoved Spintz away, using the motion to suppress her bubbling anger. Now was not the time. She couldn't act too early.

Lelion pulled herself up using the command chair, the torn skin flapping against her cheek. She ripped it off and flung it aside as a dust-filled breath flowed from her lungs in an attempt to calm her soul.

"You take command of all, now?" she asked, keeping her voice low and hard, not meeting the eyes of the emperor as she spoke.

The silence prickled at her neck.

Only once the slam of the outer bridge door echoed off the brass walls did she turn around. Through the window, she saw Tarin standing in his usual place at the bow of the soulship. The bridge crew remained motionless, their eyes only on her.

"You ..." she growled as she looked from Inhibitor to Inhibitor. "You are with me?"

All about the bridge, fists slammed against chests as one.

"All of us," replied Spintz. "We stand ready."

Lelion stared back out of the window, cold anger roiling amid her spirit. "And the captains?"

"By your offer, yes," replied Spintz. Her white eyes danced as a sliver of red seeped in.

"I share the spoils of war, understand? We will all feast upon the magi. But we do not act until the time is right. Let him weaken in battle before we strike."

"But the dragon ..."

"Is young and overstretches. Be patient." Lelion ran her fingers along the exposed bone of her cheek. "Until I say otherwise."

The admiral sat back into her command chair, allowing her anger to settle, letting logic overcome her agitated spirit. Her vision crystals told of the feeders' approach upon the breach, and the march of the Inhibitor divisions. Soon they would pour into the city. A gamble she would not have taken after the surprise attack. To the east, a field of battle that no animal or bird would normally dare feast upon, now left to the crows. The feeders had been called away. The prisoners taken were still chained together, awaiting their fate as the Inhibitors hungered.

He pushes them too hard, and into my welcoming arms.

"Commandeer any magi taken prisoner. Cut them from the herd and bring them to me. To us."

—

Popsilin sneered. The body beneath her shook as she drew their whitefire and swallowed the spirit whole. Her constant *need* had grown, the power surging through her from the last magus feeding, keening in her mind.

Tenith rose from the undergrowth, blood upon his teeth and lips, leaving a ravaged body behind amid the leaves. He had taken to the more visceral form of feeding, his mind on constant edge. The addiction she had encouraged in him pushed them both ever onwards in the hunt for more.

"How close are we to the city?" he asked, and wiped the blood from his mouth, letting it splash disdainfully upon the earth.

"Too far," she replied, looking back across the clearing to the broken wagon and the dying horses. "I say we are on our own now." She stalked over, quietly approaching the overturned carriage. Two humans lay pinned to the floor, the rest of her surviving squad feeding, sating the hunger that had taken over their minds. They were so young, and lacked the control she at least maintained. They were a liability of her making.

Tenith appeared at her side, his eyes upon the oblivious Inhibitors. "Too far," he said, as if reading her mind.

Popsilin licked her lips. The taste of their tainted souls pervaded the gap between them. It called to her, sang a song of the delights contained within her own Inhibitors. Ancient memories invaded her mind of a time after the Sundering, when Constructor fell upon Constructor. The sights and smells entranced her. Amid her lust, a hand snaked out to wrap beneath the chin of her own man. Popsilin recognised it as her own. She couldn't remember his name as she drew his neck back, only that she couldn't resist the taste of his soul any longer. Teeth bore down upon his neck, biting deep, and her mind was set alight with the tang of one of her own. A gasp at her side announced Tenith giving into the same need.

The forest stirred as the sounds of ecstasy and death echoed about the trees already emptied of life. A few yards away, ash and earth lay upon branch and twig. And beyond that, a large pile of freshly dug soil and stone.

And the pile of stone shifted, a trickle of earth that revealed a hint of glinting green metal, and the promise it bore.

71
KINST'S WRATH

ERSTENBURGH, BRANDSHOLD

Mandibles crushed the ladder, splinters flying as the segmented body rose above the stone-walled house. The first of the feeder's feet grasped the lip of the roof and, in a wave of movement, the artifice dragged half its body up top. Yanik gulped, releasing an arrow to smash into the artifice's head. Yellowfire swathed the eyes, causing the mechanised creature to thrash while pulling itself up to stretch across a second building.

"Fuck." Yanik reached for a second arrow and loosed. It spun and hit a glancing blow against another segment, the shattered crystal releasing nothing but a puff of spiritfire. More and more of the stored crystal heads had proved ineffective.

"We need to go," said Fenir, pulling at her arm. "Now."

Yanik stepped backwards. Her heels touched Roden's blood-strewn body. Shards of stone and clay peppered his limp form, his stomach missing from when the Scorpion's tail had torn into him as he made to drop the pot bomb sack. She swore, shaking her head, and stepped over the body to follow Fenir and Pulsen across the final two roofs before the market square. The ripple of the artifice's body remained prominent in her mind, sensing the scrape of crystal and metal upon stone as it pursued her. She ran for the first ladder, taking each rung at speed to cross the divide. Ahead, Pulsen was already across the next. Fenir took the first rung far too fast. His foot slipped, and the snap of bone rang in her ears. His cry pierced her heart, and she pulled up short at his look of pain and sheer terror.

A glance backwards was enough to know he was lost. If she dithered, so was she. She slung the sack towards him, dropping it beside the screaming Ranger. The cry shut off. Blood poured from his lip where he'd bitten down hard against the pain.

"Do your bloody duty!" she shouted, and took three steps back before running and leaping across to the far building. She knew she was short, but Pulsen caught her and dragged her over the lip. She'd take the bruised thigh as a reward. They ran to the next lip, and the drop to the market square. Yanik spun, swapped the bow to her off-hand and drew the handbow. The artifice had reached Fenir. Its head lifted, mandibles snapping together in anticipation of the kill. As it lurched forwards, Fenir's last act was to grasp the sack tight to his chest.

"May Justice have mercy for his sacrifice," she whispered, and pulled the trigger. The quarrel slammed into Fenir's back as the feeder's head fell upon the Ranger. He exploded, his back erupting, spine exposed briefly as the whitefire burned through to the sack beyond. The pot bombs exploded one after another, searing the wide mouth of the artifice. Metal, crystal and flesh filled the air, and the mechanised creature's screech cut through the maelstrom. It reared backwards, black smoke pouring from its mouth, only to flail and crash back down. The roof struts gave way beneath the sudden impact, and the building collapsed.

Yanik prepared her last quarrel, waiting for any sign the feeder lived. With no obvious twitch of movement, she wiped away the ash from her brow and spat out the dust in her throat. "And may Penance accept my pain as punishment a fucking 'nough."

"Yanik!" shouted Pulsen. She spun about, expecting another attack from behind. Instead, the last of her Spear pointed skywards, and towards the north. Yanik's vision filled with a metallic orange dragon, powerful wings beating at the smoke that hung heavy above the city.

"Not the Unspoken," she mouthed, "nor the Constructor's blue monstrosity."

To her surprise, the wings spread wide, catching the air with talons extended as if it would tear the square apart. A second beat of the twisted wings and its huge back feet met the ground, metal screeching upon stone, before the forelegs settled to the floor and the mighty wings pulled inwards.

"Shit," said Pulsen, bow in hand and nocking an arrow.

"No, wait," said Yanik, signalling calm.

She needed time to think, but at that moment two figures emerged from under the cover of a splintered trebuchet. Two sets of green robes fluttered in the hot wind from the city fires. The hood of one fell back as they ran, exposing the determined face of an aged meister. The woman ducked beneath a second pile, coming out with a sack Yanik knew all too well. Her eyes wandered over the square and the barrels carefully placed around it. With only the handbow ready, she aimed and fired. The quarrel landed a few feet before the meister, and whitefire flared, flinging the woman backwards. The pot bombs tumbled out of the sack. Yanik held her breath, but no explosion came.

"Kill the meister if you have to," she said, and discarded the handbow. Yanik grabbed the roof's ledge and dropped to the ground. Her knees complained vociferously as they absorbed the impact, and she rolled away. Getting up, she set off at a hobbling run towards the meister whose University robes smoked, whitefire sparking along the hem as she bent to pick up the first of the pot bombs.

"Stop!" Yanik shouted, drawing her sword. "Fucking stop!"

The meister looked her way, cheeks flushed, but with a shaking hand, she reached for a second bomb. An arrow pinged off the stone, forcing the Learned to draw back as the boy emerged from behind the meister, a dagger in his hand.

"Meister, please, stop," pleaded Yanik.

"I'm killing that bloody thing," Kinst replied. "Get out of my way."

"Do not force me to hurt you, Meister, or the boy." Yanik pointed the sword at both of them. "That dragon is hope, not death. And if you try and do what I think you're planning with the Erin's Wrath, Pulsen will take your eye out with a fucking arrow." Yanik grimaced, flicking her head back towards the roof.

"It needs to die. They took Arknold, destroyed the city. I can ..."

A shout from Pulsen cut the meister short, and all three looked back down the street. A wave of crystal armour filled it from side to side, with more upon the roofs as feeders rippled at speed towards them. Yanik's bowels heaved. Fear intruded as the mass of metal and impending death flowed towards them. Many Scorpions remained about the city, wreaking havoc and murder, yet these things plied at her nerves far more. And there were so many.

The meister glared, open-mouthed, at the artifices, then glanced back towards the dragon, whose crystalline eyes glimmered amid the fires. "If this dragon is hope, which I find hard to believe, at least let me strike a different blow." She pointed down the street. "They come for us, maybe for your precious dragon. Go, take the boy. If your Pulsen is that good, if I fail, she needs to take out one of the three barrels that stand to the east of the square."

Yanik nodded. Everyone was here to serve, meister or not.

"Boy," said Yanik, pointing away from the square and the dragon. "Run for the Houses." The knife clattered to the floor, and the acolyte ran without looking back.

Yanik nodded to Meister Kinst, and took off. Her knees complained with every stride, but felt a little less pained. She ran for the huge dragon with death at her back, and hope – she prayed – before her.

——

Laoch stepped from the dragon's chest, Justice thrumming in his hands, as smoke and spiritfire pervaded the city's air. Oisin knelt before the dragon, Fate's bow drawn. A blue arrow lit his face as he targeted the oncoming Ranger. Apparently unafraid of the metal-scaled dragon at his back, the woman's lopsided run was punctuated by the occasional shout. Amid the grime and blood that covered her, vague recognition seeped into his mind.

"Know who that is?" asked Laoch, more to himself than Oisin.

"No, but she's alive amid this madness, so she gets my salute. And must be aware of Nathair."

"Laoch!" the Ranger shouted. She slowed and peered back towards the threat that rolled down the street.

"Feeders," Ecne said as she emerged from the dragon's chest. "Nathair warns of five artifices advancing, like those we fought in Makalena. Four on the street, another along the rooftops. Too many even for her. We must go."

Laoch glanced at the Ranger who waited on the roof line, arrow nocked, covering the approaching Ranger. Old memories poured in as the familiar smell of burning assailed his nostrils.

"Ranger Laoch, the feeders come. Meister Kinst ..." The female Ranger drew in a breath, her lungs suffering from the smoke, her face battered and bruised. "Meister Kinst sets a trap. Erin's Wrath ..." She pointed back towards the market square. Laoch made out the familiar barrels and a cart.

Full circle. There are no coincidences.

"No," he said, and turned to Ecne, a twitch to his eye that he tried to ignore. "It is time to make a stand. We need to buy some bloody time. In blood, if we have to. Ask Nathair to attack from above, drive them towards Kinst's trap. Then head for the bloody Houses. You know what to do, Ecne. We're relying on you both. Oisin?"

"With you," the Handren replied. "Though I don't fancy the odds."

"Then I stay," cut in Ecne, unshouldering Wisdom.

"No, you bloody don't." Laoch pointed towards the centre of the city. "You see Renta into the House of Penance. You are that bloody moody shaman's bodyguard; I charge you with ensuring she gets into Penance's House, and her safety thereafter. There is no more important job, Ecne. Ours is to buy you bloody time. Now hurry."

"Get gone, girl. And don't die," added Oisin.

"Nor you, old man," Ecne replied, a brief smile on her lips that disappeared as the first of the feeders emerged at the edge of the square.

She hurried inside, and Nathair's roar echoed across the square as the dragon leapt into the sky. The air beat down on all three of them, their hoods rippling in the thrust of air and the smell of oil.

"Now show me ... err ..." Laoch raised both eyebrows.

"Yanik. First Ranger Yanik."

"She outranks you," laughed Oisin, who stood with a grin.

"Everyone outranks me, but not Justice. Where is the meister?"

Yanik pointed the woman out, the green robes hiding much of her among the debris of the trebuchet. She had recovered the sack, and now held something in her other hand that neither of them could make out.

"No time to get her," Laoch growled. "But Kinst would tell me where to bloody go, anyway. Track her, Oisin. If the pot bombs fail to ignite, take out the ..."

"Three barrels along the eastern edge of the square," interjected Yanik, pointing towards them. Oisin sighted in that direction. "The meister said to aim there."

"Good. We have a target."

A roar rolled across the rooftops. Pulsen flung herself down as a terrifying keening joined the swirl of noise. Orange wings appeared above the roof, beating downwards, driving Nathair onwards. As she emerged over the lip, Laoch could see three of her taloned feet were dug deep into the sides of a writhing feeder. The artifice lashed at the dragon with head and tail. Its weight forced Nathair to work hard to stay above the street, and she eventually dropped the artifice, letting it crash into the others that had paused their advance. The flailing machine tried to thrash its way upright, mandibles gnashing at the air, oblivious of the next danger. Nathair's tail whipped, and the spike cracked beneath the artifice's head, splitting the metal skull in two. Crystal armour shattered and whitefire flared momentarily. The artifice collapsed.

Wheeling about over the east of the city until she was lost to the smoke, Nathair trumpeted her success.

"One," said Oisin. "Just the four left, then."

"Big fuckers, too," said Yanik, swapping out the ragged string on her scavenged bow. "And you have a dragon, but so do they."

"Aye, well. I wouldn't say we *have* a dragon. More an ally."

Meister Kinst moved, jogging with her sack across the road to kneel beside a scattered pile of wire and wood. Laoch, peering closer, caught sight of a barrel, and possibly a fuse that poked above it. He grimaced, knowing all too well the volatility of Erin's Wrath after the attack in Smerral Clearing.

The first of the feeders returned to its task, the segmented body rippled in a wave of movement as it fully entered the square. The three others clambered over their dead compatriot mere yards behind. The meister struck at something and a light flared, only to splutter out. She tried again, the feeder now only a few yards away.

"Ready, Oisin," said Laoch. "No second chances."

The flame flared again, followed by a sparkling second as the fuse took. Kinst glanced their way, waving almost as if saying goodbye, and turned back towards the huge artifice.

"Run," whispered Laoch, more in hope. The meister stepped out in front of the machine and flapped her hands above her head. The feeder reared back for a moment, then surged forward. Kinst waited. An ineffectual arrow struck the underside of the artifice.

"Pulsen," said Yanik, her own bow ready, a final crystal-tipped arrow nocked.

The sky erupted. Whitefire morphed to orange as dragon's breath poured down the street. Nathair released a second blast, catching the rearmost feeder from behind. Momentum flung the Constructor's artifice into the next, and the dragon left a burning maelstrom raging before the meister as her wings powered her over the square and towards the Houses.

Still Kinst didn't turn and run. But Laoch knew the power stored in those barrels.

And the world, already set alight by a dragon, erupted in the fiery anger of a meister. Science tore into the thrashing artifices. Alchemy, at its pinnacle, smashed metal and crystal, twisted cogs and melted wire. The keening returned, three intertwined sounds that wavered in pitch to reach a crescendo as metal and stone cracked and popped. Laoch dragged Yanik down as the remains of the feeders crashed all around them.

"One lives," growled Oisin, Fate's light cutting through the billowing smoke. He pointed past the lead feeder, half its body gone, the other half smoking.

"Two," said Laoch, retrieving Justice and giving Yanik a helping hand. "For now. Guard our backs, Yanik. The explosions will bring the Constructors."

"Your backs?" she said.

Redfire and blue lit the air, and two Rangers went to war.

72
A CLASH OF DRAGONS

ERSTENBURGH, BRANDSHOLD

Nathair bent her wings, scooping the hot air rising from the city. Braking swiftly, she dropped down to the street. Whitefire crackled, the magic pouring from her heartstone to bolster her wings and reinforce her legs. The cost would be far larger than a normal, gentle landing, but the roar that emanated from the south had set her mind to what came next. Haste was essential.

He is here.

Conscious of the fragility of the life she contained, especially after Apso-Tran, when the pocket had nearly failed, the orange-hued dragon hit the street at a run. Her bulk smashed aside abandoned carts, and sent the soldiers who had watched her sail over the city diving for cover. Using her wings as a gentle brake, she felt the strain in her joints, but brought herself to a stop before the great Houses. The buildings appeared inert to her spirit-sight, empty. But she had learned much from Makalena, and to trust the humans who had helped her overcome the venom that had enslaved her.

'Ecne, you must act with haste,' Nathair said.

The acolyte, her bond-mate, responded with a thought.

Extending the pocket to her rib cage, the veil dragon's chest shimmered. Ecne exited at speed with Wisdom in her hands, and surveyed the area. Nathair could sense each soldier in the vicinity more as a ghost than as a full spirit, the shroud placed over the city dulling her senses at any significant range. She placed their locations in Ecne's head. Though impatient to leave, Nathair was going nowhere until she knew the acolyte and her charges were safe.

A bolt of purplefire lashed towards Ecne. Nathair sensed Wisdom react, but negated the need for the God's shield. Her foreleg flicked outwards to block the bolt's path, and the spiritfire dissipated against her scales.

'Use Wisdom's light,' she sent, and the sliver of the acolyte's God acted swiftly, as if it had simultaneously come up with the same thought. The air glowed green and Nathair pulled her leg away, exposing the acolyte to the priests' sight. The rainbow flares of spiritfire along the steps to each House winked out. With Wisdom held before her, the light intensified as Ecne ran towards Penance's House.

Nathair kept one crystalline eye upon her bond-mate, the other nervously on the sky. There was a shadow up there, assessing her more than likely, trying to decide her purpose. There was no doubt she was viewed as an enemy. The clash above Innealtóir had sealed that fate.

'Hurry, before I bring destruction down on you. The emperor nears.'

"I'm coming. Prepare Renta and the others."

Nathair chuffed, and her spirit form appeared from within the heartstone. The Schenterenta all stopped talking at once. Cat-like eyes, caught between worship and horror, locked onto hers. It soured her sense of worth, for they judged and found her an abomination despite Keran's healing.

"Ecne comes. It is time. But you must run without hesitation. Another dragon approaches." Nathair extended the pocket and pointed the way as Ecne reached her chest.

Renta acted first and strode out towards the street, her voice commanding, suppressing any argument. As the last of Sura's tribe exited, Nathair sealed the pocket and leapt into the air. Guilt swathed her as she drew upon the spirits that pervaded the air above the city, fragments of those who had died to save others. Pieces shorn off as the Inhibitors and their swords fed, or slivers the feeders had missed. Each was consumed with an apology graced with the hope she offered.

A dragon's roar cut through her thoughts, and Nathair extended the net of her senses to its limits. The feedback was a mere shadow, but as the emperor's dragon dived from above, all knowledge was welcome. The silver-blue artifice arrowed downwards, and with each beat of her wings, Nathair strived to get beyond the attack and away from the city. Another three wingbeats, and she knew it was hopeless; too much time and white-fire would need to be spent. As another screech pierced her senses, Nathair spun about, talons extended.

The emperor's dragon smashed into her chest. Talons scraped across scale and limb as the beast's momentum drove them both towards the city below. Nathair, pain running through her metal ribs, folded her precious wings and spread a curtain of whitefire across her back as they plummeted towards the buildings. Her razor-edged talons raked at the dragon's legs, shearing scales to seek the wires and cogs beneath.

Her whitefire crackled, and Nathair's back slammed into the stone buildings. The impetus drove the whitefire shield to its limit, and her vertebrae crashed into uneven roofs and stone walls, which strained under the sheer weight that pummelled her into the ground. Despite the pain, Nathair's legs heaved as she twisted onto her side and threw the silver-blue dragon off, desperate to prevent being pinned to the ground. Nathair's tail then lashed at the debris-strewn rubble. Each pulse sent agony along her spine, but popped the errant vertebrae and realigned her back scales. The cost was high. Without remorse, she drew upon whatever spirits were around.

A necessity.

The silver-blue artifice had tumbled across homes and shops to come to a stop against an inner-city wall. It rose to its feet, maw wide, trumpeting. Nathair had to move. With no time to repair the wounds upon her chest, she used her wings to roll herself back onto her feet. She had expected a face-off, perhaps a voiced challenge, followed by a battle of dragon's breath.

The old ways, when arguments arose.

But no. The artifice's talons dug into the ground, its wings beat once, twice, adding to the dragon's momentum as it powered towards her, maw glinting with malice. Nathair, forced to protect her chest, ducked her neck low, forelegs bent, eyes upon the rampaging beast. It leapt, and Nathair lashed her spiked tail, whipping it around towards the dragon's flank. To her surprise, whitefire encased the emperor's dragon, a surge of power that swung the metal beast about. Four legs caught her tail, and the talons drove into the joints, ripping and tearing. Nathair felt a sudden wrench, and lost all control of her favoured weapon. Wires snapped, cogs and pulleys whirred helplessly as they untethered. That wasn't the end, the emperor's slave careering on, its momentum heaving Nathair off her feet and across the buildings as it continued to spin. Her back spines scraped across walls and collapsed roofs, before she slammed into the rubble, landing on her side.

Trying to right herself, with one wing trapped, Nathair despaired when her tail failed to respond. The more effort she put in, the deeper she buried herself. A victory roar rolled over her, hot, oily breath swathing her prone body with the dragon's joy at her predicament. The crunch of stone underfoot heralded the emperor's approach. Slow, as if it took pleasure in each tortuous step. Nathair twisted her neck around. Her eyes caught the flicker of flame that straddled the dragon's teeth and beard. Hate, laced with joy and victory, lay behind the crystalline eyes. She tasted the breath. The Spirit Walker within tainted by the emperor's venom, and by the emperor's soul.

"The price of treachery."

The black words seared into her mind, the emperor's voice stirring hate and a distant tug of servitude. The maw widened; razor-edged teeth bared. Inside, an empty void promised an ending. The dragon would consume her spirit, feed off its power, and the world would fall. Apso-Tran would be next, and Keran's beloved family would be neither found nor avenged.

The price is high.

—

"Now. Before he drinks the Spirit Walker. He will be too strong." Lelion turned her head to look over her shoulder at her second-in-command. "Now, Spintz!"

The hand wavered, awaiting the sliver of redfire that rolled across the lieutenant's lips to seep into her mouth. The ecstasy thrilled her, white eyes streaking with its power. Spintz yanked at the lever.

A keening rose from the *Kraken* soulship and its spiritfire-laden crystals. As the intensity increased, Spintz slammed the second brass lever down.

Whitefire lit the battlefield, streaking through the breach to smash into the rear of the hated silver-blue veil dragon.

"Yes, Spintz, yes! My time is now. Take us in."

73
BLOOD AND SOULS

HOUSE OF PENANCE, ERSTENBURGH, BRANDSHOLD

"High Lord?" the queen asked, her eyes searching his. "Are you okay? Will this work?"

"I ... I need time to think," he replied, both hands resting upon his cane as he sat on the edge of a pew.

"We do not have time. You have had a thousand years to scheme and think. Now we are entering the final hours. This Ecne talks of the city as if it is in ruins, the Constructors and their infernal machines having overrun the streets. We have already called the end of times."

"I..."

But he could not think. His mind was a maelstrom of faces and words. Her smile, her anger. He let Penance ease the pain with a sliver of spiritfire.

"You say Yanik is out there, in the city?" The High Lord's words were directed to Kinst's much-changed acolyte. Wisdom's touch upon the girl's eyes and mind were obvious to his sight.

The girl nodded.

"High Lord," cut in the queen, eyes narrowing as Ecne made to speak. "Every person out there is a child of mine. My subjects, each one under my wing of protection. When you thought Yanik gone, you were prepared, as was I, to call down your fire upon everyone. This Renta and her people offer hope in the darkness, not fire."

"And if it goes wrong and the fire comes?" he said, but he knew the answer. All would die as the forbidden books stated. All, including Yanik and him. Everything he had schemed for would be worthless in the face of his own dead child.

Ecne swore as her anger boiled. Only Wisdom's calming touch prevented an explosion. "Sura died for us. Laoch and Oisin have both suffered vile torture. I was molested by a necromancer. Nathair has had the venom burned from her soul. We have all *suffered*. Yanik is out there, fighting by their sides, for this one chance – to give you the time you need. Renta left her own world to provide it." Ecne paused, the crossbow across her back pulsing in her mind. "Wisdom can feel your own God's call, your reliance upon its power."

The High Lord flinched, his dependence on the cane and the sliver of his God exposed to his mind. The wisps of power constantly fed his body, but, perhaps, had clouded his judgement. The constant call for Penance to soothe his needs, and the God's demands for punishment for his accumulated sins. The revelations to those here about the Houses' true purpose. The release of the forbidden science upon the world, then the exposure of the Eighth's true purpose and the Seven's role within it. The lies he had exposed in the hopes of saving a world.

Penance called for punishment for his failures, a final release of the burden that gnawed constantly at his soul. But it did not have to be like that for all his flock.

I miss Sneed. He would have seen my malaise.

The High Lord stood and held the cane before him. In the glow of its spiritfire, the crutch he relied upon transformed into Penance's scourge. The tips glowed a menacing purple, and he cracked the weapon across his back. Pain cut through his robes as the shock on the faces of those who watched brought a little smile to his face. A second lash was stayed by the queen, her hand upon his wrist.

"I need this," he said, and gently removed her hand. The violence of the second scourging surged through him, flaying Yanik from his thoughts. "Only the flock matters."

"You people are so strange," said Terana, and took the High Lord's arm as his legs gave.

"On that," he whispered, dropping the scourge to the floor, "we both agree. We have a lifesong to purge the true enemy, and only clarity of mind and spirit will enable such a thing." He stood and shrugged the elf's arms off with a brief grimace. Blood poured from his wounds, but he rejoiced in the pain. "Let us get to it."

—

Justice sliced into the gap between elbow and greaves, severing the Constructor's sword arm. The foul weapon the Constructor wielded spun and hit the floor of the house. Laoch carried the stroke on through to bite into the armoured hip. The blade's edge glanced off, and the Constructor's buckler struck him beneath the chin, causing him to stagger. Yanik nipped beneath the offending arm, her short sword driving up into the Constructor's neck to shatter jaw and pierce the brain. They toppled forwards. Laoch recovered enough to take the weight, and sidestepped to let the corpse crash to the floor.

Outside the remains of the shop, Oisin's arrow flew along the street to light the Scorpion's armour as it struck the hull. Spiritfire scorched the metal, rolling along the armour before fading away.

"They close," he said, glancing back towards the pile of feeders they had created, and the square beyond. "Time to go."

Laoch spat out a tooth. He ignored the bleeding cut on his chin. "Yanik, Pulsen, head for the far edge of the square. I want you to cover our retreat."

"With fucking sticks and stones," swore Yanik, and shoved Pulsen ahead of her. "Won't do no fucking good."

"We use what we bloody have, Ranger. Now piss off." Laoch turned away, half a grin on his face, wishing he'd had longer to get to know the woman.

Would have beaten the Unspoken with one hand tied behind her back.

With a scrape of metal and boot, the Rangers left. Oisin released a final arrow, forcing the advancing Constructors to take cover behind their long-limbed artifice.

"She took the sword," Oisin said, glancing over his shoulder towards Laoch. "The Constructor's weapon."

"As long as she doesn't bloody cut herself, what harm can it do? We use everything we have, like always." Laoch exited the shop and dropped behind a broken exterior wall alongside the Handren.

"Everything?" replied Oisin, nodding back towards the shop. "Because that roof looks seriously in need of a bit of Laoch care and understanding."

Laoch grinned. "You think?"

"I do."

"Who gets to be bait?"

"I'm the one with the bow, and Fate's weave." Oisin slapped Laoch on the shoulder as he stood, eyed the next building and shouldered the bow. "And yes, it took some persuasion to carry Fate. And yes, Laoch was right, as always."

"Now you bloody understand."

Laoch covered while the mountain man rapidly scaled the side of the building, easing past broken chimneys and the remains of a feeder's limb or two.

He then entered the shop and collected the severed arm of his ex-opponent. This, he threw high over the wall as the clank of the Scorpion reverberated from a few buildings down. It clattered against stone and rock. As hoped, the artifice accelerated down the street. An arrow clonked against its hull. Laoch guessed Pulsen or Yanik had taken his call for cover to heart.

The Scorpion's tail whipped savagely, and the stinger stabbed deep into the wall he hid behind, shattering the stone. Laoch threw himself deeper into the shop, his shoulder clattering against broken shelves. Springing to his feet, redfire glowed as Justice flared into life. He ran for the back exit, where the door swayed on one hinge. A quarrel smashed into the floor. The resultant burst of whitefire lashed at his boot and he staggered. Momentum sent him half out the door. He swung about, buckler up just in time, as a second quarrel struck the shield. A prayer of thanks to Justice slipped from his lips as the Constructors, swapping their spent handbows for mace and sword, ran his way amid the limbs and pincers of the angered Scorpion.

Laoch fled out the door and found himself in an alleyway half-filled with rubble. He scrambled to the summit, and turned back to hurl stones and bricks towards the doorway. The pile shifted and tumbled downwards under his weight, yet still one of the Constructors attempted to climb out.

The world was suddenly filled with the fizz of bluefire, Fate taking her turn in the battle as Oisin's arrow pierced the roof. A second and a third smashed into the stone, and it gave, dust and stone chips billowing upwards. Metal and stone collided, and as the doorway lintel gave, it pinned the Constructor. Laoch could see the Scorpion's tail still lashing haphazardly in the street. He decapitated the Constructor, and when a spark of whitefire flowed from its head, cast an evil grin and drove his boot heel into its gourd.

"No bloody way," he said, Yanik having confirmed their suspicions about the gourd's purpose. "Stay bloody dead."

A cry from the other building drew his attention – familiar, pained. He clambered back up the rubble and leapt the short distance onto the roof of the nearest building. Across the next, Oisin fought hand-to-hand with two dust-covered Constructors.

Laoch jumped onto the building's lip and Justice reformed into his trusted bow. As he pulled back on the string, a Constructor struck Oisin in the ribs with a hammer. The Handren cried out despite the armoured plate's protection.

Laoch's arrow flew, but the redfire tip didn't reach its intended target, as Oisin's second assailant stepped, unawares, into its path. It rammed into his shoulder blades, propelling the Constructor forwards and into Oisin.

Swearing, Laoch drew again despite the close proximity of his targets. The Constructor lifted the hammer up high, ready to smash the weapon down on Oisin's pinned head. With Justice's aid, the arrow flashed across the divide to crash into the enemy's arm.

The hammer still struck a glancing blow to the side of Oisin's head. The sound of its crack pierced Laoch's resolve. With a growl, he stood, arrow drawn, and released. A second winged its way before the first struck. With Oisin's aggressor smoking within their armour, he kicked at the other. The Constructor rolled onto their back and released the quarrel loaded in their handbow.

Laoch saw his death. His last thought of Sura, her eyes shining. A flash of a Ranger's cloak and he hit the roof, sliding across the debris, face scraping against the stonework. The explosion caked him in dust and blood, but only an ache sat at his hip, a weight upon his legs.

Shaking his head, he dragged himself out from beneath a bloody mess to find the first Constructor rising unsteadily to its feet in gore-splattered armour. Laoch had little time to think. A flash of scarlet at his feet gave him hope, and he plunged his hand into the blood-covered mire just as the Constructor struck with its unholy sword. Laoch drove a shoulder into their midriff, causing the soulreaver to swing harmlessly over his back. He lifted the strangely light Constructor up before slamming them back down onto the roof. Bloodied hands drove Justice under the black chest plate as he threw himself on top.

Whitefire crackled as the foul thing died, and he rolled away. The Constructor's soul boiled from its body, writhing along the armour. Panting, he tried to rise to smash the gourd. As he faltered, Yanik appeared, clambering up onto the roof. A glance to his side, and she wiped her eyes. With a snarl, her short sword swept from its scabbard to crush the gourd.

She stared at the mess the Constructor had made of Laoch's saviour and whispered, "Pulsen."

Laoch pushed himself to his feet and bent over. Breathing hard, he staggered over to Oisin. With Yanik denying the other Constructor any hope of return, he knelt beside his friend. Oisin's skin was white, the bruise red and livid along the side of his skull. Laoch lifted an eyelid, which twitched despite the wide pupil giving him little hope.

"He lives?" Yanik asked, her words low as she knelt beside what had once been Pulsen.

"He does, just. And I only live because of your friend." Laoch stood and, with a shake of the head, placed Fate back in his friend's hand.

"I hardly knew her," replied Yanik.

"Those who die at your side will always be your friends," Laoch said, eyes on the prone Handren.

The sky darkened as a shadow stretched across the rooftops. Laoch turned about, knowing what he would see and the dread it would cause. The sky ship hung above the breach, steadily spreading malevolence across the city as it floated inwards.

"Come on, Renta, Sura. End this."

A thick arc of whitefire lashed towards the centre of the city.

74

THE LIFESONG

House of Penance, Erstenburgh, Brandshold

The queen's chest vibrated. The elven song, low, insistent, filled Penance's prayer chamber with a celebration of lives lived. It tugged at her mind, caressing her thoughts. Memories flowed, some long forgotten, others cherished and forever loved. Of her father's sweetened breath. Her mother's eyes. Her first, secret kiss. The final touch of the man she had grown to care for. The adoring eyes of her subjects. The joy of winning the political dance of the court. Amid these were her wedding vows, the news of her father's death, and Sneed's self-loathing as he departed for Penance's House. A life lived.

Words spilled from her lips unbidden by her mind, plucked by the song. Their rhythm merged with that of the elves as their voices sang in celebration. She found herself on her feet, hands before her, the wisps of her soul dancing between her fingers.

Erin's eyes misted, and a light broke through the chamber. White, with a tinge of purple that blazed brightly but did not cause her to flinch or shield her eyes. Instead, she embraced it, pulling the light within herself just as those about her wrapped themselves in its warm embrace.

And there, in her mind's eye, she hovered above a lake of blood. A woman in white, ethereal, blanketed in the spirits of her people. With a touch of her finger, a wave of whitefire rippled through the lake, cleansing it of the blood, filling it with life.

—

Lady Honour gasped. Makalena's chamber sparkled with the powerful orangefire emerging from the prayer stone. It wreathed the room in its warmth, and the Schenterenta sang. Their lifesong filled the chamber, saturating the room with a joy she had felt only at Lady Death's touch. With eyes and soul alight, her heart lifted, and her eyes fell upon Ferena. The shaman shone vividly as two souls whirled in and out of her twisted body. They sang of devotion and beauty, of a love forever honoured. Her heart welled, and Lady Honour found her own words joining the throng. She celebrated her life, weaving the agony of Nesca's passing with the joy of Lady Death's kiss, the pleasure of hope in Sura's presence, and the despair spawned by the Infected horde. All were welcome. This was her song, her life. And it mattered.

—

Sura's voice filled Honour's prayer chamber. The Wyrding Stone, held aloft by the Lead of the House, emphasised the rhythm and washed the congregation with its power. Each of those who knelt, stood, or were held close to their parent's breast, took up the song and basked in Honour's light. Their words spilled out the door and mingled with the masses who waited there, each rejoicing in their own lifesong in the name of whatever God they worshipped. The voices of Seven Houses celebrated life together. The joys and depths, highs and lows. The sound built into a thunderous evocation of Ridth, filled with passion. Sura bent this to her will, and filled the Wyrding and prayer stones with its power.

Lifesong blazed from the Wyrding, piercing the roof of Honour's House to illuminate the sky in a pulsing rhythm of light. More joined, the shine of red, green, yellow, blue and purple shrouded by Death's black. Together, they broke through the clouds as the sun began to drop behind to the horizon, suffusing the world with sound written in light.

—

Light emblazoned the city below, the *Kraken*'s shadow lost amid myriad hues. Luminescence danced amid the buildings, rising, infusing the sky. Accompanying it was a familiar sound.

The hum reverberated through the admiral incarnate's mind, stirring a primal fear mired in an ancient memory. Lelion clamped her hands to her ears. Though the dreadful sound was but a murmur in her mind, the song rejoiced in the malaise and profound hatred it caused. A loathing set deep by a lack of spirit sleep, a companion that nagged constantly to be heard. She dropped to her knees, bent double, trying desperately to rid herself of it.

Spintz raced to her side, but the admiral incarnate ignored her second. Hatred for the intrusive Inhibitor bubbled in her mind. She knew it was unreasonable, that the lieutenant was now her ally in the silencing of the emperor, but the hum ... It challenged her thoughts, her logic. It whispered of past ills, of the end of all the things she held precious. And it spoke of life. Not the dust-riddled jealous immortality of her kind, but of life lived for its own sake.

And reason was lost in that sound.

She needed the sound to end, for relief to spread through her body like the warmth of a magus's spiritfire.

Spiritfire.

A salve.

Lelion shoved herself upright. Pushing Spintz away, she grabbed the magus who lay chained upon the floor. With his head between both her hands, she took his spirit. The redfire swaddled the hum, encased it within its power. Relief spread through her body, though she still shook as she took her fill.

"Admiral?" said Spintz, but Lelion ignored her again, the redfire lacing her mind, her lust rising. "Admiral. You drain too much ..." said Spintz, licking her lips.

An unexpected hand fell upon Lelion's wrist.

The admiral flinched, her white eyes afire as she turned to face Spintz, hands still clamped to the dying magus.

"I need it," she snarled.

The hum amplified, and the light in her mind brightened, shattering the inner wall created by the redfire. Hatred poured back in to ride upon her self-loathing. The decadence of her race exposed. Lelion removed her hands and clamped them on either side of Spintz's head. She tasted the fear upon the woman's spirit, the weakness of her hands as they clawed at her own.

"*I* decide when I have taken too much. Not you."

The sound hammered into her mind. A dreadful noise that coalesced into thrumming words she could not understand. They gnawed at her sense of being, urging her on. They were full of love and joy. Of life and celebration. An anathema to those that took life from others, to those whose souls were desiccated, empty of anything but greed and the need to survive, their spirits barely rooted within their long-dead bodies.

The song celebrated life, while denying she was truly alive. More a living death.

A song of life.

And the Constructors were long dead. Only their shrivelled *will* remained, entwined with whatever spirits they drank, souls they ate or lives they consumed.

Stealers of spirits.

But dead, nevertheless.

Fear struck at the admiral incarnate and she drained Spintz dry, feasted upon her shallow soul and her desperate will. She mingled it with her own, strengthening her roots so she could carry on existing, if only for a short while longer. The lieutenant's white eyes faded, emptied, and Lelion let the woman collapse to the floor. A dead shell wrapped about a void.

The bridge had descended into chaos, Inhibitor striking Inhibitor. A frenzy of desperate feeding, the need to survive driving them on as the admiral incarnate looked on, haloed by the light blazing through the window.

And the lifesong took its due.

———

The Unspoken urged An Chéad to beat her wounded wings faster. An unusual, unsettling song thrummed amid the cloud. Its sheer power inflicted a dread that snuffed out the anger and shame of her defeat. A cacophony that rippled out from the city and its shroud, which they had skirted, heading north to lick their wounds before searching for new feeding grounds. The song hit like a hurricane, smashing into the artifice, rolling down cog and wire to enshroud the pocket in its discordance of hated voices.

"Hold on," the Unspoken shouted, unable to think amid the hateful noise. The pocket gave way under the assault, and the dragon dropped like a stone. The artifice's already-ragged wings gave in as the Unspoken's will shifted to her own self-preservation. She wove a net of spiritfire, lacing it with her demand while drawing on the nearest Burners – her *need* to survive sacrificing the seemingly unaffected spirit-dolls. Yet the thrum echoed in her body, her bones shook, her dust-filled lungs expelling air as she was squeezed inwards. Sound battered at her defences and the Unspoken began to sense her spirit being drawn out – leaking, seeping towards the pull of the song.

Soul-death. Forever.

———

The Emperor, ruler of Innealtóir, the Fleshmaster, rolled about the metal floor. He crashed into the heartstone, his body afire with the agonies of the hated lifesong. Memories flooded in, those moments upon Apso-Tran when he had held victory in his grasp, only for the foul song of the Drach to rip it away. He felt that same tug at his spirit, the rending of his true life from the dead body he inhabited. The roots slid so easily from his mind and heart, their tendrils frayed.

Soul-death beckoned him for a second time.

No.

Tarin wrapped his legs about Tabharthóir's heartstone, holding his position briefly before pulling himself slowly up the crystal. Each movement screamed of Lelion's betrayal, the whitefire she had burned into him as he readied the death-stroke upon the traitorous Nathair. He had known it would come but not when, and had planned his own revenge upon the admiral incarnate when the victory was complete. But she had struck first, and opened herself up to his wrath.

"I will live ... I will tear your fucking soul out, Lelion, and burn it in the whitefire of the Seven," he growled, his ornate gauntlets gripping the heartstone. He drew upon the Spirit Walker, its own powers weak after the battles with her artifice kin and Lelion's treachery. The more he drank, the more he knew it would be the dragon's ending – at least, until Tarin could corrupt another shaman. He sensed Tabharthóir's fear, her sudden understanding of what was to come, and ignored it to drain the last of her spirit. The power wrapped about the flailing roots in his body. He refused to let the hateful song tear his soul free.

The emperor collapsed to his knees, hands still upon the now-lifeless crystal.

I am eternal.

———

Laoch dropped Oisin gently to the ground. The city glowed amid the pulses of tremendous sound and light that rippled outwards from the Houses at its centre. His world vibrated in the ebb and flow of the lifesong, a power so immense it dwarfed that of the Drach and tugged at his soul, demanding he join the throng. He fell to his knees, chest pounding, as his heart and mind fought the song. He did not share its joy; only its grief.

He knelt over Oisin, trying to protect the man, when a soft hand fell upon his neck. The touch was warm, the fingers calloused but gentle. He leant back to find the Handren standing before him wreathed in Fate's blue, and laced with venomous black. Yet his body was still laid upon the street.

Its eyes shut.

Lifeless.

"Oisin ..." he whispered. The song took his words and wrote them into the verse.

Fate's light whirled about Oisin's spirit, its pulse a drumbeat that mirrored the dance of light enveloping the city. The dreadful venom burned away, a darkness the First Ranger had fought for so long, seared from his soul. Oisin smiled, and opened his arms wide to join in the song. Each word drew Laoch's attention, and he found himself on his feet. The grief burned still, but as he turned about, the joy of seeing the whitefire pour from the writhing Constructors wrapped about the pain. Souls sullied by self-loathing and hate, masked as a drive to survive at any cost, were torn free. An end to their perpetual pain. Countless shadowed souls burned beneath the light, shredded by the song of life that cleansed the city.

Their screams were silent, and Laoch knew they were denied the song, for they took no joy other than in the death of others.

He fell to his knees, tears streaming to wet the ashes of the fallen.

75

THE SONG OF THE BETRAYED

ABOVE ERSTEN FOREST, BRANDSHOLD

It ended as suddenly as it began. The cacophony that had threatened her soul-death simply stopped.

An Chéad was spiralling downwards, wings thrashing against the air, when the Unspoken drove her will and spiritfire into the heartstone. Using the final few reserves of her energy, she infused the artifice, enabling the huge wings to catch the wind. The scarlet dragon careered along the forest's treetops, his tail dragging through leaves and branches, tearing at the earth below. Another mighty wingbeat took him above the canopy, and with a lurch, he rose a little higher, managing to maintain his height as the Unspoken withdrew to preserve the last of her precious spiritfire.

"We live," she said, her words rasping from sore lungs. "And we are betrayed. That bitch of a queen and her Union tried to kill us, An Chéad. Whatever magic that was, it was aimed at us. They tried to destroy me, my beautiful dragon, and you along with me. It appears as if our alliance ended a little earlier than I wanted. And that, I will never forgive."

A splash of whitefire to the west drew the Unspoken's attention. A calling, too weak to travel much beyond the forest, yet the pulse replaced the seeping fear caused by the lifesong with outright curiosity – and desperate hunger. The taste of the calling was oh-so-familiar, from one thought long dead.

"Leront," she said out loud. Her fingers sensed An Chéad's ill-ease within the heartstone. "It cannot be. We must see what is happening. If the emperor resurrects another veil dragon, An Chéad, we would be outmatched and forced to leave this realm. This should be *my* world to feed off. *My* humans to feast upon, to forge spirit-dolls and subjugate. Mine alone."

An Chéad responded. One wing tip rose towards the sky, the other dipped towards the forest, and the metal beast turned westwards, his spirit-sight locked on the pulsing whitefire he hungered for. As they neared a cleared section of trees – many felled, others burned in some past event – the glow's source throbbed from the dug earth and rock. Green scales glimmered amid the simple human machines. Wings were spread wide, while a long, emerald tail stretched into the woods.

The Unspoken commanded her dragon to fly over, their joint sight searching the clearing for any indication of the emperor or his Inhibitors. With a second pass alleviating her worry, An Chéad twisted his damaged wings, caught the wind, and the four sets of talons bit into the soil to settle, a little ungainly, by the broken form of Leront. An Chéad sat back, exposing his chest, and the surviving Burners exited the dragon's pocket, their wary eyes upon the horned head of the emerald dragon.

The Unspoken, her glamour in place, gracefully followed her spirit-dolls into the night. She walked with a hand upon her soulreaver's pommel, ice-blue eyes scanning the inert dragon.

"The heartstone has stopped beating," she said, turning to her Burners. With a thought, they spread around the damaged veil dragon. When satisfied, she strode towards the head, a snort slipping out alongside a little laughter as she eyed the stone door carved into the once-mighty dragon's open mouth. "Oh, how the strong have fallen, Leront." She placed her bone-white fingers upon the dragon's jaw. A warmth, gentle and limited, seeped into their tips. Raising an eyebrow, she approached the doorway to laugh once more at the intricate carving adorning the stone. A tendril of whitefire arced from her hand to lace the door. It opened, the flare of power lighting the Seven and the dragon they fought.

"They did like their theatrics," she said. "Pity the Magi declined my offer of eternal life. They tasted delightful from afar. But I will be feeding on their progeny very soon." And the Unspoken walked inside, trailing her fingers along Leront's metal neck. The inner door lay open, and beyond, a familiar light emanated from the large crystal to set the room aglow.

The Unspoken waited at the doorway, letting her senses probe the room. Only a feeble taste imbued the ether.

"Fate?" she muttered, and entered. She peered briefly at the mosaic upon the wall, guffawing at the audacity of the Seven Magi and their religion. Sigils and weapons, mere hints at the ghosts of the past.

"No," came a strangled voice. "Not Fate." A spirit swirled inside the heartstone, a taint of blue to its edges as it emerged from one facet to coalesce beside a repaired, ancient chair.

"Then who are you?" replied the Unspoken. Taking a step closer, she sent a tendril of her whitefire to taste the spirit. It didn't flinch. Instead, it accepted the touch while straightening its uniform.

"First Ranger Gowan of the Queen's Rangers. A follower of Fate – or at least I was." The eyes swirled, green seeping in. The pupils narrowed into slits as emerald-green scales emerged over the spirit's face. The inner door slammed shut. Heat and bubbling acere filled the room with an acrid tang as it sealed. "Now *I* am Leront, you traitorousss bitch, and I have a thousssand years of pain and isssolation to pour into your fucking dead Inhibitor heart."

"You? Challenge me? You are weak, Leront. The weakest of all the Spirit Walkers. And you have not fed properly for a thousand years. Your body is broken, and An Chéad waits outside to feast upon your heartstone."

The Unspoken's smile cut thin, and Gowan-cum-Leront glared back. "Challenge? No. You buried Nathair and I with your treachery. I am not trying to beat you. Just give you a tassste of our ... fate. You carry my eye around your neck like a trophy won."

The Unspoken's hand rose unbidden to her neck, and the porcelain fingers flickered into their true, husked form as she grasped Leront's Eye – the crystal she had stolen in a bloodbath from some forgotten manor house.

"There are no coincidencessss."

———

Grand Meister Arknold stumbled to the ground. The earth and stone beneath her feet lurched, twisting as if the land grumbled and complained. She picked herself up, ignoring the mud and grass that stained her meister's robes. Steely-eyed, she scanned Leront and the damaged scarlet dragon she had no name for, as well as the strange soldiers who surrounded them both. Her eyes swirled with black venom and whitefire, mirroring the fugue that had overtaken her mind. She only knew the commands Leront had written in venom upon her thoughts, and an unsettling hatred for the strange soldiers whose whitefire glow matched that of the creature who had entered Leront.

Arknold nodded to herself. "Yes. Now, I see. I know. I know." The great dragon she had spent the last months working on pushed itself upwards from the forest floor, joints screeching. The wings she had worked so hard to attach flopped lifelessly at Leront's side. Whitefire raced along the green-scaled neck to lift the head. "Now. Now. Now. I know."

She tugged the rope, and the multiple thinner strings attached to it yanked at the ballistae she had carefully oiled and smoothed. The heavy quarrels, tipped with pots of Erin's Wrath, flew clumsily through the air. But they were so close, and there were so many. Arknold ran, urging her body into movements it hardly remembered. The eruptions sounded off, one after the other, and searing heat washed beneath the trees to slam into her back as she reached the second trigger mechanism. A pull of the rope, and another set of ballistae fired. A trap she had laid for a dragon – just not this one. The explosions boiled in the clearing, flames that seared everything and anything they touched.

Arknold stayed down and rolled tight into a ball behind the set of rocks the priests had laid as their last act. All of them now just dust and bones, their souls consumed by Leront one by one as the grand meister carried out the Spirit Walker's commands. The ground shook a second time, a thunderous crash that wafted the flames and roiled heat her way. As her mind commanded, she crawled past the protective stones. Above the billow of smoke and burning leaves, two necks intertwined. Dragon upon dragon, chest to chest. Razor-edged talons slashed and gouged, tearing emerald scale from scale, exposing the skin beneath.

"Come on, come on, come on," said Arknold, and rose to her feet, ignoring her strained muscles. She ran for a pile of rock and soil her machines and the priests had dug to expose Leront. The grand meister slid to a halt. Her fingers dived into a stone pile to expose four sets of small, clay pots. Breathing hard, she waited, squeezing two in each hand.

Leront, the talons of his forelegs driven deep into An Chéad's side, powered upwards. The hind legs grasped the scarlet dragon underneath, talons tearing into her legs as he wrapped his body fully about the struggling artifice. An Chéad seemed bewildered, unable to react to a dragon that did not fight, just clung on, and responded with fury rather than reason. She continued to tear and rend whatever part of Leront she could reach, flapping her wings to beat at Leront's side.

"Now, now, now," said the grand meister, and a flash of whitefire filled the clearing. The huge green wings stiffened upon Leront's back before curling inwards, encasing even more of An Chéad. Wrapped up tight, the scarlet dragon roared and tried to turn about. Dragon's fire poured from her mouth as she bit down upon Leront's neck. With a huge twist, Leront spun them both and leaned back, letting his weight pull An Chéad slowly down towards the pit.

"Now," repeated Arknold, and she slammed the clay pots into the waiting holes one by one. A brief fizz was followed by a flash that flayed the skin from her hands, raging up her robe to sear her neck and cheeks. Her eyes bubbled, and as the skin melted from her face, the lips drew back in a charred grin.

With a roar, Leront finally pulled the scarlet dragon into the pit the Seven had dug for him, wrapped about the traitorous dragon like a vengeful winged demon. The Erin's Wrath buried deep within the rock ignited on the spark of the pot bombs. Like the precise engineer she had always wanted to be, the science of Arknold's craft caused the sides of the hole to collapse. Rock and soil tumbled down upon the struggling An Chéad until she was encased from below by vengeance, and from above, by the earth itself.

76

FOR LOVE AND FAMILY

ERSTENBURGH, BRANDSHOLD

"Laoch." The words were soft, but insistent.

She never changed.

Gentle fingers caressed his cheeks before pulling his face to hers. The lips graced his, the taste sweet, yet composed of fire and flame. He slid his hand behind her neck, drawing the woman he loved closer, and the kiss transformed into a passion that flared with spiritfire.

"Ahem," said a voice.

Sura pushed him away and lowered her head, lips to his ears. "Lady Death," she whispered.

"Seven bloody hells," he replied.

Rolling onto his front, he pushed himself up from the ground. He blinked, the darkness of the night a surprise against the last thing he remembered.

Oisin.

He spun about, to find the Handren's body gone.

"The guards took him, with Ecne," said Sura, and her hand slipped into the crook of his arm. "I thought it best."

"Best? It'll ..."

Sura placed her hand on his, silencing him. *'Ecne grieves, but our work is not done.'*

He locked eyes with her and noted the glisten of a tear that she blinked away. He nodded, and looked away to finally take in the ensemble waiting for him. Power crackled between them all, Justice responding to the slivers of Death and Hope that inhabited their weapons. Yanik waited at their side.

He bowed his head briefly.

"The shaman is exhausted, Laoch of the Queen's Rangers," said Lady Death, her silver hair streaming in the warm wind. "But she is convinced some have survived the lifesong. Perhaps the emperor himself." She pointed up towards the sky ship, which had sunk some distance since he'd last seen it. "Their sky ship dies slowly – a task for later. We seek the silver-blue dragon the emperor rode."

"Nathair fought the dragon, Laoch. The emperor was inside. Some of the guards report they saw them both fall." Lord Hope stepped forwards, pointing towards the south. "That direction."

"She is not to come," said Laoch, pointing towards Yanik. "This Ranger has done enough in the defence of this city."

"Like fuck I have," replied Yanik. "If there's a chance to have a pop at their fucking emperor, no one's going to stop me."

"Exactly the reason you can't bloody come. I need someone predictable." He glanced over to Sura, who left him with a smile as she faded away.

"Like her?" said Yanik. "Fuck that. Besides, I outrank you, remember?" She set off in the direction Lord Hope had indicated, and where Laoch assumed Sura had gone ahead.

Laoch shook his head and glanced down at the spot where Oisin had died. He sensed Lady Death's gaze. "You not coming?" he said, pointing towards the weapon she bore.

"The Houses have been emptied of their power, and we have the queen as Overseer to protect. If the emperor lives, or more of his kind, then we are her last line of defence."

Laoch stretched his battered body. Thoughts of how much Yanik must have gone through gnawed at his thoughts.

"So, it's up to us again?" With a shake of his head, he turned to run after the First Ranger. By the time he'd caught up, they were halfway down the once-wide thoroughfare. Buildings had collapsed on either side, with gouges torn into the road and side walls. It wasn't hard to work out what had happened, especially as the air was rife with the smell of hot oil.

Sura coalesced atop a pile of rubble on the central city side of the road and beckoned Laoch over, her eyes looking inwards. They stepped across the corpses of guards and Constructors, and clambered up the rubble. To the north, half buried beneath multiple dwellings, lay the scorched scales of the silver-blue dragon. The head was charred and split wide. Just the metal skeleton and its crystalline eyes remained. The lower portion bore obvious rents and tears where it poked above the rubble. And thankfully, the legs and wings remained still.

"Anything?" asked Laoch.

Sura hovered above the debris at his side. "The heartstone is dead," she said. "The Spirit Walker gone. Though if it was destroyed by the lifesong, I do not know."

"Then we go in," said Yanik, and she drew the hateful sword from her back.

Laoch grabbed her sword arm and pulled her back. "Wait."

"For fucking what?" Yanik yanked her arm away, but stayed where she was.

"For Sura," he said. The back of Sura's hand touched his cheek, and she slid away to enter the artifice's exposed upper chest.

"This death wish you're riding will get us all killed," said Laoch, turning to face the frustrated Ranger. "*All* of us."

"I am not you," she replied, but quietened, her cheeks reddening.

"Nor would I want you to be. Loss is everywhere. Oisin was special to all of us. But we must act with bloody reason, cold logic. Or we put others in a piss-poor place with our tempers. That is something I know too well."

"You don't know everything," Yanik replied, wincing as the words left her mouth amid the last of her anger. She raised her eyes from the ground. "I'm the High Lord's daughter."

"Ah. Now *that* was the bloody rumour I couldn't remember. Ack, so what? You fight like a bloody wildcat. That's all that matters." Laoch watched the inner turmoil play across her face. "Whatever it is burning a hole in your backside, it can wait."

"Sura knows," she whispered. Laoch glanced her way to show he'd heard.

Sura reappeared, her look one of disappointment.

"He's not in there. I could find no sign of a body, nor sense any spirit. I think he drank the Spirit Walker. Perhaps used it to survive the lifesong, somehow." Sura pointed towards the pile of debris and rubble to the south. A long orange tail poked out from beneath, bent in too many places to count. "Nathair."

They hurried over, digging away at the easier rocks to reveal part of the dragon's chest. Dented, shredded in places, Sura entered, and quickly returned. "She lives," she said, and dived back in.

Rocks soon shifted, and a tremble rippled the dust into circles across the building. Laoch and Yanik jogged away from the rising tide of debris, and the dragon's back emerged from the rubble, soon followed by a neck and head. There was an orange gleam to the dragon's eyes, and Laoch swore, realising the source of Nathair's newfound energy.

'*Move,*' sent Sura.

Laoch grabbed Yanik by the elbow. "Back, now!"

Nathair unfolded her wings. Kinks here and there lit with orange-tinged whitefire, and straightened amid screeches of metal. With a single beat of her wings, the dragon emerged fully and landed at the side of the hole.

The glimmer in Nathair's eye increased, and a pulse shimmered through the air. Smoke and ash danced in the spiritfire's path as it swept through the city.

A tingle in Laoch's mind signalled Sura's incoming thoughts. '*The shroud has gone, shredded by the lifesong. Nathair sent out a seeking. If the emperor is near, she should sense him.*'

Laoch raised an eyebrow as he surveyed the state of Nathair's scales. The battle must have been fraught. And close.

A roar ended the city's silence. Nathair reared her head back and dragon's fire seared the night sky. She leapt into the air, thunderous wingbeats driving her upwards. Another roar echoed as she dipped a wing, attempting to wheel back towards the sky ship. Her tail dragged limply behind, causing a stutter in her movements, but eventually Nathair flew in the direction of the ship.

"What's happening?" said Laoch. "Is he up there?"

"His family," said Sura, her spirit faded but present as she reformed where Nathair had been.

"His? Keran's?" Laoch peered up to the sky ship. "Oh shit."

———

Hate.

Hate.

Hate.

Nathair slammed into the *Kraken*, burying herself into the damaged rear. She tore at the metal, wire and cogs with tooth and claw. Not finding what she sought, the dragon clambered up the sky ship's hull to leap onto the upper deck.

Hate.

Love and Hate.

Her talons tore into the deck, dragging her weight across the domed hull.

I.

Must.

See.

One crystalline eye peered around the curve, and loathing speared deep into the dragon's heartstone. She dragged her damaged body around the deck, scales scraping over the *Kraken*'s window until death filled her vision.

Bones.

Skin.

Hollow.

Husked.

A forefoot reached out, a talon's gentle touch sweeping the hair aside. He remembered their smiles.

And hated.

He remembered their laughter.

And hated.

The first tear, kiss, touch, word.

And hated.

The artifice dragon pulled itself away, backed up, and leapt into the air. A forlorn trumpet echoing across the sky.

Lelion rose from behind her chair, the bridge strewn with the dead she had consumed. Her spirit was sour, mind and heart bleeding spiritfire as the maddening song had rent and tore at her being, at her will. But she had survived.

The admiral walked over to the rail, peering out at the city towards which her beloved soulship fell.

Glass smashed, and talons ripped into the gap to wrap about the admiral incarnate. Nathair dragged the foul thing back into the night air to slam Lelion against the brass hull beside Keran's family.

"These were mine!" she roared into the admiral's mind, tearing Lelion's spirit from its sore roots. "MINE!" She drove her words into the dead heart, shattering the foul thing into a million pieces. "And now you will suffer an ending like no other. I shall feast upon you piece by piece, day by day. You shall know never-ending *pain*."

Nathair tossed the admiral's body into the air. Teeth sawed through chest and dust-filled lungs, snapping at the head before swallowing the dry meat. But the withered spirit she did not consume. Instead, she encased the admiral incarnate in her crystal heartstone – bound and gagged – with only Keran and herself for company.

77

A QUEEN IN BLOOD

THE GODS' COUNCIL CHAMBER, HOUSE OF PENANCE, ERSTENBURGH, BRANDSHOLD

The blackened body lay stiff across the Council table, the skin cracked. Old blood dried in the wounds. An empty bottle of Khundish ale rocked gently against the cane's handle on the floor, Penance's sigil charred and inert.

The High Lord's hands were melded to the intricate glyph inlaid within the table. Flesh and metal made one by the power it contained, spiritfire gifted over a thousand years of fear and dread. Yanik placed her hand upon the withered shoulder. A tired queen stood by her side while Lady Death and Geral looked on.

"I—" said Yanik, but the words choked on her dry tongue.

Queen Erin took the woman in her arms, and let her head rest against her shoulder as sobs poured from a daughter's heart.

"He gave us life," whispered Lady Death, her eyes roaming over the High Lord's body before returning to Yanik. "Every last drop he had. He carried a burden, as all the High Lords before him had, that no one else could have borne. You will not appreciate it now in your grief, but he was a special man, and should be revered for his sacrifices."

The queen took Yanik's shoulders and eased the Ranger back to look into her eyes. "He drove me to distraction, if it helps. But somewhere in those last few weeks, he faltered at the thought of you. It was only when he realised your strength that he recalled his own."

Yanik blinked, suddenly aware she had been in the arms of the Union's queen.

"I–" was all she could manage, but stepped away with a bow of her head. Geral moved to her side and drew his niece into his arms.

"We will leave you both for a few moments, but my acolytes will come soon for his body," added Lady Death. She left, trailing the queen, and closed the door behind her.

"Erin," she said.

Her cousin took another stride before stopping and hunching her shoulders. The sobs echoed about the corridor, and Lady Death, the last of her family, took a grieving queen into her arms. Only the shared tears penetrated the silence of Penance's House. A grief at the loss of mothers and aunts, uncles and friends. For the thousands amid the rubble, and those who were nothing but ash at the gates of a distant city.

78

THE PASSING

HANDREN MOUNTAINS, BRANDSHOLD

A last melancholy horn sounded, echoing off the valley edge to stretch across the Handren Mountains in dawn's first light.

Laoch wrapped an arm about Ecne, pulling the acolyte, and his friend, in close. In the other, Sura, who leant her head against his shoulder. Her eyes shone with Honour's light. The pyre caught, and fire swept beneath Oisin's body. A stark reminder of how their time together had begun, doused in the flames of a dragon.

Sura slid her cheek gently off Laoch's shoulder, squeezed his arm, then drew Ecne in close. The tears finally came, long held back. Laoch fought his own, but in the end let them flow. It was no dishonour to have loved a man so steadfast and true. A Handren who had been his balance, a calm amid the storm of Laoch's emotions, and who'd fought the Constructor's venom when few others were able.

The smoke curled into the sky, only to be caught on the mountain winds. The ashes of Oisin's body were accompanied on their journey by the soulful mourning of a dragon on the wing. Laoch wiped away a last tear to watch as Nathair circled the valley twice more before heading south to wait for them.

Sura smiled gently towards Laoch, the flick of her head a sign for him to allow them some time alone. With Ecne in her arms, she led her away towards Oisin's village, in the lee of the valley edge. Laoch watched a while longer, sensing the presence that hovered behind but refusing to acknowledge it until he had said his goodbyes. To him, the body had long shed Oisin. He had learned much about the soul and spirits on his recent journeys, and knew he had seen Oisin depart his flesh to join the lifesong in the final battle for the realm. The body given to the pyre was merely a symbol of what it had contained, and no more.

With a final cough and wipe of a tear, he turned to face the waiting Lord. Young, but with the look of his sister, Lord Fate had shown decorum in his patience. Laoch felt a sense of pride that Oisin's achievements had been honoured by his presence. Whether the Houses still had a future was yet to be seen, but in his mind, order needed to be reinstated from the chaos left in the Constructors' wake. In this, at least, they had some part to play.

Laoch bowed his head slightly, only for the Lord to offer his hand. They clasped forearms, a moment of contact Laoch so wished Oisin could have shared.

"Thank you," he said. "Oisin never lost his faith in your House, or Fate. Though he was a stubborn bastard when it came to Fate's weapon." Laoch unshouldered the bow, the sigil glowing with a faint blue that flared brighter at Lord Fate's touch.

"Thank you for all you have done, Ranger Laoch. You, Oisin ... all of you. There are no real words to express our gratitude." Lord Fate took the bow in both hands. The weapon hummed at his touch.

"Words mean little, Lord Fate. And the sacrifices made by so many..." He paused, eyes glancing back to the pyre. "It is hard for us to understand just how bad things were here. So many dead." He shook his head, locking down the emotions that threatened to bubble over. He had heard much of what the Houses had hidden. Secrets that, to his mind, reflected potential poison at its core, exemplified by what he'd heard of their pact with the Unspoken. Yet Justice sat at his hip, and together they had fought to save a people. In his mind, he was a Queen's Ranger, and it would be the queen's words he would now live by. Wherever that would lead after they had repaid a debt owed.

—

"Here," Ecne said, and handed over the packet of acere.

"Thieves!" cried Rensta. Her weeping eye took in the young acolyte before accepting the green packet. "I would never have used it."

"You bloody would," said Laoch. "You had it in for your kidnappers, whoever they bloody were." He grinned, and the shaman smiled back.

"Whatever your methods, Queen's Ranger Laoch, in the end it was the right decision." The shaman glanced over Laoch's shoulder towards Nathair, the Spirit Walker slightly faded in the sun's light. Nathair beckoned her over, pointing to the dragon's chest with a wry smile. "Though now, at least, I go willingly. I know I will see you again. You and the amazing Sura. Our worlds are connected by pain, but our futures could be so different. I believe we may find a way to cleanse the moon pools and, in time, use those to remain in contact, instead of *dragons*."

Rensta walked away painfully, entering the dragon's chest without a glance towards the grinning spirit.

"I will be some time, Laoch," said Nathair. "But I will return. Keran needs to grieve on Mondrein, but I feel a desire to help here. It is a delicate balance, but with so many of the Constructors' artifices lying around, I sense a change coming to your world. I will be needed."

"Aye. And the bloody Unspoken is hiding out there somewhere. With the Houses broken, what reason does she have not to return to her true nature? Don't be too long. I kind of like having a dragon at my back." Laoch turned away from the Spirit Walker to let Ecne say her goodbyes.

When they were finished, the Spirit Walker entered the dragon. Before long, the mighty wings spread wide, and with a roar, the artifice leapt into the air. The earth rumbled as the powerful legs propelled the huge body towards the sky, while orange scales flashed brightly in the sun's strong light. In a few wingbeats, Nathair had guided herself up above the forest and soon disappeared out of sight.

"What now?" said Ecne, her hand upon Wisdom's weapon, though her eyes were for him.

Laoch looked along the edges of the burnt forest, though his mind was back in the valley where Oisin's charred body would remain until dusk.

"For me? Whatever Sura and the queen ask. I have two rulers in my life, and I would give my life for both." He smiled at Ecne. "And my friends."

"I keep expecting him to talk, you know. To slip in an observation, or call me *girl*." Ecne squeezed her hands together, pressing the knuckle of one to her eye. "But you are right. There is much to do, and that Handren honour would have expected nothing else but for me to do my duty."

"Yes, he was a tough bastard. And stubborn. He's left a hole no one can fill, so duty seems the best place to start. Come on, we have horses waiting. A slow ride through the forest is something we both need."

79

THE END OF THE BEGINNING

The White Palace, Erstenburgh, Brandshold

"When the meisters return, Ecne, you are to be anointed as one of them. Lord Wisdom has agreed that Seneschal Greeth shall be your liaison." The queen pointed towards the nervous-looking woman. "We are short of … of an engineer. That is the role Lord Wisdom sees for you in the future."

"Yes, my queen," replied Ecne, and she bowed low. "However, …" Ecne glanced over to Laoch, who hovered near the map table, deliberately averting his eyes. "I would prefer a commission in the Queen's Rangers."

"Denied. We are in need of your brain, young lady. Your mind. Not your ability with the bow. You have done enough fighting. We need builders and visionaries. And Laoch states you have learned much in your travels that will be of use to me. To our people."

Ecne's cheeks flushed, but the queen paid no mind, her thoughts already upon the bruised and battered Ranger awaiting her words. She wished she could be kinder, but few apart from Ridth had survived unscathed. Ecne backed away, giving a final bow and a scathing glance towards Laoch, who simply smiled in return.

"Laoch, you may approach your Queen and Overseer," announced Vianti, acting in place of the queen's assistant prime, who was among those not yet returned.

"Any news?" asked the queen, her eyes searched Laoch in hope after he had completed his bow.

"None, Your Majesty. The Rangers report the emperor's trail is cold after it left the breach. Once Nathair returns, then we may hold out more hope. Though she remains bonded to young Ecne, and they work better as a team."

"Then I charge you with the hunt, Laoch of the Queen's Rangers. Though I am loath to lend you Ecne. Will Sura-nista agree to help?"

"I have," Sura coalesced next to Laoch, a fierce smile upon her lips. "Though my duties are wide, Overseer. I am bound by Honour to her House, and the reinstatement of her faith."

"That is not my priority, nor that of the people. If we are to recover and heal, we must know the threat is ended – that the emperor is dead. And more of what happened to the Unspoken who abandoned us to our fate." The queen pushed herself up from the throne, taking each step carefully as she descended to stand before Sura. "Is there a way you can be released from this duty?" Erin placed her hands upon Sura's forearms, sensing the pulse of Honour beneath. It brought a smile to her face, and Laoch's private request to her mind. She locked eyes with the elf.

"I believe the Overseer has oversight of all Houses, Queen Weister. Your word is law," said Sura. "The High Lord and Lord Wisdom agree that upon your say, Honour is *honour*-bound to release me. That our work together would be done."

"Is that what you wish, Sura-nista?"

Sura glanced over to Laoch, a smile playing across her lips. "I wish to be my own woman, Queen Weister. I have died twice in service to this realm, and both times, Honour has intervened. Twice is enough for anyone."

Erin's lips wavered. Her yearning to give the elven spirit what she wanted – needed – was almost overwhelming. A release from duty.

But I am the queen, my hands dipped in blood. Do I relinquish warriors of both spirit and bone when they are needed?

"I will give you what you wish, but only once we know the emperor has been caught or we have proof the threat is over," she said, releasing the elf's arms as her eyes flashed with anger. "I am sorry it could not be sooner. As Overseer, I task you and Honour with helping Laoch. Once this is done, then we will speak again."

"My queen …" said Laoch, but she had turned away to ascend the steps to her throne in silence.

"My word is law, for the good of all," Queen Weister said as she turned to face him.

I am sorry. But heroes do not rebuild a world. Queens do.

80
WITH VENGEFUL INTENT

ERSTEN FOREST, BRANDSHOLD

Popsilin snapped the wrist bone, lifting the severed hand to stare at the ornate gauntlet that encased bone-white fingers. A vague memory pierced her addled mind, of the same hand gripped to a brass balustrade as a battle raged below. Though where it came from, and of whom, was too distant. As if it waited at the end of a long, dark tunnel she had no interest in following.

Scarlet glimmered off the curved ceiling, her fire's light filling the void with the pretence of warmth she did not need nor feel. But it helped her paranoia, the cloying sense of always being watched. She gnawed upon the largest finger, drawing off the metal guard and spitting it onto the husked corpse at her feet. The white eyes stared back, full of shock at their unexpected demise.

Popsilin laughed. Tenith would have enjoyed sharing the food, but he had become too strong. Had fed too much, and she was sure he had looked upon her as one would your next meal. She had, of course, got in first. But his soul had proved meagre compared to the magi she craved. And this peculiar magus had proven worthy of the effort it had taken to draw him down into her hole. A strange delicacy, one that continued to stir a distant memory, yet still a delight.

"Hah, Tarin would have been proud ... Tarin? No, Tenith would have been proud of my ingenuity." Popsilin whipped her head around, her own words taking her by surprise as they echoed back off the curved metal walls.

Tarin? Who was Tarin?

Tarin.

"The Fleshmaster," whispered the dark. *"The Emperor who brought ruin in his wake. The one whose spent soul sustains us both and husked body lays at your feet."*

Popsilin flinched and returned to her meal. The whitefire that seeped into her mouth from the finger was more than enough to see her through the day. Perhaps she'd treat herself to the whole hand, if the voice allowed.

"Not too much," came the whispered reply. *"Twice betrayed by their vicious song and their foul machinations, I need to feed, to regain my strength and beauty. You will have more than enough magi to feast upon, when I have my vengeance."*

And here ends A Queen in Blood, the final book in the Warriors of Spirit and Bone trilogy

THE WARRIORS OF SPIRIT AND BONE SERIES

Thank you for reading this final book in the series. It has always been a dream of mine to write a fantasy series, and though some would say there are elements of science fiction in Warriors of Spirit and Bone, I would argue they are there, but minor. I spent much of my late teens and early twenties exploring the worlds of the Eternal Champion with Michael Moorcock, one of my early literary heroes, and in recent years, the works of Joe Abercrombie. This final book, A Queen in Blood, is heavily influenced by both. It shifts slightly more towards grimdark (this is a war for survival, after all) yet we travel between realms on the wings of a mechanical artifice, or bludgeon through veils on a giant soulship. We explore the pain of grief and loss, the fall of the Houses, and the rise of a queen. In essence, it is the most 'human' of my books as we observe those with power fall upon each other as much as their enemy.

And of course, soul-vampires. Had to be done.

I hope you enjoyed this journey through arcanepunk fantasy, and take the time to leave a review for each of the books. There are readers out there who like their fantasy to be a little darker and different from the norm. A rating or review guides them on that path.

Thank you

About the Author

If you have read my previous books, you will know that most of my work has been in the action/military science fiction genre with the Weapons of Choice and Wrecking Squad series. These are not your usual action series as they delve into aspects of the human condition and have a reputation of being surprisingly thoughtful in their emotional depth and social conscience.

However, I have also released two standalone books in The Scorching science fiction/climate fiction series, with one more book to follow. Just Press Play is a daring take on a mystery thriller from a first-person point of view. It was a real joy to write, and though full of humour, it retains a dark undertone that will surprise. The World in My Hands is also a standalone novel exploring the Drathken who arrive to help as the Earth dies, and the humans who leave the planet to seek new worlds with a dark, secret history of their own.

You can view all my books, sign up for a newsletter and receive free books related to the Weapons of Choice and Wrecking Squad Series on my website below:

www.nicksnape.com

AUTHOR BIO

Nick Snape has been steeped in Science Fiction and Fantasy since his friends first dragged him from his schoolwork and stuck a book under his nose. Lost to the world of imagination, he became a teacher by accident, though he thoroughly enjoyed developing the joy of reading and writing in his pupils. Having retired after thirty years, he thought it was high time to practise what he preached. Nick's books feature everything from all out, heart-pounding, fast-paced action to thoughtful, character driven twists on the fantasy and sci-fi genres. Genetics to artificial intelligence, artifice dragons to soul-eating enemies, nothing is off the menu.

BOOKS BY NICK SNAPE

Weapons of Choice Series
(Amazon Only)
Hostile Contact
Return Protocol
Zuri's War
Finn's War
Alien Rebirth
Invasive Species
Legion Earth
Nemesis Earth
Weapons of Choice Box Set Vol.1 Bks 1-8

The Wrecking Squad
(Amazon Only)
The Wrecking Squad
Butcher's Folly
Warmonger's Wrath

The Scorching
The World in My Hands
Just Press Play

Warriors of Spirit and Bone
(Amazon, paperbacks widely available)

A Dragon of the Veil
A City of Ashes
A Queen in Blood

Acknowledgements

As with all authors, this book and my other series would never have existed without the dedicated friends and family who were there by my side throughout the entire process. The least I can do is give them a mention for their patience with my obsession! My Beta readers, supporters and fiercest critics for this book have been Pak and Julie. Amazing people who put that aside to make sure whatever I put out there was something they wanted to read. I have also had great support from Martin Lejeune—an author who has given generously of their time during my trials and tribulations. I would also like to thank Laurel C Kriegler, who took on the editing duties – little did she know!

Very much appreciated, and the books would not be where they are without you all.

Julie, my wife, needs a special mention. Over the past few years, she has kept me going, being there at every step through the dark and joyful times. I can't believe how lucky I am. Finally, the New Year and Pub Night Crews. Wouldn't be here without you.

Thank you all.

PRAISE FOR THE AUTHOR

'*A masterful storyteller.*' **SPR**

'*Nick Snape's creative storytelling, rich world-building, and engaging characters make this book an unforgettable journey.*' **Literary Titan**

'*Stunning series. Very highly recommended.*' **Goodreads**

'*Wildly creative*' **Self-Publishing Review**

'*I haven't enjoyed a series this much in a long time. The twists and turns keep me constantly surprised.*' **Amazon Customer**

'*A truly immersive story.*' **Amazon Customer**